JAMES BO

THE UNION TRILOGY

JAMES BOND

THE UNION TRILOGY

THREE 007 NOVELS

RAYMOND BENSON

PEGASUS BOOKS
NEW YORK

JAMES BOND: THE UNION TRILOGY

Pegasus Books, Ltd.
148 West 37th Street, 13th Floor
New York, NY 10018

Interior design by Maria Fernandez

Library of Congress Cataloging-in-Publication Data is available.

ISBN: 978-1-60598-007-2

10 9 8 7

Printed in the United States of America
Distributed by Simon & Schuster
www.pegasusbooks.com

CONTENTS

INTRODUCTION

I'M STILL PINCHING MYSELF.

Did the years 1996 to 2002 really happen? When I look back at that relatively short period in my life it seems like a dream I might have had, only to wake up to a more uneventful reality.

For seven years I was the official author of the James Bond 007 novels. I was the fourth writer in line, and the first American, to wear the shoes—and awfully big shoes they were.

Ian Fleming, of course, was the originator. He created the character that is now an international icon, one of the most recognized and admired pop culture figures of all time. But despite what my friends in Britain might think, James Bond ceased to exclusively belong to the United Kingdom many years ago. Today the entire world embraces him. It is said that one out of every three people on the globe have seen a James Bond film (although how this was measured I have no idea). The motion pictures represent the most successful long running series made by one production company in cinema history.

The jury's still out on whether my tenure as Bond author was too short, too long, or just right. Fleming would most certainly have written more novels had he lived beyond the age of fifty-six (he published twelve novels and two collections of short stories). It's a shame that Kingsley Amis didn't do more (he wrote only one, under the pseudonym "Robert Markham," in 1968). John Gardner had several wonderful entries in the series, especially during the eighties (fourteen novels and two film novelizations published between 1981 and 1996—more than Fleming!). At the time of this writing, Sebastian Faulks has been announced as the author of a single Bond novel for 2008 (the one-hundredth anniversary of Ian Fleming's birth).

I produced six original 007 novels, three film novelizations, and three short stories. I suppose that's not bad for seven years. I am now pleased to present this omnibus, which collects three novels and one short story. *High Time to Kill, DoubleShot, and Never Dream of Dying,* originally published as the third, fourth, and fifth of my original books, make up a story arc that I loosely call "The Union Trilogy." The short piece, *Blast from the Past,* was the first fiction I wrote as Bond author, and a truncated form of it was initially published in *Playboy* magazine.

Back in the spring of 1996, while I was in the throes of researching and writing my *first* Bond novel (*Zero Minus Ten*), I thought it might be a good idea to kick off my Bond tenure with a short story. *Playboy* had a long history with 007, as it was the first American periodical to publish Ian Fleming. Throughout the sixties, the magazine printed several Fleming short stories and excerpts from his novels, as well as pictorials from the films. *Playboy* had always been in bed with Bond, so to speak, but it had been thirty years since the magazine had published any new 007 fiction. So we went for it.

At the end of Fleming's novel *You Only Live Twice,* Bond's Japanese lover Kissy Suzuki is pregnant with the secret agent's child. John Pearson, in his excellent *James Bond—The Authorized Biography of 007,* took this bit of information and expanded on it, saying that the child, a boy, was named James Suzuki and was raised by his mother. That was the last that anyone ever heard of Bond's son. So, throughout the month of April 1996 I wrote the story in which James Bond discovers that his son has been murdered by his former enemy, Irma Bunt (Fleming or subsequent authors had never explained what became of her, either). I set the story in New York City because I knew the locations by memory. A subtle in-joke, known only to my friends and family who knew me when I lived in the city, was that James Suzuki's apartment on the Upper East Side was actually *my* old studio apartment—where I had written my 1984 non-fiction tome, *The James Bond Bedside Companion*.

Ultimately, the finished piece was too long for one issue and the *Playboy* editors didn't want to print it in two parts. They ended up cutting approximately one-third for space reasons, which, I felt, was a shame. The "director's cut," so to speak, was later published in Italy and France in fanzines and mystery magazines, but up until now the full-length version of *Blast from the Past* has not been printed in English. So finally, for the fans who have been clamoring for it, here it is and I hope you will overlook the minor shortcomings (that I see *now*, anyway) of my first foray into 007 fiction.

The idea for *High Time to Kill*, my third Bond novel, came to me in the fall of 1997. I had recently read the non-fiction book *Into Thin Air*, which was about an ill-fated climbing expedition up Mt. Everest. It struck me that mountaineering would make a great backdrop to a Bond adventure. Bond had never been to the Himalayas and had never done serious mountain climbing in any of the existing books or films. So I decided to set the story in Nepal and make the plot have something to do with reaching the top of one of the highest Himalayan peaks. Better yet, it would be a race—Bond's team versus the bad guys. They had to reach the summit before the other guys because . . . why?

So I came up with a "MacGuffin." (This was Hitchcock's term for the object that propels a story's characters along its path—they want the "secret plans," or the "microfilm," or the "holy grail"—it really doesn't matter what the object is, as long as it moves the plot.) My MacGuffin was a "secret formula" for creating aircraft hull material that enables planes to fly at a speed of Mach 7. Any country would kill to have that formula. So how does it get to the top of a Himalayan peak? Easy! A character smuggles it aboard a plane, and the aircraft crashes up there. 007 is ordered to go and get it before the bad guys do.

Early on I decided not to incorporate Mt. Everest, simply because it's overused. I chose Kangchenjunga, the third largest mountain in the world. Kangchenjunga, or "Kangch" as it's called by explorers, is actually considered a greater challenge because it's a more difficult climb than Everest. Another major location in the book is Belgium, and there are minor scenes in The Bahamas, Morocco, and England.

I also wanted to create something of a "trilogy," much the same way Fleming had done with *Thunderball, On Her Majesty's Secret Service,* and *You Only Live Twice,* in which Bond is battling SPECTRE and Ernst Stavro Blofeld. I came up with a new villainous organization called The Union, led by a mysterious fellow named *Le Gérant,* to figure in each of the books.

It was the easiest and quickest plot I came up with, and to this day *High Time to Kill* is my favorite Bond book. The emphasis is strongly on adventure and nitty-gritty espionage work, but I did slip in the Jaguar XK8 (which was introduced in the previous book, *The Facts of Death*), using more improbable but not impossible features that a Jaguar engineer helped me invent. (Ian Fleming always liked to say that his stories might be "improbable, but never impossible.")

The autumn of 1998 was taken up with conceiving and outlining my fourth Bond novel, which would eventually be called *DoubleShot.* As the second book of the trilogy, I wanted it to be darker and feature a James Bond who is not operating at one hundred percent. He had sustained a head injury in *High Time to Kill* and I thought it would be interesting to work with how this had affected him. James Bond is *human*—and a head injury can be very serious business. Fleming's Bond suffers all sorts of maladies, goes through bouts of depression, and is a heavy drinker. He broods a lot. He is not a happy person.

In my new story I wanted 007 to doubt his own sanity. At the beginning of the book he's having memory blackouts. Before long, he's accused of murder and is wanted by his own people. Using this plot device gave me a chance to examine how a wounded James Bond might act. I also played with the structure a bit—the novel begins with the story's ending. When all was said and done, the book contained my most complex plotting.

The locations I chose were Morocco, Spain, and Gibraltar. I figured that since Gibraltar had always been a thorn in Spain's foot, more or less, there would be a nice conflict with Britain if a Spanish villain attempted to reclaim Gibraltar for his country. It was also the first time that Bond spends a significant amount of time in Africa (nearly a third of the book). Morocco was perfect for my purposes.

Attending a *Playboy* pajama party and meeting editor-in-chief Hugh Hefner's twin girlfriends (at the time) was what influenced me to use twins as the Bond-girls in the story. It's rather surprising that this hadn't been done before. It made perfect sense to me—after all this was *Bond*. Why *not* twins?

In the autumn of 1999, I began the outline for *Never Dream of Dying*. For the final part of the trilogy, I wanted to not only bring to a close Bond's battle with The Union and *Le Gérant*, but also dig deeper into 007's character. I searched for a new way to examine his human qualities and found it by asking a question—"How would James Bond react if he were forced to kill a family member?" With that premise, I pondered what family members existed that could possibly become enemies. The only one was Marc-Ange Draco, Bond's former father-in-law. So I made Draco a member of The Union. Even better, I made him related to *Le Gérant*. My publishers absolutely loved the idea, but I wasn't sure how the fans would react. The problem was that Draco, even though he was technically a bad guy, became Bond's friend and ally in *On Her Majesty's Secret Service* (the film version especially portrayed Draco as a sweet and likable fellow). Some 007 fans found the concept controversial, but I didn't care. The fact is that Draco *is* a villain. He's a gangster, a mafia chief, a smuggler, and a murderer. We didn't see his bad side in *OHMSS*. That's what everyone forgets. Bond entered into a cordial relationship with the man for business reasons and because of Draco's daughter, Tracy. No one ever questioned what happened to the relationship between Bond and Draco after Tracy's murder. How would Draco have felt about it? Would he have blamed Bond for his daughter's death? Possibly. Actually, I thought, very likely! And that's where my premise makes complete sense.

Because Draco was involved, I set the story in France and Corsica. Specifically, the climax of the book takes place at a very glamorous public event—the Cannes Film Festival. Perfect for a James Bond story. Cannes has style, fashion, and glitz.

There's another echo back to *OHMSS* in *Never Dream of Dying*—there's a real romance in the book. It was time once again for Bond to fall head over heels in love with the heroine.

"The Union Trilogy" represents, I think, some of my best work with James Bond. There are certainly high points in the other three original novels I wrote, but the trilogy pushes boundaries and contains much more of a personal voice. There's more of *me* in these three books. I took some chances and most fans believe I was successful.

I am grateful to Pegasus Books for issuing this collection, and to my friends and colleagues at Ian Fleming Publications Ltd. for allowing the novels and story to be reprinted. And to all the Bond fans out there—I love you all!

Raymond Benson, 2008

JAMES BOND TITLES BY RAYMOND BENSON

NOVELS

Zero Minus Ten (1997)
The Facts of Death (1998)
High Time to Kill (1999)
DoubleShot (2000)
Never Dream of Dying (2001)
The Man With the Red Tattoo (2002)

FILM NOVELIZATIONS

(based on the respective screenplays)

Tomorrow Never Dies (1997)
The World is Not Enough (1999)
Die Another Day (2002)

SHORT STORIES

Blast From the Past (1997)
Midsummer Night's Doom (1999)
Live at Five (1999)

ABOUT THE AUTHOR

Besides writing official James Bond fiction between 1996–2002, **RAYMOND BENSON** is also known for *The James Bond Bedside Companion*, which was published in 1984 and was nominated for an Edgar. As "David Michaels" Raymond is the author of the NY Times best-sellers *Tom Clancy's Splinter Cell* and *Tom Clancy's Splinter Cell— Operation Barracuda*. He recently penned the best-selling novelization of *Metal Gear Solid*. Raymond's original thrillers are *Face Blind*, *Evil Hours*, *Sweetie's Diamonds*, and *A Hard Day's Death*. Visit him at his website, www.raymondbenson.com.

JAMES BOND
THE UNION TRILOGY

HIGH TIME TO KILL

For my mentors

Francis Hodge
and
Peter Janson-Smith

CONTENTS

HOLIDAYS ARE HELL

THE BARRACUDA SURPRISED THEM BY OPENING ITS JAWS TO AN ANGLE OF ninety degrees, revealing the sharp rows of teeth that were capable of tearing out chunks of flesh in an instant. It closed its snarling mouth just as quickly, leaving a half-inch gap.

Had it *yawned?*

It was easily a twenty-pound fish. One of the most dangerous predators in the sea, the barracuda is an eating machine that rivals the ferocity of a shark. This one swam lazily along beside them, watching. It was curious about the two strange larger fish that had invaded its habitat.

James Bond had never cared for barracudas. He'd rather be in a pit full of snakes than in proximity to one of them. It wasn't that he was afraid of them but merely that he found them mean, vicious, and unpredictable creatures. There was no such thing as a barracuda in a good mood. He had to be on his guard without showing fear, for the fish could sense apprehension and often acted on it.

Bond looked over at his companion. She was handling it well, watching the long, slender fish with fascination rather than trepidation.

He motioned for her to swim on, and she nodded. They decided to ignore the barracuda, which proved to be the best tactic. It lost interest after a few minutes and swam away into the misty blue.

Bond had always likened the undersea world to an alien landscape. It was silent and surreal, yet it was full of life. Some sea flowers shot down holes in the seabed as the two humans moved over them. A small octopus, or "pus-feller" (as Ramsey, his Jamaican housekeeper, called it), was propelling itself along the orange-and-brown-colored reef. Patches of sea grass hid the domains of the night-crawling lobsters and crabs.

They swam toward the beach, eventually reaching a spot where they could stand. Bond pulled off the face mask and snorkel. Helena Marksbury emerged from the water and stood beside him. She removed her own mask and snorkel and laughed.

"I do believe that fish wanted to take part of us home as a souvenir," she said.

"It wasn't interested in me," Bond said. "It was staring at you. Do you usually have that kind of effect on barracuda?"

"I attract all the meat eaters, James," she said with an inviting smile.

March in the Bahamas was quite pleasant at eighty degrees Fahrenheit. The hot summer was just around the corner, and Bond had decided to take a week's leave before then. It was the perfect time of year to be in the Caribbean. He had originally planned to spend the holiday at Shamelady, his private home on the north shore of Jamaica, but changed his mind when Helena Marksbury said that she had never been to Nassau. Bond offered to show her the islands.

"Where did everyone go?" she asked, looking around at the empty beach. Earlier, there had been a few other snorkelers and sunbathers in the area. Now it was deserted.

It was just after noon. Helena looked around for some shade and sat in the sand next to a large rock that provided some shelter from the fiercely bright sun. She knew she had to be careful not to get too much of it, as she had a light complexion and burned easily. Nevertheless, she had worn the skimpiest bikini she could find. She was most likely the only person who might notice a flaw—that her left breast drooped slightly lower than her right—but Helena knew that she had a good body, and didn't mind showing it off. It just proved that nobody was perfect.

They were on the southwest side of New Providence Island, the most populous of all the Bahamas. Luckily, Bond had found a villa at Coral Harbour, somewhat removed from the hustle and bustle of metropolitan Nassau, which is the center of commerce, government, and transportation, on the northern side of the island. Here they were surrounded by beautiful beaches and reefs, country clubs and exclusive restaurants.

"What am I supposed to wear tonight?" she asked him as he sat down beside her in the sand.

"Helena, I shouldn't have to tell you how to dress," he said. "You look marvelous in anything."

They had a dinner invitation at the home of the former Governor of the Bahamas, a man Bond had known for many years. They had become friends after a dinner party at which the Governor had presented Bond with a theory concerning love, betrayal, and cruelty between marriage partners. Calling it the "quantum of solace," the Governor believed that the amount of comfort on which love and friendship is based could be measured. Unless there is a certain degree of humanity existing between two people, he maintained, there can be no love. It was an adage Bond had accepted as a universal truth.

The Governor had long since retired but had remained in Nassau with his wife. Bond had made it a point to stop in and see him every time he went through the Bahamas, which wasn't very often. When Bond went to the Caribbean, it was usually to his beloved Shamelady in Jamaica.

Helena reclined and looked at Bond with her bewitching, almond-shaped green eyes. She was beautiful—wet or dry—and could easily have been a fashion model. Unfortunately, she was Bond's personal assistant at SIS, where they both worked. So far they had kept their affair a secret. They both knew that if they carried on much longer, someone at the office would find out. Not that there was anything particularly wrong with it, but office romances in this day and age were frowned upon. Bond justified it to himself because there had been a precedent. Several years ago he had been romantically involved with another personal assistant, Mary Goodnight. How could he forget their time together in Jamaica during the Scaramanga case?

Helena was different from Mary Goodnight. A thoroughly modern woman of thirty-three, Helena Marksbury had none of Ms. Goodnight's charming yet scatterbrained personality. She was a serious girl, with weighty ideas about politics and current events. She loved poetry, Shakespeare, and fine food and drink. She appreciated and understood the work Bond did and considered her own job just as important in the scheme of things at SIS. She also possessed a stubborn moral conscience that had taken Bond several months to penetrate before she agreed to see him socially.

It had begun in the courtyard in the back of Sir Miles Messervy's house, Quarterdeck, near Great Windsor Park. The occasion was a dinner party held there a year earlier, and the mutual physical attraction between Bond and Helena had become too much for them to ignore. They had gone for a walk outside and ended up kissing behind the house in the rain. Now, after three months of false starts and two months of cautious experimentation, Bond and Helena were dating. While they both acknowledged that their jobs came first, they enjoyed each other's company enough to keep it going casually. Bond felt comfortable with Helena's level of commitment, and the sex was outstanding. He saw no reason to rock the boat.

There was no mistaking the invitation in her eyes, so Bond settled next to her wet body and kissed her. She wrapped one slinky leg around his thighs and pulled him closer.

"Do you think we're all alone?" she whispered.

"I hope so," he replied, "but I don't really care at this point, do you?" He slipped the straps off her shoulders as she tugged at his bathing trunks.

"Not at all, darling," she said breathlessly. She helped him remove her bikini, and then his strong, knowing hands were all over her. She arched her back and responded with soft moans of pleasure.

"Take me now, James," she said softly in his ear. "Here."

She didn't have to ask him twice.

The Governor greeted Bond with an enthusiastic warm, dry handshake.

"It's great to see you again, James," he said.

"Thank you, sir, you're looking well."

The Governor shook his head. "Lord, I'm an old man, and I look like one. But you haven't changed a bit. What do you do, take frequent trips to the Fountain of Youth? And who might this lovely lady be?"

"This is my assistant, Helena Marksbury," Bond said. She was dressed in a fashionable lightweight red cotton dress with a wrap covering her bare shoulders and ample cleavage. Bond was wearing a light blue cotton short-sleeve polo shirt and navy blue cotton twill trousers. His light, gray silk basketweave jacket covered the Walther PPK that he still kept in a chamois shoulder holster.

"Do you remember my wife, Marion?" the Governor asked, gesturing to a handsome woman with white hair and sparkling blue eyes.

"Of course, how are you?"

"Fine, James," the woman said. "Come on in, both of you, please."

The dinner party was in a century-old colonial-style mansion off Thompson Boulevard, near the College of the Bahamas. The former Governor was obviously wealthy, as there seemed to be no end to the line of servants waiting to attend to Bond and his date. More than two dozen guests were already in the drawing room, which was next to a large living room with an open bay window overlooking expansive gardens. There were people outside as well, standing in clusters with drinks in hand. Ceiling fans leisurely provided a breeze.

For the first time since he had been visiting the Governor, Bond also noticed an undeniable presence of security. Large men dressed in white sport coats were positioned at various entrances, suspiciously eyeing everyone who walked past. He wondered if there was perhaps some VIP present who would require such protection.

As they were uncomfortable socializing with people they didn't know, Bond and Helena kept to themselves and went outside to the gardens. It was still bright, and night wouldn't fall for another two hours.

They approached the outdoor bar. "Vodka martini, please," Bond said, "shaken, not stirred, with a twist of lemon."

"I'll have the same," Helena said. She had actually grown to like the way Bond ordered his martini.

"This is lovely," Helena said.

"It's lovely as long as we're alone," Bond replied. "I don't relish making small talk with the Mr. and Mrs. Harvey Millers of the world," he said, indicating the other people milling around.

"Who are Mr. and Mrs. Harvey Miller?"

"Just a couple I met at a previous dinner party here."

"Ah, there you are," the Governor declared. "I see you've got yourselves something to drink, good, good. . . . How's Sir Miles doing, by the way?" He was referring to Bond's old chief, the former M, Sir Miles Messervy.

"He's fine," Bond was happy to report. "His health improved rapidly after he retired. Getting out of the job was the best thing for him really. He seems ten years younger."

"That's good to hear. Tell him hello for me the next time you see him, would you?"

"Certainly."

"How do you get on with the new M?" the Governor asked with a twinkle in his eye.

"We have a sterling relationship," Bond said.

"No problems accepting orders from a woman? I'm surprised, James! You're the one who once told me that you could marry only an air hostess or a Japanese woman."

Bond grinned wryly at the memory. "She runs a tight ship and runs it well."

"Well, that's great! I'm glad to hear it," the Governor said with a little too much enthusiasm. Bond thought he might be a bit drunk. "Listen, I'm so glad you came, really, James, because I want to—"

The Governor's attention was distracted by the head servant, a black man with gray hair and glasses, whispering to one of the security guards some fifteen feet away. The guard, a Caucasian who might have been a professional wrestler, nodded and left the scene.

"Everything all right, Albert?" the Governor called.

"Yessuh," Albert said. "I sent Frank to take a look at someone's motor scooter parked outside the fence."

"Ahhh," the Governor said. For a moment Bond thought he appeared nervous and perhaps a little frightened.

Bond asked, "You were saying?"

"Right. I was saying there was something I'd like you to take a look at. Privately. In my office. Would you mind?"

Bond looked at Helena. She shrugged. "I'm fine," she said, eyeing a large tray of peeled shrimp. "Go ahead. I'll be somewhere around here."

Bond squeezed her arm and then followed the Governor back into the house. They went up an elegant winding staircase to the second floor and into the Governor's study. Once they were inside, the Governor closed the door.

"You're being very mysterious," Bond said. "I'm intrigued."

The Governor moved around his desk and unlocked a drawer. "I think I'm in a bit of trouble, James," he said. "And I'd like your advice."

The man was genuinely concerned. The levity in Bond's voice immediately vanished. "Of course," he said.

"Ever heard of these people?" his friend asked, handing over a letter in a transparent plastic sleeve.

Bond looked at the piece of paper. It was an 8 1\2-by-11-inch piece of typing paper with the words "Time Is Up" centered in the middle of the page. At the bottom it was signed "The Union."

Bond nodded. "The Union. Interesting. Yes, we know about the Union."

"Can you tell me about them?" the Governor asked. "I haven't gone to the local police here, but I've already sent a query to London. I haven't heard anything yet."

"Is this message, 'time is up,' meant for you?" Bond asked.

The Governor nodded. "I'm heavily in debt to a man in Spain. It was a real estate transaction that wasn't particularly . . . honest, I'm sorry to say. Anyway, I received one letter from this Union, or whatever they are, two months ago. In that one it said that I had two months to pay up. I don't want to do that because the man in Spain is a crook. I got this letter four days ago. Who are they, James? Are they some kind of Mafia?"

"They're not unlike the Mafia, but they are much more international. SIS only recently became aware of their activities. What we do know is that they are a group of serious mercenaries out for hire by any individual or government that will employ them."

"How long have they been around?"

"Not long. Three years, maybe."

"I've never heard of them. Are they really dangerous?"

Bond handed the letter back to the Governor. "As a work-for-hire outfit, they have to be experts at anything from petty street crime to sophisticated and elaborate espionage schemes. They are reportedly responsible for the theft of military maps from the Pentagon in the United States. The maps disappeared from right under the noses of highly-trained security personnel. A well-protected Mafia don was murdered about a year ago in Sicily. The Union supposedly supplied the hit man for that job. They recently blackmailed a French politician for fifty million francs. The Deuxième got wind of it and passed the information on to us. One of the most recent reports that went through my office stated that the Union were beginning to specialize in military espionage and selling the fruits of their findings to other nations. Apparently they have no loyalty to any one nation. Their primary motive is greed, and they can be quite ruthless. If that letter was meant for you, then, yes, I would have to say that they are indeed quite dangerous."

The Governor sat. He looked worried. "But who's behind them? Where are they based?"

"We don't know," Bond said. "Despite all the intelligence we've gathered on them thus far, SIS have no clues as to who they are or where they make their home."

The Governor swallowed. "What should I do?"

"I can see you already have extra protection around the house. That's good for a start."

The Governor nodded. "There are so many guards around here, I can't keep track of them all."

"I'll alert Interpol and see if the letters can be traced. It's a difficult thing, though. Tomorrow I'll make a report to London and see what we can do about surveillance. It's highly likely that you're being watched. Your phones may even be tapped."

"Good Lord."

"The local police know nothing about this?"

"No."

"I wouldn't involve them just yet. The Union have an uncanny ability to infiltrate law enforcement organizations. Tomorrow let's go to Government House and file an official report. I'm glad you told me about this. We have orders to gather as much information about the Union as we can."

"Thank you, James. I knew I could count on you." He stood up, but the blood had drained from his face. He was clearly frightened. "I think we should rejoin the party."

"Try not to worry," Bond said.

They left the study and went back outside. Helena was sitting on a stone bench alone, gazing across the gardens at the house. She gave Bond a warm smile.

"Working, James? I thought we were on holiday," she said when he joined her.

"We are. Just giving a little professional advice," he said.

"Really, James, a *Japanese woman* or a *flight hostess?*"

Bond laughed. "Don't believe everything you hear."

Dinner was a magnificent feast consisting of traditional conch chowder, peas 'n' rice, Bahamian lobster, Dover sole fillets simmered in white wine, cream, and mustard sauce and topped with shrimp, and pineapple spring rolls with rum crème anglaise for dessert. Helena was in heaven and Bond enjoyed watching her eat. She savored each bite, squeezing out the juices with her cheeks and tongue before chewing and swallowing. She had one of the most sensual mouths Bond had ever kissed.

Afterward they retired to the gardens to enjoy the star-filled night sky along with several other couples. Some of the men were smoking the cigars that one of the servants had passed around. To get away from the crowd, Bond and Helena walked along a dimly lit path that circled the garden and ran around the perimeter of the grounds.

Helena sighed heavily and said, "I don't want to go back to London."

"All good things come to an end," Bond replied.

"Does that mean us, James?"

"Of course not," he said, "unless you would prefer that. I don't want to lose the best assistant I've ever had."

"Do you mean that?"

"Look, Helena, you're a wonderful girl, but you should know me by now. Entanglements can get messy, and I don't like them. I think while we're in London we need to tone it down. Being the sensible girl you are, I know that you'll agree."

They found themselves at the far end of the expansive lawn, some fifty yards from the house. A ten-foot-high stone fence separated the grounds from the street. They stood beside a toolshed and held each other.

"You're right, James," she said. "It's just that sometimes I dream of a different sort of life. One that borders on the edge of fantasy. My sister in America seems to live a fairy tale existence. She has a husband who adores her and two lovely children, and they live in an area of southern California where the weather is always perfect. She's always so incredibly happy when I speak to her that I get a little jealous." She smiled and took his arm. "But you're right, James. Let's not get morose. I want to enjoy every last minute of our time here."

He pulled her chin toward him so that he could kiss her, but her eyes widened and she gasped. "James!"

Bond whipped around to see what had startled her. A body was lying just off the path. The shadows would have completely hidden it had it not been for the moonlight reflecting off pale skin. Bond moved quickly to the corpse and saw that it was Frank, the security guard. He had been stripped of his shirt and white jacket; his throat had been cut, ear to ear. He was lying in a pool of fresh blood.

"Wait here!" he commanded. He turned and sprinted across the lawn toward the house. He heard her call behind him, "James! I'm coming with you!" as he took a shortcut over a set of stone benches surrounding a stone fountain. He ran through the gardens toward the back of the house, searching frantically for the Governor. He found the man's wife standing beside some guests.

"Where's your husband?" Bond asked.

Startled, the woman replied, "Why . . . I believe I saw him go upstairs to the office with one of those security men."

Bond left abruptly, entered the house, bolted up the stairs three at a time, and ran to the open doorway. The former Governor was lying on the floor in a ghastly pool of red. Like the guard, his throat had been slit so fiercely that his head lopped at a grotesque angle. There was no one else in the room, but two distinct footprints in blood led from the body toward the door to another bloody patch on the carpet. The killer had wiped his shoes clean before leaving the office.

Others had made their way up the stairs by this time. Bond was unable to stop the Governor's wife from glimpsing the horrid sight. She screamed loudly just as Bond pulled her away and slammed the door shut. He told one of the men to call the police and look after her, then he rushed down to the first floor. The bewildered head servant was at the foot of the stairs.

"Did you see a guard come down the stairs?" he barked.

"Yessuh!" Albert said. "He went through the kitchen."

"Would that lead to the motor scooter you saw earlier?"

Albert nodded furiously. He ushered Bond into the kitchen, where several servants were cleaning up after the huge meal. He then led him into a corridor and pointed to a door at the end.

"That's the servants' entrance," he said. "Go out of the gate and turn left. It was just down the street a bit."

"Tell the girl I came with to wait for me," Bond said as he went outside.

He found himself in a small parking area reserved for the servants. He ran to the open gate and peered carefully around to look at the street. Sure enough, a black man dressed in a guard's white jacket was on an old Vespa motor scooter. He was just beginning to pull away.

"Stop!" Bond shouted. The man looked back at Bond before accelerating down the street. Bond drew his Walther PPK and fired at him but missed. His last chance was to give chase on foot.

The man was a quarter-mile ahead of him. He had turned onto Thompson Boulevard and was headed north through busy traffic.

Bond ran into the street in front of a bus traveling in the same direction. The bus driver slammed on his brakes, throwing several passengers to the floor. The bus still hit Bond hard enough to knock him to the pavement, stunning him slightly. He got up quickly, shook his body, and continued the pursuit.

The Vespa crossed Meadow Street and zipped into the entrance of St. Bernard's Park, circling around St. Joseph's Baptist Church. Bond jumped on the hood of a BMW and scrambled over it just in time to see the assassin slam into a street vendor's kiosk that had been set up at the corner of the park. T-shirts and souvenirs went flying, and the angry proprietor shouted and shook his fist at the driver. The scooter then disappeared into the park.

It was darker off the main road. Bond kept running, panting heavily. Should he risk firing a shot? He could just see the taillight of the scooter some thirty feet ahead. He didn't want to kill the man. If he had ties to the Union, it was imperative that he be taken alive. The Vespa rounded a turn and was traveling on relatively straight pavement. It could easily speed away if he didn't stop it now. Carefully aiming the handgun at the scooter's taillight, he fired once.

The bullet hit the back tire, sending the scooter skidding across the pavement on its side. The killer landed hard, but immediately got up and started to run with a limp. Bond pursued him across the lawn. The assassin was holding his leg as he ran—he wouldn't go far.

He did, however, make it to the western edge of the park and ran across the road and into a residential street. Bond followed him, almost collided with a taxi, spun around, and fell. Not wasting a second, he leaped to his feet and continued the chase. He could see the killer hobbling along about thirty feet ahead.

"Stop!" Bond shouted again.

The man turned. Bond could see him holding something in his hand. A flash of light and the unmistakable sound of a shot forced Bond to roll to the ground. His hope of taking the armed man alive had diminished greatly.

When he got to his feet, Bond saw that his prey had disappeared. There were a couple of alleys, either of which he could have run into.

Bond sprinted to the corner and peered down one of them. Sure enough, he heard the sound of running feet. Bond hugged the wall and crept quickly toward the noise. He could see the man at the end of the alley, trapped in a dead end. Bond took cover behind some rubbish barrels.

"Give up!" Bond shouted. "You're caught. Throw down your gun."

The man turned and looked toward the voice. His eyes were wide. He fired blindly, unable to see his target. The bullet ricocheted off the alley wall.

It was now clear to Bond what had happened. The assassin had jumped the fence, killed the guard Frank, and taken his shirt and jacket. Impersonating a security man, he then persuaded the Governor to follow him inside the house. The Governor certainly wouldn't have known all the security guards by sight.

"I'm counting to three," Bond shouted. "Throw down your gun and raise your hands. I have a clear shot at your head. I assure you that I'll blow a hole in it."

The man pointed his gun in the direction of the voice. From Bond's distance it appeared to be a revolver of some kind. Another shot went off, this time piercing the garbage can next to him.

"One . . ."

The man hesitated, not sure what to do. He knew he couldn't escape.

"Two . . ."

Then the killer did a curious thing—he smiled. There was only one thing to do that made sense to him.

"You won't take *me* alive, man," the man said in a heavy West Indian accent. Then he pointed the gun at his temple.

"No!" Bond shouted. "Don't—"

The man pulled the trigger. The noise reverberated like a thunderclap in the close confines of the alley.

OLD RIVALS

"THE TRICK IS NOT IN THE AMOUNT OF FORCE YOU USE WHEN YOU HIT THE ball, Mr. Bond, but in the *negative* force," said Nolan Edwards, the starter at Stoke Poges Golf Club.

"Well then, it's perfectly clear," Bond replied with sarcasm. The ball he had just knocked ninety yards onto the putting green over-shot the hole and continued to roll into the rough.

He was frustrated by his lack of progress in mastering a difficult shot. It was called "backing the ball on the green." Pro golfers perform it successfully most of the time; formidable amateurs such as Bond found the shot elusive. He was determined to get it right, for he had always played golf with the attitude that one should incorporate new techniques and strategies to keep the game alive. This particular shot would be useful should he ever need to hit the ball into a tough pin placement. If he overshot the hole, it would roll off the green (as he had just so aptly demonstrated). However, if he could successfully put a backspin on the ball, it would roll *back* toward the hole and be in a perfect position for him to sink the putt.

Bond had been on the practice green in front of the club for half an hour. He hadn't got it right once.

Edwards, an American from Illinois and longtime Stoke Poges employee, shook his head and wrinkled his brow. "It's a tough one,

Mr. Bond. I've seen very few amateurs do it. To spin the ball with some kind of accuracy, what you need to do is combine swing speed, impact position, hand action, and acceleration into one smooth swing."

"What I need is a stiff drink," Bond said, picking up his wound three-piece Titleist ball and pocketing it.

"Any sign of Bill?" he asked.

"I believe that's his Alfa now," Edwards said, nodding in the direction of the starter shed, where Bill Tanner, the Chief of Staff at SIS, had just parked his red Alfa Romeo.

"Hello, James," he said, getting out of the car and opening the trunk. "How are you, Edwards?"

"Fine, Mr. Tanner," the starter said. Tanner pulled out the clubs and handed them to Edwards. "Mr. Bond was just practicing a very difficult shot."

"You still trying to put a backspin on the ball, James?"

Bond nodded, unsnapping the glove from his left hand. "I'm close, Bill. Damn close."

Tanner chuckled. "You're taking this *much* too seriously, James. Come on, let's go and get a drink. The others will be here soon."

Bond left his bag of Callaway clubs with Edwards and walked with Tanner to the front of the clubhouse, an impressive grade-one Palladian mansion. He had joined the club in 1993. The dues were sizable, but the splendid public and private rooms of the clubhouse, the elegant dining room and fine cuisine, the attentive staff, and the golf course itself made membership a cherished luxury. Founded in 1908, the Stoke Poges Golf Club is one of the finest in England. Located in Buckinghamshire in the south of England near Eton and Windsor, the thousand-year history of the estate is just as colorful as its surroundings. Decades of established traditions complement the clubhouse, its ancient gardens and parkland, and its world-famous course created by Harry Shapland Colt.

Bond and Tanner entered the lobby and walked past the grand staircase, which, at the time it was built, was the largest cantilever staircase in the UK. They went through the bright and cheery Orangery and into the more subdued President's Bar. Bond preferred the bar, as it was a room that was both elegant and masculine. There was a yellow marble fireplace, a well-stocked oak bar, and comfortable furniture with cream-colored upholstery. Trophies and wood plaques adorned the yellow walls, proclaiming the names of past captains and other vital historical facts about the park.

Bond ordered a bourbon and Tanner asked for a Black Label whisky. Tanner looked at his watch. It was still early in the day. "They should be here soon. Do you think it will rain?"

English weather in April is unpredictable. So far, the sun had managed to skirt around the hovering dark clouds.

"Probably on the back nine," Bond prophesied. "It never fails."

Bond had been home for two weeks. The Governor's murder had spoiled what had begun as a delightful holiday in the Bahamas with Helena. Now that they were back at the job, their relationship was a masquerade. They tried to put the romance behind them and, as much as possible, pretend that it never occurred. So far it wasn't working. The situation was further complicated by the fact that their affair had been a secret before the incidents in Nassau, but now a number of people at SIS knew that he had been there with his personal assistant. Bond could feel Helena's tension when he was at the office, so he made excuses to leave or work at home. He was extremely grateful when Tanner had suggested that he take Thursday off and play a round of golf with two other SIS civil servants.

"How is your research on the Union coming?" Tanner asked.

"Must we talk shop?" Bond snapped.

"Sorry," Tanner said. "You really do want to master that shot!"

"No, I'm sorry, Bill," Bond said. "I've been on edge lately. That business with the Governor in Nassau, and the killer who blew his own brains out . . . it's all a big mystery that I'm still trying to sort out."

"Never mind, James, it's all right." He tapped his glass against Bond's. "Cheers." Tanner knew damn well what was really on Bond's mind, but he had the tact not to mention it.

Two men entered the bar. Bond glanced up and grimaced. The taller of the men spotted Bond and Tanner and waved.

"Well, well!" he said. "If it isn't James Bond and Billy Tanner!"

"Roland Marquis," Bond said with feigned enthusiasm. "Long time."

Group Captain Roland Marquis was blond, broad-shouldered, and very handsome. A neatly trimmed blond mustache covered his upper lip. His eyes were a cold blue. He had the kind of weather-beaten face that suggested years of outdoor activity, and the square jaw of a matinee idol. He was the same age as Bond and just as fit.

He held out his hand as he approached their table. Marquis squeezed Bond's hand roughly, reminding 007 of their lifelong rivalry.

"How are you, Bond?" Marquis asked.

"Fine. Keeping busy."

"Really? I would have thought there's not a lot to do over at SIS these days, eh?" Marquis sniffed.

"We have plenty to do," Bond said with little humor. "Mostly cleaning up messes left by others. How about you? The RAF still treating you better than you deserve?"

Marquis laughed. "The RAF treats *me* like a bloody king."

The other man stepped up to the table. A man in his late thirties, he was smaller in stature, thin, and had glasses, a long nose, and bushy eyebrows, all of which gave him a birdlike appearance.

"This is my partner, Dr. Steven Harding," Marquis said. "He's with the Defence Evaluation and Research Agency. Dr. Harding, I present you James Bond and Bill Tanner. They work for the Ministry of Defence, in that gaudy building next to the Thames."

"SIS? Really? How do you do!" Harding held out his hand. Both men shook hands with him.

"Join us for a drink?" Tanner asked. "We're just waiting for our friends to make up the fourball."

Marquis and Harding pulled up chairs. "Bill, I haven't met your new chief," Marquis said. "What's she like?"

"She runs a very tight ship," Tanner replied. "Things are not that different since Sir Miles retired. What about you? I think the last time we spoke you were working at Oakhanger?"

"I've moved," Marquis said. "They've got me liaising with the DERA now. Dr. Harding here is one of their top engineers in the aeronautics division. Almost everything he does is classified."

"Well, you can tell *us*. We won't say a word," Bond said.

"You'll hear about it soon enough, I should think. Won't they, doctor?"

Harding was in the middle of taking a sip from a gin and tonic. "Hmmm? Oh, quite right. I must be sure to phone Tom after we play the front nine. We're almost there."

"Almost where? Marquis, what are you up to that you haven't told us?" Tanner asked.

"Actually we have told you," Marquis said with a broad grin. "Your chief knows all about it. Ever heard of Thomas Wood?"

"Sure," Bond said. "He's Britain's top aeronautics physicist."

At the mention of Wood's name, Tanner nodded his head. "You're right, I do know all about it, Marquis. I just didn't know that you were involved."

"It's my pet project, Tanner," he said smugly.

"Dr. Wood is my boss," Harding said.

Bond was impressed. To be working with a man of Wood's stature would require a considerable amount of gray matter. Harding must be smarter than he looked. In contrast, Bond had never thought much of Roland Marquis's brain or any other part of him. His great-grandfather, a Frenchman, had married into a wealthy English military family. The Marquis name was passed down from son to son, every one of them becoming a distinguished and decorated officer. Roland Marquis inherited his family's snobbishness and was, in Bond's estimation, an egotistical overachiever.

Ralph Pickering, the club's general manager, looked in the bar and spotted Bond. "Ah, there you are, Mr. Bond," he said. He stepped over to them and gave Bond and Tanner a message that their other two partners would not be joining them. "They said they had to go away on business unexpectedly and that you would understand. They send their apologies," he said.

"Thank you, Ralph," Bond said. He wasn't as annoyed with them for not showing up as he was with the fact that they had received orders and had probably left the country. Even after two weeks Bond was restless. He was ready to do anything to get out of London and away from Helena for awhile.

After Pickering left the room, Bond looked at Tanner and asked, "What do you want to do now? Play by ourselves?"

"Why not play with us?" Marquis asked. "I'm sure we could make it interesting. Dr. Harding and I against the two of you? Straight Stableford-level handicaps?"

Bond looked at Tanner. Tanner nodded in approval.

"I assume you're talking money?" Bond asked.

"You'd better believe it. How about two hundred and fifty pounds per man for every point by which the winners beat the losers?" Marquis suggested with a sly grin.

Tanner's eyes widened. That could be a lot of money. He didn't like gambling.

Nevertheless, the glove had been thrown. Bond took challenges *very* seriously and couldn't resist accepting it.

"All right, Roland," Bond said. "Let's meet at the starter's shed in, say, half an hour?"

"Splendid!" Marquis said, grinning widely. His straight white teeth sparkled. "We'll see you on the course, then! Come along, Dr. Harding." Harding smiled sheepishly, downed the rest of his drink, and got up with Marquis.

After they had left the bar, Tanner said, "My God, James, are you mad? Two hundred and fifty pounds a point?"

"I had to accept, Bill," Bond said. "Roland and I go way back."

"I knew that. You were at Eton together, right?"

"Yes, for the two years I was there we were bitter rivals. We often competed in the same athletic arenas. Whereas I left Eton and went to Fettes, Marquis went through Eton and Cranwell. As you know, he distinguished himself in the RAF and was rapidly promoted to his present rank."

"Didn't I read somewhere that he's a mountaineer?"

"That's right," Bond said. "He's actually quite famous in the world of mountain climbing. He made international headlines a few years ago after climbing the 'Seven Summits' in record time."

" 'Seven Summits'?"

"The highest peaks on each of the seven continents."

"Ah, right. So he's been up Everest, then?"

"More than once, I believe," Bond said. "I've run into him from time to time over the years. We still regard each other as rivals. I don't know why. It's extraordinary, really."

Tanner frowned and shook his head. "We're not going to have a boxing match out on the course, are we?"

"I'm afraid that whenever I'm thrust into a situation with Roland Marquis, it ends up that way. Cheers." Bond finished his bourbon and asked the bartender to put the drinks on his tab.

They went downstairs to the changing room. Bond put on a Mulberry golf shirt, gray sweater, and pleated navy slacks—his preferred attire for the golf course. He hung his Sea Island short-sleeve cotton shirt and khaki trousers inside a polished wooden locker and shut the door. Even the changing room was opulent, with paintings of Sir Edward Coke and Elizabeth I on the walls. Coke, one of the estate's more famous tenants, was the man who sentenced Guy Fawkes to death and often entertained the queen when she stayed at the manor house in 1601. Bond never took the splendor of Stoke Poges for granted.

"Do we want caddies?" Tanner asked.

Bond shook his head. "I don't. Do you?"

"I can use the exercise."

They walked through the corridors and an outdoor tunnel that smelled faintly of fertilizer. This led to the Pro Shop. Bond paused there long enough to purchase another set of Titleist balls with the number 3 imprinted on them, then followed Tanner outside to the beautiful course. Large, gnarled cedar redwood trees adorned the edges of the fairways. The freshly cut green grass was once prime grazing for deer, so the turf was very fine. It could hardly have been better for golf.

"They've really changed things in the past year," Tanner observed. "The fifteenth hole used to cross the main road here, didn't it?"

Nolan Edwards, who was standing nearby, answered, "That's right, sir. We actually had a couple of broken windscreens in the parking lot. We redesigned a few holes. It keeps the players on their toes."

Roland Marquis and Steven Harding were on the putting green.

Bond and Tanner retrieved their clubs and put them on trolleys. Bond had recently purchased the Callaways, which he felt were the most advanced golf clubs on the market. The set included BBX-12 regular flex graphite irons, which he had chosen because he could swing through the shot more easily with the regular flex than with the stiff-shafted clubs.

They all met at the first tee, and the game began at precisely 10:45 A.M. The sun was shining brightly behind them, although several dark clouds were moving around the sky. It was breezy and cool, which invigorated Bond. He took a moment to take in his surroundings, for he believed that in golf his human opponents were not his only adversaries. The course itself was the real enemy, and the only way to conquer it was to treat it with respect.

"Bond, I hope you brought your checkbook," Marquis said, sauntering up to the tee. Harding trailed behind him, struggling with his own trolley.

"I'm ready if you are, Roland," Bond said. He looked over at Tanner, who held two golf balls in his hand. Bond picked his Titleist 3, leaving Tanner with a Slazenger. Marquis and Harding were also using Titleist balls, with the numbers 5 and 1, respectively, marked on them.

After winning the toss, Bond was the first to tee off. He was currently delighted with the results he was getting off the tee with the Callaway firm-shafted War Bird driver. He found that a firm-shafted driver allowed him the maximum distance and, unlike many good players using firm-shafted equipment, Bond avoided hooking his drives with it.

The first hole was a gentle opening to a test of skill laid out by an acknowledged master of golf course design. It was a par 5 with a long fairway of 502 yards. Tricky cross bunkers lay 100 yards short of the green. Bond placed his ball on the tee, took his stance, concentrated, swung, and achieved an even follow-through. The ball sailed a good 225 yards to an impressive position just past the first tree on the right side of the fairway.

"Nice one, James," Tanner said.

Marquis was next. His drive didn't send the ball as far as Bond's, but it landed square in the center of the fairway. It gave him a slight advantage in that all he had to do from then on was hit the next shot to an easy lie around 100 yards out.

Tanner's drive was terrible. The ball overshot the fairway and flew into the trees on the right.

"Oh, damn," he muttered.

"Bad luck, Bill," Marquis said, obviously enjoying himself.

Harding was not much better. At least he hit the ball on the fairway, not much farther than 150 yards from the tee.

As Bond and Tanner walked together toward their balls, Tanner said, "I think the prospect of losing hundreds of pounds has got me a little edgy, James."

"Don't worry about it, Bill," Bond said. "The man's an insufferable boor. I shouldn't have accepted his wager, but it's done. If we lose, I'll take care of it."

"I can't let you do that."

"Just play your best, and we'll see what happens."

The par for the course was 72. Using the Stableford system, players received one point for a bogey, or one over par; two points for par; three points for a birdie, or one under par; four points for an eagle, or two under par; and five points for the rare albatross, which was three under par.

Bond put the ball on the green on his third stroke. If he could sink the putt in one more, then he'd have a birdie. Unfortunately, Marquis did the same and managed to put his ball three yards from the flag. Tanner's bad luck continued: On his third stroke he landed in one of the bunkers. Harding made it on to the green in four.

Marquis sunk his putt to get it out of Bond's way. Bond took the Odyssey putter from the bag and stood over his ball. It was 25 feet to the pin, so he had to give the ball a good, firm tap. His stroke sent the ball across the green, where it spun around the lip of the cup and stopped a foot away from the hole.

"Oh, bad luck, Bond," Marquis said.

At the end of the first hole Marquis had three points, Bond two, Harding two and Tanner one. At the end of the game Bond and

Tanner would combine their scores, as would Marquis and Harding. The team with the most points would, of course, win.

After the disastrous first hole, Tanner calmed down and began to play evenly. He made par on the next hole, as did the other three.

The third hole was a par 3 that Bond made in two. The other players all made par. As the four men walked over to the fourth tee, Marquis said, "Bond, do you remember the fight we had?"

Bond had never forgotten it. It had been at Eton after a grueling wrestling match in the gymnasium. The instructor, a friend of Marquis's parents, had pitted Bond against Marquis because it was well known that the two boys couldn't stand each other. Bond was obviously the better wrestler, but Marquis had surprised Bond with an illegal blow to the jaw. The instructor turned a blind eye, ultimately declaring Marquis the winner. After that a fistfight broke out.

"That was a long time ago," Bond said.

"Still smarting from that, eh?" Marquis taunted. "Just be thankful the headmaster came in to save your arse."

"I seem to remember that it was you he rescued," Bond replied.

"Isn't it funny how two grown men remember the same event differently?" Marquis slapped Bond on the back and gave a hearty laugh.

By the time they had played through five holes, the score was twenty-one to nineteen in favor of Marquis and Harding.

The sixth hole was a straight 412-yard par 4 with bunkers right and left at 195 and 225 yards from the tee. The green was uphill, small, and difficult to putt on because of its varied slopes.

Bond drove the ball 200 yards off the tee. Tanner followed suit, putting both balls in position for a straight shot over the bunkers and onto the green. When Bond made his second shot, he put the ball just in front of a center bunker about 100 yards from the green. It would be a perfect opportunity to try to back up the ball. He could hit it over the bunker, onto the green behind the pin, and hopefully put enough of a backspin on the ball to make it roll near the hole. He had to try it; otherwise making par would be extremely difficult.

When Bond's turn came, he removed the Lyconite 56-degree wedge from the bag and took a couple of practice swings.

"Come on, Bond," Marquis said patronizingly. "All you have to do is hit it over the bunker."

"Shhh, Roland," said Tanner. Marquis just grinned. He was getting cocky. Even Harding grimaced.

Bond swung and chopped the ball up and over the bunker. It fell just behind the pin but failed to roll toward the hole. Instead, it bounced forward off the green and into the rough.

"Oh, bad luck!" Marquis said with glee. Bond eventually took a bogey on the hole, while the others made par. Marquis and Harding maintained their lead.

While walking up the seventh fairway together, Tanner said to Bond, "Nice try."

"Bollocks," Bond said. "You know, I think it's taken me all these years to realize how intensely I dislike that man."

"Try not to let it affect your game, James," Tanner advised. "I agree with you, he's as obnoxious as hell."

"I can't hate him too much, though."

"Why not?"

Bond thought a moment before answering. "He's made of the same stuff as me," he said. "Roland Marquis, his personality faults notwithstanding, is good at what he does. You have to admit that he's a bloody fine player, and he's one hell of an athlete. His accomplishments in the RAF and in the mountains are impressive. He could just use some lessons in humility."

"I understand he's quite a ladies' man as well," Tanner mused.

"That's right. England's most eligible bachelor."

"Besides you."

Bond disregarded the quip. "He flaunts his dates with super-models, actresses, very wealthy widows, and divorcees. He's the sort of celebrity that bores me to tears."

"I'll bet you were rivals over a girl when you were younger," Tanner said perceptively.

"As a matter of fact, we were," Bond admitted. "He stole her right from under my nose. He engineered the entire seduction to get the better of me."

"What was her name?" Tanner said, smiling.

Bond looked at him and said with a straight face, "Felicity Mountjoy."

The chief of staff pursed his lips and nodded, as if that explained everything.

Bond got lucky on the ninth hole and made a birdie, while the other three all made par. Bond was one under par on the front nine and Tanner was two over. Marquis, however, was two under par and his partner was two over. The Stableford score was Marquis and Harding thirty-six, Bond and Tanner thirty-five.

They sat outside in back of the clubhouse to have a drink before playing the back nine. Bond ordered vodka, on the rocks, and set his gun-metal cigarette case on the table beside the glass. Tanner had a Guinness. The sound of bagpipes and drums was coming faintly over the trees from outside the chapel on the estate grounds.

"The Gurkhas are here," Tanner observed.

The Pipes and Drums marching band of the Royal Gurkha Rifles often played at Stoke Poges, for the Gurkha Memorial Garden was located near the course. Elite fighting men recruited from Nepal to serve with the British army since 1815, Gurkhas are considered to be among the fiercest and bravest soldiers on the planet.

"We're not far from Church Crookham." Bond said, referring to the regiment's home base.

Marquis and Harding joined them, each earning a pint.

"Vodka, Bond?" Marquis pointed. "That's right, I remember now. You're a vodka man. You like *martinis*." He pronounced the word with exaggerated erudition. "Vodka will dull your sense's, my boy."

"Not at all," Bond said. "I find it sharpens them." He opened the gunmetal case and removed one of the specially made cigarettes with the three distinctive gold bands.

"What kind of cigarettes are *those*?" Marquis asked.

"I have them custom made," Bond explained. Morland's and H. Simmons had gone out of business, so he now ordered his cigarettes directly from a company called Tor Importers, which specialized in Turkish and Balkan tobacco. His was a blend with low tar that he liked.

Marquis chuckled, "Well, let's try one then!"

Bond offered the case to him, and then the other men. Harding took one, but Tanner refused.

Marquis lit the cigarette and inhaled. He rolled the smoke around inside his mouth as if he were tasting wine. He exhaled and said, "Can't say I care for it much, Bond."

"It's probably too strong for your taste," Bond replied.

Marquis smiled and shook his head. "You always have a comeback, don't you, Bond?"

Bond ignored him and finished his drink, then put out the cigarette. He glanced up at the sky and said, "Those clouds don't look friendly. We had better get started."

The sun had completely vanished. Thunder rumbled lightly in the distance.

As Bond predicted, it started to rain on the thirteenth hole, but it wasn't heavy, and they continued to play. Apart from Marquis's birdie on the eleventh, everyone had made par on the first three holes of the back nine. With Marquis and Harding still in the lead, the game had become a contest of machismo between Bond and Marquis. The tension between them was palpable; it even made Tanner and Harding uncomfortable. The rain didn't help matters. Everyone but Marquis was in a foul mood when they approached the fourteenth tee.

The score remained constant after the fourteenth and fifteenth holes. Bond had to do something to better theirs. Hole sixteen had recently been redesigned. It was a par 4 at 320 yards. The old green had been tree-lined on both sides and protected by a bunker in front and a greenside bunker to the left. Now the green was farther back, closer to the small pond, so that an overshot would be a disaster. It was another opportunity for Bond to try his backspin. His tee-off sent the ball 210 yards straight down the fairway, where it landed in an excellent position. Marquis performed an equally impressive shot, dropping a mere six feet away from Bond's ball. Tanner and Harding did well enough, both driving their balls 175 yards onto the fairway. Bond approached the ball with the Lyconite wedge once again. If he could make this shot, he would narrow the gap between the scores.

The rain had subsided, so now the grass was wet and heavy. It made the task even more difficult.

"That little backspin might work for you this time, Bond," Marquis said. He perceived that Bond was about to try it again and simply wanted to rattle his nerves.

Bond paid no attention and concentrated on the ball. He shook his shoulders, rotated his head, and felt his neck crack, then took his stance over the ball. He was ready.

Tanner watched, biting his lower lip. Harding, who hadn't said more than twenty-five words all day, nervously chewed on a scoring pencil. Marquis stood with casual indifference, expecting Bond to muck it up.

Bond swung, snapped the ball into the air, and watched as it fell neatly on the back of the green. Would it roll off, away from the hole and into the pond? He held his breath.

The ball, propelled by a perfect backspin, rolled toward the hole and stopped an inch from the pin. If it weren't for the moisture on the green, the ball would have dropped in the cup.

Tanner and Harding both cheered. Marquis didn't say a word. His feathers ruffled, he knocked his ball straight into the bunker on the side of the green.

As they approached the eighteenth tee, the score was 70 to 69 in favor of Marquis and Harding. It was a par 4 at 406 yards. With a magnificent view of the mansion, the hole was uphill with bunkers on the right at 184 yards and out of bounds on the left from the tee. What made the hole extra difficult was the second shot, which had to go over a hollow just short of the green. The green was slightly elevated and bunkered on both sides, and it sloped from left to right.

Bond knocked the ball to a position nearly 180 yards from the green. Marquis made an identical shot, knocking his ball into Bond's and causing it to roll a few feet forward.

"Thanks, that's where I really wanted to be," Bond said.

"As the song goes, Bond, 'anything you can do, I can do better,' " Marquis said. He had meant to hit Bond's ball just to prove something.

All four men made par on the hole. After Harding sank the last

putt of the game, Tanner sighed heavily and looked at Bond. They
had lost the game with the score at 74 to 73. Now they had to come
up with five hundred pounds.

"Bad luck, Bond," Marquis said, holding out his hand.

Bond shook it and said, "You played a fine game."

Marquis shook Tanner's hand and said, "Bill, your game has improved
a great deal. I think you ought to have your handicap updated."

Tanner grunted and shook Harding's hand.

"Shall we meet back on the patio for drinks after changing?" Marquis suggested.

"Fine," Bond said. He and Tanner left their clubs at the starter
shed, went to the dressing room to shower and change clothes, and
emerged feeling fresher, if not altogether happy. Tanner hadn't said a
word to Bond since the game had ended.

"Bill, I know you're terribly upset with me. I'm sorry. I'll pay for it
all," Bond said as they took a seat at a table. The sun had, in inimitable English-weather fashion, reappeared.

"Don't be silly, James," Tanner said. "I'll pay my share. Don't worry
about it. I'll write you a check now and you can pay them in one
lump sum."

Tanner began writing the check and murmured, "Why the hell
does Marquis always call me by my Christian name, but he always
addresses you as Bond?"

"Because the man is a complete bastard who thinks he's a superior
being. I'm doing my best to swallow my pride and put this behind
me, but if he says 'bad luck' one more time, I'm going to punch him
in the nose."

Tanner nodded in agreement. "Too bad he's working with us, or I'd
kick him in the arse myself!"

"What is this top secret project, anyway?"

"James, it's classified. M and I are privy to it, but it's something that
the DERA have been working on for quite some time. I can tell you
more later, at the office. I had no idea Marquis was the RAF liaison
with the project."

"You've aroused my interest. Can you give me a hint?"

"Let's just say that when the project is completed, it will change the way wars are fought."

Right on cue, Marquis and Harding joined them.

"Excellent game, gentlemen," Marquis said. "I'm so glad we ran into you. It made the day so much more interesting."

Bond took out his checkbook. "Shall I make it out to you or to Dr. Harding?"

"Oh, to me, by all means. I want to watch you write my name on that check," said Marquis. He turned to Harding and said, "Don't worry doctor, I'll give you your share."

Harding smiled complacently. He gazed at Bond's check as a sparrow might eye a worm.

Bond tore out the check and handed it to Marquis. "Here you are, sir."

"Thank you, Bond," Marquis said, pocketing it. "You played admirably. Someday you just might be able to beat me."

Bond stood up and said, "That might give you an inferiority complex, Roland, and that would be so unlike you."

Marquis glared at Bond.

"Bill and I must be going," Bond said quickly. "It was good to see you again, Roland. Nice meeting you, Dr. Harding." He held out his hand to both of them. "Take care."

"Rushing off so soon?" Harding asked.

Tanner stood up, following Bond's lead. "Yes, I'm afraid he's right. We have to be back at Vauxhall before the end of the workday."

"Well, by all means, you've got to keep our precious country safe and sound," Marquis said with mock sincerity. "I'll sleep better tonight knowing you boys are on the watch."

After they said their good-byes, Bond and Tanner walked around the clubhouse to pick up their bags. As men who were quite used to winning or losing, they quickly put the loss of money and the game behind them.

Bond drove the old Aston Martin DB5 back to London, and instead of heading straight for Chelsea, went into West Kensington. The car had been kept in excellent condition, but Bond wanted something new. What he really had his eye on was the company's Jaguar XK8 that he had recently used in Greece. Sadly, it would probably be a while before Q Branch removed the "extras" and sold it as an ordinary secondhand car, as they had done with the DB5. He kept the Aston Martin in a garage in Chelsea along with the other dinosaur he owned, the Bentley Turbo R. His friend and American mechanic, Melvin Heckman, made sure that both cars were always in prime condition.

Helena Marksbury lived on the third floor of a block of flats near the Barons Court underground station. All day he had been glad to be away from her. Oddly, now he was starving for her.

Bond parked the car in front of her building, got out, and buzzed the intercom. It was just after four. He knew that she had been planning to leave the office early that day.

"Yes? Who is it?" Her voice, usually soft and seductive, sounded odd and metallic through the small speaker.

"It's me," he said.

There was a moment's hesitation, then the buzzer sounded.

Bond took the stairs two at a time and found her waiting in the doorway of her flat. Her hair was wet, and she was wearing one of his shirts and nothing else.

"I just got out of the shower," she said.

"Perfect," he said. "I'll dry you off."

"How did you know I left the office early today?"

"It was a hunch. I had a feeling that you were thinking about me," he said.

"Oh, really? Awfully sure of yourself, aren't you?"

"And I have a tension headache that needs some tender loving care."

She made a face, whispered "Tsk, tsk, tsk," and ran her fingers through his hair.

He took her by the waist and pulled her inside, closing the door behind them. Their mouths met as she hopped up and wrapped her smooth, bare legs around his waist. He carried her into the bedroom, where they spent the next two hours releasing the stress that had been dogging them both for the past two weeks.

THREE

SKIN 17

THE DEFENCE EVALUATION AND RESEARCH AGENCY RUNS, ON A COMMERCIAL basis, the research establishments that were formerly part of the Ministry of Defence Procurement Executive. With locations scattered around the UK—both public and private—the DERA is, in part, responsible for research in aerodynamics and materials used to build aircraft for the RAF. One of their larger facilities is located in Farnborough, southwest of London, at the former Royal Aircraft Establishment and home of the Farnborough air show. While most of the DERAs work is done at such official sites, which are guarded by heavy security, a few laboratories and offices are located in seemingly innocuous, unmarked buildings. Some of the agency's most sensitive and classified secrets are generated at these locations as a preventive measure, should there ever be any industrial espionage attempts against the DERA.

Not far from Farnborough is the small village of Fleet, a quiet residential community surrounded by warehouses and industrial complexes of neighboring towns. It has a railway station used daily by commuters to and from London. Its convenience to both London and Farnborough was one of the reasons the DERA hid their most secret and important project in a warehouse that appeared to be unused.

The exterior had been treated to look old. Windows were

boarded and posted signs read NO TRESPASSING. All doors were locked. It was always dark and quiet. As the warehouse was off one of the main roads, the residents of Fleet took no notice of a building that one day looked much older and decrepit than it really was. In actuality, the building contained a secret entrance, a 20-foot-by-500-foot wind tunnel, foundry equipment, a sealed pressure vessel called an autoclave, and the offices and laboratory of a small research team headed by the noted aeronautics physicist and engineer Dr. Thomas Wood.

Two years previously, the DERA had hired Dr. Wood away from Oxford to work on a classified assignment. He was an expert in ceramics, especially when it came to designing "smart skins" for aircraft fuselages.

Wood was fifty-three, a warm and intelligent man with a family. He loved his new job, for he found "government work" exciting. He had missed out on military service because of a heart murmur and other indications of an unstable condition. An insensitive army doctor had told him that he wouldn't live to see forty. He had fooled them all. Even though he was overweight, he felt great and was enthusiastic about the project. If tonight's tests on the 1\8-scale prototype were positive, and Skin 17 was indeed a success, he might be on his way to a Nobel Prize.

Skin 15 had almost worked. There were some minor flaws. The scalable autoclaved material showed possible defects in the built-in photo electrolysis that served to change the skin's resistance to abuse. The impedence sensitivity was weak. When his assistant, Dr. Steven Harding, suggested that they keep trying, Wood concurred. That had been three months ago. What they thought would be a week's tinkering resulted in a major overhaul, and out of the ashes rose Skin 16.

Wood considered that particular version of the formula to be his most brilliant creation. The team had almost declared themselves victorious; but the prototype skin failed one of several key tests. Despite the material's radio frequency transparency, one sensor was unable to transmit and receive through an aperture. There were glitches, but they were closer than ever to the goal. The biggest hurdle was always how scalable the material could be so that prototype models might be built and tested in extreme conditions. Another month's work perfected Skin 16 to Dr. Wood's satisfaction. Today he was to see the results of the tests conducted on Skin 17's prototype. If it worked, the carbon-fiber and silica ceramic that he and his small team had developed could change the world of aviation forever.

An admitted eccentric, Wood gave his team the day off so that he could work alone. He had, however, asked his second in command, Dr. Harding, to come in that evening.

Wood sat at a computer terminal, punching in data at a furious speed. Harding watched him from across the room near the autoclave, which contained a prototype of Skin 17.

"You didn't say how your golf game was," Wood remarked, still typing.

"It was lovely. We won," Harding said. "I actually made a little money."

"Splendid!" Wood said. "I hope you didn't mind me kicking you out today. I just needed to work on these figures alone. You understand, don't you, Steven?"

"Of course, Tom," Harding said. "Don't worry about it. I thoroughly enjoyed myself! Except for the bit of rain we got, it was a lovely day. I must admit that I found it difficult to concentrate on the golf. I kept thinking that you might finish it today."

"Well, Steven," Wood said as he clicked a button to execute a program that he had written himself, then sat back with his arms folded. "We'll know in a few minutes, won't we?"

Harding nervously tapped his fingers on the oval-shaped autoclave that looked like a pressure chamber used by divers. "The waiting is dreadful! I must say, this is very exciting." He looked at his watch intently. The physicist's birdlike qualities always seemed more pronounced when he was agitated or tense. His hair tended to stand up, and he involuntarily made jerking movements with his head. Wood presumed that Harding had some kind of tic.

"Staring at the minute hand on your watch will only make the time seem slower," Wood said, laughing. "It's hard to believe it's been two years since we started."

Harding got out of his seat, stepped over to Wood, and looked over his shoulder. They watched the figures appear on the monitor at an alarming rate.

"Steven, go over to the Mac and punch up the juice," Wood ordered.

Harding adjusted the level of temperature in the autoclave's chamber.

No one said anything for ten minutes as the printer began spewing out a long stream of perforated paper. It was filled with equations, letters, numbers, and symbols.

Skin 17.

When it was done, Wood peered at his monitor and a smile played on his lips. He took a deep breath, then swiveled around and faced his assistant.

"Dr. Harding, Skin 17 is a success. It's passed every test."

Harding beamed and said, "Congratulations! My God, this is bloody marvelous! I knew it, Tom, I knew you'd do it." He clasped Wood's shoulder.

"Oh, come now," Wood said. "You and the others were a tremendous help, and so were the boys at Farnborough. I didn't do it all alone."

"But it's in your contract that you get the credit," Harding reminded him.

"Well, there *is* that!" Wood laughed. "Shall we have some wine? I think there's still some in the refrigerator. Now I'm sorry I sent everyone home today. I feel our entire team should have been here."

"We were all grateful for the holiday, Tom. Jenny and Carol were both going away for the weekend, and Spencer and John had family coming to London. But they'll hear about it soon enough."

Wood got up from the desk and started to walk toward the kitchen.

"Shouldn't we save it to disk?" Harding asked.

"You're right," Wood said. "I'll burn a disk. It'll be the gold master."

Wood placed a blank compact disk into the recorder and punched the computer keypad. The entire Skin 17 formula was saved on the disk. He removed the disk and placed it in an unmarked jewel box. Wood found a red marker on the desk and wrote "Skin 17 Gold Master" on the cover.

"I better put this in the safe so it won't get lost," Wood said. "I'll make some more copies later."

"Nonsense, Tom, go and get the wine!" Harding said, laughing. "There's no one else here! Put it in the safe later."

Wood felt foolish for a few seconds, then his better judgment took over. "No, I'll just put it in quickly," he said.

He walked to a twenty-four-inch safe embedded in a wall and carefully turned the combination knob. The door swung open and Wood placed the jewel box inside.

"Now, about that wine," Wood said, closing the safe and starting to move toward the kitchen again. He was stopped by the front office buzzer. Wood looked at Harding with a furrowed brow.

"Who in hell could that be?"

Harding punched the intercom and said, "Yes?"

A voice announced, "It's Marquis. Code Clearance 1999 Skin."

Wood was surprised. "He didn't say he was coming by tonight. What does he want?"

"Shall I not let him in?" Harding asked.

"No, no, let him in. He's the messenger boy from our employers, you know," Wood said. "I just didn't want to have to share our victory with him tonight, that's all. I find him rather rude."

Harding pushed the button and a portion of the building's back wall opened just enough for a man to slip through. A passage led through a vacant ground floor that had been treated with dust and cobwebs, then up a flight of stairs to a false wall. By slightly rotating an electrical fixture hung there, a visitor could open the wall and get inside the DERA laboratory. Marquis had been there several times, so he knew the way. In a few moments Harding got up and went to the lab door to let their visitor in.

Group Captain Marquis was dressed in full uniform and was carrying a small black box. He was a physically imposing man in his own right—but when he wore his RAF uniform, he always commanded attention. The epitome of a disciplined British officer, he looked sharp, stern, and efficient.

"Good evening, gentlemen," he said. "Sorry to barge in on you like this, but I have new orders. I'll explain after you tell me about your test results, Dr. Wood."

"New orders?" Wood asked. "What do you mean? How did you know we were testing tonight?" He looked at Harding.

Harding's beady eyes widened as he shook his head.

"Dr. Harding didn't tell me," Marquis said. "I knew. It's my job." He placed the black box on a counter.

Wood looked uncertain. Marquis had visited the office a few times over the last year, but it was always during the day and with a specific administrative agenda.

"All right," he said, "but I find this highly irregular."

"Dr. Wood, you're among friends," Marquis said. "I, too, have an emotional investment in the success of your project—*our* project."

"You're right," Wood said, relaxing a little. "Steven, why don't you tell our friend what we've just learned."

Marquis looked at Harding, who grinned and said, "We did it. Tom did it. Skin 17 is a success."

"Unbelievable!" Marquis said. "Well done, Dr. Wood! This calls for a celebration," Marquis said. "Where's that wine you said you had?"

Wood pointed to the kitchen. "It's in the—" He stopped abruptly and looked at Marquis. "How did you know I said anything about wine?"

Marquis reached into his jacket with his right hand and pulled out a 9mm Browning Hi-Power pistol. He revealed a small black rectangular object with a short antenna in his left hand.

"I heard you, of course," he said. "This is a two-channel UHF receiver. And the transmitter is over there in Dr. Harding's wristwatch. I was right outside the building all the time, listening to your conversation. I only had to wait for my cue. Dr. Harding was certain you would strike gold tonight, and you did."

Wood looked at Harding, but the traitor couldn't look his colleague in the eyes.

"I don't understand," Wood said. "What's going on? Steven?"

"I'm sorry, Tom," Harding said.

Before Wood could move, Marquis shot him in the right thigh. Wood screamed and fell to the ground. Howling in pain, he writhed and squirmed on the wood floor. Blood poured from a huge hole in his leg.

Marquis calmly stood over Wood and said, "Mmmm, bad luck, eh, doctor? Now, about those new orders. Dr. Harding is to take the formula for Skin 17 and see that there are no copies left. I'm to make sure he does." He handed the gun to Harding. "He's all yours."

Harding squatted down to Wood. He waved the gun barrel at his colleague's head and said, "I'm sorry, Tom, but you have to give me the combination to the safe. I need that disk."

Wood was in agony, but he managed to spit out, "You . . . traitor!"

"Come, come," Harding said. "Let's not be like that. I'll make sure you still get the credit for developing Skin 17. It's just not going to be Great Britain that uses it first."

"Go to hell," Wood cried.

Harding sighed, then stood up. He held on to the edge of a counter for leverage, then placed his shoe on Wood's wounded thigh.

"The combination, Tom?" he asked one more time.

Wood glared at Harding but said nothing. Harding thrust all his weight onto the physicist's leg. Wood screamed horribly.

"Yes, yes, go ahead and scream," Harding said. "No one can hear you. The warehouse is closed, it's night, the street is deserted. We can go on for hours like this, but I'm sure you'd rather not." He continued to apply pressure to the wound.

Marquis stood idly by, examining the computer monitor and trying to make sense of the hieroglyphics displayed on the screen.

Two minutes later Harding had the answer he wanted. Wood curled up in the fetal position on the floor, sobbing. Harding wiped the blood from his shoe on Wood's trousers, then went to the safe. Using the combination Wood had given him, Harding had it open in seconds. He removed the Skin 17 master disk and all the backup copies of the previous versions of the specification. He placed everything except the master disk into a plastic bag, then went to the physicist's desk and rummaged for specific file folders. He found what he was looking for, took the new printout, and stuffed all of it into the bag as well.

"Make sure there are no copies of *anything*," Marquis said.

Harding went back to Wood and knelt beside him. "Tom, we have to make sure there are no traces of the formula left. Now, tell me. Do you have any copies at home? Where are the backups?"

"All the backups . . . are with the DERA . . ." Wood gasped.

Harding looked at Marquis. Marquis nodded and said, "Yes, I already got those. They've been destroyed."

"Nothing at your house?" Harding asked again.

Wood shook his head. "Please . . ." he muttered. "I need a doctor. . . ."

"I'm afraid it's too late for that, Tom," Harding said. He stood up and walked away to his own desk. He began to pack, placing personal items and other file folders that he might need in a brown attaché case. Wood began to moan loudly.

After a few minutes Marquis said, "Oh, for God's sake, Harding! Don't leave him like that!"

Harding stopped what he was doing and looked at Wood. The traitor nodded grimly, then stepped over to Wood and pointed the gun at his head.

"Thanks for all your hard work, Dr. Wood," Harding said. He fired once, and the moaning ceased. He then set down the gun on a counter and extracted a long, thin dagger from his attaché case. Harding squatted down, trying his best not to get blood on his clothes, grabbed Wood's hair, and pulled back his head to expose his neck. Harding positioned the blade against the dead man's skin as Marquis said, "Oh, *must* you do that?"

Harding replied, "It's our way. I know it seems rather superfluous at this point, but I have my orders, too." He swiftly slit Wood's throat from ear to ear. The deed done, he dropped the man's head and stepped away with a disgusted look on his face. Harding wiped the dagger on Woods trousers and put it away, then picked up Marquis's gun and gave it back to him.

Marquis holstered the pistol and said, "Doctor, make sure you delete all the files from that hard drive. Give me the master disk."

Harding handed him the disk and began to work on the computer. Marquis opened the black box he had brought with him. It was a peculiar but efficient device with a laptop computer, CD-ROM drive, microdot camera, and developer. He inserted the disk into the machine, adjusted tiny knobs, and closed the cover. He pressed a button and copied the disk's files onto the hard drive. Marquis punched in more commands, then carefully removed a glass slide from the edge of the developer. He placed it in a tray and maneuvered a magnifier over the slide. A tiny microdot, produced on positive-type film and practically invisible to the naked eye, was now on the glass. Marquis took a piece of thin, transparent film from the black box and pressed it smoothly over the glass slide. The microdot was transferred from the slide to the film. Marquis placed the film in a small plastic envelope and sealed it. He then removed the Skin 17 master disk from the machine, dropped it on the floor, and crushed it with his heel.

The next thing Marquis did struck Harding as strange. He opened the autoclave and removed the Skin 17 prototype—a small piece of rubberlike material stretched on a specimen tray. He placed it inside the jacket pocket on Wood's body.

"There," Marquis said. "The only existing record of Skin 17 is now on this microdot. Take good care of it."

He handed the envelope to Harding, who took it and said, "Right, this hard drive is blank." Harding put the envelope in his attaché case. "I'll get the petrol." He went out of the lab, down the stairs, and into a storage closet in back of the office space, where he had left two five-gallon cans of petrol. He carried them back up to the lab, opened one, and began pouring the petrol all over the floor and furniture. Marquis had placed the plastic bag full of the backup copies and printouts on the floor next to Wood.

"Make sure you get the computers and the autoclave," Marquis said, taking the other can, and he poured petrol over the other side of the room. He made sure the body and the prototype were completely covered. The smell was overpowering, but the traitors continued until the containers were almost empty.

Marquis grabbed the black box and Harding took the attaché case. They backed down the stairs, pouring petrol as they went. They made their way to the lower, vacant level, through the darkness to the exit, where they dropped the empty cans. Harding punched in the code that opened the trick door and held it open. Marquis paused long enough to remove a handkerchief from his pocket and set it on fire with a lighter. He calmly tossed it onto the floor behind him. The petrol immediately ignited and the flames spread quickly.

The two men shut the door behind them and walked to a BMW 750 that was parked twenty yards away from the building. Marquis got behind the wheel and they drove toward London. No one saw them.

Firefighters were alerted to the emergency within five minutes, but by then it was too late. The flames had spread into the laboratory, where the concentration of petrol was most intense. The building became a fireball. The firefighters did everything they could, but it was no use. Within fifteen minutes the secret DERA facility in Fleet was completely destroyed.

In the BMW, Harding reached for a mobile phone. "I need to call my headquarters," he said.

Marquis put a hand on his arm. "Not on my mobile. Use a pay phone at the station."

Marquis dropped Harding off in front of Waterloo Station. Harding took the attaché case and a bag that was already in the trunk. He had already purchased a ticket on the last Eurostar of the day to Brussels. Before boarding the train, he entered a phone booth and called a number in Morocco.

As he waited for someone to pick up, he thought about how much money Skin 17 was going to make for him. The plan had gone smoothly so far.

After several pips, a man finally answered. "Yes?"

"Mongoose calling from London. Phase One complete. I have it. Commencing Phase Two."

"Very good. I'll relay the message. You have a reservation at the Hôtel Métropole in the name of Donald Peters."

"Right."

The man hung up. Harding sat for a few seconds, tapping his fingers on the attaché case. Then he picked up the phone again, put in some coins, and made one more call before getting on the train.

The number he dialed was a private line at SIS headquarters.

EMERGENCY

JAMES BOND WALKED BRISKLY PAST HELENA MARKSBURY'S DESK ON THE WAY to his office. Usually she greeted him with a warm smile in the mornings, but today she swiveled her chair around so that her back was to him. He was sure she had heard him coming. Bond thought that their unscheduled coupling yesterday after the golf game had perhaps confused and upset her.

"It was my understanding that we were supposed to 'cool it' while we're in London," she had said. He reiterated that indeed they should do so, but he also convinced her that she was just as hungry for him as he was for her. In the privacy of her flat, what harm could be done? They had thrown caution to the wind and allowed their passion to overwhelm them.

Afterward, however, Bond brought up the subject of their relationship again. Feelings were hurt, emotions were frayed, and this time it ended in a terrible fight. Helena accused him of "taking what he wanted, when he wanted," and he admitted that there was some truth to that. She called him a "selfish bastard."

He knew then that their affair had to end, especially if he wanted to keep her in place as his personal assistant at MI6.

"Do you want to continue working for me?" he had asked her.

"Yes, of course," she replied.

"Then you know as well as I that we can't keep doing this."

"You're the one who surprised me at my door."

He couldn't argue with that. He had been a bloody fool. He had let his loins do his thinking for him once again.

They had agreed to end their romantic involvement—again—and, with tears in her eyes, she had sent him packing. Now he only hoped that they could get past it and that things at the office would be normal again, if such a thing was possible, without anyone losing their job.

He closed the door to his office and found a notice from Records indicating that the updated file on the Union was ready for his review. It was the information he had been waiting for. At least that would kill some time.

Bond sat down at his desk, took a cigarette from his gunmetal case, and lit it. Dammit all, he thought. How could he have been so bloody stupid? He should have realized that she was becoming more emotionally involved in the relationship than he wanted her to be. She would just have to get over it.

Lost in thought, he sat in the quiet solitude of his office and finished his cigarette.

One of the many improvements M made after she took charge was in the area of information technology. Old Sir Miles Messervy had been completely computer illiterate and hardly ever approved funding to update technology at MI6. Barbara Mawdsley, the new M, was all for it. The most controversial thing she did during her first year in office was to spend nearly a half million pounds to upgrade the computer equipment and network systems. Part of this money went to Records, where a state-of-the-art multimedia center was developed and built. The "Visual Library," as it was called, was a computerized encyclopedia on a grand scale. One merely had to punch in a topic and the Visual Library would find every file available on the subject and organize it into a cohesive multimedia presentation. A full-time staff maintained the various sound, photo, video, and music files so that information was constantly kept up-to-date. Hard copies of the text could be printed and distributed as well, but it was infinitely more instructive when one could sit and view information in much the same way as one watched television.

Bond thought it would be appalling, until he saw the Library in action. It was an impressive feat of design and engineering. Now he enjoyed locking himself in one of the cubicles, putting on the headset, and watching the large wall-sized monitor in front of him. All he had to do was type the commands on a keypad and watch. He didn't have to take notes; a "memo" button on the keypad automatically saved any particular segment and printed it.

After getting a cup of SIS's mediocre coffee, he made himself comfortable in one of the Visual Library booths and punched in the code for the new file on the Union. The lights dimmed as he put on the headset.

Using a mouse, Bond clicked on the "intro" main menu button. The presentation began much like a newsreel of old. There was a bit of military music, a quick series of logos and credits, and the show began.

A familiar male narrator from the BBC began to speak over a montage of famous terrorist scenes from history: Nazis with concentration camp prisoners; the American embassy crisis in Iran; a hooded man holding a gun to an airline pilot's head; the Ku Klux Klan; and Ernst Stavro Blofeld.

"Terrorists have been with us since the dawn of man. When we think of terrorists, we imagine groups of men and women who will do anything for a cause. They almost always have a political agenda and perform acts of violence to further their aims. But there is another kind of terrorist that has been cropping up more and more in the past thirty years. We have seen the rise of nonpolitical, commercial terrorists, or, to put it another way, terrorists who are in it only for the money. The difference between a political terrorist and a commercial one is important in our analysis, for the reasons that motivate these individuals are the keys to understanding them. Whereas a political terrorist may be willing to die for what he believes, a commercial one may not be so inclined. Usually very intelligent, the commercial terrorist will weigh situations as they occur and decide whether it's worth continuing in his present course of action."

Shots of large amounts of money; hunters in the wild; a soldier walking alone in a jungle . . .

"However, the lure of big money is a powerful enough temptation for the commercial terrorist to take a risk. If this enticement is combined with certain psychological factors in specific individuals, they may be persuaded to do *anything*. We believe these people possess an inherent desire for high adventure, danger, and excitement. Profit is the primary reason for their actions, but they also have a strong desire to do something that 'normal' people don't do. This makes the commercial terrorist totally unpredictable, and, therefore, extremely dangerous. The Union are the most recent group of commercial terrorists to come to the attention of SIS and other law enforcement agencies around the world. They are not the first nor will they be the last. But at the moment they could very well be the most influential."

Bond stilled a laugh. The report had been rushed. The narration was terribly clichéd, but it was the truth. He clicked on the "history" button.

"They began innocently enough." A *Hired Gun* magazine appeared on the monitor. Inside was an advertisement showing a smiling man dressed in fatigues and holding a rifle. " 'Come join the Union and be a mercenary! See the world! Earn top dollar!' These words appeared three years ago in magazines such as this one. The advertisements were printed in publications in the United States, most western European countries, the former Soviet Union, and throughout the Middle East. The union were the brainchild of an American named Taylor Michael Harris, an ex-Marine who worked as a security guard in the state of Oregon."

Taylor Harris's mug shot filled the screen. He had a shaved head and a swastika tattooed on his forehead. "In early 1995, at age thirty-six, Harris founded a small militia group who proclaimed themselves white supremacists. After the local authorities arrested several of his members during a rally that turned violent, he was run out of the state. Harris traveled to Europe and the Middle East, then came back to Oregon with a large amount of capital six months later. He had apparently gone into business with foreign investors located either in the Middle East or North Africa. With this funding, he created the Union, which certain specialist magazines touted to be a freelance mercenary outfit. Qualified men with proper military training could get a high-paying job with the Union—as long as they were willing to travel, be discreet, and show that they had the stuff. The 'stuff,' it turned out, was having the ability to commit murder, arson, burglary, kidnapping, and other serious crimes."

The visuals changed to a grainy black and white film of men in fatigues doing push-ups on a field, running around a track, shadow boxing. . . . "The ad campaign lasted six months, and men from all over the world joined the Union. This film of early trainees was confiscated during a raid, on the Union's Oregon headquarters in December 1996. The American authorities became aware of their activities after Taylor Harris was gunned down in a restaurant in Portland, Oregon, a month earlier."

The screens filled with police photographs of Taylor Harris, lying on the floor in a pool of blood and spaghetti.

"It is believed that Harris was murdered by his lieutenants, all of whom fled the country. Prior to this incident, no Union 'jobs' had ever been reported. Recruiting advertisements disappeared after the raid, and it appeared that the Union had been only a crazy whim of a deranged ex-Marine."

Maps of the world popped up on the screen. "The truth became clear in 1997 as evidence began to surface that former Union members were involved in terrorist-style operations. It is believed that unknown foreigners now control the Union, and that they are managed as an underground, networked organization. Recruitment occurs only by word of mouth. SIS is convinced that the Union already have a strong base of tough, talented men. To date, this group of criminals and mercenaries have struck around the world half a dozen times. Besides hiring themselves out to countries and governments, members often initiate their own projects in the hope that they might prove to be profitable later."

The camera focused on the Mediterranean. "The Union are a rapidly growing network of tough professionals, and it is believed that they are coordinated from somewhere in the Mediterranean region. It is estimated that there may be as many as three hundred Union members worldwide."

A man's silhouette was superimposed over the map, and a big question mark hung over his head. "The Union boss is thought to be a businessman, very wealthy and very powerful. Likely suspects are Taylor Harris's three lieutenants, all of whom fled the United States after his murder and are wanted for that crime. They are"—the monitor lingered on mug shots of the three men—"Samuel Loggins Anderson, age thirty-five, ex-Marine and former insurance salesman." He was bald, had long sideburns and crooked teeth.

"James 'Jimmy' Wayne Powers, age thirty-three, former National Guardsman who spent time in jail for armed robbery." He was thin, and had large dark eyes and black hair.

"And Julius Stanley Wilcox, age thirty-six, another ex-Marine and former forest ranger." Wilcox was the ugliest and meanest-looking, with a scar above his right eye, a hawk nose, and greasy, slicked-back gray hair.

"None of these three men has been seen since they left the United States."

A flowchart appeared on the monitor. "Like the Mafia, the Union are run by a manager or president whom they call *Le Gérant*. Beneath him are three or four trusted lieutenants—all men high in hierarchy who each control a vast worldwide network of murderers, arsonists, safe-crackers, loan sharks, prostitutes, mercenaries, and blackmailers."

Bond clicked on the "projects" button.

Another mug shot flashed on the screen. He was a small man with fear in his eyes. "This is Abraham Charles Duvall. He was arrested in Washington, D.C., after the armed robbery of the Georgetown Savings and Loan in April 1997. He kept telling authorities that he was 'Union,' and that he would never go to jail. An 'uncle' posted bail, and Duvall was never seen again. Washington, D.C., police later received a notice from individuals claiming responsibility for the robbery. They called themselves 'the Union.' "

The image on the monitor changed to that of a newspaper front page. The photograph below the headline featured American soldiers carrying a wounded man on a stretcher. "Rumors that the Union was a real organization were not taken seriously by Interpol until a car bomb killed several American soldiers in Saudi Arabia in mid-1997. What was first dismissed as a political attack on the West was later revealed to be the work of a group of individuals hired by the Libyan government. Four suspects were killed when authorities attempted to arrest them. They put up a fierce fight, and one of the dying men had this to say—"

Low-quality video footage showed an Arab in fatigues lying in the dusty street of a North African village. A medic was tending to his wounds, which appeared to be massive. The cameraman asked the man something unintelligible, but the Arab's answer was quite clear: "I am proud to die for the Union."

"Even though some members have been arrested, thus far the Union have been successful at every crime they have committed and claimed responsibility for. The world's law enforcement agencies now take the Union very seriously. It appears that they have an uncanny ability to infiltrate legitimate intelligence organizations. One of the Union's most notorious achievements was recruiting a mole in the Central Intelligence Agency."

A mug shot of a man with glasses and a pockmarked face flashed on the screen. "Norman Nicholas Kalway, a midlevel official at the CIA, was caught red-handed with classified documents. It was learned that he had provided over ten million dollars' worth of data to the Union. His story was that he had been blackmailed by the organization with evidence of unusual and felonious sexual practices (all of which came out publicly after Kalway was caught). Whether the CIA agent was a victim or not, his case is indicative of the lengths that the Union will go to in order to ensnare workers."

Another mug shot replaced Kalway's, an attractive woman in her twenties, except that she had bruises on her face and hate in her eyes.

"The Mossad experienced a similar scandal when one of their agents, Katherine Laven, was found to be Union after she had poisoned her lover, Israeli cabinet member Eliahu Digar. Digar had a number of enemies, any one of whom might have tempted agent Laven with a large payoff to get rid of him. It was this case that alerted authorities to what has been called the Union's 'signature' when it comes to assassinations. Apparently poisoning Mr. Digar wasn't enough. After he had died, Miss Laven slit the man's throat from ear to ear with an extremely sharp instrument. Other murders in which the victims' throats were cut in this manner have been reported as being Union-related."

Bond was familiar with all of the Union's alleged cases. He clicked back to the "projects" menu and clicked on the most recent addition. The picture changed again to that of Bond's friend.

"The latest notch on the Union's board is the March 1999 assassination of the former governor of the Bahamas."

The photo was replaced by one of the Bahamian man who had cut the governor's throat. "Lawrence Littleby, aged twenty-seven, was responsible for the murder. He was a troublemaker who had been in and out of the local jails on various misdemeanors. He had most likely been approached with the lure of a sizable amount of money. Investigators found ten thousand U.S. dollars hidden in the man's bedroom."

Bond clicked out of "projects" and clicked on the "exit" button.

The visuals became a full-motion montage of newspaper headlines, news photos, and newsreel footage of soldiers in various forms of combat. "We believe that the Union have become more powerful in the last year. When they cannot buy someone's services, they find other, less pleasant means to persuade them to work. They are experts at everything from petty street crime to elaborate espionage schemes. It cannot be stressed enough that the Union should never be underestimated and that they should always be considered extremely dangerous."

The presentation ended. Bond thought of his old enemies, SPECTRE. They were a lot like the Union. They had been interested

only in making money, and Ernst Stavro Blofeld had run the cabal
with the efficiency of a corporation. The Union were different in that
their tactics were more guerrilla oriented. SPECTRE had gone for
grand, world-shaking events. The Union weren't particular in the jobs
they performed. There was no social status or class prejudices in the
Union. It was one of the keys to their success in recruiting members.

The phone by the keypad buzzed. Bond picked it up. "Yes?"

It was Miss Moneypenny. "James, I thought you were in there.
You're wanted in the Briefing Room at eleven hundred sharp." Bond
glanced at his watch. It was 10:50.

"Nothing like twenty-four hours' notice, Penny," he said.

"Never mind that. This is serious. Some big brass will be sitting in.
See you there." She rang off and left Bond to ponder the empty, dark
monitor in front of him. He sighed heavily, gathered his materials,
punched the keypad so that a complete printout of the Union presentation would be delivered to his office, then left the Visual Library
and took the lift to the top floor.

The place was buzzing with activity. Secretaries were rushing back
and forth and phones were ringing. Bond caught up with Miss Moneypenny, who was walking fast and carrying a stack of folders toward
the briefing room.

"What the hell is going on?" Bond asked.

"M declared a Code Three a few minutes ago, James. You had
better get in there. The Minister of Defence and a lot of military brass
are here."

"Someone probably lost a contact lens," Bond muttered, and went
into the room.

The Briefing Room could easily sit a hundred people or more. Similar to the Situation Room, it contained large screens on the walls for
multimedia presentations, rows of school-type chairs with attached
desktops arranged in a semicircle facing the podium, and an abundance of electronic equipment. Bond eased into the room and found
a place near the end of a row of chairs. Looking around, he was surprised to see some of the people there.

M was quietly conversing with the Minister of Defence near the podium. Bill Tanner was standing by, awaiting instructions. Occupying the other chairs were various top staff members such, as Head of S., Head of Records, and Head of Counterintelligence. There were several visitors next to them, including Air Marshal Whipple, the head of MI5, and none other than Group Captain Roland Marquis.

Tanner called the meeting to order. "Ladies and gentlemen, the Minister of Defence wishes to address you first."

The Minister took the stand and cleared his throat. "Last night an act of industrial espionage and terrorism was committed against our country. A top secret formula for a hot plasma bonding process known as Skin 17 was stolen from one of the DERA's secret research facilities in Fleet. It is of vital importance to Great Britain that we track down the individuals responsible for this and retrieve the formula. Christopher Drake, a director of the DERA, will explain further."

The Minister relinquished the floor to Mr. Drake, a tall, distinguished man of fifty.

"Good morning. I've been asked to explain in layman's terms what we at the DERA were developing for the RAF. It has been a longtime goal for the UK to be the first country in the world to develop an aircraft material that could withstand a speed of Mach 7. An as-yet-unattainable speed, Mach 7 is the Holy Grail in the aerospace industry. Now, we all know that the technology has existed for years to create the power to push a plane to that speed, and the materials exist to build an airplane. Think of it. The benefits to both civil and especially military aviation are self-evident. One could fly from London to New York in forty minutes—or bomb three countries in a half hour. Two years ago the Minister of Defence ordered us, along with the RAF, to develop a material that could stand up to the wear and tear that would occur at a speed of Mach 7.

"The problem has always been that at such a high speed mere atmospheric dust is sufficient to dent and tear the skin off the plane. The way around this dilemma is found in the science of fluid dynamics. An object traveling through a fluid creates around itself a boundary layer which essentially pushes the elements of the fluid out of the way, creating a 'tunnel effect.' It's through this tunnel that the object travels relatively unimpeded. Turbulence issues abound in this science; the mathematics are extremely complicated; the engineering problems are bigger. The trick is to create 'Smart Skin' materials for the plane that would expand and alter this boundary layer, essentially forming the optimal aerodynamic configuration through which the plane would fly. This material would be a carbon-fiber and silica ceramic. But because carbon-fiber and silica do not easily bond, the DERA spent two years developing a hot plasma bonding process."

Slides began to appear on the large screens. The first was a photo of Dr. Wood.

"Yesterday Dr. Thomas Wood, whom we hired to work on the project at our secret warehouse in Fleet, successfully completed the formula— or so we believe. The DERA and the British military establishment have kept this project top secret and we were quite eager to unveil the results—giving the UK a much-needed leg up, strategically speaking, over our allies and enemies. Commercially, it is worth billions."

The slide changed to an exterior shot of the Fleet warehouse.

"Shortly after twenty-one hundred hours last night, someone infiltrated the lab in Fleet. The entire facility was burned to the ground. Records were destroyed and there was virtually nothing salvageable. We did unfortunately find the remains of Dr. Wood, who had been shot in the leg and in the head. All traces of Skin 17, the specification he created, have disappeared. The thieves were also successful in stealing backup copies of previous versions of the formula that were kept at the DERA facility in Farnborough, indicating that, I'm sorry to say, a DERA employee may have been involved in the crime. Unfortunately there are no other copies of this important work, which represents two years of intensive research and development. Needless to say, it is vital that no copies of the Skin 17 specification fall into the wrong hands."

Tanner had inched along the wall and was now standing next to Bond's seat.

"I assume this was the project you were referring to yesterday," Bond whispered.

Tanner whispered back, "Uh-huh."

The slide changed to a picture of Steven Harding.

"This is Dr. Steven Harding, who was serving as Dr. Wood's right-hand man. The rest of his team have been summoned back from various parts of the country and are here in this room. Dr. Wood had given them the day off yesterday because he wanted to make the final tests on the scalable prototype alone. We know that Wood left instructions for Dr. Harding to come to the lab at nine o'clock last night. Whether or not he did this is unknown, but we find it disturbing that Dr. Harding is missing. He is simply nowhere to be found."

Bond whispered to Tanner, "Christ, we just played golf with him yesterday!"

"I know," Tanner replied. "This is all very bizarre."

Mr. Drake said, "I'd like to call to the stand Group Captain Roland Marquis, who was the RAF liaison to the 'Smart Skin' project."

Marquis stood up and stiffly walked to the front of the room. "Before I field questions," he said, "I want to say that I am extremely proud of the work Dr. Wood and his team did on this project. Great Britain has lost a national treasure in him. Now, Minister, M, distinguished colleagues, I am at your disposal."

The Minister spoke first. "Group Captain, we understand that you saw Dr. Harding yesterday."

"Yes, sir," Marquis replied. "I played golf with him at Stoke Poges. It was around seventeen hundred hours when we said good-bye and parted company."

"Did he indicate to you what his plans were?"

"No, sir, I knew that Dr. Wood had given the team the day off, and that he was close to finishing Skin 17. Dr. Harding was quite eager to hear news from Dr. Wood. He made at least two phone calls from the club to find out what was going on. I knew that Dr. Harding would be visiting the lab later that evening, that is, last night. Other than that, he didn't say much. He's a professional and would never talk about the work outside the DERA complex, even with me."

M asked, "How well do you know this Dr. Harding?"

"Not very well. I got to know him over the last two years during the normal day-to-day administrative work I did in supervising Skin 17. One day we discovered a mutual interest in golf. That's all. Yesterday was the third time we had played together."

"How close to the project were you?" she asked.

"I had no idea what they were actually doing, technically. I mean, I knew what their goal was and I knew generally how they were going about it. But I'm no physicist, ma'am. My job was to control the budget, make sure they had what they needed, and make monthly reports to my superiors in the RAF."

"And you have no idea where Dr. Harding is now?"

"None, ma'am."

"Do you think he is capable of doing something like this?"

Marquis paused a moment before answering. Finally, he said, "I don't think so, ma'am. Dr. Harding always struck me as an introvert, a quiet type with a high intellect. I never once saw him get angry. I can't imagine that he'd have a violent bone in his body, much less be a traitor to his country. He has no criminal record. I know that stranger things have happened in our government's history with regard to spies and counterspies. Nevertheless, it is my opinion that Dr. Harding may have come to an untimely end, along with Dr. Wood."

After a moment's silence. Bond raised his hand. Marquis raised his eyebrows when he saw who it was. "Yes, uhm, Mr. Bond?"

"Have there been any communications at all claiming responsibility for this act?"

"No, not vet."

"In your opinion, do you think it's the work of a foreign power?"

"At this point, I'm not ruling out anything. MI5 is handling the investigation. However, as you will see in your briefing packet, there is a copy of a fax that was received at the DERA Fleet facility exactly nine and half months ago. Dr. Wood had shown it to me, thinking it was some kind of prank. I kept the note since the fax number at the facility had always been classified. Can we show that slide, please?"

The slide on the wall changed again to reveal a blurry copy of a faxed piece of paper. There was no mistaking the wording, however.

GOOD LUCK WITH THE SKIN PROJECT. WE ARE VERY
INTERESTED IN YOUR PROGRESS.
   THE UNION

Bond felt a chill slither down his spine.

Marquis continued. "I don't know a lot about this Union, but I was
briefed this morning on the group's recent activities. It sounds to me
like the kind of job they would pull off. Any other questions?"

When there were none, M stood up. "Thank you, Group Captain.
We'll start the debriefing with you and the rest of Dr. Woods team
after lunch."

Bond stepped into M's office to find her alone with Bill Tanner.

"Come in, Double-O Seven," she said. "Sit down."

He sat across from the woman whom he had grown to admire more
and more during the past two years. There had been a considerable
amount of friction between them when she first took over MI6, but
now they had mutual respect. Bond had especially proved his value to
her during her personal crisis during the Decada affair a year earlier.

"I understand you and the Chief of Staff played golf with Group
Captain Marquis and Dr. Harding yesterday," she said.

"Yes, ma'am."

"I want to hear what you think."

Bond shrugged. "I'm just as puzzled as anyone. I agree with Marquis's assessment of Harding—that he really didn't seem the type to
do something like this. My suspicions would be directed more
toward Marquis."

M's eyebrows rose. "Really? Why?"

"Because he's an arrogant son of a bitch."

Bond's outspokenness didn't faze her. "I know all about your history together," she said. "Please don't carry schoolboy prejudices into
this, Double-O Seven."

"Nevertheless, ma'am," Bond said, "I don't think too highly of him."

"Group Captain Marquis is a distinguished officer and a national
hero of sorts. You're aware of his mountaineering achievements?"

"Yes, ma'am. You're absolutely right, I'm allowing my personal feelings about the man to influence my opinion of him. And my opinion is that he is an ass."

"Your opinion is noted," M said, "but I'm afraid you'll need more than professional jealousy as evidence of Group Captain Marquis's guilt."

That stung.

She nodded to Tanner. He handed an eight-by-ten glossy black-and-white photograph to Bond. It was taken by a security camera and revealed a fuzzy shot of Steven Harding in a line of people. He was carrying an attaché case and a travel bag.

"We just got this," Tanner said. "It was taken last night around ten-thirty by one of the customs security cameras at Waterloo Station—at the Eurostar terminal. Dr. Steven Harding boarded the last train to Brussels."

"Why Belgium?" Bond asked.

"Who knows? We've contacted Station B to see if we can have his movements traced. MI5 have turned the investigation over to us. We believe that Skin 17 is no longer in the UK."

M spoke up. "Double-O Seven, I want you to go to Brussels and rendezvous with Station B. Your job is to track down Dr. Harding. If he has Skin 17, you're to do everything in your power to get it back. The Minister of Defence is obsessed with this Mach 7 business and with Great Britain being the first to achieve this goal. He's told me in no uncertain terms that the formula must be recovered. I'm afraid I agree with him that it would be disastrous should Skin 17 get into the hands of a country like, say, Iraq or Iran . . . or Red China. I wouldn't want the Russian Mafia to get hold of it. I wouldn't want Japan to have it. Double-O Seven, it's also a matter of principle. We developed it. Here in Britain. Dr. Wood was a brilliant British physicist. We *want* the credit for developing the process. Do I make myself clear?"

"Yes, ma'am."

"Good luck, then."

Bond stopped by his office to gather his things, then paused by Helena Marksbury's desk.

"I, uhm, have to go to Brussels," he said.

Helena was typing furiously and didn't stop to look at him. "I know. You're to pick up the Jaguar from Q Branch before you leave today. I'm making arrangements for you to use the channel tunnel so you can drive across. I thought you'd prefer that."

"Thank you."

"Station B is handling your hotel. The contact's name is Gina Hollander. She'll meet you at the Manneken-Pis at fourteen hundred hours tomorrow."

"All right."

"Good luck."

Bond placed his hand over hers to stop her typing. "Helena . . ."

"Please, James," she said softly. "Just go. I'll be fine. When you get back, everything will be . . . as before."

Bond removed his hand and nodded. Without saying another word, he turned and walked toward the elevator.

FIVE

THE GOLDEN PACEMAKER

APPROXIMATELY TWELVE HOURS BEFORE JAMES BOND RECEIVED HIS assignment to track Dr. Steven Harding to Belgium, the physicist arrived at the Midi station in Brussels and took a taxi to the Métropole, the only nineteenth-century hotel in the famed city. Located in the heart of Brussels in the Place de Brouckère, the historical center, the Hotel Métropole is more like a palace than a hotel. French architect Alban Chambon brought a mixture of styles to the interior by infusing it with an air of luxury and richness of materials— paneling, polished teak, Numidian marble, gilded bronze, and forged iron.

Most visitors find the French Renaissance main entrance and the Empire-style reception hall breathtaking, but Harding wasn't interested in the historical or aesthetic qualities of the hotel. He was tired and frightened, and he wanted to get Phase Two out of the way as soon as possible so that he could collect his money and flee to some island in the South Pacific.

"*Oui, monsieur?*" the receptionist asked.

Harding stammered, "Uhm, sorry, I only speak English."

The receptionist, used to foreign visitors, smoothly switched languages. "What can I do for you, sir?"

"I have a reservation. Peters. Donald Peters."

The young woman looked it up on the computer. "Yes, Mr. Peters. Your room has been paid for. How many nights will you be staying?"

"I'm not sure. Possibly three?"

"That's fine, just let us know. Do you have bags?"

"Just what I'm carrying."

He wrote false information on the registration card, then took the key.

"You're in the Sarah Bernhardt Room, Number 1919 on the third floor."

"Thank you," Harding said. He took the key and carried his luggage to the elevator, waving away the porter. The elevator was an old-fashioned cagelike contraption with impressive metallic beams rising up through the ceiling.

Sarah Bernhardt's autograph was engraved on a gold plaque on the door of his room. Apparently the famous actress had once lived in the suite. The hotel was indeed *the* spot for the rich and famous throughout the last century.

Harding locked the door behind him and breathed a sigh of relief. So far, so good. He hadn't noticed anyone tailing him. There were no suspicious characters lurking about. Perhaps he was really going to get away with it.

Feeling more confident than he had in weeks, Harding went straight to the minibar in the sitting room, unlocked it, and found a small bottle of vodka. He opened it and drank it straight, out of the bottle. Only then did he begin to appreciate the splendor of the hotel.

The suite was divided into two large rooms. The sitting room was equipped with a large wood desk, the minibar, a television, a glass-top coffee table, green chairs and a sofa, a closet with a full-length mirror, potted plants, and a large window that opened onto a terrace. The walls were yellow with white molding. The bedroom was just as spacious, with a king-sized bed, another glass-top table, chairs with the same green upholstery, a second television, oak dresser and cabinet, and small tables by the bed. Another large window opened to the terrace. The bathroom was in brown tile and contained all the amenities one could ask for. A frosted-glass panel covered half the area above the bathtub for showering.

"This is *great!*" Harding said aloud, rubbing his hands with glee.

He was not accustomed to such luxury. Working for the Union certainly had its perks.

The taxi driver was curious as to why Harding wanted to go to a doctor's surgery after midnight.

"They closed, they closed," the driver said in imperfect English.

"He's expecting me," Harding insisted. He handed the man one thousand Belgian francs. "Here, I'll pay you the fare when we get there. And I'll need you to wait for me."

The driver shrugged and took the money. The cab took Harding to Avenue Franklin-Roosevelt, located in an elegant area of the city near the Hippodrome. It is full of lush green parks and expensive town homes, but in the dark it looked like anywhere else.

The driver let him out at Dr. Hendrik Lindenbeek's residence. As in most European countries, doctors in Belgium usually carried on their practice from their homes.

Harding rang the bell, and Lindenbeek answered the door after a few seconds. He was a young Flemish cardiologist.

"Come in," he said in English. Harding noted that Dr. Lindenbeek's hand shook as he gestured him inside.

Lindenbeek led him through the patient waiting area, which consisted of wicker furniture in a white room, and into the large examination room. Besides the examining table, there was a large wooden desk, bookshelves, trays with equipment, and an X-ray machine with lead wall partitions.

"Is our patient ready to go?" Harding asked.

Dr. Lindenbeek nodded. "The surgery is scheduled for eight o'clock tomorrow morning. I need to get some sleep so I don't make any mistakes!" He laughed nervously.

"You had better not make any mistakes. Now, tell me exactly what you're going to do."

Dr. Lindenbeek took some stationery from his desk and drew a sketch of a man's torso. He made a small square on the figure's upper left breast. "The pacemaker will be inserted here. It's a routine operation. Takes about three to four hours, maybe less."

"Does the patient go home the same day?"

"He can, but I prefer him to remain in the hospital overnight. He can go home the following day."

Harding didn't like that. He was on a tight schedule.

"What about traveling? Will he be able to fly?"

"Sure," Lindenbeek said. "He just needs to take it easy for a few days to make sure the skin heals. The pocket of skin where we put the pacemaker might open up. It could get infected. We wouldn't want that to happen."

"No, we wouldn't," Harding agreed. "But could he handle a long aeroplane flight?"

"I don't see why not."

"Good." Harding took the sketch and opened the attaché case. He dropped it inside, then removed the envelope containing the Skin 17 microdot. "This is it. It's attached to a piece of film. Whatever you do, don't lose it. It'll be *your* neck. Remember what the Union have on you."

Lindenbeek swallowed hard. "How can I forget?" He gingerly took the envelope from Harding.

Hospital Erasme, located on Route de Lennik south of Brussels, is one of the most modern and largest facilities in all of Belgium. As it is also a university hospital, Erasme is considered to have the best equipment and technology in the country, as well as the most sophisticated and professional staff.

At exactly 7:55 A.M., a few hours before Bond would attend the Skin 17 emergency briefing, Dr. Lindenbeek walked into surgery on the second floor wearing greens, mask, and a cap. He scrubbed his hands and allowed a nurse to fit rubber gloves over them. The patient, a fifty-eight-year-old Chinese man named Lee Ming, was already on the table and was groggy from the drugs he had been given. Preparing the patient for surgery had taken nearly an hour.

A local anesthetic was applied to Lee's left side, under the collarbone. Lindenbeek examined his equipment while he waited for the drugs to work. The pacemaker was a top-line "demand" model made by Sulzer Intermedics Inc., which meant that the device sensed the heart's activity and stimulated it only when the natural rate fell below a certain level. Lindenbeek preferred Sulzer Intermedics, an

American company, not only because they had a convenient office in Belgium, but because he considered them the best.

"He's ready, doctor," the anesthetist said in Flemish.

Dr. Lindenbeek inserted a needle to find the subclavian vein under the left collarbone. After he found it, he made a subcutaneous incision to one side of the needle. He then slid an introducer over the needle, which looked like a big syringe with no plunger. The next step was to insert the pacemaker leads through the introducer down the vein into the heart. Fluoroscopy was used to visualize the lead in the patient.

"I think I'll need a stylet," Lindenbeek said. He removed the lead and placed a wire stylet on it so that it would be a little stiffer. This would aid in positioning the lead.

It was a tedious process but one that had to be performed with precision and care. The first lead took nearly an hour to position, and there was still a second one to insert. Ninety minutes into the operation, Lindenbeek was ready to go on to the next step.

The electrical status of the leads was checked to see how much energy was actually needed to pace the heart. Lindenbeek cautiously adjusted the electricity, then took the gold-colored pacemaker from the tray. He attached the leads to the pacemaker, then gave the order to check everything on the EKG.

"Looks good, doctor," the nurse said.

He nodded, then proceeded to carry on with the final phase of the operation. He carefully made a "pocket" under the incision by blunt dissection between the pectoral muscle and the skin. Once that was done, Lindenbeek inserted the sealed pacer into the pocket and closed the incision.

"Right," Lindenbeek said. "You're all finished, Mr. Lee."

Lee blinked. "I think I fell asleep."

"You did fine. We're going to take you to the recovery room now. I'll see you in a little bit. Try not to move too much."

Lee was wheeled out of surgery and Lindenbeek removed his gloves and mask. He went to the waiting room, where he found Steven Harding reading a magazine. Harding saw him and stood up.

"Well?" he asked.

"Everything's fine," Lindenbeek said. "He can go home tonight if you really want, but I recommend he stay until tomorrow morning."

Harding considered this and said, "All right. I'd rather be safe than sorry." He then lowered his voice and asked, "So . . . where exactly is it?"

Lindenbeek whispered, "The microdot is attached to the battery inside the pacemaker. I had to do it that way in order to seal the pacemaker and sterilize it."

Harding nodded. "Good. That's fine, then. Well done."

"I'm glad you are pleased. Now, will this nightmare finally end?"

Harding smiled, his beady, birdlike eyes sparkling. "I will speak to my superiors this afternoon. I'm sure they will be in touch. Thank you, doctor."

As Harding left the waiting room, Dr. Lindenbeek stood and watched him. He didn't like that man. He didn't like anyone associated with the so-called Union. At least he had done what they wanted. Now he prayed that he could get on with his life in peace.

Harding took a taxi back to the hotel and indulged himself in a fine lunch at the Métropole café. It consisted of creamed potato soup with smoked eel, salmon in flaky pastry with sevruga caviar, asparagus, and a bottle of Duvel beer. After lunch he went to the Rue d'Aerschot, Brussels's meager red light district, where he spent several thousand Belgian francs in the company of a plump but serviceable prostitute.

When he got back to his room that evening, the message light on his phone was blinking. He retrieved the message, frowned, and returned the call.

It was not good news.

"Damn," he muttered to himself. He hung up the phone, then dialed a local contact in Brussels.

"Hello?" he muttered to the Frenchman who answered. "I don't speak French. Listen, this is Mongoose, right? I've just learned that a British secret service agent is driving here tomorrow in a blue Jaguar XK8. He's on to us. He'll be on the E19, coming into Brussels, between noon and two o'clock. Is there something you can do about him?"

SIX

THE ROAD TO BRUSSELS

James Bond picked up the Jaguar XK8 from Q Branch after receiving a brief admonition from Major Boothroyd concerning a couple of new features he had added since Bond had used the car last. One of these was a supercharger, an Eaton M112, which normally delivered 370 bhp and 387-pound-foot torque. Bond had insisted on a modification to increase the boost to give 500 bhp, which Boothroyd had reluctantly made.

He took the M20 motorway to the Channel Tunnel Terminal between Dover and Folkestone and boarded Le Shuttle auto-transporter, which, in thirty-five minutes, unloaded cars at Calais. Bond skirted south toward Lille, then got on the E19, the Paris to Brussels autoroute. Recent rains and sunny weather made the landscape rich with green, yellow, and orange brushstrokes. The countryside whipped past Bond as he tested the new supercharger on the open road. It felt great to get away from England and finally make headway on the case.

The Jaguar was twenty miles from "the Ring," the busy roadway that encircled the main city, when Bond noticed two high-speed motorcycles gaining on him. They appeared to be identical dark green Kawasaki ZZ-R1100 superbikes. Bond was familiar with the vehicles and knew them to be powerful, heavy, and very fast.

Obtaining an extra boost from a ram-air system that ducted cool air from a slot in the fairing nose to a pressurized air box, they could easily keep up with the Jaguar.

A third ZZ-R1100 pulled out onto the highway from an entrance ramp in front of him just as the other two reached a point fifty yards behind Bond's car. He was certain that they were performing rehearsed maneuvers—the timing was just too skillful. Bond sat straight in the seat, gripped the wheel, and increased his speed to ninety in order to overtake the motorcycle in the right lane in front of him. It didn't help that traffic was moderately heavy.

Bond veered into the center lane so that he could pass the rider and get a good look at him. At that angle he appeared to be dressed in army-fatigues and an olive green crash helmet, neatly color coordinated with the bike. Was it a costume? Perhaps the three riders were part of some kind of auto show and weren't dangerous at all?

The motorcycle suddenly swerved into Bond's lane, preventing him from passing. Bond was forced to ease his speed down to seventy, which gave the two men behind him an opportunity to close the gap.

Now at a distance of thirty feet, the two pursuers were side by side in the same lane behind Bond. Bond swerved into the far left lane, but all three motorcycles followed suit as if they were operating by remote control.

There was no doubt now, Bond thought, these men had to be professionals. He changed lanes again, back to the center, and then to the far right, as the superbikes immediately adjusted to pin him in again.

Bond was peering at the riders behind him in the rearview mirror when he noticed a sudden puff of black smoke just below one of the windshields. He felt a series of fast, hard jolts in the back of the Jaguar.

Bond set his jaw. The bastard had fired a volley of machine gun bullets at his petrol tank.

The two riders looked at each other as if to ask "Why didn't the car explode?" Bond allowed himself a smile. The body's chobam armor was impenetrable and had reactive skins that exploded when hit, thereby deflecting the bullets. The metal was self-healing by virtue of viscous fluid.

Apparently able to communicate with each other via headsets, the riders prepared a new strategy. One of the men behind Bond pulled into the right-hand lane and sped up so that he was parallel to the Jaguar. The rider looked at Bond and mouthed what must have been an unsavory epithet.

Bond pulled the wheel sharply to the right, ramming into the motorcycle. The Kawasaki was knocked off the road and onto the shoulder, where it fell on its side and skidded for a hundred feet before stopping. Bond had hoped the cycle would be completely wrecked, but the rider apparently wasn't harmed and would be back on the road in a minute or two. He moved the J mechanism into manual mode and floored the accelerator. The Jaguar shot ahead of the front cycle, then maneuvered around slower civilian vehicles to put some distance between him and the green bikers. Bond hoped that he wouldn't have to use deadly force against these men on such a busy highway, and wondered if he should telephone the Belgian police on his mobile phone.

The remaining two cyclists darted in and out of the traffic to catch up with Bond. Road repairs had caused the far left lane to be closed at one point. Now relegated to only two lanes, the traffic was thicker. Bond sped up and soon found himself tailgating two ten-wheel lorries that were blocking both lanes. They were both traveling at unsafe speeds, attempting to outrace each other. Bond honked the horn, hoping that one would pull into the other's lane. The driver in the lorry in front of him blasted his own horn, challenging Bond to do something about it.

"Defense systems on," Bond said aloud. One of the new features that Q Branch had put in the car was voice activation for all systems—phone, audio, lighting, and, of course, weaponry. An icon flashed on the telematics screen on the dashboard, indicating that Bond's command had been executed.

"Activate flying scout," he said. An outline of the scout, a device the size of a small model airplane, appeared on the screen. It was stored underneath the chassis until it was activated from inside the car. The scout could fly out from under the vehicle and reach an altitude of Bond's choosing. It was steerable by joystick or satellite navigation.

The display changed to read SCOUT READY.

"Launch scout," he commanded. He felt a sudden whoosh behind the Jaguar as the scout ejected from its bay. The batlike vehicle soared out and up into the air, then turned so that it was traveling thirty feet above and parallel with the Jaguar. The two motorcyclists couldn't believe their eyes. One of them pointed to the scout and shouted something.

Keeping one hand on the wheel, Bond used his left hand to manipulate the joystick. He sent the scout forward and increased its speed so that it would move up beside the lorries, which were still barreling down the road neck and neck.

Bond lowered the scout slowly without decreasing its speed. Like a hummingbird, the aircraft gently positioned itself so that it was flying at door level in between the two lorries. The driver of the lorry on the right looked to his left and saw the strange contraption flying just outside his window. He gasped and almost ran off the road, but he managed to straighten the wheel in time.

The chobam armor, which also coated the scout, was quite effective for battering purposes. Bond moved the joystick so that the plane swung to the right with great force, shattering the driver's window with its wing. He pulled the scout up and out of the way as the driver then completely lost control of the lorry. It careened off the road, over the shoulder, then turned over and crashed into the ditch.

That should get the attention of the police, Bond thought. He increased the speed and shot past the other lorry, whose frightened driver had dropped his speed to forty. The scout, meanwhile, returned to its place above the Jaguar.

Surprisingly, a stretch of road ahead of Bond was relatively traffic free. He opened up, hoping that the two pursuers would follow him into the clear area. In a moment he saw them zoom past the lorry that he had left behind. One Kawasaki was gaining fast, the other dropping back a bit.

"Prepare silicon fluid bomb," Bond said. Another new feature on the car, the oil or silicon fluid explosives could be dropped from the rear bumper into the path of a pursuing vehicle. They were more direct and caused "cleaner" damage than the Jaguar's heat-seeking rockets, which were meant for heavier targets.

The Kawasaki moved into position behind Bond, and the rider fired its machine gun again. Bond felt the impact ricochet off the back of the car, then said, "Launch bomb."

A device the size of a compact disc dropped out of the bumper and rolled out onto the road. The rider on the motorcycle saw it and attempted to swerve around it, but it was too late. The device exploded with a tremendous blast, sending pieces of the Kawasaki and its rider into the air. The highway was soon littered with black smoke, burnt metal, and seared body parts.

The other rider pulled into the left lane and zigzagged around the debris, staying on Bond's tail. When he was in range, he fired his guns at the Jaguar, too.

"Ready rear laser," Bond said. The icon appeared on the screen.

The cycle moved closer, the bullets still flying. One of the back tires burst, but the car was engineered so that it could run on flats.

"Count of three for one-second laser flash," Bond said. "One . . . two . . . *three.*"

The sudden bright light confused the rider behind him. At first he thought it was glare from the sun, bouncing off a piece of reflective metal on the back of the Jaguar. Momentarily blinded, he kept the handlebars straight, hoping that his sight would clear in a few seconds—but then the pain began. His eyes felt as if they were being burned with hot pokers, and then there was nothing but darkness. The laser flash had permanently seared his retinas.

Bond watched in the rearview mirror as the Kawasaki wobbled and veered to the left. It crashed through the repair lane and guardrail, then slid into the oncoming traffic on the other side of the road. Horns blared and drivers slammed on their brakes. Several cars crashed into one another in an effort to avoid hitting the motorcycle, but the Kawasaki was run over by a van and dragged at least two hundred yards before both hunks of metal came to a stop.

Bond could hear sirens in the distance. They were coming from the city, the opposite direction from which he was traveling. He looked in the rearview mirror and saw that the third motorcycle, the one he had bumped off the road earlier, had rejoined the chase. Bond presumed correctly that this rider was unaware of the flying scout soaring above the Jaguar at a safe distance. He gently pushed the joystick so that the scout decreased speed, then made an about-face. Bond brought the scout down to a level equal to that of the cyclist, then pushed the throttle. It shot back toward the cycle at full speed.

The rider gasped when he saw the strange, birdlike thing headed straight for him. He barely had time to scream.

The scout met the cycle head-on, knocking the rider off the bike. Bond pulled the scout up and away as the motorcycle skidded on its side and eventually came to rest in the ditch.

"Prepare to dock scout," Bond said as he maneuvered the remarkable device back behind the Jaguar.

He gave the command, and the bird pulled underneath the chassis and locked into place just as Bond entered "the Ring." Blending in with heavy traffic, the Jaguar safely drove past the power plants, car dealerships, and business parks that dotted the landscape.

Bond activated the mobile speaker phone, then called out the speed dial code for headquarters in London. After the normal security checks, he was put through to Bill Tanner's office. His secretary answered and told Bond that M and the Chief of Staff were off-site at a meeting.

"Damn," he said. "Put me through to Helena Marksbury please."

In a moment he heard his personal assistant's lilting voice.

"James?" she answered. Bond could hear her apprehension. She probably had looked forward to a few days of his absence.

"Helena, we have a problem," he said. "Someone knew I was on my way to Brussels, and three men on motorcycles tried to kill me."

"My God, James, are you all right?" she asked with concern.

"Yes. I need you to get this message to the Chief of Staff immediately. He and M are at a meeting off-site." He gave her the details. "Find them and tell them that a Code Eighty is in effect." This meant that a security breach had occurred.

"Right," she said. "I'm on it now, James. Are you in Brussels?"

"Almost. I'll talk to you later."

"Be careful," she said, then rang off. Despite the awkward situation that existed between them, Bond was thankful that Helena was capable of carrying on in a professional manner.

He soon got off the Ring road and onto Industrial Boulevard, which led toward the center of Brussels, and once again offered a silent thanks to Major Boothroyd and the rest of Q Branch.

It was a beautiful, sunny, spring day. Bond parked the car in a garage near the Grand Place, the magnificent square that is considered the centerpiece of Brussels. Bordered on all four sides by icons of Belgium's royal history, the Grand Place is a dazzling display of ornamental gables, gilded facades, medieval banners, and gold-filigreed rooftop sculptures. The Gothic Town Hall, dating back to the early 1400s, remains intact; the other buildings, the neo-Gothic King's House and the Brewers Guild House, date from the late 1600s. The Brussels aldermen continue to meet in the Town Hall, the exterior of which is decorated in part by fifteenth- and sixteenth-century insider's jokes. The sculptures include a group of drinking monks, a sleeping Moor and his harem, a heap of chairs resembling the medieval torture called strappado, and St. Michael slaying a female-breasted devil. Bond had once heard a story that the architect, Jan van Ruysbroeck, committed suicide by leaping from the belfry when he realized that it is off center and has an off-center entrance.

It was nearly two o'clock. Bond put on a pair of Ray-Ban Wayfarers sunglasses that would identify him to his contact, then walked southwest through the colorful and narrow cobblestoned streets to the intersection of Rue du Chêne and Rue de l'Étuve. There, surrounded by camera-snapping tourists, was the famous statue of the urinating little boy known as Manneken-Pis. Although not the original statue (which was subject to vandalism and was removed), the current idol is an exact replica and is perhaps the most well known symbol of Brussels. Bond didn't know what its origins were, but he knew that it dated from the early 1400s and was perhaps the effigy of a patriotic Belgian lad who sprinkled a hated Spanish sentry who had passed beneath his window. Another story was that he had saved the Town Hall from a small fire by extinguishing it using the only means available. Today, "Little Julian," as he is called, was dressed in a strange red cloak with a white fur collar. Louis XV of France began the tradition of presenting colorful costumes to the little boy and since then he has acquired hundreds of outfits.

"He must have a very large bladder to keep peeing like that," a female voice said in English, but with a thick European accent.

Bond glanced to his left and saw an attractive woman dressed in a smart beige trouser suit and a light jacket. She was wearing Ray-Bans; had strawberry-blond, short, curly hair; a light cream complexion; and her sensual lips were painted with light red lipstick. A toothpick lodged at the corner of her mouth. She appeared to be around thirty, and she had the figure of a fashion model.

"I'm just glad this isn't considered a drinking fountain," Bond replied.

She removed the sunglasses to reveal bright blue eyes that sparkled in the sunlight. She held out her hand and said, "Gina Hollander. Station B."

Bond took her hand, which felt smooth and warm. "Bond. James Bond."

"Come on," she said, gesturing with her head, "let's go to the station house, then we'll get your car and take it to your hotel." Her English was good, but Bond could tell she wasn't terribly comfortable with it.

"Parlez-vous français?" he asked.

"Oui," she said, then switched back to English, "but my first language is Dutch, Flemish. You speak Dutch?"

"Not nearly as well as you speak English," he replied.

"Then let's stick to English, I need the practice."

She was not beautiful, but Bond found her very appealing. The short, curly hairstyle gave her a pixielike quality that most people would describe as cute, an adjective Bond always avoided. She was petite, but she walked with confidence and grace, as if she were six feet tall.

"Which is my hotel, by the way?" he asked.

"The Métropole. It's one of the best in town."

"I know it. I've stayed there before."

"Our target is staying there, too."

"Oh?"

"I'll tell you all about it when we get to the station house. It's just over here."

She led him into a very narrow street off Petite Rue des Bouchers, near the famous folk puppet showcase Théâtre Toone, and into a pastry shop. The smell of baked goods was overpowering.

"Care for a cream puff?" she asked.

He smiled and said, "Later, perhaps."

Gina said something in Flemish to the woman behind the counter, then led Bond through a door, into the kitchen, where a large, sweating man was loading a tray of rolls into an oven. She went through another door to a staircase that led to a second-floor loft: the headquarters of Station B.

It was a comfortable one room/one bathroom flat that had been transformed into an office, just barely large enough for an operative and some equipment. Besides the usual computer gear, file cabinets, fax machine, and copier, there was a sofa bed, a television, and kitchenette. It was decorated with a decidedly feminine touch, and there was an abundance of Belgian lace draped over the furniture.

"I don't live here, but the sofa bed is handy if I ever have to stay late," she said as they entered. "Have a seat anywhere. You want something to drink?"

"Vodka with ice, please. Before we do anything, though, I have to call London. We have a little problem."

"What's that?"

"We have a security leak. Someone knew I was coming. I was attacked on the E19."

"Really? That was *you*? I *heard* about the accidents on the road! Are you all right?"

Bond removed his gunmetal case and took out a cigarette. He offered one to her, but she shook her head.

"I'm fine, but they're not," he said. "Three men on motorcycles. Came from nowhere, tried to kill me. I'm afraid a lorry was smashed, and a few passenger cars, too. I tried to call London earlier, but everyone was in a bloody meeting."

She pointed to the desk. "I assure you there's been no security breach here. The phone is there. Please."

Bond reached for the phone and removed from the inside pocket of his jacket a device that looked like a small black light meter. He pulled out a three-inch antenna and flicked a switch. He scanned the phone with the detector.

"I do that every morning, Mr. Bond," Gina said. "With more sophisticated equipment."

"I doubt it could do much better than this little toy," Bond said, satisfied with the reading he got. The CSS 8700V Bug Alert was usually accurate. "Sorry, I had to check."

"That's all right." She went to the kitchenette to get the drinks.

Bond picked up the phone and called the secure line again. This time Tanner picked up.

"Hello, James, sorry I was away earlier. M wanted me to—"

"Never mind, did Helena give you the message?"

"Yes, she did. We're looking into it now. How many people knew you were on the way to Brussels?"

"Just you and M. Moneypenny and Helena, of course. Major Boothroyd, Head of S., Records . . . well, I suppose there could be quite a few people, Bill."

"No one outside the firm?"

"No, not even my housekeeper. She never knows where I am."

"Right," Tanner said. "Look, don't worry, we'll see if we can find the hole and plug it. In the meantime, M has new orders for you."

"Oh?"

"Since Agent Hollander has tracked down Harding, you are to observe him. Repeat, *observe* him. We want to find out who he's working for or dealing with. He must have Skin 17 or he wouldn't have fled the UK."

"Understood. You do realize that there is the possibility that he doesn't have it anymore. . . . What would you like me to do when he makes a move?"

"Use your judgment. We'd like him brought back to the UK, certainly. We're already making arrangements for extradition. If it looks like we might lose Skin 17, do whatever it takes to retrieve it."

Bond signed off and stretched back in the large reclining leather armchair behind the desk. Right on cue, Gina brought Bond's vodka and a bottle of Orval beer for herself. She sat on the sofa bed and put her feet up.

He held up his glass and said, "Cheers." He took a sip of the ice cold vodka and was pleasantly surprised. "Wolfschmidt from Riga. Well done. I think you and I will get along splendidly."

"Thanks. I save it for special occasions," she said. "I heard that Brits are hard to impress." She laughed.

"Quite the opposite. England is such a bore most of the time, so we're really quite easy. Anyway, you impressed this one. Is that the stuff made by Trappist monks?" he asked, indicating her beer.

She nodded, taking a long drink from the bottle. She managed to keep the toothpick sticking out of her mouth as she swallowed. For the first time, Bond noticed how fit she really was. Her shapely, strong leg muscles could be traced through her clothing. Her arms were also well toned. Although she was dressed as if she might be the manager of an upmarket women's department store, the toothpick in her mouth gave her an impish, mischievous quality. There was no mistaking that this woman was streetwise. She was a mature little Peter Pan with breasts, which also happened to be quite shapely.

"So, tell me about Dr. Harding," Bond said.

"When I got the alert on him from London, I ran a routine check with immigration at the Midi terminal. They caught him on camera, coming through as Donald Peters. Once I knew that, it was a matter of finding the right hotel with a Donald Peters registered there. He was at the Métropole. I waited at the café just outside. I drank a hell of a lot of coffee! He finally came out last night after dinner." She giggled slightly and said, "He went to the street where women . . . where women sell sexual favors."

Bond smiled with her. "Did he have a good time?"

She blushed. "Don't ask me," she said. "Afterward he went back to the hotel. I tipped a bellhop to phone my pager if he left. He was there all night. This morning he took a taxi somewhere . . . and I lost him. He hasn't checked out of the hotel, though."

"So there was nearly a complete period of twenty-four hours when he could have done anything."

"I'm afraid so."

"And he could be making a deal right now."

"It's possible."

"We had better go," he said, sitting up. "I want to get into his room."

SEVEN

BITTER SUITE

BOND LEFT GINA, DROVE THE JAGUAR TO THE HOTEL, AND LEFT IT WITH THE valet. She followed him and sat in her usual seat in the sidewalk café outside the building. The plan was that she would watch the front while Bond was inside.

As he checked in, he was reminded of the time he had stayed at the Métropole when he was a young man. He had become involved with a French film star who had a husband in Paris and a career in London. They would meet in Brussels to escape the press. It was a stormy, passionate affair that went on for several months before she landed a role in a picture being shot in the Far East. He never saw her again.

As a hotel catering to the rich and famous, the Métropole's staff respected the guests' privacy. It was everything Bond expected from a good hotel with tasteful luxury and unique personal character. Full of gilded coffers, Italian stucco, modern wrought iron, Renaissance-style blue stained-glass windows, and glittering chandeliers, it was a true palace. Bond was given a room on the fifth floor that he thought would do nicely. He unpacked his bag and removed an electric toothbrush. He snapped off the brush and unscrewed the bottom of the device. Next to the three C-cell batteries was a set of thin, stiff wires. Old-fashioned skeleton keys were still being used at the hotel, so Q Branch's electric pick gun would be the best tool for the job. Made of aluminum, it could pick pin tumbler locks much faster and easier than hand picks and could even open some of the pick-resistant locks that other tools wouldn't.

Bond slipped it into the pocket of his jacket, then reached for the phone. He called the front desk and asked to be connected to Donald Peters's room. There was no answer. Good. That was what Bond wanted.

He checked the magazine in his Walther PPK and slipped the gun in the custom-made Berns chamois shoulder holster, then left the room. He descended the grand staircase two floors and peered down the corridor. There was no one around. He moved quickly to Room 1919 and knocked. When there was no answer, he took out the pick gun, selected an attachment, and had the door unlocked in three seconds.

Closing the door behind him, he moved from the entry hall to the sitting room, where Harding had deposited his attaché case and other personal items. Harding had written "Hospital Erasme" on a notepad next to the phone. Bond tried the briefcase, but it was locked. He selected another attachment for the pick gun and inserted the wires into the keyholes. The snaps flipped open.

There wasn't much there. A map of Brussels, rail timetables, calculator, paper, pens . . . and a strange sketch on a piece of physician's stationery.

It was the torso of a man with a small rectangle drawn over his left breast. Bond noted the name and address on the stationery and replaced everything.

He quickly went through the cupboard and found nothing of interest, then went into the bedroom. Harding's suitcase was in the wardrobe, along with a few items of clothing he had hung up. Bond reached for the suitcase but stopped cold when he heard a rattling of keys outside the door.

He bolted forward and slipped into the small bathroom. He quickly closed the door, leaving it slightly ajar, then stepped behind the frosted glass panel over the bathtub. Bond heard the suite door open, and the approaching voices of three men.

"You have to take it easy, Mr. Lee," one of them said. Bond recognized Harding's voice. "Basil here will make sure you get on the flight. How do you feel now?"

The door closed and the men went into the sitting room.

"It's not too sore," another man said with an Asian accent. "Except when I laugh." Mr. Lee . . . Chinese, perhaps?

"Basil," Harding said, "I'm leaving Brussels now. My job is done. You follow Mr. Lee and make damn sure he gets on that flight without any problems. Understand?"

"Yeah," came a deep voice.

"Sit down, Mr. Lee, while I pack," Harding said. "You want something out of the minibar?"

"No, thank you. I'll just watch TV." Bond heard the television in the sitting room switch on. A newscaster spoke in French.

"I want a beer after I go piss," Basil said. He had a pronounced French accent, but Bond thought he might be Senegalese.

"Go ahead, it's right in there," Harding said.

Christ! There was nowhere to hide. Bond's shape could easily be seen through the frosted glass. He squatted in the tub and drew the gun.

The door swung open. Through the foggy glass Bond could see a huge bulk of a man. He was black, and was dressed in a dark T-shirt and trousers. Although the image was distorted through the glass, his shoulders looked as wide as a dam's.

Basil stood in front of the toilet and started to urinate. Bond couldn't help but think that he was looking at the evil counterpart to Manneken-Pis.

"Basil?" Harding called from the other room.

"One minute, monsieur!" he yelled.

Bond didn't wait for him to finish. He stood up slowly and stepped out from behind the glass. Basil was so busy watching his stream that he didn't notice. When he felt the nuzzle of the gun in his back, he didn't stop urinating.

"Don't say a word," said Bond. "Just finish up."

The man nodded. After a few seconds, his bladder was empty.

"Go on, give it a good shake and zip up."

The man did as he was told.

"Better flush. Someone else may want to use it."

Basil reached out and pulled the steel bulb on top of the commode.

The toilet flush was loud. Bond took the opportunity to cold-cock the man on the back of the head.

Unfortunately it was like hitting an anvil. This took Bond by surprise, and Basil took advantage of the hesitation. He swung around, using his huge girth to slam Bond against the frosted glass panel, shattering it. The Walther PPK fell to the floor of the bathroom, discharging a round.

Basil grabbed Bond by his jacket collar and lifted him as if he were paper. Now that he was face-to-face with the thug, Bond could see that he was well over six feet tall and probably weighed in the neighborhood of three hundred pounds. His upper arms had a circumference of at least twenty inches.

Like a cat with a mouse, the big man slammed Bond back and forth against the walls around the bathtub. The tiles broke off in chunks.

"What the hell?" Harding looked in the bathroom. He stood in horror for a second, then turned to Lee, who was behind him. "Come on, let's get out of here!"

Bond caught a glimpse of Harding and the Chinese man before Basil grabbed hold of his hair with one hand, then punched him in the face with the other. It might as well have been a wrecking ball. Once again Bond crashed back into the tub on top of shards of broken glass. Basil then raised his left leg and stomped on Bond's chest with his heavy boot, over and over.

Harding ran into the sitting room, gathered his attaché case and a couple of items from the bedroom, and pulled Lee out of the room. "Leave them, come on!" he shouted.

Bond was stunned, nearly unconscious. He could feel the boot slamming down on his rib cage and felt a terrible sharp pain. If he didn't get out of that tub fast, the man would kick him so hard that his chest cavity would collapse.

Blinded and in agony, Bond groped beside him and felt pieces of broken glass. His fingers wrapped around a long one with a sharp point. When the boot came down again, Bond thrust the weapon as hard as he could into Basil's calf.

The thug yelled so loudly that it snapped Bond out of the fog. He clutched the boot with both hands and shoved upward, throwing the big man off balance so that he toppled to the bathroom floor.

Bond jackknifed to his feet and leaped over the edge of the tub. He saw the Walther lying in the opposite corner, near the door. He tried to jump over Basil's body, but the brute managed to trip him and shove him against the toilet. Bond landed hard against the porcelain, striking his lower back. He felt the edge of the toilet dig into his kidneys, sending jolts of anguish up his spine.

Basil rose and put his hands around Bond's throat. He began to tighten his viselike grip. The man was so strong that he wouldn't merely choke Bond to death. The man was about to crush his windpipe, and possibly his neck.

Bond's eyes rolled into the back of head as the pressure on his neck increased. Instinctively, he reached up to the counter by the sink to his left to feel for a weapon—anything that might give him an advantage. He found it in a can of spray deodorant. With the thumb and fingers of one hand, Bond flicked the top off and positioned his index finger on the button. He aimed it in front of him and sprayed.

Basil screamed again and let go of Bond's neck.

Bond immediately brought his legs up to his chest and kicked forward, knocking Basil off him and back against the bathroom wall.

There was barely enough room for one person in the bathroom, let alone two grown men, one of whom was a giant. Bond struggled to get to his feet, gasping for air as the black man bounced off the wall. The glass shard was still in his leg. Bond scooped the rest of Harding's toiletries off the counter into Basil's face. It gave Bond just enough time to get up and leap for the gun. The black man was just as fast, though. He tackled Bond and the two of them burst out of the bathroom into the entry hall. The gun was still in the bathroom.

They had a little more room here. Bond rolled backward so that he could get to his feet in the bedroom. Basil thundered after him. Bond picked up one of the chairs and threw it at the black man, who brushed it away as if he were swatting a mosquito. The chair smashed against the full-length mirror, breaking it into a hundred pieces.

"Now look what you went and did," Bond said, completely out of breath. "Your seven years of bad luck is just beginning."

Basil made a grotesque sound that resembled the roar of a lion, then charged Bond. They both fell back onto the king-sized bed, then rolled off the other side onto the floor. Bond got in two good punches, but the man was so strong, they didn't seem to bother him at all. Bond twisted out from under him and got to his feet. He performed a neat back kick and struck Basil in the face. Basil, in retaliation, simply lifted the huge mattress off the bed as if it were a pillow. He threw it at Bond with the strength of a rhinoceros. The mattress knocked Bond into the dresser. Bond grabbed a lamp and clubbed the black man with it, smashing the lamp shade and bulb.

The fight moved into the sitting room, where they had even more space in which to move. There was an open bottle of wine on top of the wet bar. Bond took it by the neck and broke it against the wall, splashing bloodred liquid all over the place. Now he had a jagged weapon. The two men faced and circled each other slowly. Bond kept Basil at a distance with the sharp edge of the bottle.

Basil smiled, then lunged at Bond. Bond swung. The razor-edged broken bottle scraped across the black man's face, creating five even tracks of blood on his skin. Whereas any other man would have been blinded by the attack, Basil merely seemed annoyed.

Bond swiped the bottle at him again, but this time Basil caught Bond's arm and squeezed it. In pain, Bond dropped his weapon. Basil flung Bond over the writing desk and into the window. Like everything else in the beautiful hotel suite, it shattered on impact.

The desk was between him and the black man. Bond kicked and toppled it over, but Basil easily brushed it aside. Before the man could catch him, Bond spun around and dived between Basil's legs for a space on the floor behind him. This maneuver gave Bond the two seconds he needed to get back on his feet.

Just as his sense of balance returned, his opponent got up and lunged. With split-second timing, Bond grabbed the man's head and used the momentum to pull him hard and fast to his side.

Basil's head crashed into the television set that Lee had left on. It exploded with great force. There was a cloud of sparks and gray smoke as the black man suddenly tensed, then started shaking violently. After a few seconds he went limp. With the television still fitted around his head, he slumped to the carpet. It was over.

Bond took stock of the damage to his body. His lower back was screaming in pain, and his ribs hurt like hell. One or two might be broken. His kidneys might be damaged. He was bleeding from several contusions on his face and hands.

But he was alive.

He found the phone on the floor and called Gina's mobile.

When she answered, he said, "Harding and a Chinese man just left the hotel. Did you see them?"

"No. When did they leave?"

"Just a few minutes ago."

"Damn. They must have gone out the back."

"Try to find them. Call me in my room in ten minutes."

"Are you coming down?" she asked.

The pain in Bond's back was making him dizzy. "In a while" was all he could manage to say. He hung up, then opened the minibar and removed a bottle of bourbon. He unscrewed the top and took a long swig. The liquor made him cough once, but the warmth felt great.

He limped to the bathroom and picked up his gun, then left the suite. Surprisingly, no one had heard the commotion. The corridor was empty.

Bond climbed the stairs to his own floor and the sanctity of his room. He went into the bathroom and looked at himself in the mirror. There was a nasty gash above his right eyebrow, and there was a darkening bruise on his left cheekbone. He washed his hands and saw that the cuts on his knuckles were superficial. His lower back and ribs were the main problems.

He plugged the drain in his own bathtub and ran the hot water until it was steaming. He undressed, gingerly pulling off his shirt and trousers. By the time he was naked, the tub was full.

Wincing, Bond lowered his bruised and battered body into the near-scalding water and fell asleep within two minutes.

EIGHT

A TASTE OF BELGUIM

THE NEXT MORNING, BOND ALLOWED GINA TO TAKE HIM TO A PRIVATE infirmary, where he submitted to an examination. Sore and stiff from the ordeal in the hotel suite, he felt particularly irritable. His conversation with M on the phone the night before hadn't helped.

"So you let Dr. Harding get away?" she had asked.

"Ma'am, I didn't *let* him do anything," Bond had replied. "He escaped while I was fighting for my life."

"Hmpfh." She was beginning to sound more and more like her predecessor.

"And where was Ms. Hollander at the time?" she asked.

"Doing her job. Harding and the Chinese man slipped out by a back exit. We know they haven't left Brussels."

"How can you be sure? You seem to have butterfingers lately, Double-O Seven."

Bond wanted to snap at her but took a deep breath instead. "Ma'am, Ms. Hollander has unshakable connections with immigration here. We would know if they had left by plane or train."

"What about by car?" she asked. "They could get in a car and drive right out of Belgium and no one would know."

The conversation ended badly. Bond promised to do his best to find Harding, and M said something to the effect that his best wasn't enough. After he rang off, he threw a glass of whisky against the wall.

Things hadn't improved in the morning. He got up feeling as if his body had been the target of a battering ram.

The doctor spoke in French to Gina. Bond understood him perfectly. He had a cracked rib.

"I see no damage to your kidneys other than bruising," the doctor told him in English. "If you notice blood in your urine, then of course you must come in for more tests."

The doctor wrapped Bond's chest in a tight harness and told him to wear it for at least a week. It had Velcro straps, so he could take it on and off for bathing, but he should certainly wear it to bed.

As they left the clinic, Gina led him to her own car, a red Citroën ZX. "We'll go and see that doctor now," she said. She moved the ever-present toothpick from one side of her mouth to the other. "I checked him out. Dr. Hendrik Lindenbeek is a cardiologist, and from what I gather, a good one."

Bond was silent in the car as they drove southeast. Away from the central historical section, Brussels became like any other modern European city. Vestiges of the old world disappeared and were replaced by late-twentieth-century architecture, shopping malls, office buildings, and elegant town homes. Franklin Roosevelt Avenue might have been Park Lane in London.

"Don't worry," Gina said, uncomfortable with Bond's sullen mood. "We'll find him. My gut tells me he hasn't left Brussels."

"My gut tells me that I should leave this ghastly business and take early retirement," Bond said bitterly.

"Come now. Surely this isn't the first time something has gone wrong for you?"

"No, it isn't. It's just that sometimes I wonder why I bother. In the old days, the enemy was clear cut. Communism was a worldwide threat and we were motivated by ideology. Today it's different. I feel as if I've become a glorified policeman. There must be a better way to die."

"Stop it," she said, her voice stern. "You do your best. What else is there? Everyone has his or her limit."

"I've been to my limit. Many times."

"James," she said. "There will come a time, probably very soon, when you will push yourself *past* your limit. When that happens, you will come to terms with your life and this job of yours."

Bond was too weary to argue.

"What you need is an evening out," she said brightly. "A good Belgian dinner, some drinks . . . How about it?"

Bond looked sideways at her. "Are you asking me for a date?"

She grinned in her pixielike way. "Is that all right? Providing we are free tonight, of course."

Bond allowed himself a smile. "Sure."

They arrived at their destination and she parked in front of Dr. Lindenbeek's building. They got out, pressed the intercom button, and explained that they were "police." A nurse met them at the door and said that Dr. Lindenbeek was with a patient.

"We'll wait," Gina said in Flemish. She showed the woman her credentials and they were led into the austere waiting room.

"It shouldn't be long," the nurse said, then left them alone. They could hear a man's voice speaking softly through the wall. After a few minutes, an elderly woman emerged, followed by the doctor. He said good-bye to her in French, then turned to Gina and Bond.

Gina spoke in Flemish, explaining that they were from the government and wanted to ask him some questions. Immediately, Bond knew that the man was involved. Lindenbeek's eyes widened and he swallowed hard.

"Come in," he said in English, gesturing toward his office.

Bond asked, "Dr. Lindenbeek, do you recall making a sketch that looks like this?" He took a pen from the doctor's desk and drew a torso on the prescription pad. When he outlined the pacemaker position, Dr. Lindenbeek slumped back in his chair and held his head in his hands.

"Well?" Bond asked.

"Am I under arrest?" he asked.

"Not yet. But it will help if you tell us everything."

"I must keep my patients confidentiality . . ." he muttered.

Bond perceived that this man was merely a pawn. Perhaps if he scared him a bit, he would open up.

"Dr. Lindenbeek," Bond said. "We're here on a serious matter of espionage. I can assure you that if you don't cooperate with us, then you *will* be under arrest. Espionage is a major crime. It can carry the death penalty. At the very least, you would lose your licence to practice medicine. Now, are you going to talk to us, or are we going to have to take you to the police?"

The doctor almost whimpered. "Yes, I performed the operation. I was forced to."

"Why don't you start at the beginning," Gina suggested. The toothpick went from one side of her mouth to the other.

Again Lindenbeek hesitated.

Bond added, "Dr. Lindenbeek, you could also be in serious danger. The people you're dealing with are quite ruthless. They're killers."

Lindenbeek poured a glass of water from a pitcher on his desk. He offered some to his visitors, but they shook their heads.

"If I tell you everything, can you guarantee me protection?" he asked.

"Perhaps," Bond said. "It depends on how much you tell us and how helpful it is."

The doctor nodded and began to speak. "Five . . . no, six months ago, I got into a little trouble. There was a patient, a woman. I'm not married, and sometimes it is difficult for me to meet women. I was attracted to a patient and I may have gone too far. She certainly encouraged me, though. It was, how do you say, mutual?"

"Consensual," Bond said.

"Yes. But somehow photographs were taken of us, here in this examination room. I had been set up. Afterward, this woman filed charges against me for rape and malpractice. The truth is that she is a member of something called the Union."

He looked at Bond and Gina for a sign of recognition when he mentioned the name.

Bond nodded and said, "Go on."

"You know of them?"

"Yes. Please continue, doctor."

The doctor seemed relieved. "Thank God. I was afraid you would think I was crazy. This Union, they contacted me and said they could make this malpractice suit go away if I did something for them. At the time, I was defiant and thought I could prove in court that the woman wasn't raped. Then they did something horrible. I began to receive photographs in the mail—child pornography. The packets would come two or three times a week. I burned them, but the Union got in touch with me again and said that I was now on some kind of list of child molesters. If I didn't help them with a service, they would make sure that I was arrested and charged with dealing in that filth."

"How did they contact you?" Bond asked.

"Always by phone. Some Frenchman. It was a local exchange, I'm pretty sure."

"Then what happened?" Gina asked.

"What could I do? I agreed to help them," he said. Lindenbeek was sweating and his hands were shaking as he poured himself another glass of water.

"What did they want you to do?"

"I was told that a Chinese man, Mr. Lee Ming, would come to see me. He was in his late fifties and actually needed the pacemaker. His heart rhythm went up and down. I was told to schedule an operation at Erasme for this man. I was to obtain a pacemaker and have every-thing ready. The night before the operation, I was told that an Eng-lishman would visit me and deliver what they called a microdot. It would be on a piece of film. I was to put this microdot inside the pacemaker before performing the operation. As it seemed harmless, I did it."

"When was this?"

"The operation was two days ago."

"Can we see Mr. Lee's file?" Gina asked.

At first Lindenbeek hesitated, but then he nodded. "It's right here. He handed it over. Bond examined it, but there wasn't much there. "Lee Ming" could very well be an alias. The patient's address was listed as the Pullman Astoria Hotel.

"Did they ever tell you what was on the microdot?"

Lindenbeek shook his head. "I didn't want to know."

Bond believed him. The man was too scared to lie.

"Do you know where Mr. Lee is now?" Bond asked.

Lindenbeek shrugged his shoulders. "I don't know. He's a Chinese citizen visiting this country. The Englishman asked how soon Mr. Lee would be able to travel. I assumed that he was going back to China."

"And you're sure that the people who wanted this done called themselves the Union?"

"Yes."

Bond stood up. "Right. Dr. Lindenbeek, I think it would be best if you come with us. We'll want to interrogate you in more detail and show you some mug shots. This is for your own safety. If the Union are indeed behind this, and they learn that you've talked, you could be a dead man."

"I'm under arrest?"

Gina nodded. "It's better that way, doctor. You'll be safer. We'll take you to the police station downtown. Once we get this sorted out, we can move you somewhere else. We will need you for a trial if and when we catch the people responsible for this."

"You mean . . . testify?"

Bond nodded. "You're the only one who can prove that our man, Harding, gave you this microdot."

"He told me his name was Donald Peters."

"He lied. Come on, doctor. Better cancel the rest of your appointments today. Let's go."

Hendrik Lindenbeek was taken to the police station at Rue Marché au Charbon, a more than fifty-year-old dark brown brick building. The Brussels authorities had been contacted by the Ministry of Defence and were now aware of the situation. Lindenbeek would be held pending a hearing that would take place the next day at the Palais de Justice. A public prosecutor had been assigned to consider espionage charges against Steven Harding and Lee Ming, and an all-points alert had been issued for their arrest. Extraditing the suspects would be another matter altogether, as Belgium would hold its own hearings on whether or not they could indeed be sent to England. Bond figured that they would hold on to Lindenbeek, as he was a Belgian citizen. A Chinese national would probably be sent back home. Harding, however, was English, and belonged back in the UK.

Bond and Gina spent the afternoon at the police station and saw that Lindenbeek was put in a cell alone. Inspector Opsomer assured them that they would be contacted as soon as he heard something. Belgium's state security force, the Securité d'État, was taking charge of the investigation. From then on, there was nothing more that could be done.

Before leaving the station, Gina phoned the Pullman Astoria Hotel and learned that Lee Ming had checked out.

Although they had caught a big fish, Bond felt frustrated. He knew M wouldn't be completely happy, either.

They went back to the Métropole. Gina collapsed in an armchair while Bond sat at the desk to phone London. After the ritualistic security checks, he was put through to his chief.

"Double-O Seven?"

"Yes, ma'am."

"How are you feeling? I heard about your injuries," she said. Her concern sounded genuine.

"I'll live, ma'am. Just a cracked rib and some bruises."

"I dare say you've survived much worse."

"I'm afraid I don't have much to report. Dr. Lindenbeek is in custody and the matter is being handled by the Securité d'État. We're out of the loop as far as he is concerned."

"That's all right, as long as the Belgians hold on to him. For the time being anyway. No leads regarding Harding or this Chinese man?"

"None. They could very well still be in Brussels. Then again . . ."

"I understand. Double-O Seven, I want you to continue your work with Station B for at least another day. If nothing turns up, come back to England. I'm afraid I'll have to give the Minister news he's not going to like."

Bond could hear the disappointment in her voice. He had let her down. "Ms. Hollander and I are going to go through Interpol files tomorrow and try to determine who Lee Ming really is. He looked familiar somehow."

"Fine. We'll talk tomorrow."

Bond hung up and said nothing. Gina picked up on Bond's gloom and said, "Hey, remember what I said you needed tonight? Come on, let's go have dinner. The restaurant downstairs is fabulous. Change your clothes or do whatever it is you Brits do to get ready for an evening out with a gorgeous, fun-loving Belgian girl."

They met again in the hotel's luxurious bar, Le 19ème, which was laid out in the style of a gentleman's club, with Corinthian columns and deep leather chairs.

She was dressed in a low-cut, short black cocktail dress that revealed more of her legs than Bond had previously seen. The single pearl on her necklace dangled teasingly at the top of her pronounced cleavage. Her eyes sparkled.

"You look good enough to eat," Bond said.

"So do you," she said, taking his arm. He was dressed in a tailor-made Brioni dinner suit.

L'Alban Chambon is considered one of Belgium's finest restaurants. It is tastefully designed with wood floors, white walls, and intricately carved blue molding. There are mirrors on two sides of the room, creating the illusion that the room is much larger than it really is. The head-waiter showed Bond and Gina to a small round table covered by a white tablecloth on top of a blue one.

As they sat, a tall man wearing a chef's hat approached them.

"Monsieur Bond?" he asked.

"Dominique!" Bond said. He shook hands with the *chef de cuisine*. "How good to see you again. This is my colleague, Gina Hollander. Gina, this is one of Europe's best chefs, Dominique Michou."

She spoke to him in French. "Pleased to meet you." Mr. Michou kissed her hand, then said, "I would like you to try our featured special tonight."

"We'd be delighted."

"Splendid. I'll turn you over to Frederick, then. Enjoy your meal."

Michou bowed and returned to the kitchen. Frederick, the head-waiter, presented them with menus and a wine list. Bond ordered a full-bodied red wine, Château Magdaleine Bouhou.

New Age solo piano music was playing softly over the sound system. A plaintive, high-pitched male voice began to improvise lyrics over the music. Gina closed her eyes and smiled.

"You know this music?" Bond asked.

She nodded. "It's a Belgian composer named Wim Mertens. He's contemporary and does some beautiful things. I find his music very sad at times."

Bond shrugged. "If I have any taste in music at all, it's for jazz and big band. Ever hear of the Ink Spots?"

"I don't think so."

When the wine came, Bond toasted Gina and they drank together. Then he asked, "Gina, what is your cover?"

"I beg your pardon?"

"Do you use a cover? In the old days when MI6 was known as Universal Exports, and later Transworld Consortium, I traveled the world as an importer/exporter. What do you tell people when they ask you what you do?"

"My *memoir* in college was in fashion design," she said. "I really am a designer, so that's what I say. I'm partners with a friend of mine from school. She owns a dress shop in Brussels. We design things together."

"You look the part, then."

"Thank you. And what do you tell people now that MI6 is no longer an 'importer/exporter'?"

Bond smiled wryly. "Usually I say I'm a civil servant. That tends to shut them up right away."

A waiter brought them *salade d'asperges à l'oeuf sur le plat et crème d'estragon,* which was made of tender white and green Belgian asparagus with a poached egg on top and creamy tarragon sauce on the side.

"You're not like other Brits," she said after a while.

"Oh?"

"We have always seen Brits as very serious and easily shocked. Except for the ones who come over and booze it up for a weekend."

"I am neither," Bond said.

"No! You like your alcohol, but it does not seem like you would be easily shocked. Another way I've always thought of British men is that they are 'real' gentlemen. You are a gentleman."

"Flattery will get you everywhere."

"What do you think of Belgian women?" she asked, licking a bit of sauce from the corner of her mouth. Bond realized that this was the first time he had seen her without a toothpick in her mouth.

"Are you a typical Belgian woman?"

She laughed. "I don't think so. I'm not sure we can be classified, since Belgium is such a multilingual country. The French girls in the south are a little different from the Flemish girls in the north, and so on. We are perhaps not as wild and sexy as Dutch girls."

"You're not? Bloody hell . . ."

That made her laugh. "I mean, we're as sexually open as any other European girls, I suppose, we just don't talk about it. It depends on the level of education, I think. Am I making sense?"

"You're saying that actions speak louder than words?"

She knew he was teasing her. "I had better be careful," she said, wagging her finger at him. "My English is not so good. You will twist my words and make me say something I'll be sorry for later!"

The main courses came. She was having *filet de boeuf poêlé, légumes de saison frits, et sauce choron*—sauteed fillet of beef with fried vegetables and choron sauce. He tried the chef's special, *médallion de veau de lait et risotto aux légumes et parmesan*—fillet of milk-fed veal and rice with vegetables and Parmesan cheese. The rice was packed in the shape of a hockey puck with potatoes mixed in.

"This is delicious," she said, taking a dainty bite of beef.

"Monsieur Michou does it again," Bond said. The veal was light and tender, cooked a perfect medium so that the pink center was juicy and succulent.

"How important is this formula that was stolen?" she asked.

"Quite, although I think it's more important to Britain for political reasons than for scientific ones."

"Why?"

"Britain is no longer the empire it once was. My superiors believe that this process will give us more face, I suppose, and it's worth a fortune. Our Ministry of Defence have visions of profits dancing before their eyes, but it's more about proving to the world that we can still come up with technological advances."

Dessert was a Belgian specialty, one of Bond's favorites—*véritable "Café Liègeois"*—a cold, creamy coffee milk shake that left white mustaches on their upper lips. Gina gently scraped hers clean with her index finger and then licked off the excess cream. Bond found the sight incredibly erotic.

When Bond and Gina finished, it was nearly eleven o'clock.

"It is said that in Belgium, dinner *is* the evening's entertainment," Gina said. "Usually, a night out might consist of the theater or a show, or perhaps a dinner—but not both. Dinner in Belgium is a ritual to be savored and never rushed. It sometimes lasts hours. The time flew by, didn't it?" Bond could see that she was slightly nervous about how the rest of the evening might go. After they had drunk two bottles of the wine between them, she was more relaxed and flirtatious.

As they left the restaurant, he asked, "What now? Shall we take a walk?"

She wrapped her arm in his and pulled him down closer to her lips, then whispered, "No. Take me to your room."

"Why, I'm shocked! Positively shocked!"

A dim golden light seeped in from the bedroom window and splashed across the bed. She let the cocktail dress slip off her shoulders to reveal a pink, scalloped daisy lace underwired bra and thong. She gingerly undressed him and removed the rib harness, and gently pushed him back on the bed. She straddled him, then leaned over to kiss him.

Her agile tongue darted around inside his mouth. Considering that she was able to perform tricks with a toothpick, Bond wasn't surprised. He sucked it and probed her mouth with his own.

She sat back up and slipped the bra off. Her breasts were full and firm, the nipples erect and hard. He reached up and touched them, rubbing the tips lightly in the palms of his hands. She moaned softly and closed her eyes. She moved back a little so that she could touch him. Bond let her manipulate him until he was as hard as stone. Gina removed her thong and slid her wetness down over him. She rocked back and forth on his body, slowly and purposefully at first, then faster and faster in wild abandon as their passion increased. Her tight, compact body writhed and wiggled over him, sending spasms of pleasure to the very depths of their souls.

"Oh, James," she cried as she approached climax. "It's perfect . . . perfect . . ."

He could feel her spasms around him, triggering his own release. For those few moments, they were both lost in each other, melding into one living being with fire for a heart and electricity for a soul.

Perfect indeed.

NINE

COVERING TRACKS

AT PRECISELY EIGHT-THIRTY A.M., THE BELGIAN POLICE REMOVED HENDRIK Lindenbeek from his cell in Police Headquarters and prepared to take him to the Palais de Justice for a preliminary hearing. It was standard operating procedure for the police to transfer all the prisoners who were arrested during the night to the massive ornate building dating from 1883.

Bond had suggested that they transport Lindenbeek under cover, for the Union might very well attempt to assassinate him if they could get a clean shot. Inspector Opsomer, an efficient but impetuous officer, humored the British agent and assured him that they would take every precaution.

Nevertheless, Opsomer was not present in the morning. He was called away on another matter and left the transfer of prisoners to his assistant, Sergeant Poelaert.

Poelaert, who hadn't been apprised of the seriousness of Lindenbeck's crime and his importance to an ongoing investigation, put the doctor and two other prisoners in an ordinary police van. Under special circumstances, armored cars were used, but this didn't seem necessary to Poelaert, as it would have required more time and manpower.

Lindenbeek, handcuffed and in leg chains, was escorted to the garage by two gendarmes. The two other prisoners had been arrested for mugging a tourist and were already inside the olive green Mercedes van. Lindenbeek climbed in the back and sat down, nervous and frightened since his arrest. He wasn't accustomed to this kind of treatment. He was a medical doctor! He had a respectable list of patients! He hoped that all this could be sorted out quickly and that he would be sent to a safe hiding place. His lawyer was confident that everything would turn out for the best, but Lindenbeek wondered if he would ever practice medicine again.

Sergeant Poelaert locked the back of the van and got in the passenger side. He gave the signal to open the garage door.

A small seventy-year-old chapel stood less than a half block away from the police station. A window in the steeple was conveniently placed so that anyone crouched inside could see the entire street.

Dr. Steven Harding sat at the window, his eyes locked on police headquarters. He held a CSS 300 VHF/UHF radio transceiver to his face.

"Stand by," he said.

The garage door opened.

"Okay, they're coming out," he said. "Send in the bird."

"Roger that," came a voice at the other end.

The van pulled out of the garage to begin its ten-minute journey to the Justice Palace.

"It's a green van," Harding reported. "Two men in the front. Looks like there are others in the back with Lindenbeek. I can't tell how many."

"Does it matter?" came the other voice.

Harding snickered. "Not at all. A prisoner is a prisoner, right?"

The van inched along the narrow road in traffic. Aside from the normal rush hour congestion, the transfer was on schedule. Poelaert saw nothing out of the ordinary on the streets. It was going to be an easy delivery.

As Brussels is a large metropolitan city, the presence of helicopters in the air is never a cause for alarm. The Soviet-made Mi-24 Hind assault chopper had been painted white so that it wouldn't be conspicuous; in fact, it was completely ignored when it appeared in the sky over the heart of the city.

The van turned down Rue des Minimes, a wider artery, and headed southwest toward the Palace.

Harding said, "I see the bird. It's all yours now. Over and out." He pushed in the antenna and got up from his cramped position in the steeple. He quickly climbed down the steps and slipped out the back, where he had left a rented dark blue Mercedes 500 SEL. Lee Ming was in the passenger seat, his eyes closed.

Harding got in the car and pulled away from the chapel. Lee woke up and asked, "How did it go?"

"We'll know in a few minutes. Let's get out of here," Harding said.

The van progressed slowly down the large, crowded street. The helicopter hovered overhead. Armed with thirty-two 57mm projectiles in rocket pods located on the stub wings, the Hind is particularly adept at hitting small targets with precision.

When the van stopped at a red light, the driver heard the chopper and looked out the window. He pointed it out to Poelaert. The sergeant peered at the sky, but the sun was in his eyes. All he could see was the silhouette of the helicopter and that it was white.

"It's from a TV news channel," he said. "Don't worry about it."

The driver laughed. " 'Don't worry about it' is at the top of the list of best famous last words."

The light turned green and the van moved out into the intersection.

Up above, the Union member with his hand on the trigger saw that the van was clear of most of the other traffic. The timing was perfect.

Two rockets shot out from underneath the helicopter and zoomed down to the van so quickly that witnesses were not sure what had really happened. All they knew was that the van exploded with powerful force. Pedestrians screamed. Other vehicles skidded and slammed into each other in an effort to avoid the blast. For several minutes there was utter chaos on the street. When the smoke finally cleared, the only thing left of the van was a burning chassis with five charred corpses.

The Hind pulled away and sped to the south. By the time the authorities determined that the van had been shot at from the sky, the helicopter was long gone.

Meanwhile, the Mercedes SEL made it to "the Ring," and headed toward the E19 exit.

"How long to Paris?" Lee asked.

"I don't know," Harding said. "Just sit back and enjoy the scenery. I'll get you to your plane on time."

"My superiors are not happy with the change of plans." Over the past couple of days, Harding had been holed up with the Chinese man and found him to be cantankerous and annoying.

"Look, we can't help it if Lindenbeek got caught. I had to see that he was eliminated. We couldn't have him identifying us. The Union had to make last-minute changes, all right? The original plan with you flying out of Brussels to Beijing just wouldn't have worked. They've probably got both of our faces plastered on *every* Immigration desk in Belgium. You would have been arrested before stepping on the plane."

Harding sounded more sure of himself than he felt. Ever since the encounter in the Métropole, he had been a nervous wreck. Everything had begun to fall apart. Basil had been hired to guard Lee, but instead had fouled up. The Chinese thought that Lee was going to be on a plane to Beijing, but that plan had to be changed at the last minute.

"I would have you know," Harding said, "that the Union fulfilled their end of the deal. We got the formula on a microdot, and we got that microdot inside of you. It was your problem to get back to China with it."

"No," Lee said. "It was part of the Union's bargain with my people that you would see me safely into China."

"We were going to do that, weren't we? All right, so we changed the original plan. The new plan is more complicated and will take more time, but it will get you to China. Relax."

"I don't particularly want to go to India," Lee said.

"I can't do anything about it," Harding said. "These are the orders from *my* superiors. I am to take you to the Paris airport, and there you'll get on a flight to Delhi. You'll be there only a short while. Then you'll get on a plane to Kathmandu. That's in Nepal."

"I'm not stupid."

Harding shrugged. "You will be contacted by someone in Kathmandu. They'll find you at your hotel. All of that information is in the packet I gave you. Arrangements are being made to smuggle you across the border into Tibet. From there, you're home free. But you'll have to make your way to Beijing from Tibet."

"It sounds very tiresome. Don't forget I just underwent surgery."

"You could be a little more grateful, you know," Harding said. "The Union are going to all this trouble to get you to Tibet as a *favor.* We don't *have* to do this. Like I said, our obligation stopped with getting you the formula. The Union simply want our clients to be happy, so we're taking this extra step to see that you get home safely. After all, we don't get the other half of our money until you're back in Beijing."

"What about you?" Lee asked. "You are a traitor to your country. Where will you go? How much of the fifty million dollars is your percentage?"

"I can't go back to England, that's certain. Don't worry about my percentage. I am being paid enough to make all this worthwhile. I have to leave my home, my country, my job . . . I plan on retiring on an island somewhere in the South Pacific."

"Stay away from the Philippines," Lee said. "That place is no fun."

As they drove out of Belgium and into France, Harding worried about the next phase of the plan once Lee got to Nepal. At least he would be through with his end of the operation after he dropped Lee off at the Paris airport. What happened next was out of his hands, although he had helped plan it. If only that damned secret service agent hadn't poked his nose into it. What was his name? Bond? That's right . . . the golfer.

Keeping track of him would be easy enough.

James Bond and Gina Hollander sat in her office, staring at the computer monitor. Her spare laptop had been set up next to it so that they could work simultaneously. They had patched into Interpol's database using Gina's authorized password. The mug shots of Asians had been flashing on the screens for three hours and they had yet to make a match to Lee Ming.

"They're all too young," Bond said. "Is there any way we can narrow our parameters?"

"Not really," she said. "Not from here. You ask for active Chinese agents, you get active Chinese agents."

"This is getting us nowhere. We must have looked at hundreds of faces, and frankly, they really *are* starting to look alike. I don't mean that derogatorily."

"Perhaps he's not a criminal. Maybe he's an ordinary Chinese citizen. Maybe he's not from China at all," she suggested.

"Look up *inactive* Chinese agents. He's in his late fifties. He could be retired."

Gina typed on the keypad until a different set of screens appeared. As expected, the faces looked older, more seasoned.

"This is more like it," Bond said.

She typed on the laptop and brought up the same database there. "I'll take N through Z, all right?"

They worked for the next hour.

"At least there are not as many inactive agents," she said.

Bond was coming to the end of his half, when a face popped on the screen that looked familiar. He stopped and studied it closely. The man was identified as Ming Chow, a former member of China's dreaded secret police. He had retired in 1988 due to a heart problem.

"This is him," Bond whispered.

"Really?"

The photo was twenty years old, so the man appeared much younger than Bond recalled. He clicked on the "details" button and more biographical information flashed onto the screen.

Gina read aloud: "Ming Chow worked in counterintelligence through the seventies and later became an officer in the People's External Security Force. He distinguished himself with the investigation and arrest of a British spy stationed in Shanghai. MI6 agent Martin Dudley was caught red-handed with Chinese military secrets being smuggled in antiquities. Before Dudley could stand trial, he was found dead in a jail cell. Ming Chow was promoted shortly afterward."

"Of course! Now I remember why this man looked so familiar.

Martin Dudley was providing intelligence to MI6 for years when they finally caught up with him. There was quite a stink between Britain and China at the time. I was sent to China with a delegation of diplomats to testify at his trial. He was found dead the morning his trial was supposed to have begun. We were convinced he had been murdered, but the Chinese claimed he hanged himself. Ming Chow—how could I forget him?—he was the man in charge. When we suggested that perhaps Mr. Dudley had been killed, Ming Chow just grinned. 'So sorry,' he said, 'accidents happen.' I knew the bastard was lying. I could see it in his eyes."

Bond tapped the monitor with the back of his index finger. "He's older now, but our Lee Ming is Ming Chow."

"So he's not inactive at all?"

"Not necessarily. He may not be officially working for China's secret service. Many times, as you know, former agents hire themselves out for 'freelance' work."

"The Union, perhaps?"

"I smell them in this, all right. Their fingerprints are all over this case."

"We had better get this mug shot out to all the Immigration stations in Belgium."

"We'll do better than that. This fellow's face is going out all over the world," he said.

Lee Ming, alias Ming Chow, had just checked in for his flight to Delhi when his mug shot was transmitted by Interpol to all Western immigration authorities. Unfortunately, he had already cleared Customs and Immigration and was waiting at the gate for boarding to begin. As it was, he probably would not have been caught. The Interpol information accompanying the photo of the Chinese man failed to mention that the man being sought was at least twenty years older than he was in the photo.

A young British Airlines customer service representative named George Almond happened to be on break and was sitting with a sketch pad in a café across from Lee's gate. George considered himself a fairly good artist, and he especially enjoyed drawing people.

The Chinese man sitting across the way was a good subject. He had a lot of character and there was a timeless expression of world-weariness about him that George was determined to capture on paper.

It wasn't long before he had quite a decent drawing of Lee Ming.

Thirty minutes later, as Lee Ming was flying toward Asia, George Almond went back to his post in customer service. One way that he amused himself between customers (who invariably wanted to complain about the airline's food or lost luggage) was to look at Interpol's broadcasts. He liked to get ideas for sketches by viewing the mug shots. The criminals always had character.

When he saw Lee Ming's photo, his heart started to pound. He opened his sketchbook to the drawing he had done less than an hour earlier and compared the two faces.

"My God," he said aloud, then picked up the phone to call security.

The scratchy substance he had used to age and wrinkle the skin on his face had worked beautifully. Steven Harding looked at himself in the mirror and was pleased. He now had crow's-feet at the corners of his eyes and droopy bags beneath them.

For the second time, he applied spirit gum to the false mustache. He hated the smell of the stuff, and it was awfully tacky. His first attempt to disguise himself with it had failed miserably. He had used too much and it got all over his fingers. It took him a half hour to clean them with nail polish remover.

He nervously looked at the clock. He had a little less than an hour before he had to go to the Paris airport and catch his own flight.

Harding carefully pressed the mustache on his upper lip. He held it in place with the dry sponge for thirty seconds, then examined his handiwork. The mustache was straight, symmetrical, and looked great. He was pleased. Now the hair.

It was an ingenious device that the Union had given him. It looked like a small harmonica, but in reality it was hair whitener. By removing the metal comb hidden inside and running it through one's hair a few times, a person could age himself considerably. Harding did as he had been instructed to do, and within minutes he was a graying man of sixty.

After Bond and Gina had found Lee's face, both the Chinese man's and Steven Harding's mug shots were broadcast simultaneously to law enforcement agencies all over the world once again.

When the gray-haired man with a mustache and glasses approached Immigration and presented a British passport, the officer had no reason to connect him with any of the most-wanted faces that continually flashed across his screen.

"May I see your ticket, please?" the man asked. Harding complied. "Morocco, eh? It will be hot there."

"It's good for my asthma," Harding said.

"Be careful with the water." The officer, who had no idea that the passenger was wanted for international espionage, stamped the passport and handed everything back.

No one paid further attention to the small man who breezed through security, checked in at the gate with no problems, and then boarded a flight to Casablanca.

TEN

FLIGHT INTO OBLIVION

"IT'S *OUT* OF YOUR HANDS, DOUBLE-O SEVEN," M SAID SHARPLY.

"All I need to do is catch a flight to Delhi and—"

"That is all, Double-O Seven." The finality in her voice shut him up.

"Yes, ma'am," Bond said after a pause.

They stood in her office at the end of the day. He had just returned from Belgium and made his report. The meeting did not go well. Steven Harding was missing, presumably out of Europe. Lee Ming, thanks to the astute airline representative in Paris, was traced to Delhi and then Nepal.

Bill Tanner had received a report from the Delhi authorities saying that Lee Ming had come through the airport and had boarded a flight to Kathmandu. As requested, the Immigration officers in Delhi had stopped Lee before he got on the plane. They had orders to search him, but due to some unforseen bureaucratic foul-up, they had no idea what they were looking for. They searched Lee's luggage and forced him to strip anyway, hoping they would find something incriminating. They failed. Noting that the Chinese gentleman had a recent implant scar, they became confused. Had they grabbed the wrong man? He certainly seemed perfectly innocent. What should they do now?

They had let him go. Lee got on the flight and was now somewhere in Nepal. It had never occurred to the Indian authorities to hold Lee until they received further instructions.

Tanner had said, "You can't win them all, James," but it hadn't helped. Now Bond felt frustrated and angry that Steven Harding had slipped through his fingers. He was particularly sensitive about traitors. Bond had encountered his fair share of betrayal in his lifetime.

"Station I is in charge now," M said. "By the time you could get to Nepal, Lee Ming or Ming Chow—whatever the hell his name is— would be in China. We'll keep our fingers crossed that Station I is successful in stopping him from leaving Nepal. As I understand it, they've traced him to a hotel in Kathmandu. We've been told that an arrest is imminent. You're to go back to regular duty until further notice. Of much further concern, I think, is the leak from our office here. There's been a breach of security at home, and I don't like that. I don't like it one bit, do I make myself clear?"

She seemed to think that it was his fault somehow. "Ma'am, I assure you, I've treated this assignment with the same discretion that I've afforded every other one," Bond said.

"Stop it, I'm not blaming you," she said. There were times when she really did sound like a mother hen. It was as if she were upset with her eldest son and, although she still loved him, held him more accountable than her "other" children.

"It's a short list of people who knew you were going to Brussels," she said. "Do we have a traitor here at SIS? The thought is horrifying to me."

"I agree, ma'am. It's been a long time since something like that's happened."

"I don't want it happening on my watch. Mr. Tanner, tell him what we've learned."

Tanner cleared his throat and said, "An autopsy was performed on the remains of Dr. Thomas Wood. Besides being shot in the head and leg, it appeared that his throat had been cut. From ear to ear."

"That's the Union's signature," Bond said.

"Could be," Tanner agreed. "The slugs recovered from the body were nine millimeter, but they were too badly damaged to indicate what gun fired them."

M said, "Our analysts believe that Union involvement is entirely possible, especially considering that strange fax that Dr. Wood received. You know that they have recently gained a reputation for being quite good at infiltrating intelligence organizations."

"So, it's possible," Bond said, "that the Union are responsible for the breach of security."

M looked hard at him. "I'm afraid you have to play plumber for a while, Double-O Seven, and plug that leak."

Zakir Bedi, an Indian national based in Delhi, had been employed by the British Secret Service for nearly three decades. Over the years he had assisted in arresting terrorists, spied on Pakistan, smuggled Russian military secrets out of Afghanistan, and served as bodyguard and guide to visiting dignitaries. Now approaching retirement, Bedi wanted to perform one last exciting assignment for the firm before hanging up his hat. He would then go out with a nice pension and perhaps a service medal that he could display with pride.

It looked as if he might realize his goal that afternoon in Kathmandu.

It was just after lunch and he was sitting in a blue Tata jeep, one of the many used by the Nepalese police. Across the road was the famed Hotel Everest, isolated out on the Ring Road away from the central city in the section known as Baneshwar. One of the top hotels in Nepal, it was formerly the Everest Sheraton and it still maintained a very high standard with a bar, restaurants, sports facilities, disco, casino, and mountain views from upper floors.

The sergeant to his left was speaking Nepali into a walkie-talkie. Three policemen were ready to enter the hotel, burst into the room occupied by a Chinese man, Mr. Lee Ming, and arrest him for international espionage. Extradition papers had been filed in a hurry, and after intense negotiations between Britain, India, and Nepal, it was agreed that Zakir Bedi, in representing Britain, could enter the country, observe the arrest, and take charge of the prisoner.

Inside his air-conditioned room, Lee Ming lay on his bed, fighting the stomach cramps that had held him in a viselike grip since the night before. As he had become older and developed heart problems, he didn't travel well. He realized that he never should have volunteered for this assignment. Still, the money would be good if he ever made it back to Beijing.

He had been in Kathmandu a little over twenty-four hours and had slept very little. His body wasn't adjusting to the time change. After all, he had been in Belgium for three weeks and had undergone exhausting surgery. Now he was very tired and wished he could just sleep for a few hours. The problem was the edginess he felt because he didn't know when he would be contacted for the surreptitious escape into Tibet. He had to be ready at a moment's notice, which meant he couldn't leave the hotel—not that he felt like doing so.

He was just beginning to doze, when there was a loud knock at the door. Lee groaned, then pulled himself out of bed to answer it. When he opened the door, three rough-looking Nepalese men rushed inside.

"Shhh," one said, holding his finger to his lips. All three were short and stocky, and one had a black mustache. Obviously the leader of the group, he went to a window and pulled back the shades an inch. He gestured for Lee to come and look.

The blue jeep and two men were down below. One was dressed in the traditional dark blue trousers, light blue shirt, and V-necked woolen sweater with badges of rank and medals attached. He wore a faded maroon beret and black combat boots.

"Police?" Lee asked.

The man nodded. "Come with us now. We get you out of Nepal," he said in hesitant English.

Lee said, "Okay. Let me grab my—"

"No. Just come." The man spoke a stream of Nepali to his companions. One of them opened the door and looked in the hallway. He waved, indicating that it was all clear.

The men ushered Lee out of the room and to the fire escape stairs. Lee, unable to move quickly, was immediately a burden. Two of the men locked arms, picked him up, and allowed him to sit on them as they carried him down the stairs.

The Nepalese policemen entered the hotel and took the lift to Lee's floor. They arrived just as Lee and his rescuers came out of the stair-well on the ground floor and made their way toward one of the restaurants.

They pushed around a group of tourists, then went through the restaurant and into the kitchen. There, the leader spoke Nepali to one of the chefs, who gave him a large burlap bag normally used to sack potatoes.

"Put this on," the man said to Lee.

"What?"

Without wasting any more time, the man threw the bag over Lee's head. Lee began to protest, and the man said, "Shut up! Don't make a sound!"

Lee quieted down and allowed himself to go through this humili-ation. The burlap bag completely covered him. Since he was a small, lightweight man, it was easy for one of the men to pick up the bag and haul it over his shoulder—like a sack of potatoes.

The three men hurried out into an alley with the bundle. There they loaded Lee into the back of a pickup that was full of real sacks of potatoes. He grunted loudly as they dropped the bag on top.

"Quiet!" the leader said again. "You are in truck. We drive to air-port. Silence!"

The men got into the truck, backed out of its space, and took off down Arniko Rajmarg toward the Kathmandu airport.

Zakir Bedi noticed the potato truck pulling out from behind the hotel and heading southeast, but there were dozens of such trucks making deliveries to hotels in the area. He turned his gaze back to the front of the hotel, awaiting word from the men inside.

Upstairs, one of the Nepalese policeman raised his hand to knock on Lee's door but realized that it was ajar. He kicked it open to find the room empty. He swung the walkie-talkie to his mouth and shouted.

Bedi, who understood Nepali, heard the report and cursed.

"We have to find him!" he said to the sergeant. They got out of the jeep and ran inside the hotel. The two policemen met them in the lobby. They agreed to spread out and cover every conceivable exit.

Bedi was running toward the casino when he passed the restaurant. Going on a gut feeling, he asked the maître d' if he had seen a Chinese man come through there. He flashed a photo of Lee. The maître d' made an affirmative noise and pointed to the kitchen. Bedi shouted into his own walkie-talkie and ran through the restaurant.

The other policemen met him in the kitchen, where the leader questioned the chefs. Finally, one of them admitted being paid to hide the Chinese man in a potato sack.

"Potatoes?" Bedi asked. "I just saw a potato truck leave the hotel. They're headed for the airport! Let's go!"

The policemen and Bedi rushed outside to the jeep and took off in pursuit.

Tribhuvan International Airport is located four kilometers southeast of Kathmandu and is the country's single international air entry point. Built in 1989, it handles over a thousand passengers per hour, quite an improvement over the old terminal with lines trailing out the doorway and an open-air waiting lounge. Among the international and domestic flights that operated out of Tribhuvan, several private tourist agencies offered sightseeing trips from the airport.

The potato truck sped into the airport, jostling Lee Ming and the potato sacks with every bump in the road. They passed the main terminal and drove around to the private hangars. One sight-seeing operation, a British-run company called Above the Earth Flights, was preparing to send a twin-propeller plane around the Himalayas with a group of ten to fourteen British and American passengers. The truck, however, shot past the line of tourists and headed for another hangar, where a single-prop plane was fueled and waiting with the pilot on board.

The truck halted with a screech and the men poured out. They quickly pulled the burlap bag out of the back and freed their Chinese client.

"You fools!" Lee cried. "All that bumping could have opened up my chest!"

"Shut up and get in the plane," the leader ordered. "Do as we say or you'll be arrested. The police are right behind us!"

Lee grumbled and walked toward the plane. "Is this thing safe?" he asked.

Behind Lee's back, the leader looked at his other two companions and gave the signal they were waiting for.

The jeep, meanwhile, drove into the airport complex at a high speed. The sergeant contacted airport security and was told that a potato truck had been seen near the private hangars. He directed the driver to pull around the terminal. They also passed Above the Earth Flights, and then saw the single-engined four-man plane taxiing, ready to move toward the runway.

"Stop that plane!" Bedi shouted.

The jeep swerved in front of the aircraft. The three policemen jumped out and aimed FN 7.62mm self-loading rifles at the cockpit. The sergeant grabbed a bullhorn and ordered the pilot to stop.

The plane came to a halt as the officers approached it. Bedi got out of the jeep and went to the side of the aircraft. As the door opened, he leaped up the steps and stuck his head in the cabin.

It was completely empty.

Confounded, he turned to the pilot and asked where his Chinese passenger was. The pilot shook his head as if he didn't understand. Bedi drew a Browning Hi-Power 9mm handgun, the same pistol used by the Nepalese police.

"Tell me where he is or your brains will be all over your nice, clean windscreen," he said. Although Bedi had been raised a Hindu and still believed that the taking of human life was a grave sin, he had never hesitated doing so in the line of duty. As he had grown older, religion became less and less important to him. He figured that Shiva the Destroyer was on his side since he worked for law and order.

The pilot pointed to a hangar some two hundred yards away. It was the tourist company's outfit.

Bedi jumped out of the plane and shouted for the policemen to get into the jeep.

"He's over there!" he yelled, pointing to the twin prop that was just leaving the hangar.

The words ABOVE THE EARTH FLIGHTS were painted on the sides of the plane. It was beginning to pick up speed on the runway. The jeep sped after it, and the sergeant blasted orders with the bullhorn. The pilot refused to stop. The sergeant contacted the control tower and ordered them to halt the takeoff. He was told that the pilot was not responding.

Had they been able to see inside the cockpit, they would have understood why the pilot was incommunicado. The leader of the three Nepalese men was holding a pistol to his head.

"Just take off and get in the air," he commanded.

The other two hijackers were holding guns on the eleven frightened passengers, all British or American adults of both sexes. Lee Ming was sitting among them, next to a window. He didn't know what the hell was going on. Was this the Union's plan? Hijack a tourist plane? Where did they think they were going to go? Surely they couldn't cross the border into Tibet in a tourist plane!

Zakir Bedi ordered the jeep's driver to speed up, although the plane was now gaining momentum and would soon be off the ground.

"Shoot at them!" he ordered. One of the policemen aimed his SLR and fired. A bullet pinged off the tail, damaging it slightly, but it didn't slow the plane.

The aircraft reached its top speed and lifted off. It sailed neatly over the terminal and into the sky.

"Call your air force! We have to stop that plane!" Bedi shouted at the sergeant.

"Air force? We don't *have* an air force!"

Zakir Bedi put his head in his hands. After taking ten seconds to count to himself, he said, "Tell the control tower to keep track of that plane. I want to know where it goes."

Passengers were beginning to panic inside the aircraft. One of the Nepalese men told them to shut up.

The leader told the other man to keep the gun on the pilot, then went into the small, cramped cabin to address the people.

"Please remain calm," he said. "This plane is not going to look at Mount Everest as originally scheduled. We're taking a little side trip to Darjeeling. No one will be harmed if you stay quiet and cooperate. You'll be back in Kathmandu in a few hours."

Darjeeling? Lee Ming thought. Why Darjeeling? They were supposed to be going to Tibet! Was this a new, roundabout way of getting there? One of the passengers, a man in his fifties, said, "Excuse me, I'm Senator Mitchell from the United States, and this is my wife." He indicated a man and a woman across the aisle. "That's Mr. Roth and his wife. He's a Member of Parliament in Britain. I'll have you know that both our governments will not tolerate—"

"Shut up!" the leader said, pointing the gun at him. The senator complied.

Lee gestured for the leader. "What is going on? Since this is all about me, I demand you tell me what is happening."

The leader smiled and said, "I'm sorry I could not say before. We're taking you to a safe place in Darjeeling. What becomes of you there is not our responsibility."

"What do you mean? I thought I was going to Tibet."

"Plans change" was all the man said.

Smelling a rat, Lee Ming suddenly became very agitated. He felt his heart start to pound, but the pacemaker kicked in after a few seconds. Still, he felt very anxious. Something was very wrong. These men weren't Union.

Relying on old skills and the experience of a man who was in his prime, a formidable secret service agent, Lee Ming jumped out of his seat and attacked the leader. They struggled in the aisle as passengers screamed. The Browning went off accidentally. The hijacker holding a gun to the pilot's head was hit in the throat. He fell back against the controls, gagging.

The plane swerved dangerously before the pilot was able to level it and set a course for east Nepal.

The leader punched Lee hard in the face. The Chinese man fell back into his seat, unconscious. The leader told the woman next to him, "Fasten his seat belt."

He went back to the cockpit and pulled his companion out and laid him in the aisle. He was dead. The other conspirator looked frightened. Now what would they do? In answer to the unstated question, the leader said, "We continue as planned. It just means more money for the two of us, right?"

The other man hadn't thought of that. He grinned nervously and nodded.

"Keep an eye on the passengers, and especially that Chinese piece of dirt," the leader said, then went back to the cockpit.

The pilot said, "There's a storm over east Nepal. Looks like a bad one. We should not fly that way."

"Just get us to Darjeeling," the leader said.

"I can't without going through the storm. We don't have enough fuel to skirt around it. We'll have to go back to Kathmandu."

"No! Fly into the storm. We'll take our chances."

"Are you mad? We could crash into one of the mountains!"

The leader shoved the barrel into the pilot's temple, hurting him. "Get us to Darjeeling, or you're dead."

"If you shoot me," the pilot stammered, "then you will die, too."

"So be it. You want me to shoot you now and get it over with?"

The pilot hesitated, then turned the plane eastward.

A half hour later, they felt the effects of the storm. High winds, sleet, and snow battered the little plane. The turbulence bounced it up and down, frightening the passengers even more. Some of them were praying aloud, others were sobbing and holding on to their loved ones, and a few were sitting silently, staring ahead in horror. The senator from America was sweating profusely. The Member of Parliament was biting his lower lip.

They were over Taplejung when visibility became impossible. Now even the leader was concerned.

"Do you know where we are?" he asked.

The pilot shrugged. "Somewhere over east Nepal. The navigation isn't working. They shot at our tail earlier, on the ground. There's something wrong with it. I can't maneuver the plane very well. We should turn back."

"Keep going."

The pilot, who was not accustomed to anything more complicated than sight-seeing flights over the Himalayas, didn't know how to handle the situation. He was lost, and he had no clue as to which way was north or south. For all he knew, he could be flying completely off course.

The storm assaulted the plane with intensity. At one point the aircraft dipped so abruptly that the pilot thought for certain that it was all over. He managed to pull the aircraft back up into the thick white wall of horror and kept going. He didn't know that the plane was now headed northeast into the Himalayas.

"She's not responding!" he cried. "I can't get a decent reading on where we are! For the love of God, we must turn back!"

For once the leader was quiet, staring out the windshield at the whiteness. His eyes widened when he saw the summit of a large mountain materialize out of the milk-colored curtain.

"Look out!" he yelled, but it was too late.

The plane scraped the edge of the mountain and went careening off into oblivion. This time the pilot screamed as he fought for control of the little plane. He pulled the stick back as far as he could so that the aircraft would climb as high as possible. Miraculously, it worked. After a minute of sheer terror, the plane leveled.

"What kind of damage did that do?" the pilot asked the leader. The man peered out the windshield but couldn't see a thing.

"I think we hit a wing, but we're still flying," he said. Then he noticed that the right propeller was behaving erratically. "That propeller—is it all right?"

The pilot looked at his controls. "No, we're losing it. We're going to crash. There's no way we can get back to Kathmandu now."

"What about Darjeeling?"

"Forget it," the pilot said. "We're in the Himalayas. I don't know how to get there. We can try to save ourselves by turning back."

The leader thought a minute, then said, "Okay, let's try. Turn her around."

The pilot couldn't see a thing. He punched in new navigation coordinates, but something wasn't right. The controls weren't responding.

"Navigation is completely out," he said quietly.

"What do we do now?" the leader asked. His abrupt, authoritarian manner had completely vanished.

"Pray."

Through the ice and snow that was assaulting the windshield, the two men saw a dark shape getting closer. Given the conditions, it was impossible to determine how far away the peak was, but they could see that it was a monster.

The pilot reacted and tried to turn away from it. The dark shape loomed even nearer until it filled the entire windshield.

"Pull up! Pull up!" the leader shouted.

"I can't!" was the last thing the pilot yelled.

The plane hit a relatively flat ledge not far from the summit of Kangchenjunga, the third tallest mountain in the world. The wings were snapped off immediately and the fuselage slid along the rocky ice and caught fire. It smashed against a wall of rock and ice, rolled over twice, and finally settled on a slanting but near-level patch of glacier.

The impact, the freezing cold, and the lack of oxygen at such a high altitude were immediately fatal to nearly everyone aboard. Three people, however, extraordinarily survived the ordeal but were knocked unconscious. Their hell would begin shortly.

ELEVEN

THE GREEN LIGHT

THE WALTHER P99 ROARED WITH A BARRAGE OF AMPLIFIED NOISE.

The walls of the underground room bounced the crashing sound back and forth until he had emptied the magazine. James Bond remained with his arms outstretched and his grip firm, then slowly relaxed and ejected the magazine and placed the pistol on the counter. He pushed the button on the wall to his right to move the target.

The silhouette of a "bad man" slid forward on the track so that Bond could examine how well he had done. Each bullet had hit the bull's-eye inside the outlined heart.

"Not bad, Double-O Seven," the instructor said. Reinhardt was a veteran of the service, a man in his sixties who had refused early retirement and still worked part-time in the firing range in the basement of SIS headquarters. A Canadian of German ancestry, the instructor had come to England and joined the secret service during its glory days after the Second World War. Bond thought he was an excellent tutor, and at times felt that he owed his life to the man who had taught him a thing or two about weaponry.

"Not bad?" Bond exclaimed. "I blew his heart to bits, Dave."

"Not bad" in Reinhardt's book was to be interpreted as "excellent," for Bond had never received higher praise from him. Reinhardt never handed out compliments. In fact, the instructor considered 007 the best shot in the entire building, but he believed that too much praise was anathema to the soul.

"But what did *he* do to *you?* He could very well have blown your head off," Reinhardt said. He punched a button on the machine behind them. A computerized image of Bond appeared on the attached television monitor. The instructor pushed another button; the tape rewound to the beginning. Bond's silhouette could be seen drawing his pistol, taking a stance, and aiming at the camera. Flashes of white light swarmed around the gun as he fired, but at the same time, red pinpoints began to dot his torso. The instructor pressed a button and froze the image.

"There, you see?" Reinhardt said. "He got you in the . . . shoulder, the right lung, and just below the neck. Not fatal, but enough to spoil your aim on your last few rounds. You'd have to go to hospital in a hurry, or you'd be dead within the hour."

"My first shot would have killed him," Bond countered.

"Perhaps," the instructor acknowledged. He knew full well that Bond was right; he just didn't want to give him the satisfaction of a pat on the back. It was his way, and he was aware that Bond knew it.

Bond removed the Zeiss Scopz shooting glasses and Aearo Peltor Tactical 7 ear defenders, and wiped the beads of sweat off his brow. "I think that's all for today, Dave, I need to get back upstairs," he said.

"Fine, Double-O Seven. It's good to see you haven't lost your edge."

"But you're saying there's room for improvement?"

"There's *always* room for improvement, Double-O Seven. Never get it in your head that you're the best shot on the planet. Look what happened to Billy the Kid."

"What happened to Billy the Kid other than that he was shot by Pat Garrett?" Bond asked.

"He got careless and cocky. It was his downfall. That's how Garrett got to him. Never think that you're better than the other guy, or you won't try as hard. You'll let down your guard. Remember that."

"Thanks, Dave. But isn't it also psychologically helpful to have the self-confidence to believe you're going to win, no matter what?"

"Of course! I don't claim to make perfect sense when I tell you

these things!" He chuckled. "You're supposed to assimilate everything I say, even if it's contradictory!"

Bond holstered his gun and said good-bye. He normally kept the
old PPK in his shoulder holster and used the newer P99 for backup.
The trouble was that the P99 was slightly bulkier and was less easily
concealed beneath a jacket. A lot of men used the P99 in a shoulder
holster, but Bond's habits died hard. He loved the old PPK as much
as he had once adored the Beretta. He would never be able to make a
permanent switch.

He took the elevator to his floor and walked into the reception
area. Using his key card to gain access to the work space, Bond said
hello to one of the newer secretaries and made his way down the aisle
toward Helena Marksbury's desk.

Her back was to him as she typed; a phone receiver was cradled
between her left shoulder and her ear. As he walked past, he lightly
squeezed her other shoulder. She looked up at him, forced a grin, and
waved slightly. Bond walked on into his private office.

It was an awkward situation. Obviously everything wasn't back to
normal. At least he felt better physically. His body had healed quickly.
He didn't have to wear the harness around his torso any longer, and
the cracked rib was a vague memory.

The in tray held a report from Foreign Intelligence regarding the
search for Steven Harding. It was inconclusive, but preliminary findings indicated that he might have left Europe for North Africa or the
Middle East. Bond thought that this wasn't much of a leap in logic.
The Union's headquarters was rumored to be located in either of
those two places. As for Lee Ming, the last word received at SIS was
that Station I's attempt to arrest him had failed. Word on his whereabouts was expected at any time.

Helena, now off the phone, stuck her head in the door and said,
"I'm glad you're back. M wants to see you in ten minutes." She
started to leave, but Bond stopped her.

"Helena."

She paused and looked at him.

"Come in here," he said.

She swallowed, made a face of resignation, then stepped inside the office.

"Are you handling this all right? You're not thinking of transferring to another department, are you?"

She shook her head. "I'm fine. How are you handling it?" She said it with a touch of sarcasm.

The inflection in her voice was just enough to make Bond's blood rise. He hated it when relationships broke down into pettiness.

"Helena, sit down." She sat in the leather chair across from his desk and looked at him as if he were a headmaster and she, the naughty girl, had received a summons.

"Now, look. We've had a fine time, you and I. We both agreed that it was not the best idea for us to continue this affair while we're here in London. Am I right?"

"You're right."

"But you seem to be having a problem with it."

She bit her lower lip to keep from saying something she might regret, then said instead, "James, I will be fine. Don't worry about me. Now I must get back to work."

"Wait," he said. "Let's leave us for a moment. I have to ask you about the leak."

Helena regained her composure. At least she could display the facade of professionalism when she had to, even when she was suffering inside.

"They questioned me for two hours," she said. "I had nothing to tell them, of course. There is no way that the information could have been leaked out of my office."

Bond didn't say anything.

"You believe me, don't you?"

He did. "Helena, I trust you implicitly. It's just bloody disconcerting that someone knew my movements in Belgium before I made them. Do you have any idea who could have done this?"

She shook her head. "I answered that question at least twenty times, James. No. Now, can I go back to work? I have to get out a report."

He nodded, giving her permission to stand and leave the room.

Her manner was cold and abrupt. It was to be expected, Bond thought, considering the nature of their relationship now.

Why did his love affairs, whenever they became somewhat serious, always end up so messy? Salvaging them was always a problem, which is why he rarely remained friends with former lovers. It was a pattern that he had long ago resigned himself to, even though he would never grow accustomed to it. He had met few women who were able to distinguish the difference between sex and a relationship, or who could have one without the other. In his own perfect world, men would be completely happy going through life from partner to partner, loving their mates equally but not exclusively. Cynically, Bond liked to think that women invented the concept of relationships and marriage in an effort to exert control over their male counterparts.

She would get over it. It would take some time, and then perhaps they could renew their passion on another extended holiday away from England. In the meantime, though, Bond decided he must keep Helena Marksbury at arm's length until things cooled down—or warmed up, as the case might be.

"Something's up, James," Moneypenny said as he stood beside her desk, waiting to be buzzed into M's inner sanctum.

"News on Skin 17?"

"I think so. She's been with the Minister of Defence most of the day and just got back."

"That sounds interesting."

The green light flashed above the door.

"In you go," she said, giving Bond the warm smile he knew so well.

M was sitting in her black leather swivel armchair, studying images on the monitors behind her desk. Bill Tanner was standing next to her, pointing out some detail in a picture. If Bond wasn't mistaken, they were photographs of Himalayan peaks.

"Sit down, Double-O Seven," M said without looking at him. Then, to Tanner, "How can we be sure there are bodies intact inside the fuselage? It looks to me as if it was burned badly."

"Yes, ma'am, but as you can see from this shot"—Tanner pressed a button and zoomed in on what appeared to be the wreckage of an aircraft—"the entire fuselage is intact. The burn marks are back here, all over the tail end. The front is relatively damage free. The wings are gone, of course."

"You don't suppose anyone could have survived that crash?" she asked.

"Highly doubtful," Tanner answered. "If anyone did, they would certainly be dead by now. The abrupt change in altitude from a pressurized cabin to twenty-six thousand feet above sea level would kill a man quite quickly. Not to mention the freezing temperatures and the fact that it was unlikely that any of the passengers were dressed for exposure of that kind."

M swiveled her chair to face Bond. "Double-O Seven, you're an experienced mountaineer, aren't you?" she asked.

Not sure how to reply, Bond said, "Well, yes, I used to take great pleasure in the sport, but I haven't done it in a while."

"Haven't you climbed Everest?"

"Yes, ma'am, and Elbrus, too. Most of my experience has been in the Alps and Austrian Tyrol. Why?"

With pen in hand she pointed to the image of the plane wreckage on the monitor. "Skin 17 is here, in this airplane, high on one of the Himalayas' tallest peaks."

Bond raised his eyebrows. "What?"

Tanner filled him in on what they had learned that morning from Station I. Lee Ming had boarded a sight-seeing flight that had apparently been hijacked. Its final destination was unknown, but the plane was tracked eastward, into a bad storm. The aircraft went down less than two thousand feet from the summit of Kangchenjunga, located in the northeast corner of Nepal on the border with Sikkim.

"We now have a very good excuse to go up there and find Mr. Lee's body," M said. "Because the travel agency that owned the plane is British, we have a compelling reason for the Nepalese government to give us a permit to climb the mountain. There were American and British citizens aboard the flight, and their families want to salvage the bodies and see what personal belongings can be found. More significantly, the plane was carrying an MP and an American senator and their wives."

"That's normally not done, ma'am," Bond said. "Hundreds of people have died in climbing accidents over the years. Everest has claimed the lives of at least a hundred and fifty people, and their bodies have remained on the mountain to this day—no matter who they were. I'm sure there are many such corpses on Kangchenjunga."

"I understand that, Double-O Seven, but we have to tell the Nepalese something reasonable. We can tell them that we want to perform a salvage operation for humanitarian reasons so that the victims' loved ones can give their family members a proper burial. And there's the matter with the government officials being aboard. What we're really going to do is find that bloody pacemaker."

Bond's heart started to race. He knew what was coming, and he was already well aware that it would be a difficult and challenging assignment.

"The Ministry of Defence is organizing an expedition. They're arranging with the government of Nepal for permission to climb the mountain, which I understand is sacred to the people there."

"Kangchenjunga is a special case, ma'am," Bond said. "It is indeed sacred, and as I understand it, people are allowed to climb it as long as they don't summit. Many do anyway. I've always heard the mountain referred to as 'Kangch.' "

"Whatever. As I was saying, the Ministry are organizing an expedition to climb the north face, as this is a route that has proven successful in the past, and it's the best way to the plane. I think you should tag along and pick up that pacemaker for us."

Bond thought for a moment before replying carefully "Ma'am, Kangchenjunga is the third tallest mountain in the world. What is it, Bill, twenty-eight thousand feet?"

"Twenty-eight thousand two hundred and eight feet, to be exact," Tanner said. "Or eight-thousand five hundred and ninety-eight meters."

Bond continued. "Any peak over eight thousand meters is considered *extremely* formidable. Everest isn't that much taller, and it's a hell of a lot easier. Not that Everest is a piece of cake, either. Kangchenjunga is one of the most difficult climbs anywhere."

"What's your point, Double-O Seven?" M asked.

"That it's not a walk in the park. I hope the Ministry are gathering very experienced people for this job."

"They are. You're going to have some help, too. I've arranged with the First Royal Gurkha Rifles to lend you a man who is an experienced mountaineer. You're to go meet him down at Church Crookham, near Aldershot, this afternoon."

"A Gurkha, ma'am?"

"That's right. A sergeant, I believe. Comes from Nepal, of course, and happens to be an expert climber. Gets along well with Sherpas. I thought you should have Nepalese backup."

Although he preferred to work alone, Bond didn't protest. If this mission was going to be as dangerous as he thought it might be, he could use the extra help.

"Now," she said. "It's vitally important that you retrieve what is left of Lee Ming. You're to get the pacemaker with the microdot—before anyone else does. It's in the interest of Britain's national security. Not only that, the Minister has told me that my job is on the line with this one. He wants that formula and wants it bad. Do I make myself clear?"

"Yes, ma'am."

"We believe that whoever arranged to have it stolen in the first place will send their own expedition to retrieve it. If the Union are involved, our analysts believe that they will mount an expedition as well. Your job will be performed with the utmost discretion. No one on the team will know of your mission except for your Gurkha companion and the expedition leader."

"Who is . . . ?"

M leaned over to her intercom and pressed a button. "Miss Moneypenny?"

"Yes?" came the voice.

"Send in our guest, please."

Bond looked at Tanner questioningly. The Chief of Staff averted his eyes, warning him that he wasn't going to be pleased with what was coming. M watched Bond closely to evaluate his reaction.

The door opened, and Group Captain Roland Marquis entered the room.

TWELVE

NOT QUITE IMPOSSIBLE

"GROUP CAPTAIN MARQUIS? COMMANDER BOND?" M SAID. "I UNDERSTAND you already know each other. And you know my Chief of Staff."

"Right, how are you, Bond—er, James?" Marquis said a bit too warmly. "Colonel Tanner."

Bond stood halfway up, shook hands, and retook his seat. "Fine, Roland. You?"

"Good." Marquis sat in the other chair facing M, next to Bond, and placed the briefcase he was carrying on the carpet.

"Group Captain Marquis," M said, "Mr. Bond is one of our Double-O operatives. He will be accompanying you on the expedition, as we discussed. His mission to retrieve the specification for Skin 17 is classified. Double-O Seven, your cover is that of a Foreign Office liaison."

"What about the Gurkha?" Bond asked.

"Gurkha?" Marquis furrowed his brow.

"I'm assigning a man from the Royal Gurkha Rifles to accompany Double-O Seven. He's an experienced mountaineer and knows the area. He'll take his orders from Double-O Seven. Aside from you, he's the only other person on the team who will know of Mr. Bond's assignment."

Marquis flashed his white teeth and said, "The more the merrier."

Not impressed by Marquis's levity, M said, "I must emphasize that

SIS would greatly appreciate any help that you can provide Double-O Seven so that he can accomplish his mission."

"Certainly, ma'am," Marquis said. "However, when I lead a team, I must insist that safety take precedence over everything else. If I'm asked to do something that might endanger the lives of any other team members, I will refuse. An authority figure is important in an expedition of this magnitude. As team leader, we must agree that my word is final."

M looked at Bond for approval. He shrugged. "I would expect nothing less if I were leading," he said.

Marquis seemed happy with the response. "Right. I'm sure we'll get along splendidly. Bond and I are old schoolmates, isn't that right, Bond?"

Before Bond could answer, M jumped in with "Tell us about the other team members, please."

"Of course. I've managed to snare some very good people at such short notice. The team's doctor will be Hope Kendall, an experienced mountaineer from New Zealand. I've climbed with her before. She's thirty-two and very fit. Our communications officer is a Dutchman named Paul Baack. He was recommended to me by the ministry. I met him this morning and I'm confident that he will be more than adequate. He comes with some sophisticated equipment that the ministry is lending us. Two mountaineers who have worked with me before, Thomas Barlow and Carl Glass, will be my immediate lieutenants. The American State Department are sending over three well-known climbers. They'll be looking after the American interests in the expedition." He went on to name a man to be in charge of Nepalese relations and hiring the Sherpa porters and cooks in Taplejung, a famed French climber to be the equipment manager, and explained that the rest of the team would be filled out with dozens of Sherpa porters and other climbers who will assist in hauling down whatever might be left of the plane's passengers and their belongings.

"SIS will be conducting security checks on everyone, of course," Tanner interjected.

"Now, I've drawn up a preliminary schedule," Marquis continued. He pulled some notes out of the briefcase.

"Beginning tomorrow there will be three days of intense physical exercise and training, followed by a medical examination."

"Most people train for months for an expedition like this," Bond said.

"You're right," Marquis said. "But the Ministry wants this job done as soon as possible. We need to get to that plane before the monsoon season starts in June. It's already the twenty-third of April. We can't afford the luxury of a long training period. We don't want to be caught on that mountain when the storms come in."

Bond understood and nodded. "Go on."

"We'll fly to Delhi, spend the night, then go on to Kathmandu, where we'll rendezvous with the Americans and the others. We'll spend three days there acclimatizing and making further preparations for the expedition."

He unfolded a large trekking map of Nepal. A route was highlighted in yellow. "We'll fly in a chartered aircraft to Taplejung, here." He pointed to a dot in eastern Nepal. "It's normally an eight-day trek to the Kanchenjunga Base Camp from there, but we're going to cut it down to six. We'll have to push extra hard to do it, but the more time we save, the better. Base Camp is here, at 5,140 meters." He indicated an X on the north side of a triangle marked "Kanchenjunga," which straddled the border between Nepal and Sikkim.

"We'll have to spend a week there acclimatizing. No getting around that."

"Why?" M asked.

"A human being's body adjusts slowly to the change in altitude," Bond explained. "Ascent has to be taken in stages, or one can become extremely ill."

"We don't want any altitude sickness on this expedition," Marquis said. "After the week at Base Camp, we'll slowly lay siege to the mountain within three weeks." Marquis opened a detailed map of the side of the mountain. "We'll set up five camps on the north face. Camp One will be here at 5,500 meters. Camp Two is at 6,000 meters. When we get to Camp Three at 6,600 meters, we'll need to spend another week acclimatizing. I'm hoping that's all the time we'll need. There may be some of us who can't ascend as quickly to Camp Four, which will be set up here at 7,300 meters. Camp Five will be at 7,900 meters, right next to the site of the plane wreckage. We're extremely fortunate that the aircraft is on this relatively level plain. It's called the Great Scree Terrace. It's less than 2,000 feet from the summit."

Marquis sat back and looked at Bond.

Bond frowned. "It's an extremely ambitious schedule."

Marquis replied, "I agree. I'm not saying it will be a picnic. We'll have to push ourselves to the limit, but we can do it."

There was that word again, Bond thought.

"We *will* do it," Marquis continued. "I've been asked to get us up the mountain in the safest but quickest amount of time possible. I aim to do that. This schedule gives us just a little over a month. The weather will be unpredictable toward the end of May. We're sure to encounter storms as it is, being that near the monsoon season. We have to race against time."

Bond had no choice but to go along with the plan. Nevertheless, he foresaw possible personality conflicts with the expedition leader. M looked at Bond. "Well, Double-O Seven?"

"As he said, it won't be easy. But I think I'm up to it, ma'am."

"Fine. Moneypenny will draw up the details for you to attend the training sessions. Thank you, gentlemen. That will be all, Group Captain."

Marquis started to get up, then asked, "So, Bond, do you think this Chinaman, Lee Ming—or whoever he is—still has the specification?"

"We have every indication that he does," Bond replied. "Where would he have hidden it?" Marquis asked. "Do you know?"

"That's classified," M said. "Even to you. I'm sorry."

Marquis nodded and said, "Of course. I meant only that if it had been placed somewhere in his clothing or hand luggage, the crash could very well have—"

"We know exactly where the formula is hidden," M repeated. "Let Double-O Seven handle that end of things. You just get him up and down that mountain in one piece, all right?"

Marquis stood and bowed slightly. "Yes, ma'am." He turned to Bond and said, "We'll see you tomorrow, eh, Bond? Bright and early?"

"I wouldn't miss it," Bond said dryly.

The drive in the DB5 was extremely pleasant. It was a beautiful April day without a cloud in the sky. Bond almost wished he were driving a convertible, but he could never own one. They were enjoyable as a novelty every once in a while, but Bond preferred hardtops.

Church Crookham is a quiet village not far, coincidentally, from Fleet, and is the home of the 1st Battalion of the Royal Gurkha Rifles. Bond had never known any Gurkhas personally, but he had a great deal of respect for them. When M had mentioned that he would be working with a partner, Bond had momentarily stiffened. He relaxed when she told him that his companion would be a Gurkha. Bond was intrigued with the prospect of working with a member of what he considered to be the world's fiercest and bravest fighting force.

Made up of hardy hillmen from Nepal, the Gurkhas have been a part of British military history since the Anglo-Nepali conflict of 1814. Bond thought wryly of the British army at that time. He admired the tenacity with which his country had attempted to expand the empire. Britain, already in control of India and hoping to extend the border, pushed northward into Nepal. They were met with such determined, independent, and resourceful soldiers, many not more than five feet four inches tall, the British army was surprised and impressed. Britain eventually won the war, but a friendly, long-lasting relationship was created with the Nepalese government. It was agreed that the British army could recruit soldiers, and being selected became an honor to the Nepalese people. The pay a Gurkha received from the British army was considerable when compared to that of his countrymen, and he could look after his entire family with it.

The Gurkhas were later incorporated into the Indian Army, and when India became independent after the Second World War, the Gurkhas were split between the two countries. Several regiments remained in the Indian Army. Britain retained four—the 2, 6, 7, and 10 Gurkha Rifles. In July 1994, due to "options for change," the regiments were amalgamated into one regiment—the Royal Gurkha Rifles, consisting of two battalions, the 1 RGR based in the UK and the 2 RGR based in Brunei. The Gurkhas stationed in England were originally the 2 and 6 Gurkha Rifles.

As he had reviewed this history before driving out from London, Bond couldn't help but visualize the stereotypical Gurkha: a short, stocky man with legs the size of tree trunks, running through the jungle after an enemy, wearing the traditional Nepalese *topi,* a white cotton cap that was decorated with colored designs (although in battle they would wear a camouflaged jungle hat or helmet) and waving the deadly *khukri* knife. They were known to behead their opponents during hand-to-hand combat. Such was their fierce reputation that during the Falklands conflict, Argentine forces supposedly fled when they heard that the Gurkhas were coming. *"Ayo Gurkhali!"*—the famous Gurkha war cry meaning "The Gurkhas are upon you!"—was intended to strike terror in the heart of the enemy.

Bond pulled into the compound after showing his credentials to the sentry, then drove past the barracks, which were painted black with white trim. When he presented himself at the officers' mess, he was greeted by a tall young Englishman in civilian clothes.

"Mr. Bond?" he asked.

"Yes."

"I'm Captain Alexander Howard." They shook hands briefly. "Come this way."

He led Bond into a magnificent room that could have served as a museum for the entire history of the Royal Gurkha Rifles. The lounge was decorated with a blend of British colonialism and Nepalese culture. Along with the more westernized brown vinyl-covered chairs and green carpet, there were real ivory tusks mounted on a non-working black wooden fireplace with a grand carving of the Hindu god Ganesh in the front. A tiger skin covered the carpet, and there were silver trophies and ornaments all over the room. Bond took a moment to admire the famous paintings portraying the Battle for Sari Bair, Gallipoli, August 9, 1915, and the Battle of Kandahar on September 1, 1880. A portrait of Prince Charles, who serves as colonel in chief of the regiment, hung over an impressive display of *khukris,* medals, and awards. A painting of Field Marshal the Viscount Slim, the most famous Gurkha officer, was also on display. Bond greatly admired his book about the Gurkhas' exploits during World War II, which is now required reading at Sandhurst.

Captain Howard said, "Have a seat and Sergeant Chandra will be with you soon."

"I thought his name was Gurung," Bond said.

"The Nepalese automatically adopt their tribal name at birth, like you and I would adopt our parents' surname. Because there are only a handful of the main tribes, there are an awful lot of people with the same surname," Howard said. "Hence, we have several men whose last name is Gurung. A lot of Gurkhas are Gurungs. They're mostly either Gurungs or Magars, from the western part of Nepal, and there are subtribes within those. There are a few from the eastern tribes, the Rais and Limbus. We refer to the men around here either by their first names or by their numbers. It's much less formal here than in other regiments."

"I see."

"Can I get you something to drink?"

"Vodka martini, please."

Howard smiled with approval. "Excellent choice." He moved to fetch the drink, but Bond stopped him.

"Could you please shake it? Don't stir it."

Howard looked at Bond curiously, then said, "Yes, sir." He left Bond alone in the room that contained so much history: monuments and memorials to the ghosts of foreign men who had died for Britain, as well as the proudly displayed commendations and trophies for those who had survived.

The captain returned with the drink and said, "I understand that what you have to discuss with the sergeant is classified, so I will take my leave."

"Thank you, captain," Bond said. He sipped the drink and said, "You make a fine martini."

Howard gave a slight bow and left the room.

After a few moments, Sergeant Chandra came into the room. He, too, was dressed in civilian clothes consisting of dark trousers and a green pullover sweater. He was a stocky five feet two inches tall and weighed roughly one hundred and fifty pounds. He had shiny black hair slicked back on his head, and his skin was the olive brown color prevalent among the middle-Asian races who appeared to be mixtures of Indian and Chinese. What was immediately striking about the man was his huge, warm smile, which seemed to transform his entire face into a pleasant configuration of dimples and lines, especially around his sparkling, friendly eyes.

"*Namaste.* I am Sergeant Chandra Bahadur Gurung," he said in good English. *Namaste* is the traditional Nepali greeting. Gurkhas are required to learn English, just as British officers serving in the regiment are required to learn Nepali, or Gurkhali, as the military calls it. The reason for this is that many words used are specific to the army and wouldn't necessarily be part of normal conversation in Nepal.

Bond stood up and shook the man's hand. He noted that it was a firm, dry handclasp, one that was full of strength and confidence. Chandra looked to be in his thirties, and there was experience and intelligence in his eyes. Bond knew from his record that the sergeant had been in the army since he was eighteen years old.

"James Bond," he said. "It's a pleasure."

"Please, sit down." Chandra gestured to the chair and waited until Bond had sat before taking the chair across from him.

"Sergeant, I understand you've been briefed on all aspects of the mission."

"Yes, sir."

Bond put up his hand. "Let's forget the sir, all right? This isn't a military operation, and I'm not your commanding officer. As far as I'm concerned, we're equals."

Chandra smiled again. "My orders are to follow *your* orders."

"Well, yes, unless they are totally without merit. In the Himalayas, they might often be."

Chandra laughed. "You have climbed before?"

Bond nodded. "Oh, yes, but I'm no expert. I've been to the top of Everest and several big peaks in Switzerland and the Austrian Tyrol."

"Never on Kangchenjunga?"

"Never. What about you?"

"I went halfway up Kangchenjunga once. I was forced down by an avalanche and then a bad storm. I am eager to try again."

"How did you get to be such a climber?" Bond asked.

"We live our entire lives going up and down hills and mountains," Chandra said. "That's why the muscles in our legs are so big. When I was a boy I went on a climbing expedition with my father, who was friends with some Sherpas in Kathmandu. They operated one of the first trekking services there. As I grew older, I made frequent trips to the Himalayas and climbed. I guess I just like it."

"You get on well with the Sherpas?" Bond asked. Sherpas are the tribe of Nepalese hill people more prominent in eastern and northern Nepal who are expert climbers and are almost always hired to haul equipment and luggage for western tourists wishing to trek across the country or up into the mountains.

"Yes, absolutely. Although Nepal has many dialects and tribes, Nepali is understood by everyone. Sherpas have called me their 'climbing cousin' because not many Gurungs have shown much interest in mountain climbing. I am an exception. Every time I go home to Nepal, my wife gets angry with me because I take some time to go climbing!"

"She's in Nepal?"

"Yes," Chandra said. He smiled broadly, obviously pleased with the thought of his mate. "Our wives remain in Nepal. They are not allowed to visit very often. Every three years we can go home for six months. That is in addition to our normal block leave of one month and the family leave in which she was with me for two years in the Far East. So I see her every now and then."

"What do you think of Group Captain Marquis's schedule for getting up Kangch?"

Chandra shook his head. "Not quite impossible."

"But almost."

Chandra's smile said a thousand words. Then he added, "We must beat the monsoon. It's the only way."

"What do you think our chances for success are?"

Chandra looked hard at Bond. "Sixty-five percent."

Bond leaned forward and lowered his voice. "What do you know about the Union?"

Chandra frowned. "Not much. I spent most of last night reading the file your people gave me. Very interesting group of people. I am interested in their psychology."

"I beg your pardon?"

"I mean, I am interested in how their minds work," Chandra clarified. "I don't understand men who will do that sort of thing for money. I come from one of the poorest countries on earth. The concept of working hard for a living is an accepted way of life for us. To turn to crime, especially betraying one's country, is confounding to me."

"They are very dangerous," Bond said. "We'll have to have eyes in the backs of our heads."

"If they are responsible for the theft of Skin 17, then I'm sure we will encounter them along the way," Chandra surmised. "They will try to sabotage the mission."

Bond sat back in his chair and raised his martini glass to his new companion. "Oh, of that I am sure, sergeant. You can count on it."

THIRTEEN

LE GÉRANT

STEVEN HARDING HATED NORTH AFRICA. IT SMELLED, THE VAST CULTURE shock frightened him, he was suspicious of everyone he met, and it was hot. It was so hot that he was afraid the sweat would ruin the carefully applied makeup that had enabled him to get to Morocco as Randall Rice.

At least Casablanca was a bit more westernized than other places Harding had been to. By far Morocco's largest city with a population of three million, it is the country's industrial center and port, and the most attractive tourist stop in western North Africa. The famed Humphrey Bogart and Ingrid Bergman film is, in part, responsible for the attention that Casablanca receives. As it is the place to go when Moroccans aspire to fame and fortune, Casablanca has all the trappings of a western metropolis, with a hint of the decadent ambience of southern European cities. Alongside the business suits, long legs, high heels, and designer sunglasses are the willowy robes of *djellabas* and burnooses of traditional Morocco.

Wearing a suit much too heavy for the climate, Harding stepped out into the bright sunlight and donned his sunglasses. The heat was barely tolerable, and it was only midmorning. Frowning, he walked away from the Sheraton and went south on Rue Chaoui, ignoring the cluster of beggars, old and young, who reached out to people entering and exiting the hotel.

He walked along what seemed to be a fairly modern street with western architecture. The atmosphere completely changed two blocks away, when Harding entered the Central Market bazaar. Here he felt as if he'd walked into another century. As colorful and noisy as any Hollywood film depiction, the market was an overwhelming assault on the senses. Harding focused straight ahead, walking quickly through the mass of veils, fezes, turbans, and fedoras. The visual display of the distinctive customs and clothing of local tribespeople who had come to buy and sell didn't excite him. He didn't want to buy fruits, vegetables, or spices.

No, thank you, he thought as he rudely brushed past a vendor. He was not interested in the "special" on rich, golden argan oil. There was another one tugging on his sleeve. Sorry, he hadn't any money today. That flatwoven carpet is indeed a beauty, but he didn't want to buy one, thank you anyway.

Harding was drenched with sweat by the time he got all the way across the bazaar to its southeast corner, where a delapidated shanty was built against a larger stone building. A beggar, who seemed at least ninety years old, sat cross-legged on the dirt in front of the door, which was simply an open space in the wood covered by a cloth hanging from an eave. There was a bent metal dish next to the beggar.

Harding knew he had to do something specific. He reached into his pocket and found ten dirhams in coins and dropped them into the tin. The old man mumbled something and gestured to the cloth. Harding turned to make sure no one was watching, then he ducked under the drape and went inside the shack.

It stank like a toilet. Harding was forced to take a handkerchief from his jacket pocket and hold it over his mouth. Other than the rancid smell, the room was empty. Harding immediately went to the stone wall and put his hand out to touch it. He felt the ridges along a crack, searching for a catch that couldn't be seen. He found it, then pushed it with the requisite force. The secret door slid open, revealing a passage lined in steel. Harding stepped through, and the door closed behind him.

At last! Air-conditioning! And his ticket out of this dreary place.

The hard work was over. He had come to claim his reward and move on to the next phase of his life, which would resemble nothing of what he had left behind in England. He hoped that *Le Gérant* wouldn't create a problem about Lee Ming's plane being hijacked. He had done his job and that part of the operation was completely out of his hands. Harding had delivered Skin 17 in precisely the manner that the Union wanted him to. They had better not renege on the five million U.S. dollars he was being paid!

Harding knew, however, that *Le Gérant* was capable of anything. He would consider himself lucky to get out of Morocco alive.

An Arab dressed in fatigues appeared and gestured for Harding to follow him. It was unnerving, especially when the clank-clank of the man's boots on the metal floor echoed throughout the tunnel. The corridor took a right turn, and they went down eight steps to a wider, open area with a table, computer terminals, banks of video surveillance screens, and other sophisticated, high-tech equipment. Two more guards were waiting there.

"Spread your legs and arms," one of them said.

Harding did so while the other one ran a metal detector around his body.

"Look into here," the first man said. He pointed to a device that resembled a microscope. Harding stepped to it and looked in. He knew that this would identify the tattoo that had been burned into the back of his retina when he initially joined the Union. He often wondered what an optometrist might say about the tattoo during an examination. Luckily, it looked more like scar tissue than any recognizable symbol.

It was discernible only to members of the Union.

Harding felt the beam of light pass over his eye. He straightened up and looked at the guards, one of whom studied a computer terminal on the table. The other one stared at him with a look of distaste.

"All right, he checks," said the man at the computer. Harding's escort tapped his shoulder and led him around the table to a door. The guards pressed a button and released a lock. The escort pushed the door open and held it for Harding.

"*Le Gérant* is waiting," he said.

Harding nodded and grinned nervously, then went through the door.

The room was dark, long, and had a very low ceiling. The only illumination was provided by lamps hung over the seven men and three women who sat at a conference table, each with a legal pad in front of them. However, there was no light hanging over the man at the head of the table, the one sitting in shadow.

Le Gérant. The Manager.

Harding had never met him face-to-face. Very few Union members had. The inner circle, those sitting around this table, were the only individuals who were so entitled. Nevertheless, it was still difficult to discern what *Le Gérant* looked like. His silhouette disclosed that he was tall and broad-shouldered, but thin and fit. The face and hands were in shadow, but there was just enough illumination to reveal him to be Caucasian. He was more likely a Berber, a descendant of an ancient race that has inhabited Morocco since Neolithic times. Berbers characteristically had light skin, blue eyes, and often blond or red hair. Harding knew that they were famous throughout history as warriors and notoriously resistant to being controlled by any system beyond the tribe.

Le Gérant wore a beret and was dressed in dark clothing. His face was further shielded by dark glasses that completely hid his eyes. Harding had once heard a rumor that *Le Gérant* was blind. Perhaps he really was . . . .

As the doctor stepped into the room, conversation halted abruptly and everyone turned to look at him.

"Come in, Dr. Harding," *Le Gérant* said. His voice was educated and smooth, and its deep timbre sounded vaguely French. If the man was indeed a Berber, he didn't sound like one. "Sit down there at the end of the table. We have saved a seat for you."

Harding took the chair and swallowed. Now he was nervous as hell.

"It is good to meet you at last, doctor," the leader said. "We have been following your progress on the Skin 17 project with great interest. I must congratulate you on everything you've done on behalf of the Union. It must not have been easy to find the courage to betray your country and steal the specification right out from under the noses of the DERA."

"Thank you, sir," Harding said.

"You also did a splendid job getting the formula to Belgium and into our client's pacemaker. Was that your idea, planting it there?"

"Yes, sir," Harding said. He felt a thrill that perhaps the meeting was going to go well after all.

"You also acted responsibly with regard to the physician who was caught in Brussels. Having him eliminated was the right thing to do. I'm still a little confused as to how he was caught in the first place, but nothing ever goes perfectly, does it?"

"No, sir," Harding said, swallowing and managing a smile.

Le Gérant took a moment to extract a cigarette from a gunmetal case that he removed from the inside of his jacket. He kept his head straight, staring ahead at a spot on the wall just behind Harding. The man *was* blind! the doctor thought. How extraordinary! The head of the Union couldn't see a damn thing.

Le Gérant lit the cigarette with a gold-plated Dunhill lighter, took a deep drag, exhaled, and spoke again.

"That brings us to the problem of what has happened to Skin 17."

Harding involuntarily closed his eyes with dread.

Le Gérant continued. "As I understand it, Lee Ming was in Kathmandu, awaiting instructions for his transfer to Tibet. However, precisely one day earlier than scheduled, he was kidnapped from his hotel and taken to the airport. There, he was shoved aboard a tourist Himalayan sight-seeing flight that was hijacked by his kidnappers and flown into the mountains, where a storm knocked it down. Do I have the facts right?"

Harding cleared his throat. "That's what I understand happened, sir, yes, I think that's what happened."

Le Gérant took another drag on the cigarette and shifted slightly in his chair.

"This is highly embarrassing for the Union, you understand that, Dr. Harding? We've let down our Chinese clients. They want their money back. After all, the Skin 17 specification wasn't delivered as promised."

"We did our part, sir," Harding protested. "Our obligation was to get him to Kathmandu. We did that. Our people in Nepal didn't keep a close watch on Lee. Apparently the Union weren't the only ones that wanted that spec. Someone got to him first."

"But how did anyone else know he had it?"

"Perhaps the British agent who tracked me to Belgium . . . ?" Harding mused.

"Oh, yes. The British agent. What's his name? Oh, I remember now. Bond. James Bond. I think you were a bit careless leaving England, Dr. Harding. One of our first rules is to cover your tracks in such a way that no one can follow you. Unfortunately, this man did."

"It was unavoidable, sir," Harding said. He was beginning to sweat despite the cool temperature in the room. His heart was pounding and his stomach cramped.

"What about the RAF officer who helped you steal the formula? Could he have betrayed you?"

"I don't think so," Harding said. How did *Le Gérant* know about Roland Marquis? Harding had been given free rein to pick and choose his team. No one was privy to the information.

"How much was he paid?" the leader asked.

"Fifteen thousand pounds sterling," Harding replied.

"Do you believe that's enough to persuade him to keep his mouth shut?"

"Yes."

For the first time, *Le Gérant* raised his voice. There was such internal animosity in it that everyone in the room felt a chill run down their spine. "Then *who* hijacked that plane and took potentially one of the Union's biggest moneymaking ventures away from us?"

Harding was speechless. The meeting had taken a turn for the worse.

"Well, Dr. Harding?"

"I . . . I have no idea. Sir." Harding was shaking now.

"Shall I tell you, Dr. Harding?"

"Sir?"

The leader took another drag on the cigarette, then snuffed it out in an ashtray attached to the arm of his chair. He had lowered his voice and appeared to be calm once again. "Shall I tell you who foiled our plans to sell Skin 17 to the Chinese?"

"Please do, sir," Harding stammered.

"It was someone trying to double-cross the Union. Someone on the inside. Someone who thought they were smarter than we. Not delivering Skin 17 as promised makes us look bad and damages our reputation. That makes me extremely unhappy. We may be losing two other prospective deals because of this mess. Do you know anyone in the Union who may be trying to outsmart us and get away with something, Dr. Harding?"

Now there was a ringing in Harding's ears. Had he been caught? "N-no, sir. How do you know? I mean, how do you know it's someone on the inside?"

"I know much more than anyone in this room could ever dream," *Le Gérant* said. "I believe that whoever is responsible for kidnapping Lee Ming was planning to take Skin 17 for their own. Perhaps they were going to try to sell it *back* to us for a higher price. After all, we're not the only ones in the extortion business. But no one can treat the *Union* that way."

Le Gérant flicked a switch on the control panel in front of him and a bright photograph appeared on the back wall. It was a picture of the three Nepalese men who had abducted Lee Ming from the Everest Hotel and whisked him away in a potato sack.

"These are the three men who are responsible," *Le Gérant* said. "They are Nepalese, but they do not reside in Nepal."

He *knows!* Harding thought. *My God, he knows!*

"Now, help me understand something, Dr. Harding," the boss said. "We know that Dr. Lindenbeek was caught in Brussels, and he probably talked a little before he was . . . uhm, put out of action. Right?"

"Possibly," Harding said.

"How much did he know about the Union?"

"Virtually nothing. He knew that we were going to expose him if he didn't perform the surgical procedure. He was killed so that he couldn't identify me and Mr. Lee. I covered my tracks there."

"Yes, you did," *Le Gérant* said. "What about our operative inside SIS?"

"In London?"

"Where else?"

"The operative there knows very little about the Union. We receive reports on the movements SIS are making to track down Skin 17. We stay one step ahead of them, so to speak."

"And this Bond fellow. He's the one they've sent?"

Harding nodded. "He was in Belgium. I have no idea if they're sending him to Nepal. I've been traveling."

Le Gérant withdrew another cigarette from his case and lit it. "I have news for you, Dr. Harding. They are indeed sending him to Nepal to join a little expedition that the Ministry of Defence is organizing. They're going to climb that mountain and retrieve the specification."

"Well," Harding said, faking a laugh. "That gives us another opportunity, then, doesn't it? We can get it back!"

"Perhaps," the leader said. He took another moment to relish his tobacco. "Dr. Harding, do you know these men on the screen behind me?"

He shook his head. "I've never seen them before!"

"Never?"

"No, sir."

Le Gérant flicked another switch on the control panel and the slide changed. This time it was a shot at a pub, one that Harding recognized. When he saw who was in the picture, his heart skipped a beat.

The three Nepalese men were sitting with pints of beer talking to none other than himself.

"This photograph was taken three days before the Skin 17 operation went down," *Le Gérant* said. "In the Lake and Goose public house, not far from Aldershot. You know it well, don't you, doctor?"

Harding closed his eyes. It was all over.

"You hired these men to steal the specification, didn't you, Harding?" This time the voice was menacing, trembling with anger.

"No—I—it's that I . . . ." Harding was blubbering.

"Shut up!" *Le Gérant* pushed another switch on the panel and the door behind Harding opened. One of the guards came in and stood behind him. Terribly frightened now, Harding glanced over his shoulder and back at the rest of the people at the table. They were all staring at him, expressionless.

"*Le Gérant,*" Harding said. "Please, I didn't know . . . I was going to—"

"You were *going* to betray the Union, divert the formula, and make more money than we were paying you by selling it to someone else. You got greedy. Isn't that right, doctor?"

"No, sir. I mean yes, sir, it was! I didn't do this! Honest to God I—"

"You're a fool," *Le Gérant* said. "And I do not suffer fools." He gave an imperceptible nod to the guard behind Harding.

The guard roughly grabbed Harding's hair with his left hand and pulled back his head. The man produced a long, thin dagger in his right hand and with one smooth, swift stroke, slit Harding's throat from ear to ear. Blood splattered the table in front of him as he gurgled horribly. He writhed and struggled for a grip on life for a full minute before he finally slid out of the chair and onto the floor. The other Union members at the table were shocked, frightened, and speechless. None of the blood had splattered on them, but the memory of what they had just witnessed would stay with them for the rest of their lives.

The guard behind Harding lowered his dagger, stooped to the body, and wiped it clean on the dead man's clothes.

"Thank you, sergeant," *Le Gérant* said. "You can go. Have the cleanup crew come in five minutes. We'll be finished then."

"Yes, sir," the sergeant said, saluting. He turned and left the room.

The others couldn't tear their eyes away from Harding's body and the mess on the table. One woman involuntarily heaved. After a moment, though, they regained their composure and looked at the man in shadow. If there had been any doubt, he was now unquestionably their leader.

"I want Skin 17 before anyone else gets it," he said. Now his voice was controlled and even, but it was laced with venom. "We have learned that there are at least three expeditions being organized to climb Kangchenjunga and retrieve that specification. One is from England and is, of course, the one that is our most formidable adversary. Another is from Russia, manned by our friends in the Russian Mafia. The Chinese are mounting an expedition as well, with the hopes of retrieving the formula before we do—thereby giving them a reason to never pay us for the work we've already done for them. There may be more."

Le Gérant pulled another cigarette from his case and lit it. He inhaled, pausing for calculated dramatic effect. "Plans are now under way for the Union to accompany one of these expeditions to the great mountain. We *will* be the first to retrieve Skin 17. It could be the most important venture we undertake this year. Many of you will be called on to help arrange this. There will be no failure. Is that clear?"

Everyone nodded, but *Le Gérant* couldn't see them. Several of them turned back to look at the disgusting pool of red liquid dripping off the end of the table. A few felt physically ill.

"IS THAT CLEAR?" he shouted.

They quickly turned back to him and cried, "Yes, *Le Gérant!*"

Le Gérant smiled. "Good. Then let's have lunch. Is everybody hungry?"

FOURTEEN

WELCOMING RECEPTION

AFTER SPENDING ALL DAY CLIMBING UP AND DOWN STAIRCASES WHILE wearing heavy backpacks with Marquis and other members of the team on an officer's training course near Oakhanger, James Bond drove to SIS headquarters for a late meeting with Major Boothroyd in Q Branch.

"I want you to know that I postponed a very important dinner date to be here this evening," Boothroyd said, punching in the security code to let Bond into the laboratory. "With a very beautiful woman, I might add."

"Really?"

"Don't act so surprised, Double-O Seven. I may be an old man, but I'm still very healthy in that regard."

"I didn't say a word, Major," Bond said, smiling. "She is a very lucky woman."

"I should say so," Boothroyd replied. "We've been married twenty-eight years. Its our anniversary, and here I am, spending the evening with you."

"Well, let's make it brief, shall we?"

"Quite. Now, pay attention, Double-O Seven." He led Bond to a metal table that was covered with various items. "I pulled these out of storage this afternoon after I learned the nature of your assignment.

We're also working with the Ministry in supplying some sophisticated communications equipment to the expedition. The Dutchman, what's-his-name, he'll have all that."

"Paul Baack?"

"That's right."

Boothroyd went on, handing him a small tube with a mouthpiece on it. "This is similar to our underwater emergency breather, except it's for use at high altitudes. It holds about fifteen minutes of oxygen and fits into a pocket of your parka. Again, it's only for emergencies."

The major indicated a pair of boots. "These are the best One Sport 'Everest' boots with alveolite liners and built-in supergaiters. They're ultra light, and I think you'll find them quite comfortable. The unique thing about them is that they've been designed with our special field compartments in the heels. In the right boot you'll find medical and first aid equipment. In the left one you'll find a set of small tools. Screwdriver, pliers, wrench . . . they might come in useful."

Bond examined the bivouac sack made by North Face. "Ah, that," the major said. "It's a bivouac sack for when you're caught outside of camp at night. We've installed a special battery-operated power pack that will heat it up like an electric blanket. It also expands to allow room for a second person."

"How convenient," Bond said.

"You have your P99 on you?"

"Yes."

"Let me have it."

Bond handed him the Walther P99 and Boothroyd put it in what Bond hadn't realized was a fur-lined holster.

"I could just imagine you attempting to draw your gun out from under all those layers of clothing and the down parka you'll most likely be wearing. By the time you got it out, you'd be a dead man. I think this outer holster should solve that little problem. It can be worn on top of your parka, but it's still disguised to look like another pocket."

Boothroyd removed the gun and handed it back to Bond. "We'll have your own gear sent to you in Kathmandu. We've ordered all the clothing and tools you'll need, and we've spared no expense. Apparently M feels that this mission is important enough to spend a few hundred pounds on a sleeping bag. If you have any questions regarding any of it when you get there, send me a fax."

"What if I have a question in the middle of the Himalayas?"

"You can still send a fax. Paul Baack will have direct satellite linkup to the Internet, fax, and telephone. You can send me a digital snapshot from the summit of Mount Everest if you'd like."

"I'm not climbing Everest."

Boothroyd shrugged. "It's much the same thing, isn't it?"

Finally, the major opened a box and pulled out a package of plastic. "Inside this is an inflatable, portable seven-kilogram Gamow Bag. As you know, a Gamow Bag is a hyperbaric chamber used in an emergency to treat altitude sickness. This one is special because it's got its own air pump and generator, eliminating the need for another person to use bellows on it."

Bond picked up a strange contraption that looked like an oxygen regulator, but it had two mouthpieces on it.

Boothroyd smiled. "Ah, it figures that you would be attracted to that particular item."

"What is it?"

"It's an oxygen regulator, of course."

"Why two mouthpieces?"

Boothroyd shook his head. "I know you all too well, Double-O Seven. It's a two-person regulator. You both can share the same oxygen at a pinch."

"Seeing that most of the other members of the team are men, I resent that remark," Bond said.

The flight to Delhi was horrendous, and the overnight stay in the hotel closest to the airport was even worse. Even though the team arrived in the city at nearly midnight, the streets were heavily congested with traffic, pedestrians, and cows.

Symbols of India's religions were everywhere—Hindu images of

Shiva, Ganesh, and Krishna, Buddhist statues, Sikh turbans, and even crucifixes. Nepal, though, would be completely Hindu and Buddhist. In fact, Nepal officially designated itself as the "only Hindu country in the world."

Not normally a religious person, Bond respected Eastern beliefs. Even so, he had fitful dreams of these various religious icons and woke up irritable and stiff. Sergeant Chandra, with whom he shared a room, seemed to take it all in his stride. Gurkhas are typically good-natured, no matter how unpleasant conditions may be, and Chandra was no exception. When Bond awoke, the Gurkha was humming to himself, standing at the counter dressed only in boxer shorts, making coffee with a ten-year-old Mr. Coffee machine that, surprisingly, came with the room.

"Good morning, sir," Chandra said, a large grin spread over his face. "Coffee?"

Bond groaned and pulled himself out of bed. "Please. Black. Strong. Hot. I'm going to take a cold shower."

"That's all there is," Chandra said. "Apparently the hotel lost its hot water last night."

Bond told himself that he must get used to these little inconveniences. Once they had embarked on the trek to the Himalayas and set about ascending Kangch, all remnants of a civilized world would be long gone.

Shortly before lunch the party met back at the airport to catch an Indian Airlines flight to Kathmandu.

Because they were officials representing the British government, the team passed quickly through Immigration. They were met by the Nepalese Liaison Officer, an official who is always assigned to climbing expeditions. His duties include making sure proper permits and paperwork are submitted, and seeing that the expedition doesn't stray from its allotted peak.

The team piled into a rickety bus that must have been at least thirty years old. Bond gazed out the window at the streets, finally taking in that he was truly in the third world. It was such a contrast, even from Delhi. The blending of cultures in Kathmandu was striking. The traffic snaked around water buffalo pulling wagons carrying rice. There were open sewers along the sides of the roads. The people were dressed in an odd mixture of western fashions (T-shirts, blue jeans) and Nepalese and Tibetan dress. Barefoot, skinny children ran up to the bus when it stopped at a traffic light, holding out their hands and calling out, "Bonbon! Rupees! Iskul pens!" Apparently the universal English word for "sweets" in Nepal was "bonbon," and as some tourists were prone to hand out pencils and pens, the children often asked for "iskul pens," claiming that they needed them for "school."

The Yak and Yeti is one of the few luxury hotels in Kathmandu. Located on Durbar Marg, built around a wing of an old Rana palace, the lavishly decorated 270-room building is "modern" in every sense of the word, yet its history is thoroughly integrated in the design. Bond noticed that the architecture was both westernized and Nepali-Victorian.

"This hotel is a beautiful one," Chandra said as they got out of the bus. "For many centuries Nepal was cut off from the outside world. Initially it was ruled by the Mallas, but Prithivi Narayan Shah established a kingdom in Kathmandu. During his tenure, a young army general, Jung Bahadur Rana, usurped power from the monarchy and established himself as the Prime Minister, with the title of maharaja and powers superior to those of the sovereign."

Bond and the others walked into the lobby through double glass doors and onto sparkling granite flooring. To the left was a large gazebo with huge French windows. The reception desk, built with a black granite top, was to the right. A magnificent and traditional Newari wooden window, exquisitely hand-carved by local artisans, stood above Reception, where a smiling Guest Relations Officer gracefully draped in a sari sat. Beyond the reception area was a lounge furnished with yellow and green upholstered chairs. The lounge overlooked the hotel's lovely, well-manicured and landscaped lawns through picture windows.

Chandra continued. "The Rana regime lasted for a hundred and four years, until 1951, and contributed to the country's ornate neoclassical palaces. One of the reminders of this Rana period is the Red Palace, or Lai Durbar. It was built, oh, I think it was around 1855. This reconstructed palace now houses two fine restaurants—the Naachghar and the Chimney, as well as the Yak and Yeti Bar—all under one roof. Did you know that the Chimney owns the original copper fireplace from Boris Lissanevitch's famous Royal Hotel? The bar there was called the Yak and Yeti, which is how this hotel got its name. Boris Lissanevitch opened the first western hotel in Nepal."

"Fascinating," Bond said.

The strong smells from the streets were not present inside the hotel. Instead, there was the pungent aroma of curry coming from one of the restaurants.

Bond and Chandra were put in what was called a Tibetan suite. Rich silk was used to cover the walls of the room with typical Tibetan motifs in green and blue. The living room had a comfortable seating area containing furnishings of intricately carved wood. The walls and ceiling were adorned with brass and copper work. A private terrace offered a spectacular view of the Himalayan range and the Kathmandu valley. The master bedroom contained two queen-sized beds covered in silk in the same rich Tibetan colors. The bathroom was in marble with an oval-shaped bathtub and a separate shower.

"Enjoy the luxury while you can!" Chandra said, dropping his bags on the floor. "In three days we leave all of this behind!"

"Indeed. However, we're supposed to meet our man from Station I at the hotel bar in an hour. What time is our orientation with the team?"

Chandra looked at his itinerary. "Tonight, before dinner. We have the rest of the afternoon free."

"Good," Bond said. "We'll want to go to the temporary station house in Kathmandu and see what our man has for us."

Bond changed into lightweight khaki trousers and a Sea Island cotton navy shirt, while Chandra wore fatigues from his regiment. They went down to the Piano Lounge, just off the lobby, where the Mixture Trio Band were playing standards from the fifties, sixties, and seventies. Bond ordered a double vodka with ice. Chandra ordered Iceberg, the local Nepalese beer.

"Are you going to see your wife?" Bond asked.

"She is coming to Kathmandu and we'll meet before we leave for the mountain. It's a long journey for her. Most of the way has to be on foot."

"What's her name?"

"Manmeya."

"That's a pretty name."

"She's a pretty woman," Chandra said, his grin stretching across his face.

They finished their drinks just as Zakir Bedi came into the bar. He spotted Bond and Chandra and approached their table.

"Mr. Bond?" he asked.

"Yes?"

"The tour you arranged is ready. Would you like to come with me?"

"Certainly." Bond charged the bill to his room, and he and Chandra followed Bedi outside.

The midday sun was strong. The dust and heat and smell of the street assaulted Bond as they walked a mile to Durbar Square, the heart of old Kathmandu city. Clustered around the central square are the old Royal Palace and several temples designed with the multiroof Nepali pagoda style of architecture that spread to China and East Asia. Many of the temples are oddly adorned with erotic art on the roof struts. Unlike those in India, where the erotic carvings are sometimes sensuous, these are smaller, cruder, and even cartoonlike. Chandra told Bond a legend suggesting that the goddess of lightning was a shy virgin and wouldn't dare strike a temple with such "goings-on."

The square was noisy and full of life. Taxis and cows shared the same roads. Street vendors huddled around their wares, barking for attention. At least three *sadhus*, or holy men, sat on blankets in the dirt, half naked, smeared in dust, their hair and beard matted. Several women carried *dokos* on their backs. These large wicker baskets were filled with a variety of items from vegetables to firewood, and were fixed to the body by means of a *namlo*, a strap around the forehead.

The three of them walked behind the Shiva temple known as the Maju Deval, one of the larger temples in the square, and into a quieter side street. Bedi led them to an antiques shop that still bore the name Universal Exports Ltd.

"We never changed to Transworld Consortium," Bedi explained. "I rarely had to open the Nepal office, so we kept it the same. It's normally unmanned. Saves money."

Bedi unlocked the door and ushered Bond and Chandra inside. The place was musty and filled with bric-a-brac, some of which might have been worth something in the tourist trade. Most of it, however, was junk that was in place to create the illusion that the shop was legitimate.

"Please excuse the dust," Bedi said. "I had not been here for months until we tried to arrest Lee Ming. Come over here, I have something to show you."

They went through hanging drapes and into a passage leading to a door with a padlock on it. Bedi unlocked it, saying, "We're not so sophisticated in Nepal, Mr. Bond. No keycards, no electronic steel doors, nothing like that. Just an ordinary key gets you into the Nepalese branch of the British secret service!" He laughed heartily.

The "office" was a very small room containing a computer and monitor, file cabinets, a small refrigerator, a desk, and four chairs.

They had worked up a sweat simply walking across town, so Bedi opened the refrigerator and took out three bottles of Iceberg beer. The beer was refreshing, but Bond didn't care much for it. It had a curiously sweet taste, unlike some Indian beers that he enjoyed, such as Cobra.

"I've learned something about the three hijackers," Bedi said. He removed some eight-by-ten glossy photographs from an envelope on the desk. "They were Nepalese nationals who escaped from prison five years ago and were believed to be dead. They were identified by two workers at the hangar where the tourist plane was kept."

"Do we know if they're Union?" Bond asked.

"We've been unable to determine that. It's possible, I suppose, but they've been living in Nepal for the last five years. If they were Union, it seems that we would have had more evidence of their activities. We think they were living in the hills somewhere. What we did learn is that they were part of the old Thuggee cult that originated in India in the 1800s."

The "Thugs" were a religious organization that murdered and robbed in the service of a goddess.

"If I remember correctly, the British government supposedly hanged the last Thug in 1882," Bond said.

"Mostly true," replied Bedi. "But remnants of their group exist. I would think present-day Thugs would be prime recruitment candidates for the Union. You want to know the most interesting thing?"

"What?"

"They were in England briefly, shortly before the Skin 17 formula was stolen. Flew in one day, flew out the next."

"How did they get in?"

"The visas were issued for 'family reasons.' We have since discovered that their so-called families in England never existed."

Bond studied the photographs, then turned his attention to three more pictures that Bedi laid on the table. They were aerial views of the crash site on Kangchenjunga. The fuselage was plainly visible, surprisingly intact.

"Reconnaissance photos reveal that the plane is quite accessible once you get up to the Great Scree Terrace," Bedi said. "But look at this detail." He showed them another photo that magnified one of the aerial shots.

Footprints were evident around the open door of the aircraft.

"Someone survived the crash," Bond observed.

"They couldn't have survived the altitude," Chandra remarked. "They may have gotten out of the wreckage, but they wouldn't have lived long at that height. None of those people was prepared for those conditions."

"Do you have any other pictures? Where do the footprints lead?"

Bedi shrugged. "We tried to take more shots, but the winds and snow had covered the tracks by the time we went back. You can see that they went off in this direction, toward the south, but beyond that we don't know. He's right, they couldn't have survived at that altitude for very long. They hadn't acclimatized themselves at all.

Whoever it was, you'll probably find their frozen body in a crevasse somewhere."

The men went through various other documents and reports. Zakir Bedi had no solid evidence that the Union were involved in the plane hijacking. To his knowledge, the Union had not operated on the Indian subcontinent at all.

By late afternoon they were finished. Bedi offered to walk them back to the hotel and led them out of the makeshift intelligence office.

The streets were still crowded, but the heat was beginning to subside as dusk approached and they walked into Durbar Square.

High above them, inside the Maju Deval temple, a Nepalese man held a Galil Sniping Rifle, a 7.62mm semiautomatic weapon that is manufactured in Israel. Designed with battlefield reliability in mind, the Galil could score head shots at 300 meters, half-body hits at 600 meters, and full-figure hits at 800 to 900 meters. The man was a good shot, but he wasn't an expert. A sniper must have special training and technique, for bullets don't fly in a completely straight line. Gravity and friction pull on a flight path; snipers must allow for "rise and drop" conditions. Some telescopic sights incorporate range finders to help the marksman in calculations, but intense practice is necessary to get it right.

It was this factor that saved James Bond's life.

The first bullet hit the dirt at Bond's feet. All three men dropped to the ground, then attempted to determine where the sniper was located. Bond squinted into the sun, almost certain that the shot had been fired from the large triple-roofed temple in front of him.

"He's up there!" Bond pointed. He got to his feet and started to run toward the building. The other two followed him, but a passing rickshaw momentarily blocked their passage. When the man pulled the contraption away, Bedi was in front of Bond, peering at the temple.

"Is he still there?" he asked.

Up above, the sniper took a bead on Bond's head. He didn't know who the other two were. His orders were to kill the Englishman. The crosshairs centered neatly on Bond's nose, then the man squeezed the trigger. Somehow, though, the Indian man got in the way.

The bullet struck Zakir Bedi on the side of the face, knocking him back into Bond.

"I see him!" Chandra shouted, running toward the temple. Bond dropped Bedi's corpse on the ground, drew his Walther, and ran after Chandra.

The Gurkha stopped Bond at the door. "You can't come in," he said. "It's forbidden to non-Hindus."

"To hell with that!" Bond spat out.

"I'm sorry, James," Chandra insisted. "Let me go. You wait here."

"No, I'm coming with you."

Chandra made a face, then went into the temple. In Nepal, there was a fine line between Hinduism and Buddhism. A well-known Shiva lingam was inside, but the roof was topped by a pinnacle shaped like a Buddhist stupa. It was dark, and Bond almost choked from the thick incense smoke. Worshippers looked up in horror at the westerner who had run inside the sacred place with a gun.

Bond followed Chandra to a set of stairs in the back that led to the layered roof. Another shot rang out, this time inside the building. Women screamed, got up, and ran out of the temple. The men who were there didn't move, but instead watched with interest. They hadn't seen this much excitement in a long time.

Chandra and Bond saw the sniper attempting to climb onto the sloping roof so that he could jump down to the ground below. Chandra was remarkably fast, scuttling out on the roof just in time to catch the man's leg. The rifle fell as the two men struggled. Bond rolled out on the roof, halting his descent by lodging the heels of his boots in the shingles. Before he could lend the Gurkha a hand, the sniper twisted away and slipped off the edge of the roof. The man screamed as he fell, but the sound was abruptly cut short as he hit the hard ground.

Bond and Chandra climbed back into the temple and ran down the stairs. Chandra spoke Nepali to the spectators, explaining that they were policemen. Outside, they found the sniper had fallen on his head. His neck was broken.

Chandra examined him and said, "He's a local man. I can't believe that he would have had much experience in shooting people."

"That fits with Union recruiting practices, doesn't it?" Bond asked.

"In Nepal, I would say, yes. Those bullets were meant for you."

"Obviously," said Bond. "That bloody leak at SIS is getting worse. There is no way that anyone in Nepal could have known of my presence. Bedi was the only one."

They heard police sirens approaching. "Come on," Chandra said. "We don't want to get involved in this."

They ran through the crowd and lost themselves before the police arrived.

TEAMWORK

THE TEAM MET IN ONE OF THE YAK AND YETI'S IMPRESSIVE MEETING ROOMS normally used for business functions. It was seven-thirty, and dinner was scheduled for eight o'clock in the fabulous Chimney Restaurant. Everyone was tired and hungry, but there was still excitement and anticipation in the air.

Marquis sat beside Bond and Chandra while waiting for two late arrivals. He leaned over and whispered, "I hear there was an Indian found shot to death today in Durbar Square. A Nepalese, it appears, was the killer. He's dead, too. I was questioned this afternoon by police. Apparently, a Caucasian man and another Nepalese were observed fleeing the scene of the crime. Do you know anything about this?"

"Lord, no," Bond lied. "Who was it that was killed?"

"Some Indian businessman. Sorry, Bond, I had to ask. You two are the only Caucasian/Nepalese combination I know at the moment. Never mind, it's time to start."

Marquis got up as the two missing stragglers came into the room, and from the podium said, "May I have your attention, please?"

Many of the eighteen people who had assembled in the room were old acquaintances from previous expeditions and were therefore embroiled in lively conversation. There was one Nepalese Liaison Officer, sixteen male team members, and one female.

"Please, lets get on with this, so we can eat!" Marquis said even louder.

Finally everyone stopped talking and focused their attention on the leader.

"I have to keep reminding myself that I'm not addressing members of the air force," Marquis muttered, but loud enough for everyone to hear. They laughed. "Well. Its good to see old friends and nice to meet new ones. Welcome. I'm glad you all could make it. You're probably wondering why I asked you here. . . ."

There were more chuckles in the room, but less enthusiastic. Bond was put off by Marquis's manner. He projected unquestionable authority over the team, but he also tried too hard to entertain them.

"Seriously, we're on a very important mission for the governments of Great Britain and the United States," Marquis said with thin sincerity. "I'm sure we all want to get to know each other well over the next few days, but tonight we want to eat and go to bed! This is a very nice hotel, and I for one want to take advantage of it while I'm here! So, let's get on with the introductions. I'm Group Captain Roland Marquis, RAF, and something of a mountain climber in my spare time. . . ."

There was some applause from two or three members of the audience, including the girl.

"Thank you." Marquis beamed. He indicated two Nepalese men standing near the wall, apart from the others. "You all met Mr. Chitrakar at the airport this afternoon. He's our Liaison Officer. He is our contact here in Kathmandu." The man on the right smiled and gave a little bow. "Mr. Chitrakar needs to say a few words. Mr. Chitrakar?"

"Thank you," he said. His accent was thick. He proceeded to rattle off the various governmental rules and regulations the team should abide by when trekking across the countryside and when ascending the mountain.

"Of most importance," he said, "is that you do not summit Kangchenjunga. This is a very sacred mountain to our people. You may go as high as you need in order to perform salvage operations, but no higher." He smiled, and said, "You might anger the goddess who lives there."

Indeed, Kangchenjunga means "Five Treasures of the Great Snows," and is thought to be the home of Nepalese gods, as are other Himalayan peaks.

"Thank you, Mr. Chitrakar. I can assure you that none of us has any intention of summiting the mountain. Now, next to Mr. Chitrakar is Ang Tshering, a splendid *sirdar,* with whom I've worked before," Marquis said.

The man on the left smiled and waved. The same two or three people who applauded before did so again. Bond thought that Tshering looked competent. The role of a *sirdar,* or Sherpa trekking leader, was important. He would run the Base Camp while everyone else climbed.

"Now I'd like to introduce the most beautiful person in the room! She comes from New Zealand, so those of us who know her sometimes call her Kiwi Kendall. Meet our team doctor, Hope Kendall."

Red-faced, Dr. Kendall stood to the loudest applause anyone had received thus far. Bond thought that Marquis was right in one respect—she was stunningly beautiful. Hope Kendall had blond hair, green eyes, and a wide smile. She was in her early thirties and was obviously fit and healthy. She was over six feet tall, with long legs that were hidden by khaki trousers. Due to social customs in Nepal, Bond knew that he might never get a glimpse of those legs, since women revealing bare legs in shorts or miniskirts were frowned upon.

"Hello, everybody," she said. "I just have a few words to say because I'm your doctor for the next few weeks. I know you are all fit as buck rats, and you know everything I'm going to tell you now, but I'm actually required by law to give you the 'talk.' "

She managed to exert a great deal of authority over the men, and not just because of her physical beauty. Even Marquis sat down and gave her his undivided attention.

"We're going to be climbing much more quickly than any of us have ever done before. The schedule is extremely tight, and I know we all want to be off the mountain before the monsoons hit. Nevertheless, we must be conscious of any symptoms of acute mountain sickness. It can strike anyone at any time. It is each and everyone's job to recognize the symptoms in your teammates, because many times an individual cannot recognize them in himself. You must understand that the atmospheric condition at high altitude is the same as at sea level, with twenty percent oxygen, but a reduction in atmospheric pressure reduces the amount of oxygen you can take in with each breath. You're really breathing roughly half the oxygen you're accustomed to when you're above five thousand meters. The first signs are a general malaise, loss of appetite, then headache. This is followed by increasing weakness and a loss of interest in the climb. If you start to experience apathy, nausea, dizziness, or sleepiness, there's a good chance you've got AMS."

Bond knew all of this, but Dr. Kendall had such powerful charisma that he hung on every word.

"Note that these symptoms can occur at relatively low altitudes. So make sure you use what we call 'rest steps' to give your leg muscles little rests all the way up and help you maintain measured, methodical breathing. Take occasional full rest stops with forced deep breathing. Drink *lots* of water, and I mean it. Eat frequently to keep your nourishment up. Now, you should be aware of the two severe types of AMS, and these are High Altitude Pulmonary Edema, or HAPE, and High Altitude Cerebral Edema, or HACE. HAPE is when there is leakage of blood and other fluids into the lungs, restricting the air sacs in exchanging oxygen and carbon dioxide in the blood. The symptoms are similar to pneumonia. HAPE can kill you and kill you fast. Fortunately, it rarely occurs in healthy people below nine thousand feet or so. HACE, the other one, is worse. That's when there is accumulation of fluid in the brain, and symptoms begin with a severe, relentless headache that is a result of pressure due to the swelling of brain tissue. You'll soon have difficulties with physical coordination, slurred speech, irrational behavior, collapse, and eventually you die. Descent is the only treatment for these things. Forget drugs like Diamox and dexamethasone. Although they might treat the symptoms of AMS, they don't make the damaging effects go away. As your doctor, here and now I forbid the use of these drugs, got it?"

Several people in the room, mumbled, "Uh-huh."

"Finally, be aware of what we call retinal hemorrhaging. This is very serious, and it's caused by damage to the retina due to pressure changes and the tiny bundles of arteries in your eyes rupturing. If you contract it up on that mountain, you're in deep trouble. You may not regain your eyesight until weeks after descending, if you're able to descend safely at all! I'm not trying to scare you, I just want you to be aware of all this. I'll be performing routine examinations on every member of the team, so get used to it."

"I'm looking forward to that!" Marquis said with a laugh. Some of the others chuckled.

She glared at him but smiled. "Roland has told me that I have the authority to send anyone down the mountain who I think is unfit to continue the climb. That goes for you, too, Mr. Marquis!"

Bond wondered if there was something romantic between the two of them.

"Finally, I just want to say that although we're about to embark on a seemingly insurmountable task, there's an old Maori proverb that says *He nui maunga e kore e taea te whakaneke, he nui ngaru moana mā te ihu o te waka e wāhi.* 'A great mountain cannot be moved, but a giant wave can be broken by the prow of a canoe.' In plain English, that means 'Do not give up too easily—some things are possible.' That's all I've got," she said, and sat down.

Marquis took the floor again and said, "Thank you, Dr. Kendall. I'm sure we'll all put ourselves in your capable hands."

She smirked and turned red again as the others laughed.

"Right," Marquis said. He then introduced the man who was in charge of Nepalese relations. He would be working with the *sirdar* to hire the Sherpa porters once they reached Taplejung. Other climbers would be hired there to assist in the hauling once the team reached Camp Five and the aircraft.

The equipment manager was a renowned French mountaineer. Bond was aware of his talents. He was probably the only mountaineer on the team who was as experienced as Roland Marquis. He was a small man but had extremely broad shoulders and a big, bald head.

"My lieutenants on the team are my friends Tom Barlow and Carl Glass, there in the second row."

Barlow was tall, lanky, and hirsute with thick glasses, while Glass was stocky, clean shaven, and expressionless.

Marquis then introduced three men representing the Americans, who stood and said hello. One of them seemed *very* young, probably in his early twenties, and looked even younger. Bond had already heard one of the others refer to him as "the kid."

Three other men were presented as "haulers." Two were known British mountaineers. The third, introduced as Otto Schrenk, was a last-minute replacement.

Marquis explained. "Apparently Jack Kubrick was involved in a terrible accident the night before our departure from London. We had to scramble for someone else, and Mr. Schrenk here, from Berlin, volunteered to step in."

This news took Bond by surprise. He had spent quite some time studying the backgrounds of each and every team member. SIS had done a complete security check on all of them. Bond wasn't comfortable with an unknown. If the Union were going to infiltrate the team, they would do it at the last minute. Bond made a note to put in a call to SIS and have Schrenk scrutinized.

He leaned over to Chandra and whispered, "Keep an eye on that one."

Chandra nodded imperceptibly.

Marquis then gestured to them. "Over here are representatives from the Foreign Office, Mr. James Bond and Sergeant Chandra Bahadur Gurung, his assistant. The sergeant is on loan to us from the army. He's with the Royal Gurkha Rifles, isn't that right?"

Chandra grinned and nodded. His eyes wrinkled when he smiled, giving the impression that every line in his face was smiling.

Bond nodded at the others, then sat down. He caught Hope Kendall's eye, and lingered there a moment. She was studying him, attempting to figure him out with a spontaneous first impression.

"Last but not least is Paul Baack, our communications officer," Marquis said, gesturing to a tall, large man with a neat goatee and deep brown eyes. Baack stood up, immediately dispelling the notion that anyone else might be bigger than he.

"Thank you," he said with a pronounced Dutch accent. "I am happy to be here." He smiled broadly, then sat down.

In Bond's opinion, it was Baack who had the most impressive credentials. Not only was the man a top-notch mountaineer, his work in communications was widely respected in intelligence circles. Q Branch routinely consulted the Dutch engineer, but Marquis hadn't known that. Bond had never met him and looked forward to doing so.

The girl was a big question mark, Bond thought. Was she Marquis's girlfriend? They certainly flirted with each other a lot in public. She seemed capable, but in Bond's opinion, bringing a girl along with a team of men was just asking for trouble. She might insist that more effort be expended on providing her with a certain amount of privacy. On the other hand, she might be a distraction if she simply tried to be "one of the boys."

"One other thing I need to mention," Marquis said. "There are three other expeditions climbing Kangch."

Bond knew that there were two. Another must have appeared in the last day or two.

"Permits for a Chinese expedition were applied for on the same day as ours. A Russian expedition was mounted just a few days later. The Chinese are climbing the north face as well, but slightly south of us. If you ask me, they're doing it the hard way. The Russians are also coming up the north face, and at this point we don't know what route they're taking. Just a few days ago a Belgian team applied for permits. I understand that they were granted today."

Bond raised his hand and was acknowledged by Marquis.

"What do we know about them?"

"Not much. They're all experienced climbers. They came up with the money, and that's all Nepal cares about. They don't represent any specific groups. As far as we know, they're in it only for the sport."

Bond frowned.

"Right," said Marquis. "Are there any other questions?"

Otto Schrenk, the newcomer, raised his hand.

"Yes, Mr. Schrenk?"

"Why are we climbing the north face? That is very difficult." He had a thick German accent.

"It happens to be the most direct route to the aircraft. Also, the politics involved with obtaining permission to climb from the Sikkim side were too complicated. The north, west, and southwest sides of the mountain are in Nepalese territory. Of these, the north face is the safest. There have been deaths there over the years, to be sure, but several people have made it to the top."

That seemed to satisfy Schrenk. He nodded and folded his arms.

"Anyone else?"

No one said anything.

"Fine, then," Marquis said, slapping his stomach. "I'm ready to eat!"

The group stood up and stretched, picking up the conversations they had halted a half hour ago.

Bond looked at Hope Kendall, who was gathering her things. Could she really take the next seven or eight weeks being the only woman among such testosterone-heavy human beings as Roland Marquis . . . and himself?

"Just a second," Bond said to Chandra. "If I'm not back in sixty seconds, you'll have to eat without me."

He walked over to Hope, held out his hand, and said, "Hello, I thought I should come over and introduce myself properly."

She smiled warmly and shook his hand. "I'm glad to be working with you, Mr. Bond. So far the trip is a beaut, don't you think? I'm sorry, I'm afraid I don't know much about your background."

"We've been here only a day," Bond said. "The law of inevitable rubbish will descend upon us before we know it. It always happens."

"You're not going into this with a bad attitude, are you, Mr. Bond?" she asked flirtatiously.

"Not at all. As you said, we all have to keep our wits about us. Would you care to accompany me to dinner?"

She shook her head. "I'm already promised to Roland. Some other time, maybe, all right?" She smiled, gave a little wave, then turned and walked away.

Chandra, who had observed the scene, was highly amused.

"Chandra, if your smile gets any bigger, your face will split in two," Bond said.

"I think she's the wrong girl for you, Commander Bond. *Khanu paryo*," he said, meaning that it was time to eat.

Bond replied with what little Nepalese he had learned in the past few days. *"Khanu Hos."*

Contrary to popular belief, cuisine in Nepal was quite varied. In Bond's opinion, Nepalese food in and of itself tended to be rather bland and uninteresting. There was only so much *dhal bhat* one could eat, and he was going to have plenty of that over the next weeks. In Kathmandu, at least, one could get a variety of international cuisines, and the Chimney in the hotel specialized in some of the finest Russian food he had ever tasted. Founded by Boris Lissanevitch, it is perhaps the oldest western restaurant in Nepal. It took its name from the huge copper chimney and open brick fireplace that occupy the center. It was the perfect place for an intimate dinner with live classical guitar music.

Bond sat with Chandra and Paul Baack. For starters, Bond had Ukrainian borscht made from a famous, "original" Boris Lissanevitch recipe. As a main course Bond chose yogurt-marinated chicken, which was lightly spiced and served skewered with buttered rice pilaf. With it he had aubergine and sun-dried tomato Charlotte with solferino potatoes and a black-eyed-pea stew.

"This is very good," Baack said, pouncing on an oven-roasted tenderloin with an onion relish and port wine *jus.* "Why can't we just stay at this hotel for the next six weeks?"

Chandra had smoked beckti, a Bengal fish. "Yes, it is good, but the Sherpa food is better," he said, grinning.

"Ha!" Baack laughed. "Are you mad?"

Chandra said, "I'm not mad, but I can be very crazy sometimes."

The Dutchman laughed again. "What's your story, Mr. Bond? Why are you on this trip?"

"I was ordered by the men in suits over in Whitehall. They want me to make sure everything is shipshape."

"If you don't mind my asking, why do you need a Gurkha to accompany you?"

Bond and Chandra looked at each other. Chandra answered, "Commander Bond is my good friend. We always look after each other."

"Actually," Bond said, "the Foreign Office thought it would be helpful for us all to have someone here who knows the territory. Chandra has been on Kangchenjunga before."

"Really?" Baack asked. He was genuinely interested.

"Only halfway," Chandra said. "This time I'll do better. At least to the Great Scree Terrace."

"Tell me about the equipment our people gave you," Bond said.

"Ah! Very nice stuff, I can tell you," Baack said. "Of course, I helped design the satellite linkup. We have an extremely light laptop computer with enough power to last three months. It's equipped with the linkup, and that will be kept at Base Camp. With the use of cellular phones, every team member can stay in contact with each other and the outside world. We will all use the same channel, although the phones are capable of several private channels. We can even hook up to the Internet from wherever we are. I can send a fax from eight thousand meters if I want."

"Speaking of faxes, I need to send something to London. You have something handy?" Bond asked.

"Certainly. It's right here," he said, indicating a portable computer case at his side. "Would you like to do it now?"

Bond opened his own file folder containing information on the expedition and team members. He found the recently added photo of Otto Schrenk, scribbled a message on a Post-It note, stuck it to the bottom of the photo, then handed it to Baack. The Dutchman opened the case, turned on the computer, noted the phone number that Bond had written, then fed the photo into the machine.

"That should do it," he said, handing it back to Bond. "I'm in constant contact with London, Mr. Bond, so anytime you want to talk to the Foreign Office, just say so."

"Thanks. Let me know when you get a reply. And call me James."

He had a good feeling about Baack, and was pleased that he was on the team and looked forward to getting to know him better.

Roland Marquis and Hope Kendall entered the room. She had gone to the trouble to change clothes before coming in to dinner. Instead of the trousers she was wearing at the meeting, she now had on an attractive red evening gown. Marquis had put on a sleek dinner jacket but was still wearing the civilian clothes underneath.

She laughed as she walked by Bond's table. "I figured that this was my last chance to be a lady before six weeks of hell."

"Doesn't she look marvelous?" Marquis asked.

The three men muttered appreciative comments, then the couple sat at a table isolated from the others.

After a few glances in their direction, Bond decided that the two of them were indeed having some kind of love affair.

Although there was no rational reason for it, this notion gave Bond a twinge of jealousy.

SIXTEEN

THE TREK BEGINS

THE REST OF THE STAY IN KATHMANDU WAS UNREMARKABLE, AND LOCAL police never connected the deaths of Zakir Bedi and the Nepalese assassin, who might or might not have been Union, to the group of mountaineers staying at the Yak and Yeti. The remaining days were spent exercising and gathering supplies for the trek across eastern Nepal.

One of the more interesting events for Bond occurred the morning after the team meeting. Every member of the expedition had to submit to a physical examination performed by Dr. Hope Kendall. Bond reported to her in one of the hotel suites at the appointed time and found her to be cool, clinical, and objective, as a physician should be. At the same time, though, she seemed overly intrigued by his body and took her time feeling his muscles, testing reflexes, and looking into orifices. In fact, she was somewhat rough with him, pinching him here, jabbing him there. Perhaps, Bond thought, she was merely a very physical person.

"You sure have a lot of scars," she said, examining the faint mementos of Bond's illustrious career that adorned various parts of his naked body. "You're in the Foreign Office?"

"That's right."

"How does someone in the Foreign Office get so many scars?"

"I do a number of outdoor activities for sport. Sometimes you get injured," he said.

"Hmm, and I think you're lying," she said. "You're some kind of policeman, aren't you? Sorry, you don't have to answer that." He didn't. She turned to her table and put on a rubber glove. "Okay, Mr. Bond, let's see how your prostate feels."

She wasn't very gentle with that exam, either.

The expedition members flew in two Twin Otters to the Suketar airstrip near a small village called Taplejung in east Nepal. The stretch of dirt runway, located on a high ridge at 2,000 meters, is at a significantly higher altitude than Kathmandu, at 1,300 meters. The plan was to stay in crude lodges that had been erected in the village specifically for trekkers, then take a steep drop down to the Tamur Khola valley the following day. It was a more direct route to go down and north through the valley rather than east, over the alternate route to Khunjari.

The view was spectacular, and this was only the first day. The Himalayas could be seen from Kathmandu, but there they were so far in the distance that one felt they couldn't possibly be part of the same country. Here, however, it seemed as if the mountains were just over the next hill. The white-covered peaks spread over the northern and eastern sky, some disappearing into white clouds.

Their immediate surroundings were rich with the colors of spring. The hills were terraced so that farming could be accomplished on a steep surface. Bond thought it was a marvel that anyone could live their lives cultivating this difficult land. Yet, nearly everyone in Nepal did, and they did it well.

The wind was brisker here and Bond could immediately feel the thinness of the air, even at this relatively low altitude. He glanced at his Avocet Vertech Alpin watch that Q Branch had given him. It showed altitude, time, barometric pressure, and cumulative vertical ascent rates. It was three o'clock in the afternoon, but it felt later. The change in altitude made it seem as if he had already spent an entire day exerting himself. One of the Americans, Bill Scott, complained of a headache shortly after arriving. Hope Kendall examined him and told him to get plenty of sleep that night.

"I want everyone to go to bed immediately after dinner," Marquis ordered as they gathered at the small building that served as an air terminal. "We're to have dinner with the respective families who are putting us up. Remember—eat with your right hand, don't even gesture with the left, and leave your shoes at the door. Don't enter a Hindu kitchen unless invited. Let your hosts direct you to a seat. Don't touch any food unless you intend to eat it. Utensils or food is *jutho,* or impure, once it has touched your lips or tongue. Everyone eats from their own plate and drinks from their own glass. These people know that all food must be cooked, but just in case, don't eat anything that has to be washed or that isn't cooked immediately before it's served. Remember to offer a good hearty belch at the end of the meal, for that's a sign of contentment in this country."

Bond and Chandra helped the others unload the equipment. Bond carried most of his gear in a Lowe Alpine Attack 50 backpack, which was designed primarily as a functional, lightweight summit pack. A lot of the tools for climbing would be carried by the Sherpas until it was time to use them.

Perhaps the best known and most widely respected of all Nepal's ethnic groups, the Sherpas resemble Tibetans more than other Nepalese. Hundreds of years of living in east Nepal have suitably adapted them to living and working in the mountains. Ever since mountaineers discovered them to be excellent companions and workers, the Sherpas came into a hitherto unforeseen popularity and prosperity. For an expedition the size of Bond's, nearly sixty porters would need to be hired.

Chandra, Bond, Paul Baack, and the French climber, Philippe Léaud, had been assigned to a family that consisted of a toothless, smiling old couple. Bond noticed that Marquis and Hope Kendall went into a lodge together. Nepalese were generally intolerant of openly displayed affection or sexuality, and he wondered how they would get around that.

Chandra, reading his mind, said, "Marquis claimed that he and Dr. Kendall were man and wife."

Léaud made a vulgar comment in French that went over the Gurkha's head, but he got the drift when the others laughed.

Sunset came and dinner was served on a low table inside the

lodge. The food was a traditional *dhal bhat,* a lentil soup over rice. A few vegetables, or *sabji,* were served with cumin, garlic, and ginger. Hot tea accompanied the meal. By the time they had finished, Bond and Chandra were ready to turn in, the altitude and food having had a soporific effect on them. Bond unrolled his Marmot Col sleeping bag, which wasn't as warm as the more popular Cwm, but was lighter and more versatile at altitude. The wooden floor was hard, but at least there was the luxury of having a roof over their heads.

"Good night, Commander Bond," Chandra said as he slipped into his own bag. "Don't let the *kichkinni* get you."

"What?"

"The *kichkinni.* That's the spirit of a woman who died in childbirth and reappears as a beautiful and insatiable young woman intent on seduction."

"Sounds quite pleasant to me," Bond quipped.

"Ah, but her unlucky lover withers away as she saps his vital energies. The only way you can tell if she is a *kichkinni* is if you happen to notice that her feet are turned backward!"

"Just her feet?" Bond asked, struggling to get comfortable in the confines of the bedroll.

Chandra laughed loudly. It never ceased to amaze Bond that the Gurkha was always in a good humor. He enjoyed talking, sometimes to Bond's chagrin, but he had already become an entertaining and intelligent companion. He had started to tell stories of his life in the foothills of Lamjung and Annapurna Himal, a region that the Gurungs have farmed and covered with a network of trails paved with precisely cut and fitted stone blocks.

"In the higher regions of our homeland, Gurungs retain Buddhist traditions," Chandra said. "In the lower ones, they've converted to Hinduism."

"What are you?" Bond asked.

"A little of both," Chandra said. "Once you're born a Hindu, that never changes. The Buddhist religion fits neatly around Hinduism. You will find that in Nepal, many people say they are of both religions."

Baack began to snore loudly, keeping the other three men up for a while. Chandra continued to talk until finally Léaud said politely, "*Oui, oui, monsieur,* please, I need to sleep now. We have another bed-time story tomorrow night, okay?"

Chandra said, "Sure. *Shuba ratri.*"

"Huh?"

"That means 'good night.' "

"Oh. *Shuba ratri.*"

"*Shuba ratri,* Commander Bond," Chandra said, but there was silence. "Commander Bond?"

Bond was already fast asleep.

Mornings are always the most beautiful part of the day in Nepal. A magical mist accumulates in the valleys and lingers until the sun comes up and evaporates the moisture. The land is clear by mid-morning, but the sight of the fog-laden land put Bond in a reflective mood. He was truly in a land quite apart from England, exotic and mystical. The idea of one day going back to the dull office by the Thames seemed impossible.

Bond and Chandra were up early with the lady of the house, whose duty it was to take care of the family's religious obligations, which meant that first there was worship of household deities fol-lowed by a visit to the neighborhood temple with a tray of small offerings. Bond accompanied Chandra to the temple and watched him perform *puja,* an offering meant to please divine senses by scat-tering flower blossoms and red *tika* powder on images of gods and ringing bells to alert them to his presence. The Gurkha paid special attention to the idol of Ganesh, the portly deity with the head of an elephant. Ganesh is known as the creator and remover of obstacles and brings luck to those who pay special attention to him. Therefore, it was important to pray to him at the onset of any undertaking, oth-erwise he might convey misfortune and malevolence on travelers.

The Sherpa porters left with the trekking equipment very early in order to set up a campsite in Phurumba by the time the rest of the group arrived there for lunch.

"They're always so cheerful," Bond commented to Chandra.

"I would be too if my pay for the expedition would support my family and sometimes my entire village for a year or more," the Gurkha replied.

Breakfast was served in the lodge at eight o'clock, and it consisted surprisingly of scrambled eggs. They weren't cooked to Bond's specifications, but they were nevertheless welcome and he felt rested and ready to begin the mostly-downhill four-hour trek to Phurumba, the first stop on the way to the Base Camp. It would be a long, difficult day. Normally trekkers would stop overnight at Phurumba, but Marquis planned to continue to Chirwa, another four-hour trek . . . uphill.

It wasn't necessary to wear the heavy warm clothes yet. While it was cool at this altitude, the exertion of trekking could work up a sweat, especially when carrying fifty pounds or more on one's back. Bond wore a Patagonia Puffball lightweight and windproof shirt, dark denims, thick Smartwool socks, and a pair of Merrell M2 high-top boots. He would save the One Sport boots that Boothroyd had given him for the snow and ice. Water was boiled before leaving the village, and every member of the team got a full canteen and was told to conserve it. They wouldn't get more until they reached Chirwa.

The trekkers set out by nine o'clock, descending the peak into the misty valley. Dr. Kendall and Marquis walked together at the head of the group. Bond and Chandra trailed along near the back.

The views were exhilarating. They were in magnificent hills colored in brown and green, and the vast Himalayas were just beyond them. They passed farmers working with water buffalo. The men were dressed in vests and loincloths, while some women were wearing the graceful Indian sari, a five-meter length of cloth draped over a tight, short-sleeved blouse called a *choli*. The saris were always brightly colored and they fluttered like banners. Nepali women delighted in decoration, layering themselves with jewelry in carnival colors. Their long, black hair was usually braided with red cotton tassels, or they twisted it into a neat bun with a flower set in it. The essential *tika* mark made on the forehead with red *sindhur* powder was part of the daily *puja.*

"In a mystic sense," Chandra explained, "the *tika* represents the third eye of spiritual insight. For women it's a cosmetic essential."

They reached Phurumba, a drop in altitude to 922 meters, right on schedule at one o'clock. The Sherpas had lunch ready, which again consisted of *dhal bhat*. Rumor had it that there would be chicken for dinner.

After two hours' rest, the team pushed on toward Chirwa, which was a significantly more difficult walk, as the altitude would have increased to 1,270 meters by the time they arrived. Because they had already trekked a fair distance that morning, it took them nearly six hours instead of the allotted four to reach their destination.

Again, the scenery was beautiful. At one point Bond noticed a temple built high on a hill, with a single dirt road winding up to it. An old man standing at the foot of the road with a stick for a cane smiled and beckoned them forward, asking for a handout. One of the Americans gave him a few rupees.

"Right," Marquis said as they approached Chirwa. The village looked similar to Taplejung but was smaller. "Congratulations on a good day's trekking. I know we're all tired. I'm certainly feeling the effects of the altitude change. Let's get another good night's sleep and will our bodies to acclimatize quickly! The Sherpas will have dinner ready in an hour. There are not enough lodges to go around, I'm afraid. Some of us will have to pitch tents. There is room for ten people in the lodges. We can draw straws for them, if you'd like, unless someone wants to volunteer to stay in their tents."

"We don't mind," Bond said. He looked at Chandra for approval. The Gurkha shrugged.

"I'll stay in a tent," Hope Kendall said.

"Uhm, you don't have to do that," Marquis said.

"Why not? Just because I'm a woman? Stop giving me special attention, Roland. Pretty soon we'll all be in tents for a long time. It doesn't matter to me, really."

Bond could see that it was Marquis who didn't particularly want to sleep in a tent that night. Was she attempting to distance herself from him?

"Fine," Marquis said. "We'll do that, then."

"I'd rather stay in my own tent tonight, if you don't mind," she said. It was loud enough for the entire group to hear. Marquis was noticeably embarrassed. Something unpleasant must have occurred between them during the previous night.

Marquis made light of the comment, but Bond knew he was cross that she had said something like that in front of everyone. Marquis ended up staying in a lodge.

Bond and Chandra started to erect a two-man Bibler Torre tent, which was sturdy and could withstand high winds and keep the icy chill out when completely sealed. By the time they were done, a campfire had been lit and people gathered around it. The evening developed into a beautiful mild spring night. There were thousands of stars, and the silhouettes of the peaks against them produced a skyscape that Bond had seldom seen.

Dinner was an Indian-style chicken curry that the cook, Girmi, had made less spicy than usual to accommodate the western tastes. Bond was becoming accustomed to the art of eating with his right hand. The Nepalese were experts at flicking a bite of food into the mouth with their thumb. One of the Americans brought a bottle of inexpensive red wine out of his knapsack, saying that he was saving it for Base Camp but knew that drinking alcohol at higher altitudes was not wise. There was just enough for everyone to have a little in a paper cup. Philippe Léaud produced a harmonica and began to play plaintive melodies. One by one people began to wander away from the campfire and settle in for the night.

Bond walked a short distance into the darkness to answer a call of nature. On the way back, he noticed Hope Kendall's tent, which she had put up a good hundred feet away from the others. An oil lamp was burning inside, and he could see the outline of her figure against the canvas. As he walked past, roughly fifteen feet away from it, he could see that the tent flap was open. The doctor was squatting on the mat in the middle of the tent. She was still dressed in pants, but she had removed her sweater, exposing a white T-shirt. He paused a moment, anticipating a wave.

She didn't see him. Instead, she took hold of the bottom of the T-shirt and pulled it off over her head. She was naked underneath. Her breasts were larger than was readily apparent when she was fully dressed, and the nipples were erect and extended. The areolas were also red and large, almost as if blush had been applied to them. The sight of her sitting there topless was very erotic.

Then she looked up and noticed him standing there. Rather than covering herself with a start, she simply looked at him knowingly and didn't say a word. Without averting her eyes from his, she reached out and unsnapped the flap of the tent, letting it fall to cover the opening.

What the hell was that all about? Bond wondered. Was she Marquis's girlfriend or not? It was almost as if she didn't mind that he got a good look at her and was daring him to do something.

He walked back toward the rest of the camp, pondering the mysteries of the opposite sex, when he noticed Paul Baack working at a portable table. He sat on a collapsible stool, and his large frame looked comical on top of it. He was busily typing on the laptop, which was connected to a Microcom-M Global Satellite Telephone.

"How are things back in civilization?" Bond asked.

"Ah, hello," Baack said. "This is a wonderful device. It's the world's smallest and lightest Inmarsat M satellite telephone. I just got a fix on a satellite and made a call to my girlfriend."

"Where is she?"

"She lives in Utrecht. Ingrid. Nice German girl. I'm glad you came by. I just received a message for you."

Baack punched a few more keys and brought up an e-mail written in code. "I can't understand a word of it, but you might be able to."

Bond leaned over to look at the monitor. It was in a standard SIS code that used word associations to get its message across. Bond frowned as he read it, then said, "Thanks. You can delete it."

Baack shrugged and said, "I hope it's not bad news."

"It's good and bad," Bond said. "Good night."

"Good night, Mr. Bond."

He walked back to his own tent, where Chandra had just boiled some water with a Bibler hanging stove. It hung from the tent roof to keep the floor clear, minimizing spillage.

"Want some tea?" he asked. "It's special herbs from Nepal. Help you sleep."

"I normally despise tea, but I'll have some," Bond said. "I just got a message from London."

"Oh?"

"No word on Otto Schrenk. SIS confirms that he is known to be a serious mountaineer, but they're still doing a background check. More interesting is that Dr. Steven Harding is dead. His body was found washed up on the shore at Gibraltar. His throat was cut. There was a note in his pocket that said, 'Your traitor has ceased to be useful. We hereby return him to you.' It was signed 'The Union.'"

Chandra gave a low whistle. "Then they are on to us, I expect."

"Have you observed anything unusual so far?"

He shook his head. "Only that Group Captain Marquis and Dr. Kendall aren't sleeping together tonight!" He chuckled.

Bond avoided that subject and said, "I have a sneaking suspicion that someone from the Union is here."

"I feel that, too. If not among us, then they are nearby. Perhaps with the Chinese or the Russian expedition?"

Bond removed his boots and put on Patagonia Activist Fleece sleeveless bibs, perfect sleepwear for chilly high altitudes.

"It's possible. Let's just be on our guard. Maybe you and I will take a side trip and take a look at the Chinese group."

"Okay commander."

"Chandra?"

"Yes?"

"You can call me James."

"Fine, James."

Fatigue must have hit the Gurkha harder than on the previous night, for he was asleep within ten minutes. Bond, however, was wide awake. Sometimes it is difficult to sleep at high altitudes; insomnia is a common malady among mountaineers. Bond often experienced it himself, and he knew it would get worse as they kept ascending. Insomnia, however, wasn't what was keeping him awake tonight.

His mind was racing with thoughts of Steven Harding, the Union, the dangerous mission they were undertaking . . . and Hope Kendall's magnificent breasts.

SEVENTEEN

ELIMINATING THE COMPETITION

THE TEAM WERE IN RELATIVELY GOOD SPIRITS WHEN THEY AWOKE AND prepared for the second day of trekking. The day's goal was to reach Ghaiya Bai, which was at an altitude of 2,050 meters—not much of an increase, but it was a good six hours' hike to get there. The Sherpas left early, as usual, and Bond and Chandra enjoyed a light breakfast of yogurt, known throughout the subcontinent as curd. The buffalo milk curd of Nepal was surprisingly good, Bond thought, but he also imagined that sending overweight people on a trek across Nepal for a month would be an excellent way to diet.

The team met in the center of Chirwa at eight-thirty. The sky was overcast, causing a drop in temperature. Everyone was dressed in more layers—sweaters, jackets—some were even wearing their parkas. Chandra preferred to dress in combat equipment marching order, which basically consisted of a bergen, or rucksack, topped by what he called a "grab bag." This contained essential bits of kit that he might need in a hurry; such as a radio, small gas stove, articles of warmer clothing, and a waterproof jacket. Ever present was the Gurkha staple, the outstanding *khukri* knife. It was carried at his waist in a shiny black leather sheath. Two smaller knives, the sharp *karta* and the blunt *jhi*, were also part of the *khukri* package, and these were used to light fires and peel fruit. The larger knife, which was eighteen inches long, was made of tempered steel with a handle of buffalo horn.

"The boomerang-like shape symbolizes the Hindu trilogy of Rama, Vishnu, and Shiva," Chandra explained when Bond asked him about it. He pointed to a little nick in the blade near the handle. "You know what this is for? It's to catch your enemy's blood as it runs down the blade and keep it from reaching your hand!"

Hope Kendall barely glanced at Bond. It was as if the voyeuristic episode of the previous evening never happened. As the team set off, she began by striding beside Roland Marquis, but after an hour she had dropped back and was walking and talking with one of the Americans. Marquis seemed to be most friendly with Carl Glass, who occasionally looked at Bond as if the "Foreign Office representative" were an outsider and didn't belong on the expedition. Bond expected a certain lack of acceptance from the other climbers, but Glass in particular looked down his nose at him.

Otto Schrenk always walked alone and rarely said much to anyone. Bond attempted to engage him in conversation, but the man was tight-lipped.

"How did they find you on such short notice?" he asked.

"In eight-thousand-meter climbing, one's reputation is known," Schrenk said, as if that explained everything.

A sudden downpour made the second hour into the trek less than pleasant. Everyone scrambled to put on rain parkas, but they kept moving.

Paul Baack caught up to Bond and said, "Hey, Mr. Englishman, where's your umbrella?" He laughed loudly.

"I left it at home with my bowler hat," Bond replied.

The rain stopped in thirty minutes, but it left the ground wet and muddy. Marquis gave the order to halt for fifteen minutes to air out the wet parkas. Magically, the sun appeared from behind the clouds and the rest of the day promised to be beautiful.

Bond sat on a rock near Hope Kendall. She was brushing her hair, which glistened in the new sunlight.

"I don't know about you," she said offhandedly, "but I'll be ready for a full aftermatch function when we're through today, providing I don't bust my boiler getting to camp."

"Oh, you like to drink?" Bond asked, referring to her kiwi jargon.

"I'm a doctor, I'm not supposed to drink," she said. "But I enjoy a pint or two. When I was in college it would make me chunder all the time, but not anymore."

"How long have you known Marquis?"

"Roland? Uhm . . . six years? I was on an expedition to Everest with him. We met again when he climbed Mount Cook in New Zealand. What about you?"

"Oh, we're old rivals from Eton. It was a long time ago."

"I *thought* there was something between you two," she said. She began to apply sunblock to her face and other exposed skin areas. "You have to admit that he's a good head sherang. He always goes for the doctor in everything he does. He's a hard case."

"Does that appeal to you?" he asked.

She shrugged. "I like men who are boots and all."

"I beg your pardon?"

"Sorry, I meant that I like men who give it everything they've got. You haven't been to New Zealand much, have you?"

"I'm afraid not. Once or twice."

"Where did you go?" She finished brushing her hair and began to reorganize her pack.

"Auckland, mostly."

"Ah, well, that's where I live and work," she said. "It's the big smoke of New Zealand, isn't it? I was born in Taupo. It's a fairly well-to-do place. I got out of there as soon as I could. I didn't like the snobbery."

Bond had thought that she might have come from money. She had an aristocratic air about her that bordered on being snooty. Somehow, though, she had risen above the stereotype and seemed to be a genuinely friendly person. Perhaps it was the medical profession that had changed her.

"I lived for a while on the west coast of the south island, where everyone is basically pretty weird," she said. "People say it's a lot like

California there. I spent some time around Mount Cook—that's where I learned to climb."

"What made you become a doctor?"

"That's a long story. I was pretty wild when I was young. Hell, I'm still young. When I was *younger,* I should say. All I wanted to do was live in the outdoors, go camping, climb mountains, that sort of thing. And, uhm, there were men." She shook her head, whistled, and smiled. "I had a huge men problem. I thought there was something wrong with me! I couldn't get enough . . . hell, I don't know why I'm telling you this, I hardly know you!"

Bond laughed. "We're spending the next few weeks together, so I wouldn't worry about that. As a matter of fact, I sometimes think I have the same problem. With women, of course."

"Well, I had it with women, too," she said under her breath and rolling her eyes. "I didn't think there could be such a thing as sex addiction, but I had it bad. When I was treated for it, I became interested in psychology, and that in turn led to medicine. I hadn't gone to college yet, so I did a complete turnaround. The wild child became a serious student. I moved to Auckland to study to be a doctor, and now I can name every part of your body and spell it, too. I turned the interest in sex into a specialization in sexology for a while—you know, sexual dysfunction and all that—but then I became more attracted to general practice. I suppose you could say I find the human body a very interesting machine. I'm fascinated by it, the way a bloke knows how to take apart a sports car and put it back together. I like to test the body's limits."

That explained the rather rough physical examination he experienced the other day.

"And how's that addiction now?" he asked.

She stood up and put the pack on her back. "Like any vice, as long as it's in moderation, it can't be too bad." She winked at him and walked away.

She was a "hard case" herself, Bond thought. He knew that he shouldn't bother attempting to figure her out, but he found that he was very attracted to her. Hope obviously exhibited a great deal of energy and intelligence, but she also possessed a distinct and unsubtle animal magnetism that was inviting.

They reached the picnic site set up by the Sherpas at approximately one o'clock. There was still another two hours or more to go before they reached the day's stop. Lunch was *tama*, a Nepali soup made from dried bamboo shoots. Bond found it less than satisfying, but it would have to do.

As they rested for a half hour, Bond wandered over to Paul Baack and asked, "Any new messages from London?"

"Nothing," he said. "I'll let you know. I check the e-mail three times a day. I did receive a note from our liaison in Kathmandu. He says the Chinese are only a mile to the southwest of us and are gaining ground. If we stay on the same schedule, we'll still beat them to the mountain. But if they happen to double their efforts and attempt to pass us . . ."

"Noted," Bond said.

The team prepared to leave the site as the Sherpas packed up. The three Americans were standing on a ledge looking at a glorious view of a terraced hill that farmers were plowing. When they turned to join the others, Bill Scott, one of the Americans, tripped over a stone and fell. He cried out in pain and held on to his foot. Hope Kendall rushed to him.

"Now what?" Marquis muttered. He wandered over to the huddle and listened to what the doctor had to say.

Bond and Chandra joined them. Hope had unlashed Scott's boot and was examining his ankle. It was already swelling badly.

"It's broken," she said finally.

"Aw, hell," Scott said. "What will that mean?"

"You can't continue on," she said. "I mean, you could try, but you're going to be in a lot of pain. Once we reach Base Camp you'll certainly be in no condition to climb the mountain. I really think you should go back."

"Go back? Where?"

"To Taplejung," Marquis said. "You'll have to wait for us there."

"For a month?" Scott was angry and humiliated. "Aww, man . . ."

"One of the Sherpas will take you back. You'll just have to stay put there until we return, unless you can get a flight back to Kathmandu. That's possible, I suppose."

Hope did her best to wrap the ankle so that he could hobble. One of the Sherpas found a tree branch that could be used as a crutch.

"It's going to take you a long time, so you had better get going," Marquis said. "Bad luck, old man."

"Yeah." Scott said his good-byes to the rest of the team and his fellow Americans, then he and Chettan, one of the Sherpas, began the long trek back.

When they were out of earshot, Hope addressed everyone. "I was afraid that would happen. He had been complaining of headaches. He had a mild case of AMS and wasn't totally with it. It just goes to show you that accidents can happen quickly and unexpectedly."

"Can AMS really strike at this altitude?" the young American known as "the kid" asked.

"It varies with the individual," she replied. "We're really not very high yet, but that doesn't matter. Some people experience symptoms of AMS just driving a car up to a higher elevation than the one they're used to. Others have difficulty riding an elevator to the top of a sky-scraper. Everyone is different. That's why you've got to be aware of the symptoms."

"Fine, fine," Marquis said impatiently. "Well, we've lost one team member, let's not lose any others, all right? We had better push on."

They picked up their gear and continued on the faint path that must have been trampled by a few hundred people over the last fifty years.

The next hour was a tough one. The terrain changed, and although the altitude increase was minimal, the ground was rockier and more difficult to walk on. One of the Sherpas said that a rock fall from the neighboring "hill" had caused the problem.

They eventually got to a smoother path, and Bond caught up with Roland Marquis, who was dressed in khakis and a wool flannel shirt that was embroidered with RAF insignia.

"Hello, Bond," he said, steadily marching as if he were on a treadmill. Keeping up with him meant not lagging for an instant. "Come to see how it feels to be leader for a while?"

"No, I came forward to see what that horrible smell was coming from the front of the team," Bond said with a straight face.

"Very funny. I suppose you think you can do better, eh?"

"Not at all, Roland. Can't you take a joke? I think you're doing a splendid job. I mean it."

"By Jove, Bond, it almost sounds as if you really do. Well, thanks. It's not easy, this. You know as well as I that the schedule is damn near impossible," Marquis said quietly. It was the first time Bond had ever heard him say anything without his macho facade.

"I can't believe that fool American tripped and broke his bloody ankle," he continued. "Somehow, when a member of my team gets hurt, I feel responsible."

"That's only natural," Bond said.

"But what happened was stupid. I should have looked at his credentials more carefully."

"Roland, I'm concerned about the new man, Schrenk," Bond said. "There wasn't time for SIS to completely clear him. What do you know about him?"

"Nothing, except that he doesn't say a bloody word to anyone. I wondered when you were going to mention him to me. I had no choice but to bring him on, Bond. He was the only one. Now with Scott gone, we'll really need the extra manpower. Besides, it was SIS's job to check him out, not mine. I reviewed only his mountaineering credentials, which were excellent, so don't complain to me."

They walked on in silence. Both men were breathing at the same rate, moving with the same speed, and thinking identical things about each other.

"I do love climbing," Marquis said after a while. "If I didn't love it so much, I certainly wouldn't be the leader. But it takes someone with experience to be leader, I suppose. Have you ever led an expedition, Bond?"

"No."

"No, of course you haven't. You don't make the sport a habit, do you."

"Not like you, Roland. I go climbing only once every three or four years."

"That's too long a gap. What if a golfer played only once every three or four years? He wouldn't be a very good golfer."

"It's a bit different."

"I'm just making a point, that's all," Marquis said.

"What is it?"

"That climbing isn't a sport for you. You're an amateur. You're a *good* amateur, don't get me wrong, but you're still an amateur."

"You haven't seen me in action yet, Roland."

"True, I suppose I should wait until we're at seven thousand meters before I make that assessment."

"Everything has to be a contest with you, doesn't it, Roland?" Bond said rhetorically.

Marquis laughed aloud. "Admit it, Bond, you've always been a little jealous of me. I beat you too many times on the wrestling mat back when we were boys."

"Once more, I seem to remember it the other way around."

"There you go again distorting history," Marquis said.

"I wouldn't think of it." It took everything to keep Bond from losing his sense of humor. They walked for ten minutes in silence again.

Finally, Marquis asked, "So, Bond, what do you think of our good doctor?"

"She seems capable," Bond said tactfully.

Marquis laughed. "Oh, she's a fine doctor. I meant, what do you think of her as a *woman?*"

Again, Bond said, "She seems capable."

Marquis snorted. "I think she's simply amazing."

Bond normally didn't like to discuss other people's relationships. He was curious, though, to see what Marquis might have to say about her. He was the type of man who enjoyed boasting and had a loose tongue when it came to sexual exploits. The trouble was that his kind of man also tended to exaggerate.

"I know what you're thinking, Bond," Marquis said. "You're

wondering what kind of relationship I have with her. We're not lovers, if that's what you think. We were once, a few years ago. We tried to rekindle it at the beginning of this little venture, but it didn't work out. We're just friends now."

"Are you saying she's fair game?" Bond asked.

Marquis stopped dramatically in his tracks. Bond almost stumbled, then halted and looked at Marquis, who had a glint in his eye that was full of menace.

"She's *absolutely* fair game, if you can manage it," he said. There was, however, an implicit warning in the voice.

At that moment Hope walked up and stood between them. Her long, golden tresses blew in the wind and around the pack on her back. Even with no makeup and none of the normal day-to-day personal conveniences enjoyed by western women, she was wholesomely attractive.

"I expected to find you two arm-wrestling up here," she said. "Roland, you look like you're ready to hit your friend, here. Did he say something mean?"

"It's nothing, my dear," Marquis said. "Bond and I go way back, that's all."

"So I've heard. You two had better behave. The smell of testosterone over here is overpowering. I don't want to have to patch up either of you after you've beaten each other into a pulp."

"We're not fighting," Marquis said.

"Not even over me?" she asked facetiously, but Bond thought she was more earnest than she let on.

Marquis turned to her and said, "Yes, Hope, my dear, that's *precisely* what we're doing. We're fighting over *you.*"

She didn't rise to his anger at all. She turned up her nose flirtatiously and said, "Well, in that case, may the best man win." With that, she moved back toward the others, who had all interpreted Marquis's stopping as a signal for them to halt and rest.

"What are you doing sitting on your arses?" he shouted at them. "We've had our rest already! Get up! There's still about an hour to go before we reach camp."

Irritably, he turned and began trekking forward. Bond let him lead on and waited until Chandra caught up with him. Hope passed him, glancing at him out of the corner of her eye but not saying a word.

Bond thought that she was the biggest tease in the Eastern Hemisphere. Normally he disdained women of that ilk, but with her, the come-on was more of a challenge. He was beginning to understand her better. By her own admission, this was an intelligent woman who liked to get physical. She was unable to separate her rough, clinical manner as a medical practitioner from the rather coarse nature of her individual sexuality. Just as she liked to see what made human beings tick, she was stimulated by the primal rituals between males and females. She enjoyed the mating game in its purest sense. Perhaps this explained her love for the outdoors and for adventure. Bond was convinced that she probably had a healthy percentage of testosterone in her own body. He wondered what she might be like in bed. . . .

Bond continued up the path with Chandra and Paul Baack. The camp was a welcome sight when they finally reached it at four o'clock in the afternoon.

The overnight stay in Ghaiya Bai was uneventful, and the team had settled into a daily routine that would vary little until they reached the Base Camp. The goal for the day was to reach Kyapra, at 2,700 meters. The following day the team would ascend to a relatively major village called Ghunsa, located at 3,440 meters. Normally, a few days would be spent there acclimatizing, but that wasn't in Marquis's plan.

Bond stayed with Chandra most of the morning, purposefully avoiding any contact with either Roland Marquis or Hope Kendall. He had enough to worry about without getting into a match of wills with one or the other. Instead, he concentrated on the day's goal and tried to enjoy the scenery. They were seeing fewer and fewer signs of civilization as they ascended above 2,500 meters.

At lunchtime Paul Baack approached Bond and said, "The Chinese are less than a mile that way." He pointed toward the southwest. The big man handed him a pair of binoculars. Bond stood on a rock and looked through them.

He could see a group of at least ten men moving slowly across the side of a hill toward a site where many Sherpas had set up their own lunch stop.

Marquis climbed on the rock and asked, "What do you see?"

"We have company," Bond said. He handed the binoculars to Marquis so that he could look, then asked, "I think Chandra and I should leave you here and do a little reconnaissance. We'll meet you in Ghunsa tomorrow afternoon."

"What, you'll do a bivouac tonight?"

"That's right," Bond said, "we'll go without a tent. We both have bivouac sacks. We each have copies of the trekking route. We'll be fine. We'll catch up with you tomorrow."

"I don't like the idea of you wandering off, Bond," Marquis said.

"Sorry, Roland," Bond said. "We're going." He jumped down from the rock and went to explain the plan to Chandra.

Roland Marquis frowned to himself. He needed Bond in one piece, at least until they found Skin 17.

Bond and Chandra slipped away from the others and made their way as surreptitiously as possible toward the Chinese expedition. They got within one hundred meters of them, close enough to make an assessment of their group.

"There are eleven of them," Chandra said, looking through binoculars. "And a lot of porters." He scanned each man carefully and noted, "At least three of the men are carrying rifles. Why would anyone want a rifle on an expedition up Kangchenjunga?"

"Unless they were planning to do someone some harm when they get there," Bond suggested. "Come on, they're moving."

Chandra moved stealthily, and Bond followed. The Gurkha was a superior mountaineer. He also knew tricks and techniques to move around the hills unseen. Bond gladly turned over the leadership of their side venture to him.

Shortly before sundown the Chinese set up camp not far from Kyapra. They pitched tents and were settling down for the night. Bond and Chandra took up a position above them, nestled in an array of rock formations surrounded by a few trees.

"We'll wait until dark, when they're asleep," Bond said. "Then we'll see what there is to see."

Chandra grinned. "I haven't had this much fun since Bosnia."

"Bosnia was fun?"

"Yes, sir! Any kind of action is better than sitting in England twiddling our thumbs. I've been to Zaire. The Gulf War was interesting. I had never been in that part of the world. I'm still waiting for the chance to use my *khukri* the way my ancestors did."

"You mean that you haven't killed anyone with it yet?"

"That's right," Chandra said. "I've chopped plenty of fruits and vegetables with it, but no enemy necks. Someday I make a good tossed salad with heads, and I don't mean lettuce, eh, James?"

"You Gurkhas have a morbid sense of humor, did anyone ever tell you that?"

"All the time."

"Chandra, if you're part Buddhist, how is it that you could kill if you had to?"

"That's a good question, James," the Gurkha said. "Buddhists are not supposed to kill any living creature. However, I am a soldier and a Gurkha. We are here to preserve the dignity and freedom of man. I know it's a contradiction in terms, but the Gurkhas have been a contradiction in terms for nearly two hundred years!"

Nightfall finally came, and they waited until the last embers of the Chinese campfire died. Then, slowly and silently, they crept down the hill toward the site. Bond had observed the group carefully so that he could pinpoint which tents held humans and which ones only equipment and food supplies. The portable kitchen, similar to their own, was built near there. The Sherpas were sleeping in tents close to this area, and Bond knew that they would probably be lighter sleepers than the Chinese.

Using a penlight, Bond found sacks of rice and lentils. Another group of bags held tea. There was a sack of dried figs and other fruits. He whispered to Chandra, "They seem fairly ill equipped, wouldn't you say? I'm afraid we have to play a dirty trick on them and contaminate the food somehow. Then they'll have to turn back to resupply themselves, and by then they'll be too late to catch up. Got any ideas?"

Chandra whispered back, "That's easy!" He removed the *khukri* from its sheath, then neatly slit open the bag of rice. He did it so swiftly that it didn't make a sound. The rice poured out onto the ground. The next thing he did flabbergasted Bond. The Gurkha unzipped his fly and proceeded to urinate all over the spilled rice. He grinned at Bond the entire time.

"Hand me your knife," Bond said, stifling a laugh. Chandra handed it over, still relieving himself. Bond slit open the other bags of food and poured the contents onto the pile of freshly sprayed rice. He took a stick and mixed it all up. Chandra zipped up, then removed the two tiny knives from the *khukri* sheath. He squatted down and rubbed the two blades together on the burlap sacks. A spark flew, then another, and another. After four tries, the burlap caught fire.

"I think it's time we run now, James," Chandra said.

A gunshot startled them, and they turned to flee. They heard several men shouting in Chinese. The flames grew in intensity as they climbed away from the camp. More gunshots whizzed past them, but by that time they were in the dark. The marksmen were firing blindly. Some of them retrieved torches and cast the beams over the hill, but they were ineffective. Bond could hear at least three men scrambling up the rocks after them. After more gunshots, the entire camp was up, running about and shouting. The Sherpas were busy trying to put out the fire, which had engulfed all their supplies. Bond and Chandra climbed back into their niche in the cliff and watched the chaos below. The pursuers had given up and returned to the campsite to help salvage what they could.

It took them half an hour to extinguish the fire. Bond and Chandra had achieved their goal. The Chinese expedition was completely sabotaged. They could hear them arguing and shouting at one another. The Sherpas began to argue as well, and Chandra could pick up a little of what they were saying.

"The Sherpas are very upset that the Chinese fired guns here. They say the gods will not be pleased and will bring misfortune on them. They refuse to go farther. They are now without any food. They are turning back in the morning."

The Chinese calmed down after an hour. Someone had apparently brought out a couple of bottles of alcohol, and that did the trick. Eventually, they crawled back into their tents, leaving just one man with a rifle on guard.

Bond opened his North Face bivouac sack and secured it behind a large stone, where there was just enough room for him to stretch out. Chandra found a hole where he could curl up in his own sack.

"*Shuba ratri,* James," Chandra said quietly.

When they awoke the next morning, the Chinese expedition had given up, packed, and left.

EIGHTEEN

TENSIONS RISE

WHEN BOND AND CHANDRA SAW THE VILLAGE OF GHUNSA PERCHED ON THE side of a snow-covered peak, they breathed a sigh of relief. The ascent to 3,440 meters had taken its toll on them, and Bond found himself becoming winded quickly and having to stop and rest more often. Chandra, on the other hand, seemed to be unaffected by the altitude.

There were some yak herders living there, and Bond admired how people could live this high in the mountains and make ends meet. The villagers stopped and stared at the two of them, more curious about the man who was obviously a Gurkha soldier than the Caucasian encroaching on their land.

They rounded a bend and saw a campsite some two hundred meters away.

"That must be us," Bond said. "I hope lunch is ready, I'm starving."

They climbed up a slick wet rock face to a ledge. It wasn't necessary to use climbing tools yet, but they knew they would be employing the ice axes soon enough. The trek from Ghunsa to the Base Camp was substantially steeper. The next two days would be more strenuous.

Bond and Chandra turned to continue toward the camp, when a bullet whizzed past them and struck the snow. Both men instinctively dived to the ground. Two more shots hit the snow around them.

Chandra rolled next to a rock for better cover. Bond crawled on his belly to a large tree stump that must have been hundreds of years old.

"Do you see him?" Bond whispered.

Chandra carefully raised his head and looked about. "I don't see anything."

Bond looked up and saw a whiff of smoke on a cliff face overlooking the village. He pointed. "He's up there. See?"

Chandra squinted and nodded. "What do we do?"

"I suppose we wait."

"Who could it be?"

"Obviously someone who knows we're here and doesn't want us to rejoin our group."

"The Chinese?"

Bond shook his head. "I don't think so. There was no trace of them this morning. They went back the way they came."

Chandra took a good look at their surroundings and pointed to a ledge fifty meters away. "If we can make it to that ledge, we can climb down, go around the cliff here, and come up on the other side of the camp."

"Good thinking," Bond said. "Let's go together. It'll give the sniper too many targets to aim for. On three. One . . . two . . . three!"

The men leaped from their cover and scrambled toward the ledge. Two more bullets zipped into the snow at their feet. Chandra reached the edge first, squatted, put his hands on a sturdy rock, and hurled himself over the side. Bond did the same thing, although not as gracefully. Together they hung for a few seconds, then gained a foothold on the side of the rock face. Carefully, they inched down ten feet to level ground.

"That was an impressive move," Bond said, completely out of breath. He coughed, then collapsed into a sitting position.

"Are you all right?"

He coughed again. "Yeah, I've already got climber's cough. You know how it is. I'm surprised I'm getting it so soon." He took slow deep breaths for a few minutes.

"Do you have a headache?" Chandra asked.

"No, thank God. It's not that bad. Come on, let's go."

"Are you sure?"

"Let's go, dammit!" Bond was annoyed with himself. He wanted to be as resilient as his partner, but there was no competing with a native Nepalese, especially a Gurkha.

They skirted around the cliff and found another place to ascend. They came up on the other side of the camp and wandered in, keeping an eye on the cliff where the sniper had been. There was no sign of any movement there now.

Roland Marquis was deep in conversation with Carl Glass when he saw them coming and waved. "We were about to give up!" he called. "We have to make it to Kambachan before sunset."

"Christ," Bond said. "How far is that?"

Marquis shrugged. "Four and a half hours. Why? You're up to it, aren't you, Bond?"

Bond coughed and nodded.

"Sounds as if a night in a bivouac didn't do you much good," Marquis said. "Bad luck." Bond noted that there was a certain degree of pleasure in the man's voice. "What did you find out about our Chinese friends?"

"They won't be bothering us anytime soon. Is there anyone from the team missing?" Bond asked.

"You mean right now?"

"Yes."

"Uhm, three or four people are in the village. They're supposed to be back"—he looked at his watch—"any minute now. The plan was to leave at twelve-thirty. It's twelve-fifteen."

"Who's gone?"

"Why?"

"Never mind, Roland, just tell me!" Bond snapped.

Marquis's eyes narrowed. "Careful, Bond. Don't forget who's leader here."

Bond grabbed the man's parka and pulled him forward. Chandra interceded, saying, "Hey, hey, stop it. Move back, commander."

Bond let go and stepped back. "Roland, you're the leader, but you also have orders from SIS to assist me. Now, who went into the village?"

Marquis relaxed a little, then said, "Dr. Kendall, Paul Baack, Otto Schrenk, and the American kid."

Schrenk, Bond thought. The sniper was Schrenk.

At that moment Baack and Hope were seen coming down the path toward the campsite. Baack was wearing a bright, distinctive yellow and green parka that he hadn't worn earlier. Bond sat down on a collapsible stool and coughed some more. Hope approached him and said, "Hey, you already got the cough."

"Thank you, doctor," Bond said. "I appreciate the diagnosis. Where have you two been?"

Hope looked at Marquis and Baack. "You feeling all right, James?"

Chandra said, "We've had a rough night and day, that's all."

Baack said, "I was bartering with one of those yak herders for a gourd." He held it up. "It's supposed to taste like pumpkin. The good doctor appeared just in time. The old man must have had a thing for Caucasian women, for he went down in price when he saw she was with me."

Hope held up a necklace. "And I traded five packs of chewing gum for this. Not bad, eh? It's probably worthless, but it's pretty."

"Hey!" a voice called. They all turned to see Otto Schrenk running slowly toward them. He, too, was out of breath and had to stop every few steps. Finally, he got to the site and collapsed onto a tarp. He began to hack and it was several seconds before he got his wind back. Finally, he said, "The kid . . . he's dead . . . he's been shot."

"What?" Marquis and Hope said simultaneously.

"Where?" Bond asked.

Schrenk pointed to the cliff where the sniper had been. "Just below that cliff there. Come, I'll show you."

As they walked toward the site, Bond wondered where Schrenk might have hidden his gun. It had to have been a rifle. Where in his gear could he have stashed it? Did he abandon it on the cliff?

"The kid," whose name was David Black, was sprawled on the path where snow had given way to mud. Blood was seeping onto the ground where he lay.

Hope Kendall got on her knees to examine him. "Help me turn him," she said.

"Shouldn't we leave the body alone?" Baack asked.

"What, do you think the police are going to come and seal off the area?" Marquis said.

"Actually, there is a Nepalese police post in Ghunsa. They will be coming to check our permits before long," Baack replied.

Bond helped her turn Black over. The bullet had entered the center of his chest.

"This was done at point-blank range," Bond observed. Hope nodded in concurrence.

His eyes met Chandra's. They both knew what had happened. David Black had most likely stumbled upon or had heard the sniper fire. He was eliminated because he had seen the sniper.

The trek to Kambachan was called off and the team settled to spend the night at Ghunsa. Marquis was sullen and frustrated with the turn of events. Bond and Chandra took care of removing the body from the site and also spent some time on the cliff looking for evidence. Chandra found a 7.62mm shell and showed it to Bond.

"This is from a semi-automatic. A sniper rifle. A Dragunov, maybe?" Bond surmised.

"I fired an L1 A1 rifle once. It used ammunition like this." The L1 A1 was the British version of the Belgian FN FAL, one of the most widely used modern self-loading rifles. It was gas operated and held a twenty-round magazine.

"Chandra, I think you might be right."

"It has to be one of our team. No one living in Ghunsa would have this rifle," Chandra said. "Should we search Schrenk's belongings?"

"We might have to. Come on, let's make our report."

The team was bewildered and shocked that David Black had been murdered. When Bond announced that the killer was possibly one of their own, several of them protested.

"Are you out of your mind?" a climber named Delpy asked. "Why would any of us want to do such a thing?"

"Is there something about this expedition you're not telling us?" asked Doug McKee, the sole remaining American on the team.

"Calm down," Marquis said. "We're on a salvage mission, and that's all there is to it."

"Who would want to shoot at us, then?" Philippe Léaud asked.

"The Russians," Paul Baack answered. They all looked at him. "I just got word that their team will reach Base Camp tomorrow. Maybe they think there's something up there at that plane."

Everyone looked at Marquis. "Is there?" Hope asked.

"Just bodies," he said. "British and American ones."

Bond considered the possibility that the Russians might be involved. Could their team be Union members? They had been known to deal with the Russian Mafia. What if that entire expedition was made up of Union criminals?

"Are we in some kind of danger?" Tom Barlow asked. "I mean, danger from human beings, not danger from the elements."

"Of course not," Marquis said, attempting to reassure them. "I think what happened to Mr. Black was some kind of freak accident."

"How can being shot at point-blank range be a freak accident?" Baack asked. "I have a bad feeling about this."

"Me, too," another said.

"And me," one more ventured.

"Fine!" Marquis shouted. "Then you can all turn back. Look, you were hired to perform a mission and you're being paid bloody good money for it! Now, tomorrow morning, I'm going on to Kambachan, and then I'm going to push to Lhonak so that I will be at Base Camp the day after tomorrow. I'll be happy to lead whoever wants to join me!"

Hope cleared her throat. "From here to Lhonak is an increase in altitude of a little over a thousand meters. That's going to be difficult."

"We all knew this would be difficult," Marquis said. "You all knew the risks. If anyone wants to turn back, he's welcome. I for one am going on. Who's going with me?"

No one said anything until Bond raised his hand. "The way I see it, there's altitude sickness, HACE, HAPE, avalanches, frostbite, snow blindness, and dozens of other catastrophes that could happen. What's a little gunfire aimed in our direction?"

A few people snickered. Chandra spoke up then. "In the Gurkha forces, we have a saying in Gurkhali: *Kaphar hunu banda, marnu raamro.* It's our motto. It means 'It's better to die than be a coward.' I shall go with you and Commander Bond."

"Me, too," Hope Kendall said. "Besides, I have a feeling you'll need a good doctor up there."

Paul Baack shrugged. "Hell, I've come this far. Why not?"

The others ultimately agreed. Only Otto Schrenk was silent. They all looked at him, waiting for an answer. Finally, he said, "I'm in."

Keeping the murder from the Ghunsa police proved to be easier than they expected. Hope Kendall submitted a death certificate claiming that David Black had received a "puncture wound" when he fell on some equipment. Luckily, the police were accustomed to dealing with accident-prone westerners and allowed the team to take care of the matter without their interference. Permits were checked and the team were cleared to move on.

The Liaison Officer volunteered to take David Black's body to Kathmandu and attend to the appropriate bureaucracy involved. After he left with the corpse on a wagon, the Sherpas performed a token prayer service for the dead climber.

As night fell, the entire team went to their tents in silence. They attempted to put the events of the day behind them, but there was no escaping the feeling that impending disaster was just around the corner.

The trek grew more difficult after the overnight stop in Lhonak. Everyone on the team was feeling poorly. The ascent was overly ambitious, and even Roland Marquis was coughing and breathing heavily when they finally reached Base Camp, six days after leaving Kathmandu.

It was located on the north side of the great mountain at 5,140 meters. Remnants of past expeditions were still there—broken tents, rubbish, *puja* shrines, and, most conspicuous, a few gravestones that had been placed to honor those who had perished on Kangchenjunga.

The peak itself was massive, extending up into the clouds. It was a spectacular behemoth of rock, ice, and snow. Winds dangerously whipped around it. Billows of what appeared to be white "smoke" occasionally exploded off the upper regions. This was really snow and ice being thrown about by the high winds. From the base of the mountain, this phenomenon was beautiful to look at; but to be up there *in* it would be extremely hazardous. There, it would be a terrible blizzard. It was no wonder, Bond thought, that the Nepalese believed the gods lived at the top. The sight was so overpowering that his first instinct was to bow to it, proclaim himself unworthy to be in its vicinity, and then turn around and go home. The facts were well known to him—the mountain is eight miles in length and five in width, and its main summit is at 8,598 meters, or 28,208 feet, making it the third-highest peak in the world. Although Everest receives most of the attention in the Himalayas, Kangchenjunga is considered more difficult and "mightier." Many people have attempted to summit the Kanch from the north side. It wasn't until 1979 that three men made it to the top via the "north ridge," bypassing the lower glacial shelves. The Japanese were the first to summit via the north face in 1980.

"All in all," Marquis said as they approached the Base Camp, "there have been over twenty-five expeditions up this mountain, using seventeen possible routes. I've never tried the Kanch. I've always wanted to."

"We're not here to summit," Bond reminded him.

"If we get our job done and there's time, I'm bloody well going to do it," Marquis said with finality in his voice. "And you can't stop me, Bond."

"Some of the Sherpas might."

"Besides, I'd like to see Hope get to the top. Not many women have done it."

Dr. Kendall overheard this and said, "Unh-unh. As much as I'd like to, Mr. Bond is right. We're not here to set world records."

Marquis looked at them both with disgust and walked away from them.

In three hours the camp was set up and operational. Ang Tshering organized it quickly and efficiently. A tent was erected for Girmi to store the food supplies and cooking equipment. Paul Baack was in charge of expedition HQ, which consisted of all his various communications devices, cots, lamps, and other supplies. A portable satellite dish was constructed just outside the HQ tent, and it wasn't long before he was in communication with the outside world.

Nearly everyone was wheezing and coughing. As the altitude change was now quite serious, people retired to their tents immediately after dinner. Most of them weren't very hungry and had to force themselves to eat something.

The temperature was another factor that affected the team. At the Base Camp it was below freezing, and the windchill made it even worse. At subzero temperatures, Bond would wear a Marmot 8000 Meter down parka and trousers. Equipment and clothing weight is always something to consider, and Bond had chosen the parka because it weighed around one kilogram. His hands were kept covered by OR Promodular gloves, which were very strong, supple, and warm. Even inside the Marmot sleeping bag, he was constantly aware of the chill.

The next morning Bond felt better and found that others did, too. He was eager to get up the side of the mountain, but he knew that a week had to be spent at the Base Camp so that the body could properly acclimatize. He joined the others for the traditional *puja* ceremony in which the Sherpas and Chandra built a small shrine out of rocks and hung prayer scarves on it. Prayers were said, as it was believed that they had to ask permission to climb the mountain. They made offerings, and a live chicken that Girmi had brought along in a wooden cage was sacrificed for just this purpose. Supposedly, this would appease the gods at the top, and the climbers would be looked upon favorably.

"It is important not to take the climb lightly," Chandra told everyone. "Always respect the mountain. The mountain is far more powerful than you will ever be. The gods don't like men to be overconfident. They despise anyone who thinks he can get the better of the mountain. Misfortune will most certainly fall upon anyone who believes they can 'trick' the mountain."

Everyone listened attentively, but Bond noticed Marquis holding back a snicker. He whispered to Bond, "You don't believe that mumbo jumbo, do you, Bond?"

"It's not a question of belief, Roland, it's a question of respect."

Marquis shook his head. "You always liked playing by the rules, didn't you. . . ."

Afterward, Marquis addressed the group. "Right. I hope you all had a good night's sleep. I know I didn't. But as our bodies acclimatize, the sleeping will improve, isn't that right, doctor?"

Hope said, "Well, for most people it should. Sleeping is automatically impaired at high altitudes. That's why it's important to take frequent rests. I should also remind you to drink lots of fluids."

"Now," Marquis continued, "all this week we'll spend the time doing just that. However, beginning the day after tomorrow, some of us will commence short excursions up the face. Each day we'll climb a little higher and return to Base Camp the same day. I'll be watching you all to see how you do, and on that basis I'll select those climbers who will accompany me in the Lead Team." The Lead Team was the group that had the most difficult job. They had to install the hardware that helped other climbers get up the mountain—ropes, anchors, ice screws, pitons, carabiners, runners, and the like.

After the meeting the team broke up for "free time," which Bond considered a joke, as there was absolutely nothing to do. He had brought two paperback books to read—an old thriller by John le Carré and a new nonfiction book about criminal profiling, written by a former FBI agent. Several of the men had brought playing cards and portable chess and checkers sets, and Paul Baack even had a television that picked up a few channels by satellite.

Base Camp life was long and dull in Bond's opinion, and he found himself becoming restless and agitated by the third day. Marquis didn't pick him to go on the first climb, but he did select Otto Schrenk. Bond thought he would use the opportunity to take a look inside Schrenk's tent.

He got Chandra to stand watch as he slipped inside. Typically, Schrenk had insisted on pitching his own tent and bunking alone.

There were the usual accoutrements necessary for survival—a hanging Bibler stove, climbing gear, sleeping bag, clothing—but nothing that remotely resembled anything like a sniper rifle. The only weapon he found was an antique but beautifully preserved dress dagger that the Nazis wore as an item of uniform. They were special to each branch of the service, and this one was naval. It was not hidden but was lying in plain sight with a pile of other tools. A Union weapon perhaps?

Bond crept out of the tent and shook his head at Chandra. Perhaps they could find a way to search everyone's tent before the actual ascent began.

Two days later Bond was attempting to nap in his tent after lunch. Gunshots woke him, so he leaped out of the sleeping bag and slipped on his boots. He ran outside, where it had begun to snow.

The shots were coming from behind the mess. Three or four people were standing around, watching something. Bond pushed through and saw that Roland Marquis had set up targets of bottles and tin cans and was practicing his aim with a Browning Hi-Power handgun. The Sherpas were quite agitated with this behavior, and Bond understood why. The gunfire would displease the gods.

"Roland, what the hell are you doing?" Bond snapped.

"What does it look like, Bond? I'm keeping my trigger finger up to snuff."

"You're upsetting the Sherpas. Stop it, now."

Marquis turned and looked at Bond. "I don't give a damn what the Sherpas think. I'm the leader here, and if I feel like target practice, by God, I'm going to do it. Care to join me?"

"Hell, no. Put the gun away."

Marquis shrugged and laid the pistol on a rock. He picked up an ice ax that was at his side. "All right, how about a little game of ice ax throwing? Come on, Bond, aren't you bored, too? We'll throw ice axes at the targets. The Sherpas won't mind that."

Bond shook his head. He didn't want to get into this kind of brawl with Marquis. More team members had heard the noise and had by then ventured to the area. Hope Kendall was among them.

"Come on, Bond, it's all in fun. Don't tell me that our Foreign Office rep is afraid of being beaten?" Marquis said it loud enough for everyone to hear.

"You're acting like a schoolboy, Roland."

Without warning, Marquis flicked the ice ax at Bond. It struck the ground an inch away from his right foot. The tool perfectly embedded in the snow with the handle sticking straight up.

Whether it was the effects of the high altitude, the relentless boredom, or his lack of sleep, he didn't know; but this angered Bond to such an extent that he reached down and removed the ice ax, saying, "All right, Roland. Let's do it."

"Now you're talking, Bond!" Marquis laughed aloud and looked around for another ice ax. He got one from Carl Glass and then said, "Carl, go and set up those bottles and cans again, would you? What shall our stakes be? I'm sure you didn't bring much money with you, so we can't have a replay of our Stoke Poges match."

"This was your idea, Roland, you name it."

Marquis grinned and looked around at the crowd. He spotted the doctor looking at him with wide eyes.

"Very well. The winner gets to sleep with Dr. Kendall tonight."

"What?" she blurted out. "What the hell are you—"

Bond held up his hand. "Come on, Roland, that was out of line, and you know it."

Marquis gave her a little bow. "I'm sorry, my dear. Just a little joke."

"Screw you, Roland," she said, then walked away.

Marquis shook his head and said, "Tsk-tsk, the fairer sex. I suppose they can't be saints and sluts at the same time."

It took all of Bond's willpower to keep from slugging him. He knew, though, that it wouldn't be good for morale to do so in front of the team. The man was behaving as badly as Bond had ever seen him.

"Well, never mind. We won't play for anything except the satisfaction of being the best. Is that all right?" Marquis asked.

"Fine."

"Shall I start?"

Bond gave a slight, mocking bow. "By all means."

Marquis sneered at him, then turned to face the targets. There were five bottles and five cans set on various objects—portable tables, rocks, canvas bags. . . .

Marquis raised the ice ax and tossed it. It knocked the first bottle cleanly off its base.

He smiled and said, "Your turn, Bond."

Bond took a position, tossed the ice ax from hand to hand to get a feel for its weight, then flicked it forward. The second bottle shattered.

"Oh, nice one, Bond! Do we get extra points for breaking the target? I think not."

Carl Glass retrieved the ice axes and handed them back to the players. The other members of the team were enthralled by the display of antagonism between the two men. Even Hope returned out of curiosity.

Marquis took a stance, raised the ice ax, and threw it. The tool whizzed past the third bottle, missing it by two inches.

"Oh, bloody hell," he said.

Bond took his place, raised his own ax, then tossed it. He knocked the third bottle into the snow.

The axes were retrieved again, and Marquis took his place for a third try. He flung the ice ax and missed the fourth bottle by a hair.

"*Goddammit!*" he shouted. He was losing his temper. In fact, Bond thought, he was acting quite irrationally. Could he have AMS?

Bond knocked down the fourth bottle, which only angered Marquis more. Luckily for him, Marquis succeeded in demolishing the fifth bottle.

By the time they were into the tin cans, Bond was ahead by one hit. There were only two targets left. Bond had hit every object he had thrown at except for one, which had allowed Marquis to catch up a little.

Marquis took aim, threw the ax, and knocked off the can. One to go.

Bond stood his ground, aimed, and threw. The pick missed the can. There was an audible gasp from the spectators.

"Oh, bad luck, Bond," Marquis said, cocky as hell. He took the retrieved ice ax and aimed carefully. He raised his arm slowly, then threw the ice ax hard. Instead of hitting the can, it struck the rock it was sitting on. The force of the blow, however, was enough to dislodge the can, causing it to fall into the snow.

"Ha! It's a draw!" Marquis shouted.

"I don't think so, Roland," Bond said. "You didn't hit the can. You hit the rock."

"The bloody thing got knocked off, though."

This time Carl Glass intervened. "Well, since I'm the unofficial referee here, I have to side with Mr. Bond on that one, Roland. You didn't hit the can."

"Who the hell asked you?" he shouted at Glass.

"Let Bond have another go," someone in the crowd said.

"Yes, that should clinch it."

Marquis was fuming. "Very well. Bond, if you hit it, fine, you win. But if you miss, I win."

"You'd still be tied," Glass reminded him.

"Shut up!" Marquis snapped. "Whose side are you on, anyway?"

"Fine, Roland," Bond said. "If I miss, you win." Bond took the ice ax, concentrated on the tin can that had been reset by Glass, then threw the tool. It spun around, hit a nearby rock, bounced off it, and struck the can. The spectators applauded and shouted.

"Whoa, fancy move!"

"Well done!"

Marquis glowered at Bond. "You cheated."

"How? It was your bloody game. There were no rules."

He stuck his finger into Bond's chest and said, "I never liked you, Bond. Not back at school, not when we were in the service, and not now. Someday you and I will really have it out."

Bond stood there, silently taking it. He couldn't jeopardize the mission by getting into a fight with Marquis now. They had to get to the plane, and Marquis was the only one who could adequately lead them up the mountain.

It was Hope who defused the situation. "Roland, I want you to go to bed. You're exhibiting AMS symptoms."

"No, I'm not."

"One of the first symptoms is denial that you have them."

"I agree with Dr. Kendall," Bond said. He attempted to control his anger and speak calmly. "Look, this was just a game. We'll do it again sometime if it will make you feel better. But the doctor is right. You're not thinking straight."

Marquis looked around him and saw that the entire team was staring at him. He began to protest, then backed down. "Fine," he said. He seemed to relax a little. "But you wait. I'm going to prove to you all that there's no one else who can summit this mountain faster than me."

"We're not summiting the mountain, Roland," Hope reminded him.

"Oh, believe me, I will," he said. "I haven't come all this way just to pick over a bunch of dead bodies in a plane wreck. I don't give a shit about your 'secret mission,' Bond."

That did it. Bond grabbed him by the parka. He whispered through his teeth, "Listen to me, *Marquis,* you had better start behaving. Might I remind you of your duty and of M's instructions? I will not hesitate to exercise my own authority to have you replaced. I can do it, too."

Hope Kendall was the only one who heard him. She said, "Come on, Roland. Lets go to the medical tent. I want to take a look at you. Let's check your blood pressure." She gently pulled him away from Bond. Marquis glared at his adversary but allowed her to take him away.

NINETEEN

KANGCH AT LAST

A WEEK PASSED AND ROLAND MARQUIS PICKED A SMALL TEAM TO PREPARE the temporary camps up the north face of Kangchenjunga. The plan was to ascend the mountain over two weeks, with several days spent acclimatizing at the halfway mark. Camp Five would be set up at the crash site on the Great Scree Terrace.

Bond expected Marquis not to pick him, and when Marquis announced that the Lead Team would consist of himself, Philippe Léaud, Carl Glass, Tom Barlow, Otto Schrenk, Doug McKee, and two Sherpas, Bond protested.

"Let me and Chandra go with you," he insisted.

"Sorry, Bond, only professional climbers are allowed to be in the Lead Team. It's the rule."

"Bollocks, Roland. You know damned well I can do it. So can Chandra."

Marquis thought for a moment. He was quite aware that Bond was properly acclimatized simply from observing his ability and stamina during the trek from Taplejung.

"All right, Bond," he said patronizingly. "I suppose we can use you."

Climbers usually work in pairs so that one can belay the other and take turns making pitches, so Marquis could not exclude Chandra.

Bond put on Boothroyd's One Sport boots and made a thorough

inspection of his equipment. His various ice tools—axes, ice screws—were made by Black Diamond, among the finest available. His snow pickets, the stakes used as anchoring devices, were MSR Coyotes. He had chosen the Deadman model simply because he liked the name. He examined the points on his Grivel 2F crampons to satisfy himself that they were sharp enough. Crampons are necessary for ice climbing, allowing the climber to gain a solid foothold on hard ice and snow. They were hinged so that they would bend naturally. He used the Scottish method of strapping them to his boots—a strap with a ring in the middle is permanently connected to the two front posts of the crampon; a strap then runs from one side post through the ring to the other side post, with a rear strap wrapping around the ankle from the two back posts. He knew it was a rather old-fashioned way of doing it, but it was how his father had taught him when Bond first started climbing at the age of five. Like everyone else, he carried Edelweiss 9mm Stratos ropes, made with polyamide braid in fifty-meter sections, and fixing ropes, which are different and made of 7mm Kevlar cord in one-hundred-meter sections.

Marquis and Léaud set off in the lead, followed by Barlow and Glass, then Bond and Chandra. The two Sherpas, Holung and Chettan, who had come back to the Base Camp after leaving the injured Bill Scott in Taplejung, were next, and Schrenk and McKee brought up the rear.

To get to Camp One at 5,500 meters, the team had to walk up a moraine and across a low-angle rock and ice glacier. They had made such a trip at least once during practice runs the previous week, so they were familiar with the path. Unfortunately, the wind was now blowing hard and the temperature had dropped significantly.

The first part of the ascent was relatively easy. The French had developed a widely used technique for ice climbing called "flat-footing," which requires the climber to keep his feet as flat against the ice as possible at all times to keep all crampon points on the ice. The Germans developed a technique known as "front-pointing," in which the climber kicks the front crampon points hard into the ice and then steps directly up on them. In both techniques, climbers must progress by moving their weight from one point of balance to another, supporting themselves as much as possible on their legs, and planning several moves in advance. Bond liked to call it "climbing with one's eyes." Climbers learn to rely on surface features, seeking out buckets and protrusions for handholds, footholds, and ice-tool placements.

Technical expertise was needed once they reached the upper glacier. One man climbed while his partner belayed. The belay had to be connected to an anchor, the point of secure attachment to the rock or ice. The belayer paid out or took in rope as the climber ascended, ready to use one of the various methods of applying friction in case the climber fell. Marquis took the lead, belayed from below, and moved up the rock face to the next desirable spot to set up a new belay. The last climber would take apart the belay and climb up, belayed from above. The distance between belays is known as a pitch. The climbers leapfrogged their way up so that the one who went first led all the odd-numbered pitches, and followed second on all even-numbered ones. The leader attached hardware—called "protection"—to the rock or ice on the way up.

All along the way the team pitched flags and ropes, marking the route so that the others would have less difficulty ascending. It was a strenuous four hours, but Bond felt great to be climbing again. It reminded him of his youth in the Austrian Tyrol, when he first fell in love with the sport. The cold air that burned his lungs was a painful yet exhilarating sensation.

As he and Chandra pitched their tent at Camp One, though, he got the disconcerting feeling that he was in grave danger. He felt that the Union could raise their ugly head at any time.

At dawn Bond and Chandra were awoken by the Sherpas, who brought them hot tea. The tea was welcome, but he would have given a year's salary just to have a plate of his housekeeper May's scrambled eggs. He also would have killed to have a cigarette, but this was truly a situation when having a cigarette would have killed him.

He rose stiffly from the sleeping bag, coughed and hacked for several minutes, then sipped the tea. Chandra sat up, said "Good morning" but was otherwise atypically speechless. The climb was getting to them both. Bond had slept fitfully, with very vivid, disturbing dreams, which was quite normal at high altitude. What was worrying was that the conditions would worsen as they got higher. That day they were ascending to 6,000 meters. It wouldn't be long before they would require oxygen.

The team met at Marquis's tent, which would remain as Camp One HQ.

"Right," Marquis said, breathing heavily. "Today's climb is another five hundred meters up the ice glacier above us. It's a relatively easy jaunt. First we have to climb through that small, low-angle icefall to get to the main glacier. We'll set up Camp Two there."

"There are some short ice steps we'll have to fix rope on," Philippe Léaud said. "How big are they, Roland?"

"Ten to twenty meters. No problem. How does everyone feel?"

They all mumbled, "Fine."

"Lets go, then."

The team kept the same formation as the previous day, with Marquis and Léaud leading. The ropes were attached easily enough, and they trudged up the slope in silence. As the air grew thinner, their strength diminished with each step. It took twice as long to travel a few feet as it would have at sea level.

They got to Camp Two midafternoon, totally exhausted. Tom Barlow fell to his knees, gasping for breath.

"Chettan, take a look at him," Marquis told the Sherpa. "Make sure he's all right. The rest of you, set up the tents. The sooner we get this done, the sooner we can collapse."

Barlow regained his wind after a few minutes. So far no one except Marquis had shown any signs of AMS. They erected the tents and huddled in two of them to eat. Bond found himself in a tent with Chandra, Marquis, and Léaud. Marquis brought out his cell phone and punched the memory dial.

"Camp Two to Base, Camp Two to Base," he said.

"Hello? Roland?" It was Paul Baack.

"Paul, we're here. We're at Camp Two."

"Congratulations!"

"How are things down there?"

"Fine. We're all restless, but we just watched *Gone With the Wind* on television. Uncut. No commercials. That passed the time."

"Frankly, my dear, I don't give a damn," Marquis said, laughing at his own joke.

"Hope wants to know how everyone is feeling," Baack said.

"Tell her we're fine. Tom had a few moments of breathlessness, but he's all right now. Tomorrow we'll push on to Camp Three and wait for you to join us. In the meantime, can we order some Chinese takeaway?"

"Sorry, we're all out of Chinese food. You don't want Chinese food tonight. Why don't you order a pizza?"

"That sounds fine, too," Marquis said, laughing. "Over and out."

He put away the phone as they began to eat Alpine Aire freeze-dried rations, which were types of casseroles made of vegetables and/or meat. Sealed tightly in waterproof plastic bags, the rations were lightweight and easily boiled to produce a high-calorie meal with no dishes to clean.

"Hey, come out here!" a voice called outside.

"Who's that?" Marquis asked.

"Sounds like McKee," Bond said. He stuck his head out the tent flap. Doug McKee was standing a few feet away, pointing at something.

"Come look at this," he said. The others were gathered around a dark object in the snow.

Bond and his group climbed out and stomped through the ice and snow to see what the fuss was about.

"I wonder how long he's been here," McKee said, pointing to the thing frozen in the ice.

It was a man's skeleton, fully dressed in climbing gear.

Bond's dreams that night were filled with unholy terrors. He thought that an avalanche had buried him at one point and that he was suffocating and freezing. As he dug frantically in the snow with his bare, frostbitten hands, he came upon the frozen skeletons of an entire expedition. The skulls were laughing at him. One addressed him in Roland Marquis's voice: "Oh, bad luck! You never were the best, Bond. But you tried to be, didn't you? Now look at you!"

He awoke with a start. Chandra was shaking him. "James, there's a fire. Wake up!"

"What?" Bond snapped out of it, groggy and disoriented. The first thing he noticed was the biting, cold air attacking his lungs. He coughed hard and wheezed for a few seconds.

"One of the tents is on fire!"

Bond leaped out of the sleeping bag, slipped on his boots, and followed Chandra outside. The sun was just rising, casting an eerie orange glow over the ice around them.

Three men were stomping on a tent that was ablaze. Bond had to think a moment to remember whose tent it was.

"Schrenk?"

"He got out. He's over there." Chandra pointed. Otto Schrenk was one of the men putting out the fire. They were using snow shovels and blankets to snuff it out. Bond and Chandra jumped in to help, and within minutes it was extinguished.

"How did this happen?" Marquis asked, stumbling up to the scene. His voice was hoarse.

"The goddamn stove in my tent," Schrenk said. "I was trying to boil water, and the tent caught fire. Look, it's all ruined."

"What gear did you lose?"

"I'm not sure yet. My extra clothes, I know." Schrenk began to rummage through the blackened fabrics and pulled out some tools that were still intact. "There are these, thank God."

"He can borrow some of my clothes until we reach Camp Three," Philippe Léaud said. "You're my size, Otto?"

"I think so, thanks."

The team settled down for breakfast and attempted to get their wits about them. No one was thinking particularly straight. They gathered by Marquis's tent as he pulled out a map of the route.

"Today we come to our first big obstacle. After we cross the glacier, we come to the so-called ice building. Now, we have a couple of options. The normal route is to climb six hundred meters on a steep ice slope to the left of the seracs of the ice building. We would then traverse right across the first snow plateau to make Camp Three at sixty-six hundred meters. Now, this is very steep ice climbing, which we will fix rope on. I know that an American team who did this claimed it wasn't that difficult, just extremely tiring. The other possibility is to do what the Japanese did and climb directly through the ice building. This would be easier going technically, but it could be dangerous. This ice building is really the key to the north face—how to get around it. A serac collapse in the area killed a Sherpa in 1930. It's pretty scary, I must say, and different teams chose different strategies for getting around it."

"What do you recommend?" McKee asked.

"I say we should try the Worth method from 1983 and climb the ice-wall to the left of the ice building. Above that we would go right across the glacier back to the north face."

"You're the boss," Léaud said.

"Now, when Schrenk—where is Schrenk?" Marquis asked, looking around. Only then did everyone realize he was the one member of the team missing.

"Maybe he's putting his gear back together?" McKee suggested.

They looked around and found Schrenk walking toward them with his gear packed and ready to go.

"Sorry," he said. "Did I miss anything?"

"It's all right," Marquis said. "Just follow us. Let's go, everyone! I want to start climbing in ten minutes!"

Bond and Chandra rushed back to the tent and packed quickly. Bond slipped on his crampons and joined the party outside. The wind had died down, the sun had risen, and it was a relatively beautiful day considering the fact that they were on the side of the third tallest mountain in the world. They were already higher than many of the peaks around them. This was what Bond truly loved about mountain climbing. It was a vigorous, dangerous sport that, when one achieved the goal, gave one a sense of accomplishing the impossible. Here one really was the king of the world.

The "ice building" is a beautiful but frightening formation that is virtually a tunnel of ice. It could have been used as a shortcut up to the plateau, but, as Marquis said, the possibility of icefalls is very high.

Instead, Marquis led them up the ice slope to the left, which was at a steep angle ranging from forty-five degrees to seventy. Slowly and carefully, they worked their way up a gully that proved to be quite strenuous an operation.

They were nearly halfway up the gully when it was Bond's turn to make the next pitch. Chandra belayed while Bond used the ropes already set in place by Marquis and Léaud, who were a hundred meters above them.

Just when the angle was at its steepest, Bond's crampons suddenly slipped off his boots. He lost his footing and began to plummet. He slid backward on the ice and attempted to stop himself with his ice ax, but he was unable to obtain a secure hold with it. Chandra jumped into action and held the belay rope tightly.

Bond fell thirty meters and was jerked to a halt by the rope. His back felt as if it had snapped in two. He yelled in pain as he dropped his ice ax.

"Hold on, James!" Chandra called.

Bond swung limply on the rope. The others became aware of what happened and stopped climbing.

"What happened?" Marquis called from above.

"James?" Chandra called. "Are you conscious?"

Bond lifted his hand and waved.

"Can you swing yourself to the wall and get a foothold?"

"I'll try," Bond called. He began to swerve and kick, gaining enough momentum to rock himself back and forth on the rope. Finally, he hit the wall of ice but couldn't find a handhold. He kicked away once again, attempting to maneuver himself toward an anchor that had been set a few-feet to his right. After two more tries he grabbed hold of it and slowly worked his way down the rope to the ledge where Chandra was.

"What happened? Are you all right?" Chandra asked.

"Yes. Gave me a hell of a fright, though. Bloody crampons. They slipped right off my boots!"

"How could that happen?"

"Where are they? Did you see them fall?"

"I think so. Over there somewhere." They moved carefully along the ledge and found one of them. The other had fallen into oblivion.

Bond picked it up and examined it. The ring that the straps went through was bent and had a two-millimeter gap in it. Bond removed his goggles for a moment to look at it closely.

"This ring was filed," he said. "Look, it has serrated edges there. Someone tampered with it!"

"When was the last time you looked at them?"

"Well, last night, I suppose. But they were in my tent all night. Who could have . . . ?"

He thought a minute. "Schrenk. He was missing at the team meeting over breakfast. He could have had time to slip into our tent and do the damage."

Chandra nodded. "It's possible. Maybe that fire was something he set on purpose to cause a diversion."

At that moment the two Sherpas caught up with them. Schrenk and McKee were not far behind at the rear. When they appeared on the ledge, Bond cheerfully addressed them.

"My crampons slipped off. Anyone have a spare pair?"

McKee said, "I do. I'm not sure if they'll fit you. What happened?"

"I don't know. They came undone somehow." Bond looked directly at Schrenk, who averted his eyes.

McKee pulled off his backpack and dug into it. He found the two extra crampons, which were wrapped in cloth to protect the other gear from the sharp spikes. Bond tried them on. They were a little small but would do the job.

"Thanks. I'll make sure the others bring up more when they meet us at Camp Three."

"What the hell is going on down there?" Marquis called. He was quite some distance away.

Chandra waved the okay sign and they began to climb again.

Four hours later they reached the plateau, 6,600 meters above sea level. Everyone was coughing and attempting to take slow, deep breaths.

"What about oxygen?" McKee asked Marquis.

"We don't need oxygen until we're higher up. If you need it now, you're going to use it all up. How many canisters did you bring?"

"Three, but the Sherpas have the team's entire supply."

Marquis nodded. "But we have to conserve it. We'll need the oxygen at Camp Five, where the plane is. We don't know how long we'll be there. Try to make do without it, okay?"

McKee coughed and nodded.

Marquis looked at Bond. "What the hell happened to you down there?"

"Nothing," Bond said. He thought it best not to alarm anyone about the tampering. "The crampons slipped off. I must not have fastened them very well. My fault."

"Don't let it happen again, Bond. As much as I can't stand you, I'd hate to lose you."

"Thanks, Roland, that's comforting."

Marquis walked away toward his tent. Bond and Chandra looked over at Otto Schrenk, who was helping Doug McKee erect a tent for the two of them.

Was it Schrenk? Or could it have been someone else?

At least they were safely at Camp Three, where they would spend the next week acclimatizing. The rest of the group would be joining them over the next few days.

Bond knew, though, that someone on the team definitely wanted him out of the picture.

HIGHER AND HIGHER

THE OTHERS FROM THE BASE CAMP BEGAN TO ARRIVE IN GROUPS THE following day. Paul Baack was one of the first, carrying the lightweight laptop satellite phone with his own equipment. Hope Kendall had partnered him, and insisted on examining the Lead Team—but not until she had had a night's sleep. Bond thought she didn't look well, but then he remembered how he had felt on reaching Camp Three.

The next day Bond visited the doctor in her tent. They sat cross-legged opposite from each other as she examined him. Bond thought she seemed much better, but he could see that the climb was taking its toll. She wore no makeup, of course, had dark circles under her eyes, and looked thinner.

"How are you feeling, James?" she asked, listening to his breathing with a stethoscope.

"I'm fine now. When I first got to Camp Three, I felt like hell."

"I know what you mean," she replied. "I haven't been sleeping well."

"You should heed your own advice and get plenty of rest, then."

"This is my job," she said. "Cough, please."

He did. It was a horrid, dry croup.

"That cough's a beaut. Does your throat hurt?" she asked.

"Yes."

"I'm going to give you some lozenges. You need to drink more water. Are you drinking water?"

"Yes." He coughed again.

"Then drink more." She reached into her bag and gave him a packet of vitamin C and eucalyptus lozenges. "Otherwise, you're fit as a buck rat."

"I'll take that as a compliment."

She smiled, but then rubbed her forehead and shut her eyes tightly. "Damn," she said. "I can't shake this headache."

"You need to take it easy," he said. He put a hand on the back of her neck and massaged it. That brought the smile back.

"Mmm, that's nice," she said. "Would you just do that for the next twenty-four hours?"

"Seriously," he said, "are you all right?"

"Yeah, I think so," she answered but wasn't very convincing. "Go on, now. Send in your cuzzy."

"My what?"

"Your cuzzy, your cousin, your brother, your mate . . ." she explained. "It's Maori talk. Chandra. Send him in. Please."

Bond let it go and crawled out of the tent.

It was about three hours later when he noticed Marquis rushing to Hope's tent. Paul Baack was standing outside it, looking as if he were lost and didn't know what to do. Bond approached him and asked, "Is something wrong?"

"Yes," Baack said. "Dr. Kendall is sick."

Bond stuck his head in the tent. Marquis was kneeling by Hope, who was lying on her sleeping bag. Carl Glass was with them.

"We have it under control, Bond, you can leave," Marquis said rudely.

"It's all right, he can stay," Hope mumbled. "God, just let me die now."

"She's got acute altitude sickness," Glass told Bond.

"My head feels like it's going to explode," she said. "Goddammit, this has never happened to me before!"

She coughed loudly and gasped when she attempted to breathe deeply.

"My dear Hope," Marquis said, "you yourself said it could strike anyone at any time. You're no exception. Now, please, let me take you down to Camp Two. You need to descend as quickly as possible. I can carry you on—"

"Shut up, Roland!" she snapped. "I'm not going anywhere. This will pass. Stop fussing over me. I hate it!"

"I'm only trying to—"

"Please just leave me *alone!* Get out of here!" she screamed.

Marquis stiffened, embarrassed and angry. He moved away and, without a word, glared at Bond and left the tent.

"What should we do?" Glass asked her.

"I'm sorry. He's right, dammit," she said. "I need to go to Camp Two but I just don't have the strength. For three days I haven't slept, haven't eaten, haven't peed . . . I'm constipated as hell. . . ." She was on the verge of tears, but she didn't have the energy for it.

"Wait, I'll get the Gamow Bag," Bond said.

He left the tent as she mumbled, "Why the hell didn't I think of that?"

Bond retrieved Major Boothroyd's modified device from the Sherpas and brought it back to the tent. She climbed into it and sealed it up after thanking Bond and telling everyone to let her be for a few hours. Since the bag had its own generator to pump air into it, it was inflated within minutes.

A Gamow Bag artificially reproduces the pressure of a lower altitude. It temporarily cures symptoms of AMS, but the victim normally has to descend anyway to recover fully.

Bond looked up through his goggles and saw that the sun was still high in the sky, so there was possibly time for her to get down before nightfall, as descending wouldn't be as time-consuming as the trip up. He then found Paul Baack and asked to use the satellite linkup. The Dutchman gave him the privacy of his tent.

Alone, Bond phoned London. After several rings the voice-messaging service kicked in.

"You have reached Helena Marksbury. I'm sorry that I am away from my desk . . ."

It was almost a surreal experience. Here he was, halfway around the world, on the side of a fierce mountain and isolated from civilization, yet he was able to hear the voice of a lover, albeit a former one.

"I'm halfway up Kangch," he said after the beep. "Camp Three. Where are you? I'll switch over to Bill. It was nice to hear your voice."

He quickly pressed the code sequence that transferred him to Bill Tanner's office. Christ, Bond thought. He was thankful that she hadn't picked up after all. It would have been awkward. He hoped that she was not still upset about their relationship.

There were a few pips, and Tanner picked up. "James?"

"Hello, Bill. I'm calling from sixty-six hundred meters. Nothing on Schrenk?"

"No, but we received some interesting intelligence from our new man in India. His name is Banerjee. He's Zakir Bedi's replacement."

"What's that?"

"They intercepted Union communications to Kathmandu. The man who tried to kill you there was indeed employed by the Union. An accomplice was snatched, a go-between apparently, and he confessed that the Union have infiltrated your expedition. It's someone in your party, James."

"I've suspected that all along. Thanks for confirming it."

"Any idea who it might be?"

"I've been thinking it's Schrenk."

"If we find anything that ties him to the Union, I'll certainly get a coded message to you. We also learned that the Russian expedition is being financed by certain military authorities in Moscow who have files in our offices a mile long. They have strong ties to the Russian Mafia. There can be only one reason they're up there."

"Thanks for the tip. I had better go. I don't want the Ministry of Defence complaining about the phone bill."

"There's one other thing, James."

Bond detected hesitation in his voice.

"What's that?"

"Helena is missing. She's been gone for two days and hasn't

phoned in. As you know, our security procedures are such that when someone in her position doesn't call in, we—"

"I know," Bond said, "you send someone to her flat. And?"

"She wasn't there, either. The flat had been ransacked."

Oh, no. Bond squeezed his eyes tightly shut.

"James," Tanner said. "We concluded our investigation into the leak at MI6."

Bond said it before the Chief of Staff could. "It's her."

Tanner's silence confirmed it.

"She's probably in trouble if she's mixed up with the Union," Bond said.

"James," Tanner said gently. "She's probably dead. But we'll keep looking. Try not to worry about it. Concentrate on the job at hand."

Right. Bond gripped the phone tightly and said, "Keep me informed."

"Watch your back, James."

Bond rang off and stepped outside the tent. Paul Baack was standing there, shivering.

"All done?" he asked.

"Yes, thanks. Better get inside and get warm."

"I will. You might tell the same thing to our illustrious leader over there." Baack gestured toward Marquis's tent, then went inside his own.

Bond found Marquis throwing his ice ax at a solid boulder of ice. He seemed to be in a trance. He threw the ax, walked over and retrieved it, returned to his position, and threw it again. And again.

Bond felt like joining him but decided not to bother.

Three hours later Hope Kendall emerged from the Gamow Bag and announced that she was going down to Camp Two for a couple of days. Bond offered to accompany her, but she said it wasn't necessary. Marquis knew better than to volunteer, but he insisted that a Sherpa go with her.

Two days later Bond was in his own tent, having just completed reading the criminal profiling book, when Paul Baack stuck his head inside.

"I must show you something, James," he said. Bond got up and followed the Dutchman back to his tent. There was a blurry photograph displayed on the monitor of his laptop.

"It's a satellite photo," he said. "It's the north face of the mountain as seen from space, but magnified many times. Look, this is our camp here." As he pointed to objects on the screen, Bond began to comprehend what he was looking at.

"Over here is something that wasn't there yesterday." He pointed to another mass of dark objects, slightly east of them. "Those are the Russians."

"We knew they were close, but what is that, a thousand meters?" Bond asked.

"Less. Maybe eight hundred. They set up their equivalent of Camp Three there. To get there you would have to climb up and over the *Bergschrund*, see?" He pointed to a deep slit that delineated a glacier's upper terminus. It was a phenomenon that formed as the body of ice slid away from the steeper wall immediately above, leaving a gap between glacier and rock.

Bond nodded. "We have to cross that to get to Camp Four," he said.

"But then, to get to the Russians, you have to go down this way here. That's quite a hike, at least an eight-hour journey. I don't think we have to worry about them making a sneak attack on our camp."

They're probably waiting for *us* to make the next move, Bond thought.

"Thanks," Bond said. "Keep an eye on them. If they show signs of activity, let me know."

"Will do." Bond started to leave, but Baack stopped him. "James?"

"Yes?"

"What was Roland talking about the other day when he said you were on a secret mission? I mean, I *know* you're on a secret mission. I have known all along. They wouldn't have given me all this *stuff*. Ministry of Defence . . . a Gurkha assistant . . . I mean, what's going on? I have a right to know, I think."

Bond sighed and clapped the big man on the shoulder. "Sorry, it's classified, but I appreciate your hard work. Let's just say I have to find something on that plane and bring it back to England."

Baack nodded and said, "Well, you can count on me to help how-ever I can."

"Thanks. You're doing a great job already," Bond said, then he left the tent.

The news about Helena still hung heavy on his heart. He had done his best to put it aside, but there was no denying that he was worried. What he needed was a different sort of distraction.

On the way back to his quarters, he saw Hope Kendall.

"Well, hello. When did you get back?"

"An hour ago," she said. She pointed to her new tent. "I'm over there."

"You sound much better."

"I feel a *lot* better," she said. "I guess I needed the extra two days at Camp Two before coming up here. This time the ascent didn't bother me at all. I did it in less than four hours."

"I'm glad you're back," Bond said.

"Hey, and thanks for that Gamow Bag. It saved my life."

"Don't mention it. Can I buy you dinner? I know a great little Nepalese takeaway in the neighborhood."

She laughed. "You never give up, do you?"

Not now, Bond thought.

Roland Marquis finally deemed the Lead Team adequately acclima-tized to ascend to Camp Four. Marquis, Glass, Léaud, and Barlow had all made practice runs and reported that it would take two, maybe three days, one pitch at a time, to get to Camp Four.

The first day went relatively well. On the second day they had to cross thirty-degree snow slopes that ended at the rock wall over the *Bergschrund*. The Sherpas had hauled an aluminum ladder that could extend across the crevasse. Roland Marquis, belayed by more than one person, carefully crossed the ladder and fastened anchors on the opposite side. He looked back at the others, then saw something in the *Bergschrund*.

"There's a person down there," he called, pointing. One by one they all crossed the ladder and were in a position to see. It was indeed a corpse, a woman, with a blanket wrapped loosely around her. Bond thought that she looked well preserved.

"She has to be one of the plane survivors," Bond said. "Look, she's hardly dressed for climbing."

Both Marquis and Bond thought it best to attempt to retrieve the body. Using an elaborate system of belays and anchors, the Sherpas climbed down into the *Bergschrund* and tied a rope around the woman's shoulders and upper arms. They gave the signal and she was brought up to the ledge.

She was wearing blue jeans, tennis shoes, a sweatshirt, and the blanket. The woman had been a tourist in a comfortably pressurized plane. She had obviously survived the crash and had attempted to climb down the mountain. Now she was frozen stiff.

Bond broke the ice surrounding the blanket and pried it away from her body. He searched her pockets and found an American passport.

"Cheryl Kay Mitchell, from Washington, D.C.," Bond read. "She's the American senator's wife."

It was also apparent that her skull was cracked and the head and shoulders were horribly misshapen. Her clothes were torn in some places, and there were cuts and bruises on exposed patches of skin.

"Poor woman," Léaud said softly.

"She fell," Marquis surmised. "From a great height, too. Her body must have bounced and bounced and slid all the way down here from the crash site. There is absolutely *no way* she could have survived this far. Look at the way her body has frozen. I would bet that she has a million broken bones."

"If she didn't fall immediately, then I suspect she died within an hour or two after leaving the plane and *then* the body slid off the edge up there somewhere," Bond said. "She was probably desperate to do something and knew she wouldn't survive inside the plane. . . ."

"We'll take her back to Camp Three tonight. Let's leave her here for now. There's nothing else for us to do but press on."

The discovery cast a pall over the group, but they continued over the rock band in silence. It was the most technically difficult climbing they had done so far.

Camp Four was finally reached, and the next day the group began the assault to the final stop—the Great Scree Terrace at 7,900 meters. They had to climb 250 meters of a rock band via a snow gully and 100 meters of rock wall to reach an upper snowfield at around 7,500 meters. Tom Barlow and Doug McKee began using oxygen, something the Sherpas liked to call "English Air."

On the thirty-first day of their journey, with five days left in the month of May, the Lead Team finally made it. The Great Scree Terrace was a bizarre, sparkling-white, gently sloping plateau that seemed to be out of place at such a high altitude. The remainder of the mountain, only 686 meters of it, towered over the plateau like a malevolent sentinel.

The Sherpas began to set up Camp Five while Bond, Marquis, and Chandra examined the wreckage spread out before them. One broken wing was half buried in snow and ice. Forty meters beyond that were pieces of the tail. Sixty meters farther was the fuselage, remarkably intact. The other wing must have been completely buried or blown off the plateau. The cabin door was wide open. Any footprints that might have led from the plane had long been covered.

"I have to go in there first, Roland," Bond said.

Marquis said, "Be my guest."

"Come on, Chandra," Bond said as he trudged through the knee-deep snow toward the aircraft.

TWENTY-ONE

THE MISSING BODY

BOND TURNED ON A FLASHLIGHT AND STEPPED INTO THE COLD, DARK CABIN. Light filtering in from windows had a ghostly, incandescent quality that was unnerving even to him. Ice and snow had built up through holes in the fuselage, so it appeared that the passenger seats had been built in snowdrifts. An eerie whistling sound echoed throughout the cabin.

Nearly all the seats contained a body each.

Bond shined the light at the cockpit. The pilot and copilot were slumped forward in their seats, frozen in a macabre still-frame of death. Another man was lying in the aisle between the cockpit and cabin. He didn't appear to be dressed like the crew.

"Help me pull this one up," he said to Chandra.

Together they tugged on the hard, stiff body and turned it so that they could get a good look at the man's face. Ice had formed a grotesque transparent mask across half of it. There was a bullet hole in his neck.

Bond recognized him from Station I's mug shots. "This is one of the hijackers."

Chandra nodded. "I remember."

"Come on, let's look back there." Bond stepped over the body and moved back into the small main cabin. He counted the corpses.

"The plane has twelve seats for passengers. The crew consisted of the pilot, copilot, and an attendant." He indicated a woman sitting in a single seat facing the other passengers. "Here she is. There were ten tourists booked on the flight, which would have left two empty seats, right? I count nine bodies."

"The woman we found near Camp Four would make ten," Chandra said.

"But Lee Ming and the three hijackers would have made fourteen. One hijacker is accounted for, making eleven. That means there should be eleven bodies in here. Where are the other three?"

"Wait, here's someone not sitting in a chair," Chandra said, shining his light in the back of the cabin. It was another man, dressed similarly to the hijacker they found in the cockpit.

"It's one of them," Bond said, examining him. "All right, that means there are two missing. Let's see if Lee Ming is one of these people."

They each took a side of the plane and shined their flashlights on the faces one by one. The dead were all Caucasian men and women of varying ages. At least three had their eyes open, fixed in a frosty expression of fear.

"He's not here!" Bond said through his teeth. "Damn!"

"Hold on, James," Chandra said. "If that woman survived and got out, maybe Lee did, too. And the other hijacker. They couldn't have got far. They must be in the vicinity."

"Unless they dropped off the face of the mountain like that woman did. They could be *anywhere!*"

Chandra knew Bond could be right. "What do we do?"

"Nothing *to* do except search the area. Let's look at the ground outside again. Maybe there are some faint traces of footprints or something."

They came out of the plane and found Marquis and Glass waiting patiently. Paul Baack was standing anxiously nearby, and Otto Schrenk was not far behind him.

"Well?" Marquis asked Bond.

"He's not in there," Bond said quietly. "We're going to have to search the surrounding area. Chandra and I will do that. You go on with the salvage operation."

"Not in there? Are you sure?" Marquis looked as if he might panic.

"Quite sure."

"Oh, for Christ's sake!" Marquis said. He threw the ski pole he was holding against the side of the aircraft. "That's just great."

"Why are you so concerned, Roland?" Bond asked. "You did your job. You got me up here."

"I just . . . I just wanted you to succeed in your mission, that's all. I want Skin 17 back in the UK as much as you do."

For a brief moment Bond thought that Marquis might be the Union operative. Could that be possible? Usually Bond's instincts were sharp, but at such a high altitude all his senses and reflexes were numbed. He suspected everybody and anybody.

"We're going to see what we can find," Bond said, and walked away.

Marquis composed himself and turned to the others. "Right, let's help set up camp."

By the second day Camp Five was completed and the rest of the parts had made it up to the site. The salvage operation began, with the first stage being the removal of the corpses from the plane and hauling them down to Camp Four, one at a time. The plan was to start a convoy, assembly-line fashion, with some workers stationed at each of the four lower camps. The *sirdar* arranged for a yak herd to pick up the bodies at the Base Camp and take them back to Taplejung for a flight to Kathmandu. It was an expensive, time-consuming, dangerous, and absurd thing to do, Bond thought. The families and governments paying for this needless operation should have left the remains on the mountain. It would have been a different story had they been alive. But to go to all this trouble for the dead? At least it made a somewhat feasible cover story. Bond was thankful that he had a different job, although it was one he was afraid he wouldn't be able to complete.

After three days Bond and Chandra had found no traces of Lee Ming or the other hijacker.

The physical changes one experiences at 7,900 meters are remarkable. Bond felt that every move he made was in slow motion. It was quite like being underwater in a JIM diving suit. He was packed in solid warm clothing, every inch of skin covered, with an oxygen canister on his back and a hose running to his mouth. He was concerned that the team might not have brought enough oxygen to last for the next few days. Even with oxygen, the team still found that they were able to perform only a few seconds of work before having to stop and catch their breath.

Bond sent a message to London via Baack's laptop that Lee's body wasn't in the plane. Tanner came back with M's instructions to keep looking until Marquis's job was finished. If Lee wasn't found by then, there was nothing to do but come home. Bond read between the lines of the coded message and saw her disappointment. He hated to let her down.

There was no news about Helena.

Tired and frustrated, Bond left the tent and found his companion.

"Dammit, Chandra," Bond said. "If you stumbled out of that plane onto this plateau, where would you go?"

"I'd try to find my way down . . . over there," he said, pointing to a gradual slope on the south side.

"That's the first place we looked, remember?"

"Maybe we should look again. There were crevasses down that way that we didn't examine. Maybe they fell in one."

"You could be right. The ice seemed very unstable when we were there the other day. Freezing to death in a crevasse isn't very appealing," Bond said.

"It is not the way in which one dies that is important," Chandra said. "It is the reason. Let's look again."

Bond knew he was right. "We also haven't looked over there on the east side of the plateau. Let's try there first. I want to find that bloody body and go home. All right?"

They had begun to trudge through the snow, when they heard Marquis calling.

"Damn," Bond said. "Come on, let's see what he wants now."

They turned around and went back to the camp HQ, where everyone had gathered. Marquis had already begun talking.

"—with the extra men we hired for the lower camps. The yaks are in place at Base Camp now, and we shouldn't have too much more to do. Oh, there you are, Bond. I was just saying that our time here is being cut short and we're trying to determine how much more we can do before we have to get out of here."

"Why? What's wrong?"

"Storms coming," Baack said. "I got the weather report a few minutes ago. Two successive storms are on their way and will reach the upper altitudes of the mountain by tonight."

"Bad storms?"

"Severe. Monsoons. One today and one tomorrow."

"Right," said Marquis, "and they can be quite deadly up here. We either have to take shelter for several hours or get down."

"I can't go yet," Bond said. "I haven't come all this way just to turn around. Our tents are built to withstand a storm. I'll risk waiting the two storms out."

"I figured you would say that. However, I must offer the option to everyone on the team of going down now. Some of you can make it all the way to Camp Three before the storm hits, or at the very least Camp Four. The next day you can descend to Base Camp. Just remember that you'd have to come all the way back up so we can finish the job."

"How much is left?" Léaud asked.

"We've estimated it to be at least two more days, not counting the rest of today. That would completely clean out the plane. At the rate we're going, we can send down only three bodies a day. There are six left."

"What about you?" McKee asked.

"I'm staying," Marquis said.

"So am I," Hope Kendall said.

"No, you're not," he said.

"Look, I don't—"

"I don't want to argue with—"

"I'm *staying!*" she said forcefully.

Marquis glared at her. "Very well. Who else wants to stay? It would be less wear and tear on you, I think. We'll just have to hunker down in our tents when the storms hit. But I can't guarantee we'll live through them."

When all was said and done, everyone decided to leave except for the core group, which consisted of Marquis, Bond, Chandra, Hope, Baack, Léaud, Glass, Barlow, Schrenk, and three Sherpas. Those who elected to descend promised to be back in two days. Some of them were going to stay put at Camp Three rather than go all the way down.

One thing was certain, Bond thought. The Union man had to be one of those who had elected to stay.

An hour after the others left, the wind began to pick up.

Bond was looking on the far east side of the plateau for any traces of the missing men, when his cell phone rang. Digging it out of the parka pocket with the gloves was clumsy, but he managed to get it open.

"James, I think I found them!" It was Chandra.

"Where are you?"

"Where I said they would be. In a crevasse. Come down and look."

The plateau was large enough that it would take him an hour of strenuous walking to cross it. "All right, I'm on my way. Mark your position and meet me at the top in an hour."

It was midafternoon when Bond got to the slope that Chandra had pointed to earlier. The Gurkha was waiting for him, bundled up like a polar bear. The wind was stronger now, and dark clouds were forming in the sky. They hadn't much time left.

Chandra led him a hundred meters over one crevasse to a second one that had a natural ice bridge at one end. Fifty feet down, wedged in tightly, were two bodies.

"Chandra, I could kiss you, but I don't think I can find your face," Bond said. "We're going to need some help getting them out of there."

Bond got on the phone to Marquis and Léaud, who arrived on the scene just as the snow started falling. With the windchill, the temperature dropped to eighty degrees below freezing. Bond pointed out the bodies to them, and Marquis said, "You had better wait until tomorrow, after the first storm passes. Paul said we should have ten to twelve hours of clear weather between the two storms."

"I'm going down now," Bond said. "We have at least an hour. Help Chandra belay me."

"You're mad, Bond, but all right. I'm as curious as you are at this point."

It took Bond forty-five minutes to get down to the bodies. They had set up a Z-pulley system, which offers a three-to-one mechanical advantage through the use of two pulleys. The result was an ingenious method of hauling heavy objects safely on what could possibly be unstable ice.

Bond had his back flat against one wall of the crevasse, and his feet pushing against the opposite one. He inched down to one of the bodies and used the ice ax to free it enough to turn it over. It was the corpse of the third hijacker. The other body was five feet below. Chandra gave him more slack as he inched down into an even tighter squeeze. When he got to the body, Bond had to work for another twenty minutes chopping ice away from around the head and shoulders so that he could pull it up.

"The wind is getting stronger, Bond," Marquis said over the phone. "You had better come up."

"I'm almost finished," Bond said. "Five minutes."

Finally, he tore away the frozen blanket covering the man's face. It was Lee Ming.

"All right, I got him," Bond said into the phone. "I'm going to fasten the harness around him." Since Lee was dead, Bond didn't have to worry about fashioning a comfortable harness. He wrapped the rope around the man's shoulders and arms and tied a Prusik knot.

The storm hit with frightening strength just as Lee's body was near the top of the crevasse. Marquis, Chandra, and Léaud were pulling as hard as they could, but the wind proved to be a formidable opponent. Getting Bond up was much easier, as he could help by using his crampons to "walk" up the side of the crevasse as they pulled.

"We have to get into the tents as quickly as possible!" Marquis shouted. He could barely be heard over the howling wind.

They threw Lee's body onto a plastic sled, then all four men fought their way to the camp. They were in a full-scale blizzard now, and they could barely see where they were going. Bond directed them to his tent, where they laid down the corpse on a sleeping bag. Hope Kendall had provided Bond with some sharp instruments and tools, although she didn't know what he needed them for.

"I'll stay in here," he told them. "You all go back to your tents, and hurry. Chandra, keep the phone handy."

Marquis nodded and the others left the tent. Bond closed the flap, but the noise outside was so loud that he could barely hear himself think. He didn't particularly relish the thought of spending the night with the corpse, but he didn't want to take the chance that the Union operative might get to the body if he left it alone.

The cadaver was frozen solid. Bond lit the Bibler stove, which generated a little heat. He took the standard-issue chemical hot packs, normally used when activated to treat frostbite, and placed them on Lee's chest. He lit them, melting away the ice that held the man's clothes in a solid straitjacket.

In ten minutes Bond was able to cut away Lee's shirt and expose his chest. The skin was cold and hard. He carefully examined the area above Lee's breast and found the pocket of skin where the pacemaker had been inserted. It was still intact. Now all he had to do was wait awhile for the skin to thaw.

The storm raged outside. To pass the time, Bond took a snow shovel, opened the tent, and spent fifteen minutes clearing the entrance. It was quite common for climbers to find themselves buried inside their tents by huge snowdrifts after a big storm. Anyone caught inside without their shovel might never get out.

Bond came back into the tent and examined Lee's skin. It was now a bit like rubber, not totally fleshy, but soft enough to cut.

He took a scalpel from Hope's tools and began to carefully cut a square out of the man's chest. It was tough, almost like cutting leather. Once the square was outlined, he used scissors to grasp a corner and pull it up, revealing bluish pink inner flesh and a gold-plated pacemaker.

Bond breathed a sigh of relief. He removed his oxygen mask so that he could get a better look. He snapped the leads with the clippers, then, with his bare fingers, wrenched it out of the now-pliant, liquidless flesh.

He had it! It was in his hand! Bond clutched the device triumphantly, ready to pick up the phone and call Chandra. He dialed his number and started to speak, when he felt a sudden sharp, heavy blow on the back of his head. The tent spun chaotically as everything went black.

Bond fell forward on top of Lee's mutilated cadaver, dead to the world.

TWENTY-TWO

LOVE AND DEATH AT 7,900 METERS

OTTO SCHRENK HAD WATCHED BOND'S PROJECTED SHADOW FROM THE outside of the tent, waiting until it was in the ideal position. Not wanting to kill him yet, Schrenk used a stone to knock Bond unconscious. He then tore open the flap, crawled in, and squatted over the two bodies. He rolled Bond off Lee, pried open the clenched fist, took the pacemaker, and reached for his mobile phone.

"You there?" he spoke into it.

"Yes," came a voice from the other end. The storm made the connection tentative.

"Where are you?"

"I'm at our agreed rendezvous. Where else would I be in this storm? Do you have it?"

"I have it."

"Good. Make sure Bond doesn't wake up."

"Ja." Schrenk rang off, put the phone away, and drew the Nazi dress dagger from the inside of his parka. He grabbed Bond's black hair and pulled his head back, exposing his neck. Schrenk placed the blade against Bond's neck and was about to slit his throat, when a bullet shot through the tent.

Schrenk's blood and brain matter splattered over Bond's body as the German slumped over to the side.

Roland Marquis crawled into the tent, lowered his Browning 9mm, then wrenched the pacemaker from Schrenk's hand. He put it in his pocket, then aimed the gun at Bond's head.

The phone that Bond had dropped suddenly spurted to life with a burst of static. "James? Are you there?" Marquis thought it sounded like Chandra's voice, but it was difficult to tell because of the noise. "If you can hear me, I'm on my way!" the voice said.

Damn, Marquis thought. He quickly put away the gun, covered his head, and left the tent.

Chandra, fighting his way through the blizzard, pushed forward toward Bond's tent. He never should have left him alone. It was a good thing he had been watching with his Common Weapon Sight, which greatly intensified images. He had seen a figure enter the tent, followed by another.

He plowed ahead, barely able to see even through his goggles. There was a dark shape ahead, and it was moving toward him. It was a person. Chandra moved closer until they were face-to-face. He recognized Roland Marquis.

Chandra started to speak but saw that Marquis was pointing a pistol at him. He reacted quickly, turning away just as the weapon flashed. The bullet caught Chandra in the shoulder and spun him around. He fell to the snow and lay still. Marquis looked around to make sure he wasn't seen, but everyone was safely in tents. The gunshot was muffled by the intense sound of the wind.

Chandra felt the cold snow on his face and opened his eyes. He could just see Marquis's silhouette turn and walk away from the campsite. The Gurkha managed to pull himself off the ground. His quick defensive move and the thick layers of clothing had luckily helped to deflect the bullet so that it hadn't entered his chest. Nevertheless, he was in an immense amount of pain. Chandra breathed deeply from his respirator, savoring the oxygen contained in the canister on his back, then began to follow Marquis.

"Wake up, damn you!"

The slaps came hard and fast on his face. Bond's vision was blurred and his head was pounding. Someone was crouched over him, and the voice was decidedly feminine.

"James? Wake *up!*"

He groaned, felt a rush of nausea, then rolled to his side and stopped himself from vomiting. After a moment he turned on his back and looked up at Hope Kendall, who began to wipe his face and forehead with a cloth.

"Are you all right?" she asked. "You were out cold. You have a nasty bump on the back of your head. Answer me!"

Bond nodded. "I think I'm okay."

"Can you sit up?"

He did so, slowly. His hand went to his head and felt a lump there.

"I was afraid you were dead. Everyone else is!" she said. He realized there was pure terror in her voice.

"What did you say?" She was terribly upset and in tears.

"Everyone—Philippe, Tom Barlow, Paul Baack, the *sirdar*—well, I can't find *everyone,* but there are six people dead up here. James, they've been *murdered!* Their throats were cut! And look at him—" She pointed at the body of Otto Schrenk. "He's been shot in the head!"

The news brought Bond out of the fog. The years of experience and living on the edge had long ago honed his ability to shake away pain and discomfort and focus on the matter at hand.

"Who's missing?" he asked.

"Roland, Carl Glass . . . I'm not sure who else, I'm not thinking straight," she said.

"What about Chandra?"

"I haven't seen him, either."

The storm was still raging outside. Bond peered outside the tent. It was night, and there was absolutely no visibility. He turned back and surveyed the scene in the tent. Lee's body lay where he had left it. Schrenk was crumpled up next to him. The Nazi dagger was lying by his side. There was a bullet hole in the tent.

"I think I know what happened," he said. "Schrenk. He hit me with something from outside the tent. He got the pacemaker."

"The what?"

"Something I need," he said. "He got it but was shot by someone else. Whoever shot him took the pacemaker."

"What pacemaker? What are you talking about?" she asked.

He pointed to Lee's body. She lifted the bit of clothing covering his chest and recoiled.

"Christ," she said. "Someone dug a pacemaker out of this guy?"

"Yes, I did. That was my whole purpose for being on this expedition. You might as well know. Some classified military information was hidden inside it. I have to return it to England. Come on, let's make some more room in here. Help me get rid of these bodies."

He began to drag Schrenk's corpse toward the opening. She got hold of the legs and helped push the cadaver out into the snow. They did the same with Lee, making the tent comfortable enough for two people.

"We're going to have to wait until morning," Bond said. "The storm is too severe to go out. At least we can stretch out now."

"I don't understand," she said. "What was in this pacemaker?"

"Military secrets. The entire reason this expedition was put together was for me to retrieve them."

"You mean—this whole thing, I mean, this 'salvage operation'—was just a cover story?"

He nodded.

She sat back and folded her arms. "You son of a bitch," she said. "Why the hell am I here? I'm lucky I'm not dead, too! You mean to tell me that you risked the lives of all these climbers and Sherpas just so your government could get hold of these so-called secrets? Are you out of your mind?"

"Look, Hope," he said. "I'm a civil servant. I do what I'm told. I've always thought it was a crazy, almost suicidal mission. Sometimes I'm ordered to do some very unpleasant things. Often there are other lives at stake. I'm sorry you got involved."

She was flabbergasted and, Bond thought, possibly in shock. She sat there, shivering, despite the layers of clothing she had on.

"Now tell me about the dead people," he said. "Start at the beginning."

She took some breaths from her oxygen canister, coughed, then began the story.

"After you and the others brought back the body of that guy from the plane, Roland told us all to get into our tents, use a tank of oxygen and try to sleep through the storm. So that's what I did, except I didn't go to my own tent. I went to the supply tent, where I had set up medical HQ. I got into the bedroll there, mainly because it was warmer in there with all that stuff than my own tent. I think I got about two hours of sleep, but I woke up restless. I decided to go out and grope my way to Roland's tent. I found it empty."

"Who was he sharing the tent with?"

"Carl Glass. He was gone."

"Go on."

"I then went over to Philippe and Tom's tent, and that's where I found them. They were both dead, their throats cut. I don't know, I guess I panicked. I went to the next tent, the Sherpas', and found them dead, too. Same thing, throats cut. All of them. Paul Baack was lying in his tent covered by that parka of his . . . blood all over the place. Then I came here and found you. I thought you'd been killed, too, until I examined you. You have a slight nick on your neck, there's dried blood there. Then I noticed the bump on your head."

"It's a good thing you weren't in your own tent," Bond said. "You might be dead now, too. Have you tried reaching anyone by phone?"

"Yes, and it's impossible to make a connection in this storm. All I get is static on all channels."

Bond considered the story. Had Schrenk committed the murders? He examined the Nazi dagger and saw that there was dried blood on it. Schrenk had most likely been in the act of slitting his throat when he was shot, but by whom? Could it have been Marquis? Was Marquis working against all of them? If so, which of them was Union? And if one was Union, whom was the other working for?

He then noticed his own mobile phone lying in the corner of the tent, still switched on. He picked it up, made sure it was working, and dialed Chandra's number. A message appeared on the digital display that read "No Connection."

"I told you that you'll never get anything in this weather," Hope said.

"I had to try," Bond said. He put it away and closed his eyes. His head was throbbing.

"How important is that thing you're after?" she asked.

"Important enough for it to be essential to keep it from the wrong hands. It contains technology that could upset the balance of power."

"War stuff," she said.

"I suppose." There was silence for several long moments.

"Have you ever killed anyone?" she asked softly.

The absurdity of the question caught Bond off guard, but he was too weary and cold to laugh. Instead, he simply nodded.

"I should have known," she said. "I did know, instinctually, I guess. It's why I found you attractive."

"You're attracted to killers?"

"That's not what I meant. Is there any water in that thermos?" She pointed to one in an open sack. Bond shook it, heard a splashing sound, and handed it to her. She took a long drink, then said, "Remember I told you that I like to see how far a human being can go? Killing is related to that. I've always wondered how someone can kill another human being. You see, in my career, I try to save lives. We all lose patients, of course, but I vividly remember a particular one. It was a Maori woman, a mother who died during childbirth. She was brought into the emergency room at the hospital where I worked. She had an ectopic pregnancy. I did everything I could to save her. The baby lived, but she died. I always blamed myself for her death."

Bond put his hand on her leg and said, "It wasn't your fault. Surely you know that?"

"Of course, but still . . . Actually once I knew that she wasn't going to live, I used her to satisfy something in myself. I was so goddamned *curious* about her condition. I wanted to *see* it. Remember I told you that I look at the human body as a machine? I wanted to see if I could fix it. What I tried didn't work. She would have died anyway, but I think I might have helped her along. And to tell you the truth, I was horrified and saddened, but at the same time excited by the thought that I had that power. Do you understand what I'm saying?"

She took a breath of oxygen from the respirator hanging over her shoulder. She coughed a couple of times, then continued talking. Bond thought she might be exhibiting shell-shock symptoms.

"When I think of us up here where God never intended humans to be, the concept of life and death becomes such a trivial thing. Any one of us could die quickly and suddenly. Some of us already have. In the grand scheme of things, we're just like bugs. Are we ants that wandered too far from home? I mean, here we are, stuck in this tent, sitting under God's microscope—a male and female of the species. What kind of experiment is waiting for us? What kind of test?"

She looked at him and laughed, but it quickly turned into coughing. She grabbed the respirator again and took some deep breaths of oxygen. Then she said, "I'm babbling. Don't pay any attention to me. Hey, you know, it's medically advisable that one snuggle with a partner to keep warm at high altitude. Would you like to do that?"

Bond moved closer to her, and she clutched him tightly.

"Wait," he whispered. He loosened her grip, then pulled out the bivouac sack with the built-in electric heaters. He unzipped and held it open. She laughed again and slipped her legs inside. He got in with her and zipped it closed.

They held each other for what seemed like an hour as the wind howled outside. Their bodies gradually warmed, and soon their hands were exploring each other. Her face, ashen and dirty, never looked more beautiful. Bond ran his hand through her blond hair and brought her head closer to his. Their mouths met in a passionate kiss, then they broke away, breathless. They read each others thoughts, then kissed again . . . and again. She unzipped his parka and slipped her hands inside so that she could feel his chest through his shirt. He did the same, running his fingers slowly and sensually around her firm breasts. They kissed some more, then he felt her hand exploring between his legs, encouraging his arousal.

They were breathing heavily, fighting for air. Bond managed to say,

"We're going to asphyxiate if we continue this way. Wait, I have another toy. Just a second . . ."

He reached for his bag and removed the dual respirator that Major Boothroyd had given him, then attached it to his oxygen canister.

"Oh, my God," she said when she figured out what he was doing. He slipped the respirator on her face and attached the other to his own. Then he slipped his hands underneath her sweater and shirt and felt her nipples harden beneath the bra she was wearing. She moaned slightly, then moved in to kiss him, forgetting that they were both wearing respirators. They bumped and she laughed.

He expertly removed her bra and pulled it out from under her clothes. Then he began to work on her trousers, slowly inching them off, while her hands were busy with his clothes. It was awkward and clumsy, but in ten minutes they had undressed each other inside the bivouac sack.

It was a first for Bond . . . sex at 7,900 meters.

They used up the precious air in the canister quite quickly, but it was worth it.

TWENTY-THREE

BLOOD, SWEAT, AND DEATH

CHANDRA DID HIS BEST TO FOLLOW ROLAND MARQUIS ACROSS THE PLATEAU. The wind was so fierce that it was an effort to place one foot in front of the other. Marquis's footprints were covered within minutes of his making them, so Chandra had to force himself to keep moving or he would lose the trail. Using an ice ax as a walking stick, Chandra pulled himself forward one step at a time until he came to a rock face. Anchors and a rope had been affixed there, and there was no other possible route. Marquis had gone farther up.

Chandra found climbing the rock face surprisingly easier than walking against the wind. Here, the wind pushed him snugly against the wall. It took him nearly an hour, but he finally made it to the top, where a blast of wet snow and ice hit him in the face. He nearly lost his grip and fell, but he hung on for dear life and willed one leg to swing up and over the lip. Chandra slammed his ice ax into the rock and ice, using it as a lever to pull himself up. He lay there, totally exhausted, dangerously exposed to the vicious elements. He said a silent prayer to Shiva and breathed through his oxygen respirator for several minutes, trying to regain some strength.

After an eternity, he knew he had to move or he would freeze to death. He rolled over and crawled away from the ledge, searching for some kind of shelter.

Through the blinding snow he saw a tent set up some forty meters away. That was where Marquis had holed up, Chandra thought. He wouldn't be going anywhere until the storm let up, so the Gurkha figured he must find a bivouac for the night.

There was a *Bergschrund* to his left. His father had taught him how to enlarge a crack in the ice big enough to crawl into. It was his only hope. Mustering every ounce of strength, Chandra got to his feet and slowly moved forward.

He raised the ice ax and let it fall over and over as chunks of ice flew about him. It was tremendously hard work, and he had to stop every minute or so to take deep breaths of oxygen. His legs were beginning to feel numb, but he kept chopping.

Eventually, it was done. He had made a hole that he could crawl inside and assume the fetal position. He did so, closed his eyes, and was immediately asleep.

He awoke with a start. The storm had stopped, and the light of the new day was beginning to spread over the mountain. Chandra was stiff and cold, but alive.

Then he noticed his left hand. Somehow he had lost his glove during the climb or while he was digging the hole. His hand was completely frostbitten. The fingers were dark blue and the rest of the hand was purple. He tried to flex his fingers, but they were paralyzed. The skin was insensitive to touch.

He crawled out of the hole and stood. The rest of him appeared to be in one piece. With his good hand he slowly ripped off his backpack, opened it, and dug around for anything he could wrap around his hand. There was a prayer scarf that his father had given him when he was a boy, so he used that. It didn't help much. He knew it was entirely possible he would lose the hand when they got back to civilization.

Never mind! he told himself. Get on with the job! He repeated the Gurkhali motto to himself, over and over: It is better to die than be a coward . . . it is better to die than be a coward. It served as a mantra of sorts. He found a bar of chocolate in his pack and ate it for energy, then put the pack on again and tromped forward toward Marquis's tent.

Chandra flattened himself on the snow when he got around the glacier. Roland Marquis and Carl Glass were together, packing the tent. He decided to stay back and see where they went rather than confront them.

Soon they were off, moving toward the north ridge of the great mountain. What were they going to do? Summit? Were they mad?

Chandra followed them over the ridge, which was one route to the summit taken by many explorers over the years. But Marquis and Glass didn't continue the ascent. They went over and down to a level plane, where four tents had been set up.

The Russians.

Chandra held back, got out his CWS and peered through it, watching Marquis's every move.

Roland Marquis and Carl Glass had spent a rough night in the single tent. Marquis was anxious about the coming negotiations with the Russians, not sure if he wanted to go through with the deal he had arranged. In the early hours of the morning he had decided what he was going to do and made a plan with Glass.

They trekked to the Russian encampment, where they were greeted by two men with AK-47s. The sentries ushered them into a tent, where the leader, a man named Igor Mislov, was waiting.

He looked a lot like Joseph Stalin, with a thick black mustache and bushy eyebrows.

"Mr. Marquis!" he hailed in English. "Have some hot tea?"

"Thank you, Igor," Marquis said. "It's nice to meet face-to-face after all this time, eh?"

"Indeed, indeed." Mislov looked curiously at Glass.

"Oh, this is my associate, Carl Glass," Marquis said. "Igor Mislov."

The men shook hands and sat down.

One of the guards served the tea, and it warmed Marquis considerably. Finally, he said, "Right, I have the specification for Skin 17. It is worth . . . billions."

"Well, let's see it!" the Russian said.

"It's in the form of a microdot. The goddamned Union have been trying to get their hands on it, and they almost did. I got it first, and I even kept it from the Double-O agent who was on our team!"

"Ha!" Mislov roared. "Double-O agent? I didn't know they still existed! When the KGB disbanded, I thought there was no more use for those guys."

"One would think so," Marquis agreed, humoring the man. "But I'm afraid SIS keeps them around to keep tabs on the Russian Mafia, too."

Mislov dismissed the label with a wave of his hand. "Don't call us that, it's an idiotic name. We're businessmen, that's all. Russian Mafia—phooey! The Mafia lives in Sicily. We live in Moscow. That's a long way from Sicily!" He laughed boisterously.

"Whatever you say, Igor," Marquis said. "Now let's talk business. I've come a long fucking way to get here. You picked one hell of a rendezvous spot."

Mislov shrugged. "I know how valuable Skin 17 is. I knew the Union were after it, too. We found out one of our team was working for them. He . . . uhm, met with an unfortunate accident. They are everywhere these days, those goddamned Union. I've done business with them, but they have no loyalty to customers. Hey, I saved you the trouble of having to carry Skin 17 all the way down the mountain. Who knows what might have happened to you? This is a dangerous place. That was some storm last night, huh?"

"There's another one in about eight hours," Marquis said. "We'd like to get going before it hits. Now—we had agreed upon a starting price of one billion dollars. We both know it's worth more than that. What are you prepared to offer now?"

"Two billion American dollars. We can pay you fifty thousand dollars in uncut diamonds right now. The rest you'll get in Kathmandu after we get out of here."

"Are you mad?" Marquis asked. He had been afraid of this.

"Am I mad? What do you mean?"

"You think I'd let this go for only fifty thousand in diamonds?"

"Are *you* mad?" the Russian asked. Suddenly there was a heavy tension in the air. "You don't think we would carry two billion dollars in cash up Kangchenjunga, do you? It was difficult enough carrying these goddamned diamonds."

"Where are they?"

Mislov nodded at one of the two guards, who produced an ordinary water thermos. He unscrewed it and showed the contents to Marquis. It was full of off-color stones. Marquis recognized them as uncut diamonds. He nodded, and the guard replaced the lid.

"I'm afraid it won't be enough," Marquis said carefully. "Perhaps the Union will pay more."

"Mr. Marquis, we, too, came a long way for this. You will sell us the specification, or things will get unpleasant."

Marquis turned to Glass and gave him a well-rehearsed signal. "I don't know, Igor, but it seems that since we last talked, the demand for Skin 17 has skyrocketed. The Union want it, my country wants it back, the Chinese want it . . . I understand there's a few Belgians that want it . . ."

Glass heard the code word "Belgians," pulled a Glock out of his pocket with lightning speed, and shot the two guards neatly and efficiently. Marquis drew his own Browning and held it to Mislov's head. Glass picked up one of the AK-47s and aimed it at the tent flap. Two more men rushed in but saw that their leader was in danger.

"Tell them to drop their guns," Marquis said. Mislov spoke to them in Russian, and they did as they were told. Marquis then nodded to Glass, who calmly blasted them with the automatic weapon.

"Now, Igor," Marquis said. "You're all alone. How much is the *Russian Mafia* willing to pay me now?"

Mislov swallowed hard, then stammered, "Two . . . two billion now, and two more when we reach Kathmandu."

"You have it?"

"In diamonds, yes."

"Where?"

Mislov gestured to a bag. Glass looked inside and found several more water thermoses. They were each filled with uncut stones.

"Why the hell didn't you offer us these diamonds before?"

Mislov shrugged and laughed nervously. "I'm a businessman. I was going to tell my superiors that we paid you the diamonds, but, of course, I would have kept the rest."

"I see. Well, thank you, Igor. I accept your offer," Marquis said, then pulled the trigger. The side of the Russian's head exploded as the bullet slammed through it.

They were alone in the camp now. After a moment of silence Glass said, "Christ, Roland, we're rich." He began to stuff half of the thermoses into his pack. Marquis took the remainder and put them in his own.

"Come on, let's go."

They left the tent and started to move up the slope toward the north ridge. As they passed an icewall, Chandra Gurung jumped from a perch and tackled Carl Glass. Glass dropped the AK-47, and it slid on the ice toward the edge of a cliff and into space.

Both men got to their feet. Chandra slugged Glass hard in the face with his good fist, knocking him into Marquis, who was in the process of drawing the Browning. He, too, lost his grip on the gun, and it sailed into the air and lodged in a snowdrift behind Chandra. The Gurkha backed off and stood between the two men and the drift.

They were dangerously close to the precipice.

"You are both under arrest," Chandra said. "You must accompany me back to Camp Five."

Marquis laughed. Glass, not sure how to react, laughed with him.

"Oh, really!" Marquis said. "*You* are going to arrest *us!* I tell you what. How about we pay you twenty rupees to porter our bags for us?"

"Give me the pacemaker," Chandra said. "And I will let you both live."

"Carl, throw this stinking Gurung off the mountain."

Glass, a sizable and very strong man, rushed Chandra. The Gurkha, however, was far better trained and much faster.

"*Ayo Gurkhali!*" Chandra shouted as he drew the *khukri* from the sheath at his side.

With one swift movement Chandra swung the *khukri* evenly and neatly. All it took was one stroke. Carl Glass's head separated from his shoulders, spun around in the air, and sailed off the edge of the cliff.

The body stood there a moment, trembling, blood gushing from the gruesome wound at the top.

This so unnerved Marquis that he turned to flee. Chandra knocked Glass's body over the cliff and ran in pursuit.

A slick rock face stood in Marquis's path, but that didn't stop him. Using an ice ax in one hand, he began to ascend, finding footholds and handholds where he could. There was no time to use hardware—this was climbing using brute strength and skill.

Chandra stood at the bottom of the wall and looked up at the figure who was already thirty feet ahead of him. He didn't know if he could do it. His left hand was useless. How could he climb with only one good hand? Should he let the traitor go?

The mantra reemerged in the Gurkha's head: It is better to die than be a coward.

With determination Chandra swung his ice ax at the rock, lodged it in tightly, and pulled himself up. His boots found edges in the rock to hold his weight as he hugged the wall. He pulled out the ax, almost losing his balance in doing so, but swung it back into the rock just as quickly. It was slow going, but he managed to ascend a few feet with every try. Marquis, on the other hand, was rapidly approaching the top of the ridge.

Chandra had climbed twenty feet when the air in the respirator noticeably changed. The oxygen canister was empty! He winced, spat the respirator out of his mouth, took a lungful of cold, biting air, and kept going.

He looked up at his prey and saw that Marquis was sitting on the ridge, watching him. The man had something shiny and metallic in his hand. Marquis let it go, and the tool fell straight for Chandra. It was a carabiner, and it struck the Gurkha on the shoulder. The surprise almost caused Chandra to let go of the ice ax.

He had to get down. He couldn't climb farther or he would surely die.

Marquis extracted an ice screw from his pack, held it in the air, and dropped it.

The object struck Chandra on the head. He clung to the handle of the ax, hugging the wall, praying that his feet wouldn't slip. He was breathing in gasps, and never knew that pain could be so severe.

A few seconds later, another ice screw struck him on the forehead, successfully disorienting him enough for him to lose his balance.

One foot slipped. He struggled to hold on to the ax handle, but it was wet and slippery now. He reached with his dead left hand, but this proved to be the fatal handicap. The other boot lost its footing as his hand slipped away from the ax. He fell backward into thin air and bounced off the edge of the cliff.

Instead of screaming, the Gurkha was aware of the words running through his head as he plummeted to the vast lower depths.

It is better to die than be a coward . . . it is better to die than . . .

Roland Marquis cursed the fact that Carl Glass had been carrying half of the diamonds. He didn't know how much he had in his own pack, but it wouldn't be enough to buy his way out of England and into a foreign country where he could hide behind a false identity and live out the rest of his life in splendor. That had been the plan, such as it was.

If only the Union hadn't interfered. Nevertheless, this was still *his* show, and he wasn't going to let anyone wreck it—not them, not the Russians, not the damned Gurkha, and certainly not James Bond.

He could still find a buyer for Skin 17. Perhaps, he thought, perhaps he could sell it to the Union! They wanted it badly enough. Their incompetent minion, Schrenk, had been unsuccessful in getting it. Perhaps they would pay *him* a handsome fee. After all, they had employed him before to help steal it in the first place. It was only a matter of finding the right person to talk to. He hadn't known who Steven Harding's contact was. When Harding had approached him several months before with the Union's pitifully low offer, he could see that the doctor was a greedy bastard and could be turned. He had talked Harding into going along with the Union's orders, but instead of delivering the specification to them, Harding and he would "lose" it, sell it to the Russian Mafia, and make even more money together. Harding had been afraid of the Union, but Marquis was able to ease his fears. They had worked together. They had stolen the formula and were successful in diverting it from the Union. Now he had it and could name his price.

Would the Union seek revenge on him? Would they refuse to deal with him? He thought not. They wanted it too badly. They were probably the most likely buyers. The Chinese would offer too little. He didn't know who was behind the Belgian team, but he didn't care. They were probably being funded by a European consortium of some kind.

The trick would be contacting the Union before *they* found *him*. He wasn't sure how he would do it, but he had plenty of connections. He would go back to Camp Five, keep the pacemaker under wraps, and try to avoid Bond at all costs, if he was still alive.

He looked up at the sky. Dark clouds were beginning to form again. The storm was probably three or four hours away. He had to make it back to camp before then. It wasn't very far. The trouble was, he was exhausted and had a splitting headache. Marquis checked his oxygen canister and saw that it was nearly empty. That must be the cause of the headache, he thought. He found his last canister and attached the respirator to it. The new air felt good. That was another reason to risk going back to Camp Five. He needed more oxygen. He took another five minutes to eat two granola bars and drink some water from his canteen, then he set off toward the camp. Now if he could only avoid running into 007.

James Bond and Hope Kendall had spent the morning looking around the camp for any signs of the missing people. The storm had completely covered any tracks, so they thought it best to stay put and see if anyone came back. They had decided that they would perform crevasse burials for the dead, stay put through the coming storm by sharing the bivouac sack again, and begin their descent the following day. Bond hated to give up, but there was nothing else to do. Attempting to search the upper reaches of Kangchenjunga for people who might be lost or buried was foolhardy. To hell with Skin 17, he thought. If it had been created once, it could be created again. Britain had plenty of intelligent physicists. If Marquis had indeed stolen the specification and had found a way down the mountain, then so be it. If it fell into the wrong hands, it was beyond Bond's control at this point.

He was past caring.

Hope pulled Barlow's and Léaud's bodies out of their tent so that they could be buried. Bond went into Paul Baack's tent, looked at the bright yellow and green parka covering the body, and sighed. It was too bad. He had liked the Dutchman. Before pulling him out, though, Bond decided to get a message to London on Baack's satellite phone.

Reception was surprisingly good. He got Tanner, who put him through to M herself. She agreed with Bond's plan to descend the following day if the missing climbers failed to show up. As for Roland Marquis, an all-points warrant was issued for his arrest. If he dared to show his face at any western airport, he would be nabbed.

"Don't worry, Double-O Seven," M said. "I've explained to the Minister what has happened. He was furious, but he'll get over it. You did your best."

"I'm afraid I didn't, ma'am," Bond said. "I feel as if I let you down. I'm also very concerned about Sergeant Gurung. If he died up here, I would—"

"If he died up there," she interrupted, "he died for Britain. That was his job. He knew the risks. Now put it behind you. That's an order, Double-O Seven."

"Yes, ma'am. Uhm, any news on Miss Marksbury?"

"Nothing. Not a trace of her. Now, finish your own job and get home safely."

He rang off and sat there a moment. Had he tried hard enough? Had he pushed himself to the limit? Had he gone the distance? And what about Helena? Had there been a clue of her betrayal—some sign that he may have missed? Bond suddenly experienced a crushing feeling of guilt and anger. What could he have done better?

He stood and prepared to drag Baack's body out of the tent but then decided to let it go. He would do it later. At that moment he felt like taking a good look at the Himalayan range and cursing the gods.

He emerged from the tent and called for Hope. There was no answer.

He walked back to his own tent, calling her name.

"Over here!" she yelled. She was busy digging out the snow from the front of the plane fuselage. Bond joined her, took another shovel, and began to help.

"We should have buried the plane passengers in the first place instead of trying to haul them down the mountain," he said. "How many are still in the plane?"

"I don't know, five or six," she said. They would have to make do with giving the victims crevasse burials, which meant that they would simply haul the bodies to the nearest crevasse and throw them in. This avoided having to dig in the ice and snow, which was a major expenditure of energy.

They worked hard for several minutes, then stopped to take a break. They sat on rocks, breathed oxygen, and drank from their water bottles.

"I'm hungry," she said. "How about I boil up some freeze-dried?"

"Why, I haven't had a dish like that in such a long time. By all means!"

She laughed and started to get up, but he surprised her by standing quickly, shoving her out of the way, drawing the P99 from his outer holster, and firing into the distance. She screamed.

"Stop right there!" Bond shouted, holding the gun level. Hope turned to look and was shocked by what she saw.

Roland Marquis was fifty feet away, his hands raised.

TWENTY-FOUR

A BETTER WAY TO DIE

MARQUIS STOOD HIS GROUND, NOT MOVING. BOND WALKED TOWARD HIM, the Walther still in hand. Hope stood spellbound, watching the two of them.

"Put the gun away Bond," Marquis said. "I'm not the bad guy."

"How do I know that's true?" Bond asked.

"I saved your miserable life, you fool. It was Carl Glass and Otto Schrenk. They were working together. They tried to kill you and take the pacemaker."

"What happened to the pacemaker? Where have you been?"

"I saw Schrenk and Glass enter your tent. It was a good thing I was watching with a CWS. I didn't like the look of it, so I went over to the tent but stood outside. I heard a gunshot and rushed in. They had already hit you on the head, and Glass had just shot Schrenk. I don't know why Glass turned on Schrenk. I suppose he got greedy. Anyway, I surprised him, and Glass panicked. He knocked me down running out of the tent. I chased him over the north ridge."

The story was plausible but something wasn't right. "Go on."

"Not much else to tell except that Glass fell. I never did catch up with him. He was near a precipice and lost his footing. He saw that I was behind him and he got careless. The weather was bloody horrific. I was mad to go after him, but I thought you would appreciate it if *someone* did."

"So the pacemaker . . . ?"

"It went down with Glass. It's gone forever. Can I put down my hands now?"

"I'd feel better if you empty your pockets and throw down any weapons you might be carrying," Bond said.

"I assure you that I've lost my Browning. I tried to shoot Glass, but I dropped the bloody thing. Couldn't find it."

Bond approached him and patted the pockets on his parka. He looked through the goggles into Marquis's eyes, attempting to judge whether or not something there would betray him. All Bond saw, though, was the familiar hatred eminating from his old school rival.

"All right, Roland, but don't try any sudden moves. I've got an itchy-trigger finger."

Marquis lowered his hands. He looked around and said, "Where's everyone else?"

"They're dead," Hope said, walking up to them with an ice ax in hand. "Everyone is accounted for now that you're back and you've confirmed why Glass is missing. Except for Chandra."

Bond said, "We don't know where he is. Do you?"

Marquis shook his head. "No. I haven't seen him since we brought up Lee Ming's body. Everyone else is dead? The Sherpas, too?"

"Yes," Hope said. "They were all murdered in their tents. We think Schrenk did it."

"So you're burying people? That's what you're doing now?"

"Yeah," Hope said. "We were going to stay here tonight, sit through the storm, and go home tomorrow."

"Well, then," Marquis said. "I'll help you. I'd like to go home, too. I daresay we'd be safer traveling together, don't you think?"

"You're no longer our leader, though," Bond said. "I take no more orders from you, Roland."

"Fine, Bond. If it makes you feel victorious or something, then you be the leader."

Bond didn't comment. He lowered the gun and said, "We had better hurry and finish the job with these corpses. The storm is coming." He put away the Walther but was still wary. There was something about Marquis's story he didn't like.

They walked back to the hole that Hope had begun to dig. She asked, "Have you had food? Do you need something before we get to work?"

"That would be very nice," Marquis said. "Some hot tea would be quite welcome indeed, Hope."

Bond stopped her and said, "Wait. Roland, did you happen to run into the Russians?"

Marquis replied, "As a matter of fact, yes. Just saw their campsite, is all. It was over on the other side of the ridge. We steered clear of it."

Bond's eyes narrowed. *"We?"*

Marquis flinched. He knew he had said the wrong thing. Without a moment's hesitation he lashed out at Hope, grabbed her ice ax, and swung it at Bond. The point buried itself in Bond's right shoulder. He cried out in pain as Hope screamed. Marquis pulled the ax out, turned, and ran the way he had come. Bond fell to his knees and clutched his arm. Blood was pouring out of the wound. Hope squatted beside him and tried to examine the injury.

Bond watched Marquis running, or, rather, trudging through the snow toward the rock face. The bastard had done it. He had betrayed his country and the security of the western world. Bond couldn't let him get away with it. Not Roland Marquis. Not the only son of a bitch at Eton who believed he beat Bond at wrestling. All this time Marquis had been in denial that in reality, Bond had gotten the better of him back then. Everyone watching had known that Bond had been the victor. The bloody instructor gave the match to Marquis and the bastard never let Bond forget it.

"Stay here," Bond said to Hope. He struggled to his feet.

"You can't go after him, you're hurt!" she cried.

"Stay *here!*" Bond said firmly, then set off after Marquis.

Neither man was wearing a backpack. Bond had his weapon and an ice ax, but no oxygen canisters. Chasing Marquis at this altitude was complete madness, but he was determined to catch the bastard. Bond hoped that Marquis was telling the truth when he said he hadn't eaten. Perhaps he would be more fatigued than Bond and that would slow him down.

Even so, Bond was under extreme physical stress. He was already breathing so rapidly that he was afraid he might hyperventilate. The wound in his arm didn't help.

Marquis scaled the wall like a lizard. It was uncanny the way the man could climb. Bond conceded to himself that his rival was indeed the superior mountaineer, but it was time to push himself further than his body could go.

Bond found handholds in the rock wall and attempted to follow along Marquis's route. He felt as if he were moving in slow motion again. He was gasping for air, and every move he made was torture.

Thirty minutes later Marquis was over the wall. Bond was not far behind, but he was ascending at a snails pace. When he got to the top, he collapsed onto his back as his lungs screamed for oxygen. He felt dizzy and disoriented. If he stood up, he would surely fall.

If only he had brought an oxygen canister! He had been about to put one on his back when Marquis had hit him with the ax. He should have heeded Hope's admonitions to stay put. This was madness indeed!

The sky was darkening above him. He felt cold, wet drops on his face, reminding him to cover his skin with the muffler. The wind was picking up again and the snow began to fall in earnest.

His lungs were on fire. Could he make it back down the wall without falling?

Wait! How could he have forgotten? He reached into the side pocket of his parka, praying that Major Boothroyd's little tube was there. Bond grabbed it and brought it to his mouth.

The emergency air breather was a godsend. The oxygen was cold and dry, but it sent bursts of energy into Bond's veins. He took several deep breaths, willing the clouds of confusion from his mind. He would have to conserve the air, though, and use it only when necessary. After a few minutes he put it away, got to his feet, and continued the chase.

They were climbing a snow gully of mixed rock and ice that cut through a rock wall to reach the West Ridge, which was a hundred meters from the summit. Marquis was climbing without oxygen at

all, something that many professional mountaineers dared to do.
Bond had never attempted an 8,000-meter peak without oxygen, but
he had known men who had. They were usually like Marquis, cocky
and egotistical, believing that they were invincible against the might
of the mountain. Perhaps this time, Bond thought, the gods would
not look favorably on Marquis. Perhaps his arrogance would be his
downfall.

As he climbed higher, Bond lost sight of Marquis. He stopped and
looked around frantically, wondering what had happened to the man.
Had the falling snow somehow obscured his escape?

Suddenly Marquis leaped from a ledge, jumping on Bond and
knocking him to the rock. He raised the ice ax and attempted to
smash it into Bond's head. Bond grabbed Marquis's arm and held it
tightly, forcing it back in a life-or-death arm wrestle. Marquis, too,
was wheezing loudly, fighting for air. Bond shoved with all his might,
rolling the man off him. Without giving him time to counter, Bond
jumped on his opponent and hit him twice in the face. The thin air
inhibited the blows' effectiveness, for the degree of force behind the
punches was nowhere near what Bond perceived it to be.

Marquis slammed the side of the ice ax against Bond's head, stunning him. Bond fell over and was momentarily helpless. His vision
blurred and he began to gasp for breath again. He expected the point
of the ice ax to come crashing down into his chest, but it never did.

. He forced himself to shake away the stars and stand up. His vision
returned, but his head was pounding. Marquis had run. He was
climbing farther up the mountain—toward the summit. Bond took a
few more breaths from the emergency breather, then continued the
ascent.

The snow fell faster as the wind blew harder.

Marquis, doing his best to move in rhythm, felt like hell. He was
totally exhausted from the climbing he had already done that day. He
was hungry and thirsty, and his headache had increased by the minute.
It was so excruciating that he wanted to scream. He was certain that he
had developed High Altitude Cerebral Edema. The symptoms were
quite evident. If he didn't descend soon, he might have a stroke.

He *had* to get over the top, he thought. His only hope was to go up and over the summit and descend Kangchenjunga into Sikkim. He could easily lose himself there if he could get away from Bond. That's what he would do, then!

Roland Marquis might have recognized the symptoms of HACE, but he didn't realize how delusional he was. He had completely forgotten that he was without supplies, a tent, a sleeping bag, or any other necessities for spending a night on the mountain, much less surviving a monsoon and attempting to descend to the bottom. He didn't think about the fact that it would take three or four days, or more, to get to the Sikkim-side Base Camp. He was convinced that he was going to reach the top of Kangch and escape.

He made it to the West Ridge. All he had to do now was scramble a hundred meters to the summit, then he would be across the border and over. Marquis thought he was running, but in reality he was taking two steps every ten seconds. To him, everything around him was a blur. He had to concentrate on the goal . . . the top of the third highest mountain in the world.

Why did it seem like he was on a treadmill? It felt as if he were not moving any nearer to the summit. He had to push harder. Run, dammit! he told himself.

I *will* conquer this mountain! he screamed in his head.

"To *hell* with you, Kangchenjunga!" he yelled, but he was so breathless that it came out as a whisper.

The Nepalese believe that the gods see and hear everything, and what happened next might have been attributed to this faith. Through the heavy snow Marquis thought he could see the markers, prayer flags, and spikes that other climbers had left on the summit. It was within reach! He crawled forward on hands and knees, and then suddenly went blind. It was an unexpected, horrible sensation. This was followed by a searing pain moving through his skull. He thought his head was going to explode.

Marquis screamed and fell to his knees.

Hope had warned them about retinal hemorrhage. It had struck him hard in both eyes. Simultaneously, he experienced severe symptoms of

HACE. He writhed on the ground and beat his head, trying to knock the pain away. It was no use.

He continued to crawl forward, feeling his way to the summit.

Breathe . . . breathe . . . !

His lungs couldn't take it. His heart was pounding in his chest.

Just a little farther . . .

He reached out his hand and felt a flagpole. He had made it— 8,598 meters! Marquis collapsed and lay still, trying to breathe the thin, precious air.

He could rest here, he told himself. He deserved a reward for making it to the summit. He could afford the rest he needed. Whoever was following him would surely never make it. It was *he* who was king of the world now. He was Roland Marquis! He was . . . invincible!

Then James Bond caught up with him. He, too, fell beside Marquis in exhaustion, fighting for air. He removed the emergency breather from his pocket and inhaled. The Himalayan range spread out before him in all directions. It was as if he were in an airplane but without the plane.

"Who's there?" Marquis gasped.

"It's your old friend from Eton," Bond managed to say between breaths. He put away the breather.

Marquis was confused. Who?

"Oh . . . right," he said. "Bond. I almost forgot who I was running from," he whispered. "We're at the top, aren't we?"

"Yes."

"How . . . how are you?"

"I'm alive," Bond coughed. "You . . . you don't look so good, Roland."

"No," he agreed. "I probably don't. I can't see a damned thing. Bad . . . bad luck. You have any air?"

"Yes."

"You wouldn't want to give me some, would you?" Marquis pleaded, but with dignity. "For old time's sake?"

"Where's the pacemaker?" Bond asked coldly.

Marquis coughed and choked. The spasm lasted for nearly a minute. Finally, the officer caught his breath and said, "See what happens when I try to laugh?"

"It's an honest offer, Roland," Bond said. "Oxygen for the pacemaker."

"You bastard."

There was silence. The storm was getting worse. The wind was screaming, and Bond could feel the subzero temperatures penetrating his parka. They had to get out of there.

"Come on, Roland, I haven't got all day."

Roland reached into a pocket. Bond caught his hand. "It's all right, Bond," Marquis said. "There's no gun there."

Marquis brought out the gold object and held it in his palm. Bond took it, verified that it was indeed Lee's pacemaker, and put it in a pouch. He then removed the emergency breather and placed the mouthpiece to Marquis's lips. Marquis choked on the air but was soon breathing steadily.

"How much was the Union paying you?" Bond asked.

Marquis tried to laugh but coughed again. He said, "I'm not Union, Bond. I never was. It was Steven Harding, not me." He began to tell the story slowly, between breaths. "The Union got to him and paid him something to steal Skin 17. . . . He came to me and offered me an insulting fifteen thousand pounds to help him. . . . I, of course, would remain a silent partner because of my high profile in the RAF, but I was the ideal person to bring in on the job because of my proximity to the Skin 17 project. . . . Even though the money was ridiculous, I thought about the scheme's potential. I talked him into double-crossing the Union and helping *me* sell it to the Russian Mafia. . . . You see, I've done business with them before. . . . I convinced Harding that he would make a lot more money. . . . Besides, better the Russian Mafia get it than the Chinese, which is whom the Union wanted to sell it to. . . . We were just eliminating the middlemen and their commission!"

"Then the business with the pacemaker, and Lee Ming . . . ?"

"That was the Union's plan all along. . . . When you interfered in

Belgium, the Union changed the scheme. . . . They decided to reroute
Lee's journey to China through Nepal and Tibet. . . . Since I had con-
nections in Nepal, I came up with the plot to hire hijackers, kidnap
Lee from his hotel, and whisk him away to an airfield in Sikkim. . . . .
There he would have been picked up by my people and hidden. . . .
Harding made most of the arrangements. . . . After selling the formula,
Harding and I were going to split the money, but he was careless. . . . I
knew the Union would eliminate him and then the fortune would be
all mine. . . . Unfortunately, the damned tourist plane crashed on this
. . . fucking mountain . . . it was carrying a goddamned MP and an
American senator. . . . I knew that the Skin 17 microdot was somewhere on Lee Ming's body, but exactly where was one piece of information that was withheld from me. You knew where it was. . . . I
needed you to find it for me. And now . . . here we are."

He returned the emergency breather to Bond.

"You had better get going," Marquis said. "That storm is getting
worse."

"You're coming with me," Bond said.

Marquis shook his head. "I don't want to be court-martialed. I
couldn't face it. I don't want to die in prison. No, this is a much better
way to die. Leave me here. Let me die at the top of the world."

"What happened to Chandra?" Bond asked.

"He did his best to stop me. He fell. He didn't die a coward, that's
certain. Unlike me. I'm sorry, Bond."

Bond became aware of another person climbing toward them. At
first he thought it might be a supernatural being—a yeti or a ghost.
But it was only Hope Kendall. She was carrying a backpack and had
oxygen. She dropped the respirator from her mouth and yelled,
"Christ, what the hell are you two *doing* here? We have to get *down!*"

"Hope . . ." Marquis said. "Congratulations . . ."

"What?"

"Congratulations," he gasped. "You can count on one hand the
number of women who have summited Kangchenjunga."

That news surprised her. She involuntarily laughed, then dropped
to her knees beside Bond.

"Well, I'll be damned," she said. "I was in, boots and all, and didn't even think about that. I just wanted to catch up with you two."

"Both of you," Marquis said. "Go. Leave me. I'm staying here."

Bond pulled on Hopes arm. "Come on."

"What?"

"We're leaving him."

"We can't leave him!" She struggled against Bond. "Let's give him oxygen. We can get him down the—"

But Marquis gasped, choked a moment, and went limp. Hope examined him, reached for his wrist, and felt for a pulse. She put her head to his chest.

Bond gently tugged on her arm again. "The storm is getting bad," he said.

She finally raised herself, nodded, and got to her feet. She helped Bond stand, but his legs were very weak. She reached into her pack and brought out an extra oxygen canister. "Here, put this on," she said.

The new air helped tremendously, and they began the torturous descent back to Camp Five. Bond paused to look at the figure of Roland Marquis, lying amid the prayer flags and country markers. He might have been a great man, Bond thought, but his pride got him in trouble. The gods disapproved of it. He had not shown the mountain the proper respect. As he had betrayed his country, he had betrayed his pact with the deities who controlled the elements in this cold hell, high above the living earth.

"Come on," Hope urged.

She helped him as he stumbled along, trying to keep his balance on the West Ridge. He hadn't realized how wrecked he was until he started moving. The wind was intense and was getting worse by the minute. If they stopped at all, they would perish.

The storm hit full force when they were a hundred and fifty meters from camp. Hope could see the Great Scree Terrace below them. All they had to do was climb down the rock wall.

Bond took one look and knew that he couldn't do it. Like Marquis, he was ready to give up and die.

"Get up, damn you!" Hope cried. "You're not wimping out on me now! You're coming down with *me*."

Bond attempted to wave her away.

"Breathe, dammit! Breathe the oxygen!" she yelled.

Bond took some breaths, but he could barely find the strength to inhale.

"Fine, I'll have to do it the hard way," she said.

Working as quickly as she could, Hope removed anchors, rope, a harness, and a pulley from her bag. She got the harness around Bond, who was barely conscious. She drove the anchors into the rock with her ice ax, fixed the pulley and threaded the rope through it. She then attached the rope to the harness and pushed Bond over the wall.

She slowly lowered him, belaying his body as he bounced like a marionette against the side of the rock. When he reached the bottom, he crumpled as if he had no skeleton.

Hope then began her descent, holding on to the bits of rock and ice, praying that the wind wouldn't blow her off. It was more difficult than she had thought it would be, but she kept going without looking down.

After what seemed like an eternity, her boots touched the plateau. She fell against a snowdrift and rested for a minute, then pulled Bond to his knees.

"Get up, you bastard," she yelled at him. "We're almost there!"

Bond mumbled something. He was completely out of it. He could barely stand and lean in to her. She helped him along, acting as a crutch.

"Right foot . . . left foot . . ." she called, telling his brain what to do, for it had ceased to function. Nevertheless, he understood her commands, moved his feet forward, and marched with her.

"That's right," she said. "You're doing great! Right foot . . . left foot . . . !"

They continued in this manner until they reached the tents. She opened the flap, pushed Bond inside, then crawled in after him.

This time, the Q Branch bivouac sack saved their lives.

TWENTY-FIVE

HUMAN MACHINES

"ARE YOU AWAKE?" SHE ASKED HIM.

They were both inside the bivouac sack. Bond moved slowly and groaned. He had slept the sleep of the dead.

Sunlight oozed through the top of the tent. Hope didn't know how long they had been asleep, but it was obviously the next day. She put on her boots and opened the tent to inspect the damage. The entrance was completely blocked by snow and ice. She took a snow shovel and began to dig her way out.

Bond heard the scraping and sat up. "What year is it?" he asked. His voice was hoarse.

"It's the year they'll put on our tombstones if we don't dig ourselves out of here and get moving, what do you say?" She continued to scrape. "How do you feel?"

"Terrible. How did I get here? The last thing I remember was leaving the summit." He then noticed a large bandage wrapped around the wound that Marquis had made with the ice ax.

"Your fairy godmother took care of you," she said. She stopped and put down the shovel. "I suppose I should boil some water before exhausting myself."

The few hours of sleep had worked miracles. Bond recovered quickly.

His shoulder was extremely sore, but he could manage. He pulled his down jacket over him and together they cleared the entrance to the tent. While Hope continued to drag bodies out of the fuselage, Bond dug his way into Paul Baack's tent to use the satellite phone. He wanted to make another call to London before they made the descent to Camp Four. He also wanted to alert Ang Tshering at the Base Camp that they were on the way.

As soon as he entered, Bond felt a burst of adrenaline.

The satellite phone was not sitting on Baack's portable table. Someone had been in the tent before the storm had hit.

The body was still there, covered by the brightly colored parka. If he remembered the tents contents correctly, there was a pack missing, but the rest of the Dutchman's belongings seemed to be intact.

On an impulse Bond stooped over Baack's pack, which had been stored in the corner of the tent with other things. He dug in the clothing and found pieces of a rifle: a stock, barrel, telescopic sight— and 7.62mm cartridges. It was a gas-operated sniper rifle much like a Belgian FN FAL.

A chill slithered down Bond's back. It couldn't be! This was the weapon used to shoot at Bond and Chandra during the trek. The gun that killed young David Black. The sniper had been Paul Baack!

He turned to the body on the tent floor. Bond took hold of the parka and yanked it off the corpse.

It wasn't Baack at all. It was a Sherpa, one of the new men who had come up from the Base Camp to help haul. His throat had been cut, like all the others.

Bond leaped to his feet and ran outside.

"Hope?" he called. She wasn't out by the plane. Bond tromped as fast as he could through the deep snow. He could now clearly see another set of footprints other than Hope's around the fuselage.

Paul Baack was standing in the open hatch, holding a Hechler and Koch VP70 to Hope's head.

"Hello, James," he said. "Raise your hands. Now. Where I can see them."

Bond did so. Carefully, his gun still trained on Hope, Baack ordered, "Dr. Kendall, please take Mr. Bond's pistol out of that little pouch on the side of his parka. Pick it up with your thumb and index finger, please."

She did as she was told and held it gingerly.

"Throw it over there," Baack commanded. Bond watched as his Walther sailed several feet away, landed with a plop, and sank into a soft snowdrift. Baack pulled her next to him again and repositioned his gun to her head.

"I heard you were still at Camp Five," Baack continued, "so I thought I'd pay you a visit. It's a pity that Otto didn't kill you and our good doctor like he was supposed to."

"Let her go, Baack."

"No, James, I have to finish the job that Otto botched up. He was working for me, you see. I hired him. In the eyes of my superiors, if he fails, then I fail. I have to make sure they don't see me as a failure. It could damage my reputation. That damned Roland Marquis. I didn't count on *him* being a free agent in this mess. He screwed up my plan."

"So that's it," Bond said. "I didn't count on *two* Union operatives infiltrating the team. Schrenk was the muscleman and you were the brains, right?"

"If you say so," Baack said. "I'll take that as a compliment."

Bond's eyes narrowed. "And you had constant contact with London. You knew my every move. You hired the hit man in Kathmandu and had me followed."

"He was a disgraceful amateur. I apologize for that," Baack said.

"You knew where we were going to be and when. Where were you hiding all this time?"

"I went down to Camp Four to wait for Otto, but he never showed. As you say, I overheard your conversation with London that you were still alive. That's the problem with mobile phones. They're very easy to eavesdrop on. I waited for you and Hope to descend, but you insisted on staying here through those dreadful storms. So I came up here to surprise you this morning."

Bond was furious. "Did you recruit my personal assistant? Do you know what's happened to her?"

Baack laughed. "Miss Marksbury? I had a part in recruiting her, yes. As for her whereabouts, do you think I'll tell you? Forget it. If she's not dead already, she will be soon. Now give me the pacemaker."

"It's gone," Bond lied. "Roland had it. It went down the mountain with him."

Baack studied Bond's face. Finally he said, "That's very disappointing. And too bad for you. Now let's march to the edge of the plateau over there. You two are going on a thrill ride that beats anything they have at Disneyland."

"Why don't you just shoot us?" Bond asked. "Or cut our throats? Isn't that the Union's preferred method of disposal?"

"Oh, this will be much more fun," Baack said with a smile. "I want to hear that wonderful scream that fades out when someone falls, like you hear in the movies. You know, *Aaaaaaaiiiiiiiieeeeeee!*" He laughed at his sound effect, then wiped away the smile. "Now, move."

Bond turned and walked through the deep snow toward the edge. Baack shoved Hope out of the plane but kept hold of her. "Follow him," he said.

When they got to the cliff, Baack said, "It's high time to kill, James. You first."

"You're making a big mistake, Paul," Bond said. "How are you going to get down the mountain by yourself?"

"I'm an experienced mountaineer. I'll be fine. You'll get there before me, though. You're going headfirst."

Bond turned to face him. Baack was still holding the gun to Hope's head.

"You're going to have to push me," he said.

"Either you jump off the edge, or you get to see me blow a hole in her head. Which is it?"

Bond looked at Hope and peered through the goggles. He could see a flicker of understanding in her eyes. Bond blinked twice.

Hope raised her right boot and kicked Baack hard in the shin. The sharp points of the crampon dug through his clothing and into his skin.

Baack screamed. Hope pushed the gun away and dropped to her knees. At the same time, Bond lunged for the big man. They fell together and rolled. The VP70 arced through the air and made a deep hole in the snow.

Bond hit Baack hard in the face, cracking the goggles. Baack roared like a bear, grabbed Bond's hood, and pulled it off. The cold air felt like needles on Bond's skin and head. Baack's large hand fixed on Bond's face, his fingers digging into the skin and pushing him back.

There was genuine strength behind Baack's size. Bond fell backward, giving his opponent time to regain his balance and stand. He kicked Bond hard in the chest, the crampons ripping the fabric like tiger claws. The boot came down again, but Bond grabbed Baack's ankle and twisted it sharply. Baack yelled again and lost his balance. He toppled over, dangerously close to the edge of the cliff.

Bond wasted no time counterattacking. He leaped on top of the big man and attempted to roll him over. Baack lodged his shoulder against a rock to brace himself, but it was very slippery from ice. As he started to slip over it, he took hold of Bond's parka and said, "You're coming with me!"

Hope jumped into action and held Bond's legs. "I've got you!"

Bond kept pushing and hitting the man, forcing him closer to the dropoff. Finally, Baack's waist went over, pulling his legs with it. Now he was hanging on to Bond's shoulders for dear life. His weight was dragging them both over the cliff. Hope dug her crampons into the ground, trying her best to keep Bond from sliding forward.

Bond was face-to-face with Baack. Now there was terror in the man's eyes, but he wasn't about to plead for mercy.

"Going down, James?" he said through clenched teeth. "First floor . . . lingerie?"

Bond dug his fingers into Baack's hands, trying to wrench them away from his parka.

"Christ!" Hope said, gasping for air. "I can't . . . hold . . . much . . . longer!"

Bond felt his torso slipping forward. Except for his head, shoulders, and arms, Baack's entire body was now over the edge.

"The Union . . . will . . . crush . . . you," he spat out between gasps.

A blast of cold wind reminded Bond that his hood was off, and that sensation prompted Bond's next action. He slammed his forehead into Baack's, inflicting the hardest possible head-butt he could give. Baack's eyes rolled up into his head as his hands loosened their grip. Bond broke free, sending the man off the cliff and into space.

"Aaaaaiiiiiiieeeee . . . !"

Bond inched back onto the ledge and held Hope in his arms as the scream faded into thin air.

"Just like in the movies . . ." he said.

It took them three days to get to the Base Camp, where Ang Tshering met them with open arms. Since he had heard nothing by mobile phone, he was convinced they were dead. He had resolved to wait a few more days before leading the surviving team members back to Taplejung.

That night they built shrines to the men who had died on the mountain. Bond spent two hours scratching Chandra's name on a stone, then drove a piton in above it and attached a white prayer scarf through the eye. When Hope made a stone for Roland Marquis, he made no objections.

They began the long trek back to civilization the next morning. Bond had regained much of his strength after descending the mountain, and the rest at Base Camp worked wonders. Bond and Hope were inseparable, ignoring the disapproving looks of the Sherpas. The Nepalese, shaking their heads, would never understand the decadent ways of the west.

The couple made the seven-day journey a memorable one, if not by day, then certainly by night. They made love for hours every evening after dinner, knowing full well that they might never see each other again after they left Nepal.

One night, as they lay naked in the sleeping bag at the Gunsa campsite, Bond lit his first cigarette in weeks, coughed loudly, then said, "You realize that we've been to the brink of disaster and lived to tell the tale."

"What has it taught you?" she asked. "Other than that you really should give up smoking."

"No way," he said, taking another drag. "Actually, I've been thinking about our earlier conversation concerning limitations.

Despite what my government thinks, I'm just a man. You don't realize how mortal you really are until you're fighting for your life at eight thousand meters."

"In my opinion," she said, "you're the finest specimen of a man I've ever seen. Speaking as a medical doctor, of course."

He smiled. "Hope, you saved my life up there. More than once. I'll be forever grateful."

"Don't mention it. I've learned a lot as well."

"Such as?"

She sighed. "I don't think I have something to prove anymore. Hey, I summited the third tallest mountain in the world, right? I now know that the capabilities of the human machine are far greater than I could ever have imagined. I need not concern myself with limitations anymore, because there are no such things."

"Doesn't one's mind have a lot to do with it as well?" he asked. "Without the will, the body doesn't have much of a chance."

"Quite right," she said. She reached between his legs and held him. "Speaking of will, *will* you please make love to me again?"

She didn't have to ask him twice.

They said good-bye at the Kathmandu airport. She was flying to Bangkok, then on to Auckland. He was traveling in the opposite direction, to London by way of Delhi.

As her flight was called over the intercom, she said, "Take care of yourself, James. Keep in touch."

"I'm not very good at that," Bond admitted. "But we can try."

Hope placed a hand over his face and let her fingers run smoothly over the faint scar on his cheek. She gazed into his clear blue eyes, then pushed the comma of black hair off his forehead. She leaned up and kissed the cruel mouth she had come to know so well. Without another word she turned away, picked up her bag, and walked toward the gate. Bond watched her as a wave of melancholy washed over him. It was a familiar friend, a bittersweet companion for his wretchedly solitary life. Hope handed her ticket to the flight attendant, then went through the door to board her plane.

She never looked back.

TWENTY-SIX

THE COLD STONE HEART

M LOOKED HARD AT BILL TANNER AND SAID, "I DON'T CARE HOW LITTLE time you've had. I want your new proposal for security procedures on my desk in the morning!"

"Yes, ma'am," Tanner said. He stood, glanced at Bond, and left the office. M turned to Bond, took a breath to redirect her thoughts, then said, "Needless to say, the Minister is very happy with your work on this case. Skin 17 was returned to the DERA and they have some new people working on it. I must admit I had my doubts about this one, Double-O Seven, but you pulled through. Well done."

Bond sat stiffly across from his chief with a frown on his face. He wasn't used to such praise. It disturbed him. There also seemed to be an edge to her voice that wasn't quite right.

"I'm supposed to extend an invitation to you," she continued. "The Minister asked that you come to a dinner tonight. Black tie. Ministry of Defence dining room. Seven-thirty. You're to receive a commendation, Double-O Seven."

Bond didn't think he had heard right. "Ma'am?"

"A medal. You're going to get a medal." She looked at him, waiting for some kind of response.

"Ma'am, I've never accepted commendations in the past, not even a knighthood. Your predecessor knew that. I thought you did, too."

"The Minister thought you might reconsider this time," she said.

"I'm sorry, ma'am, but please give the Minister my thanks and my apologies. I have an engagement."

M knew he was lying. She was silent for a moment, then said, "It's just as well. I must admit I didn't approve of you receiving it, either."

Bond now knew what was coming.

"Double-O Seven," she said. "I have to turn down your request for two months' leave. I want you around London in case the Union retaliate. Although you did a fine job in Nepal, I'm extremely unhappy with what has occurred with Miss Marksbury."

"I understand, ma'am."

"No, you don't," she said. She leaned closer to him and narrowed her cold blue eyes. "Your relationship with that girl nearly cost you your life. It caused a massive security breach in our organization. Didn't you ever learn that you cannot be romantically involved with colleagues at SIS? *Especially* your bloody personal assistant! What the hell was the matter with you?"

"I'm sorry, ma'am."

"Yes, well, of course you are. Now she's probably lying at the bottom of the Thames and the Union have a good idea of how we work. This better not happen again, Double-O Seven, do you follow me?"

"Yes, ma'am."

"That's all. Take a week, then we'll talk about how we can go after this Union."

"Yes, ma'am. Thank you," he said, then got up and left the room. Barbara Mawdsley sighed and shook her head. She should have taken disciplinary action and had his head on a platter.

But that was something she could never do to her best agent.

Bond sat in the sitting room of his flat off the King's Road, a double bourbon in hand and a cigarette hanging from his mouth. He had sent May away so that he could be alone with his demons. Sometimes they were the only things that could comfort him.

The white phone rang. He was tempted to let it go, but he

inexplicably detected an urgency in the pips that forced him to pick up the receiver.

"Yes?"

"James! Thank God, you're there!"

It was Helena Marksbury.

Bond sat up abruptly, completely alert. "Christ, Helena, where are you?"

"I'm . . . I'm in a hotel in Brighton. I came here a few days ago. I've been hiding. I assume you know—"

"Yes, Helena. I know."

"Oh, God, James . . . James . . ." She started to cry.

"Helena," he said, attempting to control his rising anger that he knew would be inappropriate. "Tell me what happened. From the beginning."

She sobbed uncontrollably. "Oh, James, I'm so sorry, I'm so sorry. . . ."

He waited a few moments for her to get it out of her system. He was unable to detect that any of it might be pretense; her sorrow was genuine.

"It's best if you tell me everything, Helena," he said.

She gained control of herself and slowly began the story. "They got in touch with me the night we had that fight, after your golf game at Stoke Poges."

"The Union?"

"Yes."

"Go on."

"They must have been watching my flat. They waited until you left, then two men came to the door. At first I wouldn't let them in, but they convinced me they were from SIS. But they really weren't."

"Who were they? What did they look like?"

"One was English. The other was Dutch or Belgian, I think. They told me that they were from the Union. They showed me . . . oh, God, James . . . they showed me photographs . . ."

"Of?"

"My sister. In America. Her two children. Photographs of her dropping them off at school. The men threatened their lives if I didn't cooperate with them."

"What did they say?"

"Only that my nephew and niece would meet with a horrible accident, and that my sister would suffer terrible torture."

"What did they want from you?"

He knew that she was trembling. Her voice shook as she answered him. "They said they wanted to know everything you were going to do with regard to Skin 17. I had to report to them where you would be and when. I had to tell them what the Ministry of Defence were planning at all times. I had to answer any questions they asked."

"For how long?"

"As long as they deemed necessary, they said. Oh, James . . . I didn't want to do it. It was extortion, you see that, don't you?"

"Of course I do," he said. "But I'm not sure how the Ministry of Defence will see it. You could be in a lot of trouble, Helena. How would you contact them?"

"I wouldn't. They contacted me."

"At the office?"

"They had my private number, somehow. They would call and demand to know everything. I tried to put a trace on the calls, but it was never any good. They had some kind of block on the line. They warned me not to alert anyone about them or my sister and her children would die."

"And you believed them?"

"Of course I believed them! I had no choice but to believe them!"

"They could have been bluffing."

"I thought about that, but there were the photos. They seemed to know exactly what my sister was doing at any given time. Oh, James, I've been a nervous wreck. I've been horrible to you. You could have been . . . killed! It would have been my fault!" She broke down again.

Now he knew that her treatment of him those days before he left on assignment had nothing to do with their relationship. He had selfishly thought that she was upset about *him,* when, in fact, she was in torment over what she was being forced to do.

He might have taken her in his arms, but his heart was quickly cooling toward her. Betrayal was something that never sat well with him.

"I'm in danger," she said quietly.

"I should think so."

"A blue van is parked outside on the street. It's been there for two days. A man has been watching the hotel. They know I'm in here."

"Is he there now?"

There was a pause as she peered out the window. "The van is, but it doesn't look like anyone is inside now."

"Listen to me, Helena," he said. "Tell me where you are. I'm coming to fetch you. You have to turn yourself in. It's the only way out of this mess. It's the only way to protect you."

"I don't want to go to prison," she choked.

"Better that than lose your life. We'll make sure that the FBI in the States is contacted so that they can get your sister and her family to a safe place."

"Oh, James, will you help me? Please?"

"I'll do what I can, Helena. I must warn you, though, that there will be a question of treason. Only the courts can answer that one, I'm afraid."

He heard her crying again. The poor girl was in agony.

"Helena, you have to surrender. It's the only way. I'll take you straight to headquarters."

After a few seconds of silence she said, "All right." She gave him the address.

"Don't do anything stupid," he said. "I'll be there as soon as I can."

He hung up the phone and rushed out of the flat. He drove the Aston Martin recklessly across the river and down to the popular seaside resort, where there are literally hundreds of small hotels. He quickly found the street she had mentioned in the less fashionable part of Brighton some five minutes' walk from the seafront.

He parked in front of the building and looked around. The blue van was nowhere in sight. He got out and went inside the building.

Ignoring the elderly woman at the reception desk, Bond rushed through the small lobby as a feeling of dread poured over him,

He took the stairs two at a time to the second floor, drew the Walther, and peered carefully around the landing. The hallway was clear. He quietly moved to the correct room and listened at the door. A radio inside was broadcasting the second movement of Beethoven's Seventh Symphony. Bond raised his hand to knock but realized it was slightly ajar. He slowly pushed it open, his gun ready.

Helena Marksbury was lying in the middle of the floor in a pool of blood.

Bond entered and shut the door behind him. He quickly checked the bedroom to make sure he was alone with the corpse, then kneeled down beside her.

The Union had gotten to her first. Her throat was completely severed.

He took a moment to collect his thoughts, then picked up the phone and dialed the emergency number at headquarters. After ordering a cleanup crew, he sat down in a chair and stared at the body of the beautiful girl he had once made passionate love to.

The music filled the room as the orchestra on the radio reached an emotionally charged climax.

He was sorry for her, but he no longer felt any affection for the girl who had been a wonderful part of his life for some time. Just as he had always shut his heart to other women who had betrayed him in the past, Bond forced Helena out of his life then and there.

As he took out a cigarette and lit it, Bond wondered what was colder—the cruel realm of espionage that had victimized and ultimately destroyed Helena Marksbury, the icy summit of Kangchenjunga, or his own hardened heart.

DOUBLESHOT

For Randi

CONTENTS

PROLOGUE

PASEO

DRAMATIS PERSONAE

THE CONVENT'S SECURITY OFFICER GASPED WHEN HE SAW WHAT CAME UP on the computer screen. Domingo Espada's British bodyguard had given his name as "Peter Woodward," but he was positively identified as James Bond, agent 007 of SIS.

"Better have a look at this, sir," he said to the aide-de-camp, a tall young captain from the Gibraltar Regiment.

The captain looked over the officer's shoulder at the monitor and recognized the face—it was indeed the man who had walked into the Governor's Residence that morning with Espada and the rest of his Spanish entourage. He was now upstairs with the other delegates, politicians, and their aides.

"I'd say he has a lot of nerve coming here like this," the captain said. "He knows we can't arrest him because he's here with diplomatic immunity. I had better get on to London and let them know about it. You're sure he passed through the metal detectors all right?"

"Yes, sir."

The aide-de-camp frowned. "I don't like it. The man's a menace. 'Peter Woodward' indeed. How long before the Governor and the PM arrive?"

Another officer was just hanging up a telephone. "The PM's plane just landed. I would say half an hour."

The Convent, the Governor of Gibraltar's official residence on Main Street for over 250 years, was a hive of activity. As they were under a "Red" security alert, it was crawling with extra men from the Gibraltar Regiment. VIPs from several neighboring countries were upstairs, awaiting an important summit meeting between Britain's Prime Minister, Spain's Prime Minister, and others who had an interest in the Gibraltar conflict.

Another security officer rushed to the captain with a piece of paper. "This urgent fax just came in, sir."

The captain read it. It was from the Ministry of Defence headquarters in London.

"My God" was all he could manage to say after he had absorbed the message.

Upstairs, Nadir Yassasin looked across the long table in the Banqueting Hall at the man the aide-de-camp was worried about. The man *was* the British secret agent, wanted by his own people, suspected of having turned terrorist, and one of the most dangerous men on the planet. There was no mistaking the face—from the three-inch scar showing whitely down the sunburned skin of his right cheek to the black hair, parted on the left and carelessly brushed so that a thick comma fell down over the right eyebrow. The gray-blue eyes were set wide and level under straight, rather long black brows. His jaw was firm and strong. His mouth was wide and finely drawn; Espada's aide, Margareta Piel, had been correct in describing it as "somewhat cruel."

Yassasin took a deep breath and congratulated himself for having finally arrived at this fateful moment. It had not been easy, but the project would surely go down as his finest hour. Everything had fallen into place, and he was confident that his new assassin would come through and perform his final task without hesitation. The man was already a cold-blooded killer. After undergoing the necessary "remodeling" and reconditioning, the Brit was now under Yassasin's total control. The fool would do anything for him.

Yassasin almost allowed himself a smile. It was all going to happen in a few minutes, and agent 007 would take the blame. History would be made today, and Nadir Yassasin, the Union's most accomplished strategist, would have a part in it. Yet, if all went according to plan, no one would ever know that he had even been in the room. Today, he was "Said Arif," a Moroccan representative from a United States agency. He would leave the Rock under the same alias. It was sad, Yassasin thought, not to be remembered as he deserved for his role in the day that Gibraltar was besieged.

Never mind, he thought. His reward was that he had planned the entire operation, and that it was going to succeed.

Jimmy Powers glanced for the fifth time at the *Gibraltar Chronicle* sitting on the table beside him. The headline screamed, "PM TO MEET ESPADA TODAY," beneath which was a picture of the Spaniard, standing at a podium with a painting of Franco behind him. His fist was raised and he was shouting to the throngs of people who would do anything he ordered. He certainly had something of Franco in him—not to mention the deadly charisma of a Hitler or a Mussolini. Another story on the front page announced, "Spanish Mob Gather at Border—UN to Mediate."

"Gather" . . . that was funny, Powers thought. "Ready to erupt" would be more accurate. There were a couple of thousand men, armed and dangerous, waiting for the signal to storm across the border between Spain and Gibraltar. The Gibraltar Regiment and the Gibraltar Services Police had lined up a battery of weapons and were more than willing and ready to take them on—but this was a question of numbers, not strength. With the reinforcements from the U.K. delayed, the "Rock" didn't have a chance. They had underestimated the power that Domingo Espada held over his people. More important, they also had no idea that the Union was behind the brilliant plan that would topple the British colony and make them look foolish. This was one time that history would not repeat itself. The most impenetrable fortress in the world was about to be assailed— from the *inside*.

Powers moved his right hand surreptitiously to his waistband and felt the Browning 9mm, waiting for the fateful moment when it would be called into play. According to the plan, he was not supposed to do anything unless something went wrong. If all went according to plan, then he would walk out of the Convent alive. If not, well . . . he would die killing as many people in the room as he could.

No one could detect the Spanish 9mm Super Star inside Margareta Piel's jacket pocket, for she was unusually adept at moving with grace and poise. After all, she was one of the most accomplished equestrians in Spain.

Margareta took stock of the room and what was about to happen in it. She was beginning to have doubts about the Union's choice of an assassin. If her suspicions were correct, then the entire operation was blown. She would have to do what she could to save her own skin and get out of the room alive.

Margareta scanned the others' faces and carefully considered who might be a threat when the shooting began. The Spanish Prime Minister and the other politicians from the U.K., America, Gibraltar, and other U.N. representatives posed no danger. The only additional woman in the room was an Arab, dressed traditionally in a caftan and a veil, which hid her face entirely except for a shadowy slit for her eyes. Margareta was confident that she wouldn't be any trouble either.

Margareta had to admire Espada, who at sixty-two looked more like fifty. He had made a fortune and won the hearts of the people during a three-decade bullfighting career. Now a businessman and politician, Espada was a staunch supporter of those who repeatedly called for Gibraltar, that "pebble in Spain's shoe," to be ceded back to his country. He hated the British. He had used his considerable power and influence in the Costa del Sol region of Andalucía to bring about what history would someday call a revolution. The government in Madrid didn't like it, but there was not much they could do because of his popularity. Many of his followers called him *El Padrino*—"Godfather." This was appropriate, for Domingo Espada was perhaps the most efficacious racketeer in the Mediterranean area.

Margareta turned her attention once again to the killer next to her.

Her lover. The incongruous Brit, sitting among the group of Spaniards at the table. He certainly *had* become a different man in the last three months. She studied his features, the broad shoulders, and his unbelievably relaxed demeanor. . . . The name "James Bond" fitted him nicely. It was blunt and masculine, just as he was.

But things were not as they seemed. What should she do? She *had* to speak to the assassin.

The gun was warm in the pocket near her breast. She squeezed her legs tightly, forcing waves of pleasure to jolt up through her spine and into her brain. The sudden stimulation brought her focus back to the task at hand.

She patted the warm metal in her pocket once more for inspiration, then prepared to make her move.

For his part, Domingo Espada looked upon the day's political meeting as a formality that must be suffered before the day's real business could begin.

So far everything had gone smoothly. The British PM and Governor were on the way. This would be a day long remembered in Spain's history. Screw the politicians in Madrid, he thought. Espada was satisfied that they were, quite simply, afraid of him. He had single-handedly amassed more support and power from the lower and middle classes than any other Spaniard in the twentieth century except Franco. It was only fitting that the millennium launch a new era of Spanish dominance in the Mediterranean.

Domingo Espada was quite prepared to die for his cause. Even if the plan failed, he would be happy to go down in history as the instigator of the Great Siege of the Millennium.

Today, Gibraltar. Tomorrow . . . ?

The man who had been identified by the Convent's security apparatus as James Bond was ready for the assignment at hand. He mentally checked his body to make sure that the Walther PPK was in place in his waistband. He was now itching to get the act over and done with.

For the hundredth time, the hired Union assassin went over the details of the plan. When the PM entered the room, the killer was first to take out the Double-O agent serving as the PM's bodyguard and then the Governor's bodyguard. The next target was the PM himself, who would die with a single bullet to the head. Before anyone else had time to react, the Governor of Gibraltar would be shot. By then, Espada, Agustin, and the woman would have sprung into action. They would draw their own weapons, kill any guards who might be in the room, and then hold the rest of the delegates hostage. The Spanish prime minister would be executed if he didn't agree to Espada's demands. Yassasin and Powers were to use their weapons only if something went wrong. Otherwise they would maintain their covers as diplomats, become "hostages," and eventually be released. Espada would declare himself the new Governor of Gibraltar, and the signal would go out for his men to storm the border and take over the colony.

It seemed easy enough. He knew he could handle it.

Finally, the door opened and the aide-de-camp stepped into the room. "The car has just arrived," he announced. "The prime minister and His Excellency are just entering the Convent now. They should be here any moment."

It was time. The Union members in the room shared a quick knowing glance as the captain stepped out and closed the door.

The man identified as James Bond gripped the gun at his waist and waited for the door to open again.

TERCIO DE VARAS

TWO

SUICIDE MISSION

As THE SUN HAD RISEN OVER NORTH AFRICA TWO WEEKS EARLIER, THE plaintive morning call to prayer had floated out over the rooftops of Casablanca. Mixing verses from the Koran and a traditional beckoning for religious Muslims to offer the first of five obligatory prayers to be performed each day, the melancholy voice was one of the few things that the people of Morocco's largest city could count on. While the new king and the government did their best to keep the population content, the country was suffering from vast unemployment and, as a result, crime. This was especially true in the larger cities such as Casablanca, Rabat, and Tangier. Casablanca, far from being the exotic and romantic locale for the famed Humphrey Bogart film, exhibited an odd conflict of traditional Moroccan culture with the trappings of a modern, metropolitan business center. The latter was winning, even though the city's poor and needy were evident on every corner. Wherever there was money to be made in the face of outright poverty, a criminal element naturally gestated.

Even so, the awe-inspiring Hassan II Mosque, towering over the city like a benevolent sentinel, served to remind the people that Morocco was well ahead of its Muslim neighbors in terms of economic stability and that all was right with the world. In a way, the mosque represented a blending of the modern Muslim world's idealism and its desire to exist on an equal basis alongside the West.

The ambitious leader of an organization that held its meetings not far away from the great monument shared this view.

As the religious faithful hurried to mosques and those who held honest jobs commuted to their places of employment before the early morning rush of business, the worst of Casablanca's criminal element were also preparing for the new day. Several very different businessmen and women gathered to begin their day's work in a high-tech conference room decorated in reflective sheet metal. It was not an ordinary meeting room in that it was located two hundred feet below street level, beneath the old Central Market, which ran the length of a city block along Rue Allal ben Abdallah. The room was part of an immense, private, underground complex that extended northwest nearly a mile from the Market to the old *medina,* the centuries-old section of town that consisted of narrow, winding passageways where shopkeepers sold produce, arts and crafts, clothing, and souvenirs.

The complex had been built in the mid-nineties by a consortium represented by a powerful Arabic law firm. As most of the construction was below ground, very few Casablancans knew of its existence. In fact, the only two entrances to the complex were well hidden behind seemingly innocent stalls in the market and *medina.* A loading lift was also located in the market behind what appeared to be a rubbish skip. Much of the vast structure was empty. Workers inhabited perhaps a fifth of it, while supplies and weapons occupied another fifth.

The consortium that owned the property was made up of three banking firms—one located in Morocco, another in Switzerland, and one in Monaco. An offshore oil corporation with assets all over the Mediterranean and in North Africa was also a major shareholder in the property. Silent partners based in the Middle East and France were involved. Mostly, though, the funding came from a private individual who was now calling a meeting to order in the darkened, chilly·steel chamber that was the conference room for the international criminal organization known as the Union.

"Are we all here?" *Le Gérant* asked.

The others casually spoke in the affirmative. As usual, *Le Gérant* was sitting in shadow, wearing dark glasses. Today he wore an Armani suit that fitted snugly over his rather large frame. This meant that today's meeting would be strictly business. *Le Gérant* would stick to a memorized agenda, keep things moving along briskly, and discuss the all-important money issues.

Sometimes he wore a traditional *jellaba,* a gownlike garment with a hood. Although no one could pinpoint exactly why, the meetings were always different when *Le Gérant* dressed in Moroccan clothing. His considerable charismatic powers were somehow more intense when he embraced his mother's ancestral Berber culture. Those in his presence felt an elusive aura of self-confidence and enlightenment, and this had a significant effect on his powers of persuasion and leadership. Meetings became lessons in philosophy or Union ideology, and money was never discussed. One *commandant* had said that *Le Gérant* became more "mystical" when he wore the *jellaba.*

Le Gérant never used or took notes. Everything was in his head. Always. He pulled sophisticated facts and figures from the air. He never needed to be reminded of anything. Anyone who had the privilege of meeting him always came away impressed by his profound intellect.

He was usually fair and generous with the Union's profits. The other people in the room, the *cercle fermé,* were all millionaires thanks to their work for the Union. Each man or woman was a *commandant* responsible for a geographical area somewhere in the world, and employed anywhere from fifty to several hundred people, depending on the needs of the district. It took a lot of money to keep several hundred people happy and the Union was able to provide stability. That kept the *commandants* loyal.

Fear was also a major factor in keeping the *cercle fermé* faithful to *Le Gérant.* If for any reason he believed that someone had cheated him or attempted to do something behind his back, he became furious. He could extract a confession easily and punishment was, as a matter of course, swift and merciless. *Commandant* Jimmy Powers had seen a man's throat cut in this very room.

The twenty-six *commandants* were required to take notes and be prepared with any documentation *Le Gérant* might require. Their leader was very strict, even compulsive, about the appearance of everything. He insisted on cleanliness and order. He dictated what kind of pens and paper would be used in the conference room, and what coffee was served and in which cups. He liked everything to be in its place. A desk light was essential at every station at the table, because *Le Gérant* kept the room so dark. The *commandants,* although they were used to them, never liked these policies and wished *Le Gérant* would change them. Why should they matter to him?

After all, *Le Gérant* was blind.

A servant entered the room with a tray full of tall glasses filled with hot mint tea. A Moroccan tradition, the tea was served with mint leaves floating in the narrow glass, and each person had the option of adding sugar or not. It was yet another part of the ritual *Le Gérant* insisted upon.

Jimmy Powers disliked mint tea intensely. It was something he put up with, though, for he had to admit that the Union had brought him more wealth and interesting things to do than the founding Union boss, Taylor Harris, could ever have hoped to offer. He had been wise to stick with *Le Gérant* after Harris was killed in Oregon. The original Union broke up after that, but *Le Gérant's* reformed Union rose from the ashes. While the original Union made a show of being an organization of mercenaries willing to perform any paramilitary task for the right price, *Le Gérant* transformed the group into something far more serious. Once *Le Gérant* had outlined what the new Union could do for him, Jimmy Powers turned coat as well and left America for Morocco. He had been there for three years, acting as one of *Le Gérant's* most trusted *commandants*.

Julius Wilcox, the other American charter member, was the ugliest and meanest-looking *commandant* at the table. He had a particularly gruesome scar above his right eye, a hawk nose, and greasy, slicked-back gray hair. He was, perhaps, the Union's most accomplished executioner. He, too, was happy that he was working for *Le Gérant* rather than the temperamental Taylor Harris.

Powers scanned the faces of the other *commandants*. He had never made a point of getting to know any of them personally—it was against the rules. He did, however, know who each of them was and which districts each controlled.

One of the men who intrigued him was Nadir Yassasin, a black Muslim from Morocco . . . or perhaps Mauritania . . . he wasn't sure. Yassasin was known as the Union's "strategist." If anyone could be called *Le Gérant*'s right-hand man, it was he. Powers had been promised that he and Yassasin would work together very soon.

The other *commandants* were from other areas of the globe—Great Britain, France, Spain, Belgium, Germany, Russia, Israel, Argentina, Taiwan, Japan, Australia, Sudan, Lebanon, Syria, Egypt, Libya, Algeria, and the United States. Collectively, they controlled thousands of Union members worldwide. In the six short years of its existence, the Union had grown into a powerful, deadly force that kept Interpol, the CIA and FBI, MI5 and MI6, Mossad, and other law enforcement agencies on alert for any information pertaining to the capture of Union leaders. The organization's accomplishments were impressive. The Union were responsible for several audacious terrorist attacks, political upheavals, high-profile blackmail and extortion cases, murders-for-hire, drug smuggling, prostitution, and arms dealing. The only major failure had occurred within the last two months: the one involving the disastrous Skin 17 project. Powers knew that this had been a thorn in *Le Gérant*'s side since that fateful day in the Himalayas.

As green and black olives were served with the tea, *Le Gérant* decided it was time to begin. He spoke in English, with a French accent.

"I am happy to report that several of our latest ventures have been successful. Thanks to people working day and night in our communications department, we have penetrated nearly every intelligence agency in the world. If we are not already inside them, then they are not worth bothering with."

The group applauded politely.

"Mr. Wilcox, could you please inform everyone of our financial status?"

Wilcox sat up and cleared his throat. "Yes, sir, here we are," he said, thumbing through his notes. "Total income for the last fiscal year was twelve billion dollars in U.S. funds."

The group applauded once more, this time a little more enthusiastically.

"The distribution of the money will occur by the end of this month," Wilcox continued. "You are all aware of your percentage. If you have any problems, see me."

"And recruitment?" *Le Gérant* asked.

"Up fifteen percent," Wilcox replied. "The payroll indicates that we now employ over ten thousand people worldwide. Like McDonald's, we'll soon have a Union franchise in every major city."

Some of the *commandants* laughed.

"Very good," *Le Gérant* said, obviously pleased. It couldn't be said that he didn't have a sense of humor. "I believe our efforts to escalate the war in the former Yugoslavia were what put us back on track after the failure of the Skin 17 project. We have our strategist, Mr. Yassasin, to thank for that."

Again, there was applause. Yassasin merely nodded. He was always given the most "impossible" jobs and always managed to pull them off with finesse. Besides being an expert in computers, electronics, physics, and disguise, Yassasin was a master planner. Like a chess champion, he could predict every possible move and countermove in any job he undertook.

"Which brings us to new business," *Le Gérant* said, shifting the tone of his voice to something more akin to that of a disapproving parent. "The Skin 17 failure cost us much more than the money we invested in it and the lives of the operatives we lost. We had promised to sell the formula to the Chinese. Not making good on that promise left us with bad credit in the Far East. All of the markets in Asia have dried up, and we're having difficulties keeping up our operations there. This is seriously affecting our business, not only in the Far East, but everywhere. When the word got out that the Union slipped up on a major job, it made our clients less enthusiastic about working with us. It damaged our image and reputation. We must work on repairing that damage."

Le Gérant finished his mint tea, then paused to light a cigarette. He never once moved his head as he performed these simple tasks with his hands. His sense of touch was highly amplified to compensate for his lack of sight. Some *commandants* believed that all of his other senses overcompensated for his disability. It was said that *Le Gérant* could hear a mouse flitting about in a room on the other side of the complex and that he could *smell* whether a person was telling the truth or not.

"As you no doubt know, a famous ex-matador in Spain is stirring up trouble with the British. Has everyone seen the latest news? Domingo Espada is very busy with his little revolution that he's organising just north of us. Now, I'll be quite open here, and I trust that nothing I say will leave this room. Domingo Espada, the head of a considerably successful Spanish mafia, refused to join the Union when we first invited him. He has considerable influence in areas we would like to penetrate, such as South America. Ladies and gentlemen, Señor Espada has come back to the Union and offered us an intriguing project for which he will pay a considerable amount of money. Aside from the monetary considerations, Espada has agreed to help the Union access those areas in which we have no influence. His personal organization controls them now.

"Of even more interest to us is the fact that Great Britain is the target of Señor Espada's proposal. Espada has had long-standing issues with the U.K. for political reasons. As you all know, the failure of the Skin 17 project was largely due to the interference by Britain's MI6. Their SIS and Ministry of Defence made fools of us, and I do not take kindly to that."

Jimmy Powers shot a glance at the *commandant* for the district that included Great Britain. The man shifted uncomfortably in his seat.

"One agent in particular," *Le Gérant* continued, "a Double-O, was the man most responsible for the project's failure. Therefore, Espada's proposal is of great interest to me because it may give us the perfect opportunity to exact revenge for Britain's unforgivable meddling in our business. I would like to see this British agent suffer the tortures of the damned for as long as possible, then die a humiliating death that will make world headlines."

Le Gérant paused, taking a couple of drags from his cigarette before extinguishing it in the ashtray in front of him. He knew exactly where it was sitting without feeling for it.

"Espada's plan is really quite insane. It's a suicide mission. When I first heard about it, I told him quite frankly that no one would walk away from it alive. He said that he was willing to die for the cause. But, if we can pull off his proposal, the Union will be the most powerful criminal network in the world. We will be able to demand any price from any country for the merest threat. The name 'the Union' will be so feared that we will have more influence on the world's economy than the New York Stock Exchange. Therefore, I have decided that Señor Espada's suicidal project is worth attempting. And *we,* my friends, *will* walk away from it alive.

"What I would like to do," *Le Gérant* continued, "is to kill two birds with one stone. We will agree to help Espada, for the money, of course, but at the same time, we will exact revenge on Great Britain. When it is revealed that the Union was behind the catastrophe that Espada wants to instigate, the entire world will bow to us. It will solidify our place in history."

"How do you plan to do this?" Powers asked.

Le Gérant smiled and said, "I detect excitement in your voice, Mr. Powers. Is this something you'd like to work on?"

"I'll do whatever you want, *Gérant.*"

"Fine. I've asked our strategist to come up with a plan. And I'd like you to serve as his eyes and ears, since you're so good at that sort of thing."

A chance to work with Yassasin! Powers was pleased.

Le Gérant turned to Yassasin. "Would you like to tell us about it, Nadir?"

Yassasin leaned forward so that the desk lamp cast an eerie light on his face.

"The plan is already in progress," he said. "In fact, it began shortly after the collapse of the Skin 17 project."

The others sat up, alert, waiting to hear what the strategist had to say. Everyone was thrilled that they were about to participate in another Nadir Yassasin project. He was the most respected man in the room, other than *Le Gérant.*

"One of Domingo Espada's closest colleagues and confidantes is a woman named Margareta Piel. We need her help, so we have offered her membership in the Union. She works for Domingo Espada in many capacities and lives at his private ranch in Spain. She is well known in Spain as an equestrian instructor and performer, but she has quite a dark side. She's a vicious homicidal maniac. Her skills at stealth, theft, breaking and entering, seduction, and murder are top quality," Yassasin continued. "Her nickname is *Mantis Religiosa,* or 'Praying Mantis,' because it is rumored that she disposes of her lovers after she has had her way with them."

"My kind of gal," Julius Wilcox said. There were some chuckles, but *Le Gérant* abruptly snapped, "Silence!"

After a pause, Yassasin continued. "She will be an integral part of the plan. Whether or not she turns against Espada remains to be seen, but I think she is enticed by the financial possibilities of being a member of the Union.

"I have also enlisted one of our top mercenaries; he had been working for us in Africa. He's Welsh, a man by the name of Peredur Glyn. He was a former football hooligan who was convicted of murder a few years ago. The Union helped him escape from prison in the U.K. and he has lived underground ever since, working for us. He's in excellent physical shape and he's a formidable killer. Most important, he possesses the necessary physical attributes that will suit our plan perfectly."

"Has he agreed to the fee?" *Le Gérant* asked.

"He has agreed to the payment of a half-million U.S. dollars," Yassasin confirmed. "Besides, he feels that he owes us a service for helping him get out of prison."

"Good. Tell us about the remodeling and reconditioning."

"Glyn went through the remodeling well over a month ago, and it was more successful than I had hoped it would be. He is now currently undergoing reconditioning and training." Yassasin smiled. "We won't have a problem with him. He is a very gullible man. Very susceptible to our techniques. Not very bright, but eager to please. In two weeks' time, Glyn will be ready. Everything is in place for the plan to proceed. We will be on a very strict schedule."

"Very well," *Le Gérant* said. He looked at the *commandant* for Great Britain. "What is the latest on attempts to replant an operative inside SIS? It was unfortunate what happened to that girl at MI6 . . . what was her name?"

"Marksbury," the man answered. "Forget her, she was insignificant. We are still working on replacing her. These things take time."

"Perhaps you need to step up your efforts," *Le Gérant* suggested with the slightest hint of menace in his voice.

The *commandant* swallowed hard and continued. "But, *Gérant,* with all due respect, you are aware that our primary operative in the U.K. has been in place for two years and continues to provide us with valuable information on MI6 personnel."

Yassasin spoke up. "And this operative will continue to play a part in our plan," he said, cutting through the tension with equanimity. "As you know, the information that was furnished to us was the catalyst for the scheme. When we learned that our target was on an extended medical leave since the events in the Himalayas, we felt that the opportunity was too good to pass up. He is still currently off duty and therefore extremely vulnerable."

Le Gérant nodded. "Will the *commandants* in charge of the British, Spanish, and North African districts meet me in precisely one hour in my office. We must commend Mister Yassasin, for he has come up with a truly ingenious and highly imaginative plan, albeit a risky one, to exact revenge on Great Britain, as well as eliminate the Union's number-one enemy—James Bond of Her Majesty's Secret Service."

THREE

FORTUNE COOKIE

MEETING YOUR DOUBLE MEANS CERTAIN DEATH.

James Bond blinked and read the fortune again.

Odd, he thought. He had never seen such a downbeat fortune cookie in a commercial Chinese restaurant before. That, on top of the havoc raised by the crying toddler who had just been in the restaurant with his rude and demanding father, had brought back Bond's headache.

"Harvey!" he called. The fat Chinese man wearing a messy apron stuck his head out of the swing door that led to the kitchen.

"What now? You not full yet?" he asked in his unintentionally belligerent way. Bond had known Harvey Lo long enough to know that he was never *really* perturbed by his customers. It just seemed that way.

"Come here," Bond said, motioning him over. Harvey looked over his shoulder. "Read this."

"It fortune."

"I know it's a fortune. Read it."

Harvey took the little piece of paper and squinted, reading and whispering to himself. He furrowed his brow. "This not our fortune," he said.

"What do you mean?"

"I never see this fortune before. I know all the fortunes. There are twenty-five fortunes, all the same, all mixed up in cookies. This not one of them."

Bond retrieved the slip of paper. "I think I'll keep it as a souvenir, Harvey," he said. "Maybe it's a lucky fortune."

"Does not sound lucky to me. Sorry about that, Mr. Bond."

"Not a problem." Bond dug into his trousers and found a ten-pound note. "Keep the change."

"Thank you, thank you." Harvey beamed. The only time he smiled was when he was paid. "How was food? You like?"

"Same as always, Harvey. Not quite spicy enough." Bond had ordered shrimp and cashews, Szechuan style, with a bowl of hot and sour soup. "When I say I want it so hot I can't eat it, I mean it."

Harvey laughed boisterously. "Aw, you not serious, Mr. Bond. Remember that time I made it so hot? You really could not eat it!"

"That was because it was burnt, not spicy. You overcooked the vegetables and they came out black!"

"Okay, next time, I make it good and spicy. I make tears in your eyes, you will like."

Before leaving, Bond took a small pill case out of his pocket and swallowed two of the white tablets that Sir James Molony's colleague had prescribed for him. The headache was becoming worse, and he was damned if the pills had any effect.

Bond got up and left the cozy neighborhood place tucked away in an alley off the King's Road, just down a flight of stairs. The Ho Ho Lo Restaurant was marked on the street only by a posted menu. It mostly did a takeaway business, but Harvey provided three tables for eat-in customers. As it was a ten-minute walk from his flat, Bond had become a regular over the years when he was home alone during the week. But he had never seen a fortune like the one he had just received.

Bond got to the street and glanced at his Rolex. It was just after 1:00. Should he take a walk farther into Chelsea and browse through a sports shop he knew, or should he go back to the flat and start the day's drinking?

Damn it all, he thought. He was bored to death. He hated being between assignments, and he especially despised medical leave. It was particularly frustrating because he hadn't had a decent mission since the Skin 17 affair two months ago. M had ordered him off the duty list for a minimum of three months because of the injuries he had sustained in the Himalayas. Bond believed that she was actually using that as an excuse to punish him for the indiscretion with his personal assistant, Helena Marksbury.

Although he had initially suppressed his feelings for Helena, her death had begun to weigh heavily on his mind. He desperately wanted to track down the Union members who were responsible for blackmailing and terrorizing her.

Naturally, he blamed himself—mostly for not recognizing the warning signs.

M had sent him away for two weeks' holiday, so he had gone to his winter home in Jamaica, the house he called Shamelady. There, he had gone on a binge, drinking himself into a solitary oblivion, brooding and staring at the calm, blue Caribbean. Things grew worse. By the time he got back to London, he was a mess. He felt terrible, had no energy, and was still physically sore from the ordeal in Nepal. That was when he went to see Sir James, the neurologist who acted as a consultant to SIS, to ask about the incessant headaches that he had been experiencing since the end of his last mission.

Bond began to walk up the King's Road, thinking back to M's admonishment after she had seen the way he looked.

"You're in no condition to take this matter into your own hands, Double-O Seven," she had said. "I wouldn't allow it even if you were. You're too emotionally involved in the case. Scotland Yard is handling it as a murder, and until they find the culprits, then there's not a lot that SIS can do about it. Our own antiterrorist teams are working on locating the Union members and their headquarters."

Bond had protested, arguing that he owed it to Helena to find her killers. He wanted to go after the Union himself. M wouldn't hear any more and ordered him off duty "until further notice."

"Besides," she had added, almost as an afterthought, "I expect my people to be in top physical shape. And you're nowhere near that."

Now he was doubly anxious to get back into action. It was the

only thing that could shake him out of the malaise . . . the depression
. . . that he felt himself drowning in. It happened to him every once
in a great while. Bond had seriously slipped off the deep end once,
after the murder of his wife, Tracy. The previous M had been forced
to send his top agent for psychiatric evaluation and then off to Japan
on a mission in the hopes that Bond would pull himself out of the
well of despair he had fallen into.

If only he *felt* better. The damned headache had crept up on him
and was now excruciating. The events in the Himalayas had certainly
taken their toll on him. Besides the fatigue, which never seemed to
improve, he suffered from various aches and pains. Worst of all were
the frequent headaches, which tended to begin midday and continue
well into the night. His sleep patterns were disturbed, he had fitful
dreams, felt bouts of inexplicable anxiety, and had taken to drinking
more. He also felt unusually paranoid for the first time in his life.
Ever since returning from Nepal, Bond had sensed that he was being
watched, although he had used every trick in the book to determine
if that was true. So far he hadn't been able to substantiate his suspicion and he was afraid he was imagining things.

The most alarming event was the blackout incident that had
occurred while he had been recuperating in Jamaica. He had been
about to take a leisurely swim in the private cove behind Shamelady,
when he suddenly felt disoriented. His heart had begun to pound
mercilessly and a blanket of dread enveloped him. For a moment he
thought he was having a heart attack. He had stumbled back to the
shore and had collapsed onto the sand. The next thing he knew,
Ramsey, his Jamaican housekeeper and cook, was shaking him.

At that point, Bond had known there was something seriously
wrong with him. He had immediately made arrangements to return
to London and see Sir James.

Bond approached Royal Avenue and sat heavily on a bench, staring
at the street, watching the buses, taxis, and people go by. Bond felt
removed from the scene, almost as if he were floating out-of-body. It
was an unfamiliar, disconcerting sensation.

Should he go back to the doctor? Sir James was still away on some kind of tour, so he would have to see Sir James's colleague, Dr. Feare, again.

Bond remembered the appointment with the neurologist a month ago. When he had arrived at Molony's office on Harley Street, he was surprised to find that Molony was on an extended, worldwide lecture tour as a guest neurologist. Miss Reilly, the unpleasant, middle-aged woman who served as the clinic's nurse, informed Bond that he would have to see Molony's relatively new assistant, who had intro-duced herself as Dr. Kimberley Feare. Bond was taken aback, for Dr. Feare was petite, blond, and extremely attractive.

"How long have you worked for Dr. Molony?" he had asked.

"Not long. I was lucky to get the job. Sir James is probably the best neurologist in the world. He's in India at the moment, and he's working his way west toward Africa," she said in a girlish, playful voice. Bond liked her immediately. "Now, what can I do for you, Mr. Bond? I understand your file is classified. You're with SIS, am I right?"

"That's right."

"Then the only other person outside this office who shall see my report will be your chief," she said, making a note in the folder. "As you know, we're very careful about confidentiality with government civil servants."

Bond went through the examination, X rays, an EEG, and returned a day later for a CAT scan. After he had described his various Himalayan injuries to Dr. Feare, she suspected that he might have some damage to his skull. At one point during the expedition up the third tallest moun-tain in the world, Bond had been hit on the head and knocked uncon-scious. Exacerbated by the oxygen deprivation at high altitude, the injury could be the cause of the headaches; there might be a blood clot, a crack in the skull, or any number of ailments associated with a blow to the head. The tests came back with somewhat alarming news. The EEC had picked up a lesion on the temporal lobe of Bond's brain. Dr. Feare was of the opinion that it wasn't terribly serious, but the blackout in Jamaica was probably a result of "post-traumatic epilepsy." Although it was a rare condition, it wasn't extraordinary. It was possible, however, that it could occur again without warning.

"With this kind of thing, we could perform a little surgery and remove the lesion with a laser," she had said. "But that's a last resort. I think we should first try to get rid of it with medication and rest. Pure and simple."

Dr. Feare gave Bond an additional diagnosis of "too much stress," and recommended to M that he take it easy—for at least three months. She had prescribed carbamazepine and painkillers and told him to take two tablets at lunchtime and two before bedtime. Dr. Feare warned him that if things hadn't improved in three months, surgery might be the next step. The worst thing about it was that he was forbidden to drive. He wasn't supposed to drink alcohol, either, but Bond ignored that directive.

Unfortunately, the pills didn't work at all. Bond had been struggling with the intense pain in the back of his head for months now, and it was driving him mad. There was only one thing to do—go back to see Dr. Feare.

Bond stood and continued the stroll toward the square lined with plane trees, where for many years he had owned a comfortable flat on the ground floor of a converted Regency house.

He was convinced that a mission was the only thing that could bring him back on track. It had always worked in the past. The only way he could put the demons to rest was to go after the Union and, if possible, destroy the entire organization. If M wouldn't put him on the assignment, then by God he would just have to do it himself. It wouldn't be the first time he had deliberately disobeyed orders. It would be for the good of SIS and Britain. The Union was the most evil menace to threaten international law and order since his old enemies, SPECTRE. Its members had to be smoked out and exterminated like pests.

But Bond knew that he was not in good shape, and it made him irate. He was well aware that the Union was out there, waiting for the right moment. Bond was probably the number-one man on their hit list after what he did to their organization in the Himalayas. He should be prepared for a surprise attack, and he wasn't. It could occur at any time. Bond knew that if he didn't do something about his vulnerability soon, he just might be spending his next holiday in the morgue.

Lost in thought, Bond ambled up the street, closer to his home, when he suddenly noticed a familiar woman walking toward him. She had shoulder-length golden hair, blue eyes, and shocking-pink lips. The woman looked past him and kept walking, but Bond was paralyzed with shock.

It was his dead wife, Tracy!

Bond closed his eyes tightly and opened them. He turned to watch her walk away from him, and then realized that it wasn't her after all. Of course it wasn't. How could it be?

Shaken by the experience, Bond continued his walk, but he felt his heart pounding. He was perspiring heavily, and it was not a warm day. What the hell was wrong? he asked himself.

He had imagined it. That was the only explanation. He chalked the hallucination up to his fatigue, stress, and the headaches. He had been thinking a lot about Helena, and that was probably the catalyst. Sure, that was it.

Best to get home and have a nap.

Bond increased his pace until he was a block away from his street. He was stopped at the intersection by a traffic light. He glanced at his wristwatch again: 1:33. He had taken twenty minutes to walk what normally took him five. He had better snap out of it!

While waiting for the light to change, Bond casually looked across King's Road to the other side of the street. A man was standing on the corner, staring right at him. He was tall, had dark hair, and . . . NO!

Bond suddenly felt dizzy and disoriented. His heart felt as if it was going to push itself through his chest. His mouth grew dry and he had trouble swallowing.

The man across the street was himself, or at least he looked like himself. He wasn't moving; he just stood staring right at Bond!

A bus passed by, momentarily blocking Bond's view of the opposite side of the street. When the bus had gone, Bond saw that there was now no one on the corner. Bond ran across the street, dodging traffic, and began to look for the man, but he didn't see anyone remotely resembling him.

His head was throbbing in pain and he felt sick.

Bond's mind flashed briefly on the fortune cookie from the Chinese restaurant.

Meeting your double means certain death.

His eyes were playing tricks on him, he told himself.

Bond stumbled as he attempted to cross back to his side of the street. A taxi almost hit him and the horn blared loudly. A very unpleasant, suffocating feeling of anxiety rushed over him and locked around his chest cavity. He gasped for breath, felt a sharp pain in the back of his head, and reached out for a phone box for support.

Instead, he crashed to the pavement.

When Bond opened his eyes, he was in his favorite armchair in the sitting room of his flat. The old-fashioned white and gold Cole wallpaper and deep red curtains gave him a feeling of serenity at first, but then he bolted upright in fright.

How the hell did I get here?

His hands were shaking now. He carefully stood and tested his balance. Nothing wrong there. The dizziness he had felt earlier was gone. He looked at his watch.

It was 2:47.

My God! He had lost over an hour!

Had he walked home and let himself in without remembering any of it? He had heard of people having these extended blackouts and not recalling anything that happened during the period of time they were "out of it." In actuality, these people carried on mechanically, often finding themselves in a different location from where they were when the blackout first occurred.

Bond immediately went to the cupboard, removed a bottle of Scotch, dropped two ice cubes into a glass, and filled it. He took a long, burning draught, then sat back in the armchair.

Now he knew something was really wrong with him. He had just had a second blackout and didn't have a clue what had happened in the interim.

FOUR

CHASING CLUES

BOND RECALLED HIS APPOINTMENTS WITH DR. FEARE. HE HAD ANSWERED ALL her questions negatively, including "Have you had any other fainting spells or perhaps hallucinations since the incident in Jamaica?"

At the time, his answers had been the truth. But now? He had experienced both in one day!

And what about the man he had seen on the street? Had the man really looked like him? Had he been a hallucination, like the woman who had resembled Tracy?

Bond was aware of the supernatural concepts of doubles, or *doppelgängers,* and that supposedly they were apparitions of living persons. Popular occult theory held that a double was a projection of an astral body. English and Irish folklore called the phenomenon a "fetch," and, as the fortune cookie warned, seeing one's fetch indeed meant that one was going to die. Legend had it that Shelley saw his double before his death by drowning.

But Bond never bothered with superstitions. There had to be another explanation.

Dr. Feare had told him to come back and see her if there were any change, especially if he began to have new symptoms or if the headaches got worse. Bond had to admit that both of these conditions were true.

Bond was very concerned, playing possible scenarios in his head. His mind raced frantically as he considered every alternative for the future and simultaneously attempted to calm down. But what if it was all in his mind and he was finally going mad after all these years of living on the edge?

Bond threw the glass of whiskey across the room. The glass shattered against the wall.

To hell with it! All he needed was an attitude adjustment.

He decided to go to the office and dig into Helena's case and track down the Union members who had recruited her in London. That should keep his mind focused. First, though, he would call Dr. Feare.

He paused a moment as he considered a positive aspect in having to go to the doctor again. Dr. Feare—Kimberley—was a gorgeous woman. Perhaps all he needed was some female companionship for a night. Since Helena's death, Bond had been celibate. Two months is a long time. His close friend in America, Felix Leiter, would have simply advised, "James, my boy, all you really need is to get laid."

He looked up her number and picked up the phone. When Miss Reilly answered, Bond asked to speak with the doctor personally.

"Dr. Feare is in surgery. You'll have to leave a message," the nurse snapped.

"Will she get it today?"

"I should think so."

"Fine. This is James Bond. I saw her a little over a month ago. I would like to see her again. It's rather urgent."

"Would you like to make an appointment? If so, I'll have to call you back."

"Please. As soon as possible." He left the phone number for his answering service.

Adhering to the no-driving rule, Bond took a taxi to SIS headquarters on the Thames and arrived at 3:30 in the afternoon. When he walked past the security officer and through the X ray, Bond suddenly realized that he must look terrible. He hadn't bothered to shave that morning, and his casual clothes—a Sea Island cotton shirt, navy trousers, and a light-gray jacket—were a bit wrinkled.

Bond ignored the guard's stare and went straight to the lift. He strode onto his floor and was grateful that no one was about. It was fortunate that the offices were rarely occupied, as Double-O agents were usually abroad, and the secretarial pool was very small.

Bond slipped into his small, uncluttered office, and sat at the desk. Two folders from Records were sitting on top of his "IN" tray. Bond took them and saw that they were an update on the investigation into Helena's murder and the latest file on the Union. The former hadn't been sealed, but it was hardly helpful. Everything had been turned over to the Metropolitan Police, who were in charge of the case. Bond noted the contact name at New Scotland Yard and picked up the phone.

"Howard," the man answered.

"Detective Inspector Howard?" Bond asked.

"Yes, who's calling?"

"This is James Bond at SIS."

"Oh yes, Commander Bond, how are you?" Detective Inspector Howard had met Bond while investigating the murder of M's friend, Alfred Hutchinson, a while back.

"Fine, thanks. I'd like to have a word with you. It's rather urgent. Are you free this afternoon?"

Howard paused to check his diary. "I could see you at five o'clock, but I'll only have fifteen minutes or so. Will that do?"

"That's fine, I'll see you then. Thank you."

Bond hung up and felt somewhat gratified that at least someone capable was on the case. Stuart Howard was a good man.

He turned his attention to the other folder, which was actually a thick binder containing a hard-copy collection of information, images, and the latest intelligence from SIS's Visual Library file on the Union.

There hadn't been much progress in unveiling the Union's mysteries since Bond first became involved in their cases. The report reiterated what he already knew: Taylor Michael Harris, an American militant in Portland, Oregon, created the Union circa 1993–1995. A self-professed white supremacist, Harris was arrested in 1993 for disturbing the peace during a rally that became violent and was run out of the state. He returned six months later with a large amount of capital, and with this money he founded the Union. Harris had apparently gone into business with unknown partners from the Middle East and North Africa.

He used specialist magazines to advertise for "mercenaries" to carry out dangerous jobs in Third World countries. Surprisingly, a great deal of men applied, looking for work as soldiers of fortune. After a six-month advertising campaign, it was estimated that nearly a thousand men had joined the organization. They trained at the Oregon facility, but no jobs were carried out before the FBI raided the place in December 1996 for illegal arms possession and distribution. Taylor Harris had been gunned down, gangland-style, in a Portland restaurant a month earlier, believed to be murdered by his own lieutenants. These three men, Samuel Anderson, James Powers, and Julius Wilcox, fled the country, and at least one of them was a suspect in the murder. The killer had paused in the restaurant long enough to slit Harris's throat from ear to ear: an act that became the Union trademark.

Harris's organization, however, lived on. Whether or not the three lieutenants were responsible for keeping it going, no one was certain.

It became a more sinister organization after publicly taking responsibility for several serious terrorist acts committed between 1997 and 1999. No longer merely a band of "soldiers of fortune," the Union became an international network of spies, killers, and militants. They were particularly adept at infiltrating intelligence organizations. The Union quickly became one of the most dangerous organized crime syndicates in the world, on a par with the Italian and Russian mafias, Chinese Triads, and SPECTRE. SIS had experienced a serious encounter with the Union within the last year, and Bond could attest to their loyalty, tenacity, and dangerousness.

Discovering the location of their headquarters was a top priority for SIS, the CIA, and other intelligence organizations. Recent reports from America indicated that the Union was probably located in North Africa, perhaps in Morocco or Algeria.

Bond did find something new in the folder. Interrogation of a Union member who had been arrested in France after a nasty bank bombing revealed that the Union's leader was someone they called *Le Gérant*. The prisoner claimed that no one knew whom he really was, not even the "commanders" who made up the "inner circle" of underlings. The Union was structured much like a mafia, with an executive boss, a number of immediate subordinates—the *cercle fermé*—and branches of groups and leaders extending from there. It was valuable information, but before any further interrogation could be performed, the prisoner had managed to hang himself in his cell.

Bond had a thought and picked up the phone. He quickly consulted his Rolodex and found Felix Leiter's number in the States. His longtime friend, formerly with the CIA, Pinkerton's, and the DEA, was now working as a freelance intelligence agent out of his home in Austin, Texas.

A woman with a lovely Spanish accent answered the phone. "Hello?"

"Manuela?" Manuela Montemayor was Leiter's live-in companion and a formidable FBI agent.

"Yes?"

"James Bond calling from London."

"James! How are you?"

"I'd be better if you were standing in front of me, but I'm fine. How are you and Felix?"

"We're great. It's so nice to hear your voice! Wait a second, I'll put Felix on." Bond heard their Dalmatian barking in the background and Manuela shushing him. After a moment, Bond recognized the easy drawl that he knew so well.

"James! How the hell are ya, my friend?"

"Hello, Felix. I'm fine. And you?"

"We're happier than pigs in slop. Hey, I increased the horsepower in my wheelchair so that it now goes seventeen miles an hour!" Leiter was referring to the Action Arrow power chair he had been using for the past couple of years since the deterioration of his leg muscles.

"That's impressive, Felix, but I hear the Texas highway patrol just loves to give speeding tickets."

Leiter laughed. "What's up? You coming to the States?"

"No, but this *is* a business call, I'm afraid. I need some information."

"Sure, how can I help?"

"The Union. I need everything you have on them."

Leiter whistled. "You and everyone else. Those guys are just gettin' to be too damned popular, you know what I mean? Why, are you havin' more trouble with 'em?"

"Something like that. I'd like to see if your government has any updated information about them—the suspected location of their HQ, leadership, the organization and . . . I'd be interested in any leads you can track down in the Portland area, where Taylor Harris was killed. Are there any Union members left there? Where did his three lieutenants go? What became of them?"

"Hold on, Manuela is just handing me a file," Leiter said. "You know about their leader? He has a French name. . . ."

"*Le Gérant.* I've just read about him."

Bond heard him turning pages. "The lieutenants. You talkin' about Samuel Anderson, James Powers, and Julius Wilcox?"

"Yes."

"Right. According to the file we have here, those three guys left the U.S.A. in 1996 and haven't been heard from since. But I'll see what I can do. I have a contact in Portland. I'll get the latest from Washington, too."

"Great, Felix. It's always a little slow-going for other intelligence agencies to share information. You know how it is."

"You bet I do. When do you need this stuff?"

"The sooner the better. Can you fax whatever you find to my office?"

"Sure thing. Give me two or three hours, is that all right?"

"That's better than all right. Thanks, Felix."

"Take care, James."

Bond hung up the phone and rubbed the back of his head. The headache was manageable now, but it was still a nuisance.

A blinking red light on the auxiliary telephone caught his

attention. This was the line he used for incoming messages, usually filtered through a number of security checkpoints. He picked up the receiver, punched in the code, and listened.

"Hello, Commander Bond, this is Deborah Reilly at Dr. Feare's office." Bond detected a distinct, punctilious *sniff*. "I've had a chat with the doctor. I'm afraid she can't see you today. She will be tied up for the rest of the day in surgery. This evening she will be attending a meeting at the hospital and will be having dinner at The Ivy with some colleagues at around eight o'clock. She asked me to tell you that if this is an emergency, I can page her, of course. Otherwise you can expect a call from her in the morning."

Snooty bitch, Bond thought, as he erased the message and set down the receiver. She must have thought that mentioning the doctor's plans to dine at a fashionable restaurant would elevate her feeling of self-importance.

Glancing at his "IN" tray again, he noticed the corner of a brown padded envelope beneath several sheets of interoffice memorandums. He pulled it out and saw that it was addressed to him, marked "Personal," and had been sent through the post. SIS had stamped it "Cleared by X Ray."

He tore it open, found a paperback book inside, and was shocked and puzzled by its title: *Helena's House of Pain*. It was a pornographic book, with a cover illustration showing a dominatrix spanking an "innocent" schoolgirl on the bare bottom. Inside the book was a sales receipt for £5.99 from a shop called "Adult News," with an address in Soho.

Scrawled in ink on the back were the words "She had it coming."

What kind of sick joke was this? Who would send this to him?

Once again, the all-too-familiar waves of nausea and dizziness enveloped him. Was he about to black out again? He felt a rush of warmth to his face and perspiration under his arms. He thought he was about to be sick. . . .

Bond gripped the side of his desk, shut his eyes, and willed the uncomfortable sensations away. Again, his heart was pounding in his chest and he felt suffocated by a blanket of anxiety.

"Are you all right, James?"

Bond opened his eyes and saw Bill Tanner, M's Chief-of-Staff, standing in the doorway. He was holding a stack of files and looked concerned.

Bond nodded grimly. "Just feeling a bit under the weather," he managed to say.

"Well, you look bloody awful," Tanner said, coming into the office. "Should you go to the infirmary?"

Bond shook his head. "I'll be all right in a minute. Just something . . . I ate, I think."

Tanner sat down in the chair on the other side of Bond's desk. "You're supposed to be on leave anyway, James. What are you doing here?"

"I can't stay away, Bill. If M isn't going to put me on the case, I'm doing it myself."

"I didn't hear you say that."

"The bloody Union is still out there, Helena's murder isn't solved, and I'm a bloody sitting duck here in London. I should be out there looking for them, Bill! I'm no good doing nothing. You know that. Isn't there anything you can say to M?"

"Actually, I've tried, James," Tanner said. "She's quite adamant about you staying away for a while. For one thing, you're on medical leave. You have to be cleared for duty. And she also feels that, and I'm afraid I agree with her, you wouldn't treat the case objectively. You're too close to it, James."

"But that's what makes me the best man for the job!" Bond spat, slamming his fist on the desk. "I'm beginning to know these people—the Union. You have to get close to them to understand them. Damn it, they want *me* as much as I want them! One has to be emotionally involved!"

"James," Tanner said gently. "Don't turn this into an obsession. You know the Union is a very high priority, but right now we have our hands full with the Gibraltar situation. You've heard what happened this morning?"

"No."

"Domingo Espada's supporters threw rocks and bottles at the Immigration officials at the La Linea border. There was gunfire. We don't know if anyone was hurt yet. It's becoming ugly. Espada's a menace."

Bond vaguely remembered reading the memorandum on Espada. He was a Spanish millionaire, a businessman with a political agenda. He had recently made a loud noise in southern Spain with renewed calls for the U.K. to give back Gibraltar. He was even at odds with the government in Madrid but apparently had an enormous amount of influence in the country.

"Go home," Tanner said. "You look terrible and obviously need some rest. Don't let M see you like this. Please. Do yourself a favor."

Bond shut his eyes again and took a deep breath, forcing the headache to subside a little. Finally, he nodded.

"Good," Tanner said. He got up. "Call if you need anything."

After the Chief-of-Staff had left the room, Bond slipped the Adult News receipt into his pocket, threw the book into a desk drawer, and made his way to the lift.

Bond rarely had a reason to visit New Scotland Yard, the imposing and unsightly twenty-story structure that seemed to be made of nothing but windows. Since MI6 dealt with cases outside the U.K., the Metropolitan Police at Scotland Yard or the people at MI5 usually handled crimes that were committed within the boundaries of Great Britain. Most of the time this jurisdiction was strictly enforced. Nevertheless, Bond had never paid much attention to protocol. If he needed information from one of SIS's sister organizations, he wasn't afraid to go and get it.

Bond took a taxi to 10 Broadway, not far from Westminster Abbey, and gave his credentials to the guard at reception.

"Detective Inspector Howard will see you now," the man said after calling upstairs.

Bond took the lift and was met at the floor by Stuart Howard, a medium-built man in his forties with a mass of curly brown and gray hair.

"Commander Bond," he said, offering his hand. He squinted when he saw 007's unkempt appearance.

"Hello, Inspector. Please excuse the way I look; I've been working round the clock."

"I hate it when that happens," Howard said, chuckling. "Come on down to my office."

They walked past a dozen secretaries, both male and female, and into a private office that was cluttered with files, papers, photographs, and faxes.

"It may look like a mess, but I assure you I know where everything is," Howard said. "Do sit down. Would you like some coffee?"

"That would be fine," Bond said. "Black, please."

"Right. Be back in a sec . . ."

Bond sat and rubbed his temples, glancing around the room for anything pertaining to Helena's case, but the only things that stood out were various unrelated gruesome crime scene photos tacked to the bulletin board.

Howard returned with the coffee and sat behind his desk. Bond took a sip and said, "You fellows must use the same coffee vendor as SIS."

"Well, it's not the gourmet stuff," Howard said, smiling. "Now, what can I do for you?"

"Helena Marksbury. I'd like you to tell me how the investigation is progressing."

Howard frowned.

"Please."

"Commander Bond, this is slightly irregular, wouldn't you say?"

Bond leaned forward. "Inspector Howard. Helena was my personal assistant. I had a nasty scrape with the Union a few weeks ago, as you know. I just want information. I'd like the peace of mind of knowing what is happening with the case. That's all."

Howard studied the disheveled man in front of him and, against his better judgment, said, "All right. I don't suppose there can be any harm in telling you what we know. It's confidential, of course."

"Of course."

Howard dug into a pile of folders on his desk and found the appropriate one. He opened it and scanned two or three pages quickly.

"I'm afraid we haven't got very far," he said. "Whoever killed her at that hotel in Brighton left no traces. No fingerprints. Nothing. The blue van that was seen outside the hotel was abandoned at Heathrow. It had been stolen."

"I suppose you've investigated her background?" Bond asked. "She had family in America."

"Yes, with the help of the FBI in California, we were able to locate them. No leads there, but we've arranged for their protection. We conducted interviews with Miss Marksbury's neighbors, people listed in her address book, and her landlord. No clues there either. . . ."

Bond held out his hand. "May I?"

Howard shrugged and handed the file to him. Bond scanned the typed pages of interviews. There were two or three girlfriends who all stated that Helena never mentioned anything unpleasant, and several neighbors and a building maintenance man who reported that they barely knew or rarely saw her. Bond stopped at the interview with the owner of her building in West Kensington. His name was Michael Clayton.

"You won't find anything there," Howard said. "The landlord seemed clean enough. He claimed he had never met his tenant. A superintendent looks after the building and an estate agent handled the lease."

"English?"

"I beg your pardon?"

"This Michael Clayton. Is he English?"

"Yes. Owns a number of residential buildings, a pub, and some bookshops in Soho."

This news shook Bond. "Bookshops?"

"Yes, what does he say down there near the bottom? About his business partner?"

Bond read further and found the passage Howard was referring to. Michael Clayton had a partner named Walter van Breeschooten. They owned the various properties jointly.

"His partner is Dutch?" Bond asked.

"That's right. Kind of a sleazy character, but we did a background check and he came up spotless. The bookshops are the adult variety. They sell pornography, you know, videos, magazines, books . . ."

Bond did his best to keep the excitement of this discovery to himself. Helena had told him before she died that the two men from the Union whom she had "dealt with" were English and Dutch. She had always spoken to one of them on the phone and had never met them until that fateful day in Brighton.

Bond closed the folder and gave it back to Howard.

"I'm sorry there isn't anything else, Commander Bond," Howard said. "We're doing our best."

"I understand. I am sorry to have troubled you."

"No trouble."

"Do me a favor, please, and keep me informed, would you?" Bond asked.

Howard nodded. "Certainly."

Bond got up, shook the inspector's hand, and left the building. Rather than going back to Chelsea, however, Bond grabbed a taxi and told the driver to take him to Soho.

FIVE

ESPADA

THE WOMAN WHISTLED SHARPLY SO THAT HER GLORIOUSLY WHITE Percheron stallion performed a neat *elevada,* a trick in which the horse rose high on its back legs. She gave him a gentle kick with her boots, and the horse leaped into the air, executing a flawless *cabriola,* one of the most impressive stunts the animal could do in front of an audience. The horse literally jumped up and kicked out with all four legs, suspended in midair for a moment. Its beautiful, sleek rider completed the picture by holding her hat high above her coal-black hair that was tied neatly in a bun.

When the horse was safely back on his hooves, Domingo Espada applauded from the other side of the bullring.

"Bravo," he called. "You got him to do it!"

Margareta Piel reached around and stroked the horse's neck. "I knew you could do it, my darling." She pulled the reins and the horse trotted back to the bullring entrance, where Espada was standing.

"You have your new star," she said. "I think he's ready for an audience."

"I think you're right," Espada said. He opened the large wooden door that led to the *pasillo,* the area beneath the seats that encircled the bullring. He then turned and watched with interest as Margareta, who had been riding sidesaddle, slid to the soft ground. Her

tight-fitting pants with a slit at the bottom, worn by female equestrians, were especially flattering of her firm, rounded buttocks and
muscular legs. She wasn't a tall woman, but she had a body that most
men would die for. Ironically, this was often the case. He had heard
stories that claimed she could be a cruel mistress in bed, although
he had never had the pleasure of finding out. Domingo Espada knew
better than to make love to the *Mantis Religiosa.*

Margareta flicked her wide-brimmed hat, which sailed neatly, like
a discus, onto the fence post. She then undid the bun, shook her
head, and let her long, straight hair fall around her shoulders.

"Has our guest arrived?" she asked.

"Not yet. I expect him soon. We should get back to the house."

"Let me take care of Sandro," she said, leading the horse toward
the second set of doors beneath the stands, to the stable in the expansive building that was part of Espada's estate. Besides having room for
a dozen horses, the annex, as it was called, also had facilities to stage
a modern bullfight. There was the regulation-size bullfighter's practice ring, which, oddly, Espada had covered with a roof after he had
retired from professional bullfighting, a bullpen, facilities for bullfighters and their teams, including a chapel and infirmary, and, in a
more remote section, a slaughterhouse.

Not far from the annex was a smaller house that was referred to as
the "compound." It was off-limits to anyone except Margareta and a
few other select employees, and trusted guests.

They left the annex and walked out into the bright Andalucían
sun. Domingo Espada's estate was ten miles north of Marbella, the
Costa del Sol's smartest, most expensive resort. Espada had built the
property in the hills just beyond Conch Mountain, which overlooked
the city and faced the Mediterranean. The rich and famous all came
to Marbella for holidays. Wealthy organized crime moved in as well.
A "Spanish Miami Beach" of sorts, Marbella became the crossroads
for smuggling in the Mediterranean area. Far too many drug and
arms dealers had been caught in Marbella, simply because they
couldn't resist the urge to flash their money.

Domingo Espada had never needed to do that, for everyone in

Spain knew who he was. He could probably get a free meal in any restaurant he walked into. Everyone knew the face of the bullfighter who had simply gone by the name "Espada" in the bullring. His portrait was usually featured on the walls of tapas bars and restaurants along with the photographs of Spain's other legendary matadors. He, too, was a national hero. But in Marbella they affectionately called him *El Padrino,* paying tribute to the efforts he had made to boost the area's economy. With the fortune he had earned as a matador for twenty years, Espada had invested wisely in several ventures, including tourism (in the form of casinos, hotels, and clubs) and had helped bring Marbella back from the decline in popularity it had suffered in the 1980s. He also owned and managed three bull-breeding ranches, acted as manager of several successful matadors, and had considerable influence in the world of bullfighting. The fact that he was often linked to organized crime did not lessen Domingo Espada's popularity.

Although he had aged considerably since his bullfighting days, Domingo Espada still cut a commanding figure. At exactly six feet, he exuded an authority and self-confidence that demanded attention. At sixty-two, he remained devilishly handsome, with dark wavy hair, now streaked with gray, and a bushy mustache that covered a sullen mouth. His chin was adorned with a short, pointed salt-and-pepper beard. Women virtually swooned when he stared at them with his piercing brown eyes that seemed to be both hot and cold at the same time. The twenty-two-year-old scar that extended from the outside edge of his left eyebrow to just over the cheekbone also served to give him a sinister, Mephisthophelean appearance.

His boots made crunching sounds on the tiny gravel as Espada and Margareta walked up the path to the magnificent ranch house he had built on the property. It overlooked a small artificial lake stocked with fish. Typically Spanish in its design, the house took additional elements from some of the more modern structures in Marbella, such as the palace built by the financier and arms broker Adnan Khashoggi. The main building consisted of a single level, but a unique guard tower rose four stories high so that sentries could spot approaching vehicles from miles away. The entire estate was over six hundred hectares in size, was surrounded by a high stone wall, and was protected by state-of-the-art security equipment.

The grounds contained an Olympic-sized swimming pool, a tennis court, a garage for several vehicles, and a putting green. Beyond the annex and the compound was an enclosed field, where dozens of *Bos Taurus Ibericus* roamed free. The beautiful black bulls, the special lineage that were bred for one purpose—to die in a *corrida*—lived a luxurious life eating the best food and mating with the best cows until the fateful day when they were chosen to meet their destiny. Sometimes Espada enjoyed walking in the field amongst the animals, admiring their power and pride. The bulls usually left him alone unless he came too close to the calves or made sudden moves. From birth, they attacked instinctively when they felt cornered or threatened, but in an open field they turned and walked away.

Espada and Margareta stepped onto the open patio, where a young female servant met them and asked what they wanted to drink. Espada looked at her and snapped harshly, "Where is Maria?"

The girl jumped at his bark and shyly said, "I don't know, sir. They asked me to fill in for her today."

"Is she ill?"

"I don't know, sir."

"Very well." He asked for a bottle of Barbadillo Solear, a sherrylike wine made in Sanlucar de Barrameda. The girl gave a subservient bow and went inside.

Agustin, Espada's loyal *mozo de espadas,* the title of a matador's dresser and keeper of the swords, now Espada's most trusted right-hand man, came out of the house to deliver a message.

"Where is Maria?" Espada asked him.

"She is gone, Domingo," Agustin said with a stern face. "She has escaped."

"Escaped?" Espada nearly choked with surprise. He looked at Margareta. She stared at Agustin and asked, "How could that be possible?"

"When we sent for her this afternoon, we learned that she had left with a man. One of the other girls told me."

"Who?"

"She didn't know him."

"Where is . . . who was guarding them? Where is Carlos?"

"Carlos was on guard all day. Would you like to speak with him?"

"Yes! Go and fetch him." Espada was trembling.

"Yes, sir," Agustin said. "By the way, your visitor has arrived," he said. "They're parking his car. Shall I bring him outside, sir?"

"Keep him waiting until after I talk to Carlos."

Agustin nodded and went inside.

Margareta had never seen Espada so upset over the disappearance of one of his girls. He refused to admit that several had escaped with his guests in the past, despite efforts to keep them in the compound. Margareta had been lobbying for tighter security measures. She had worked for Espada for a few years; her job was to train and look after his secret harem residing in the compound. She knew that he often obtained the girls from poor families in Spain and Morocco. After they spent some time learning their "trade," the girls were sent out to points abroad that were managed by Espada's organization. If they were lucky, they became high-class call girls and earned a lot of money. If not, some of them simply disappeared.

"She must have been a favorite," Margareta observed. "Was she particularly good at something?"

"Shut up," Espada said. "Maria was the freshest, most beautiful girl I've ever found. She was the best. So pure, so . . . tight . . . I cannot believe she would leave!"

"Why not? You *do* keep them prisoners. . . ."

"But they have a great life here . . . it's paradise . . . all the food and sun and . . ."

". . . *sex,* whether they want it or not," Margareta continued.

"Part of this is your fault!" Espada said.

"Oh, please, Domingo," she said. "I train them and patch them up after you get too rough with them, but I don't guard them."

Carlos, a large man in his late twenties, came out onto the patio. He appeared nervous, fingering the Beretta M92 that hung on his belt.

"You wanted to see me, sir?" he asked.

"Did you see Maria today?" Espada spat.

"No, sir."

"What time did you come on duty?"

"Eight o'clock this morning."

"And the girls were in their quarters all day and night?"

"Except for those with chores, sir. Maria wasn't scheduled to work until this afternoon," Carlos explained.

"You must have seen something."

"No, sir, I swear," Carlos said, shaking his head.

Espada looked at him hard. Agustin stood behind the guard, waiting for a signal from his boss. Espada glanced at his lieutenant and gave him the slightest of nods.

"Very well," Espada said to Carlos. "You may go."

"Thank you, sir," Carlos replied, then went inside.

"Agustin," Espada said. The lieutenant stopped. "Have him interrogated. In the meantime show our guest outside. I'd like you to join us, too."

"Yes, sir."

"Oh, Agustin?"

"Yes?"

"What are the enrollment figures for today?"

Agustin cleared his throat. "I've just checked on that. We're up to about one thousand four hundred."

"Only fourteen hundred men? We must do better than that!" Espada turned abruptly, holding his arms up in frustration.

"If we had a little more to spend on recruitment . . ." Agustin suggested.

Espada rubbed his chin a moment, then turned back to his friend and confidant. "All right. Call the accountant and tell him to release another three million *pesetas*. We have to reach our goal of two thousand five hundred men quickly."

"Yes, sir." Agustin went back inside as Espada and Margareta sat in comfortable lounge chairs with a view of the green, manicured lawn and the pool twenty meters away.

The servant girl brought the wine and poured glasses for the couple.

Margareta looked her up and down, admiring the girl's youth and wholesomeness. She was probably no more than fifteen. After she had left, Margareta said, "You sure know how to pick them, Domingo."

Espada held up his glass and said, "*Salud.* Yes, I certainly do. I've been picking them all my life. That one, she's from Granada. My men found her in a particularly poverty-stricken area. Her parents were quite happy to accept the money that was offered for her."

"And how has she worked out in the bedroom?" Margareta asked with a wicked smile.

"I haven't had the opportunity to try her out yet. I was still breaking in Maria," Espada said, twisting his mustache. "You're a fine teacher. So are the other girls. They all do whatever I want. Damn, that upsets me about Maria."

"Tell me, Domingo. What would the police say if they knew you were keeping sex slaves against their will?"

"Nonsense. I give these poor girls a wonderful life. They are treated like queens. They eat the best food, live in a nice home, and have access to the outside world through the miracle of television and video. A far better life than they had before."

"They also have to submit to you anytime you want."

Espada laughed and said, "You're jealous! You would like your own harem of young men, I think!"

"And tell me, Domingo. What do the police say when a body is washed up on the shore near Marbella? It happens, what, every other year or so?"

"You don't know what you're talking about."

"Oh, I don't, Domingo? Young girls, most of them unidentifiable, runaways, street kids . . . There's a steady stream of them being found up and down the Costa del Sol."

"You're imagining things. Besides, the local police turn a blind eye when they see me coming. I have them all in my pocket."

"There *is* a high turnover rate of your girls, Domingo."

"That's because they get jobs within my organization—as expensive call girls. There is no better training ground than here. They travel to exotic locations like South America or Mexico to work."

Margareta looked sideways at Espada. "Not all of them. Come on, Domingo. What do those girls have to do to incur so much wrath that you dispose of them in so . . . ignoble . . . a fashion?"

"Look who's talking." Espada wagged an accusatory finger at her, then shrugged. "That only happens when one of them disobeys me. It's not often."

Agustin returned with a tall, dark man in a suit and fez and said, "Señor Nadir Yassasin, sir."

Espada didn't get up, but instead motioned to the chair next to him. "Welcome, Nadir, sit down. Did you have a pleasant journey?"

Yassasin gave a slight bow and replied, "Yes, thank you, Señor Espada. It's a pleasure to be here."

"How are things in Casablanca?"

"The same. As you know, the *cercle fermé* met last week."

The servant girl returned and poured the wine for Yassasin, then left. The Arab pulled a thin cigar from his jacket. "Mind if I smoke?"

"Go ahead." Agustin leaned over with a lighter and lit the Arab's cigar. Yassasin held it pretentiously, close to his face with his hand bent, palm upward. Margareta thought this enhanced his stereotypical image as a mysterious North African spy. Agustin sat down and pulled his chair closer.

"Now," Yassasin said. "*Le Gérant* has given me instructions to thank you for your generous and impressive offer of five million dollars to the Union. The territories you control are profitable."

"It's my pleasure," Espada said. "However, I do hope that *Le Gérant* realizes the tremendous risks I take to keep operations going. South America and Mexico are still quite new and require a lot of payoffs. Law enforcement is particularly strong when one gets near America. The drugs are doing well, but I've lost several men. Some were arrested, others killed by the police. It's becoming more difficult."

"We can all appreciate that," Yassasin said. "It's time to discuss your proposal."

Espada brightened. "So *Le Gérant* has agreed to help me? Is he committing Union resources to my cause? I thought he said it was a 'suicide mission.' "

"He still believes that, but . . . that's where I come in."

"Oh?"

"*Le Gérant* has taken into consideration your generous offer, your enthusiasm, and the opportunity for the Union to even the score with an enemy. So, yes, the Union will become involved in the Gibraltar project."

"That's very good news." Espada lifted his glass and finished the wine.

"There are some conditions."

"What are they?"

"*Le Gérant* will supply the necessary manpower to accomplish your goals. The North African district will be employed, under my supervision. You will be in charge of the Spanish district, but you must follow a plan that I have formulated."

"You? What plan?"

"These are *Le Gérant's* specific instructions. We will go into the details after dinner. Suffice it to say that my plan will accomplish much more than the siege of Gibraltar. You want to be the first Spanish governor of Gibraltar in over two hundred years? The only way you will see that happen is if you follow my orders to the letter."

Espada's eyes narrowed. No one ever talked to him in this manner.

"Why should I?" he asked. "I could still do this without the Union."

"Domingo," Margareta said gently, putting a hand on his arm.

"That wouldn't be advisable," Yassasin said. "Turning your back on the Union after we've offered to help is not very . . . sporting. You should know that."

Espada grumbled, calming down. "I don't like taking orders from someone else. No offense, Nadir. I know you're supposed to be a brilliant planner, but I've always gone my own way."

"This is *Le Gérant's* condition. Take it or leave it. Why don't you hold off on your answer until you hear what the plan is. It is . . . risky . . . but very clever, if I do say so myself."

"All right. But before we eat, give me a hint. What happens? How does it end? I like to know the result before the setup."

Yassasin smiled and said, "When the operation is completed, Gibraltar will be the property of Spain. You will be the new governor. The British governor will be dead, along with the British Prime Minister."

"The Prime Minister? We're going to kill him?"

"That's part of *Le Gérant*'s revenge against the United Kingdom for their interference in our previous major project."

"Sounds dangerous . . ." Espada rubbed his chin and looked at Yassasin with doubt in his eyes. Then he grinned broadly. "I love it already! Yes! Let me hear what you have to say after dinner."

"Very well. The important thing now is for you to build up your group to intimidating proportions. One of our concerns is how the government in Madrid will react to your revolution. They may strike you down."

"They wouldn't dare. They may be putting up a good face with Britain over Gibraltar, but they want it back as much as I do. I think they'll let me get away with it."

"And if Great Britain declares war on Spain?"

Espada rubbed his hands with glee. "What could be more exciting? Two NATO powers going at it, *mano a mano!* What a way to start the new millennium!"

"You could be killed, Domingo," Margareta said.

Espada shrugged. "I have been prepared for that for a long time. I'm sixty-two years old. If I can make a difference in the history books . . . if I can take Gibraltar for just *one day* . . . then I will die fulfilled."

"I take it, then, you agree to the plan? I have full control?" Yassasin asked.

"Yes."

"Then I'm happy to tell you that the plan has already been put into effect, and in less than a week it will all be over. I am here to set up command central at your home, for it will all culminate here. My lieutenant is in Britain as we speak, keeping watch on things as they progress. His name is Jimmy Powers, an American."

"Command Central? Here? What the hell? What if I had said no?" Espada asked, incredulous.

"You don't want to ask that, Señor Espada."

Espada was silent a moment, then eyed Yassasin and said, "If I did not know you and have respect for your reputation, Nadir, I would have killed you just now. But I know enough about you to trust that you know what you're doing. *Le Gérant* must have a good deal of faith in this thing as well. All right, I agree. Let's hear your brilliant plan."

"After dinner," Margareta said, pulling on Espada's arm.

Much later, after a luxurious dinner and a tense two-hour meeting, Yassasin was put up in a guest room and Espada retired to his study. Espada liked time alone in this room, which also served as a library of sorts and a place in which he could display the many trophies, posters, and photographs from his bullfighting days. He also enjoyed putting on a costume, red-and-black traditional matador garb, the *traje de luces,* or "suit of lights"; although it wasn't the same one he had worn when he was younger. This one had been made especially for a man who had gained a bit of weight since that time, even though he was physically fit and in good shape. Agustin had laid the clothes on a long wooden table, each item in placed in the requisite order.

There was a knock at the door.

"Come in."

Agustin entered the room and saw that his boss was back in the past once again. He had pledged undying loyalty to Domingo Espada, but he did think that his benefactor lost touch with reality every now and then. Once a *torero* retired from the bullring, he was never supposed to put on the costume again. Not *Espada* . . . he could not let go of his past and still longed for the cries of *"Olé!"* and the exhilarating feeling of being carried out of the ring on the shoulders of his friends and relatives after a successful *corrida.*

Some nights, Agustin would find Espada alone in the study, dressed in the costume, standing and staring at the stuffed bull heads that were mounted on the walls as trophies. They were all missing at least one ear, signifying the reward Espada had received after the fight. One ear was cut off for a good fight, two ears for a better one, and both ears and the tail were for the best. Espada had collected more ears and tails than he could count. He had kept some of them, but most of the time he had thrown the trophies to fans in the audience—usually beautiful *señoritas* who he knew would accompany him to his hotel or villa for the night.

This evening, Espada stood in the center of the room, holding the *estoque,* the thin sword used to thrust into the bull's withers and through the vital organs for, hopefully, a quick kill. Espada extended the sword at one of the bull heads, his arm straight, concentrating, as if he were readying himself for the moment of truth.

"Domingo," Agustin said.

"Yes?"

"We got Carlos to confess. Roberto Rojo paid him five hundred thousand *pesetas* to help him free Maria. She has run off with Roberto."

"*Roberto?*" Espada cried. "How could he do this to me? That ungrateful . . . !"

"We will catch up with Roberto," Agustin said.

"Roberto is one of my star matadors! He and his brother have glorious futures ahead of them. Why would Roberto choose to ruin it by stealing this girl from me?"

"Carlos said that Roberto was in love with her."

"Damn him! He shall pay for this," Espada said, pacing the room.

"What about Carlos?"

"He must answer for his betrayal."

"In that case, the prisoner is ready."

"I'll be there in a minute."

Agustin nodded and left his friend and master alone with his memories . . . and his madness.

Domingo Espada entered the practice bullring and raised his hat to the throngs of people sitting in the stands. He could hear the tumultuous applause and cheers, he could see them saluting him, standing for him. . . .

None of them were really there, of course. But to Domingo Espada, it was all real. The empty stands projected the same amount of noise and excitement as if they had been packed full of spectators.

Agustin and two other men stood inside the 1.2-meter-high *barrera,* the fence that enclosed the working area of the ring, near the *burladero,* the "trick" shields built slightly out in front of the openings in the fence. Bullfighters stood behind these to escape the charging beast. Agustin approached Espada and handed him the brightly colored *capote,* the cape that was red on one side and yellow on the other—traditionally used in the first two acts of a bullfight.

Once Espada was ready, Agustin gave the signal to the man at the *puerta del toril,* the door out of which the bull would charge. It swung open, and for a moment there was silence. Espada waited patiently, the excitement and anticipation just as powerful as it had been in the old days.

Then the object of the *corrida* came out into the ring. He stumbled on two legs and appeared to be lost. Carlos, badly bruised from beatings, was wearing a dirty white shirt and black pants. In his hands was a pair of bull's horns, the kind used in training bullfighting beginners. Another person would "act" as the bull, charging the student so that he could practice with his cape.

Agustin announced loudly, as if he were projecting his voice so that the people in the very top seats could hear him, "Carlos Rodriguez, you have been found guilty of the crime of betraying your employer. Therefore, you must fight for your life in the bullring against the supreme matador, *Espada!*"

Carlos looked at Espada standing there in all his glory. The cape twirled with a flourish. Espada called to him as if he were a bull.

"*El toro!* Come!"

When Carlos realized what was about to happen to him, he turned to run back through the open doors, but they slammed shut in his face. He turned to face Espada, his eyes wide with fear. He backed up against the wooden doors, dropped the bull's horns on the ground, then fell to his knees.

"Please, Señor Espada, have mercy!" Carlos cried. "I beg you! I'm sorry!"

Espada ignored the man's pleas and simply waved the cape. "Come!"

After a minute, Espada saw that Carlos wasn't going to "play." He nodded to Agustin, who picked up a picador's lance, and walked toward the helpless man. As Carlos cowered on his knees, kissing the dirt, Agustin brutally thrust the lance into the man's back and withdrew it. The sharp point had been shortened so that it would not mortally wound the man, but merely cause him pain.

Carlos yelped in pain, then rolled over. Agustin spoke to him calmly, telling him that his fate would be far worse if he didn't get up and fight.

"Who knows," Agustin said. "If you show great courage and spirit, the matador may grant you an *indulto*." This meant that the bull's life would be spared. "Now get up and charge!"

Carlos finally realized that he had no other choice. He got up, gave a frightening war cry, and ran at Espada. The matador performed a neat *verónica* with the cape, sidestepping the man. But, unlike a bull, the human could not be fooled. He swung at Espada with his fists, ready to jump on his opponent and beat him to a pulp if he had to. Espada, though, was prepared for the attack. Using the cape to protect himself, he managed to keep the bleeding, angry man from connecting his punches.

The "fight" went on like this for several minutes. Carlos was obviously becoming tired as his lunges at Espada grew less inspired. Not one of his blows had connected. Espada eventually walked away from the man, who collapsed in the middle of the ring, out of breath. Blood soaked his clothes.

Espada took two *banderillas,* short spikes used in the second act of a bullfight to further weaken and enrage a bull, and calmly walked back toward his victim.

Carlos saw what Espada had in his hands and knew that he could do only one thing. He pulled himself to his feet and started to run away, toward the edge of the ring. But before he could make it behind a shield, one of Agustin's assistants pulled a switch located behind the fence.

All of the shields in the ring mechanically moved in a few feet until they were flush against the fence, blocking off any possible escape for the prisoner. All of the regular doors were shut tight.

The prisoner gathered every last bit of strength that he could muster, then charged at Espada, screaming.

Espada deftly thrust the two spikes neatly into Carlos's back as he sidestepped the charging prisoner. The man screamed and fell to the dirt. The spikes hung grotesquely out of his back. He reached around and managed to pull one out.

Espada walked away from him, approached Agustin, and took the *estoque* and *muleta,* the sword and smaller red cape used in the final act of a bullfight. He approached the cowering, wounded man.

"*El toro!* Come!"

He waved the cape, the deadly sword positioned behind it.

Carlos picked up the spike he had pulled out of his back and held it like a spear. He slowly got up and faced the matador. Then, cursing, he charged, the spike out in front ready to plunge into Espada's chest.

Like a dancer, the matador executed a smooth *pase de trinchera,* a low pass performed with the right hand. Carlos missed Espada entirely, falling to the dirt again.

Espada moved around to the man's front, then held the sword at arm's length.

Carlos, further enraged and desperate for the ordeal to be over, got to his feet and charged at Espada with the spike one last time.

The sword pierced Carlos's chest and went cleanly through his heart.

Domingo Espada had at least one more ear to add to his collection.

SIX

LIVE GIRLS, ETC.

LODGED BETWEEN THE BUSY THEATER DISTRICT TO THE SOUTH AND THE shops of Oxford Circus to the north, Soho was unusually quiet for a late weekday afternoon. The commuters had left and the theater crowds had not yet arrived. The streets were only moderately crowded with tourists and curiosity-seekers who were gawking at the sex shops, the "modeling studios," and the "Live Girls!" dives that pervaded the area. While it tended to come alive at night, in daylight Soho was undeniably seedy.

James Bond found the Adult News shop on Berwick Street and stood across the road to observe the building for a few minutes. Men of various types went in and out—mostly white middle-class businessmen in suits and ties—and Bond saw nothing unusual. It was a small, ground-floor establishment with a neon sign proclaiming that the shop sold "XXX Videos, Magazines, Books."

Bond perked up when a middle-aged woman in a business suit emerged from the shop and began to walk north toward Oxford Circus. He did a double take, for he could swear he knew her. Tall, rather severe. Not the type one would expect to see in an adult bookshop. Who was she? Damn! The headaches had clouded his normally photographic memory. Bond rubbed his eyes and looked again, but the figure had disappeared into the crowd.

He crossed the street going north in an attempt to catch sight of her again, but she was gone. She had slipped into a side street or got into a taxi. Had his eyes been playing tricks on him again?

Bond walked back to his position across from the bookshop and decided to make his move. He crossed the street and entered through the strings of beads hanging in the doorway. The shop was devoid of customers at the moment, and there was a large, obese man with greasy, stringy hair sitting behind the counter and watching a portable television. Bond pretended to browse at the skin magazines for a moment, then approached the counter.

"Excuse me, but is Mr. van Breeschooten here? He's the manager, isn't he?" he asked.

The big man eyed Bond without moving his head.

"Yes, he's the manager, and, no, he's not here."

"Can you tell me when he might be available?"

The man turned his head to look Bond up and down. Not many people asked for the manager.

"Are you a cop?"

"Of course not. I'm a salesman. I wanted to talk to him about a new line of videos my company is selling. Amateur stuff. Hard-core, of course. Very high quality."

"He's at the office. You'll find him there."

"Ah. Thank you. Might I have the address?"

"Down near Brewer Street." The man rattled off a number.

"Right," Bond said. "Many thanks." He turned to leave, then hesitated, as if he wanted to ask the man something but was too shy.

"Is there anything else?" the man asked.

"Uhm, yes, I couldn't help but notice that pretty woman who came out of here a few minutes ago. Does she come here often?"

Now the man really thought Bond was some kind of pervert. "I don't know who you're talking about. Lots of women come in here. Men with their wives, couples, lesbians, you name it . . ."

"Right," Bond said sheepishly. "Well, thanks." This time Bond hurried out of the place.

He walked south and found the office on the ground floor of a seedy-looking building. The upper floors presumably contained residential flats. A plaque on the door read: "Clayton Enterprises." Next to it was the residents' entrance to the building. An intercom and listing of the tenants with buzzer numbers was attached to the alcove. He scanned the list and found a "van Breeschooten" in number 302.

Bond knocked on the office door, but there was no answer. He tried the knob—it was unlocked. He went inside and found a cluttered room that smelled of stale coffee and cigarette smoke, but there was no one there. It contained a desk, computer, telephone, coffeemaker, and stacks of papers all over the place. The ashtray overflowed with cigarette butts. Behind the desk was another door that was ajar. Bond peered inside and saw that the rest of the ground floor had been gutted to make a storeroom for the boxes of products carried by van Breeschooten's shops. Two men were inside, packing videos into padded envelopes for posting. They both had Cockney accents, were heavily built types, and appeared to be in their thirties. They were probably strong-arms in van Breeschooten and Clayton's organization. He was surprised to see from the bulges at their waists that they were both armed.

". . . But then he said that the money would be bloody good, and it was!" one of them said.

"Last month's check was a nice surprise, I must admit," the other said.

"The company must be doing well. We'll get the details on the new job any day."

"If the money is as good as last time, I'm there!"

"Where is Walter, anyway?"

"Upstairs in the flat. Clayton is with him."

The first man snorted. "Couple of poofters, they are . . ."

Bond left them alone and turned his attention back to the cluttered office. The papers were invoices, packing slips, order forms, and the like. He opened a desk drawer and found an unsealed envelope from a travel agency addressed to Walter van Breeschooten. Bond looked inside and found airline tickets for both Clayton and van Breeschooten to fly from London to Tangier, Morocco, later that night.

Interesting, Bond thought. The Union's headquarters was believed to be in North Africa.

He replaced the tickets and envelope in the desk, gave the other drawers a cursory search, and decided there was nothing else of interest.

Bond slipped out of the office and tried the door to the residential part of the building. It was locked, so he pressed the button marked "Deliveries." After a moment, someone buzzed him in. The building's narrow stairwell smelled of garbage and dirty nappies. He could hear a baby crying in one of the flats above him. Bond quietly crept up to the first floor and listened at the landing. No one was about. He went up two more flights to the third and top floor. He could faintly hear the voices of two men talking behind the door of number 302, which was next to a window that opened out onto the fire escape.

Bond raised his left foot and pried off the heel of his field-issue shoe. Major Boothroyd had recently added an ingenious listening device to the equipment inside the shoes, which included a first-aid kit, escape tools, and other odds and ends that were neatly packed in the hollowed-out spaces. The device was a high-power UHF transceiver the size of a two-penny coin. A suction cup/microphone was attached to the side so that the device could stick to any surface. Bond licked the suction cup and placed it firmly on the door. He then pulled out the earpiece that was attached to a tension wire embedded within the device. With the earpiece lodged firmly in his ear he could hear the voices clearly.

". . . And the process will continue with the distribution of the latest payments. But the new project will bring in a lot of money. I think we'll do very well."

"I've heard that it's very risky."

"It is, what I know about it. They're keeping the details under wraps for now. You know as much as I do."

The first voice was Dutch, all right, so that must be van Breeschooten. The other voice was decidedly English. Michael Clayton.

The Dutchman sighed loudly and said, "I sure don't want to have to go back to Morocco again. I hate it there."

"I'm looking forward to it," the other man said. "It will be nice to get out of London for a change."

Bond waited, hoping that one of them would reveal something that might implicate them as Union members.

"Well, let's just hope that tonight goes as planned," van Breeschooten said. "Your cousin's news was encouraging."

"Yes. Everything is in place. We'll make the bloke wish he'd never been born."

"How come your cousin's always so cross?"

"I don't know," Clayton said. "Been that way forever."

A noise in the stairwell distracted Bond. He heard the front door open downstairs. Someone was on the ground floor and was beginning to ascend. Bond willed whoever it was to stop at one of the lower floors. He was determined to hear as much of the conversation as possible.

A Cockney voice boomed out from the stairwell, "Get your own bloody sandwich. I'm going upstairs. Back in a minute."

Damn! It was one of the storeroom workers. He was coming up here!

Bond listened intently to the two men inside the flat. Come on, he thought, say something about the Union. . . .

"Did I tell you what happened at the meeting three months ago?" van Breeschooten asked.

"A *commandant* was killed?"

The footsteps were growing louder. The man was at the first floor.

"Throat slit, ear to ear. Right in front of us."

"What did he do?"

"Cheated the company. The boss doesn't like that."

The ascending worker was at the second floor. In a few seconds he would appear and Bond would be trapped.

"The boss doesn't like a lot of things, from what I gather."

"He's quite a character," van Breeschooten said. "I admire him a great deal. You know he's given the orders to move the headquarters out of Casablanca."

"Where are they moving?"

"I don't know yet."

The Cockney was a few steps from the landing. Bond was ready to pull the listening device off the door when the Englishman in the flat said, "Do you think I'll really get to meet *Le Gérant* this trip?"

That was all Bond needed. He tugged the device off the door just as the Cockney thug appeared around the corner. He saw Bond and yelled, "You there! What are you doing?"

Not giving Bond time to explain, the man pulled out a .38 Special. Bond immediately went on the offensive and kicked his right leg out and up, sending the handgun flying. Unfortunately, it discharged a round when it hit the floor and the noise reverberated in the stairwell.

The thug swung at Bond, but 007 dodged the punch and delivered one of his own to the man's chin. Bond felt his knuckles burn as the man fell backward and crashed into the wall. The entire building seemed to shake. Bond didn't stop there. He lunged into the man, punching him twice in the stomach, then once more across the face. Blood splattered from the man's nose.

The noise attracted the attention of the tenants, several of whom opened their doors and peered out into the hall. Van Breeschooten and Clayton also looked out to see what was going on. Bond turned in time to catch a glimpse of both men, who were staring at him, wide-eyed and mouths agape. The taller of the two, probably van Breeschooten, was middle-aged, had white hair and blue eyes, and fair skin. Clayton also had a pale complexion, appeared to be a bit older, had brown hair streaked with gray, and brown eyes.

One of the other tenants yelled, "I'm calling the police!" and slammed the door.

The distraction gave the thug the time he needed to recover from Bond's attack. While his head was turned, the muscleman slammed his fist into Bond's face. The impact sent bolts of lightning into Bond's skull, and he fell to the floor but rolled just as the big man tried to kick him in the ribs. Bond managed to grab hold of the man's foot and twist it hard. The man yelped and lost his balance.

Bond jackknifed to his feet, spun on one leg, and kicked with the other, causing the man to fall into van Breeschooten's open doorway, knocking them all down as if they were bowling pins. Bond immediately ran for the stairs as a bullet whizzed past his head. The other man from the storeroom was below him, on the second landing, pointing a revolver at Bond.

"Don't move!" the man shouted.

Bond did the opposite, jumping back out of the line of sight, just in time to meet the first thug head-on. It was then that Bond realized how physically out-of-shape he really was. The man hit him hard, causing the corridor to spin. For a moment, Bond thought he was going to collapse, but he was able to steady himself on the edge of the stair railing. He was truly stunned.

Van Breeschooten shouted, "Don't kill him!"

The big man paid no attention. He lifted Bond by the shoulders and threw the limp body at the fire escape window. Bond crashed through the glass and fell onto the metal platform just outside the building, and he couldn't stop himself from rolling off it. He tumbled down the steel stairs, blindly reaching for the nearest solid object that could prevent him from falling three stories to his death. Luckily, it was the railing around the intermediary landing above the second floor fire escape.

Above him, the first thug leaned out of the broken window and fired his gun. Bond ducked and pressed himself against the glass. Bond drew his Walther PPK and returned fire, shooting through the holes of the third-floor fire escape landing.

He heard police sirens squealing in the distance and they were growing louder. He had to disappear, and quickly. He didn't dare risk going back into the building.

More gunfire zipped around his head and he heard Clayton and the Dutchman both shouting, "Don't shoot him! Let him go!"

Bond heard the men arguing above him but couldn't make out what they were saying. He looked around him and saw that the adjoining building was one story shorter than the one he was in. There was a gap of approximately ten feet. He wouldn't get much of a running start on the little fire escape platform. Nevertheless, Bond holstered his gun, carefully calculated the distance, and leaped.

He landed hard on the edge of the other roof, and it knocked the wind out of him. He held on, gasping for breath until he was able to suck in some air. He swung his legs up and over the side, fell to the roof, and lay there for a few seconds before peering over at the other building.

The men had disappeared from the third-floor fire escape. The police sirens were just moments away.

Bond got up and ran to the other side of the roof. It was another ten-foot gap to the next building. Now that he had more room, Bond performed a broad jump and this time landed on his feet. He kept going, looking for a way down. A metal-rung fire escape ladder extended from the roof to the pavement below.

Bond swung his body over the top of the ladder and began to descend, when he felt a sudden jolt in his chest and a searing pain knifed through his head. For a moment he thought he had been shot.

His heart pounded frantically and the world was spinning. Bond wasn't sure if he was standing up or falling. He thought he was going to die, right then and there.

Fight it! he commanded. Bond continued to descend, but in his state, he lost his footing on a rung. He slipped and attempted to catch the ladder, but instead he missed and slid down, crumpling with a slam onto the ground below.

In pain, Bond rolled over and sat up. His vision was blurred.

The wind was cool on his face. He reached up and rubbed his eyes and pressed the sides of his aching temples. As his eyesight returned, he could see a man and woman staring down at him. They appeared to be Japanese tourists. When they saw that he was stirring, they quickly ran away.

He had fallen into an alley, some twenty feet from a pedestrian-filled street.

After a minute, Bond slowly got to his feet and looked around, disoriented. His head was still pounding, but the awful nausea and dizziness had disappeared. He had a few aches and pains from the fight, and his jaw hurt, but otherwise he was in one piece.

Bond made his way to the street, not far from the Adult News bookshop. He walked south, back to the apartment building where the office was located, and saw a constable patrolling the pavement in front.

Rather than make any more trouble for himself, Bond decided to get away from Soho. He had two hours before he could catch Kimberley Feare, and there were still a few things he needed to take care of.

Of least priority to Bond was his state of mind.

As he hailed a taxi, three men watched him from the third-floor flat in the building overlooking the street. One of them was on the phone.

"That's right, he's fine. He just got in a taxi. Right."

Walter van Breeschooten hung up and said to Clayton, "Come on, let's get going. We have to get to the airport."

The third man waved them on. "Go on, get out of here. I'll keep close tabs on our boy," Jimmy Powers said.

SEVEN

DAZED AND CONFUSED

BOND TOOK THE TAXI BACK TO SIS. THE SETTING SUN SHONE BRIGHTLY OFF the green reflective surfaces of the building, suggesting that it might belong more in the Emerald City of Oz than in London.

He took the lift back to his floor, slipped past the few secretaries, and entered his office. There were no new messages, but there was a fax from Felix Leiter. Bond snatched it from the machine and read it.

Dear James—

Not much luck. Probably things you already know. Taylor Michael Harris left no relatives in Portland. What leads we have on the three lieutenants are sketchy and speculative. One of them, Samuel Anderson, was confirmed dead just two months ago. His body was found in Algeria, riddled with bullets. The other two, James Powers and Julius Wilcox, are thought to be alive and stationed somewhere in North Africa. *Le Gérant* is believed to be an Arab, citizenship unknown, although a Mossad report claims that he might be French. It's possible that *Le Gérant* was the business partner of Taylor Harris when he first solicited financing for the Union. The FBI believe that Julius Wilcox was the man who killed Harris at the restaurant in Portland. Eyewitnesses identified his mug shot. Wilcox was an ex-Marine and forest ranger before joining the Union. Immigration reports that he made several trips to Morocco before disappearing from the U.S. for good. Will overnight further information on the Union. Hope this helps.

—FELIX

Bond picked up the phone and dialed Detective Inspector Howard. He got one of the deputy inspectors, who said that Howard was in a meeting.

"Tell him it's James Bond, and it's urgent."

He waited three minutes, then Howard came to the phone.

"Commander Bond?"

"Inspector Howard," Bond said. "Sorry to interrupt your meeting but I have some information for you."

"Yes?"

"Michael Clayton and Walter van Breeschooten are both Union members."

"How do you know this?"

"I overheard them talking about it just a couple of hours ago."

"You what?"

"I paid a visit to their office in Soho. I overheard them talking about a job that was going to occur tonight . . . and they definitely have ties to *Le Gérant*. I think you need to pick them up."

He heard Howard sigh. "Commander Bond, to be frank, I don't appreciate you taking this matter into your own hands. You spied on them without authorization."

"It needed to be done. You were overlooking them."

"Commander Bond, I have a mind to inform M about this. You're out of order. Now, is there anything else?"

Bond decided against telling him about the plane tickets to Morocco.

"No. But I still suggest that you pay a visit to their office tonight." He gave Howard the address.

"I'll see what I can do. Now let us do our job, Commander."

Howard rang off and left Bond holding the phone. He slammed it down and cursed aloud.

He paced the floor a minute, considering his options. Finally, he picked up the red phone and dialed Miss Moneypenny's line. It was possible she had left for the day, but . . .

"Executive Director's office."

"Moneypenny, it's James."

"James! How are you? You're in the building? At this hour?" Miss Moneypenny had long been an ally of Bond's, through thick and thin. He could depend on her.

"I was just going to say the same thing about you. It's past six."

"This intelligence racket never stops, didn't you know that, James? M's got me looking into this Spaniard's background. You know who I mean?"

"Espada?"

"That's right. He's stirring up trouble in Spain."

"I know. You say M is in the office?"

"She's here, but not for long. Why?"

"I'm coming up." He hung up before Moneypenny could protest.

Five minutes later, he entered the outer office of M's sanctuary. Moneypenny was standing at the filing cabinets, digging through folders. When she turned and saw Bond, her mouth opened.

"My God, James, where have you been?" she asked, concerned.

"Why?" he countered sarcastically.

"You look like you've been up for days. What's wrong? Are you ill?"

"I'm fine. I . . . haven't slept much lately. Didn't shave this morning, that's all."

Bond strode toward M's office.

"Wait, James, I don't think—"

But he was already at the door, opening it. He gave a cursory knock and stuck his head in.

M was behind her desk, wearing reading glasses, intently poring over a tall stack of legal documents.

"Ma'am?"

She looked up and blinked. "Double-O Seven?"

"May I disturb you a minute?"

M gave a brief smile. "You already have. Come on in." The smile dropped and her eyes widened when she got a good look at his appearance. He closed the door and sat down in the comfortable leather chair in front of the desk.

"How's your leave going?" she asked with a slight hesitation in her voice.

"Fine, although I'm quite ready to come back to work," he said.

"You look . . . tired."

"I'm very restless, ma'am," he slapped his hands on the arms of the chair in frustration. "You should know how inactivity is the worst thing for me. I need an assignment. I need to be on the Union case. Please, I'm asking you. I need the work."

M leaned back in her chair. She obviously saw something in her top agent that disturbed her.

"What is it you're not telling me?" she asked.

"I can't keep away from the case," he replied. "I've been doing some digging of my own."

"Double-O Seven, you are not assigned to the—"

"I know, ma'am . . . please, hear me out."

She folded her arms and raised her eyebrows, indicating that he should go on.

"Helena Marksbury's landlord, a man named Michael Clayton, is a Union member and is probably the man who recruited her. He's a partner of a Dutch fellow, Walter van Breeschooten. Together they own some residential buildings, adult bookshops in Soho, and some nightclubs. They're into some shady business, and in fact I think they have something planned for tonight."

"Like what?"

"I have no idea. I think they're planning to kill someone."

"How do you know all this?" M asked. She wasn't particularly impressed with the information, but was perturbed that Bond had knowledge of it.

"I overheard them this afternoon. I . . . happened to be near their office so I did some eavesdropping."

"Double-O Seven, I must say that I don't approve of this. The Metropolitan Police are handling the case. MI5 are involved as well."

"Ma'am, with all due respect, I am quite prepared to pursue this alone, with or without your blessing."

"You're too emotionally involved in it!" she snapped. "I can see that from here." She attempted a softer approach. "You look terrible, Double-O Seven. Are you getting enough rest? How's that head of yours?"

"You're not the first person to tell me that I look terrible today."

"Well, you do. You look ill. What's the matter?"

"I need an assignment!"

The intensity in Bond's voice frightened M for the first time since she had known him. She waited a beat, then leaned forward and looked Bond in the eyes.

"James," she said. "I care about you a great deal. We all do. You're under a great deal of stress. We can all see it. You know what your medical report from June revealed. You've been ordered to get at least three months' rest and this is only the first Tuesday in August. Now . . . I know you're troubled about Miss Marksbury. I understand. I felt a great deal of guilt when Alfred was murdered. I'm sure that what you're feeling is not at all dissimilar. Now I want you to *go home,* and get some rest. I don't want you thinking about this. We have a team working on the Union night and day. MI5 and the Metropolitan Police have Miss Marksbury's case. We must let them do their job."

The sincerity in M's voice calmed him down. Bond looked away from her, feeling ashamed of his behavior.

"All right," he said.

"Good. Why don't you come back in two weeks? Go back to your place in Jamaica for a while."

Bond nodded grimly, stood up, and started to walk out of the office without another word.

"Double-O Seven?"

He stopped and looked back.

"It's for your own good. Surely you know that." He forced a smile, nodded, and left the room.

———•———

Damn her and everyone else!

He paced the floor of his little office as he mulled over what M had said. The events of the day had frightened and infuriated him, but he had no intention of giving up now.

Bond refused to believe that there was anything "wrong" with him. It was just not a possibility, he told himself. The blackouts—stress related, surely. But what about the hallucinations? The stress and headaches probably brought them on. That had to be it. Perhaps Dr. Feare could tell him more. He didn't want to wait another day to see her. Bond thought that the best thing to do would be to track her down at The Ivy that night.

Nevertheless, Bond was convinced that he could beat whatever mental or physical ailment he might have by simply getting back into action. That was the key to clearing his head.

He sat at his desk and turned on the computer. He got into the airline schedules' program and found what he was looking for.

British Airways had one flight a week to Tangier, and Clayton and van Breeschooten were on it. It was also completely booked. Luckily, Royal Air Maroc had two flights a week, and one of them was the next morning.

He glanced at his watch: 6:50. He had an hour to go home, get cleaned up, pack a bag, and try to find Kimberley Feare at the Ivy. Before leaving, though, he wanted to stop by Q Branch.

Major Boothroyd had left for the day, but technicians worked round the clock in the little laboratory in the basement of the building. Located near the gun practice range, Q Branch was accessible only to privileged members of SIS, a group that included Double-O agents. Therefore, Bond had no problem walking in through the security check.

"Can I help you, Double-O Seven?" the man at the front desk asked.

"No, thank you," he replied. "I'm just inquiring about a piece of equipment I left for repair. Be right back."

The official let Bond through the doors, not thinking anything of it.

Bond went to the small-arms cage and said hello to the attendant.

There it was, in the glass case with the other semi-automatics. Bond liked the new Walther P99 in .40 caliber S&W, but he hadn't yet talked Q Branch into issuing him one. Certainly more powerful than the standard 9mm, it looked the same, was designed the same, but used more potent ammunition. This resulted in a slow round, due to its added weight and size, but packed a stronger punch at the other end. With laser sight and flashlight accessories, the new P99 was a powerful handgun, but not ideal for hiding under a jacket. Bond had used the earlier model P99 and preferred to keep it in his luggage or automobile as backup. When he did wear it, Bond used an ISP-3 slotted-belt attachment holster, custom-made for the P99 by Del Fatti Leather.

When the attendant wasn't looking, Bond took the gun from the case and put it in his waistband. He then grabbed the holster and thrust it into his pocket, turned and said, "See you later," to the attendant, and left the building.

He hailed a taxi and directed the driver to a travel agency. There, he booked a one-way trip in economy on the Royal Air Maroc flight to Tangier. He paid with cash and gave his name as John Cork. The Cork identity, one of several aliases he used, was one that even SIS didn't know about.

Bond felt better as he entered his flat minutes later. He showered, shaved, and put on a clean white shirt, a navy jacket, red and blue tie, and dark trousers. Underneath the jacket was the Bianchi X15 leather shoulder holster and Walther PPK, still his choice of weapon for concealment. He had loaded the magazine with prefragmented ammunition. He chose Glaser Silvers for better penetration.

Bond packed a bag for the trip to Morocco and left instructions for May, his housekeeper.

At 7:45, he left the flat and took another taxi back to the theater district.

THE HEAT OF THE MOMENT

THE IVY IS A CHIC, OLD ESTABLISHED RESTAURANT FREQUENTED BY THE theater community, and by professionals in television, film, publishing, advertising, and journalism. In many ways, it is a modern, living Poets' Corner. Located at the junction of West and Litchfield streets in London's busy theater district, the Ivy's history dates back to 1917, when it was a modest café that quickly gained a reputation among the theater society.

But it was not James Bond's kind of place. While he appreciated the food at the Ivy, which was always excellent, the idea of going to a restaurant to see and be seen was not his style. He preferred anonymity and quiet. The Ivy can be a noisy place when it was crowded, which it usually is. Tables have to be booked weeks, if not months, in advance.

When he entered the Ivy shortly after 8:15, the maître d' asked, "May I help you, sir?"

Bond peered past him. "I'm meeting someone. May I take a look and see if they're already here?"

"What is the name?"

"I'm not sure whose name the reservation was under. They're doctors."

The maître d' shrugged and gestured toward the dining room as if to say, "Be my guest." Bond nodded and walked past him. He entered the crowded dining room that was buzzing with noise and excitement. London's favorites were out in force, all deeply animated in conversation and luxuriating in culinary delights. At least a half-dozen people were on their feet talking and laughing with diners.

He finally spotted her at a large table conversing with two other women and two men. Bond guessed that they were all physicians.

Dr. Feare was the youngest and most attractive in the group. She had bright blue eyes, a long but pretty nose, thin lips that seemed to be always on the verge of a sexy smile, and shoulder-length blond hair. Bond had found her to be good-looking, but the clinical atmosphere of a physician's office tends to neutralize any thoughts of sex. Here, in the restaurant's golden illumination, Kimberley Feare looked marvelous.

Bond turned and slipped out of the room. As he passed the maître d' he said, "Wrong restaurant. Sorry."

He went outside and quickly crossed the street. Luckily, the light was fading; loitering in the shadows would be less noticeable. Bond took a position under an awning, leaned against the building, and waited.

The pounding in his head seemed to mark the seconds. . . .

At one point, Bond felt that he was being watched. He scanned the street and buildings around him, but he couldn't see anything out of the ordinary. His nerves were acting up again, he told himself.

It was nearly an hour later, long after the sun had vanished, when Dr. Feare emerged from the restaurant. The others were with her. They noisily said good-bye to one another, shaking hands and hugging, then all went their separate ways. Dr. Feare got into a waiting taxi.

Another taxi pulled around the corner. A stroke of luck! Bond hailed it and got inside.

"Follow that taxi, please," Bond said.

The driver accepted this as a challenge and said, "Right."

After a brief uneventful drive, Dr. Feare's taxi pulled up in front of her building on Harley Street. It was the same building in which Sir James Molony kept his office, as well as his own flat. A battery of doctors who all had private offices in the building shared the ground-floor waiting room. A few of them lived there as well.

Bond instructed his driver to stop fifty feet behind it. He got out, paid, and approached the doctor just as she was completing the transaction with her own driver.

"Dr. Feare?" Bond asked.

She looked up, startled, but then she relaxed when she recognized a familiar face. "Yes?"

"james Bond. I saw you a few weeks ago. . . ."

"Right! My nurse told me that you had called. Mr. Bond, how are you?" She smiled.

"I was hoping that you could tell *me*," Bond said. "Please excuse the invasion of your privacy, but I simply had to see you."

The cab drove away and left them standing in front of the building. The porter was just inside the glass windows, watching them.

Her expression changed to one of concern. "Oh dear, what's wrong?"

"I'm leaving the country tomorrow morning on classified business. There wasn't time to make a proper appointment."

Dr. Feare frowned. "I thought that you were off-duty. Medical leave."

"Never mind that," Bond said. "Please, is there somewhere we can talk?"

She looked at him closely, noting the amount of stress his face revealed. "You're right, you don't look well, Mr. Bond. You have dark circles under your eyes."

"Sleep deprivation," Bond said. "It's the bloody headaches. They're becoming worse, and I don't think those pills you prescribed are doing anything for me. And . . . well, I seem to have experienced another episode of blacking out."

"What do you mean?"

He didn't want to mention seeing the double just yet. "I got a feeling of overwhelming anxiety—almost like I was having a heart attack—as well as a pounding in the head. Suddenly, I passed out. I woke up an hour or so later, and I couldn't remember what had happened. The odd thing is that I'd moved. I wasn't in the same place I was when I blacked out."

"Mr. Bond, you should have called me immediately," she said. "How long has this been going on?"

"Just today."

"I see. Perhaps you should come upstairs. Let me have a look at you."

He followed her into the building. She greeted the porter and led the way through the luxurious marble-floored lobby area. The clinic's waiting room was to the left, now closed and locked, of course. He followed her straight ahead into a lift, where she pressed button number 5.

Dr. Feare's flat was a modest one-bedroom with a living room, kitchen, bathroom, and a dining alcove. It was tastefully decorated in green and white, but it was also decidedly feminine, and very comfortable. A large rug covered the living room floor. A glass-top coffee table was the focus, and a green leather couch and two chairs surrounded it. A television and stereo system stood in the corner, near the window.

She took off her jacket and flung it over a chair. "Have a seat in the living room, Mr. Bond. Make yourself comfortable. I'm going to make some coffee. Would you like some?"

"That would be lovely," he answered.

She went into the kitchen. Bond removed the jacket, followed by the shoulder holster, and draped them over a chair. He then stood idly in the living room, glancing at the various knickknacks and pieces of art on the walls. Dr. Feare evidently liked to collect miniature elephants, as she had at least two dozen of them on a silver tray. All of them were posed so that they had their heads raised, trunks in the air. The elephants were made of various substances: glass, silver, wood, onyx, even gold.

"When the trunks are raised like that, it means good luck," she said, bringing out a small tray with cups and a bottle of mineral water. She placed it on the coffee table and approached him.

"First of all, do you have your medication with you by any chance?" she asked.

"Yes," Bond said, sitting on the sofa. "And please call me James. I haven't taken this evening's dose yet. I thought I should talk to you first."

"Let me see your pills."

He took the small container out of his pocket and handed it to her. She opened it, poured a few into her palm, nodded, then replaced them. She handed the container back to him. "Just checking to see that you had the right pills. Go ahead. Take four tablets instead of two."

"Now?"

"Yes, James."

Bond swallowed four pills with the water.

"Good," she said. "I'll be right back."

He watched her move back to the kitchen, admiring the shape of her hips. She was a lovely woman. Despite her youth, there was something comforting about her. Bond found her very attractive.

A few minutes later, she brought in a coffeepot and they sat on the couch together.

"Black, please," he said. She added a little cream to hers, but no sugar.

"Is the headache worse before these episodes?" she asked.

"Yes. I've had only one other blackout, if you recall. Three months ago. What could have caused it?"

"It could be a number of things," she said. "We don't call it a blackout; we call it poriomania, a condition in which the patient suffers a loss of cognizance, yet his body continues to function normally. It's uncommon, but it happens, especially with raging alcoholics and people who might have post-traumatic epilepsy, which we considered before. Normally it occurs six months or later after an injury, but in your case it was much sooner."

Bond didn't like the sound of that.

"James, I suggest that we run some more tests. I'd like to do another EEG. That lesion in your head may not be shrinking like we hoped. Must you leave the country tomorrow?"

"Yes. It will have to wait until I return."

"But James, you have a dangerous condition. You might never know when you'll have another episode of poriomania."

"I promise not to drive. Last time you told me that my symptoms could be stress-related. I'd like to believe that. I'm convinced that if I get out of this bloody rut I'm in and get back on the active duty list, I'll be fine."

He realized that he inadvertently gave away the fact that he was indeed still on medical leave.

"I see," she said. "Then you *don't* have to leave tomorrow."

"It's personal," he replied. "I need to go."

"I'm not sure that's what you need, James. You must take this seriously," she said, placing her hand on top of his. She hadn't meant for it to be an intimate gesture, yet neither of them could deny the electricity they felt. Encouraged by the look in her eyes, Bond raised the charm a notch by turning his hand and squeezing hers.

"Or perhaps I need a different kind of diversion," he suggested. He gave her a smile that penetrated her defenses.

Whether or not it was due to the wine she had consumed earlier, or perhaps to the immense amount of charisma that he had, Kimberley Feare suddenly felt vulnerable. She tried to tell herself that he was, after all, a patient, but his overwhelming masculinity instantly crushed that delineation. He was one of the most attractive men she had ever met, and she was alone with him in her flat.

Bond knew enough about women to recognize when the barriers were down. The seduction of a woman had everything to do with attitude, not looks or wit. Bond reflected—just for a moment—how unprofessional it might be for her to sleep with him. Most women in her position would have resisted going this far. Bond chalked it up to her youth and enthusiasm, and, giving himself a small boost to his ego, to his experience with the opposite sex.

He turned to her and put his arms around her. She looked up at him, her mouth parted. Her lower lip trembled a bit, and he could feel her shaking.

Bond brought his mouth down on hers and roughly held her against him. She submitted with a soft moan, then opened her mouth to receive his tongue. They kissed passionately until she finally, gently, pushed him away.

"Mr. B—James, please," she said, breathlessly. She took a sip of coffee, then said, "Uhm, tell me more about your, uhm, condition. You said you haven't been sleeping well?"

"That's right," he said, lightly brushing a strand of blond hair from her face.

"Any hallucinations?"

Bond hesitated.

"Seen anything unusual? Things that shouldn't have been there?" she asked.

"I'm not sure," he replied truthfully.

She reached up and rubbed his eyebrow slowly with her thumb, as if to brush away something caught there.

"Feelings of paranoia?"

Bond closed his eyes as she continued to massage his forehead with both thumbs. "Mmm hmm," he answered.

"James, we have to do another EEG."

She rubbed his temples with care for another thirty seconds, then stopped. She was unsure how to handle the situation or her desire.

After a few sips of coffee in silence, she looked at him and tried to smile. He took this as an invitation and leaned in to kiss her again. She nearly spilled her cup setting it on the saucer, then pulled him down on the couch on top of her. Her hands ran through his hair, pulling it, clawing the back of his neck with her fingernails. With his mouth firmly on hers, he brought his right hand up the side of her left leg, pushing the skirt up until it was above the tops of her nylon stockings.

They rolled off the couch, crashing into the coffee table and spilling the coffee. They didn't notice, though—such was the unexpected passion that had overtaken them.

They lay naked on the carpet next to the overturned coffee table. Bond had lit a cigarette and was using a saucer as an ashtray. The sex had been intense, as if neither of them could get enough of each other. The world outside could have been on the brink of disaster, but they would not have known it. The first time had been rushed and anxious, almost a selfish race to pleasure themselves rather than climax together. The second time was more relaxed and slower, but just as fierce. There was more give-and-take, and they had focused their energies on each other. They were by now exhausted.

Now she snuggled next to him, her firm breasts pressed up against his rib cage. She was still attempting to catch her breath and said, "Just so you know, I don't do this with all my patients."

"I'm so glad to hear that," he said. The throbbing in his head had just returned, and he rubbed his brow.

"I think it was your brooding angst that was so dreadfully attractive," she said with a laugh. "What's wrong? Head again?"

He nodded.

"I tell you what." She sat up. "I'm going to the loo. When I get back, I'll give you a proper massage. We'll see if I can work out some of that tension."

He closed his eyes as the warmth of her body disappeared. When he heard the bathroom door shut, he tried to sit up, but found that he couldn't. The room was spinning again, just like when he had been on that rooftop earlier in the day.

So he lay there for a few minutes with his eyes closed. When he thought that he heard something at her front door, but wasn't positive, he tried to sit up again.

Bond cursed aloud and reached for one of the leather chairs nearby. He managed to pull himself up to his knees, but now the pain in his head increased tenfold. This was accompanied by the dreaded anxiety that flooded his senses. Once again, his heart began to pound, bringing on that horrible feeling that he was about to die.

"Kimberley . . ." he tried to call, but his voice came out in a whisper. Exerting every bit of strength in his body, he pulled himself up against the chair and got to his feet.

The room went dark as he lost his balance and fell over the glass coffee table.

He was aware of a cold sensation on his right cheek. It was hard and wet.

A tile floor. Shards of broken mirror.

He opened his eyes and saw a toilet. But something was wrong. The normally white appliance was streaked in red.

Blood.

Bond felt a burst of adrenaline as life poured back into his body. He groaned and rolled over.

He was lying in Kimberley Feare's bathroom, naked. He coughed and put his hand to his face so that he could rub the haze from his vision. He got a jolt when he saw that his hand was covered in blood.

He sat up quickly, alarmed.

There was blood all over the bathroom and on his body. The mirror had been shattered. He examined himself and found several cuts on his arms, legs, and torso. He vaguely remembered falling into the glass coffee table.

He gingerly got to his feet and looked in the broken glass around him.

My God.

Dozens of ghosts stared back at him.

His skin was pale, frosty white. Streaks of blood went from his face and down his chest. Looking around the bathroom, he saw that the door was closed and noticed that his hand and footprints were all over the place in blood. On the floor by the door was a large bloody kitchen knife. He already knew that his prints probably covered it.

"Kimberley?" he called.

Dreading the worst, he opened the door and looked out.

The living room was a shambles. The glass coffee table had been broken. The cups, saucers, and coffeepot were on the rug. Their clothes lay in heaps on the floor, some of them torn. The collection of elephants had been scattered, some broken.

The green-and-white design scheme of the flat had been smeared with red.

"Kimberley!"

Bond stumbled to the open door of the bedroom and gaped in horror at the gruesome tableau before him.

Kimberley Feare was lying on the bed, naked, covered in blood. Her throat had been slashed, ear to ear, and she had been stabbed several times.

NINE

SUNRISE IN THREE COUNTRIES

JAMES BOND RARELY PANICKED, BUT HE WAS ON THE VERGE OF DOING SO NOW.

Did he kill this woman? What the hell was going on?

Trembling, he stepped into the bedroom to take a closer look. The multiple stab wounds suggested rage on the part of the killer. The blood trails on the carpet indicated that the body had been dragged from the living room and placed on the bed. She had probably been killed in the other room. Bond suspected that the throat-cutting had probably been done in here, postmortem.

But who could have done it? Not he! He might be a professional killer in the line of duty, but he was incapable of doing this to a person.

Or was he?

Bond backed out of the room, frantically going over everything that had happened in the last few hours. He looked at the clock in the living room: it was 2:48 in the morning. He had been unconscious for a long time.

He moved to the front door and saw that it was still locked.

My God, what the hell happened here? Was he losing his mind?

Shaken by the turn of events and the uncertainty of his mental condition, Bond began to act irrationally. He rushed into the bathroom, grabbed some towels, and started wiping up the blood. He mopped up the hand and footprints, cleaned off the knife, and

scrubbed down the walls and broken mirror. After ten minutes, the
towels were soaked in blood, and the place was still a mess.

What the hell am I doing? he thought. *I DID NOT DO THIS!*

He sat on the toilet seat.

Think . . . think . . . Calm down . . .

Wait a minute . . . he thought. The throat slashing . . . that was the
Union's way of killing! The Union murdered Kimberley Feare! It was
the only possible explanation. But how did they get in? And why kill
Kimberley? If the Union were inside the flat that night, why didn't
they kill him, too?

Were they trying to frame him? His prints were everywhere. He
had been seen with her that night. How could he prove that he didn't
kill her? Perhaps that was it. They wanted to pin a murder on him.

Bond buried his face in his hands and took a deep breath.

Right. Let's get cleaned up, he decided.

He found some clean towels in the linen cupboard and got into the
shower. He washed himself thoroughly, rinsing the blood down the
drain. The wounds on his arms and legs were superficial, but one on
his arm was still bleeding. He probably needed a stitch or two, but he
wasn't about to bother with it.

He stepped out of the shower and looked inside the medicine cabinet. He found some adhesive bandages and put one on the cut. He
then gingerly stepped out of the bathroom, avoiding the broken glass
and blood spots, and picked up his clothes. He dressed quickly, even
though a couple of buttons were missing off his shirt. He thought he
should get on his hands and knees and search for them, but the
carpet was such a mess that he would probably have made a bigger
one had he done so.

The shoulder holster was still on the chair where he had left it. He
put it on and surveyed the scene.

The flat looked like the devil's workshop.

He glanced at the telephone and considered calling the police.

Not a good idea at this point.

He needed to find out who had done this terrible thing and make
sure he could clear his name.

Bond refused to believe that he had done it.

He put on his jacket, opened the door to the flat, and looked into the corridor. All clear. He turned back to the flat and whispered, "I'm sorry, Kimberley," then shut the door.

As he left the building, the porter watched him suspiciously.

The thought kept nagging at Bond: *What if he* had *done it?*

He walked the streets in a daze.

For a moment he thought that someone was following him. He turned quickly, but didn't see anyone.

Get hold of yourself! He was jumping at shadows.

The obvious thing to do would be to contact Bill Tanner. Bond should tell him everything—about the blackouts, the hallucinations, and Kimberley. On the other hand, if he did that, he would be detained and questioned by the police. He would be in the middle of an inquiry, and would end up being the prime suspect. M would suspend him from duty indefinitely, and he would *never* get to the bottom of this.

No, even if it was totally imprudent, Bond knew that he had to keep quiet.

Bond was unsure of where to go and what to do. He flagged down a taxi on a main street and decided that his flat was the safest place to go. In the cab, he kept telling himself what he wanted to believe. *The Union was responsible.*

He had to get closer to them. It was the only way. If he could track down Helena Marksbury's killers, he would probably also find Kimberley's murderers. If he could face his enemy, he would come to grips with what was happening to him. It just *couldn't* be anything physical. He hadn't much faith in psychiatry, either, so he was loathe to seek out additional help.

Bond made a vow to beat this himself. The only way to do it was to go after the Union with guns blazing. Leave no stone unturned. Flush them out and smash them like insects.

When he got to his flat, it was nearly dawn. His flight to Africa was looming.

He double-checked the bag he had packed and looked at the message he had left for May. He had written that he would be out of the country for a while. Bond scribbled an additional sentence—that he didn't know when he'd be back. That was good enough.

He caught another taxi outside and went straight to Heathrow. Using his alias "John Cork," he went swiftly through Immigration and boarded the Royal Air Maroc flight to Tangier.

As the sun rose on the southern coast of Spain, Royal Gibraltar Police border control officer Captain Brian Berley eyed the group of protestors with understandable apprehension. This was the largest group he had ever seen, and he had been stationed on the border between Spain and Gibraltar for nearly fifteen years. The mob had appeared the previous night in the sleepy town of La Linea, just north of the border. They had arrived in buses and cars, and on bicycles . . . and had stayed in hotels or camped out in their vehicles. As soon as the sun rose, they were out in force.

Berley picked up the phone and made a call.

"Commissioner, I think the situation down here looks extremely bad. They're becoming quite noisy, and if they decide to storm the border, we're outnumbered twenty to one. We need MACA immediately." MACA stood for Military Assistance to the Civil Authorities.

He was assured that military police were on the way, but that the border should be closed until further notice. Berley issued the instructions to the Immigration officials, who lowered the barriers and told pedestrians and people in cars that there would be no entry into Gibraltar. Besides, the mob had all but blocked the road in and out of the colony.

The hundred or more protestors were bunching up as close as possible to the gates. Many of them were carrying signs that read, in Spanish and English, "Gibraltar Is Spanish, Not British!" Some signs proclaimed, "Espada—Governor of Gibraltar!" While the inhabitants of the British colony were accustomed to protests and demonstrations, having dealt with this kind of thing for centuries, the recent turn of events had them a little worried. The U.K. had been slow in sending reinforcements and, in fact, the decision to do so was being held up for political reasons.

Berley had read the newspaper reports with cynicism. The U.K. Prime Minister was attempting to find a peaceful settlement with Spain. The Madrid government's official line was that they "disapproved" of Domingo Espada's actions, but they were making no attempts to curb him. Berley thought that this was merely a public relations ploy and that they were in fact rubbing their hands with glee. If an upstart like Espada could take back Gibraltar without the "approval" of Spain, then the Spanish government wouldn't be blamed. Seemed pretty simple.

A truck carrying twenty Gibraltar Services Military Police officers drove across the Gibraltar airfield's runway, which was inconveniently located just south of the border (people entering or leaving the colony had to cross it!), and stopped at the Immigration building. The men, carrying SA-80 5.56mm assault rifles, leaped out of the truck and formed a line at the border. This prompted more shouting and abuse from the protestors, who had by now pushed themselves up as far as they could get to the border.

When the rocks started flying, Berley made another call to his superiors. The Royal Gibraltar Regiment was being dispatched as well.

The security alert at the Governor's Residence went from "black" to "amber." The Governor made an urgent call to London, again requesting assistance. Unfortunately he was told that rock-throwing did not constitute a threat of "serious violence" and that NATO's European Rapid Reaction Force, which was drawn from Allied Command Europe Mobile Force Land (ACE), would not be dispatched. NATO were discussing the situation in Brussels, but these things took time. However, the U.K. was sending the 1st Battalion of the Parachute Regiment based in Aldershot. They were expected to arrive by midday.

The Governor gave the order to secure the airport and allow only the reinforcements from Britain to land. All other traffic in and out of Gibraltar was to cease.

Captain Berley was told to keep calm and stand his ground. Help was on the way, but it wouldn't arrive until midafternoon.

The mob was becoming ugly. The shouting and insults were increasing by the minute. The police were doing their best to keep cool and not retaliate in kind. The situation was a powder keg, ready to ignite. Rocks broke one of the windows in the Immigration office. Berley wondered if he should employ tear gas in an attempt to disperse the crowd.

Suddenly, a deafening explosion rocked the Immigration building. A fireball engulfed the surrounding area. Chaos erupted as some of the Spanish crowd cheered, while others screamed and ran. Several soldiers had been caught by the blast and were now lying on the pavement, dead or seriously wounded.

Berley ran out of the smoking building and ordered the men to fire warning shots to disperse the crowd. As the guns went off, the Spanish mob thought they were being fired upon.

Several Spaniards pulled their own guns and began to fire at the police.

Berley was horrified. He dropped to the ground, avoiding the gunfire, and crawled for cover just as a second bomb detonated at the gate.

This one created a huge explosion, killing several people on both sides.

Berley cursed aloud. He was now in the middle of a shooting war.

The events that morning at the Gibraltar border prompted a major panic in the governments of Britain and Spain. By noon, fingers were being pointed, tempers had flared, and both sides were blaming each other for the catastrophe.

The morning sun had also brought life to the streets of Casablanca. As the merchants and shopkeepers and bankers and beggars went to their respective places of business, the Union subordinates had already been working round the clock, packing various files, pieces of equipment, weaponry . . . it wouldn't be long before they had finished.

Le Gérant rose from his magnificent Louis XIV four-poster bed. He reached for and felt the silk robe hanging on the hook by the bed. Putting it over his naked body, he wrapped the sash snugly around his thick waist. *Le Gérant* wasn't fat, but he was what is often referred to as "stocky."

Knowing the exact path to the bathroom, he walked in his bare feet across the tiled floor. Even if something unexpected had been placed in the way, *Le Gérant* would have sensed the obstacle's presence and moved around it. He had been able to do it since he was very young. He possessed some kind of sixth sense that allowed him to "see" when he couldn't do so physically. His mother had noticed that he had a gift, and she believed that he was a messenger from Allah. A Berber woman with a strong tribal heritage, she came from a group of Riffians in the eastern part of Morocco, near the Algerian border. He had lived with her as a child until he was ten years old, when she unexpectedly died. His Corsican father fetched him out of Morocco and brought him to Paris so that he could be educated in the Western ways. There was also hope that a cure could be found for his blindness.

Le Gérant returned to his mother's people in the Rif Mountains for a brief period of time as an adult. Even though he had adopted the ways of the West, he was accepted warmly, for many people remembered him.

From the moment he returned, the other Riffians regarded *Le Gérant* as some kind of divine being. They were amazed that he could navigate his surroundings so easily. Some wondered if he were truly blind. When he was able to call them by name before they said a word, the people were so impressed with "the Western Berber" that they became his loyal followers.

Le Gérant was a man from two countries and two cultures.

In the bathroom, *Le Gérant* splashed water on his face. He would miss the Union quarters here in Casablanca, but it was time to move on. Discovery of the base was imminent, and it was too costly to maintain the complex. By the end of the day, the Union would be gone. Vanished, without a trace.

Le Gérant had thought long and hard about where to move the

central headquarters to. He thought that the authorities would temporarily ignore Marrakesh. That was where they would go for the
time being. He thought that perhaps he should move the operations
to Europe. But where to? France? He would have to think about it
some more. Marrakesh would do for now.

He heard the buzz of the telephone. He walked back through the
bedroom to the study. He sat in a large cushioned chair and picked
up the phone.

"Yes?"

"*Gérant,* it's Nadir, I hope it's not too early."

"I've been expecting your call. I trust you are on a secure line."

"Most secure, sir."

"Very well. What have you to report?"

Yassasin said, "Everything has worked as planned. James Bond is
behaving exactly as we had hoped. He is on his way to Morocco now."

"That's excellent news. What about the *commandant* from
London?"

"Mr. van Breeschooten and his colleague Clayton will also arrive
this morning, sir. They have instructions to go to the training camp
in the mountains, as you wished."

"And you're sure Mr. Bond will find them?"

"If he picks up the clues we left for him, he will. He's smart enough
to find them."

"And Clayton's cousin?"

"Still in place and under cover. An excellent operative, I must say."

Le Gérant was pleased. "How is Señor Espada feeling this
morning? He must be fairly happy."

Yassasin allowed himself to smile. "He is thrilled that the confrontation at the border is going as well as it is. Just enough people
have died to make the various politicians sit up and take notice. After
tomorrow's events, he is certain that his proposal to the governments
of Britain, Spain, and Gibraltar will be accepted. The Governor of
Gibraltar has already expressed an interest in hosting the summit
meeting."

"Perfect. Nadir, you continue to amaze me."

"It is my pleasure to serve you, *Gérant.*"

"Tell me, Nadir, does Espada suspect anything?" *Le Gérant* asked.

"I don't think so. He isn't aware of anything but his own selfish dreams. He is becoming careless."

"I'm not so sure that will matter much in a few days."

"Oh?"

"I've decided that when he becomes the Governor of Gibraltar, his tenure shouldn't last very long. When we gain control of his operations, it would be best if he wasn't in the picture."

"I understand. I have already built that option into the plan. His tenure will last . . . say . . . a minute?"

Le Gérant smiled. "You are a genius, my friend."

"No, sir," Yassasin said. "You inspire me to do my best. How is the moving going?"

"Smoothly. The next time you see me, we'll be in Marrakesh."

"*Ma' as-salaama,* then," Yassasin said.

"*Ma' as-salaama* as well."

Le Gérant hung up the phone. He felt very pleased with himself. Before long, the Union would be as powerful as any country on the face of the earth, and he was its rightful leader. It was *he, Le Gérant,* who had made the Union what it was today. He had the business sense of a metropolitan Westerner, but the spirituality and tenacity of a Berber tribesman.

As the first phase of the plan came to a close, everything was in its place. Domingo Espada believed that he had employed the Union to do his bidding, when, in fact, he was but another chess piece in the grand game that Yassasin and *Le Gérant* had concocted.

The best moves were yet to come.

ACT TWO

TERCIO DE BANDERILLAS

ON THE RUN

AT NOON, THE ROYAL AIR MAROC FLIGHT TOUCHED DOWN AT TANGIER'S tiny Boukhalef airport, fifteen kilometers southeast from the town center. James Bond disembarked and immediately felt the cultural shock of being on another continent. North Africa was indeed a completely different world from Europe. Sights, sounds, art, food, and religion all contributed to making the way of life in the Muslim world distinctly unique. In many ways, English-speaking Westerners were the least at home in *al-Maghreb al-Aqsa,* the "land of the setting sun." They were treated with a certain degree of suspicion, although this was less so in Morocco than in some other Muslim countries.

Signs printed only in Arabic and French pointed the way to baggage claim and the exit. Porters descended upon Bond before he'd cleared Immigration. He waved them away, nearly barking at one persistent one, and made his way outside to the taxi stand. He carried a small holdall containing necessities and a box wrapped in brown paper. Its label was addressed to "Mr. Latif Reggab" at an address in Tangier, and a Customs label claimed that it contained machine parts. The official who had cleared it spoke to Bond in French, saying, "Oh, you're friends with Mr. Reggab? He's always importing or exporting something." In fact, the box contained Bond's two firearms, carefully masked by X ray–proof material perfected by Q Branch.

Bond negotiated a price of two hundred dirhams for the taxi driver
to take him to Tangier. It was a twenty-minute ride, and the landscape was atypical for what one might expect from a port city like
Tangier. The countryside was hilly and green, dotted with the occasional shepherd in the distance. There was surprisingly little development out this way, but the city was suddenly upon them. Bond felt
the change in the atmosphere, for Tangier was famous for its unique,
decaying character of the post-Interzone days.

People from all over the world have inhabited the port for over
2,500 years. During the days when resident diplomatic agents of a
number of countries controlled Tangier, it was known as an "international zone." Then, every kind of dubious activity developed in the
port, including money laundering, smuggling, currency speculation,
arms dealing, prostitution, and slave trading. It was also a fashionable resort haven for artists, writers, refugees, exiles, and bankers.
When Tangier was reunited with the rest of Morocco in 1956, this
notoriety fell by the wayside, but the legends lived on.

Bond had been to Tangier a number of times and he was always put
off by the amount of hustling that went on. The trick, Bond had
learned, was not to act or look like a tourist. Because Bond had black
hair and a relatively tanned complexion, it wasn't immediately obvious
that he was British. A glare from his cold, steely eyes also worked to dis-
suade faux guides from offering to "show him the medina."

The driver let him off in the Grand Socco, a poor imitation of the
famed Djemaa el-Fna in Marrakesh, where snake charmers, musicians, storytellers, makeshift shops, and food stalls filled the air with
smells, noise, and spectacle. Outside the chemist's was a group of
tattoo-faced Berber women dressed in traditional *izars* or *haïks*,
hoping to secure a housecleaning job. A Moorish horseshoe arch led
from the Grand Socco into the medina, the city's oldest quarter. Navigation by foot, bicycle, motorcycle, or donkey cart were the only
options in this labyrinth of narrow passages and winding paths.

Bond walked into the medina, shaking his head at a man who
wanted to "show you something special, my friend," and moved past
the numerous shop fronts where anything and everything was sold.

The small streets were full of donkeys and cats, beggars and children, hawkers and tourists. It was the smell of the place, in particular, that seemed to be a common trait with all of the medinas in Morocco. The fresh fish, meats, and spices combined with the surrounding humanity to create a confusion of odors that, to Bond, smelled of rotten eggs mixed with incense and urine.

Bond made his way deep into the medina to the busy little square known as the Petit Socco. Children were kicking a ball back and forth between the constant movement of carts and wagons, women dressed in caftans and veils who were buying the day's produce, and "students" looking for tourists to befriend. He passed the Pension Fuentes, which had been one of Tangier's luxury hotels at the end of the nineteenth century. At that time, the medina was the sole center of activity and the city's administration was established there. Important international offices had once resided in the medina, such as the old American Legation, which was now a museum. This all came to an end when the ville nouvelle was built at the beginning of the new century.

At first Bond thought he might have taken a wrong turn, but then he recognized some landmarks and continued on his way up Rue de Almohades to a three-story Berber house. Built around a courtyard, the square structure had high ramparts and corner towers. Magnificent, colorful, handmade carpets hung on the outside, and the ground floor was covered with arts and crafts, from textiles to pottery and ceramics. Brass and copperware were abundant, and jewelry, woodwork, and basketware dominated the premises. Everything was of very high quality.

A teenage boy approached Bond, saying in English, "Come in, sir, come in. *Español*? American? We have best prices in Tangier. You like carpets? Please, we give you free demonstration."

"No, thank you," Bond said. "I'm here to see Latif Reggab. Is he here?"

"Yes, sir, he is always here. Please, come in and look around. I will find him for you."

The walls and floor of the room were decorated in the intricate and exquisite tile work that was prevalent in Moroccan architecture. The smell of incense was stronger inside, covering the foul odors of the medina. A few American tourists were haggling with a shopkeeper over the price of a black leather jacket. Some Spaniards were admiring the precious stones that were protected in a glass case.

"*As-salaam 'alaykum,* may I help you?" said a familiar voice behind Bond.

He turned to see a rather short man in his fifties. He was dressed in the traditional white *jellaba,* wore glasses, had dark, curly hair flecked with gray, and large brown eyes with an unusual bluish tint. His skin color was light, as was common among indigenous Berber people. When the man saw who it was standing in his shop, he beamed.

"Well, Allah be praised. I don't believe it!"

"Hello, Latif," Bond said. "It's been a long time."

"James Bond, as I live and breathe. Welcome!" Latif Reggab laughed heartily and embraced Bond warmly, planting kisses on both cheeks. "Why didn't you let me know you were coming?"

"I couldn't, for security reasons," Bond said, quietly, as he glanced around to make sure no one was listening. "Latif, I need your help. I need a place to stay while I'm here, and no one must know about it."

"Of course, of course! No problems. You are always welcome here. Consider this your own personal *funduq.*" Latif was referring to the smelly "motels" used by caravans.

"And," Bond added, "I would also appreciate it if London didn't know I was here as well."

Latif grinned conspiratorially and said, "Oh, are we up to some kind of international intrigue? Are you in pursuit of dangerous terrorists? Has the spy network returned to Tangier?"

Bond laughed. "Not quite. Let's just say that I'm on a personal mission. So, tell me, Latif, how are things in T Branch of Station NA? How is your family?"

"Come upstairs, James, please, and I'll tell you." He led Bond up the flights of stairs, past the carpet and rug gallery on the first floor, upward beyond the living quarters, and onto the flat roof, where several carpets had been hung or laid out to dry in the sun. On the way, Latif had barked an order in Arabic to a young man on the second floor.

They could see the entire medina from this height. It looked much as it did hundreds of years ago, with the crowded clusters of flat rooftops, hanging laundry, and the occasional minaret. The only difference was that now most of the rooftops were sprinkled with television aerials or satellite dishes.

"My family is wonderful," Latif answered. "My wife is still beautiful and my children are almost all grown. My eldest has already made me a grandfather. You met my youngest son earlier. That was Hussein."

"My lord, the last time I saw him, he was—" Bond held his hand at his waist to indicate the boy's height.

"Yes, they grow like wildflowers, these kids."

"Grandpa, eh?"

"Yes, it's a blessing," Latif said, smiling broadly, revealing large, yellow teeth. "Anyway, they're all fine, and the branch is fine, too. To tell the truth, I am very bored with intelligence work. Most of the time these days I simply run my shop and sell beautiful carpets to tourists. There is hardly anything for me to do anymore. Most of the North Africa station's activity is concentrated in Egypt now; we never have any excitement in Morocco. I'm hoping you have some excitement up your sleeve and that you will allow me to have some of it."

The second boy appeared, carrying a tray with two glasses of hot mint tea.

"Please, James, have some tea," Latif said.

Bond wasn't a big admirer of tea in any form, but he knew that it was customary to accept the offer of mint tea in Moroccan households. It was way too sweet for his tastes, but he made a show of drinking it.

They sat in two wooden chairs overlooking the medina. Just to the north, they could see the coastline. A European cruise ship had just put in to the port, which they could plainly see to the northeast.

"We're getting all the cruise ships that were supposed to stop in Gibraltar," Latif said. "Sticky situation there, eh? Anyway, so tell me what this secret mission of yours is."

"I need to locate two men who flew here from London last night on the British Airways flight. An Englishman named Michael

Clayton, and a Dutchman named Walter van Breeschooten. Can you get on to your contacts at Immigration?"

"Sure, no problems. They can tell us if they passed through Immigration all right. But they could be anywhere in the country by now, you know."

"It's essential that I find them."

"Perhaps they wrote their Moroccan address on their Immigration card," Latif said facetiously.

"That would be the headquarters of the Union."

Latif raised his bushy eyebrows. "I see. That's what this is about, then."

"What can you tell me about them? Do you have any idea where the Union keeps its main base?"

"As you know, we have an ongoing directive from London to gather information on the Union. I have a little, not much."

"Then I'd like to get started as soon as possible."

"We'll have some lunch and can talk," Latif said. "Let me show you to your room."

Bond found his room modest but comfortable. It was small, with a single bed, a tiny window, and a dresser. The bathroom was down the hall, and he would be sharing it with Latif's extended family. He didn't plan to stay long.

He went into the bathroom and stared at his hard face. It didn't reveal the torment he was feeling inside. He looked tired, but otherwise seemed fit and alert. In fact, he felt like hell. He was still jittery after the shock of discovering Kimberley Feare's body. He hadn't had a proper night's sleep in days. The headache was stable but persistent.

Bond did what he could to make himself look presentable, put on his shoulder holster and PPK, and covered them with a light sports jacket. He also put on the ISP-3 holster for the P99. The handgun was bulky, but he felt it would be better to keep both guns on him at all times. He rejoined Latif in the family room on the second floor, where a woman in a caftan was setting the dining table.

"You remember my wife, Maliza?" Latif asked, gesturing to her.

"Of course," Bond said. "Thank you for your hospitality," he said to Maliza. She smiled and nodded at him, then scurried out of the room.

"She doesn't speak English," Latif said. "Sit down, my friend. Tell me more about this mysterious mission you're on."

Bond sat down in a wooden chair as Latif offered him an ashtray. He removed the gunmetal case that was as much a fixture on his person as his beloved Walther, removed a cigarette with the three distinctive gold bands made by Tor Importers, and held the case open for Latif. The Ronson lighter appeared and lit both cigarettes.

"The Union killed someone close to me," Bond said flatly. "They almost killed me. They've made it personal. I want them. That's all."

Latif looked at Bond a long time before saying, "My friend. You realize that when they make it personal, it becomes too dangerous. You lose objectivity. That's when you need to step back and let someone else handle the job."

"I hear you, Latif, but I can't do that. That's not all. Last night, I'm pretty sure the Union tried to set me up for murdering a woman in London—a doctor."

Latif's eyes narrowed. "So let me understand this . . . you're on the run?"

"You might say that," Bond said. "I'm looking for answers."

"Do you even know what the questions are?"

"I'm making them up as I go along."

That caused Latif to smile. "My friend, James. Don't worry. You can trust me. I will help you in any way I can."

After a bit of silence, he spoke again. "You know, I read somewhere . . . I think it was on the Internet . . . that if we could shrink the earth's population down to a village of precisely one hundred people, with all the existing human ratios remaining the same, the results are quite extraordinary. I was so struck by the revelations that the numbers are permanently imprinted on my brain. There would be fifty-seven Asians and twenty-one Europeans. There would be only fourteen people from the entire Western Hemisphere, both north and south. There would be eight Africans. Of these hundred people, fifty-two would be female, forty-eight male. Seventy would be nonwhite, thirty white. Seventy would be non-Christian, thirty would be Christian. Eighty-nine would be heterosexual, eleven homosexual. Fifty-nine percent of the village's wealth would be in the hands of only six people, and all six would be Americans. Eighty people would live in substandard housing. Seventy would be unable to read. Fifty would suffer from malnutrition. One would be near death, one would be near birth. Only one person would have a college education, and only one would own a computer."

Reggab let that sink in, then said, "When one considers our world from such a compressed perspective, the need for both acceptance and understanding becomes glaringly apparent."

Maliza brought food to the table and beckoned to the men. They sat down to a meal of chicken curry with rice, served with bottled sparkling water. Bond knew that Latif, purportedly a devout Muslim, didn't keep alcohol in his home. He wasn't adverse, though, to slipping into bars with Bond for the occasional drink.

"I'll tell you what I know about the Union," Latif said. "Everyone is becoming scared of them. They are the number-one priority with Interpol. The Union have gained a lot of power in the past couple of years."

"Yes."

"I think they're in Casablanca. It makes sense. It's the financial center of Morocco. It's a port and has the largest airport."

"Do you think *Le Gérant* is Moroccan?"

"Yes. Partly, anyway. I've been waiting for some more information before I submit my report on the Union to London. I think I know who *Le Gérant* is."

Bond's heart skipped a beat. "Do tell."

Latif shrugged. "I'm not sure yet. You see, I'm a Berber. My people came from the Rif Mountains. I have heard talk of a man, a Westerner, whose mother was Berber. He came to the mountains some years ago and was regarded as some kind of prophet. The word was that he had a French father who had once served in the government here during the Second World War. Anyway, this man, they say, is blind, but he possesses extrasensory powers that normal human beings do not have. He had tremendous influence over some of the tribes in the mountains. He took many people with him and disappeared back into Western civilization."

"Do you know his name?"

"If it's who I think it is, his name is Olivier Cesari."

"A French name? Corsican?"

"Corsican. Although he was born into the Berber tribe, he was raised and educated in France by his father. He probably has a Berber name as well, but I don't know it."

"How did you find this out?"

"Well . . . for one thing . . ." Latif said, smiling devilishly, "I went to university with Olivier in Paris."

"Really?"

Latif nodded. "It's true what they say about him. Tremendously gifted. He was an excellent student, extremely intelligent. He studied law, as I did, but changed to economics. And I remember him walking on campus with a stick, never bumping into anything. Once I came into the classroom and he was the only one in there. I didn't say anything, and after a few seconds, he greeted me by name. Uncanny."

"Why do you think this man is *Le Gérant?*" Bond asked.

"I don't know," Latif said. "As I said, I've heard these stories from the Riffians about this so-called prophet. In fact, that's what they called him in the mountains. *Prophet.* Unfortunately, no one has seen him in fifteen, twenty years."

"We should go ahead and have London investigate him."

"They already have. I put in the request a long time ago. According to official records, Olivier Cesari disappeared from Paris when he was in his twenties."

"Which was . . . what, thirty years ago?" Bond surmised.

"Right. Olivier is my age, roughly, which is fifty."

Reggab's mobile rang. He answered it, speaking in Arabic. After a few short exchanges he hung up and said, "Your two men came through Customs last night, all right. So they're in the country."

"How do we find them?"

"My source at the airport said that they took a taxi toward Tangier. That's all we know. But don't worry. I have eyes and ears all over this country. Let me make some calls this afternoon."

Latif's youngest son came in with an overnight courier envelope. "This came for you, Papa."

"Thank you, son," Latif said. He examined it, his brow wrinkling. "Now what is . . . ?" He opened it and found a large brown envelope inside. "Ah. It's for a case I'm working on. These are the photos I was expecting."

"Anything interesting?"

"In a way. There's a strange campsite in the mountains, between the villages of Chefchaouen and Ketama. It sprung up there about a year ago on some land that's owned by a private company. A bank. Anyway, it's like a compound—they have it surrounded by barbed wire and the dirt road leading to it is guarded off the main highway. It looks like soldiers are in training there, but no one has got close enough to make sure. I've been ordered by London to find out if it's some kind of terrorist training camp."

Latif shared the photos with Bond. They were eight-by-tens in black-and-white and looked as if they had been shot with a camera hidden in someone's clothing. The lighting was bad, as they were obviously night shots and had depended on the little illumination made by a couple of spotlights at the scene.

"These are quite good, considering the location of the camera," Latif said. "We had to put it in Rizki's *tarbouch*. He's one of the men who helps me. I had him stationed on the hill above the entrance to the camp. It's quite a way off the main road. He was to take photographs of everyone going in and out."

The photographs, obviously blown up from a smaller size, showed various figures at a checkpoint gate. Bond could make out tents, lean-tos, and campers within the compound. Among the figures in the shots were men in military fatigues sitting in a jeep, being waved through by two guards dressed in traditional Berber *jellabas*. The guards were carrying automatic weapons, but it was difficult to discern what they were.

Bond flipped through the photographs and stopped at the last one. It showed two Caucasians in business suits getting out of a taxi at the gate.

They were Walter van Breeschooten and Michael Clayton.

"Latif, when were these photos taken?" Bond asked.

"Last night. Rizki got them to me quickly, he's a good—"

Bond slapped the photo. "These are the men I'm looking for!"

"Really?" Latif took it and stared. "That's incredible!"

"How soon can we get to this camp?"

"We'll have to go after dark. Is tonight soon enough?"

For the first time in days, Bond smiled and breathed a sigh of relief.

ELEVEN

SWIFT SETTLEMENT

IT WAS MIDAFTERNOON WHEN M RANG OFF WITH THE PRIME MINISTER AND Miss Moneypenny buzzed.

"Yes?"

"Chief-of-Staff is here and would like a word."

"Send him in."

M was still thinking about the conversation that she had just had when Bill Tanner came into the office and sat down. He was carrying a folder and had an odd expression on his face. M sat up, instinctively sensing that something was wrong.

"I have some disturbing news, ma'am," he began.

"What is it?"

"Have you heard about the murder of the young doctor in Harley Street last night? The police and building superintendent found her body this morning. . . ."

"I heard something on the news. What about it?"

"She was one of ours."

"What?"

"Dr. Kimberley Feare. She was a colleague of Sir James Molony. He's away and Dr. Feare had taken over some of his cases."

"I remember her name on some reports."

"I've just had a look at the police report. Ma'am, it was a particularly brutal murder. There is one detail in particular that concerns me."

"What is that?" M was a bit shaken by this news.

"Her throat had been cut, Union-style."

"My lord, what could they want with a girl like her? She was young and new, wasn't she?"

"Just the type the Union go for. If she was involved with the Union, we could have some security problems again."

M cursed. Bill Tanner rarely heard her do it, but this wasn't the first time and it surely wouldn't be the last.

Tanner shifted in his chair.

"There's something else, isn't there?" M snapped.

"Yes, ma'am," Tanner said. "It's Double-O Seven, ma'am."

"What about him?"

"He may be involved."

"What do you mean?"

"Dr. Feare's nurse reported that Bond had called her office yesterday, insisting on an appointment. Preliminary investigation has shown that he was seen with Dr. Feare last night in front of her building."

"Is that true?"

"Well, we don't know. The porter at the building remembers her coming home in a taxi and being approached by a man on the pavement. He accompanied her inside the building and he matched the description of Double-O Seven."

The expression on M's face indicated that she simply didn't know what to say.

"As you recall, Dr. Feare diagnosed Bond's condition after his return from the Himalayas. That's all we know, except that Double-O Seven doesn't call back when we page him," Tanner said. "We think . . . we think he's missing."

Finally M burst out with, "I don't believe a bloody word of this."

Tanner tapped the folder. "It's all here in the police report. MI5 is being brought in to the case."

"Who alerted the police in the first place?"

"It was an anonymous phone call. Someone called the police and said that a woman had been murdered. They gave Dr. Feare's address and hung up."

"The real murderer, no doubt. Where was Double-O Seven?"

"The porter saw him leave the building after midnight, if that's what you mean. There is one puzzling piece to the porter's statement."

"What is that?"

"He says that after he had seen Dr. Feare and the man enter the building, an hour or two later he saw the same man, alone, coming into the building with a key. The porter thought that he had probably missed seeing him leave the building the first time, perhaps on an errand to fetch a bottle of champagne or something, and that Dr. Feare had given him a key to use upon returning."

"What do you mean?"

"If it *was* Double-O Seven, he was seen going into the building twice. Once with Dr. Feare, and a second time alone and with a key. Doesn't that sound strange?"

"Indeed. The porter was mistaken, I should think. How long has Bond been seeing this woman on a social basis?"

"I have no idea. This is the first I've heard of it. He met her when he visited Sir James's office."

She tapped her fingers on the desk a moment. "Well. There he goes again, mixing business with pleasure. I shall have his hide."

"I'm afraid the government will have more than that if he's charged with murder, ma'am."

She looked at him incredulously. "You're not serious. James Bond is *not* a murderer. Not that kind. Surely you agree that he could *not* have done this?"

Tanner nodded. "Absolutely, ma'am. It's extraordinary."

"They can't possibly realistically suspect Double-O Seven. . . ."

"He's wanted for questioning, ma'am. We have to try and find him." Tanner frowned again and added, "There's something else that disturbs me."

"What?"

"The attendant in the small arms cage down in Q Branch reported a firearm missing this morning. A Walther P99, along with its holster and some Glaser ammunition. The last man seen in the cage yesterday was Double-O Seven."

"Are you implying that Bond stole a gun?"

"I'm afraid that's what it looks like."

M shut her eyes and rubbed her brow, attempting to take it all in. Finally, she pushed her chair back from the desk. "On top of all that, we have to deal with the Gibraltar situation. I was just on the phone with the PM. He has decided to accept the offer to go there for a meeting with this Espada fellow, the Spanish Prime Minister, and the Governor of Gibraltar. We're to send someone to accompany him as an extra bodyguard."

"I'll take care of it," Tanner said. "I think Double-O One is free." He got up to leave, still carrying the police report. M stopped him and held out her hand.

"Oh, right," he said, handing it to her. He, too, was disturbed by what the day had brought.

After he had left the room, M began to study the contents of the folder with trepidation.

Set astride the awesome hundred-meter-deep El Tajo gorge amid the beautiful Serranía de Ronda mountains, the enchanting village of Ronda bathed in the rays of the late afternoon sun. About an hour's drive north of the southern Spanish coastline on a winding, mountainous road that cut through forests of cork and *pinsapo* trees, Ronda is said to be the birthplace of the art of bullfighting. Indeed, the oldest bullring in Spain, Ronda's Plaza de Toros, serves as a monument and symbol of the quaint community. Ernest Hemingway and Orson Welles (whose ashes were spread over Ronda per his wishes) loved the town. One of Spain's most prestigious matadors, Antonio Ordoñez, had his ashes scattered *in* the bullring, in accordance with his desire to give the bulls the pleasure of stepping on his remains after he was dead.

Today, the bullring was filling up with spectators. Even though it was Wednesday and not Sunday, an exciting *corrida* was scheduled for 6:30 P.M., and one of Spain's rising stars had top billing. Everyone in town had turned out for the bullfight and many fans from Marbella and Málaga had made the trip to Ronda.

However, before the bullfight, the audience was subjected to a political speech delivered by Domingo Espada. As promoter and manager of the most influential matadors in the country, he was able to do things that no one else dared to. He had been traveling through the provinces and making impassioned pleas to the people to join his party, demand that Gibraltar be ceded to Spain, and reform the current government. The people didn't mind. To them he was a legend. He was *Espada.*

A surprising number of men always volunteered to join Espada at these political rallies. It helped that Espada pretended that matadors all over Spain gave him their full support.

Just southeast of the bullring stands the magnificent Parador de Ronda Hotel, perched on the edge of the gorge. Just beyond a railing, the cliff plunges down steeply to the valley of the Río Guadalevín far below. The best rooms in the five-star complex featured balconies looking out over the dazzling view. It was the most fashionable place to stay in a town where celebrities often went for a little quiet and beauty.

Margareta Piel walked across the plaza in front of the Parador, where tourists and locals sat at tables having drinks and tapas. A large number of police were positioned there as well, for the matadors staying at the hotel were on a par with rock stars; very often fans could become a nuisance.

All of the men turned their heads to look at Margareta as she walked through. She was dressed in a sleek black bodysuit that showed off her every curve, and was wearing a dark backpack and sunglasses. She knew that people, and the police, would notice her entering the hotel. They always noticed her.

There was still an hour to go before Espada's speech. She would have preferred to perform the business at hand under the cover of darkness, but time did not permit it. She strode into the lobby as if she knew where she was going, past the bellboy, who stopped and stared, and snaked around the lounge to the lifts, got into an empty one and pressed the button for the second floor.

Inside room 214, a deluxe suite built on two levels, like a townhouse, a naked man and woman were finishing a pleasurable primal ritual.

Roberto Rojo rolled off the girl, who had said her name was Maria. The sweat was beaded around her forehead, and she was still breathing heavily, her breasts moving up and down with the heaving of her chest as her heartbeat began to subside. Rojo sighed, "Oh man, oh man," then pulled her closer. She snuggled up to him, wrapping one slinky leg over his torso. Maria had been extremely lucky that Roberto Rojo had taken a liking to her at Domingo Espada's ranch. While leaving her family to "work" for Espada had seemed, at first, like a good idea, it had turned out to be a nightmare. She had become his concubine and he could do whatever he pleased with her. It was horrible and degrading. One day, Roberto Rojo and his brother, Javier, came to visit Espada. They were two of the most popular matadors in the country. At twenty-three, Roberto was fast becoming a superstar. His sultry looks had been plastered all over the covers of the major Spanish magazines, and his private escapades often found their way into the tabloids.

"I'm not letting you go," she said playfully. "Forget the bulls tonight, all right?"

Rojo just laughed. "Are you kidding? I will make a million *pesetas* tonight. Providing I'm not killed, of course."

"Aren't you frightened?"

"Certainly. But not of the bull. I get stage fright. I'm afraid of the people in the audience. I don't like to be booed."

She laughed. "They never boo you. You're a hero to them."

He shrugged, "Yes, well . . . Still, it's more of a challenge to go out there in front of all those people than to face a charging bull."

The phone rang. He groaned and picked it up.

"Sí?"

The voice on the other end was muffled. "Señor Rojo?"

"What is it?"

"You have something that belongs to your manager," the voice said. "Señor Espada asks that you give it back."

Rojo sat up, nearly knocking Maria off of the bed. "You tell that son of a bitch Espada to leave me alone! He's a crook and a liar and a madman. He has single-handedly given the art of bullfighting a bad name. After tonight's *corrida,* I'm through with him. I'm changing managers."

"We beg you to reconsider, Roberto. Your life may depend on it."

"Is that a threat? Are you threatening me?" Rojo was furious. How dare they call him here! "How did you find me, anyway? How did you know what room I was in?"

"That doesn't matter now. So, do we take it that your answer is no?"

"That's right, it's no!" He slammed down the phone. "Bastards," he muttered.

"Who was it?" Maria asked, a little frightened at the show of temper.

"Someone who works for my ex-manager," he said. "Espada knows you're here. I don't know how he found out, but he did. He wants me to give you back."

Her eyes widened with fright.

Roberto kissed her. "Don't worry. I won't." He kissed her again. "Espada is trying to control his matadors in ways that he shouldn't. It's part of his grand plan to get his party elected. I'm supposed to be there in time for his speech and stand up there with him. He thinks that if the matadors are part of his political machine, then the rest of the people will follow him, too. Most of the *toreros* I know can't stand him. He's double-crossed them, cheated them, and disgraced the art."

Rojo got up and slipped on the terry-cloth robe that the hotel supplied. He opened the doors to the balcony and stepped outside. He deeply inhaled the fresh air and used the serenity of the landscape to help calm down.

"Want to take a shower together?" Maria called.

Rojo thought that was an agreeable suggestion. There was still time before he had to get to the bullring.

He went back into the bedroom and gazed at the naked girl on the bed. Perhaps he had time for one more. . . .

"Let's do it again first."

She laughed. "Roberto! You are a machine! No, thank you. You have worn me out. I'm taking a shower."

Maria got up and went into the bathroom. Roberto was about to follow her, but there was a knock on the door downstairs.

"Christ, who could that be?" he muttered. He bounded down the wooden stairs into the living room. Without bothering to look through the peephole, he unlatched and opened the door.

An absolutely stunning woman with long, flowing dark hair stood in the hallway.

"What do—oh, hello," he said.

"Roberto Rojo?" Margareta asked, smiling seductively.

Oh, he thought. She was a fan. She probably wanted his autograph.

"How did you find me?" he asked. "The hotel is supposed to keep autograph seekers like you away." He didn't recognize her, as Margareta had never met him when he had visited Espada's ranch.

"I was very determined to see you," she said.

"Well. Normally I would turn you away, but since you are so beautiful . . ."

He held the door open and gestured for her to enter. She sauntered in, pausing to run her index finger along his chin as she walked by him.

"Oh, I see you're not alone," Margareta said, indicating the sound of the shower upstairs.

"Uhm, no," Rojo replied. "Another fan. You know how it is."

"I sure do," she said. "Now. I want you to sit down in this chair while I take my clothes off for you."

"What?"

"You heard me. Sit in this chair." She pointed to one of the living room chairs facing the television.

"But what about . . . ?" he asked, pointing upstairs.

"We'll ask her to join us," Margareta said. "If she's not interested, then she can leave."

Rojo laughed and practically jumped into the seat. The terry-cloth robe parted, revealing his tight, muscular body. Margareta moved around in front of him and let the backpack slip off to the floor. Then, she slowly pulled down the zipper on the front of the body-suit, from her neck all the way to her crotch. The suit parted, revealing her shiny, tan skin. She was wearing nothing underneath.

Rojo's eyes bulged as he swallowed loudly.

Margareta stepped out of the suit, kicked it behind her, and then straddled his lap. She ran her hands up and down his chest and leaned in to kiss him.

As he closed his eyes and explored her mouth with his tongue, Margareta guided him into her. Rojo's grunts and moans quickly covered the sound of the shower upstairs as the strange woman rocked back and forth on his lap; leisurely at first, then faster and harder.

Margareta allowed herself a cry of pleasure as she climaxed with him. They remained motionless for a minute, clutching each other.

"What is your name?" he asked breathlessly. His eyes were closed.

She slowly disengaged from his body as the sound of the shower stopped. She reached down to the backpack and unsheathed a knife that was fastened to it. She brought it out and readied it.

"Some men call me *Mantis Religiosa*," she said.

Rojo opened his eyes. "Why?"

She paused a second, holding his chin up in her left hand. "Because of what those insects do to their mates. Oh, I almost forgot. I'm here to deliver a message from Domingo Espada."

With that, she swiftly drew the knife across Roberto Rojo's throat. Blood shot out in an arc, drenching them both.

Rojo's eyes bulged in horror. His hands grabbed at his neck as he fought for air and made horrible gurgling sounds. Margareta stood back as he slipped off the chair onto the floor, gagging and struggling for life. Margareta placed her foot on the back of his head and kicked it into the floor. That shut him up. He would die in silence.

Then she realized that she had unintentionally killed him the "Union Way." Margareta had heard stories of how the Union would sometimes make a statement by leaving a victim with a cut throat. Would this be interpreted as such? She smiled. It would be a good joke on Espada. Why not? She would soon be a full-fledged member of the Union. She was merely "between jobs."

She had forgotten about Maria until there was a scream on the stairs behind her. Margareta turned to see the wet, naked girl, recoiling in horror at the bloody sight.

Margareta slowly ascended the stairs as Maria fell to her knees on the steps, trembling with fright.

Margareta silenced the girl with one swift slash of the knife.

She then stepped over the body and went into the bathroom. She paused long enough to step into the shower and wash the blood off her body. Back downstairs, she dressed quickly and put on the backpack, then returned to the bedroom and walked through the open balcony doors.

It would not do to stroll back through the hotel lobby and outside in full view of the police.

The valley was one hundred meters below. It was a breathtaking vista.

Margareta reached behind and pulled straps from the backpack, fastened and adjusted them, then stepped up onto the balcony edge. She held herself steady and concentrated on what she was about to do.

BASE-jumping was illegal, but many daredevils liked to attempt it. A BASE rig allowed one to jump from a low altitude, such as a building or a cliff, and use a parachute to land. Margareta's rig was a Precision Dynamics "Super Raven 4" canopy, which was especially well suited for BASE-jumping. The low aspect ratio chute had been free-packed to ensure against "bag spin" or "bag lock" and enhance the odds of a straight-ahead opening. Even so, she had made sure the rig was set with deep and multiple brake settings so that it would fly slowly. That would buy her time to react if the canopy were to open pointing her toward the deadly cliff face. The slider had been removed to give almost instantaneous inflation of the canopy, but to soften that opening jolt, the chute was made of nonzero porosity fabric.

Margareta raised her arms wide, holding the rig's pilot chute in her right hand. She leaped from the balcony as far out as possible and dropped into the abyss. Once she was in midair, she threw the pilot chute out into the air stream. The nine-foot bridle line was long enough to ensure that the pilot chute would easily clear the burble of air. As the bridle line snapped taught, it dragged the canopy out of the pack.

The chute snapped open before Margareta had fallen one hundred feet. The seven-cell, ram-air canopy allowed her to glide like a hawk. She floated down to the valley, where a white Percheron stallion was waiting for her. He was tied to a tree, saddled and ready to go. Margareta flared the chute steeply and lightly touched down in seconds. She stripped off the backpack, and untied the horse. She took a moment to pat his neck and whisper quiet endearments in his ear, then she mounted the beautiful beast.

She looked up at the hotel on the edge of the cliff. Now the sky was a bright orange and blue, as the last rays of the sun streaked across the panorama. It would be ten minutes or so before the bodies were found. By then, she would be long gone. The bellboy and other eyewitnesses might recall seeing a beautiful woman dressed in black come through the hotel lobby . . . but they wouldn't be able to say whether or not they saw her leave.

Margareta jabbed the horse with her heels, and it galloped away into the hills.

TWELVE

THE CAMP

JUST BEFORE THE SUN SET, LATIF REGGAB AND JAMES BOND DROVE OFF IN A Land Rover on the main road that led southeast out of Tangier. As they drove toward the Hispanic-Moroccan city of Tetouan, the landscape became more hilly and green. It was a two-lane road populated by numerous slow-moving lorries, and Reggab muttered a prayer under his breath every time he attempted to pass them. After about half an hour the road became steeper and more twisting as they traveled higher into the Rif Mountains. Occasionally the hillsides were spotted with groups of stone houses and clusters of goats or sheep herded by *jellaba*-clad men. Bond noticed that the only landmarks along the road were petrol stations and the occasional checkpoint, where officers in gray uniforms, the *gendarmes,* sometimes stopped vehicles to look for drugs or check identity cards. Taxis were often targets for these random stops, due to regulations that restricted where certain types of them could go.

"Take a good look before it gets dark," Reggab said. "Very beautiful scenery driving into the Rif. Unfortunately, there are all these slow trucks."

Bond noticed that a *gendarme* waved the Land Rover through a checkpoint.

"They all know me," Reggab explained. "It is sad that such beautiful country is the main source for *kif.*"

Kif, Moroccan slang for marijuana, was the region's biggest export.

"Smoking that stuff is an ancient tradition in northern Morocco," Reggab said. "The cultivation is tolerated because it's the only way the people there can make a living. The government is searching for alternative crops, but until then . . ." He shrugged.

They came upon Tetouan an hour after they had left Tangier, but Reggab took the road south, higher into the mountains. Twenty minutes later, Reggab pulled over and stopped at a group of white buildings. The sun had nearly set, but Bond could see some activity behind the structures.

"This is a souq," Reggab said. "It's closing down for the evening, but there's a man here I need to see. It concerns our mission, tonight. We won't be long."

Bond was grateful to get out and stretch his legs. The headache was holding steady, even though he had miraculously caught three hours of sleep that afternoon in Latif's spare bedroom. He had washed and shaved after the nap, then prepared for the evening's excursion by dressing in dark clothing, strapping a Sykes Fairbairn commando knife to his shin, and carrying the P99 in a holster at his waist and the PPK under his arm, plainly visible.

The souq's "parking lot" was filled with mules. The flea market itself was made up of dozens of tents, *berrakas* (canopies supported by four poles), and lean-tos. The Berber tribes had come down from their various mountain homes to sell their wares. Many of them were packing up now, as the business day was finished.

Reggab led Bond through the crowd, shaking his head at the veiled women who were holding and offering live chickens. They came upon a tent where a man in a *burnous* was pouring spices into containers. Reggab and the man spoke Arabic and embraced each other, and then Reggab introduced Bond.

"This is my friend Khalil."

"Hello . . . how . . . are . . . you?" Khalil said in rehearsed English.

Reggab and Khalil continued to speak in Arabic. Reggab reacted to some news with dismay. The conversation continued as Bond wandered a few feet away to gaze upon the extraordinary sights of the souq. Only in countries like this could one see a market that was no different now than the way it was hundreds of years ago. Once one got away from the major cities, Morocco offered such cultural diversity that it would take Bond years to discern between the various tribes and ethnic groups.

Reggab took Bond's arm and said, "Let's go."

When they got back in the Land Rover and drove on, Reggab said, "I just heard some upsetting news. Rizki, my man in the mountains, was found dead this afternoon. They think he was seen taking those photographs last night, and whoever runs that camp was responsible."

"I'm sorry," Bond said. "They killed him for taking the pictures?"

"The strange thing is that he had been dead at least twelve hours. A courier sent that envelope this morning. That means someone other than Rizki took care of sending me the photos."

This revelation sent off alarms in Bond's mind. "You have no other people in the Rif?"

"No. Rizki was the only one."

"Then the enemy must have made sure you got those photos. Why?"

"I don't know. Maybe we'll find out."

A little less than an hour later, they arrived in the quaint village of Chefchaouen, which was known as the "blue city." This was because the walls of the buildings were painted blue four or five times a year. The blue paint supposedly kept the interiors cool in the summer and warm in the winter.

"Chaouen is one of my favorite places in Morocco," Reggab said as he pulled the Land Rover onto a main artery entering the city. "I think I will retire here. We are going to stop a moment, all right? I need to pay respects to Rizki's family."

The blue-washed houses were built up a gentle slope that culminated in a magnificent mountain overlooking the entire village. In the moonlight, they appeared to be ghostly, luminescent structures floating above ground level.

Bond followed Reggab into the medina, which was now sparsely populated and dark. The odors of the day's produce lingered, and Bond wondered if they ever went away. After a couple of twists and turns in the path, they came upon a baker's quarters. Reggab knocked on the door. When it opened, an older man almost said something nasty to the stranger who was disturbing the family's grief, but he recognized Reggab and embraced him warmly.

As is common in Morocco, the door was set into a frame in the wall so that one had to step over a sill to enter the building. A family of six or seven men and women were inside, all mourning the loss of their loved one. Reggab spoke quietly with the older woman, whom Bond presumed to be Rizki's wife. Mint tea was offered, and Reggab and Bond felt obliged to stay for a while. Bond was sorry for the family's loss and that one of Latif's operatives had been murdered, but he was anxious to get to the campsite.

Finally, Reggab made his excuses and stood up to leave. He embraced each family member and led Bond away with a loaf of bread in each hand.

On the way back to the Land Rover, he said, "Rizki's body was found on the side of the road near the camp. His throat had been cut."

The men exchanged glances, knowing full well what that implied.

The journey continued eastward toward Ketama, which was supposedly the hub of *kif* activity in Morocco. At one point, an intimidating black Mercedes appeared from nowhere in front of them, moving slowly. Reggab slowed down and was forced to follow closely behind the Mercedes. The narrow, winding road was treacherous in the dark, and even the most courageous of drivers would think twice before overtaking. Before Reggab could attempt it, the Mercedes stopped abruptly. Reggab slammed on the brakes and turned the wheel to avoid ramming the back of the car. Three rough-looking characters got out of the Mercedes and approached the Land Rover.

Bond was ready to draw his gun. Reggab put his hand on his friend's arm, indicating that he had it under control. He leaned out the window and spoke quickly to the men in Arabic. Reggab spat words at them, after which they appeared to apologize, bowed, got back into the Mercedes, and drove away.

"What was that all about?" Bond asked.

"They wanted to sell us a kilo of *kif*," Reggab replied. "If we hadn't agreed to buy it from them, there was a possibility that we would have been forced to do so. They thought I was a guide bringing a tourist into the mountains. When I explained that I was a 'policeman,' they decided to leave us alone. Don't worry; it happens all the time. You just have to know how to handle these characters."

An hour later, the nearly full moon cast a chilling glow over a dark landscape filled with large, ominous black shapes. They were in the very heart of the Rif Mountains.

"We are almost there," Reggab said. He peered through the windscreen, concentrating, as the road was inadequately illuminated by the headlamps. Finally, he pointed and said, "There. That's our landmark."

In the brief moment in which it was visible, Bond had seen a *berraka* built on the side of the road. At least one mule was hitched to the side and there had been a light—a campfire?—just in front of the *berraka*. It had been impossible to see how many human beings might have been there. Bond guessed two.

"They look like a couple of shepherds. The sheep are over there, on the side of that hill, you can barely see them in the moonlight."

Bond said, "I see them."

"They are really some kind of lookout for this camp. The turnoff is up ahead."

"Won't they report having seen you?"

Reggab shook his head. "This is still a major highway. The amount of traffic that comes through would not be worth keeping track of."

"Unless what you're trying to hide is important enough," Bond suggested.

Reggab grunted in agreement and made a sharp right onto a pitch-black dirt road. It wound around a mountain and eventually came to a bridge. Reggab slowed and parked the Land Rover beside the entrance to the bridge.

"The camp is just on the other side of the bridge, about a kilometer away. There's a gate there with at least two guards. Now. We're going to get out here and climb this mountain. Up there you can get a good view of the place. There's no fence on that side of the camp. The mountain serves as the barrier."

"Lead the way," Bond said. Before getting out of the Land Rover, he took four of Dr. Feare's pills. The headache gauge was climbing upward toward the "excruciating" mark.

Without the moonlight, climbing the mountain would have been impossible. They settled on a ledge near the top. The camp was approximately forty meters down the south face of the hill. Several campfires were burning amidst tents, *berrakas,* and some portable buildings. A number of jeeps, four-wheel drives, as well as horses and mules, were set off to one side. Bond could faintly hear Moroccan folk music coming from the largest tent, which was big enough to hold a circus ring. Reggab handed him a pair of field glasses. Bond put them to his eyes and adjusted the infrared brightness. He could now see men walking about. They were dressed mostly in army fatigues. Many of them looked European or North American. Others were dressed in traditional Arab or Berber clothing. They all carried guns.

"Latif, I think you're right about this being some kind of terrorist training camp," Bond said. "Those men are armed. How do the police let them get away with this?"

"It's private property," Reggab whispered. "Whoever owns it apparently has more influence over these parts than the government. If the Union is behind it, then there is a lot of money to throw around. Morocco is not a wealthy country, so it's very easy to bribe the officials. Look, that big tent is where they feed everyone. It serves as a mess during the day and a bar at night. We know that prostitutes are brought in some nights, and they leave in the mornings. If we could get some hard evidence that they are harboring heavy arms, we could maybe do something. So far, though, all the weapons you see are legal." He pointed to a relatively flat area. "Sometimes helicopters land there in that field. It's used during the day for training; the men are always out there exercising. Some target practice goes on, and we really can't get them for that."

"I'm going down to take a closer look," Bond said, handing back the glasses.

"I can't let you do that, James. It's too dangerous."

"You can't stop me, Latif. Look, meet me back at the Land Rover in thirty minutes. I have to try and find these men. I'll be as discreet as possible."

"If they catch you, you will be on your own. I am sorry."

"I understand. You must protect your cover. Now go on, I'll be all right."

Reggab hesitated, then shook Bond's hand. "Good luck, my friend. I shall see you soon."

Bond didn't wait for Reggab to leave. He moved swiftly down the rocks, darting from one shadow to another. Seven minutes later, he was at the base of the hill, near a dilapidated shack that smelled of excrement. A man in fatigues came out of the shed, buckling his pants. It was obviously the latrine.

Bond stealthily crept behind the shed, then followed the man by scrambling from tent to tent, keeping to the shadows. A laundry line was stretched behind one *berraka.* Bond pulled off a dark *jellaba* and put it on. If they caught him, at least he would look the part. The man ultimately got to the big tent, where the music was much louder. There were at least thirty men out in front with drinks in their hands, and inside the place was packed. Hoots and catcalls could be heard over the live band.

A festive bar atmosphere just might provide the camouflage Bond needed. Determinedly, Bond put the hood on, then walked right through the crowd and into the tent as if he knew exactly what he was doing. The men ignored him as they talked in Arabic and laughed.

A makeshift stage had been erected at one end of the tent. A four-piece band was performing behind a buxom belly dancer who attracted the gaze of every eye in the bar. One man played the *amzhad,* a single-chord violin made of wood and goatskin; two musicians played typical Arab and Berber drums, the *darbuka* and *tebilat.* The fourth man played the Arab lutelike instrument, an *oud.*

Bond wandered through the crowd, scanning the faces for someone familiar. After five minutes, he was about to give up and try somewhere else when a tall blond man came in and went to the bar. It was the Cockney from London—one of the thugs from the adult bookshop's office!

Bond waited until the brute had bought four bottles of beer, then followed him outside. He was almost certainly taking them to his bosses. . . .

The man crossed through the tents toward one of the small portable buildings. Bond took a detour around the latrine and came up behind the building. He was in luck—a window was open. Bond positioned himself at the edge and carefully looked inside.

The man had just delivered the bottles to Walter van Breeschooten and Michael Clayton. They were sitting at a card table playing poker. Wads of dirham notes were piled in front of them.

"Thanks, Rodney," Clayton said. The blond man grunted and left the little building. Bond waited and listened.

"I still don't understand why we couldn't stay in a hotel in the city," the Englishman said.

"This is only for tonight. Will you shut up?" van Breeschooten replied.

"I just don't know what we're doing here!"

"All will be clear tomorrow. We can't leave until . . . you know . . ."

"Until he shows up, I know . . ." Clayton said. "How do we know he will?"

"The strategist is always right," the Dutchman answered. "Now. We'll be splitting up tomorrow. You have the address in Casablanca?"

"Yes, I have it written down. It's in my pocket."

"Don't go to the Central Market. That entrance is closed. You have to go to the medina."

"We've been over this already."

"I just don't want you to get lost. We have to be there at eight in the morning, sharp. Day after tomorrow."

"I know, I know. I have to go and piss."

"Hurry back."

Bond heard Clayton leave the building, then crouched below the sight lines of the windows and moved to the edge of the building. Bond stepped out onto the path, assuming a normal stride behind his prey as he headed for the latrine. When Clayton went in, Bond followed him.

The man went into the smelly stall. Bond reached down and unsheathed the commando knife, which he had previously bound to his shin. He waited until Clayton was finished. When he stepped out of the stall, Bond grabbed hold of him and put the blade to his neck. He shoved him into a dark corner of the latrine.

"Mr. Clayton," Bond said. "Do you know who I am?"

Clayton's eyes were wide with fear. He nodded.

"I want the address of the Union headquarters in Casablanca. Give it to me or I'll carve out your Adam's apple and feed it to the mules."

"It's . . . it's in my pocket," Clayton stammered.

"You get it," Bond said. "No tricks."

The man reached into his trousers and pulled out a slip of notepaper. Bond took it and noted the address.

"Thank you," Bond said. "Now you have to answer for Helena Marksbury."

"Oh, God, please, no!" the man cried. "I didn't do it, I swear! It was Walter. My partner. He's the real Union man. He's one of the *commandants.* I just work for him. I swear. It was all his doing. I just followed orders."

"And did you kill her?"

"No, I swear," Clayton pleaded. "It was Walter. He did it. He does all the dirty work like that. He . . . he *likes* it! Please, don't hurt me!"

"And what about Dr. Feare?"

"Dr. Feare?"

Then Bond remembered. Clayton and van Breeschooten had already left London by the time Kimberley had been killed.

"Do you know who killed her?" Bond applied a little more pressure with the knife. The blade made a small nick in Clayton's neck.

"I don't know anything about Dr. Feare! I swear!"

The man seemed to be telling the truth. He was too frightened not to.

"*Why* was she killed? Was she Union?"

"I don't know! Maybe my cousin does! Please have mercy!"

"Who's your cousin?"

Bond heard voices approaching. At least two men were on their way inside. He had run out of time.

Clayton heard them and started to scream for help. Bond savagely sliced the man's neck, then stabbed him in the heart.

"There's your mercy. I made it quick," Bond spat.

Clayton gasped, his eyes bulging, then fell to the floor. Bond wiped the knife clean on the man's clothes, then walked out of the latrine just as the two men were stepping inside. One of them said something in Arabic and Bond grunted.

As soon as he was outside, Bond began to run. He heard shouts behind him, and the two men ran out of the latrine in pursuit. Bond zigzagged through the groups of tents and headed toward the hill. Shots were fired, and then a siren wailed.

A big man appeared in front of him and shouted, "Hey!" It was Rodney. Bond kicked, swinging his foot in the shape of a crescent moon. There was a discernable *crack* as he connected with Rodney's jaw. The man screamed and fell to the ground. Bond leaped over him and kept running.

Two floodlights snapped on and began to sweep the area. Men were running about in a state of confusion. What's the trouble? What happened? An intruder? Where?

Bond made it to the cliff just as a floodlight beam passed over him. There was more shouting, and two bullets whizzed uncomfortably close and ricocheted off nearby rocks. He didn't stop, praying that he could stay ahead of the light. It found him anyway, and it stayed with him as he ascended.

Bond turned with the Walther in hand to aim at the floodlight, but realized that he was out of range. More bullets chopped up the earth around him. He tried to roll out of the spotlight and keep climbing, but the light followed him to the top. Fortunately, he was up and over before any of the men could stop him.

He ran for the bridge, crossed it, and was never so happy to see a Land Rover waiting for him.

"Are you all right?" Reggab asked.

"Yes, let's get out of here!"

They jumped into the vehicle and fired it up. Reggab spun the wheels and took off. They heard more gunfire behind them. Bond looked back and saw three pairs of headlamps.

"They're right behind us. Step on it!"

"I'm going as fast as I can!" Reggab shouted.

The Land Rover made it to the main highway. Reggab swerved out of the dirt road and skidded on the gravel, straightened, and sped west toward Ketama. As they passed the landmark *berraka,* two men with automatic rifles stepped out into the middle of the road and began firing in their direction. Bullets broke the back window and took out a taillight. The three pursuing vehicles were gaining fast. They appeared to be jeeps, but it was really too dark to tell for certain.

Bond leaned out of the window and fired the Walther at them, but the road had too many bends. He couldn't get a good bead on them.

He sat back in the cab and said, "We're just going to have to outrun them."

"No problem," Reggab said, clutching the steering wheel. "Better fasten your seat belt."

But one of the jeeps had gained ground and was not far behind. More bullets slammed into the back of the Land Rover. There was a loud boom, the recognizable sound of a blowout. The Land Rover swerved and screeched as Reggab struggled to gain control. To avoid sailing off the cliff into a dark abyss, he pulled the wheel toward the mountain. The Land Rover sideswiped a rough patch of rocks, causing it to topple onto its side. The vehicle slid for twenty feet and crashed into the mountainside.

Bond was dazed. The first thing he was aware of was the sound of the Land Rover's blaring horn. Then he smelled the petrol leaking out the back. Bond looked over at Reggab. His friend was slumped forward, his head bent grotesquely. There was a bullet hole at the base of his skull.

Without another thought, Bond kicked at the passenger door above his head. He got it open and struggled to pull himself out. The three jeeps had stopped thirty yards away. Men with guns piled out and stood watching him.

Bond fell to the ground and crawled away from the Land Rover. He fought to get to his feet, but the sudden pain in his head and chest prevented him from doing so. He reached up and felt the sticky, wet blood in his hair. He collapsed on the road just as the Land Rover's petrol tank exploded behind him and the sudden waves of heat rolled over his body.

One of the men in uniform ran to him and dragged him across to the side of the road. Bond was woozy, unable to fight back. He felt his shirtsleeve being unbuttoned and rolled over. There was the prick of a needle, and in a moment he felt nothing.

THIRTEEN

ALL-POINTS ALERT

JAMES BOND OPENED HIS EYES.

Three alley cats were eyeing him suspiciously. When they saw that the human was awake, they scurried away.

The smell of urine and rotten eggs was overwhelming.

It was dawn. Bond could hear roosters crowing in the distance. His surrounding were bathed in the dim light of the new day.

He was lying on something scratchy.

Bond rose carefully. His head was spinning wildly, and he had a massive headache. Where the hell was he?

It was a street. A medina. He was lying on a pile of hay used to feed mules. Bond recognized Latif's shop across the little street and down a few doors.

He was back in Tangier! *How did he get here?*

Bond got to his feet and found that he was steadier than he expected. He took stock of his body. To his surprise, the Walther PPK was in the shoulder holster and the knife was in its sheath. His passport was in his pocket.

Hold on . . . the P99. It was gone. The holster on his belt was empty.

There were some cuts and bruises and a crusty wound on his head from the Land Rover wreck, but otherwise he seemed to be in one piece.

Again.

What the hell?

How did he get here? Could the Union have brought him here? If so, *why?* Wouldn't they have left him to die, or better yet, made sure of it?

Then he remembered the needle. He had been drugged.

Bond was convinced more than ever that something extraordinary was going on. Someone wanted him alive. In London, he had distinctly heard Clayton and von Breeschooten order their thugs not to shoot at him. After the Land Rover crash outside the terrorist training camp, he remembered seeing several vehicles and armed men surrounding him before he had succumbed to his injuries. They had put him to sleep and then carted him back to Tangier. It was the only possible explanation.

Bond wearily stumbled to Latif's shop and went inside. Reggab's son Hussein was shocked at Bond's appearance.

"I'm sorry," Bond said. "I have something I need to tell your mother."

The boy knew what the problem was just by looking at Bond's face. He immediately embraced Bond and sobbed. Bond held the boy and stroked his head before going inside to break the news to the rest of the family.

An hour later, Bond was back on the street, dressed respectably, and feeling as refreshed as he possibly could. He walked out of the medina so that he could catch a taxi to the railway station. Once again he examined the piece of paper he had taken from Michael Clayton. The slip said: "14 Ville de Casablanca." The Union headquarters.

As he entered the Grand Socco, he noticed that there was a high concentration of police cars circling the square. There seemed to be excitement in the air. People were rushing about and shouting. Something had happened.

He caught a Westerner and asked in French, "What's going on?"

"Terrorists on a ferry," the man said. "Some men shot a bunch of British tourists last night."

"What?"

"That's all I know. They're looking for the gunman."

Bond went to the nearest newsstand and bought an English newspaper.

He couldn't believe what he saw on the front page. *It was madness! Utter madness!*

The headline read: "TERRORISTS KILL BRITISH TOURISTS!" What was more disconcerting was a police drawing of a suspect who had fled the scene of the crime.

The man in the drawing looked just like Bond.

Bond quickly scanned the article to glean the details. Apparently, the ferry was on its way from Spain to Tangier. Sometime in the late evening hours, three armed men had taken control of the ship. Witnesses described them as "two Spaniards and an Englishman." The men entered the dining room and called for everyone with a British passport to come with them. There were ten in all—six men and four women. The men marched them to the front of the dining room. The British terrorist announced to the crowd, in English, that what they were doing was in the name of Domingo Espada of Spain. The man then called for an immediate surrender of Gibraltar, or war would break out between Spain and Britain. He then said, "This is the first strike." With that, he shot each and every British tourist, one by one. The two Spaniards held the rest of the crowd back with their weapons.

After the murders, the three men ran out of the room and hid somewhere on another deck. When the ferry got to Tangier, the police stormed the boat. Panic ensued as gunfire erupted all over the ship. The two Spaniards were killed, but the Brit slipped away unseen. He might have escaped with the crowd of frightened passengers who rushed the gangway after the incident.

Eyewitnesses described the unidentified Briton and the police were looking for the man shown in the drawing.

Bond dropped the paper in a dustbin and kept walking.

Christ! he thought. This was all becoming too bizarre.

As he couldn't possibly have done that horrible deed, someone was obviously impersonating him. The Union was behind it. That had to be the answer. It was some kind of diabolical plot, and he was a part of it. The only way to uncover this mystery was to go to Casablanca and find the Union headquarters. He would kill everyone in the place if he had to. Walter van Breeschooten would be number one on the hit list.

"SmeH leeya! Inta!"

Bond looked up and saw a policeman ten feet away, walking toward him. Without a second's hesitation, Bond turned and ran. The policeman called on him to halt in Arabic and French and the chase began. Bond crossed the square and ran up stone steps that connected to a major avenue, Rue de la Liberté. The traffic was heavy, and Bond used this to his advantage by darting in and out between cars. Horns blared and drivers shouted at him as they slammed on the brakes to avoid hitting him. Bond glanced back and saw that the policeman was still in pursuit. He forged ahead, running down the avenue to the Place de France roundabout, then turned southeast onto Boulevard Pasteur and ran across a bridge overlooking the Grand Socco below. Another set of stone stairs led back down, so he took them three at a time. Bond ran past men selling piles of silver, smelly fish, then slipped into a crowd of veiled women. They screamed as he pushed through and turned a corner, finding himself in a narrow alley. He stopped and pressed himself against a wall, attempting to catch his breath. He waited, hoping he had lost the policeman.

"Put your hands up!" The voice came from the other end of the alley. It was the policeman. He must have known another way around. He held a handgun and was calmly walking toward Bond.

Perhaps the smartest thing he could do at this point was surrender, Bond thought. He should let London handle it. Surely Bill Tanner would believe that Bond had not committed those crimes.

Bond slowly raised his hands. The policeman had a glint in his eye. He had caught the terrorist!

A gunshot rang out, reverberating in the narrow alley. Bond was confused—at first he thought that the policeman had fired his gun. Instead, the officer stumbled and dropped his firearm. A red splotch spread across the man's chest, and he fell to the ground. Bond looked around frantically, trying to pinpoint where the shot had come from. There were some windows in the building overlooking the alley, but they were dark.

He scanned both ends of the alley. They were clear. Rather than ask questions, he decided to keep running. He backed out of the alley and ran back to the square, and then climbed up the stairs to Boulevard Pasteur. He hailed a taxi and told the driver to take him straight to the railway station.

The station was crowded with commuters coming into the city from the outskirts. Bond bought a one-way first-class ticket to Casablanca. His timing was perfect. He could catch a rapid-service train in one hour. Now he only had to stay unnoticed in the waiting area.

At least three policemen were patrolling the station, probably looking for him. Bond went into the gift shop and purchased a pair of cheap sunglasses and an American-style baseball cap with "Morocco!" stitched on the front. It wasn't much of a disguise, but it would have to do for now.

Bond spent the rest of the hour in the small snack bar, where he had a mediocre breakfast of eggs and yogurt. Nevertheless, the food made him feel better, and he thought that perhaps he could get some sleep on the train. If only the damned headache would go away . . . as well as the nagging feeling that he was being watched.

He took his time with the breakfast, then made his way out to the platform, where the ONCF express to Casablanca sat waiting. The trains in Morocco are modern and reliable. They are painted red and yellow with black tops, and the compartment classes are clearly marked on the outside. Bond got into the only first-class carriage and found his compartment. For the moment he was alone, but there were five other seats. He had purposefully asked for a nonsmoking compartment, thinking that it might be less crowded. If he wanted a smoke, he could go out into the corridor or stand on the platform and look out the back of the train.

Before long, the train began to move. The conductor came by and punched his ticket without saying a word. Bond settled into his seat and silently watched the scenery.

He felt more alone than he had ever felt in his life.

—◦—

"It can't be him," M said, looking at the police sketch of the terrorist suspect.

Tanner shook his head. "I don't believe it, either."

"We need to determine if Double-O Seven really went to Morocco. Still no answer from Station NA?"

"No, ma'am. I've left three messages. If Mr. Reggab is anywhere around, he should have got back to me."

The intercom buzzed. M pushed the button. "What is it?" she snapped.

"An urgent communication came in from Cipher. I'm sending it through on your PC," Moneypenny said.

"All right, thank you," M said.

Tanner looked over M's shoulder as she punched the keyboard and Bond's coded message came up.

> LATIF REGGAB, STATION NA, KILLED BY THE UNION.
> PLEASE MAKE ARRANGEMENTS FOR HIS WIDOW ASAP.
> WILL REPORT WHEN I KNOW MORE.
>   007

M punched the intercom again.

"Moneypenny, where did this message come from?"

"Somewhere strange," her secretary said. "Wait a second . . . here it is. Thailand."

"Thailand?!"

"Cipher thought that it had been routed through several countries so that we wouldn't know where it originated from."

"Thank you."

Tanner sighed. "Well, I doubt it came from Thailand."

"He's obviously in bloody North Africa!" M said. "You were right. That fax from Felix Leiter indicated as much. Double-O Seven's going against my orders and is off on a mission of personal vendetta."

Tanner sat down in front of the desk. He had found Leiter's fax in Bond's office, as well as the other documents concerning the Union.

"I think you need to look at it from his perspective, ma'am," he said gently.

"I understand his perspective!" she spat. "It doesn't mean that he can compromise SIS and my orders. Have you spoken to Inspector Howard today?"

"No, ma'am. As far as I know, Double-O Seven's still the number one suspect in Dr. Feare's murder."

The red phone rang. M picked it up and said, "Yes?" She listened intently for a moment, then said, "Thank you," and hung up.

Tanner waited for her to speak. She looked at him with concern and said, "A group of Spanish tourists were attacked in London a couple of hours ago. An angry mob surrounded them in Piccadilly. One man was killed."

"My God."

"The PM has asked that the summit meeting in Gibraltar be moved up. We're waiting on the exact date and time, but it will probably be in a day or two. In the meantime, NATO and the U.N. are urging restraint."

The intercom buzzed again. "Now what?" M asked.

"Captain Hodge is here. He says it's urgent," Moneypenny said. Hodge was the head of the antiterrorism section at SIS.

"Well, send him in. I can only imagine . . ."

Captain Hodge, a tall man in his fifties, walked into the room.

"Good morning, ma'am, Chief-of-Staff," he said.

"What do you have for us, captain?" she asked.

"It's not good, I'm afraid." He held up a videocassette. "Something you ought to look at."

M gestured to the VCR and monitor on the cabinet to her left. "Be my guest."

Hodge popped in the cassette and turned on the monitor. The picture was grainy and black-and-white, shot from a security camera. Numerals indicated the date and time of the recording.

"This was recovered from the ferry's camera in the dining area where the shootings occurred. It happened on Deck Seven, also known as the 'boat deck.' "

They could make out a number of people dining at tables. There was a bar in the background.

"The Comarit ferry left Algeciras, Spain, at approximately seven o'clock last night. There were fifty-three passengers and eight staff. Most of them were Spanish or Moroccan citizens. The ten British citizens were businessmen and women in the hotel industry. You can see them sitting together at that table, there." Hodge pointed to a large round table. "Now watch carefully."

Three men came through a passage and entered the dining room. Two of them were strangers, but the third appeared to be James Bond. The trio produced automatic weapons and began to shout. There was no sound on the tape, so M and Tanner had to imagine what was being said. The reactions of the people in the room told all. Many of them ducked down under the tables. Finally, the British citizens stood warily and produced their passports to Bond. He then ushered them to the back of the room. The two Spaniards forced them to stand against the bar, their backs to the room. James Bond then stood behind them and opened fire, killing them in cold blood.

"My God," M muttered.

As soon as the deed was done, Bond turned to the room and said something else. Then he did something strange. The killer placed his handgun on the counter. Hodge froze the frame, pressed a button, and zoomed in on the gun.

It was a Walther P99.

"Is that your missing handgun?"

Tanner squinted. "It's a P99, all right."

"The killer left it there on the counter, its magazine empty. We should have the serial number in an hour or two and we'll know if it's a match," Hodge said. Then he manipulated the frame and zoomed in on the terrorist's face.

Up close, there was no mistaking those features.

"We've positively identified the man as Double-O Seven," Hodge said. "We think that after the shootings the three of them went down two levels, past the saloon deck, to the car deck. They probably hid inside a car or lorry until the ferry docked at Tangier. There were very few personnel aboard the ferry, so there was nothing they could do. Once the boat got to Tangier, the police boarded, but someone started shooting. It's still not clear what happened. The two Spaniards were killed, but Bond was nowhere to be found."

"Damn it, it's got to be a mistake!" M said. "Someone must be impersonating him!"

"Bond wouldn't do this, Captain," Tanner said.

"Nevertheless, I urge you to bring him in," Hodge said.

"Is there anything else?" M asked.

"Yes." Hodge handed a report to Tanner. "These are the police records on the two Spaniards. As you can see, they have a history of terrorist acts. If you'll look at the most recent information on the ugly one, you can see that it's unlikely that these men were working for Domingo Espada."

Tanner and M read it together. One of the men was wanted in Israel for a bombing. The Union had later claimed responsibility for it.

"The Union," M said flatly. "Of course."

"They're trying to stir things up between Britain and Spain," Tanner suggested.

"But why? What's in it for them?"

Tanner shrugged. "Revenge?"

"We need to get this information to the PM and to Spain. It might help alleviate the tension if they know that the Union was behind this attack, not Britain," M said.

"I'll get on the phone right away," Tanner said.

"What about Double-O Seven?" Hodge asked.

M set her jaw. "We have to hope that all of this is a tremendous error, but we also have to assume the worst. We must accept the possibility that Bond has joined the Union. They've been successful in recruiting our people before. I would be remiss in my responsibilities if I didn't issue an all-points alert for the apprehension of Double-O Seven."

FOURTEEN

JOURNEY BY RAIL

THE TRAIN ROLLED OUT OF TANGIER AND HEADED SOUTH ALONG THE coastline toward Rabat. Bond stared wearily at the passing scenery, which grew flatter as the journey progressed. For the first time in hours, he had a chance to sit and mull over the events of the past two days. He wished that he could relax, but he was wound up like a coil.

It wasn't long before he craved a cigarette. He got up and left his compartment, made his way through the narrow corridor and stepped out onto the rumbling platform at the back of the train. He removed the gunmetal case, took a cigarette, and lit it.

Had his career finally come to an end? he asked himself. Was it time to give it up? Had he begun to pay the price for living on the edge for so long? He had seen it in other agents. Something in them finally snaps and they have to put in for early retirement. Was this happening to him? Was he absolutely certain that he could beat this thing on his own? What if he really *was* going insane?

Stop it! he commanded himself. Don't be ridiculous. It's some kind of Union plot . . . it's obviously some kind of Union plot. . . .

Bond's thoughts were interrupted when an attractive blonde opened the door and joined him on the platform. She didn't look at him or speak; she dug into a handbag, found her own cigarettes, and attempted to light one.

"Allow me," he said. He produced the Ronson lighter and cupped the flame close to her face.

She got it lit and said, "Thank you."

For a moment, they stood there in the open air, enjoying that exhilarating sensation of watching the tracks rush away from the train.

"I get claustrophobic on trains," she said. "Smoking in the corridor isn't cool even though everyone does it. I'm in a smoking car, but it's just too crowded. I like to smoke but I don't like to live in a cloud of it. I had to get some air."

She had an American accent. She seemed to be in her mid- to late twenties.

"I know what you mean," Bond said. "You're welcome to join me in my compartment. It's nonsmoking, I'm afraid, but there's no one else in there."

She eyed him up and down, then smiled. "That was the quickest pickup line I think I've ever heard."

"Forgive me," Bond said. "I didn't mean it that way. My name's Cork. John Cork."

She looked him up and down again, then smiled once more. "Hello, John Cork. My name is Heidi Taunt."

"It's a pleasure," Bond said. "What brings you to Morocco from the States?"

"How do you know I live in the States?"

"I assumed that you're American."

"I'm a California girl, born and raised, but I don't live there," she said. "We live in Tokyo."

Hell, Bond thought. She was married.

"My sister and I," she added. Heidi looked back through the window into the corridor. "What about you? You sound English."

"I live in London," Bond admitted.

"You don't look English."

"How does one look English?"

"I don't know," she said. "I just meant that you don't look English *here,* in Morocco. You have that 'dark, handsome foreign stranger' quality." She shrugged and smiled.

She was flirting with him!

Heidi Taunt was tall and well built. She was wearing designer jeans, which tightly outlined her long legs without revealing too much and offending the social sensibilities of the Moroccans. She had on a white blouse with the sleeves rolled up. The top two buttons were undone, exposing substantial cleavage.

Her shoulder-length blond hair was fine and straight, parted in the middle. She had dark brown eyes that exhibited intelligence and a sense of humor. Bond found her incredibly sexy.

"So what brings you from Japan to Morocco?" Bond asked.

"My sister and I are travel guide writers. We've done a series of books on various countries. Perhaps you've seen them? The *Small World* books?"

"I can't say that I have. Sorry."

"That's all right," she said. "We've only done four. This is our fifth. We're published in America and Britain."

"That sounds like a fun job."

She finished her cigarette and tossed the butt onto the tracks. "It is. It's more work than you think, though. It's not just traveling to exotic places. The business side of it is overwhelming. But you're right, it's great fun to travel. We hope to visit every country in the world, my sister and I."

"That's quite an ambition."

"I know, it's impossible, but we like to imagine it."

"Where are you going? Rabat?"

"No, to Casablanca. To Marrakesh after two nights. Rabat on the way back. What brings you here?"

"I'm an importer and exporter," Bond replied.

"What do you import and export?"

"Junk, mostly. A whole lot of nothing."

She laughed.

Bond offered the cigarette case to her, but she shook her head. "No, thanks, I'm going back inside. It was nice to meet you, Mr. Cork." She held out her hand. Bond took it.

"Call me John. It was a pleasure, Heidi. Where are you staying in Casablanca?"

Her hand was smooth and cool. She allowed him to hold it.

"The Royal Mansour Meridien."

"What a coincidence!" Bond said. "That's my hotel, too."

"Small world," she said, smiling wickedly.

Actually, Bond hadn't thought about where he would stay, but he knew the hotel. It was one of the best in Casablanca. Staying at a large five-star hotel like that might be what the authorities looking for him would least expect him to do. And if he happened to have a girlfriend . . . ? A perfect cover, one the police weren't looking for . . .

She withdrew her hand, turned and opened the door. "Maybe I'll see you there."

"Heidi," Bond said, stopping her. "Would you care to have dinner with me at the hotel tonight? It has a lovely Moroccan restaurant."

"Why, thank you, John, that sounds terrific. I'll see you later, then."

And she was gone.

Bond congratulated himself. His way with women had not changed. Screw the headache, he thought. There was desire in that girl's eyes!

Bond finished his cigarette and went back inside the train. He made his way back to his compartment, which was still empty, and he collapsed heavily into his seat. He put his feet up on the opposite seat and looked out the window at the passing rows of cacti, which seemed to be more plentiful as the train went farther south. The color of the earth changed, too, as the climate became hotter and more arid.

He shut his eyes and felt merciful waves of drowsiness pull him toward unconsciousness. The movement of the train, combined with physical exhaustion, lulled Bond into a fitful but badly needed sleep.

When he opened his eyes, the train was still rocking and rumbling toward its destination. He felt another presence in the compartment with him.

Heidi was sitting across from him, with a seat between hers and the one where his feet were propped. She was reading a romance novel and had on reading glasses; otherwise she was still dressed in the tight jeans and white blouse.

"Hello there," Bond said, sitting up and straightening his jacket. "I must have dozed off."

She glanced at him and gave a cursory smile and nodded, but kept silent. Her eyes went back to the book.

Odd, Bond thought. What was the matter with her?

"So," he said, "what time are we having dinner?"

The blonde looked up at him over her glasses. "I beg your pardon?"

"Dinner? Tonight? At the hotel? What time?"

Heidi opened her mouth as if she had just been insulted. She closed her book and stood. "I think I'll go back to the compartment I was in before." She opened the door and stepped into the corridor. Her parting words were, "You have some nerve, asshole." Then she walked on.

What the hell? Bond rubbed his eyes. Did he dream that?

He felt foolish and confused.

Dizzy woman, he thought. Well, she had admitted being from California. She had probably grown up on the beach, wearing skimpy bikinis and giving all the teenaged boys inflexible frustration. To hell with her . . .

The train stopped in Rabat, Morocco's capital. There was a half-hour wait before it departed, so Bond took the opportunity to don his sunglasses and baseball cap and stretch his legs. Rabat station is larger and has more amenities than the one in Tangier. He scanned the newspapers in the gift shop but couldn't find one in English. A French paper proclaimed that war between Britain and Spain was imminent. There was a photo of Domingo Espada, surrounded by bodyguards, giving a speech at a bullring. Several matadors were standing beside him.

Bond recognized one of them. Javier Rojo was a young bullfighter whom Bond got to know by accident just a few years ago at an art gallery in Lisbon. Bond's date had been a friend of the artist. Apparently Javier's date was, too. They had met at the bar, where Bond was busy with a vodka martini in an effort to avoid the small talk of the art crowd. Rojo was having a soft drink, and he turned to Bond and said, in English, "The only alcohol I drink is wine at dinner."

"Why?" Bond had asked.

"You have to be sober to do what I do."

He was a handsome, fiery young man in his mid-twenties, and he had come from a long line of bullfighters. His grandfather had been one of the most famous matadors in Spain until he was killed in the ring. Rojo's father was also a very successful bullfighter who had passed the torch on to his two sons when he retired. Javier Rojo was wealthy, popular, and as much a celebrity as one could be in Spain.

Bond blinked when he saw the headline of a related story on the inside of the paper. "ROBERTO ROJO MURDERED."

That was Javier's younger brother!

Bond read with incredulity how the young matador and the body of an unidentified young girl had been found slain in his hotel room in Ronda. According to the police, the bullfighter's "throat had been cut."

It was the Union way. Could it be a coincidence? Bond wondered.

He thought back to the beginning of his friendship with Javier Rojo.

That night in Lisbon, Bond and the young bullfighter had struck up a conversation and found that they got along well. Bond had always held the art of bullfighting at arm's length until Rojo had enlightened him. Like most non-Spaniards, Bond was of the opinion that bullfighting was both cruel and archaic. This notion changed after Rojo convinced Bond to come to a *corrida* and watch him fight. Rojo had taken the time to teach Bond the history of bullfighting and its traditions, and why the Spanish were so passionate about it. After a week as Javier's guest, Bond began to see why men like Ernest Hemingway and Orson Welles had become fascinated by bullfighting. Bond grew to appreciate the art and drama behind the spectacle, and he admired the courage of the matadors who risked their lives to face a charging bull.

Bond studied the newspaper carefully. So Javier Rojo was in with Domingo Espada now. Bond wished that he didn't have the Union to deal with. Otherwise, he could be in Spain, seeking out Espada and stopping him from instigating this idiotic conflict between their two countries. Perhaps Rojo could be of help.

Bond sighed. He couldn't think about that now. He had other, more important things to worry about. Britain would deal with Spain. If war broke out, it would be over quickly. NATO or the U.N. would negotiate a settlement. Bond didn't have to worry.

Or did he? The terrorists aboard the ferry in Tangier—they had claimed that they were working for Domingo Espada.

The police sketch of the suspect was also on the front page. The caption said that the "British terrorist was still at large." Although he hadn't been identified yet, there was some speculation that he was with British secret intelligence.

Wonderful, Bond thought. He wagered that the press would know his name within a day.

He rejoined the train after eating a dry roast beef sandwich and drinking a Spéciale Flag beer. His compartment now had three new people in it—a man, his veiled wife, and a small boy, who was already fussing over a toy that his father had taken from him. Bond wasn't about to stand for that, so he excused himself and went back out to the corridor as the train pulled away from the station.

He went to the rear of the train to smoke another cigarette and watch the remnants of Rabat disappear. Trains were Bond's favorite means of traveling if he couldn't drive a fast car. There was something old-fashioned and romantic about train travel. Airplanes simply dropped a person in the middle of a location. With trains, one was injected into the bloodstream of a country, and enabled to see the people and places and cultures. It took more time to get around, but it was far more gratifying.

The door to the corridor opened behind him and Heidi Taunt came out to join him.

"Hi there," she said, brightly. She was smiling broadly, as if the earlier encounter in the train compartment had never happened. "We've got to stop meeting like this."

Bond didn't say anything, wondering what her game was. He did offer her a cigarette, which she took.

"Thanks," she said. "Hey, what time do you want to meet for dinner?"

Even more confused, Bond said, "Eight o'clock?"

"Fine," she said. "The Moroccan restaurant. I can't wait to see the King Hassan II mosque. I hear it's one of the wonders of the world. Have you seen it?"

"Yes, it's lovely," Bond said. "But I must say that Casablanca is not my favorite city in Morocco."

"I hear it's not so great," she concurred. "Marrakesh is supposed to be *the* place to go. I hear Fes is nice, too."

"You're right on both counts." Bond finished his cigarette. Why was she so friendly now, when just a little while ago she had treated him with disdain?

Without warning, she said, "Excuse me," and reached up to remove Bond's sunglasses. She peered at his face, studying it. "I just wanted to see your eyes. They're very sexy." She handed back the sunglasses. "Here you go."

She stubbed out her cigarette and tossed the butt into the air. She squeezed his arm lightly and said, "See you tonight, handsome." She reentered the train, leaving Bond dumbfounded.

Bond took the time to smoke another cigarette, then went back inside. He didn't feel like sitting in his compartment, so he walked through the first-class car and entered the adjoining second class. It was very crowded. He moved through the people standing in the corridor and went on into the next car.

He saw Heidi coming toward him, holding a soft drink she must have purchased from the food and drink cart.

"We're going to be in the gossip magazines if we keep bumping into each other like this," Bond said with a smile.

Heidi looked at him as if he were the rudest man alive. "Stop following me or I'll call the conductor," she said much too loudly. She pushed past him, opened a compartment door, and went inside.

Bond squinted and rubbed his brow. What the hell was going on here? Why the hot and cold treatment? Was she some kind of nut?

His old friend, the headache, was returning. He rubbed his temples, turned around, and went back to the first-class car. He rejoined the family in his compartment and sat in his seat, glumly looking out the window.

After six hours, not including the stop in Rabat, the train pulled in to Casablanca Voyageurs station, located four kilometers east of the city

centre. It was midafternoon, and the place was buzzing with
activity—commuters were trying to get home, tourists were catching
the next express to another destination in Morocco, porters and
guides were attempting to hustle business. . . .

Bond got off the train and looked around for Heidi. He didn't see
her in the mass of people. The train had filled up at Rabat, and now
there was a rush of passengers trying to get on for the next leg of the
journey.

He went outside into the warm air and hailed a taxi. The driver
took him to Le Royal Mansour Meridien on Avenue des FAR, easily
one of the most exclusive five-star hotels in the city. Ten stories high,
it lay in the heart of the city's business center and bore the name of
Ahmed Mansour Addabhi, the most glorious line of Saadi monarchs.

Bond registered as John Cork in the circular reception space. The
lobby was a large open hall, much like a cloister, with blue square
divan pieces surrounding a thick marble column. The lobby was very
bright, accentuated by the mirror panels set in a geometric pattern
around the room. An indoor waterfall at the back and numerous
potted plants created a garden atmosphere.

There was a message for him at the concierge desk. It was hastily
scribbled on hotel stationery and read, "Dinner at 8:30 instead of
8:00. OK? Heidi."

Fickle woman, Bond thought. He had a good mind to stand her up.

He took the lift to the third floor, where his suite was located.
Bond was impressed with the size and tastefully decorated room. The
suite contained a functional office, sitting room, bedroom with twin
beds, and a bathroom tiled in white marble.

This would do nicely, Bond thought, but he needed a drink. His
head was still pounding and he needed to unwind.

Rather than use the minibar, Bond took the lift to the ninth floor.
La Terrasse, a bar overlooking the city, offered a superb view of the
vast flat rooftops with antennas and satellite dishes, the splendid
Hassan II Mosque, and Casablanca harbor. Bond ordered vodka with
ice and sat at one of the tables to gaze upon the metropolis.

Bond didn't like the city, but he appreciated its history. Originally called the port of Anfa, Casablanca had been created by Berbers. From the mid-nineteenth century onward, Casablanca became one of the most important ports in Africa, and once the French Protectorate took over in 1912, it had the biggest harbor in Morocco. Casablanca is now the fifth largest city on the continent.

Bond whiled away the remaining hours watching CNN in his room. The news was full of the British/Spanish conflict. Spanish tourists had been mobbed in London. The border between Spain and Gibraltar had been declared a no-man's zone. All traffic across the border had been stopped. The Royal Navy patrolled the waters of the Mediterranean. The U.S. president had offered to broker a settlement. At the center of it all was the man who had sparked the trouble—Domingo Espada. He was seen in parades, marching with his supporters, calling for the return of a Franco-inspired government. The administration in Madrid had finally spoken out against Espada, claiming that he was a "rebel." They were sitting on their hands, though, choosing to wait and see what was going to happen.

Plans for the summit meeting in Gibraltar had gone awry when the Spanish Prime Minister refused to sit at the same table with Espada. The king of Spain was intervening, and it looked as if the meeting would finally take place in four days, on Monday. Attendees would include Espada, the Spanish PM, the British PM, and several United Nations representatives from interested countries in the area.

It all seemed so far away and unimportant to Bond. At the forefront of his mind was the Union, the score he needed to settle, and the nagging fear that he was going mad.

Never mind, he thought. His rendezvous with Walter van Breeschooten was tomorrow morning.

At 8:30 sharp, Bond went down to the restaurant, Le Douira, which was designed as two distinct representations of Moroccan culture. One side was in a genuine caïdal tent, and the other was decorated in intricate blue and white tile work, like the inside of a traditional Moroccan palace.

Bond had decided he would confront Heidi about her erratic

behavior on the train. He wasn't about to put up with games, no matter how attractive a girl might be.

He waited for ten minutes and finally heard Heidi's voice behind him.

"Here we are, sorry we're late."

Bond turned and blinked. He thought he was seeing double.

"John," Heidi said. "I'd like you to meet my sister, Hedy."

Now everything was clear. Hedy was Heidi's identical twin.

FIFTEEN

"AS TIME GOES BY"

THE TWO GIRLS HAD IDENTICAL FACES, BUT HEDY HAD SHORT RED HAIR, which Bond quickly decided was really a wig.

"*This* is the guy?" Hedy asked her sister.

"Hedy, this is John Cork," Heidi said, beaming. "It's okay that my sister came along, isn't it?" she asked Bond.

Bond couldn't help but laugh. "I believe we've already met but didn't realize it. You weren't wearing the wig on the train, were you?"

"No," Hedy said. She folded her arms and looked at Heidi with a frown.

Heidi said, "Oh *no*, not again! This happens all the *time!* Damn it, Hedy, that's why we never have any boyfriends."

"You'll pick up *anyone,* Heidi! He made a pass at *me* out of nowhere. I thought he was a pervert," Hedy said, glaring at Bond.

"I'm sorry, John," Heidi said. "It really *does* happen a lot. Men have a problem telling us apart. It's a sore subject with us both. That's why we sometimes take turns wearing the wig. It's not that we compete with each other, it's just that whoever we happen to be dating always ends up hitting on the other one, usually by accident."

"Sometimes *not* by accident," Hedy added.

Heidi agreed and nodded. "It can be a problem. I guess we should have used the wig on the train."

She was right. Hedy was an exact copy of Heidi in every respect.

They were both wearing full-length, relaxed fit-and-flare sundresses made of ribbed cotton, buttoned in front down to their knees. The only difference was that Heidi was in gray and Hedy was in black.

"Well, the wig helps, but have you considered dressing differently?" Bond suggested wryly.

Hedy looked at Heidi and said, "He's a wise guy, too, Heidi." She turned back to Bond and asked, "How do we know you're not a serial killer?"

"Ladies, please," Bond said. "My apologies, Hedy, if I offended you earlier today. It was not intentional. As you say, you do look uncannily like your sister. Now, if you're saying that your dilemma is that the same man falls in love with both of you, I can understand why. Might I suggest a reasonable solution to your problem? That would be to agree to share the man, and I'm afraid that's just what you'll have to do this evening. Let's have dinner, shall we? I'm starving."

Heidi laughed, but Hedy remained unreceptive. She followed along grudgingly when the maître d' asked them to first wash their hands, the Moroccan way, with a pitcher and basin. They were then shown to the tented side of the restaurant, where they sat on cushioned seats at low tables. Heidi commented on the beautiful décor and Hedy said, "Let's hope the food warrants it."

As it turned out, the food was excellent. For starters, they shared *panaché de briouates aux crevettes,* a variety of puff pastries stuffed with shrimp, chicken, and minced meat. Bond had *tagine de kebab maghdour aux oeufs,* a traditional Moroccan dish of meat kebab in a spicy paprika sauce with a fried egg on top. It was served in a *tagine,* the Moroccan pot shaped like an inverted top. Heidi had roasted rack of lamb, and Hedy opted for chicken with couscous. The girls insisted on drinking cold beer, so it was Spéciale Flag all around.

"So does this meet your expectations?" Heidi asked her sister.

"It's pretty good," Hedy admitted, finally cracking a smile.

They exchanged the usual sort of small talk that occurs when people are meeting one another for the first time. The girls talked about growing up in California, as Bond suspected, on the beach. They had been models when they were children, doing print and television ads for a variety of products.

"We were cute kids," Heidi said.

"You still are," Bond added.

"But we decided to join the real world when we became teenagers," Hedy explained. "We both liked the traveling part of the modeling jobs, so that's what we decided to do. We're pretty good travel writers, if I say so myself."

"I do most of the PR because Hedy says I'm more bubbly than she is," Heidi said. "Hedy does the lion's share of the writing. We both do the research. We make a good team."

"We've always been inseparable," Heidi explained. "We do everything together."

"Everything?" Bond asked.

"Not everything," Hedy quickly answered.

"If we ever disagree on something, we flip a coin. Heads I win, tails she loses."

"Very funny," Hedy said.

There was a moment's silence before Heidi said, "Mr. Cork says he's an importer and exporter."

"Oh?" Hedy asked. "And what exactly does that mean?"

Bond shrugged. "I make sure things go in and out. Smoothly."

Heidi grinned at Bond. Hedy caught the exchange and frowned.

"Seriously," he continued, "I work for a firm in London that deals with arts and crafts. Carpets, mostly. There's a man in Tangier we buy from. I need to see someone in the medina tomorrow. I arrange the deals and let others deliver."

"You were in Tangier last night?" Hedy asked.

Bond nodded.

"Did you hear about what happened on that ferry?"

Bond felt a sudden stab of paranoia. Had she been reading the papers? Had she recognized him?

"Yes, I heard about it this morning."

Heidi shook her head. "It was terrible. . . ."

Looking at Bond, Hedy said, "I hope they catch the guy who did it."

"Me, too," Bond said, meeting her gaze. She was studying him intently. Had she seen the drawing in the newspaper? Was it safe to be in their company?

The girls shared a piece of chocolate cake for dessert and they all had coffee. A live band had begun playing traditional Moroccan folk music. Finger cymbals rung throughout the restaurant, casting a mesmerizing and exotic charm over the diners.

"Do you go back to London after you're through here, John?" Hedy asked.

"I think so," Bond said. "I may . . . I may be sent somewhere else. I'm not sure yet."

"What should we do now?" Heidi asked cheerfully. "The night is young, as they say." She winked at Bond.

"The night is quickly fading," Hedy said. "Come on, Heidi, I want to hit the sack."

"Hedy! It's so early!"

"We have to get *up* early, remember? We have that guided tour of the city. . . ."

"Big deal. I'd rather stay up and hang out with Mr. Cork." Heidi was a little tipsy from the beer.

"I don't think so, sis. I'm sure Mr. Cork needs to go to bed early, too," Hedy said.

"Hedy, don't be rude," Heidi said. "I know, let's flip for it."

"Please, Heidi."

Heidi looked at Bond, shrugged, and shook her head, as if she were asking, "What am I going to do with her?"

"As a matter of fact," Bond said, "I am a bit tired. Bit of a headache, too. I think Hedy has the right idea. I'm sorry, Heidi, but I'm afraid I will be retiring after dinner, too."

"Well, shoot," Heidi said. "Here I am in the city where 'As Time Goes By' came from, and I have to go to bed early."

"Heidi, *Casablanca* was made in Hollywood," Hedy said, rolling her eyes.

Bond insisted on putting their meals on his bill, for which Heidi was overly grateful and Hedy seemed resentful. He bid good-bye to the girls as they walked to the lift.

"We're in room 415, if you can't sleep," Heidi said with a giggle.

"Heidi . . ." her sister groaned.

Bond got off at the third floor and went to his suite. He had enjoyed the girls' company, but there was something odd about them that he couldn't quite place his finger on. The wig business was a bit strange. He didn't completely buy their explanation for their taking turns wearing it. Hedy could be a problem, but he wasn't going to worry about her. He didn't think she would try to turn him in to the authorities, even if she did suspect him of the terrorist attack. It was too bad he couldn't have found a way to be alone with Heidi. She seemed rather spirited . . . but after further thought he knew that he needed to rest. She probably would have kept him up all night. . . .

Bond undressed, took a warm bath, took four of Dr. Feare's tablets, and got into bed naked, his Walther PPK safely underneath his pillow. He fell into a deep, troubled sleep and dreamed fitfully about his double. The other Bond was pointing a gun at him and smiling malevolently. Heidi and Hedy were on either side of him, laughing. The gun went off and Bond thought he was falling into a dark, bottomless pit.

That's where he stayed until the alarm clock woke him at six o'clock.

At 7:45, Bond stood on the street called Ville de Casablanca inside the medina, watching the exterior of the address on Clayton's piece of paper. The door was part of a large building with several shop fronts. *Berrakas* had been built in around several of them, including number 14. Various wares were displayed for sale, but number 14 was curiously empty. The door itself was cloaked in shadow and couldn't be seen.

A beggar sat cross-legged just on the outside of the *berraka*, a tin plate with a few coins in front of him. He didn't look particularly homeless; on the contrary, he was dressed in a clean *jellaba* and appeared healthy. A watchman, perhaps?

Bond had arrived at the scene fifteen minutes earlier. The night had not given him the rest he had hoped for, so he had begun the day with the persistent headache and a nervous energy that bordered on anxiety. He had eaten a light breakfast of eggs and toast in the hotel (and hadn't seen the twins, thank God), then walked the quarter mile to the medina. Now, though, as he watched the old quarter of town come alive with the noise and smells of the day's bartering, Bond felt a little better. The anticipation of something happening, of some possible revelation, brought back the welcome rush of excitement and interest.

A man in a business suit stepped up to the *berraka,* tossed a coin into the beggar's plate, then went under the covering. He disappeared into the shadows, and ultimately into the building. In fact, it appeared that the man had gone into the *berraka* and walked straight into the brick wall. Bond was pretty sure that he didn't see a door open.

Now more curious than ever, Bond thought he should get a closer look at the inside of the *berraka.* Playing the tourist, he wandered over to the beggar. Instead of holding out his hand and pleading for a handout, the beggar sat still, staring straight ahead. Was he waiting for some kind of signal?

Bond reached into his pocket, grabbed a couple of ten-dirham coins, and dropped them into the plate. The beggar nodded and muttered something in Arabic. Bond went under the *berraka,* and, as he suspected, found himself facing a brick wall. The number 14, which was displayed outside on the *berraka,* was also painted on the bricks. But there was no door.

He reached out and ran his fingers along the edges of the bricks, searching for a trapdoor catch. He knew it had to be there somewhere.

Bond looked at his watch. It was now nearly 8:00. He backed out of the *berraka* and walked across the street. The beggar looked up once at him, then continued his stare into space. Bond resumed his station, where he was partially hidden by a fruit cart.

Right on time, Walter van Breeschooten came walking down the narrow street. Bond drew the PPK, put it in his jacket pocket, and then smoothly joined the Dutchman in his stride. He leaned in close, nudging the barrel into van Breeschooten's side.

"Keep walking, up this way," Bond said, gesturing past number 14 to another narrow street full of vendors.

"You!" van Breeschooten said. He was clearly shocked.

"Shut up and walk," Bond said.

They maneuvered in and out of the crowd of people, turning several corners and up a small flight of steps. Bond escorted him to an out-of-the-way passage where no one was about. He then frisked the man roughly and found a Smith & Wesson Model 60 .38 Special. Bond threw it on the ground away from them.

"I don't know anything!" van Breeschooten pleaded, falling to his knees.

"I don't want to know anything," Bond said with murder in his heart. "I already know that you slit Helena Marksbury's throat." He pulled out the gun and aimed it at the Dutchman's head. "Empty your pockets. Slowly."

Van Breeschooten took a stuffed envelope out of his jacket and dropped it.

"You're making a big mistake," he said.

"How is that?" Bond asked menacingly.

"The Union are after you in a big way."

"What else is new?"

James Bond exercised his licence to kill and pulled the trigger. He felt no remorse, but it didn't give him any satisfaction either. He felt absolutely nothing. Bond had once again transformed himself into the blunt instrument of death, something which he had been able to do at will ever since he began his career in government service. When he did it, Bond shut himself off from every possible emotion and performed the task coldly and objectively.

As for van Breeschooten, his last, terrifying thought was that he now realized that the Union had set him up to die this way. He had been a piece of Yassasin's plan all along. This was his punishment for the failure of the Skin 17 project.

Looking down at the corpse's face, Bond used his foot to roll the dead man facedown.

The stuffed envelope was still on the ground. Bond picked it up and opened it. Inside was a map of the Málaga province of Spain, which included the Costa del Sol cities of Málaga, Marbella, and Torremolinos. There was an "X" marked slightly north of Marbella.

Also in the envelope was a ticket to a bullfight in Málaga, scheduled in two days. It was paper-clipped to a flyer announcing a "public rally" by Domingo Espada to take place before the *corrida*. Bond noted that the headlining matador was Javier Rojo.

Bond holstered his gun, put the envelope in his pocket, and slowly walked away from the bloody scene. He considered what had just happened and the implications of the envelope's contents.

They meant that the Union were involved with Domingo Espada in this conflict with Britain. Otherwise, what would van Breeschooten have been doing with a ticket to Espada's rally?

Bond's thoughts were rocked by the deafening sound of an explosion. It wasn't far away, just a few streets over. He looked up and saw a billowing black cloud above the rooftops. Bond ran out of the deserted street and retraced his steps back toward Ville de Casablanca. People were running and screaming in sheer panic.

He got to the site of chaos and saw that it was the Union's building that had been bombed! The *berraka* was completely gone, replaced by burning rubbish. He could hear sirens approaching, but as the streets were so narrow, the authorities would be running in on foot. A small police cart, however, quickly appeared on the scene. Two officers got off it and immediately began to set up barriers to keep people away.

Bond took refuge behind the fruit barrow he had used earlier and watched the unfolding drama with confusion and wonder. What the hell had happened here?

What was particularly strange, Bond suddenly realized, was that no one was coming out of the burning building. In fact, it appeared to be completely empty.

More officers arrived on the scene and were talking to a few witnesses. Bond recognized the beggar in the crowd of onlookers. The beggar wasn't watching the building; he was looking right at Bond.

The man then approached one of the officers and said something, pointing at Bond. The policeman spotted Bond and shouted. The other officers looked up and in his direction. All of them drew their weapons and aimed them at him.

Faced with no other choice, Bond slowly put up his hands.

SIXTEEN

CHANGE OF PLANS

BOND PUSHED UP ON THE END OF THE FRUIT CART, CAUSING THE ENTIRE contents to topple to the ground. Oranges, apples, grapefruit, and assorted vegetables spilled across the street. He then shoved the entire cart forward on its wheels, toward the police, blocking their sight lines and giving Bond just the right amount of confusion he needed to make a run for it. A policeman fired his gun, but the bullet zinged off one of the walls. People screamed and parted the way for Bond as he rushed through the crowded bazaar.

Two teenage boys, trying to help the police, attempted to grab him as he ran by. One of them caught Bond's legs, tackling him; the other one jumped on his back to pin him to the ground. Bond didn't want to hurt them, but he didn't want to be captured either. He rolled hard, knocking the boy off his back. He then kicked his legs wildly, preventing the other boy from holding on. Once he had freed himself, Bond got to his feet and continued to run. By now, though, the police had nearly caught up with him.

Bond took a sharp turn through a group of Berber women selling live chickens. The chickens squawked and fluttered, which prompted the women to shout at him and point the way for the police. The Berber men joined the chase, ready to make the rude foreigner pay for what he had done.

Bond ducked into a doorway and found himself in a shoemaker's shop. The place was covered with all manner of footwear, from Moroccan *cherbil* slippers to the latest American athletic varieties. Bond looked around quickly and noted a large rack of shoes next to the front door and another door at the back of the shop. The policemen's shouts were coming closer.

The shoemaker, who was sitting and working on the floor, looked at Bond with bewilderment. Bond said, "Forgive me," then pulled down the rack of shoes, blocking the front door. He then leaped over the shoemaker and ran to the back door.

It emptied into another part of the twisting medina. Bond ran outside and turned a corner as quickly as he could. Now he was truly lost in the maze, so he simply kept running, turning this way and that, hoping that he could lose the police. Up ahead was a small mosque with scaffolding on one side. Bond tried to go inside the building, but a man standing in front blocked his entrance. Only Muslims were allowed in the mosque.

Bond didn't have time to argue. He heard the police running at the end of the street, so he leaped onto the scaffolding and began to climb. Another shot rang out, barely missing him, as the police arrived at the foot of the scaffolding. Bond got to the roof and ran across, jumping over a large hole where repairs were being made. At the edge of the building, he found that he could make another leap to the top of the adjoining building.

The horrible smell there was overpowering. It reminded Bond of manure and vomit mixed with chemicals . . . turpentine or something. A stone staircase led down into a courtyard that was revealed to be part of a small tannery. The pungent odors were coming from the vats where men were up to their knees in red and orange liquids, scrubbing hides. The exotic ingredients used in the process included pigeon dung, cow urine, fish oils, animal fats and brains, chromium salts, and sulphuric acid.

Bond held his breath and leaped over the vats, one by one, causing the men to shout at him in anger. He ran past a wall of hides that had been hung up to dry after they had been scraped of the hair and extraneous flesh and soaked in the putrid dyes. Not seeing a convenient way out, Bond took a running jump and gained a handhold in the cracks in the wall. He swung one leg up and over, but unfortunately wiped the front of his body over one of the wet hides. He dropped down the other side of the wall and was in another street full of people and mule carts.

Bond pushed his way through, slowing his pace so as not to attract too much attention. He could see a horseshoe-shaped arch at the end of the street, one of the medina's exits. He made his way toward it, but three policemen suddenly appeared there. They were looking intently at the crowd. Bond turned around abruptly and merged with a group of men in *jellabas* marching in the opposite direction. As soon as he could, Bond rounded a corner and got off the street. Unluckily, it was a dead end, with a wall much too high to climb.

He looked back around the corner and saw that the three policemen were headed his way. Surely they would notice a Westerner emerge from the passageway if he attempted to do so.

A rope suddenly dropped and dangled beside him.

"Up here!" whispered a female voice. Bond looked up. It was one of the Taunt twins! She was standing on the roof of the building and was holding the rope.

"Don't just stand there. Climb!" she ordered.

Bond did as he was told. He climbed the wall and bolted onto the roof just as the policemen reached the street and inspected it. All they saw was a rope being pulled up the building.

"Am I glad to see you," he said. She was wearing the same tight blue jeans, but was now dressed in a red silk blouse with the sleeves rolled up.

"Hush up and follow me," the girl commanded. She ran across the roof to the other side. Bond accompanied her, dazed by this sudden turn of events.

"Which one are you?" he asked.

"I'm Hedy." She took a sniff and grimaced at the stains on his clothing. "Lovely smell. Come this way." She took a running start and leaped across the eight-foot gap between buildings, then turned and shouted, "Don't just stand there. Come on!"

Bond mimicked her action, then they both ran across the second rooftop.

"Where are we going?" he asked.

"Just shut up and don't stop. We're trying to save your ass."

She led him across two more rooftops until she pointed to a fire escape. "Down, mister. Go in the open window, first floor down."

Bond climbed down the stairs and slipped into the window. He was in a bedroom with Western furnishings. Hedy slithered inside behind him. She led him out of the bedroom, down a hallway, and into what was some kind of office. Heidi was dressed identically and sitting at a desk, looking at a computer monitor. Neither of them wore the red wig. Filing cabinets, a fax machine, a copier, telephones, and other pieces of high-tech equipment dominated the room.

"What the hell is going on?" Bond asked.

"Welcome to the Casablanca headquarters of the CIA, Mr. Bond," Hedy said.

Bond's jaw dropped.

Heidi pointed to the monitor, where a satellite image of the medina was magnified hundreds of times. "We thought they had you there for a second. It's a good thing you found us."

"I found *you*?"

Bond dropped into a chair. He was trying to project some semblance of composure, but he was, nonetheless, dumbfounded.

Heidi laughed when saw the expression on his face. "We got you good, didn't we?" Then she noticed the stains. "Pee-uuu . . . ! What did you get on you?"

"Someone better start explaining. I'm in no mood for jokes," Bond said.

"We *are* travel writers," Heidi said. "But that's just a cover. Hedy's a senior agent with the CIA. I'm a junior agent. We don't live in Japan. We live right here, in this building."

Hedy added, "I'm the one who went into the CIA first. When they found out I had an identical twin, they came up with an unorthodox plan and made us a proposal."

"As far as official records go, I don't exist," Heidi said.

"And neither do I," Hedy continued. "But there does exist a *Hillary Taunt*, CIA agent, who works in the North African sector. Either one of us can pose as Hillary during the course of our work. The boys in Virginia figured that Heidi could be used as a decoy in special cases. We rarely travel together, which is why you never saw us at the same time on the train. We rode in separate cars on purpose. We confuse a lot of people, especially conductors and flight attendants."

"If we have to be seen in public together, one of us wears the wig," Heidi said. "The only people that know that *we* aren't Hillary Taunt are our bosses at the Company. If, say, your own organization at SIS wanted to find out information about CIA agent Hillary Taunt there would be nothing in her file to indicate she might be an identical twin. This can be very advantageous in the field."

"I can see that," Bond said. "So you've known who I am all along."

"Sure," Heidi said. "We were sent to track you down. We got lucky and made contact with you on the train. If you hadn't found us this morning, we would have had to come after you. You're in a lot of hot water, mister."

"Tell me about it," Bond said. "I'm not sure what happened back there. The Union headquarters was blown up. Someone made it look like I was responsible."

"To hell with Union headquarters," Hedy said. "What about that doctor in London and the ferry in Tangier? What do you have to say about those things? You're a wanted man. Your chief has put out an all-points alert for your arrest."

Bond winced. "I didn't do any of those things."

"Tell it to the judge," Hedy said. "Our orders are to escort you to London. We've already checked you out of the hotel and we have your things." She pointed to his holdall on the floor in the corner. "Now, you have to hand over your weapons. All of them." She held out her hand.

Bond was aghast. "You're not serious."

"Please don't make me use force," Hedy said. "I'm pretty good at what I do."

"I believe you," Bond said. He reached into his jacket.

"Carefully," Hedy commanded.

Bond froze, then continued in slow motion. He brought out the PPK and tossed it on the desk.

"The knife?" she asked.

"Oh, right," Bond muttered, and took the sheath off the back of his belt. "This really isn't necessary, you know. I'd much rather be arrested by you two than the Moroccan police. I'll be a good boy."

"We're just playing it safe," Hedy said. She was definitely the "bad cop" of the two.

"I seem to have lost a Walther P99 in Tangier," he said.

"Yeah, you left it on that ferry after killing those civilians," Hedy said.

"No, I didn't. I wasn't there."

"Sure," Hedy said with a sneer.

"I'm sorry, James," Heidi said with sincerity. "We might have had some fun together."

"We still can," Bond said. "It's a long way to London."

"Hush," Hedy snapped. "We've got a car outside. We're going to take a drive to the airport. There's a plane that leaves in three hours. But first you're going to shower and change out of those stinky clothes."

"I must know what you think is going on," Bond said.

"We don't know what's going on," Hedy said. "All we know is that we have to escort you to London and hand you over to your chief."

"You *do* know that was the Union headquarters that blew up this morning?" Bond asked.

"We had come to that conclusion but didn't have proof," Hedy replied. "Actually, our suspicions were focused on another part of town, the Central Market, southeast from here. Maybe what you found this morning could have been another entrance. Anyway, we were already in the process of coordinating a raid on the Central Market entrance with Interpol and the Moroccan police when all this business with you and the ferry happened. I guess that sorta screwed up our plans."

"Sorry."

"We were told that you had gone renegade, had joined the Union," she added.

"That's why you were in Casablanca, we thought," Heidi said.

"Well, it looks like the Union might have suspected something and got the hell out of Dodge," Hedy continued. "That building was completely empty. The police reports are still coming in. They've begun to explore it and apparently there's some kind of underground complex. If I didn't have to deal with you, I'd be one of the first officials in there to find out if it really was Union headquarters." Hedy looked at him out the corner of her eye. "You *sure* you're not Union?"

"I'm not a member of the bloody Union," Bond said.

"I'd like to believe you," Hedy said.

"I believe you," Heidi added.

Hedy rolled her eyes. "My sister has a one-track mind."

"Look," Bond said. "There's something . . . there's something going on. Some kind of plot that the Union have cooked up. I'm a part of it. I can't explain it, though. Not yet. If you take me to London, something terrible will happen. My hunches are usually pretty good."

"We don't know what you're talking about," Hedy said. "Better hit the shower so we can get going."

"Wait a minute," Bond insisted. "Listen to me. For the past few days, I've felt as if I've been knocked here and there like a pinball. Whoever committed those crimes in London and Tangier—he's some kind of double. I think I've seen him. Once, in London. He looks just like me and he's certainly Union. I'm also pretty damned sure that I'm being manipulated by them; to what end, I don't know, but I would bet my life that there's something monstrous behind everything that's happened. The murder of Dr. Feare . . . the shootings on the ferry . . . the explosion in the medina today . . . They're all connected somehow, and I think that this Spaniard, Domingo Espada, is involved."

Heidi and Hedy looked at each other. "What do you mean?"

Bond reached into his pocket and pulled out the envelope he had taken from van Breeschooten. "I got this from one of the Union's top men. He was responsible for recruiting—and killing—someone close

to me at SIS. I tracked him from London to the very location where
that explosion occurred this morning. As you can see, he had something to do with Espada."

The girls looked at the bullfight ticket and the map. "What's this
'X'?" Hedy asked.

"I don't know yet."

"It's not far from Marbella," Heidi observed. "Domingo Espada's
home is just north of there. I think that 'X' marks the spot."

"Hey, I think you're right, Heidi," Hedy said. They gave the material back to Bond. "The U.S. government is very concerned about
Espada. We've been on alert ever since he started all the ruckus in
Spain over Gibraltar. We're afraid your people might get into a nasty
scuffle with Spain over it."

"We're all afraid of that," Bond said. "You've got to give me the
benefit of the doubt. If I'm taken out of the picture, we'll never know
what's going on. I'm a part of it, don't you see? The Union *needs* me
for something. If I don't follow this scheme through to the end, then
we'll never know what it is."

The girls were silent. Finally, Hedy said, "I want to talk to Heidi in
the other room. Don't try anything."

"I wouldn't dare leave," Bond said. "Being with you two is the
safest I've felt in days."

When the girls went into the bedroom, Bond shut his eyes and
tried to relax. They returned, and Hedy sat down in front of him.
Heidi draped herself on the desk, one long leg bent like an inverted V.

"All right, James," Heidi said. "We're going to play it your way. But
we're going to have to clear it first."

"You have to call your boss," Hedy said. "You have to convince her.
If she gives us the okay, then we'll trust you on this one."

"Give me the phone," Bond said. He fought a wave of panic. Could
he convince M that he was sane and not guilty of the crimes he was
accused of? Would she allow him to continue this possibly aimless
wild goose chase?

Hedy handed him a white phone. "It's a secure line."

Bond dialed the number and was put through to Bill Tanner.

"My God, James, are you all right?" The Chief-of-Staff sounded very alarmed.

"Yes, Bill."

"I'm glad to hear that. We were very relieved a few minutes ago when we got the message that the CIA had found you. You have to come back, James. You know you do."

"Bill, I didn't do those things, and you know it."

"I believe you. But . . ."

"No 'buts,' " Bond said angrily. "You have to trust me. I'm on to something and must speak with M."

"Certainly," Tanner said. "I'm sure she'll want a word."

Bond waited a moment. He looked at the twins, who suddenly felt uncomfortable and exchanged glances, but didn't bother to get up and give him some privacy.

"Double-O Seven." The voice was hard.

"Ma'am."

"Well? Are you on your way back to London with Agent Taunt?"

"Agent Taunt?" Bond asked.

"That's what it says here, Double-O Seven, agent Hillary Taunt."

"Are you listening, Bill?" Bond asked. He knew that Tanner monitored some of M's phone calls when she gave him the order, and he was sure that this would be one of them.

"Yes," came the voice, after a beat.

"I'm with . . . er, Miss Taunt, now," Bond said. "If you insist on it, ma'am, yes, I will come back to London. However, I must ask that you hear me out first."

"Very well."

"I may have evidence that Domingo Espada is linked to the Union."

That got her attention. "Go on."

"I disobeyed your orders, ma'am; I freely admit that," he said. It was one of the most difficult things he had ever confessed in his life. "But I had to go after the Union. If not for Britain, then I had to do it for myself. I swear to you that I'm not responsible for Dr. Feare's murder, or the terrorist attack on the ferry. I identified and traced Helena Marksbury's recruiter and killer to Casablanca and almost got into the

Union's main headquarters. The CIA here was on to them, too. The Union must have suspected discovery, so they left. Vanished."

"What's this about Espada?"

"The man I followed here had a map on his person with the location of Espada's home marked on it. He also had a ticket to a political rally and bullfight at which Espada is speaking."

"When is that?"

"The day after tomorrow."

"Interesting," M said. "The summit meeting in Gibraltar has been scheduled for the day after that."

"Who's going to this summit meeting?" Bond asked.

"The PM. Spain's PM. Espada . . ." Tanner answered.

"Ma'am, all this is connected somehow," Bond said. "I'm sure of it."

"But you have nothing, Double-O Seven. What does a ticket tell you? Perhaps this man simply likes bullfighting."

"*Liked,* ma'am," Bond said. "He's, uhm, no longer with us."

"I see."

"Why would he have a road map to Espada's house? This man was *Union!* It either means that the Union is involved somehow with Espada, or that they are interested in him for some reason. Maybe someone has paid the Union to kill him! I think I should try to meet Domingo Espada before the summit meeting and see what I can determine." He then presented M the same argument that he had given the twins—that he believed he was a cog in the Union's plan. If he were taken out of it, something awful might happen.

"Agent Taunt . . . and I . . . would like your permission to pursue this," he said.

M was silent. After a moment, she said, "Hold the line, Double-O Seven."

Bond heard a click. She was conferring with Tanner, and probably the Minister of Defence.

She was back in three minutes. "Double-O Seven."

"Yes, ma'am."

"I've just spoken to my opposite number in the CIA. I should probably have cleared this with the PM, but I'm not going to. You are to stay in Agent Taunt's company at all times. You are under house arrest, although you'll be mobile. You are not to attempt to escape, do I make myself clear?"

"Yes, ma'am."

"You can go to Spain. I realize that you're interested in this because you think it will bring you closer to the Union. Be that as it may, I think you might be on to something with regard to Espada. Providing you can get close to the man, you are to gather any information that you can that might link him to something as reprehensible as the Union. He's already a controversial figure in Spain, but I think that would all but destroy the people's confidence in him. It would give us more bargaining power. At the same time, we wouldn't want any harm to come to him before the meeting in Gibraltar. It's the most important thing on the government's plate right now. We can't have it jeopardized, but we can certainly have it slanted in our favor. Do we understand each other, Double-O Seven?"

"Clearly, ma'am."

"Very well."

"One more thing. One of the Union recruiters I tracked to Morocco—Michael Clayton—has a cousin in London who is connected to the Union. You might want to investigate that."

"Noted. Now let me talk with Agent Taunt. Good luck."

Bond thanked her and held the phone up for one of the twins to take. Hedy grabbed it and listened, occasionally replying, "Yes, ma'am." Then she said, "I'll call him right now. Thank you."

She rang off and said, "I have to call my chief in the States." She received the same instructions, and then she hung up and looked at Bond.

"Well. Looks like we'll be spending more time together after all. Heidi, I think we should use the yacht to get up to Spain, what do you think?"

Heidi nodded. "That's the safest. We can't risk bringing him through Immigration anywhere."

Hedy explained. "The Company has a boat in a hidden marina on the coast not far from Tangier. We can use it, but we'll have to drive to Tangier."

"Let's go, then," Bond said, standing.

"Oh boy!" Heidi cried, jumping up. "This is going to be fun!"

"Just watch it, pal," Hedy told Bond. She patted the Browning 9mm at her side. "I'm pretty good with this. And we also carry extra-strength, high-powered OC pepper spray that will stun an elephant. So don't try anything that would be considered conduct unbecoming of a gentleman."

"I wouldn't dream of it," Bond replied.

"Now go shower and get dressed," Hedy ordered.

"Wow," Heidi said. "I just thought of something."

"What?" Hedy asked.

"That for the next couple of days we get to baby-sit a British Double-O agent who's suspected of being a terrorist!"

"So?"

"It doesn't get much cooler than that!"

SEVENTEEN

MOUNTING EVIDENCE

MARGARETA PIEL TOOK A SIP OF WHITE WINE, AND THEN STRETCHED LAZILY, providing the men on the dock a spectacular view of a superbly built, beautiful woman in a skimpy bikini.

"You have an audience," Espada said, lighting a Havana cigar. He, too, was wearing swimming attire. Agustin was asleep on a recliner behind them, dressed in bathing shorts and a T-shirt.

"I always have an audience." Margareta sighed. "They just won't leave me alone."

They were on the deck of Espada's yacht at Puerto Banús, the chic Marbella harbor where the rich and famous liked to be seen. He owned an American-made 70-foot Cheoy Lee MY, a high-tech luxury boat with extensive extras. Like many of the other boats in the harbor, it was registered in the tax-free paradise of the Cayman Islands. Espada had rarely used the yacht for sailing. Mostly, he simply liked to lounge about on the deck half-naked with half-naked females waiting on him. It was the one public place where he didn't mind being a bit of an exhibitionist, and that was simply because he liked to show the other millionaires that docked at Puerto Banús who was on top. The area had become quite fashionable with Marbella's rise in tourism. Consisting of long stretches of beach clubs, shops, restaurants, and bars, the harbor was always alive with people. Even now, at noon, a group of male tourists were standing at a bar on the other side of the dock, gawking at Margareta. By nightfall, Puerto Banús would be packed.

"Roberto Rojo's death is causing quite a stir," Margareta said casually. "Have you seen this morning's paper?"

"No."

"At least three prominent matadors have announced defection, claiming that you are mad."

"Who are they?" Espada demanded.

She told him. Espada threw his drink at the edge of the dock, shattering the glass.

"They will turn public opinion against you," she said. "You can't afford that right now."

"Would you shut up?" he snarled. "Who made you my spiritual adviser?"

Margareta laughed. "Oh relax, Domingo. I'm teasing you. We all know you're unstoppable."

"I will have those three taken care of," he said. "Tomorrow night's *corrida* in Málaga will solidify my position with the matadors. When the people see me in the ring with men like Javier Rojo, they will follow me to Gibraltar."

"Don't you think the king will have you stopped?"

"He hasn't made a sound yet," Espada noted. "They're all afraid of me in Madrid. They're scared that I might actually run for office and win."

"We have company," she interrupted, gesturing to the dock. Espada squinted and saw his prize matador, standing near the boat.

Javier Rojo was tanned, muscular, and nearly six feet tall. His long black hair was combed back behind his ears and flowed down around the back of his neck. Margareta, like most warm-blooded women in Spain, found him very attractive. At twenty-six, the older of the two Rojo brothers, Javier was easily the most dynamic and charismatic in the bullring. Now, however, he was staring at Espada with hatred in his eyes.

"*Hola*, Javier," Espada called. "Come aboard and join us!"

Rojo hesitated, but then stepped over the railing and jumped onto the deck. He strode over to Espada and stood before him.

"How are you, Javier? You know Margareta, don't you?" Espada asked. "Have a drink."

"I didn't come to drink with you, Domingo," Rojo said. "I have come to ask you something."

"What is it, *mi amigo?*"

"My brother. Did you have him killed?"

Espada made a show of pain. "Mother of God, Javier, you can't possibly ask *me* that. Do you really believe I would do such a thing? I loved Roberto as much as I love you. He was such a promising young matador. Did your mother receive the flowers and the money I sent?"

"Yes, she did, and she thanks you. But Domingo . . ." Javier said, narrowing his eyes. "The talk is that Roberto did something to displease you. What was it? The police are baffled by the murder. Who was that girl he was with? I think you know something and are not telling me."

Espada looked at Margareta and shook his head. She continued to look at the young man, admiring his build.

"Can you hear this, Margareta?" Espada asked. "He is accusing his manager of murder. I am like an uncle to him."

"He's upset, Domingo," Margareta said, stone-faced. "Surely you understand that."

Espada acknowledged this with a nod of his head. He turned back to Rojo and said, "Please, Javier, sit and have a drink. I share your sorrow, believe me. I promise you on the soul of Pedro Romero that I had nothing to do with your brother's death."

Javier blushed and relaxed a little at the mention of the famous bullfighter. "I'm . . . I'm sorry, Domingo," he said, now feeling foolish. "You're right, I *am* upset. It's just that no one seems to know what really happened."

"Sit down, have a drink, Javier," Margareta repeated.

"No, thank you," the matador answered. "I must go and rest. I am fighting tomorrow, remember?"

"Of course I know that," Espada said. "And that is precisely the thing to get your mind off of this terrible tragedy."

Javier turned to leave, but stopped and looked back. "If I ever find out who was responsible for this," he said, "I will kill him with my bare hands."

With that, he jumped off the boat, walked down the wharf, and disappeared.

Espada looked at Margareta and rolled his eyes, Agustin had woken during the exchange and was applying suntan lotion on his shoulders.

"We'll have to be careful about him," Espada said. "I don't want him flying off the handle."

"I thought you came out here to get away from business, Domingo," Margareta said a half-hour later. "Look who's here now."

Espada looked up and saw Nadir Yassasin standing on the dock.

"Permission to come aboard, sir?" Yassasin asked.

Espada waved him on, and the man climbed over the rail and took a seat on the deck. Agustin sat up in his chair, alert and ready to serve his master.

"Get yourself a drink," Espada said, gesturing to the bar.

Yassasin poured a glass of sparkling water from a bottle that was sitting in a bucket of ice.

"Everything will fall into place tomorrow night after your rally and bullfight, Domingo. The plan has succeeded beyond my wildest dreams. Each step has proceeded exactly as I predicted. Tomorrow night at dinner you will meet the assassin we have chosen."

"How do I know he's any good?"

Yassasin smiled. "Because he's an ex-British SIS agent. He's now a member of the Union."

"Who is it?"

Yassasin pulled a photograph out of his jacket pocket, and handed it to Espada.

"His name is James Bond," Yassasin said. "He's a very formidable killer. He will be one of your bodyguards at the summit meeting on Monday. That's how we get him inside the Convent."

"He'll do this for me? Betray his country?"

"It is inevitable, *señor*," Yassasin said, slightly bowing. "Jimmy Powers has been on his tail for the past several days, reporting his movements to me. He should be arriving in Marbella later today."

"If this guy is as good as you say, he'll spot the tail," Espada said.

"No one spots Jimmy Powers," Yassasin said. "You know that."

Espada shrugged, unconvinced. "What else?"

"The Union has put together a force of new recruits—a thousand men from North Africa. They will unite with your men at La Linea as of tomorrow morning. We're counting on you to recruit at least one thousand men tomorrow at the rally. If that happens, combined with the number you already have, you will be four thousand men strong."

"That's incredible!"

"Now. The meeting. The British Prime Minister is coming, as well as several United Nations delegates. Of course you are allowed to bring as many people with you to Gibraltar as you wish, but only three bodyguards or assistants may accompany you into the banqueting hall of the Convent, where the talks will take place. One of those will be Mr. Bond, who will use an alias, of course."

"Agustin will be my lieutenant," Espada said. "Margareta will also accompany us." He turned to Agustin. "Make the necessary arrangements when we get back to the ranch."

Agustin nodded in compliance.

"That's what we thought you would say. Mr. Powers and myself— we have secured false documentation as U.S. State Department officials. I am a Moroccan citizen working in America. We will be there to make sure everything goes smoothly. In essence, Jimmy Powers will be there to protect you if things get out of hand."

"What about weapons?"

"Powers will be going to Gibraltar tomorrow to make those arrangements. Everything will be in place before Monday."

Espada was impressed. "It sounds as if you have everything under control. I feel so helpless. It's a disconcerting feeling, but I suppose I must commend you."

Yassasin produced a rare smile and lifted his glass. "Well then. Here's to our continued success. I have no doubt that when you take over as the new Governor of Gibraltar, the government of Spain will have no choice but to acknowledge your power as a political leader."

"Detective Inspector Howard is here, ma'am," Moneypenny said into the intercom. The green light above the door illuminated. "You can go on through, inspector," she told him.

Detective Inspector Howard found M with Bill Tanner. She was sitting behind her desk, and he stood alongside her like a sentinel.

"Sit down, Inspector," M said. "Can we get anything for you?"

"No, thank you, ma'am," Howard said. "I'm sorry to disturb you on a Saturday."

"That's all right, we were here anyway."

"Yes. Well, I'm afraid I have some rather serious news."

"I gathered that from your telephone call. What do you have to tell us?"

"It's your man, Bond. He killed Dr. Feare. The forensic evidence is irrefutable. We found his blood at the scene, buttons from his shirt, hair. . . . I'm afraid we have to find him, and find him quickly. He's going to be charged."

"What if I don't believe you, Inspector?" M asked.

"Ma'am?"

"I cannot believe that Double-O Seven would do something like that unless he had a damned good reason. It's not his style."

"Ma'am," Howard said. "We've obtained information that he was seeing Dr. Feare as a patient. He had an evaluation and tests performed two months ago. For psychiatric evaluation and other complaints. You were aware of that?"

"Of course I was," M answered.

"We'd like to know the results of those tests. I was hoping you might have copies."

"We have a summary report that the doctor sent to me after seeing Double-O Seven," M said flatly. "I can let you have a copy of that. But let me ask you this, Inspector. Do you really think Double-O Seven would commit this crime and flee?"

"All of the evidence leads us to believe that Mr. Bond is very unstable," Howard said. "Look what he did on that ferry, for God's sake!"

"There is no proof that the man responsible for that horrible act was Double-O Seven!" M said sternly. "That is still under investigation."

"Well." Howard sighed, realizing he was fighting a losing battle. "I'm here to deliver this arrest warrant for James Bond. He's officially wanted by the police for murder."

Tanner took the documents.

"Thank you, Inspector," M said. "If we find Double-O Seven, we'll make sure he gets them."

"We'll let you know as soon as we hear anything," Tanner said.

Howard nodded, stood and walked toward the door. He turned and faced M again. "Ma'am."

"Yes, Inspector?"

"You wouldn't be protecting Double-O Seven, would you? For some . . . reason?"

"He's a Double-O, Inspector," M answered. "He doesn't need me to protect him."

The Inspector smiled grimly and walked out.

M and Tanner exchanged glances.

"Bill, could it possibly be true?" she asked him.

"No, ma'am," Tanner said, shaking his head. "It's not James. It can't be."

M gripped the pen in her hand and stared straight ahead. "He sounded quite lucid when we spoke, I'll give him that. God, I hope I've made the right decision. I could lose my job over this."

"We have to let James work it out," Tanner assured her. "He always does. When he's on to something, he's usually right."

M repeated her Chief-of-Staff's words in her head a few times, then said, "Right. Let's move on. Double-O Seven and the CIA agent will arrive in Spain at what time?"

"Certainly by this evening," Tanner said. "They're traveling to Marbella by boat."

Moneypenny buzzed again.

"What is it?" M asked, punching the button.

"It's Captain Hodge. He's here and says it's urgent."

M winced. "Send him in," she said, simultaneously pressing the button that lit the green bulb outside her office.

Hodge came in stiffly and approached the desk.

"Yes, Captain?"

"Ma'am, we've just received the guest list for the summit meeting in Gibraltar. As you know, everyone entering the Governor's Residence is screened in advance. This information is made available to all of the countries involved."

"Yes?"

"Domingo Espada's entourage will consist of two assistants and a bodyguard. They're all Spanish except for the bodyguard. According to the documents, he is a British exile now residing in Spain. His name is Peter Woodward. Have a look at his photograph."

He handed her a file with a black-and-white head shot attached to it. She inhaled deeply when she saw who it was.

"It's Double-O Seven," she said.

"Yes, ma'am."

Tanner leaned in closer to get a better look. He furrowed his brow. "It certainly looks like him," he concurred.

"We're going to have to arrest him as soon as he shows his face in Gibraltar," Hodge said.

"You can't," Tanner said.

"Why not?"

M answered for him. "Because he'll have diplomatic immunity. With Spain."

Hodge was horrified. "My God, I hadn't thought of that. What are we going to do?"

M said, "Captain, would you allow me to confer with my Chief-of-Staff privately? For a few minutes?"

"Of course, ma'am," Hodge said, standing. "I'll be outside."

After he had left, M looked at Tanner and said, "This changes things, doesn't it?"

Tanner looked unsure.

M asked, "What about Double-O One?"

Tanner nodded. "He's been briefed and is all set to accompany the PM to Gibraltar. They leave early Monday morning."

"Then you had better give him additional orders."

"And they are?"

"If Double-O Seven really accompanies Espada to this meeting, then Double-O One should be prepared for anything. He is to keep close watch on Double-O Seven. If Double-O One determines that Bond is dangerous, he should respond appropriately."

"Do you mean . . . ?"

"Yes, I mean," M said. "If the need arises, Double-O Seven must be eliminated."

ACT THREE

TERCIO DE LA MUERTE

EIGHTEEN

THE YOUNG MATADOR

"LOOK AT THAT MOUNTAIN!" HEIDI EXCLAIMED AS HEDY DROVE THE 1998 BMW 320i onto the so-called Golden Mile of five-star hotels and resorts in Marbella. Conch Mountain hovered over the city, a magnificent backdrop for the seaside resort.

"It's a great town if you like golf," Hedy commented. Among Marbella's numerous golfing establishments was Europe's only night course; it was floodlit so that golfers could play after dark.

Hedy pointed to a huge estate on their left and said, "The king of Saudi Arabia built all that." Beyond expansive gardens was a sparkling white mosque and a mansion that was an exact replica of the White House in Washington, D.C. A large outline of a scimitar made of white stone was embedded in the grass.

"Wow," Heidi said. "Pretty cool, huh, James?"

Bond was in the backseat, where he was happy to be. It was a pleasure not having to drive or constantly look over his shoulder for a change. It was nice not having to *think* for a few hours. They had picked up the BMW, apparently a CIA company car, in a discreet garage not far from Tarifa, at the most southern point of Spain. They had stored the boat and had driven up the coast, past Gibraltar, and on to Marbella. Bond couldn't sleep because of the persistent throbbing in his head, but he was thankful for the rest, even though the twins talked about the scenery along the way. He took four of Dr. Feare's pills in the hopes that the headache wouldn't grow worse.

They drove past the restaurant owned by the famous Italian singer Tony Dalli, and Marbella's hot discotheque, Olivia Valere, and soon pulled in to the entrance of the Marbella Club Hotel on Bulevar Principe Alfonso von Hohenlohe. One of the finest resort hotels on the beach, the Marbella Club offered everything from bungalows to simple rooms.

"Are you sure this guy is here?" Heidi asked Bond.

"When I phoned, he said to look for him on the beach," Bond answered. "He likes to relax the day before a bullfight."

"Yuck," Hedy said. "I can't imagine why anyone would want to *watch* a bullfight, much less participate in one."

"Don't be so quick to condemn it," Bond said as they parked and got out of the car. "It's an integral part of Spanish tradition and culture. It's not a sport. It's an art."

"Yeah, right," Hedy said. "Tell that to the bull."

Bond decided not to argue. They checked in to the hotel, where the girls had reserved an exclusive bungalow with two bedrooms, two bathrooms, a shared living room, and an enclosed patio. They walked through the grounds, which were surrounded by lush foliage and palm trees. When they entered the bungalow, Heidi was ecstatic.

"Now *this* is the life!" she purred. "We need to get the company to send us on business trips more often."

"We'll take this one," Hedy said, gesturing to the bedroom with twin beds. "You're in the other one, Mr. Bond. Don't try any funny stuff. We're going to guard you in shifts tonight."

Bond shook his head. "I keep telling you that you don't need to guard me at all," he said. "I'm not going anywhere."

"Whatever. Let's go find your matador."

"Since we're going to the beach, can I put on my swimsuit?" Heidi asked.

"Jeez, Heidi," Hedy said, rolling her eyes.

Ten minutes later, all three of them were dressed in beachwear. Bond was wearing a pair of navy shorts, a white polo shirt, sunglasses, and flip-flops. He had asked the girls for his gun, but Hedy refused to give it to him.

Heidi was wearing a yellow and white bikini that revealed just how shapely and athletic she really was. Her muscle tone was perfect and she had an hourglass figure. Hedy chose to wear a red and black bikini, and for the first time, Bond was able to tell them apart. Hedy had a small, sexy mole on her left breast, whereas Heidi had one to the right of her navel. Otherwise, their figures were exactly alike.

"Wait a second," Hedy announced as they were ready to leave. "One of us should stay here. We have phone calls to make. And we probably shouldn't be seen together if you're meeting someone who's close to Espada."

Bond saw the logic in that. "So . . . who's coming with me?"

"Do we have to flip for it?" Heidi asked her sister.

Hedy waved her hand. "You two go on. I'll be the responsible one. I'll get some sun on the patio while I make calls."

So Bond and Heidi left her, strolled across the hotel grounds, through the beach club and shops, and onto the warm, soft sand. The Mediterranean was calm, creating a flat, blue horizon of serenity. The beach was populated with hotel guests lounging on recliners while staff fetched towels or drinks from the bar.

"Do you see him?" Heidi asked.

Bond peered up and down the beach, and finally spotted a tanned young man lying alone on a lounger some fifty yards away from the rest of the crowd. He was wearing swimming trunks and sunglasses.

"*Hola,*" Bond said as they approached. Javier Rojo turned his head and smiled. He immediately jumped off the lounger and removed his sunglasses.

"James Bond!" he said enthusiastically. "How are you, my friend?"

They shook hands and embraced.

"I'm fine, Javier, it's good to see you," Bond said. "I'm very sorry to hear about your brother."

Javier lowered his head. "Thank you. I am trying to come to terms with it."

"Any ideas on how it happened?"

The matador shook his head. "The police are clueless."

Noting Javier's unease, Bond quickly changed the subject. "Allow me to introduce you to . . . Hillary."

Javier smiled warmly at the beautiful woman. "I should have known that you would be in such company! I'm very pleased to meet you, *señorita*."

Heidi was speechless. Javier was a superb specimen of a Latin male. He had large, round brown eyes and a wicked smile that could melt any woman's reserve.

Javier held out his hand to Heidi and she took it gingerly, as if she were in a trance.

"Hi . . ." she muttered.

"Sit down," Javier said, gesturing to some empty loungers nearby. "Pull them over here. I was trying to stay away from the crowd so no one would recognize me."

Bond dragged the lounger next to Javier's and they sat, facing the sea.

"Where have you traveled from?" Javier asked.

"We came from North Africa," Bond said.

"Ah, that's a different world over there," Javier commented. "Nice place to visit, but I wouldn't live there."

"I do," Heidi said.

"Oh? Do you enjoy it?"

"Sometimes," she answered.

"So, James, how long has it been? Three years?" Javier asked.

"Something like that. Four perhaps?"

"I don't know. The time, it is flying. Ever since I got my *alternativa,* the world has been spinning," the handsome young man said.

"What is that?" Heidi asked.

Bond explained. "It's like a graduation, when a *novillero,* or novice, bullfighter becomes a full-fledged matador. It occurs at a special *corrida,* and the novice is proposed and seconded by senior matadors. It's almost like a christening."

"Very good, James," Javier said. "You remember!"

Bond shrugged. "Javier, I asked to see you because we need some information about Domingo Espada."

Javier nodded. "I thought so. What do you want to know?"

"Tell us your impressions of him. How close are you to him?"

"Domingo is my manager," Javier said. "He manages several matadors. In the beginning, he was like an uncle. He was a friend. He looked out for his matadors, and I was no exception. He took on my brother when he was a novice. He has a lot of power in the world of bullfighting. Alas, sometimes he misuses that power. I think he bribes bullring owners. I know he bribes the regulators and the presidents at bullfights. He can make sure that the bulls he breeds are sold for *corridas*. At the same time, as a manager, he can dictate which bulls his matadors will fight. He is a good manager, but I sometimes question his ethics. Lately, he has started demanding that his matadors publicly support his political causes. I don't particularly like that."

"Why can't you just leave?" Bond asked.

"It's dangerous to leave Domingo Espada. They call him *El Padrino* down here. I don't mind telling you; he's a crook. He has been linked with organized crime for many years. I never used to pay any attention to it. But now . . . I have reason to believe he's a murderer. I think he may be responsible for Roberto's death."

"Why?" Heidi asked.

"Because Roberto crossed him. I'm still trying to piece together what happened. You see, I know that Domingo Espada also deals in prostitution. He finds young girls from poor families and literally buys them and trains them to be high-class whores. Sometimes special guests are allowed to 'try them out' before they go out to work for real. Espada keeps this all very quiet, of course, and he's got judges and policemen on his payroll. Anyway, I think Roberto—he was, you know, a ladies' man, as you say—I think he fell for one of Espada's girls and helped her to escape from the ranch where they are kept as prisoners. They went to Ronda, where Roberto was supposed to fight in a *corrida*. Espada was there, doing one of his rallies to recruit volunteers for his army."

"Excuse me," Heidi said. "How come he's allowed to do that?"

Javier shrugged. "Because he's Espada. He *runs* the *corridas*. He can do what he pleases."

"Go ahead," Bond urged. "What happened to your brother?"

"He and the girl were found dead in his hotel, minutes before the *corrida* was supposed to have begun. His throat had been cut. No one knows how the killer got away. The hotel had only one entrance—the front."

"When you say his throat was cut, do you mean ear to ear?" Bond asked.

Javier nodded, swallowing. "I swear, if I find out that Espada was responsible, I will kill him. I'm thinking of killing him tonight."

"Javier, don't do anything rash. Have you ever heard of the Union?" Bond asked.

"Which union?"

"Not a bullfighting union, but a criminal organization called 'the Union'?"

"I don't think so."

"They're like a mafia, only they operate worldwide. We think Domingo Espada may be associated with them. As you know, he's stirring up trouble between my country and Spain over Gibraltar. If we can prove that the Union is backing Espada before Monday's summit conference in Gibraltar, we may have a chance of bringing him down."

"Being Spanish, I have mixed feelings about that situation," Javier admitted. "Gibraltar is a part of Spain and always has been."

"Not according to treaty, Javier," Bond said. "Gibraltar rightfully belongs to Great Britain until we decide otherwise. You wouldn't want a war to break out over it, would you?"

"Of course not."

Heidi interrupted. "We think Espada and the Union might be planning something catastrophic for Monday. It could affect everyone in this region . . . Spain, Gibraltar, Britain, North Africa . . . the whole Mediterranean."

"What's he going to do?" Javier asked.

"We don't know. We'd like you to find out, if you can."

"Me? What can I do? I'm not *that* close to Domingo. I'm beginning to hate him. I can't believe that I've treated him like family for years.

I feel betrayed. The more I think about it, the more certain I am that he killed Roberto."

A sharp pain shot though Bond's chest. The look on his face must have given it away, for Heidi asked, "James? What's wrong?"

It was the suffocating anxiety again. He suddenly felt disoriented and nauseated. He shut his eyes, willing away the uncomfortable, dreadful feeling.

"I'm all right," he whispered. He rubbed his brow and lay back on the lounger.

"You don't look so good," Heidi said. "Maybe we ought to go back to the room?"

Bond shook his head. "It will pass. Keep talking, Javier. How about it? Will you help us?"

"James, I'm twenty-six years old. My entire career is ahead of me. I can't afford to cross a man like Espada. I have a fiancée. We plan to get married next year. If Espada doesn't kill me, he could make things very difficult for me. I might not get to fight at all, and that's my livelihood. But . . . Domingo has given the art of bullfighting a bad name lately."

"All we need is some kind of evidence that Espada is with the Union," Heidi said. "We need it before Monday. Can you get to his ranch and snoop around?"

"Somehow that seems more risky than killing him," Javier said. He was obviously frightened, but he took a deep breath and then said with resolve, "It was Pedro Romero, the father of modern bull-fighting, who said, 'El cobarde no es hombre y para el toreo se nece-sitan hombres.' 'A coward is not a man, and for bullfighting you need men.' I'm certainly not a coward in the bullring, and I'll be damned if I will be with this. He deserves to die!"

"We have to keep him alive for the time being, Javier," Bond said, sitting up again and looking at him. "He's part of some Union plot and I'm sure that it has to do with the summit meeting on Monday. Please . . . wait. Don't do anything yet. If not for the sake of Spain, then for the sake of the future of bullfighting."

Javier looked out to sea. He knew that his British friend was right and nodded. "I'll see what I can do. Maybe I can go to the ranch tonight. I can't promise anything, James. If I find out that he did kill my brother, I cannot say what I will do or not do."

"I understand. Can we meet before the bullfight tomorrow?" Bond asked.

Javier shook his head. "Not before. After. There's a café across the street from the bullring in Málaga. It's called Bar Flor. I'll try to sneak away from the crowds and meet you there immediately after the *corrida*. Again, I can't promise anything."

"That's all right, Javier," Bond said. "I have a ticket to the bullfight, by the way. Only twenty-six, and you're already the senior bullfighter on the roster. Congratulations."

"I still don't see what the big deal is with this bullfighting," Heidi said. "It's not really fair to the bull, is it?"

Bond shot her a look, but Javier was used to such comments. "That is a common misconception among non-Spaniards. You see, the fighting bull is specially bred *just* to fight in the ring. It is a species that would otherwise be extinct if not for bullfighting. You must understand that the bulls live a glorious life on the ranches before their day of destiny in the bullring. They are treated as gods. The bull is a very special animal in Spain. We respect them because of their courage and their will to fight."

Javier became even more introspective as he gazed out over the Mediterranean. "There is a kind of duality that occurs between the matador and the bull. The entire *lidia* is a dance in which both the matador and the bull size up each other. They look into each other's eyes. The matador must know what the bull is thinking at all times, and this he must detect simply by watching the bull from the moment when he first enters the ring. The matador must *become* the bull, and in many ways, the bull does the same thing—he attempts to outthink the matador as the *lidia* progresses. With every pass of the *capote,* with every charge, the bull learns from his mistakes. If he misses the matador by two inches because the man performed a flawless veronica, the bull will remember it and charge a little closer next time. It is up to the matador to predict what the bull is going to do and then meet the mighty beast at the halfway mark. It is a dance. In the ring, the bull becomes the matador's mirror image."

Javier glanced at the wristwatch lying on the little table next to his lounger. "I must go now," he said. "I will see you tomorrow."

"Good luck," Bond said, shaking his hand again. "It was great to see you."

"You, too, James." He stood up and shook hands with Heidi. "And, *señorita,* you are as beautiful as any woman on earth." With that, he walked away toward the hotel grounds.

"Is it a requirement for all bullfighters to be gorgeous hunks, or is it just him?" Heidi asked.

Bond laughed. "Come on, let's go back to the hotel."

As they walked away from the beach, Jimmy Powers made a call on his mobile. He had been lying on a lounger some fifty feet away, his nose buried in a magazine. He was sure that Bond had not noticed him at any point over the last few days. Jimmy Powers learned his special ability while growing up first in the swamp country of Louisiana and later in the forests in Oregon. He wasn't known as the Union's best tracker and expert in shadowing a target for nothing.

When Nadir Yassasin heard what Powers had to say, the Moroccan made a quick decision. "Bond's contact with the bullfighter is dangerous. It was unforeseen that he would be a friend of the young matador. I think we need to take care of this situation before something unexpected happens. We're too close now, I don't want anything to derail the plan. Do you know who the girl is yet?"

Powers answered, "Preliminary search reveals that she is a CIA agent. Name of Hillary Taunt."

Yassasin smiled. "Good. She will have reported Bond's whereabouts to SIS in London. They know he's in Spain now. Things couldn't be better. You ought to return to the ranch, Jimmy. I am confident that Bond will appear at the bullfight tomorrow, right on schedule. We need to talk about what we're going to do about the matador, and then get you on your way to Gibraltar. I think there's a way we can use Bond's friendship with the matador to our advantage."

NINETEEN

DEATH IN THE AFTERNOON

J AVIER R OJO ARRIVED AT THE E SPADA estate at 7:00 ON S UNDAY MORNING.
He told the guard at the gate that he had been invited to breakfast on
the morning of the *corrida*. Since Javier was a familiar face at the
ranch, the guard let him in without verifying the appointment.

He drove the Porsche around the annex and parked at the back.
He quietly entered the house from the back door, which he knew
would be unlocked. Javier thought that if Espada were really
involved in criminal activities, then he should have better security!

He heard people talking in a room beyond the kitchen. They were
indeed having breakfast on the patio, located off the immense living
room. If he could creep into the living room and hide behind some
furniture, perhaps he could hear their conversation.

Javier started to sneak into the room, but the sound of footsteps in
the corridor to his right stopped him. He quickly moved back and
stood behind a tall cactus in a painted clay pot.

He couldn't believe what he saw.

A man came out of the corridor and went into the living room,
obviously headed for the patio.

It was James Bond! What the hell was *he* doing here?

In confusion, Javier stepped out from behind the cactus, hoping to
get another look before the man disappeared outside.

"May I help you?"

It was the woman. Margareta Piel. She must have been just behind Bond.

"*Hola,*" Javier said. "I thought I saw someone I knew. . . ."

"Were you invited here this morning, Javier?" she asked.

"Well, no, but I thought that . . . considering that today . . . tonight . . ."

"Domingo isn't here," she said. "As much as I'd like to say I would love to have breakfast with you, Javier, it's just not convenient this morning. I'm sorry. You'll have to leave. Besides, Javier, you need to be ready for tonight! Go on! You know Domingo wouldn't like it if he saw you here, anyway. You're supposed to be preparing for the *corrida!*"

"Fine," Javier said. Now he wasn't so sure that he had seen what he had thought. Perhaps his eyes had been playing tricks on him. "I'm sorry to disturb you, *Señorita Piel.*" He said it as if he were spitting on her.

She flared her eyes at him as he left the way he had come in.

Jimmy Powers stepped out of the corridor. He had been listening just a few feet away the entire time.

"I hate to say I told you so," he said to Margareta. "He came looking for something, all right. What did he see?"

"I'm not sure, but I think he saw Peredur," she replied.

"Well," Powers said. "Please tell Nadir. Someone needs to keep an eye on the kid and make sure he doesn't go near our friend in Marbella before tonight. I'm off to Gibraltar."

Powers left the room. Margareta turned and went outside to the patio to find Yassasin.

"Nadir, I need to speak with you," she said. She led him to a corner of the patio and whispered softly. Peredur Glyn watched her, totally absorbed by the gorgeous woman he had spent the night with. When they came back to the table, Margareta sat in the chair next to him and squeezed his thigh.

Margareta told the servant what she wanted, then turned to Peredur. He was one of the most handsome men she had ever met. Dark. Cold. She liked that.

When Peredur Glyn had arrived at the ranch yesterday, she knew she had to sleep with him. He was terribly good-looking. The fact that she knew he was going to die tomorrow excited her even more.

They killed time in Bar Flor, the sidewalk café directly across the street from Málaga's *Plaza de Toros La Malagueta*. Bond sat with Heidi at one of the sidewalk tables, while Hedy, wearing the red wig, a scarf and sunglasses, sat inside the cafeteria, apart from them. She could hear their conversation by means of an earpiece and a small microphone attached to a button on Heidi's blouse.

It was a busy little place, crowded with anxious spectators waiting for the doors of the bullring to open. The two slot machines made a tremendous racket, and the air was buzzing with patrons' exuberance. These were people who loved bullfighting, and bullfighting is as widely discussed there as football is debated in Britain.

The throngs of people outside the bullring fascinated Bond and Heidi. They were all dressed in traditional garb for *corridas*—the women wore large, colorful dresses and headpieces, and carried fans. Every man was equipped with a cigar, and groups carried *botas*, pouches full of wine. While the atmosphere was not as festive as during the annual August *feria*, which had occurred a week earlier, there was still enough excitement to generate anticipation in even the most jaded person.

Bond wanted to catch Domingo Espada's speech before the bullfight, so he finished the sherry and took one last bite of pork.

"Hedy doesn't like the idea of you going in there alone," Heidi said.

"Hedy, don't worry," Bond said, directing his voice at the button on Heidi's blouse. "Something is destined to happen here. I just wonder if the Union are expecting me. And . . . thanks for giving me back my gun."

Hedy had handed it over before they reached Málaga. "I'm giving this back to you on one condition," she had said. "That you promise not to run away from us, do anything rash, shoot us, or kill more tourists."

She had gradually warmed to Bond over the last twenty-four hours. While Heidi was the consummate flirt and continued to show the most obvious interest, Bond was beginning to find Hedy the more attractive of the twins. He liked her style.

"I suggest you follow me at a very safe distance," Bond said to Heidi. "No doubt I'm being watched. You know whom to call if something goes wrong. I'm going to do my best to obtain a face-to-face meeting with Espada. Hopefully this ticket will be for a seat somewhere near him."

He stood and left some *pesetas* on the table. He leaned over and kissed Heidi on the cheek. "That was for you, too, Hedy," Bond said to the button.

"Good luck," Heidi said.

Bond crossed the street and joined the masses of people entering the beige bullring. While not as old as the one in Ronda, it is a beautiful, historic landmark. It is the site of not only bullfights, but also rock concerts, motorbike shows, operas, elections, and political rallies. The city had grown around it; tall apartment buildings stood on all sides of the ring, offering spectacular views for tenants owning binoculars.

The energy around him was palpable as Bond entered the *pasillo* and walked past the refreshment stands. Much like at an American sporting event, hawkers sold sweets, sunflower seeds, beer, and soft drinks during the *corrida*. Bond stopped and bought a beer, and then swallowed four of Dr. Feare's tablets, noticing that he was running low. What would he do when he needed to refill the prescription?

The place was filling up quickly, so Bond made his way to the *tendidos*. His seat was in one of the best sections, the *tendido sombra*, where patrons are able to sit in the shade. Next to it was the *apoderados* section, where managers and other bullfighting regulators sat. Some prime seats there had obviously been draped and reserved for VIPs, presumably Espada and his team. The president of the *corrida* and his aides sat in a section a few rows higher than Bond. Directly across the ring was the orchestra, the members of which were settling down, ready to begin the music. The fight was completely sold out; the roar of the spectators grew louder as the seats filled, section by section. The seat next to Bond's, however, remained empty.

Bond looked around the place with interest. Ever since he had met Javier and learned a thing or two about bullfighting, he genuinely enjoyed the spectacle. It was already an assault of colors, noise, and expectation—and the bullfight had yet to begin! He noted that the flags of Spain, Andalucía, and Málaga's local provincial government hung over the *puerta de cuadrillas,* where the procession of matadors and their teams would enter. Banners or advertisements, prominently displayed during concerts and other events, were prohibited at bullfights.

He didn't notice Hedy Taunt taking a seat in one of the sections above him. She could get a good view of Bond with a pair of opera glasses she had brought.

"I see him, Heidi," she said into her microphone. "So far, nothing unusual."

Bullfights, miraculously, always began on time. At exactly 6:25, Domingo Espada walked out to the center of the ring, carrying a microphone, ready to make the most of his five minutes. The crowd immediately gave him an ovation. Espada smiled broadly and waved, then raised the microphone to his mouth and began to speak.

"My friends, ladies and gentlemen, welcome to Málaga's *Plaza de Toros.* I will not take up too much of your time, for we have an exciting *corrida* today. You probably know that I am scheduled to go to Gibraltar tomorrow morning to meet the Prime Ministers of Spain and Great Britain, and the Governor of Gibraltar. I have pledged the remainder of my life to raising public consciousness regarding the Gibraltar issue. I have no idea what tomorrow will bring, but I am asking any able-bodied men to come with me and join my security force. The pay is very good. We have nearly two thousand men already. My goal is to increase the size of the force to twenty-five hundred. I need to show the other side that Domingo Espada's party is powerful and has the will of the people behind it. You will find recruitment centers located at the exits. If you are over eighteen years of age, please, I would love to have you work for me. If you want to see Spain become a major force in the politics of the world again, you will support my cause. I need you. The people need you. Spain needs you.

"And now, I salute the brave men facing the bulls tonight!"

This brought a loud cheer from the stands. Espada waved again and began walking toward the fence. Bond noted the man's natural charisma that carried even at this distance. If he was as articulate and intelligent as he was supposed to be, Bond could see why so many people wanted to follow him.

At that point, a strikingly attractive woman with long black hair moved into the aisle and sat down in the seat next to Bond's. She was dressed in a green traditional *flamenco* dress with a yellow and orange flower pattern.

"Hello," Bond said.

"*Hola,*" she said, not smiling. She settled into the chair, then looked out over the heads as if she were looking for someone. Bond glanced at her every few seconds, but she seemed to be ignoring him.

"You're not Spanish," she said, finally, still not looking at him.

"No, I'm not," Bond answered. At last. He was getting somewhere.

"Where are you from?"

"Britain."

He saw the hint of a smile at the corner of her mouth. Bond was fascinated with her face. She had classic Spanish features, but there was something very cold in her dark eyes. The woman exuded a worldliness that was immediately attractive. She had exquisite poise, as if she had stepped out of a painting.

"My name is Margareta Piel," she said. "What is your name?"

"John Cork."

"Pleased to meet you, Mr. Cork. Do you enjoy bullfighting?"

"Yes, I do. I find it fascinating."

"I'm surprised," she said. "Most people who are not Spanish do not like it."

"It's because they don't understand it."

"Quite so," she agreed.

The band suddenly struck up the *pasodoble* and the bullring gate swung open, right on time.

A *corrida* always begins with a *paseo*, or procession, of the three matadors who are fighting, followed by their *cuadrillas*, the teams made up of *banderilleros*, picadors, and *mulilleros*.

Javier Rojo, as the senior matador, was walking in the middle. He would fight the first and fourth bulls of the *corrida*. All of the men, grouped together in their colorful costumes, made a spectacular vignette on the field.

After the procession, the field was rapidly brushed by men wielding *rastrillos*, the wooden brooms used to smooth the dirt.

Bond felt a twinge of anxiety as he watched Javier prepare for the entrance of the first bull. One never knew if a matador would live or die in the ring. It is a far more dangerous "sport" than most people realize, although it is no sport to the Spanish. Javier assumed his position near one of the shields in front of the fence. The music ceased and the crowd grew quiet. The moment at which the bull entered the ring was among the most dramatic in a bullfight. It was then that a matador could see exactly how brave and strong the bull was.

The gate swung open and a huge, black beast thundered into the ring. The first act, the *tercio de varas*, had begun. With the help of his *banderilleros*, the bullfighter would now test the bull by having him charge at the capes. One of the *banderilleros* called to him, waving a cape. The bull immediately charged the target, but the man stepped inside a shield in the nick of time. The bull's horns slammed into the wood. The crowd cried, "Olé!"

Another *banderillero* called to the bull and waved the bright red cape. The bull turned, snorted, and rushed toward him. Again, the man stepped inside a shield, barely escaping injury.

At last, it was Javier's turn. He stepped out into the ring and called to the bull. Much of the appeal of a bullfighter was the way he carried himself. The more arrogant and egotistical he was, the more popular he would be. There was a great deal of posing and grimacing involved in being a matador, but even that required skill. Javier did it well, simultaneously displaying pride, honor, and a demand for respect.

Somehow, the bull knew that this was the man who was his true enemy. The bull pawed the dirt in front of him, then charged. Javier performed a neat *verónica* and sidestepped the bull. The crowd went wild.

"This matador is one of the best," Margareta said. "Have you seen him before?"

"As a matter of fact, I have," Bond said.

The picadors entered the ring on horseback. It was their job to wound the bull with lances called *varas* without causing injury to the horses, even though coverings made of cotton and steel mesh protected the animals to some extent.

At this point, Domingo Espada and two men entered the stands and sat down in their seats not far away from Bond and the girl.

"He's also quite an orator," Bond said.

"And very popular with the people," Margareta agreed. "At one time he was a great matador. Now he is a great politician."

"It sounds as if you admire him," Bond said.

"I have to. I work for him."

"Do you? Why, I'd really like to meet him. As an interested expat, of course."

"Of course," she said. "I can arrange that. After the bullfight."

"I'm beginning to believe that our rendezvous was no coincidence," Bond said.

"You might be right," she said seductively, as she rubbed her leg against his.

Out in the ring, the bull had been stabbed twice with lances. A good deal of blood was streaming down the animal's side.

Before the third lance, Javier spent several minutes in the middle of the ring, taunting the bull. The bull would rush him, but the matador deftly countered with the cape in a series of maneuvers. His movements were pure and smooth as he stood, feet together and back arched. Bond could appreciate that a matador's dance with the bull was very sexual; it was no wonder that bullfighters were considered sex symbols. It was almost as if the matador was seducing the bull. As Javier had said, the two living things—man and beast—had become one in the ring. With the cape, the matador had molded the animal's wild charges into something of beauty.

Javier gave way so that the picador could gallop his horse around the ring, leading the bull into a charge. The horse turned sharply, heading off the bull so that the picador could thrust the lance into the bull's withers, the hump on its back that was the gateway to its vital organs.

The signal was given for the change in acts, to the *tercio de banderillas*. The *banderilleros* were older men, usually matadors who never made it to the top. They strutted out into the field, each holding a pair of the colorful spikes called *banderillas*. Again, each man had to taunt the bull to charge and, as it came within inches of his body, accurately thrust both spikes into the bull's withers. It was one of the most dangerous parts of the bullfight, since the bull, at this point, was in pain, angry, and ready to gore anything that moved.

The bull charged Javier's first *banderillero,* who was standing alone and unprotected near the center of the ring, the sticks held high above his head, back arched, and raised on tiptoes. He neatly sidestepped the animal and stabbed it with the spikes. The crowd cried out in approval. After the second pair of spikes was delivered, Javier motioned to the *corrida* president that he would opt to administer the third pair.

Javier moved to the center of the ring and beckoned to the bull. The animal was now wary of the men in the colorful costumes. He was learning and adapting his strategy for attack. Without warning, the bull charged and brushed against Javier, knocking him to the ground. Javier dropped the spikes and rolled to avoid being gored. The spectators gasped loudly. Javier jumped to his feet before the bull could turn and charge again. Forced to retreat to the fence, Javier brushed off the accident and picked up two more spikes.

This time, Javier boldly moved to the center of the ring and called to the bull. He arched his back and held the sticks high. It charged and the matador perfectly administered the spikes. The spectators roared.

It was time for the third and final act, the *tercio de la muerte*. The president gave his permission for the bull to be killed, something that was always traditionally asked for by the matador. Javier then looked around the bullring for someone to dedicate the bull to. Matadors would often pay tribute to a woman, a visiting dignitary, a friend or relative, by offering his hat to that person. If he wished to dedicate the fight to the entire crowd, he would throw the hat into the ring.

Javier strode toward the section where Bond was sitting. Their eyes met, and Javier flung the hat up and over the heads of the people in the first rows. Bond reached and caught the hat as the audience applauded. Javier smiled at Bond, then took his cape and sword from his assistant.

The matador has a time limit in which to kill the bull in the third act. It has to be done with precision, for no one likes to see the bull suffer. Aimed correctly, the *estoque* would sever the bull's spinal cord and other vital organs, killing it quickly. If it were still alive after falling to the ground, a member of the team would stab it in the back of the head with a short knife. Death was then instantaneous.

Javier stood in the middle of the ring, daring the bull to come closer and closer with each charge. He expertly twirled the cape, holding back the sword so that the bull would not expect it. This is the point at which a matador indulges in his most risky maneuvers, allowing the bull to get as near to his body as possible. With each pass, the crowd cried, "Olé!" and cheered. The music started up again and the first bullfight was quickly approaching its climax.

The dance of the matador and the bull became a ballet as Javier created beautiful flourishes with the cape, sometimes dropping to one knee to accept the animal's charge. He enthralled the crowd by performing a kneeling pinwheel maneuver. In this vulnerable position the matador moved the cape to one side, crossing his body with his arm. Then, once the horns passed, he spun in the opposite direction to the bull's charge, wrapping the cape around his hips. It was a decorative pass, but it was necessary with a quick-turning bull such as this one.

Finally, Javier faced the bull and dropped to his knees again. He called to the bull, daring it to charge a defenseless man on his knees.

"He is brave, that young man," Margareta said.

At that moment, one of the *banderilleros*, the only one dressed in red, stepped out of the shield directly behind the bull, in Javier's view. He stood there a moment, as if waiting for some kind of reaction from Javier.

Bond could see that something was wrong. Javier stood and, for a moment, he looked at the *banderillero*. He rubbed his eyes and

appeared disoriented. The bull sensed the man's hesitation and
charged.

The crowd screamed as Javier was picked up by the bull's horns
and thrown over the animal's back. Javier landed with a thud on the
ground. The rest of the team ran toward him, shouting, attempting
to attract the bull's attention, but the animal wasn't to be distracted.
It turned and plunged its horns into the matador's body. There were
more screams from the spectators. Bond stood in alarm, clutching
Javier's hat.

The *banderillero* in red had disappeared.

The men brought out a stretcher and rolled Javier's body onto it.
The blood on his side was quite evident. In the meantime, one of the
other matadors came out to finish the job. Taking a cape and sword,
the new man stood in front of the bull and held the sword out in
front, taking careful aim. Then, just as the bull charged, the matador
lunged forward and thrust the sword into the bull's back. It was a
perfect kill. The crowd cheered wildly as the bull collapsed, the blood
pouring out if its wound.

Bond began to move out of the stand. "I have to see about Javier,"
he muttered to the woman.

She followed him down the stairs into the *pasillo*, where a number
of people had already gathered to see about Javier Rojo's condition.

Hedy stood and spoke into her mike. "He's on the move, and that
woman who was sitting with him is right behind him. Damn, he's
getting lost in the crowd." She shoved her way out of the row and
attempted to keep sight of Bond, but the swarm of spectators blocked
her view.

Bond pushed through the crowd, running toward the *enfermería*, a
fully equipped emergency room.

What the hell happened out there? Had he imagined it?

He got caught up in the mass of people, and suddenly Bond's head
started to spin and he felt pressure in his chest.

"Let me through!" he tried to shout, but no one could hear him.

Someone cried, "Javier Rojo is dead!" There were screams of
despair from the crowd.

Bond's vision blurred and he stumbled, but he felt a soft hand take his.

"Come with me," Margareta said.

Bond let her lead him out of the crowd and into the chapel, often called the "place of fright," because that's where the matadors left their fear before entering the bullring.

Bond collapsed to his knees.

"You don't look well, Mr. Bond," Margareta said.

"Who . . . are . . . you?" Bond asked, but the words came out as gibberish.

Margareta walked around him and opened a side door. The *banderillero* in red entered the chapel and began to remove his costume.

Bond looked up through the hazy film in his eyes and attempted to focus on the man who had killed his friend.

"Murderer . . ." Bond gasped.

The vision became a little clearer.

The *banderillero* was the double—the man who looked like Bond! Javier had become fatally distracted when he saw his "friend" in the bullring!

Margareta slammed the butt of a pistol down on the back of Bond's head.

Hedy made her way into the *pasillo* and frantically searched the faces of the crowd for James Bond. It was pandemonium, as the media had already descended into the area to find out more about Javier's condition.

"Heidi, I've lost the bastard," she said.

"Keep looking," Heidi instructed. "I'm watching the street."

Hedy was near the chapel when the door opened and the woman with the dark hair emerged. Hedy spotted her and watched as the woman directed a couple of men to follow her. They were carrying a stretcher, upon which lay a body covered by a sheet. Hedy moved forward, but then she saw James Bond come out of the chapel and bring up the rear of the little group.

Hedy followed them out of the *pasillo* toward the VIP parking area. There, the men loaded the stretcher into a red minivan. The woman got in the back with the stretcher, and James Bond took the passenger seat. In a moment, the van backed out of the parking space and was on its way.

"Damn!" Hedy said. "Heidi, get the car, quick!"

James Bond became aware of a low rumbling sound as he opened his eyes. He was on a stretcher in the back of a vehicle—a van perhaps? His wrists were bound behind him and his head felt as if it were on fire. Then he noticed that his clothes had been removed and exchanged for a white cotton shirt and dark trousers. Margareta Piel sat across from him with a Glock in her hand.

"Just stay calm, Mr. Bond," she said. "We're going to your meeting with Domingo Espada."

Bond squinted and saw that another man was riding in the front with the driver. It might have been the *banderillero,* but a shaded barrier made it impossible to tell.

"Women who point guns at me usually regret it in the end," Bond said.

"Is that a threat, Mr. Bond?" she asked.

"Just a warning."

"You're awfully handsome, Mr. Bond. I like dark men like you. You don't have any Spanish blood, do you?"

"Not that I know of."

"Pity." She crossed her legs, inviting him to gaze at her.

Instead, Bond looked out the window and saw that the minivan had entered the motorway, heading west toward Marbella and the home of Domingo Espada.

TWENTY

THE MAN WHO CAME TO DINNER

THEY WERE SITTING IN THE BMW, WHICH THEY HAD PARKED NOT FAR FROM the bullring. Hedy was driving and the car screeched out of the parking space onto the main avenue.

"How far are they ahead?" Hedy asked.

"They're pulling onto the expressway," Heidi replied.

Hedy accelerated, shooting past the slower-moving vehicles. "I sure as hell hope he didn't skip out on us."

"I don't think he would do that," Heidi said.

"How do you know?"

"I think he likes us."

Hedy snorted. "Then he'd better be hot on Espada's tail."

"It looks like they're heading for Torremolinos . . . and Marbella is just beyond that. How much do you want to bet he's headed for Espada's ranch? You know, the 'X' on that map he had . . ."

"If we lose him, we'll have hell to pay."

They drove silently for a few minutes, and then Hedy asked, "You really think he likes us?"

Heidi turned to her sister and smiled. "Sure. Can't you tell?"

Hedy shrugged. She had a mischievous look in her eyes. "I think he likes *you*."

"Isn't that the same thing?"

"Heidi, we're not going to get into another situation like that, are we?" Hedy asked.

"Don't you like him, too?" Heidi asked. "I think he's a hunk and a half."

Hedy acknowledged her sister's remark with an approving grin. "All right, I admit it. He's not bad."

"Not bad, are you kidding? The guy oozes sex." Heidi squinted at her sister. "You *do* like him, don't you?"

Hedy refused to answer, but instead observed, "You saw him first."

Heidi shrugged. "Well, you're the one who's undersexed. We can work that out later. . . ."

The tension in the air over Gibraltar Town's Main Street was palpable late on Sunday afternoon. Nevertheless, the shops had remained open, their proprietors hoping that at least one tourist would venture in and spend some money. But it was not to be. Gibraltar's ports were closed, and the airport open only for official governmental business. It would seem that the inhabitants should panic and flee in fear of a Spanish takeover. Instead, the stalwart Gibraltarians chose to put their faith in the existing government. After all, the Rock had been threatened many times in the past, and it had a long history of surviving.

With or without tourists, the King's Chapel was always open to the public at the weekend. Officially a part of the Convent, the Governor's private residence, it dated back to 1533. The original Franciscan Chapel had been built in the shape of a cross, although a portion was later appropriated for the Governor's residence. The shape is more or less retained and today is used by both the Church of England and by Roman Catholics.

Jimmy Wayne Powers sighed, finishing a pint at one of the Angry Friar pub's sidewalk tables, perfectly situated across the street from the Convent and the chapel. He noted the heightened security around the front of the Governor's residence. On a "black" security code day, there would be at least one guard from the Gibraltar Regiment standing outside, whereas, on an "amber" code day, there might be four. Today was a "red" code day, and Powers counted eight men outside the Convent. There was no telling how many more were inside.

Powers thought this whole thing was crazy, but he didn't attempt to question it. If Nadir Yassasin claimed it would succeed, then he had to believe him.

Time to get to work.

He left some money, picked up his brown briefcase, and crossed the street. The soldiers eyed him suspiciously, but they treated everyone that way. He went straight into the King's Chapel and found himself in a surprisingly quiet and peaceful room furnished in exquisite elegance. The front of the chapel was on the east end of the "cross." A locked white door led to the Convent at the south end. The congregation sat in the western portion, and the entrance and memorial hall lay in the north section.

He was alone.

Powers was good at this kind of work. He excelled in stealth skills and was an expert in sabotage. Why, he had tailed the great James Bond for over a month and the fool never knew it! Powers was pleased that he could supply such reliable information about the Union's target.

Now he had something different to do.

He quickly opened the briefcase, working silently at high speed. He removed six white silk bags and a roll of tape. Each bag contained a firearm: three of them Spanish 9mm Super Star automatics, two Brownings, and one Walther PPK.

Powers spent the next five minutes taping the bags under various pews in the chapel. When he was done, he put the tape back in the briefcase, closed it, and made his way past the memorials to the entrance. He paused long enough to sign the guest book.

In it, he wrote the date and "Richard Bunyon—Washington, D.C."

He glanced at his watch. By now, Union killers would have pulled off a relatively simple job in the United States capital. The limousine driver for two State Department officials, the real Richard Bunyon and an Arab named Said Arif, would inadvertently get lost on his way to Dulles Airport.

The two men would never check in for their flight to Gibraltar. By the time their superiors discovered they were missing, it would be too late.

Powers walked out of the chapel onto Main Street, ignored the guards as he strolled past the front of the Convent, then climbed the hill to the Rock Hotel, where he would spend the rest of the evening enjoying dinner and a good book.

The minivan zipped through Torremolinos and made it to Marbella in an hour. The sun was setting as the van turned north to drive into the hills. Margareta had stayed silent during the trip, but the way she stared at Bond unnerved him. She had a glint behind her eyes that he recognized all too well. He had seen it many times before, and it meant bad news. This woman was a killer. His experience had taught him how to identify that particular trait in a person. She might be beautiful and refined, but Margareta Piel was probably as dangerous as they come.

When the minivan pulled into the drive in front of the ranch, two guards peered inside. They saw Margareta and waved the van through as they opened the gate. Bond was impressed with the spread. It was a beautiful location here, up in the hills overlooking the Mediterranean. They drove past enclosed fields full of bulls, and a large barnlike structure that looked as if it was some kind of slaughterhouse. Bond noted the circular annex to the building, and guessed that it was probably a practice bullring of some kind.

The dirt road curved up and around a small hill, and the main estate loomed ahead of them. It was a splendid mansion built in a Roman tradition with Arab influence and Mudéjar decoration. It was a flat-roofed structure common in *cortijos,* built of earth, mud, and lime. Wood was only used as a framework for the walls, for the roof, and as beams. The windows and doors were framed. The overall impression was that it was a modern version of an eighteenth-century neoclassical palace.

The minivan turned and drove on a side road around behind the barn. Eventually the driver stopped at the back of the building, out of sight from the main road.

Margareta leveled her gun at Bond and said, "Get out. No funny stuff." The driver opened the door for him. The other passenger had already got out and walked into the building before Bond could get a good look at him. He could have sworn that the man had been wearing Bond's clothes. Was he really a double, or had Bond's eyes been playing tricks on him again?

The woman marched him inside, through a passageway, and into a small room furnished with a table, chairs, and a television. The walls were covered with old bullfight posters.

"Sit there," Margareta said, pointing to the largest chair in the room, facing the television.

"You're not so cruel that you're going to make me watch Spanish television, are you?" he quipped.

"Shut up." The driver shoved Bond into the chair and then secured him to it with leather straps.

"So, señorita, how long have you been with the Union?" he asked.

Margareta expected that he would know and would have been disappointed if he had not figured it out. "Not long. In fact, I won't officially be a member until after tomorrow. That's when I get my tattoo."

"Your tattoo?" Bond asked.

Margareta drew a sharp intake of air. She suddenly wasn't sure how much Bond knew about the Union. The laser-implanted tattoo on a new member's right retina was a part of the initiation. How secret was it?

"I thought I told you to shut up," she said.

"What happened to our bullfighting friend?" he asked. "I'm afraid I didn't catch his name. . . ."

"You'll meet him formally in a while. First, though, you've been invited to have dinner with Señor Espada. Unfortunately, you won't get to taste the wonderful food his chef prepared for tonight's feast. However, you *do* get to watch it on TV."

Margareta turned on the television. It was a closed-circuit picture of a dining table. A servant girl was placing silverware and glasses at the settings.

"Virtual dinners, I love them," Bond said. "Low on calories.".

Margareta stepped closer to him and took his chin in her hands. "You won't be making jokes too much longer, Mr. Bond. This is the end of the line. I'm sure you've been traced here, which is exactly what we want. You've walked right into the trap. It won't be long before your people in London know that you're at Domingo Espada's home."

"So?"

Margareta smiled. "In time you will know all. . . ." With that, she leaned over and kissed him hard on the mouth. He let her do it, but he didn't reciprocate at all. When she was done, she licked her lips and said, "Mmm, not bad, Mr. Bond. You taste . . . like fresh meat."

She turned to go. The driver held open the door for her.

"Don't try to escape. You're heavily guarded. I'll be back after dinner," she said. "Enjoy the show."

With that, she left. The driver slammed the door shut and Bond heard the locks turn.

Heidi and Hedy pulled over about a mile away from Espada's ranch.

"He's there, no doubt about that," Heidi said. "What do we do now?"

"I wish we knew if he went willingly or not." Hedy thought for a moment. "Should we call for backup?"

"Who's gonna come?" Heidi asked. "Our operatives are in Madrid, Barcelona, and Seville. By the time anyone gets here, the show, whatever it is, will be over."

"You're right." Hedy opened the glove compartment and removed a pair of binoculars. She got out of the car, adjusted the glasses for infrared vision, and put them to her eyes. She had a fairly good view of the entire estate, save for a portion of the main house that was blocked by the large annex.

"I see some men at the gate," she said. "I don't see the minivan. It might be behind that barn." She scanned the buildings and then said, "Oh no."

"What?"

"I see him," Hedy said. "It's James. He's walking from that other building to the main house. Look." She handed the glasses to Heidi.

Sure enough, James Bond was entering the front door, accompanied by other men and the Spanish woman.

"Goddamn him!" Heidi said. "Do you think he really *is* in cahoots with Espada? He walked in there like he owned the place! And that woman! Who the hell is she?"

"Heidi, I think he fooled us."

Heidi looked as if she might cry.

Hedy took back the binoculars. "I wonder if there's another way around. You know, an approach from the back."

Heidi peered at the road ahead and pointed. "Look," she said. "There's some kind of trail there. See? It leads down to that valley. You think maybe there's another trail that leads up and around?"

"I don't think the car will make it. I'll have to go on foot. Let's split up."

"Why you? I should go."

"No, I'll go."

"Let's flip for it."

"Forget it, Heidi, I'm going!"

"Well, what's our plan?" Heidi asked. "We gotta have a plan."

"I'm making it up as we go along," Hedy said. "You stay here. Is your communicator still working?"

"Of course."

"If you see anyone come out of the house, let me know." She handed the binoculars to her. "If you get into trouble, just press the panic button. I'll do the same thing. Either way, we come running, all right?"

"How the hell will I know where you are?"

"I'll scream," Hedy said, shrugging. "If nothing happens, let's meet back here at midnight. If he's not out by then, we'll call London."

"Okay," Heidi said hesitantly.

Hedy checked her weapon and ammunition, and gave her sister a peck on the cheek. "Don't worry. I'll be fine." Before Heidi could respond, Hedy had set off down the road toward the trail.

The pain in James Bond's head had increased tenfold since he had been tied to the chair, exacerbated by the recent blow. He had to force himself to concentrate on his surroundings and search for a way out of his predicament. The bindings were terribly tight, but he could scoot the chair across the floor if he wanted to. That wouldn't do much good, unfortunately. Perhaps it was best to let them play out the game. They had some kind of a plan in mind, and he was part of it. He couldn't intelligently plot a course of action without knowing what it was.

Something started happening on the TV monitor. Margareta Piel entered the picture, accompanied by a tall, black man in a fez. They sat at the table as Espada's voice boomed out of the speakers.

"Sit, sit," he said. "We have some wonderful *paella* tonight."

Espada and another man, a bit older, entered the frame and sat at the head of the table. "Wonderful *corrida* in Málaga, although it was unfortunate about Javier." He shook his head and made a "tsk tsk" sound. "I am sorry to lose him."

Bond couldn't help but catch the glance that Margareta gave the Moroccan.

"So, Nadir, are we on schedule?" Espada asked him.

"Yes, Domingo, everything is prepared. Jimmy Powers is in Gibraltar and was successful in planting the weapons in the chapel. We will leave here tonight after dinner. I suggest that you leave only a skeleton force here, for we will need every competent man with us," the man called Nadir said.

"I was planning on it. Now, what about the assassin?"

Margareta spoke up. "He should be here any minute. He had to change clothes and wash. Oh . . . here he is now."

Espada stood and looked toward the camera. A man entered the frame, his back to Bond.

"Domingo Espada, I'd like you to meet James Bond, formerly with Her Majesty's Secret Service in Great Britain."

Bond's jaw dropped when the man turned to reveal his profile and shake hands with Espada.

"Welcome, Mr. Bond," Espada said. "I have heard great things about you. Despite my hatred for your homeland, I welcome you here." He gestured to the other man at the table. "This is Agustin, my *mozo de espadas.*"

"Thank you, sir, I've already met Agustin," the imposter said. "It's a pleasure to be here."

My God! The man *was* an exact replica of him! He hadn't been imagining a double at all . . . there really was one! How had they done this? The man didn't completely *sound* like him, Bond thought. The speech was a little off . . . in fact, the accent was Welsh. People close to Bond might detect the slight differences in inflection, but for all intents and purposes, the man on the television was James Bond.

Beads of sweat began to form on Bond's forehead. He knew that the science of plastic surgery had advanced by leaps and bounds in the last few years. The best in the field could literally do anything short of cloning a person. That was what they must have done. But . . . why? Just to frame him? To set him up as a criminal? Surely London would see through such a ploy. . . .

A servant girl poured wine, and then the *paella* was served. As a first course they had *tortilla de patatas,* an omelette made from potatoes. Bond felt his stomach rumble as he watched them eat.

"So, Mr. Bond, what are your feelings about what we are about to do tomorrow?" Espada asked, picking up a crawfish with his hands and biting into it with a crunch.

The look-alike made an offhand gesture that Bond instantly recognized as his own way of dismissing an idea. The man, whoever he was, had done his homework.

"I have felt for years that my country has been extremely selfish with Gibraltar," the pseudo-Bond said. "I am half Scottish, so I can sympathize with anyone who takes issue with who runs their government, who owns their land, and what constitutes a fair treaty."

"Why did you leave your country? Why do you want to help me?" Espada asked.

"British intelligence is no longer interesting," the man said. "In the past decade, SIS came out of the woodwork, so to speak. We . . . er, *they* used to be a secret organization. No one knew where our headquarters were located in London. Our covers were solid, all around the world. Nowadays, SIS is in plain sight, in that ugly building on the Thames, and the newspapers print photographs of the leading personnel. Foreign intelligence networks seem to have an uncanny knack of identifying agents. The Union infiltrates them and embarrasses the company. While the work was always political in nature, the mere machinations of *playing* at secret agent have become political. It got to where I couldn't make decisions on my own. Too much red tape. Too much bureaucracy."

Bond shook his head in disbelief. The imposter had him nailed. While Bond was nowhere as cynical in his opinions, he *had* entertained similar thoughts recently.

"Mr. Bond," Espada said, "I suppose what I really want to know is if you are prepared to perform the task which Nadir Yassasin and Margareta Piel here tell me that you have been hired to do. You are about to betray your country, commit treason and murder."

The imposter Bond smiled and replied, "I have no love for Britain anymore. I have lost . . . people I have loved . . . because of my work for the British government. One was my wife. It is time for me to pay them back. What have they done for me? My salary was adequate, but compared to what a hit man in the Italian Mafia makes for an assassination, I'm a pauper. Killing people has always been a part of my job. It's time I was paid properly for doing it. That's why I joined the Union."

Espada seemed pleased with the answers. He turned to Yassasin and said, "I believe you were right, Nadir. This man will do nicely. I like him." He raised his wineglass, and the others followed suit.

"To James Bond," he said. "May you perform your deed tomorrow morning with finesse and accuracy."

So that was it, Bond thought. The Union was going to use a double to assassinate someone—someone important—and *he* would get the blame.

Hedy made her way into the dark valley, trying her best not to stumble over a rock or a fallen branch. The area was thick with oak trees, and the half-moon barely penetrated the leaves. Nevertheless, she finally made it to the path leading up the hill and soon found herself back in the pale illumination of the night sky.

She crept over a ridge overlooking the estate and crouched in the shadows. The back of the annex was visible now, and she could see the minivan parked by a few other vehicles. She wondered what the circular section of the building might be, not realizing that it was a bullring.

The main house was well lit, and she could see at least two guards pacing the grounds around it. A barbed-wire fence surrounded the entire property.

What the hell should she do now? she wondered. She spoke into her microphone.

"Anything happening over there?" she asked in a whisper.

"Nothing," Heidi answered. "What about you? Where are you?"

"I'm above the main house, on the hill looking down into their backyard. I see a swimming pool, tennis courts, a garden . . . the van's behind that barn and there are . . . two, three, four other vehicles parked there. There's another parking area at the side of the house, and I see at least a half-dozen cars over there."

"So if there's one person per vehicle, then we're outnumbered," Heidi said. "Assuming that there are at least two people per vehicle, we're *seriously* outnumbered."

"We can't just go rushing in there like the cavalry, either. We have no grounds, no warrant. Espada is expected at a major political to-do in the morning, and who are we to screw that up?"

"Maybe we should just make a report and get instructions," Heidi suggested.

"You're probably right. You do it. I'm going to stay—" She screamed when a torch beam flooded the area around her. A voice commanded her in Spanish to stand up and raise her hands. Without thinking about the consequences, she went for her gun. A blow on the back of her head put a stop to that, and she fell over.

Espada apparently liked to talk, and he dominated the dinner conversation.

"Reclaiming Gibraltar for Spain has been an ambition of mine since my days with Franco. Bless his soul, he shared my views on the matter. I made a promise to him that one day I would do something significant to further our cause in that regard. Tomorrow, that dream will be fulfilled. It is Spain's destiny. And . . . I am willing to die for the cause, if that is the final outcome."

"Don't be ridiculous, Domingo," Margareta said. "Mr. Bond here is a professional. He will not miss his targets. And Nadir, Jimmy, and I will be there, too, just in case something goes wrong."

"And I will not let anything happen to you," Agustin said, "if I can help it."

What the hell were they planning to do? Bond wondered. Keep talking! What were the details of their terrible scheme?

But before he could learn more, a guard entered the dining room and whispered something to Espada.

"Bring her in, let's have a look," Espada said aloud. The guard went out of the room. "It seems we have another guest. An uninvited one."

After a moment, the guard brought in Hedy. The wig was gone. Her blouse was torn, revealing a white bra, and her hands were tied behind her back.

Oh no! Bond thought. Which one was she? Heidi or Hedy . . . ?

The guard held her as Espada addressed her in English. "Who are you, my dear?"

She kept silent.

"Oh, not talking are we?" The guard tossed some things onto the table. They were her identification, microphone, and earpiece. Espada picked up the ID.

"Hillary Taunt. Travel writer," he read. "What makes you want to spy on my house, eh? You're not really writing about a private property, are you?"

The girl continued to glare at him.

"She's with the CIA," Yassasin said. "We know all about her. She's based in Casablanca."

"She's beautiful," Margareta said. "So blond . . . nice figure . . ."

"Yes, indeed," Espada agreed. "CIA, eh?" He addressed the guard.

"Take her to the compound. I think I might keep her a while. She's a little older than what I'm accustomed to, but she might provide some amusement for a few nights before she's discovered missing. After that . . ." He shrugged.

The guard pulled her away and out of the room. Espada turned to the imposter Bond and asked, "Perhaps you would like to try her out tonight? She will be my gift to you in appreciation for what you are going to do for me tomorrow."

The imposter Bond smiled lecherously and said, "Why, thank you, Señor Espada. I might just do that."

Nadir Yassasin cleared his throat. "Whatever happens, we must not be late for the boat. Domingo, you and Agustin and the rest of the men are expected in La Linea by midnight. We have some final preparations to do with Mr. Bond, and he and Margareta will join you in the morning for the border crossing into Gibraltar. Jimmy Powers and I will arrive separately. Remember, when we're all together at the Convent, you do not know us."

"I'm no fool," Espada said. "Very well. Shall we go?"

He stood and held out his hand to the imposter Bond. "I will see you in the morning, then."

"Thank you, sir, for this opportunity," the double said.

Espada said good-bye to Margareta and Yassasin, then started to leave the room. He turned back and addressed them all. "Mr. Bond can have his way with that girl tonight, and then we'll get rid of her. I don't need a blond American in my harem."

After Espada and Agustin left the room, Margareta looked at the camera.

"Dinner is over, Mr. Bond," she said, addressing him. "It's time for dessert."

TWENTY-ONE

DOPPELGÄNGER

THE LOCKS RATTLED AND THE DOOR SWUNG OPEN. MARGARETA PIEL AND the Moroccan entered the room. She was carrying a leather briefcase, which she set on the table.

"Did you miss me, Mr. Bond?" she asked. "This is Nadir Yassasin. Say *hola*."

The tall man bowed slightly. "It's a pleasure to meet the real James Bond after all this time. You have my respect, sir, but not my benevolence."

Bond spat an obscenity at them both.

"Tsk tsk," Margareta said, closing the door. "How was the television program? Did you get it all, or would you like someone to explain it to you?"

"Who is that imposter going to kill?" Bond growled.

It was the man who answered. "The Union have worked very hard these last three months in order to humiliate and embarrass your country and your feeble intelligence agency. The leadership decided that you, specifically, had to pay for a certain past Union failure."

"We call Nadir the 'strategist,' " Margareta said. "He came up with an absolutely brilliant scheme to lure you here so that we can pull a . . . what do the Americans call it? . . . a 'Switcheroo'?"

Yassasin began to walk around the room, his hands clasped behind his back. "Think about it, Mr. Bond. Think back to how you felt when you returned from the Himalayas. We knew that you would want to go after us just as much as we wanted our hands on you. Lucky for the Union, you had some medical difficulties. Am I right?"

Bond didn't answer.

"You see, Mr. Bond," he continued. "We knew you were on medical leave. This made you particularly vulnerable. Mr. Bond, I profiled you the way the FBI in America profiles serial killers. I got to know you *personally*. I studied your history, I had you followed, I know what you like and don't like. . . . We even knew what *medications* you were taking for your condition. Let's just say that . . . we tampered with them a bit."

Bond squinted at Yassasin. *Tampered with the medicine? How? What had they done to him?*

"You became so psychologically unstable that you were able to play right into our hands. By the power of suggestion, we provided you with hints as to how you could avenge your personal assistant's death. As a result, we were able to lay a trail for you to follow and make it appear that you were doing all the work. You sniffed out every bread crumb we dropped in front of you. It all began with the visit to your neighborhood Chinese restaurant, didn't it? Our best surveillance man, and one of the Union's founding members, had his eye on you for a month after the Himalayan business. We learned your daily habits. When you were followed to lunch that day, the fortune you got was planted by a cantankerous customer."

Bond remembered the rude man with the screaming toddler. He would never have known. . . . Now he realized that his feelings of paranoia and of being watched, which he had dismissed as part of his ailment, had been genuine.

"We sent you the book that led you to Walter van Breeschooten's shop in Soho. We let you follow him to Morocco. It was only logical that you would contact your friend in Tangier. The photos of your prey were sent to him just in time for you to see them. That, in turn, led you to the Union training camp in the Rif Mountains. We allowed you to uncover just enough information to lead you to Casablanca, where, of course, we threw Mr. van Breeschooten to you." Yassasin shrugged. "He had displeased the Union's management, so he was dispensable. But not before you received the ticket to the bullfight. I knew that you would be headstrong, stubborn, and reckless. I knew that you would show up, one way or another. I honestly didn't think you'd pick up a ride to Spain with the CIA, and I must say that was very resourceful. We had a more complicated plan to abduct you from the bullfight, but when I learned that one of the bullfighters was your friend, I thought of something better. It was . . . easy to get you out of the crowd and down below the seats where we could take care of you. Poor Javier . . . such a fine young matador. Seeing *you* standing there, dressed as a *banderillero,* distracted him so much that he became careless. The bull took advantage of that. It's a pity."

Bond seethed in anger.

"While all this was going on, a man named Peredur Glyn created the public impression that you were causing all kinds of trouble," the Muslim explained. "After it had come to my attention that a Union mercenary working in Africa was a dead ringer for you, we had extensive photos made. No, you weren't identical twins by any means, but Glyn was the same weight and height; he had the same body type, and he had similar enough features that one might mistake him to be a member of your family.

"So we turned to Dr. Iwan Morelius, a Swedish plastic surgeon who is known for his high-priced and elite clientele in Beverly Hills and Hollywood. Perhaps you have heard of him? No? Dr. Morelius arrived in Hollywood with a very unique talent. He's a true artist, this Dr. Morelius. He is a master of dermabrasion, in which outer layers of skin are removed by "sanding off" or abrading the layers with a carbon dioxide laser. Morelius is an expert with the laser—he can precisely "sculpt" a face. He has such a skilled hand that he can quite literally mold a person's face into any shape or likeness. He got into a bit of trouble with the Screen Actors Guild when he created two uncanny look-alikes of famous movie stars. The real film stars sued and Dr. Morelius was forced out of business. Luckily for him, the Union learned of his talents and employed him. Dr. Morelius performed the rhytidectomy, or face remodeling, on Glyn. It was expensive, but certainly worth it. Dr. Morelius will no doubt be useful for the Union in the future.

"Glyn needed a fairly major overhaul for the outcome to be totally believable. Besides a complete dermabrasion, he was subjected to blepharoplasty and rhinoplasty. Fat tissue was removed from his cheeks to make them less full, and from his lips to make them thinner. The remodeling did the trick. Using computer-generated three-dimensional models of your head, adapted from Union file photographs, Dr. Morelius performed a Hollywood miracle.

"After six weeks, the face had healed. Glyn went through the next three weeks learning to be you—he memorized your daily routine, based on reports provided by Jimmy Powers. It didn't matter that his voice is dissimilar to yours. It's the visual effect that counts."

"He is a murderer," Bond said.

"And you're not?" Yassasin asked. "Yes, you're right. First, he murdered poor Dr. Feare, who had the unfortunate luck of being your girlfriend for the night."

"You're all bastards," Bond muttered.

"Now, now, Mr. Bond," Yassasin said. "There's no need to insult my family. The next thing Mr. Glyn did was to shoot a few British tourists on a ferry. Again, you were blamed. By then, your people were surely convinced that you had become renegade. You had disappeared, disobeyed orders, and are now wanted for a number of crimes. Therefore, it will come as no surprise to the world when 'James Bond' commits a few more terrible crimes tomorrow morning." He nodded to Margareta. She opened the door and the man whom Bond had dreaded meeting walked in.

"Mr. Bond," she said, "meet James Bond."

The man glared at Bond, the cruel mouth turning into a snarl.

Bond stared back and examined the imposter's features up close and in bright light for the first time. The clear blue eyes, the black hair, the scar on the right cheek . . . it was all correct and flawless. Anyone who actually knew Bond would most assuredly perform a double take if they saw the imposter.

"How does it feel to meet your double, Mr. Bond?" the man asked.

"Your doppelganger? And you know what they say happens to you when you meet your doppelgänger, Mr. Bond? It means you're going to die." With that, he punched Bond hard in the face. Blood spurted out of Bond's nose and ran down his mouth.

"How does it feel to be hit by you?" he asked, laughing.

"That's enough, Peredur," Margareta said.

"Stop it with that Peredur crap. I'm James Bond now," Glyn said roughly.

"Of course, James," Yassasin said, humoring the imposter. "That will be all. Meet us in the ring in ten minutes."

The imposter smiled coldly at Bond, then left the room.

Yassasin seemed pleased with himself. "As you can see, the results are most extraordinary. With the aid of a little brainwashing, Mr. Glyn will now do anything I command. He would perform a suicide mission, if he was told to do so."

Yassasin stared fiercely into Bond's eyes. "And he *was* told to do so."

"Who's he going to kill?" Bond asked, fighting back the horrible anxiety that was beginning to envelop him.

Yassasin nearly smiled. "The primary targets are two men. The Governor of Gibraltar and Britain's Prime Minister. And their body-guards, of course. He will kill the Spanish Prime Minister if he has to, for he will then follow Domingo Espada's orders. Espada will make demands, such as the ceding of Gibraltar to Spain and his appoint-ment as the new Governor. If the Spanish Prime Minister doesn't sign the pact with Espada, he will die, too. The rest of the U.N. delegates, including me, will be held 'hostage' until Espada gets what he wants. We'll make sure Miss Piel gets out alive. If the antiterrorist forces manage to free the hostages and kill Espada, so be it. The foolish man is willing to die for his cause."

"Domingo has a martyr complex, that's for certain," Margareta said. "He doesn't like becoming old. It's what he really wants."

"Domingo wants to make a political statement that will be heard the world over," Yassasin said. "That's all he cares about. That's enough for him to justify the enormous amount of money he raised to finance his coup."

"You'll never get away with it," Bond said.

"Correction, Mr. Bond," Yassasin said. "Peredur Glyn will never get away with it, but he doesn't know that. He thinks the escape plan is foolproof. Such is the power of suggestion. It is expected that he will die in that room in Gibraltar tomorrow. In fact, someone that he least expects will kill him. As for the rest of us, we will be released as soon as we provide our statements as to what happened. Diplomatic immunity is a powerful weapon. At any rate, after tomorrow 'James Bond' will be a blight on the history of British intelligence."

"They'll know he's not me," Bond said. "Anyone examining his corpse will know."

Yassasin conceded. "Oh, you're absolutely right. Fingerprints and dental records cannot be changed. But it will be at least a day or two before someone from London identifies the body, or rather, fails to identify the body. By then, though, the damage will be done."

"All we have to do now is to make sure that there is no trace of you," Margareta said.

"We thought we'd leave that unpleasant task to Mr. Glyn," Yassasin continued. "He's convinced that there can be only *one* James Bond, and you're not him. Therefore, he wanted to see you perish personally."

"Let's go, *amigo*," Margareta said. "You have an appointment with destiny."

Heidi moved as silently as possible toward the barbed-wire fence. After she had lost communication with Hedy, she abandoned the BMW and crept in the dark toward the front gates of the estate.

She had to roll into the ditch when she heard several vehicles start their engines. Headlights shone on the road ahead, and the guards ran to open the gate. Heidi raised her head just enough to watch as two Land Rovers, a Rolls-Royce, and the minivan drove out of the compound. It looked as if everyone in the place was leaving!

Of course, Heidi remembered. They were going to Gibraltar.

The guards were about to close the gate behind the caravan. Heidi crawled back to the road and walked calmly toward them. She drew a Heckler & Koch USP45 and held it loosely in her right hand.

The two guards looked up and were momentarily confused by the sight of a beautiful blonde walking up the road. Before they could speak, Heidi asked, "Where's my sister, creeps?" and then raised her arm and shot both men in their chests. They flew backward, landing with thuds on the ground.

Heidi walked through the open gate and went inside.

TWENTY-TWO

BULLRING

THEY LED HIM THROUGH THE BULLRING ENTRANCE AND SHOVED HIM TO THE soft dirt in the center of the bullring. With his hands still tied behind his back, there was not much that Bond could do to fight back. Peredur Glyn, the man who looked like James Bond, stood against the fence. Three Spanish guards were at the shields, watching Bond intently.

"This is Domingo's practice bullring," Margareta said. "It's a marvelous facility. The annex is equipped with everything one needs to breed fighting bulls. Domingo also uses part of the complex as a slaughterhouse. Have you ever seen what those vats of acid do to the remains of animal parts, Mr. Bond? The acid melts the skin right off the bones, and before long, the bones disintegrate as well. You get to experience this once-in-a-lifetime sensation firsthand!"

Yassasin addressed Glyn. "After you've had your fun, make sure there is nothing left. Report to Margareta when you're finished, then you can have your blond American."

"Yes, sir," the imposter Bond said, not taking his eyes off the man he was going to kill.

Yassasin turned to Margareta and said, "I'm off to Gibraltar. Needless to say, make sure he makes it to the meeting on time." He indicated Glyn.

"Don't worry," she replied. "That American girl will keep him occupied. We'll set off bright and early."

The pair began walking back through the door. Yassasin turned and said, as an afterthought, "Good-bye, Mr. Bond." The door closed and Bond was alone with his double and the three men.

Bond struggled to his feet and looked at his captors. What now? he wondered. He prepared himself for a beating, for he was certain they would want him alive when they were ready to use the acid. Bond scanned the ring for any sign of an escape. The shields were well covered by the guards.

One of the men said something in Spanish that Bond didn't catch. Glyn nodded, then all of them moved behind a shield. One man remained in the ring, moved to the bull's gate, and opened it.

A full-grown, fighting-mad black bull charged into the ring. The guard closed the door behind the animal, then quickly ran to the safety of the shield.

Bond froze, knowing full well that if he moved, the bull would charge. The bull was agitated. It ran to and fro, looking for a way out of this strange pen. Then it saw Bond, standing in the middle of the ring. Bond held his breath, but it was no good. The bull sensed the human's fear, and it charged at full speed.

Bond broke into a run across the ring, but the bull was fast. It attempted to slam into its moving target, but Bond sidestepped the animal just in time. The bull dug its front hooves into the dirt and skidded to a stop. It turned around and charged again. This time Bond ran to a shield, but the guard there thrust a spike at him. The sharp barb jabbed Bond's shoulder, causing him to recoil in pain. He fell back against the fence, only to see the bull charging straight for him. Bond spun around and away just as the bull's horns smashed into the fence. The men laughed and taunted Bond in Spanish. Peredur Glyn shouted, "If I were you, Mr. Bond, I would let the bull kill you. That would be preferable to watching your skin fall off in a vat of acid, don't you think?"

The bull recovered from the missed attack, then charged at Bond again. Bond ran along the fence, searching for anything that might cut the binds around his wrists.

Suddenly, the bullring entrance opened, and a picador, carrying a pair of lances, entered on horseback. The bull, seeing the horse, forgot about Bond momentarily and charged at it. The picador expertly maneuvered the horse around the bull and successfully thrust a lance into the bull's withers. The bull snorted and bellowed, becoming even angrier.

Bond could feel the bull's immense power even from across the ring. There was no other beast quite like it. It was a galloping locomotive weighing over a thousand pounds. It had one intention, and that was to destroy what it perceived to be its enemy.

The picador galloped his horse around the ring, leading the bull in a chase. Bond managed to get out of the way, but the bull's concentration was on the horse at the moment. In a surprise turn, the picador doubled back and threw the second lance into the bull.

The bull, confused and angered by the pain, stopped to take stock of its situation. The gate opened again, and the picador rode out, leaving the bull alone with Bond again.

It turned to Bond, breathing heavily. A crimson stream flowed down its side.

Bond turned his back on the bull and walked slowly toward the fence. As long as he didn't make any sudden movement, perhaps he could continue to avoid the bull until it tired out.

But he had no such luck. The bull pawed the dirt, snorted, and bolted toward him. Bond ran to the shield, but he heard Glyn shout something in Spanish. The sound of machinery echoed in the ring as the shield suddenly moved back into the fence, blocking off the safety zone. In fact, all of the shields in the ring had slid back and were now flush with the fence. There was no way out.

Glyn and the others were now behind the fence, whistling and taunting Bond.

Bond ran along the fence, the bull close on his heels. Bond zigzagged, attempting to throw the bull off its concentration, but the animal stayed with him. He ran faster, but he could hear the pounding of the bull's hooves on the ground coming closer and closer behind him.

The force of the impact took Bond by surprise. He felt a hammer-like slam in the small of his back, and for a moment he was in midair. The bull had butted him and thrown his body into the air like a paper cup. Bond landed hard on the ground, knocking the wind out of him. The bull turned and charged with its head down and horns pointed forward.

Bond rolled out of the way with split-second timing, avoiding a terrible goring.

The men laughed and jeered.

Bond got to his feet and stood in front of the bull, attempting to adapt a matador's stance. He stared at the bull, daring it to make another move. The bull hesitated just a moment, then charged again. This time Bond was ready. He allowed the bull to broadside him close enough so that Bond could perhaps grab one of the lances sticking out of the bull's back. It was an awkward maneuver with his hands tied behind him, and the first time he tried it, he missed. Bond beckoned to the bull again, and this time he spun around as the bull passed him and took hold of the lance with his right hand.

The bull, confused by the additional pain of having the lance's barbs tear out of its wound, stopped. It trotted to one side of the ring, staking out what was called a *querencia,* an area of the bullring where the bull felt secure. Many times in a real bullfight, a bull might retreat to this area and refuse to leave. It was up to the matador to draw it out to fight.

Bond used the momentary lull to thrust the lance's handle into the soft dirt, with the point sticking up. Even with his hands behind him, Bond managed to angle the lance so that he could reach the barbs with his wrists. He rubbed the bindings against the barbs.

"Hey, that's against the rules!" Glyn shouted.

The other men shouted at the bull, trying to provoke it into attacking before Bond could cut the binds.

The barbs cut into his hands as he did it, but Bond was finally successful in freeing himself before the bull charged. Somehow, it had sensed that Bond was about to gain an advantage over it.

Bond pulled the lance out of the ground and pointed it at the bull. Now aware that the strange polelike object brought pain, the bull slowed its charge and moved away.

The men booed the bull. One of them climbed on top of the fence and sat on it, his feet dangling over the now-flat shield.

A gunshot rang out, reverberating in the enclosed bullring. The jeering stopped as the men looked around.

The man on the fence clutched his chest and fell over into the ring.

The others immediately jumped into action, pulling out their weapons and looking around the seating sections.

"James!" came Heidi's voice. "Here!"

An object flew down from the darker area of the upper stands and landed on the dirt near Bond. He picked it up and found that it was her high-powered OC pepper spray canister.

Peredur Glyn fired his weapon into the stands but missed the girl.

"Get her! Don't let her escape! I'll deal with the prisoner!" he shouted.

The two other men raced up the stands as another shot ricocheted around the ring. Bond could now see Heidi as she ran from the seats to the exit, into the *pasillo*.

Meanwhile, the bull, frightened and confused by the sudden loud noises, seemed to pick up a second wind. It charged full speed at Bond.

Bond opened the canister, aimed, and sprayed the bull head-on.

The bull bellowed and tripped on its own front legs. It fell over with a crash, blinded and in pain. It managed to pull itself up, shaking its head, then sauntered around the ring in a daze. The fight had gone out of it for now.

Peredur Glyn jumped into the ring from the top of the fence. He was holding the thin sword that could pierce the hide of a thousand-pound bull. Running it through a human being would be like slicing butter.

Bond readied the lance as he came face-to-face with his mirror image.

Meanwhile, Heidi had run into the *pasillo* and around to the passage she had found when she had come looking for a way in. She ran through it as bullets whizzed past her. She turned and fired her USP45, but it was too dark to see anything. She kept running and eventually found herself in the slaughterhouse.

The stench was overwhelming, and the place was a nightmare of hanging carcasses, animal body parts—bulls, cows, horses—and slimy, foul vats where the beasts were dismembered and skinned.

Heidi searched frantically for a way out, but the sound of the men behind her forced her to duck between two hanging bull carcasses.

The men entered the room, muttering to each other in Spanish. They paused a moment, then split up. One man moved to the right, the other to the left, so that they could cover the entire room in a circular sweep.

As soon as one man was in her sights, Heidi aimed and squeezed the trigger. The blast knocked the man into a table covered in offal and blood. She ducked just as the remaining guard leveled his gun and fired a succession of shots in her direction. The bullets penetrated the hanging carcass with a *thump-thump-thump*. Heidi ran, keeping low, but a burning, knifelike pain shot through her left shoulder as one of the bullets connected. She fell back into a carcass and bounced. The gun slipped from her hand and slid across the concrete floor.

Heidi was in terrible pain. The bullet had entered her body just below the collarbone. It was a perilous wound. She didn't know if her lung had been pierced or not. Using every bit of strength that she could muster, she reached down to her calf and took hold of the object that was secured to her leg. Then she lay very still.

The guard cautiously approached her, gun in hand. Was she dead? He stepped up to her body and nudged it with his foot. Blood was spreading all over the floor and her eyes were closed. She had to be dead.

He made the fatal mistake of bending down to see if she was still breathing.

The hunting knife swung up and perforated the man's heart. His gun discharged into the air as he fell over next to her.

Heidi attempted to sit up, but the room was spinning. The pain was unbearable. *God, don't let me die here,* she prayed.

She tried to stand, but couldn't. Blood was pouring out of her wound like tap water.

The last thing she was aware of before blacking out was that she had still not found her sister.

—•—

Back in the bullring, James Bond and Peredur Glyn circled each other with their respective weapons. The bull, curious but wary of the two humans, stayed at the edge of the fence to let them fight it out. It was still smarting from the pepper spray.

Bond thought it was one of the most unsettling sensations he had ever felt. Here he was, facing an enemy that was, to all outward appearances, himself. If ever he had needed a clear head, it was now. Unfortunately, the throbbing in his head had taken over and his heart was pounding from the exertion and anxiety.

Glyn charged at Bond like the bull, the sword held straight in front of him. Bond feinted, swung the lance, and caught the imposter in the stomach. Glyn doubled over and dropped the sword. Bond broke the lance over Glyn's head, but the man merely fell to his knees and shook it off. He reached out, grabbed Bond's legs, and tackled him.

They rolled together on the dirt, their hands clutching at each other's throats.

Glyn managed to get on top. Bond was exhausted from the ordeal with the bull, and his increasingly disorienting condition was not making it any easier.

The man who looked like Bond whispered through his teeth, "When you see . . . your double . . . it mean you're . . . going to die. . . ."

Both grips tightened as each man attempted to strangle the other before their strength gave out.

Then the hazy dark cloud that had been plaguing Bond for months began to descend again.

No! Not now! Bond screamed to himself. I *mustn't* black out now!

His enemy's fingers dug into his throat. The lights in the ceiling spun above the imposter's head, bringing on nausea and the inevitable feeling that death was mere seconds away.

Bond fought the blackout with every ounce of willpower he could summon from the depths of his soul . . . but it was no use.

The dark curtain fell with a crash and then there was nothing.

TWENTY-THREE

BLOOD AND LUST

MARGARETA PEERED THROUGH THE PEEPHOLE AND SAW THE BLOND WOMAN sitting in a corner of the room, her knees folded in her arms. With the guards accompanying Espada to Gibraltar, the compound had been left unattended for a night. Margareta wanted to make sure that everything was secure and that none of the girls could escape. Everything appeared to be all right, she thought.

The rest of them were in their rooms, quietly enduring the long hours of waiting for the times when they would be called upon to perform their duties. Some of them who were literate would read books, others might sew. Some slept, some watched television, while others simply sat and stared at the wall, wondering if they would ever see freedom again. Some of them looked forward to their new life away from poverty and hunger, but most of them knew that they had been sold to a fate worse than their most horrid nightmares.

Margareta was satisfied that the girls were safe. She closed and locked the door, then went through the corridors and out of the foyer. She relocked the front door of the compound, then crossed the yard to the house. It was hauntingly quiet with everyone gone. In just a few hours, she, too, would leave with the assassin and join the others at the border.

She went to her room and checked the bag that she had packed.

Now she would take a quick shower and get ready for bed. Sleep would probably be elusive, though, for she felt tense about the upcoming events. She needed something to relax her, so she pulled a bottle of red wine off a shelf, uncorked it, and poured a glass.

Margareta undressed and went into the bathroom to start the water. She waited until it was hot, filling the room with steam, then she got in the shower stall.

Margareta had finished washing her hair when the knock startled her. Someone was in the bedroom, just outside the bathroom door.

"What is it?" she called.

"It's me," came the voice. Peredur Glyn.

"Just a second," Margareta said. She rinsed, turned off the water, and stepped out of the stall. She wrapped a towel around her body and opened the bathroom door.

The imposter was standing in the middle of her room. There was a cut above his eye, and red marks were evident around his neck.

"What happened to you?" she shouted. "You look terrible!"

He laughed. "It was the prisoner," the man said in the distinctive Welsh accent. "We had a scuffle. It's all right, though. You won't be hearing from him anymore."

"What happened?"

"The guy passed out in my hands," Glyn said. "Just fainted dead away. I said, 'To hell with this,' and let the others handle it. I left him with them, they were going to take him to the slaughterhouse. The job should be finished by now."

"You need to get cleaned up. It won't look right if your face is messed up tomorrow," she said, leading him to the bathroom. She ran water in the sink, took a washcloth, and dabbed the wound on the assassin's head.

She smiled as he winced. "That plastic surgeon did an incredible job. I have to admit that James Bond was a handsome man."

"You mean *is*. That's who I am now," Glyn said as he slipped his hand inside the towel, feeling her firm breast.

"Right," she said, ignoring the gesture. He wondered if that, in itself, was an invitation to continue.

Instead, though, he said, "Sorry, Miss Piel, but tonight I have a date with a certain American blonde, if I remember correctly." He withdrew his hand.

"Hmmm," Margareta said. "I suppose you do. Well, don't overdo it. You need your wits about you in the morning. Don't stay up all night."

"I can come back and do you again after I'm finished," he suggested.

"Last night was lovely, dear, but I do need my beauty rest," she replied. "But if I can't sleep . . ."

Glyn grinned lecherously, then left the room.

The phone woke her two hours later.

Margareta grabbed it and answered, *"Que?"*

"Something bad has happened." It was the imposter. He sounded out of breath.

"What's the matter?"

"She's dead."

"What? Who?" Margareta had to fight the clouds of drowsiness away.

"The girl. The blond American."

"Dead? How?"

"I don't know. . . ." he stammered. He sounded upset. "I didn't mean to hurt her. . . . It was an accident. . . ."

"I'll be right there." Margareta slammed down the phone and put on a silk robe over her naked body. She removed the Glock from her bedside table and stormed out of the bedroom.

By the time she got to the compound, she could hear the cries of the girls. They were bemoaning their predicament in Spanish. One was demanding to know what had happened to the "new girl."

Margareta told them to shut up, then went straight to the American's cell. She gasped when she opened the door and saw the bloody mess that was inside.

The imposter Bond was sitting on the bed with an odd expression on his face. He looked like the naughty boy who had just been caught with his fingers in the cookie jar, and his hands and chest were covered in blood.

The blond girl was lying on the floor. She was wrapped in a red-soaked bedsheet.

"Peredur, what happened?"

"My name is James Bond," the man said, choking back a sob.

"Fine, James, tell me what happened."

"She wouldn't cooperate," he said. He held up a bloody knife. "I only wanted to scare her with it. She fought me. When I forced her to . . . you know . . . she pushed herself against the blade. She stabbed herself. It made me very angry. So I . . . stabbed her some more. . . ."

"You damned fool," Margareta said. "What's the matter with you?"

"I'm sorry," he said.

"Domingo won't like this. You have to get rid of her. Clean up this place. Take her body to the slaughterhouse and get rid of it. Throw her into the vats. Do you hear me?"

The imposter nodded.

"Get one of the others to help you. Where are they?"

Glyn shrugged. "I suppose they're still in the annex. Don't worry, I'll take care of it. I'm sorry I disturbed you."

"Never mind that. Just get her out of here. Then get cleaned up. I think I had better keep my eye on you for the rest of the night. We have to leave very early tomorrow. Come to my room when you're finished."

The man stared at the body on the floor.

"Do you hear me?" she demanded.

"Yes," he muttered.

She walked out and slammed the door closed.

It was after midnight when the knock came.

"It's open," Margareta said.

Glyn walked in. He had showered and was dressed in a terry-cloth robe. The earlier persona of little-boy helplessness had disappeared. Now he was all man, handsome, virile, dangerous. . . .

"Well?" she asked.

"It's done," he said, sitting on the sofa. "The place is clean. There is no trace of her."

"There had better not be. What made you do that? You really are one sick *hombre*."

He shrugged. "I kill. It's what I do."

Despite the savagery of his act, Margareta couldn't help but feel a twinge of excitement as she gazed upon his magnificent body. His animalistic nature appealed to her and she felt the stirrings of desire. The compulsions that had given rise to her nickname of *Mantis Religiosa* were not about to dissipate anytime soon.

He was a lot like her, this Union assassin. Sex and murder were intrinsically linked in their psychological makeup. Margareta knew full well that she and Peredur Glyn weren't . . . normal.

Margareta loosened the sash around her robe and let it fall open. She stood in front of him, then ran her fingers through his hair.

"That's not all you do well, Peredur," she said.

Glyn looked up at her and replied, "My name is James Bond now."

"Yes, that's right," she said. "Mr. Bond."

A smile played around his lips. He slipped his hands inside of her robe and felt the soft warm flesh. His right hand snaked around her waist and rested on her buttocks. He squeezed a cheek, then pulled her closer to him. He nuzzled his face between her breasts, kissing them, licking them. . . .

Margareta sighed as she straddled his lap. Men who had the capacity to kill had always excited her. Her first lover had been a Spanish bandit who was notorious for robbing grocery stores and murdering the staff. She had accompanied him on a few of his sprees, but the police had never caught up with her. She had been fourteen years old at the time.

She took the assassin's chin and raised his mouth toward hers. Their lips met, then she pushed him back on the sofa.

They both needed a relief of tension to prepare for the big day. . . . She climbed on top of him and took the initiative. She found that the anticipation of the next morning's violence served to enhance her pleasure.

It was unlike anything she had felt before.

TWENTY-FOUR

BACK TO THE BEGINNING

THE RECEPTION WAS SCHEDULED FOR 10:00 A.M.

Margareta Piel and the assassin left Espada's estate at 6:30 and drove into Marbella, and then on to La Linea, where Espada and Agustin were waiting for them. Jimmy Powers was already in Gibraltar. Nadir Yassasin was making his way to the Rock by way of Tangier. They would assume the identities of the slain delegates from Washington.

During the journey, Margareta had struggled with a dilemma that had risen overnight. She wasn't quite sure how to deal with it. If her suspicions were correct, it could mean that the Union's plan might end in disaster. On the other hand, it was possible that she could be able to use her newly gained knowledge to her own personal advantage. She had been eager to break away from Espada for a long time. The opportunity to join the Union was a welcome one. This could be her chance to show them her resourcefulness. She decided to play it by ear, see how the morning progressed, and make her move when the time was right.

A Governor's aide, an attractive brunette who might have been a Miss Gibraltar at one time, met them at the airport. The four Spaniards and the man from Britain piled into a limo and then went to the Convent. Main Street had been closed, blocked off to all traffic, both pedestrian and otherwise. It was 9:45 by the time they stepped through the impressive brick facade that framed the main entrance to what was at one time an old Franciscan convent. The name had stuck.

Security was extremely tight. Officers from the Gibraltar Regiment were everywhere. The four of them were directed to produce their papers, walk through a metal detector, and submit their bags to be searched. The assassin's passport and documents bore the name "Peter Woodward." One of the security officers spent a long time examining at the passport. There was a moment when Margareta doubted if any part of the Union's plan could be pulled off. Finally, the imposter Bond was allowed to go through.

After signing the guest register, they were led up the red-carpeted wooden stairs to the first floor and upper Cloister. Margareta noticed a copy of the original Grant of Arms to Gibraltar by Queen Isabella of Castille in 1502. The first British Governor of Gibraltar later used these arms, which were eventually adopted as the castle and key symbols on the coat of arms of the City of Gibraltar. The colony's flag, of course, grew from this.

They were led into the ballroom, where a number of people had already gathered.

It was a lovely room, surrounded by a collection of royal portraits of British monarchs commencing with Queen Victoria. Sparkling chandeliers hung from the high ceiling, and large mirrors reflected the illumination. There was a stage at one end with a string quartet playing Mozart; at the other end was a table set up as a bar.

Margareta saw Nadir Yassasin near the bar, standing alone. Should she tell him about her suspicions? Their eyes met briefly, but she then made a point of ignoring him throughout the remainder of the reception.

Jimmy Powers was in an animated conversation with two other men who appeared to be American. She slowly made her way toward them so that she could overhear what they were saying.

"Mr. Bunyon, I've been with the State Department for ten years," one gray-haired man was saying, "and I simply can't recall your face. Forgive me. I thought I knew everyone in the Bureau of Mediterranean Activity."

Powers chuckled and said, "Sir, I've been around since the Reagan administration. I'm often out of the country."

Margareta was satisfied that Powers could handle the grilling. She moved on and asked a servant behind the bar for a glass of orange juice. A couple of men smiled at her, probably hoping she would introduce herself to them. One man staring at her was the Spanish Prime Minister. She gave him her best come-hither look and watched him swallow visibly.

An Arab woman in a full-length caftan and veil was sitting alone, near the quartet. Every part of her body was hidden, except for her brown eyes. Margareta decided to approach her and say hello. The woman introduced herself as a delegate from Morocco, but she didn't offer much more information than that. Margareta made an excuse to continue mingling.

Espada, Agustin, and the assassin sat down near the bar and surveyed the room. Espada sat with his arms folded as if he were bored and annoyed with the entire proceedings.

What if she didn't report her suspicions to Yassasin? Would the Union punish her if something went wrong? The important thing, she thought, was to save her own skin if it did.

To hell with it, she thought. She had better speak to Nadir. She approached him casually and said, "Hello, I'm Margareta Piel. I'm with Domingo Espada. I saw you standing here alone and thought I would introduce myself."

He shook her hand. "Said Arif. I'm from Morocco, but I live in America."

"I think we need to talk," she said, lowering her voice.

His eyes narrowed. "Are you mad? What about?"

Before she could answer, a heated exchange in Spanish was heard in Espada's corner of the room. The Spanish Prime Minister was standing in front of him. Everyone in the room turned to look at them, especially at the man who had caused all this trouble. Espada stood and glared at the Spanish PM and for a moment there was complete silence. Finally, the Spanish PM muttered something to the effect that he hoped their differences could be resolved today, and then he walked away.

Margareta had to admit that Espada looked splendid. He was wearing a uniform of his own design that closely resembled that of a

Spanish officer at the time of the Second World War. Agustin, at his right, and the imposter James Bond, at his left, were dressed in smart Brioni suits. The assassin looked comfortable and relaxed, if a bit out of place as a bodyguard to Espada.

Espada noticed that he had the room's attention. He cleared his throat and managed to say in English, "Thank you all for coming. I am happy to be here."

The room seemed to relax then, and the conversations resumed. Margareta watched the assassin as he stayed close to Espada and kept his eyes on everything.

Perhaps she was wrong? Margareta wondered.

"What was it you wanted to say?" Yassasin asked.

"Never mind," she said.

The aide-de-camp entered at 10:00 and made an announcement.

"We have arranged a small tour of the Convent for you that will commence at this time. If you do not care to join the tour, you may remain here. His Excellency the Governor and the British Prime Minister are due to arrive at ten thirty, at which time we'll move into the Banqueting Room."

Margareta slid next to the Americans from the State Department and introduced herself as they walked out of the ballroom to follow the brunette who had picked her up at the airport. Yassasin, Powers, and Espada's entourage joined in as well.

The group of nearly twenty people paraded downstairs, passed the main entrance, then down another five steps to the open-air ground-floor Cloister. The square was surrounded by an arched covered way, and a well had been built in the center. A black wooden statue of General Sir George Eliott, the Governor of Gibraltar during the Great Siege, was the dominating ornament in the Cloister. All around the square were samples of different kinds of shells and shot used during Gibraltar's various skirmishes. The gardens were especially beautiful, boasting the largest "dragon tree" in all of Europe. Planted in 1484, the dragon tree has a skinlike texture and bleeds red sap when poked with a sharp stick.

The brunette lectured in English but was able to answer any questions in a variety of other languages.

The tour went through the Duke of Kent Room, back upstairs to the Drawing Room and Billiard Room, then back down to the main entrance. At this point, the group turned north, went through a small white door, and entered the King's Chapel.

The guide told the tour participants that they had ten minutes to wander freely around the chapel and examine the various memorials and artwork. She even encouraged them to use the time for silent meditation. Some of the guests remained to do so, while others chose to go back upstairs.

Jimmy Powers casually sat in a specific pew, reached down, and removed the white silk bag he had planted there the day before.

Margareta walked slowly around the back of the chapel and sat down on a pew, pretending to examine a stained-glass window. She, too, groped for and found the bag that was meant for her.

Nadir Yassasin had become engaged in a discussion with delegates from the Middle East. He tactfully led them to the pew where his weapon had been planted, and they sat there for a moment. Just as the tour guide announced that the ten minutes were up, Yassasin retrieved the silk bag and put it in his waistband.

Espada and Agustin were also successful in picking up their planted weapons. It was easier than Espada had imagined. With so many delegates in the chapel, no one was paying any attention to what the others were doing.

The man who had entered the building as "Peter Woodward," obviously an expat now working as a bodyguard for Espada, found his weapon under the designated pew. The weight was familiar—it was the Walther PPK. He placed the bag in his waistband under the jacket. As he walked back up the stairs to the first floor of the Convent, he carefully undid the string on the silk bag and removed the gun. Once he was led back into the Ballroom, the Walther was loose in his waistband with the safety off, ready to be fired.

There was still another ten minutes before the British PM and the Governor were scheduled to arrive. Nadir Yassasin found Jimmy Powers by the string quartet and spoke to him.

"They are wonderful, aren't they?"

Powers shrugged. "If you like that kind of music . . . me, I prefer good ol' American rock 'n' roll."

Yassasin lowered his voice, even though the music was loud and the acoustics of the large room assured that they would not be overheard. "So, this is the moment of truth, yes?"

Powers shrugged again, as if he were hedging on a political opinion.

Yassasin seemed to be talking to himself, as Powers certainly knew the drill. "Timing is crucial. First, the assassin takes out the PM's and Governor's bodyguards, then immediately shoots the PM and Governor. Espada and Agustin will draw their weapons and shoot any other guards in the room. They believe that they will secure the room and hold everyone else hostage until the Spanish Prime Minister signs a pact with Espada. Unfortunately, that's not going to happen."

"Has the alternative plan been approved?" Powers asked.

"Yes. *Le Gérant* has given the order. Espada is to die. The assassin will kill him as soon as the PM and Governor are dead. Then Miss Piel will kill the assassin if the remaining guards in the room don't blow him away first. The fool really thinks he's going to get away with this."

Powers shrugged again. "Such is life."

"No, my friend," Yassasin replied. "Such is death."

At 10:30, everyone moved into the exquisite Banqueting Hall. Espada, Agustin, Margareta, and the assassin sat at the east end of the table. Espada took the seat at the head of the table. Agustin was on his right, the assassin on his left. Margareta sat next to the imposter Bond. The other delegates took various seats, but left designated chairs for the PM and Governor.

Margareta eyed the man sitting next to her and struggled once again with the resolve to make herself known. The man was a killer. He was unpredictable. If she didn't defuse the situation right now, there was no telling what kind of carnage might erupt.

A minute went by, and she finally decided to confront the assassin with what she suspected.

Now.

TWENTY-FIVE

FAENA

MARGARETA LEANED OVER AND WHISPERED IN THE ASSASSIN'S EAR. "ALL right, Mr. *Bond*, I know it's you. You think I can't tell the difference between you and Peredur Glyn in bed? You gave yourself away last night with the one area of your body that the doctor in Hollywood didn't alter."

Nadir Yassasin was looking at the two of them with a furrowed brow. Bond swallowed but remained stone-faced. He had to keep his cover or the entire operation would be blown.

"Now, here's the deal," she continued as he felt the gun barrel digging into his kidney. "You're going to do exactly what you're supposed to do. Kill the PM and the Governor, as planned. If you don't do it, I'm going to shoot you in the back, and then my cohorts will do it anyway. My job here was to kill Peredur Glyn after the assassinations. Whether it's you or him makes no difference to me. That's my ticket out of here. I'll be the hero. You will lose, no matter what, the PM will be dead, and the Union's plan will succeed. This isn't about Espada. This is between the Union and your pitiful country."

She sat back in her chair. An avalanche of doubt fell on Bond and smothered him.

She knew! Was the plan ruined?

He suddenly felt his heart accelerate as a wave of panic enveloped him. The pounding in his head was excruciating. Masses of darkness clouded his vision.

No! he willed. *I must not black out now!*

The aide-de-camp remained in place by the open door. Activity could be heard in the corridor as the PM, the Governor, and their bodyguards approached. Two Gibraltar Regiment soldiers entered the room, armed and alert.

Bond clenched his fists and shut his eyes, struggling against the attack.

The operation could still work! Concentrate, damn it!

Espada looked at Bond in anticipation, but Yassasin could see that something was terribly wrong. He glanced at Powers, who was also narrowing his eyes at Bond and Margareta. He reached for his weapon, ready to draw it at a second's notice.

Bond opened his eyes as a tall, distinguished gentleman with white hair entered the room—the Governor of Gibraltar. Right behind him was a man in a suit whom Bond recognized as 001. Their eyes found each other and they shared a quick and silent acknowledgment, even though 001 could see the pain in Bond's eyes.

The British Prime Minister stepped into the room and stood beside 001. He was a short man with a bright face and charming smile. He virtually lit up the room.

The aide-de-camp announced, "His Excellency, the Governor of Gibraltar, and the Prime Minister of Great Britain."

The door had remained open. Another figure entered the room and stood beside the Prime Minister.

She was one of the Taunt twins, dressed in a smart business suit.

Margareta, Yassasin, Espada, and Agustin gasped simultaneously.

Agent 001 shouted, "Everyone down!" and time suddenly seemed to stretch into a slow, dreamlike eternity.

In the first second, 001 pulled the Prime Minister to the floor. At the same time, the soldiers tackled the Governor. Some of the delegates began to scream. Powers drew his gun, not sure whom to shoot first.

During the next second, Bond slammed his upper body forward

onto the table as he pulled the Walther from his waistband. This maneuver provided a clear view of Margareta Piel. Nadir Yassasin began to draw his weapon.

At the beginning of the third second, the veiled Arab woman sitting across the table from Bond swung her right arm out from under the caftan. She was holding a Heckler & Koch USP45. A single round caught Margareta in the chest and threw her backward.

Halfway through the same second, Bond, still leaning forward over the table, angled his body onto his right shoulder and shot Powers with one bullet through the man's right temple. Powers fell against the State Department delegate, who shrieked in horror. By the end of the third second, some of the delegates jumped out of their seats and dived for the floor. The others were frozen in fear.

The fourth second. With a bloodcurdling scream, Margareta crashed through a stained-glass window and fell to the cloister below. Espada and Agustin, momentarily frozen by the sudden turn of events, jolted into action at the sound of the shattering window. Their guns were in hand, but Bond was faster. Bond swung his arm across the tabletop and shot Agustin in the forehead at point-blank range. Yassasin, his hand shaking, aimed his Browning at Bond.

Five seconds. Espada leveled his Super Star at Bond, but the Walther exploded first. The round caught Espada in the cheek and the man fell back in his chair. Yassasin's gun erupted, but the bullet whizzed past Bond's head and into the wall. The Taunt twin was immediately behind the strategist, a Beretta M93R poking the back of his head. She ordered Yassasin not to move. "Drop your weapon on the table," she commanded.

Yassasin did so and slowly raised his hands, and time equivocally returned to its normal rate of duration. Only six seconds had elapsed since 001 had shouted the order to launch the operation.

Bond knelt beside Espada, who was choking and splattering blood all over the carpet.

"That was for the matadors," Bond said through his teeth.

Espada's eyes exhibited fear and hatred, but eventually they rolled up into his head as the choking ceased.

Bond finally stood and said, "It's all over, everyone." The waves of nausea and panic were subsiding. He had fought against them and had won.

The Taunt twin turned to the aide-de-camp and indicated Yas-sasin. "He's all yours, sir." The Regiment soldiers immediately hand-cuffed the Union strategist and frisked him. The Governor, the PM, and the other delegates were slowly rising to their feet and wiping their brows. Suddenly the room was full of chatter, tears, prayers, hugs, and relief.

Agent 001 gave Bond a thumbs-up. Bond nodded at him, then looked at the blonde.

"Nice work, Hedy," Bond said. He turned to the Arab woman in the veil and whispered, "You too, Heidi."

The debriefing took place in the Governor's Drawing Room, where the day's participants could relax in a friendly environment after the terror of the morning's events. Present were the Governor, the British PM, the Spanish PM, 001, Hedy Taunt, and James Bond.

Hedy was attempting to explain how she escaped from Espada's compound without blowing "Hillary's" cover when the Spanish PM interrupted her. "Wait a second. I'm confused. I thought Double-O Seven was a captive. What happened to the double? How did you get off the property?"

Bond spoke up. "If I may? I'm not sure what happened during the fight with Peredur Glyn, but I had another one of the blackouts I have been experiencing. I continued to function, however, even though I have no memory of it. When I came to, the imposter was lying dead on the ground, strangled. I collected myself and went back to Espada's house. I thought I might be able to fool anyone still there that I was Peredur Glyn. I succeeded, except for, er, one minor detail that eventually gave me away."

Hedy almost laughed and averted her eyes.

Bond continued. "After convincing the Piel woman that I was Glyn, I went to the place they call the compound and found H— uhm, Miss Taunt. Since Peredur Glyn was reputed to be some kind of homicidal maniac, we concocted a rather unique plan to get her out. I went to the slaughterhouse to fetch a bucket of blood—animal blood."

He neglected to say that he had also found Heidi Taunt there. She was bleeding badly from the bullet wound in her shoulder and was drifting in and out of consciousness. Bond had administered first aid as best as he could, then told her to sit tight and that he would be back with her sister.

"I took the bucket of blood back to the compound and we staged Miss Taunt's death. The Piel woman ordered me to get rid of the body, as I suspected she would, so I carried Miss Taunt out of the compound and went straight to the slaughterhouse."

Again, he left out the sequence in which he and Hedy helped Heidi out of the slaughterhouse and into one of the Land Rovers that was parked outside.

"We were lucky that almost the entire staff had gone with Espada. The guards at the front gate were dead. We quickly made a plan. Miss Taunt drove to Marbella and I went back to the house to see the Piel woman."

Hedy took over the narrative. "I got on the phone to Washington and London. It took some doing, but I finally convinced Double-O Seven's chief to allow us to go ahead with the plan." This was, of course, after Heidi's bullet had been removed and she had received a blood transfusion, but Hedy didn't mention that. Heidi had insisted on coming along to the Convent, disguised in the veil.

"I must say, it sounded terribly risky to me," the PM said.

"M wasn't happy about it," 001 concurred.

"But," the PM conceded, "it was perhaps the only way we could avoid any further bloodshed. I agreed to go along with it. So did the Governor. We got word to the aide-de-camp here just in time."

The Spanish PM asked, "What would you have done if Mr. Bond's true identity had been discovered?"

No one had an answer to that.

"I'm afraid Señor Espada might have got his way," the Governor said. "By the way, what's happened to his army?"

"When they heard that Espada was dead, they dispersed," the Spanish PM said. "Our forces arrived after the King decided that he had had enough of Domingo Espada. He wasn't about to let our country go to war with Great Britain."

"I'm glad to hear that," the British PM said.

"We have sent a special task force to Espada's estate. The girls being held captive there will be freed and given financial and housing assistance. We will do our best to find them suitable and legal employment. As for Gibraltar . . ."

The Spanish PM looked hard at the British PM and then smiled, saying, "We will discuss the matter another time."

The two Prime Ministers stood and shook hands as the Governor of Gibraltar looked on.

Bond rubbed his eyes. The bloody headache was taking control once again. It had been threatening to do so all morning. Agent 001 looked at him and said, "Come on, Bond. We have to go to hospital. Someone is waiting for you there."

"What's going to happen to that Arab guy?" Hedy asked. "Yassasin."

"We're going to interrogate the bloody hell out of him," 001 answered. "We want to find out as much as we can about the Union. They've gone too far this time. SIS have declared an all-out war against them."

"Well, when you're done, just make sure you lock him up and throw away the key," Hedy said.

"You can be sure of that," 001 replied.

The two PMs and the Governor turned to Bond as he stood. "Thank you," the Governor said. "For everything."

Bond smiled, nodded, and shook their hands without saying a word. He felt curiously numb now that the crisis was over. He quietly allowed his colleague to lead him out of the room as Hedy followed close behind.

TWENTY-SIX

AFTERMATH

"Sir James Molony is here," Miss Moneypenny announced on the intercom.

M pushed the button for the green light as Bill Tanner continued his report.

"The FBI in America picked up the plastic surgeon, Dr. Morelius, in California. Unfortunately, he never actually broke the law. He was paid by the Union to perform a legitimate service. The FBI had to let him go."

"But he's insignificant in the grand scheme of things," M replied.

Tanner nodded. "The director of the FBI assured me that the doctor had the living daylights scared out of him. He's being placed in their Witness Protection Program. Hopefully he will identify his employers, and if he's lucky he can have a legitimate practice in another state."

Sir James Molony opened the door and entered. M remained seated and said, "Good morning, Sir James. Please sit down. How was your flight from Gibraltar?"

"Fine, thank you," Molony replied, sitting across from her. Tanner pulled up a chair after offering the staff neurologist a coffee.

"I appreciate you cutting short your lecture tour to attend to Double-O Seven," M said.

"Believe me, madam, it was a blessing in disguise," the doctor answered. "I can't tell you how bored I was after two months of talking to young people all over the world who had no interest at all in what I was saying. I was quite ready for something to interrupt it."

"How's James doing?" Tanner asked.

"He's doing quite well. The operation was a complete success. He should be feeling himself by now. We discharged him from hospital yesterday and he's recuperating at the hotel there. I expect that he'll fly back home in a day or two."

"Tell us exactly what was wrong with him," M prodded.

Molony sipped his coffee and placed it on the edge of the large glass-topped desk.

"As you know, Double-O Seven had a lesion on his temporal lobe. This was probably caused by the injury he sustained in the Himalayas three months ago. It was the source of his headaches, as well as what I would clinically diagnose as panic attacks. Dr. Feare, may her soul rest in peace, had originally detected the lesion with an EEG and pre-scribed a medication, carbamazepine, which might have cured him without the need for surgery. However, when I examined the pills he had been taking, I discovered that he had the wrong pills. They had been disguised as the correct ones. He was taking haloperidol, which is often used as a treatment for a number of psychoses. But if used improperly, it can make some conditions worse. As a result, Bond suffered from post-traumatic epilepsy. He would hallucinate, have delusions of paranoia, and even experience poriomania, or black-outs. This sometimes happens with hard-case alcoholics. They'll pass out somewhere and wake up in a completely different location. How they get from one place to the next is a mystery to them. The same thing happened to Double-O Seven. More than once. I'm still trying to determine how he got the wrong medication in the first place. Dr. Feare's prescription was correct."

"I think Mr. Tanner can answer that one," M said.

Tanner cleared his throat and said, "Sir James, I'm afraid I have to inform you that one of your employees is a traitor. Double-O Seven alerted us to the fact that Michael Clayton, one of the Union members he first encountered in London, had a cousin who was also well connected with the organization. After we further investigated the man's background, we determined that he did indeed have a cousin—Deborah Reilly."

Molony's eyes bulged. "Good Lord, that's my nurse!"

"I'm afraid so," Tanner said. "MI5 arrested her yesterday. She was pretty tight-lipped until we confronted her with all manner of evidence. She confessed to switching Bond's medication, even disguising it as the proper pills. We believe she was instrumental in setting up Double-O Seven for Dr. Feare's murder."

Molony shook his head. "It's extraordinary. She's been with me for several years. How could this have happened?"

"She was obviously promised money. She was apparently terribly devoted to her cousin. He probably got her involved. When she learned that he was dead, she broke down and told all," Tanner explained.

"So, you see, the Union was on to Bond all the time," M said. "Your nurse provided them with the information that he was not well. When we told Double-O Seven that we had found her, he remembered that he had seen her in Soho the day before he left for Africa. She had paid a visit to one of her cousin's adult bookshops, apparently to deliver information or something to Clayton. Bond couldn't place her at the time."

"She wasn't a terribly pleasant person, I must say," Molony admitted. "She was an excellent nurse, though. She correctly prescribed what kind of medication would, at the very least, have some kind of psychological effect on the patient."

Tanner continued. "From what we've gathered from preliminary interrogation of this fellow Yassasin, one of the Union's founding members, an American, James Powers, was also responsible. Apparently he was a brilliant surveillance expert. He had been watching Double-O Seven from the moment he had returned from the Himalayas. Powers even followed Bond to Jamaica and back. He got to know Double-O Seven's daily routine. Quite frightening, really."

"How effective will the surgery be?" M asked, veering the conversation back to 007's health.

"One hundred percent, we hope," Molony replied. "James has been through a lot, but he has a strong reserve. I believe he'll pull through with no lasting side effects. He just needs some time."

"Thank you, Sir James," M said.

She glanced at Bond's medical records on the table in front of her. She found a photograph of him and picked it up. "The Union really came up with something extraordinary, didn't they?" M asked rhetorically, shaking her head.

Tanner nodded. "They led Bond by the nose and made him think that he was the one making discoveries and finding clues. They even had *us* for a while—we really thought he had gone off his rocker and joined the Union."

"It was what they wanted us to think," M said. "But the Union underestimated one thing," M said, running her index finger along the edge of Bond's photograph.

"What was that, ma'am?" Molony asked.

"My belief in him."

Further south, on the continent of Africa, another man was touching a photograph of James Bond, but he couldn't see it. Somehow, though, he was able to absorb the subject's essence simply by holding the object in his hands. He could sense that this man was a far more complex and resilient human being than any of the Union's analysts could have guessed.

Le Gérant sat in his new quarters in Marrakesh, a plain, sun-baked stone building not far from the *Djemaa el-Fna*. When he had received the news that the Gibraltar operation had failed dismally and that his chief strategist was in captivity, he had dismissed the *cercle fermé* and retreated to his study. He had asked not to be disturbed and had remained in his private quarters for twenty-four hours.

Le Gérant usually had a finely tuned sense of humor. His father had taught him that, along with keen business acumen, a ruthless efficiency in dealing with obstacles, and organizational skills that commanded respect and discipline from every division of his domain. *Le Gérant* was very good at what he did. Still, he could remember his father repeatedly driving the point home: a businessman should never lose his sense of humor, no matter what happened.

At this point, however, *Le Gérant* knew that he had lost it and wondered if he would ever get it back.

Twice now this Double-O agent had made the Union look foolish. *Le Gérant* was not going to let it happen again. If it was a war that MI6 wanted, then it was a war they would get.

Le Gérant angrily crumpled the photograph with one hand and tossed it across the room, where he knew it would drop neatly into a dustbin.

As others spoke about him, James Bond didn't feel his ears burning as he lay in bed in the sea-view room in the Rock Hotel in Gibraltar. He wouldn't have been able to scratch them anyway—the bandage on his head covered them completely.

CNN was reporting that the Spanish/British crisis was over. The two governments had put aside their differences and had held a conference in Brussels to quash any further misunderstandings. The Spanish Prime Minister had, for the first time, publicly denounced Domingo Espada and his tenets. Espada's followers had staged a protest march in Madrid, but they quickly realized that it was a lost cause. The majority of the population quickly came to the opinion that Espada was a madman. When many prominent *matadors* saw fit to denigrate Espada's actions and speak out against him, the people completely turned against him. When it was reported that he had been linked to the deaths of the Rojo brothers and had kept kidnapped sex slaves on his estate, Espada was forever cast as one of the country's most notorious villains.

There was a knock on the door. Bond switched off the television with the remote but didn't get up. He called, "If you have a key, come in."

The only people who had a key to his room were a nurse . . . and the Taunt twins.

"We're the candy stripe girls and it's time to party!" Heidi sang cheerfully as they entered his bedroom. Hedy was carrying a bottle of

Taittinger. They were both dressed identically again, in white blouses and tight-fitting designer jeans. Heidi's arm was in a sling.

"We're here to make you well," Hedy said.

Bond indicated the champagne. "I'm not supposed to drink, you know."

"We know that," she answered. "This is for *us!*"

"Remember that first night at dinner in Tangier? You made a suggestion about sharing," Heidi said with a smile.

Hedy began working on the bottle. The girls laughed at Bond's suspicious glare, poured glasses of champagne, and then sat on either side of him.

"Who's first, Hedy?" Heidi asked. "Or do we have to flip for it?"

NEVER DREAM
OF DYING

For Max

CONTENTS

THE NEW WAR

A TINY BEAD OF SWEAT APPEARED AT THE COMMANDANT'S RIGHT TEMPLE and lingered there, waiting for the moment when it would drop off and trickle down the man's high, scarred cheekbone.

James Bond knew that the French commandant was nervous. He empathized with the man, for he, too, never went into a situation such as this one without feeling some amount of anxiety. It was normal. It was healthy. It kept one sharp.

They peered around the edge of the carpenter's shop. It was night and the studio had kept the buildings' exterior lights on. Besides providing plenty of illumination, this created the illusion that the film studio lot was in reality another village with its own paved roads, buildings and community. The palm trees, standing like sentinels around the property, tended to further perpetuate the notion that this was a Hollywood-style studio, even though it was located in the south of France. The trees, Bond had heard, were not indigenous to the country. They had been imported from Africa by Napoleon in the nineteenth century.

Bond focused his attention on the two bungalows near the sound-stage. The lights in the windows had not changed.

"Are you absolutely sure that they're in there?" Bond asked Commandant Malherbe in French. "They might have left."

"We have been watching them all day and never saw them leave," Malherbe whispered, taking a moment to wipe his forehead with his sleeve. It was a mild January day, nothing unusual for the Riviera at this time of year.

Bond surveyed the scene once again. The two bungalows, used by the studio as dressing rooms, stood quietly at the dead end of a road between two soundstages. One of the soundstages was currently in use, even at 9:45 in the evening. According to the French police's sources, a television movie was being filmed and was behind schedule. They were making up for lost time. Every once in a while, a technician or actor stepped outside the stage door for a cigarette. Signs of use were everywhere—several cars were parked nearby and a good deal of equipment had been stacked near the loading doors—crates, boxes and petrol drums. For special effects, perhaps?

There were no vehicles in front of the bungalows. Bond was still not convinced that the Union thugs inside were planning to move the arms tonight. If there really *were* arms.

Bond felt compelled to speak. "As an official observer for the United Kingdom, I have to give you my recommendation not to carry out this raid. There are too many civilians about, in my opinion."

"Noted, but I have my orders, Commander Bond," Malherbe said. "We are not to let them leave. We are to catch them with their hands dirty. They've got millions of francs worth of guns in there. Do you really want them to get away with that? Surely you must have a rather personal score to settle with the Union yourself?"

Bond chose not to answer him, but merely nodded grimly and moved back around the empty building to where Mathis and the others were huddled.

Bond's long-time French colleague and friend, René Mathis, was quite happy to observe from the sidelines and let the French RAID officers do their jobs. Mathis thought that they looked much too young for this sort of job, but then again, nearly everyone in this business was younger than he was.

Bond crouched beside him and said, "René, I have a bad feeling about this."

Mathis hesitated a moment and then said, "Me too."

"Call it off."

"I can't."

"Your information could be wrong."

"It often is."

Mathis looked hard into Bond's eyes and then grinned with a sardonic gleam in his eyes. Bond's old friend was being stubborn.

Bond studied Mathis' eyes. He and Mathis had a long history together. The Frenchman had even saved his life once. He owed the man a lot. Bond had to trust him and his organisation.

The logic behind the plan seemed sound enough. For some time, Mathis' outfit, the DGSE, which had swallowed up the old Deuxième Bureau years ago, had been gathering reliable intelligence on the whereabouts of Union arms depots ever since France had been the target of a Union bombing spree. No doubt the criminal organisation had been funded by one of the country's independently minded terrorist groups, for the Union purportedly never took political sides. They were only in it for the money.

And made money they had. In the last three years, they had grown from a small group of terrorists and mercenaries based in Morocco to an international network of criminal enterprise. The Union's mysterious leader, *Le Gérant,* remained an enigma and his location was unknown. The organisation had moved its headquarters out of Morocco over a year ago; discovering its current location was the priority of several nations' law enforcement divisions. The CIA, FBI, SIS, DGSE, and Mossad had declared the Union to be the world's most dangerous threat.

It was true that Bond had no small reason to hate the Union. He had been involved in two of the syndicate's more dangerous schemes and had personally been the target of one of them. The Union had been responsible for the deaths of several people Bond had been close to. He had seen the organisation stop at nothing to invest time, energy and manpower into seemingly impossible stratagems that ultimately ended in the destruction of its target and the immediate satisfaction of its current employer.

At SIS it was known as "the New War," meaning that the conflict between the Union and the world's law enforcement and intelligence agencies had become akin to a war with an unfriendly foreign power. As in a real war, guerrilla tactics were used to gain information and strike at the enemy. Known safe houses all over the world, for both sides, were bombed. Lives were lost. But money talked and agents were turned. Retaliations were frequent. In seven months the New War had reached a stalemate.

Finally, word had come from René Mathis. When Bond had learned in Morocco that *Le Gérant* might possess a Corsican surname, all investigations had focused on France and her headstrong island in the Mediterranean. Bond re-established contact with Mathis, who normally worked out of Paris. As it happened, the DGSE had placed Mathis, once the head of the Deuxième Bureau, on its own Union task force; thus the two old friends were able to share information.

One of Mathis' agents had been following the trail of Julius Wilcox, known to be one of *Le Gérant*'s top lieutenants, or "commandants," as they were called in the Union's inner circle.

Wilcox was reportedly working with Union arms dealers operating through Western Europe. He had been sighted several times in the Côte d'Azur, mostly around Nice and Cannes, and occasionally in Monaco. When his movements were traced to the old Bisset film studios in west Nice, the DGSE convinced SIS and the CIA that the Union was storing illegal arms there.

Until quite recently, the film studios had only been in partial use. Originally constructed in 1927, they had been the home of many famous motion pictures. But after the heyday of the sixties, the studio facilities had fallen into disrepair and were now terribly outdated. Most of the buildings, long abandoned, stood rotting on the lot. Only areas essential to small films currently in production were kept functional.

A well-known French film producer and director had purchased the studio a month ago. Mathis had told Bond that although the man was a celebrity, the DGSE were keeping their eyes on him. Léon

Essinger, an influential but controversial figure in French cinema, had a rather shady past. Mathis had spent some time attempting to link Essinger to the Union, but had come up empty-handed. At any rate, with Essinger's purchase, the film studios, now re-named Côte d'Azur Studios, were scheduled to see a vast facelift within two years.

Commandant Malherbe appeared and whispered to Bond and Mathis. "I have the go-ahead. This is it, gentlemen. Are your vests secure?"

Bond tugged at his bullet-proof vest and replied, "Mine's secure, but I'm just an observer, remember?" He smiled at the French officer.

Mathis said, "Commander Bond is concerned about the number of innocent civilians about, and I agree with him."

"We'll do the best we can," Malherbe said. "But if we wait any longer, the Union may attempt a getaway. That could create chaos all over the studio grounds and that's infinitely more dangerous. At least we can control a raid ourselves." The commandant adjusted the microphone on his headset and spoke into it. "Lieutenant Busnel? Are you ready?"

The French officer listened and then gave a thumbs-up sign. He turned to a sergeant at his side and barked an order. Four men picked up a metal battering ram and prepared to rush forward. Malherbe directed other men to their positions, guns drawn.

Bond felt helpless as he crouched beside Mathis. He had his Walther on him, but technically he was prohibited from using it here. This was a French government operation. To hell with that, he thought. He would damn well use it if he had to.

The commandant gave the order and the four men with the battering ram rushed toward the door of the bungalow on the right.

Later, survivors would swear that the four men were instantly vaporized by the fireball that suddenly engulfed the area. It was a tremendous explosion, one that rocked the ground and shook the buildings. The noise was deafening.

Bond pulled Mathis to the tarmac as waves of searing heat passed over his head. He could hear shouts of pain and terror from the men near him. Then came the gunfire. Bond looked around the corner.

Through the smoke, he could vaguely see men on the roof of the soundstage. They were firing at the RAID officers.

It had been a trap. A typical Union trap.

"Roll over to the edge of the building!" Bond shouted at Mathis. The Frenchman was cursing and drawing his own gun, a 9mm Smith & Wesson, but he managed to do as he was told. Bond rolled with him, ultimately pushing himself against the side of the building. He crawled slowly on his belly so that he could get a better view around the edge of the building at the mayhem in the street between soundstages.

There was nothing left of the first bungalow and the other bungalow was on fire. Both had obviously been empty. Several RAID men were lying face down on the street. The others were scrambling for cover as bullets sprayed the area from above. RAID men were falling left and right. The assault was a disaster.

Bond rotated his body so that he could get a clearer view of the soundstage roof. There were three men with machine guns, blasting at anything that moved on the ground. Bond drew the Walther, took a bead on one of the killers, and squeezed the trigger. The man's head jerked and then his body rolled forward and sailed smoothly off the roof. The other two men looked around, trying to determine where the shot had come from. One of them spotted Bond and pointed. Bond jack-knifed to his feet, scrambled across the road so that he was beneath the shooters and hugged the wall. Unfortunately, there were three more men with machine guns on the roof of the building he had just left. They began to fire at him. Bond leaped for cover behind a large crate, but a bullet seared the top of his thigh and sent a burning shot of pain down his leg. Once under cover, he examined the wound and saw that it was superficial, but it hurt like hell.

The noise and chaos had attracted the attention of the production people inside the soundstage. A stage manager stuck his head out the door, saw the horror and immediately slammed the door shut. Alarms sounded.

Bond noticed two RAID men pinned down behind crates twenty feet along the wall to his left, unable to move away from the gunfire. He aimed at the men on the roof and fired. Both of them spun around and fell. The two RAID men waved at him and emerged from behind the crates, firing their guns.

A white van tore around the corner and sped down the street toward the burning bungalow. As it screeched to a stop, the back doors opened. Two more men with sub-machine-guns jumped out and sprayed the area with bullets. The remaining Union men on the roofs jumped onto the crates, then slipped off to their feet—obviously professionally trained for such stunts. They ran and climbed inside the back of the van as the two shooters continued to spray the road.

Bond looked around frantically for a better weapon. One of the RAID men lay dead in the road about ten feet away from him. An MPL sub-machine-gun was by his feet. Bond tempted fate and simply bolted out into the rain of gunfire. He hit the tarmac hard and rolled like a log toward the body. He grabbed the MPL and, on his belly, aimed it at the men by the van. The machine gun vibrated hard in his arms as the bullets found their targets. The men slammed back against the van and fell to the ground. The others inside the vehicle attempted to close the doors, but some of Bond's bullets penetrated the metal. One of the men fell out as the van began to move backward. The vehicle turned and backed up against the soundstage, near the barrels of petrol. The driver was attempting to turn around so that they could speed out of the studio lot.

Thinking quickly, Bond aimed his gun at the petrol drums and fired. The bullets pierced the metal and ignited the petrol. The van was sent flying in the ensuing explosion. It rolled twice and settled on its side as the passengers scrambled to get out. But they were too late . . . the van's petrol tank exploded, killing them all.

Bond got to his feet as three RAID men ran toward the soundstage. The exploding petrol barrels had set the building on fire. Mathis, out of breath, ran to Bond and said, "We have to get those people out of there!"

The wooden building was very old and the fire spread quickly. Burning support beams collapsed and covered the door, trapping the people inside. The burning van was pushed up against the loading doors, eliminating that as a possible exit.

"Is there another way out?" Bond shouted.

"God, I hope so," Mathis said.

Bond ran down the road to circle the soundstage. On another side of the building, black smoke was pouring out of a broken first floor window. He could see a woman there, her face frozen in terror. He called to her in French to jump, but she couldn't bring herself to do it.

He had never seen a fire spread so quickly. These studio buildings were firetraps waiting to happen. They probably should have been condemned and flattened years ago, he thought.

More frightened faces appeared at the broken window. One man did jump, landing hard on his ankle. He cried out in pain, but he was alive. Bond ran and helped him away just as the RAID men ran forward with a steel ladder. They propped it near the window and beckoned for the people to descend. The first woman finally found the courage to step through the broken glass and climb onto the ladder. She was followed by another woman who nearly slipped off the first rung, then managed to regain her balance after several tense seconds. At this rate, evacuating the victims would take forever.

Bond continued his survey of the other sides of the soundstage. The fire must have spread rapidly inside, probably igniting the flammable paints and canvas used to make scenery flats. Curtains on stages were notorious fire hazards. Old ones might not have had the asbestos treatment used in later structures.

He heard glass breaking above him. A man and a woman were at another high window, crying for help. The black smoke billowed out around them. Bond looked around him and noticed a pile of metal piping with pieces of varying lengths and a stack of bricks lying next to them. He quickly rummaged through the piping and found a piece that might just be long enough to reach the window. It wasn't terribly heavy, so he took it along with two bricks and ran with them back to the side of the building.

He called in French to the man in the window, "Secure the end if you can!" Bond used his foot to hold one end of the pipe on the ground and then levered it up until the other end was near the window. The man grabbed the pipe, tore off his shirt, and used it to tie the pipe to the window sash. Bond placed the bricks such that they would prevent the pipe from slipping on the tarmac. He signaled to the man that he was ready and held on to the pipe. The man pushed the frightened woman out of the window first. She tentatively climbed out onto the pipe, held on to it like a fire fighter, then slid down the pole. Bond caught her as she landed.

"*Merci!*" she cried.

The man was next. He climbed out onto the pole and slid to the ground after calling to others behind him.

Bond could see a procession of other panicked people in the window, waiting their turn. He turned the job of holding the pole over to the man, said, "Good luck," and ran back around to the other side of the soundstage to find Mathis.

Sirens grew louder. At least the fire-fighters were on the way. They would know what to do.

Mathis was bending next to Commandant Malherbe, who was lying against a crate with a bloody wound to his head. The blaze on the soundstage was reaching inferno proportions.

"We have to get these men out of here!" Bond shouted, waving his arm at a couple of other wounded RAID men lying on the road.

Mathis said, "Help me!"

Together they dragged Malherbe away and down the road to a place of safety. He had been hit at least three times and was bleeding profusely. They went back for the other men just as two fire engines roared onto the scene, followed quickly by an ambulance.

"Better tell them they'll need a few more ambulances," Bond said to Mathis. Mathis sprinted toward the emergency vehicles, ready to take charge.

Bond, covered in grime and sweat, backed away from the smoke and heat as the roof of the soundstage completely collapsed. He moved to a safe distance, sat on the ground, and watched the catastrophe unfold. He knew that there was nothing else he could do. People were dying inside the burning hellhole. Had it been his fault? If he hadn't shot the petrol barrels, this wouldn't have happened. But then, the van full of Union killers would have escaped.

—•—

As a result of the failed raid, nineteen people died inside the destroyed soundstage, including two women and an eight-year-old child actress. At least twenty others were injured, some seriously. They were all innocent professionals working on the television film: actors, technicians, stagehands, designers, grips . . . The building itself was completely ruined and had to be leveled after the city had made its investigation into the fire. The media had a field day, blaming the tragedy on the French police, the DGSE, and "unknown foreign intelligence officers" who had been present.

Léon Essinger, the new owner of the studios, was outraged. A flamboyant character, he appeared on national French television and expressed his anger at the authorities. He was mortified that accusations had been made claiming that a criminal organisation was using the studio as a storehouse for illegal arms. "The notion is ridiculous," he said. "All these allegations turned out to be completely false." When asked who the men were that attacked the assault team, Essinger started to bluster. "It has not been proven that there *was* a group of attackers. I think the government made them up to justify its actions!" He vowed to get to the bottom of the incident and make sure that "those responsible would pay."

The raid did not go down well with the French government, either. Fingers were pointed in every direction. The French police blamed the DGSE and vice versa. René Mathis was given two months' suspension from duty, even though it wasn't his fault that the intelligence he had been given was incorrect. Nevertheless, Mathis vowed to continue his pursuit of the Union on his own, pay or no pay. Bond told Mathis to keep him informed and promised to help if needed. They put together an informal method for communicating with each other about the case and bid each other *au revoir* and *bonne chance*.

James Bond was recalled to London. SIS was formally ordered by the DGSE to back off. They would handle the case and keep other agencies informed from then on. Bond not only understood the firm's embarrassment, but he shared much of the guilt. Over the next few nights, he relived his shooting at the petrol barrels in his dreams. Each time he lifted the gun and aimed at those barrels, an inner voice warned him that lives would be lost. And each time, Bond ignored the warning and squeezed the trigger. The noise of the explosion was always overshadowed by the screams of the people inside the sound-stage. The cacophony of horror and death never failed to wake him with a jolt.

Bond was quite accustomed to guilt. It was part of his profession. In his business people lived or they died. It was that simple. His actions always had consequences, and bearing the weight of those repercussions was just another part of the job.

The trick was learning to live with it.

THE BLIND MAN

APPROXIMATELY FOUR MONTHS LATER, RENÉ MATHIS FINISHED HIS CUP OF *café au lait* in The Louis XV restaurant, which adjoined the opulent Hotel de Paris in the proud, tiny principality of Monaco.

Mathis had always found Monaco an anomaly. Located on a beautiful piece of shoreline on the Côte d'Azur covering just under two square kilometers, it is surrounded and protected by France, yet it remains fiercely independent. Its roughly 5000 citizens never pay taxes, and they have their own flag and traditional dialect. Monaco even looks different from France. The buildings, when seen from a distance, look an ochre color immediately distinguishing them from the structures in, say, Nice. Mathis likened the architecture to Lego blocks, as if a child had assembled the buildings with pre-existing pieces so that they appeared jagged and irregular. Since there was no room to expand the principality by land, buildings were built high and even below ground. Despite the seemingly haphazard construction of the community, it was beautiful to look at. Mathis enjoyed coming to Monaco every once in a while to gamble in its famous casino. Tonight, however, he was in the principality on important business.

Mathis raised his hand at the waiter and said, *"L'addition, s'il vous plaît."* He paid the bill and walked out of the restaurant into the Place du Casino. The magnificent casino was brightly lit. It was still early: the place wouldn't be buzzing until after midnight.

Mathis went inside, presented his identification for entry, and stepped into the luxurious palace that was designed by Charles Garnier, the same man who had created the Paris Opera House. The gold inlay and marble pillars gave the impression that this was indeed a royal castle from the nineteenth century. The beauty of the interior, the high-class ambience, and the sight of beautiful women in designer evening gowns always impressed Mathis.

He made his way into the *Salon Privé*, which was separate from the main center of the casino where most of the tourists gambled. Only those well known by the casino staff or players who have given proof of a serious intention to play for high stakes were allowed inside. Luckily, Mathis had an informant at the casino, and Dominic was at his usual place by the door.

"*Bonjour,* Dominic," Mathis said.

"*Bonjour,* Monsieur Mathis," the young man said.

"Is our party here as scheduled?"

"Monsieur Rodiac arrived ten minutes ago. I'm sure he's at the table now."

"*Merci.*" Mathis went past Dominic and made his way to the little crowd around the *chemin de fer* table where the blind man liked to play.

He was an interesting-looking man, and it was very difficult to tell what nationality he might be. There were definitely swarthy Arabic features, perhaps Berber, but there was also a European softness about him. He wore a fashionable dinner jacket and dark sunglasses, and he smoked what appeared to be an American brand of cigarette that he kept in a case inlaid with ivory. The usual goons were around him . . . his helper was sitting to his right, and two bodyguards who looked like professional wrestlers stood behind him. As the man was blind, his helper would whisper into the man's ear and tell him what was on the cards. The man would then make the appropriate bets, ask for a card, or whatever.

He always seemed to win.

"Ten minutes. He is already doing well," Dominic said as he slipped in beside Mathis.

Mathis grunted affirmatively as he watched the blind man, who went by the name of Pierre Rodiac, play various challengers around the *chemin de fer* table.

It was a relatively simple game, a cousin to baccarat, except that the house served as "referee" instead of as banker. The casino supplied the room, the equipment and personnel, for which it charged a five percent commission on the winnings of the bank hands. The banker-dealer was whoever could put up the highest amount of money. He had to relinquish the deal to the player on his right if he lost a hand; otherwise he could quit at any time. All other players at the table bet against the bank. One hand was dealt to the "player," the cards usually controlled by whichever player had put up the highest bet against the bank. If the banker won the hand, the amount of money in the bank could be doubled, creating a good deal of suspense for the players who wanted to continue the game.

Pierre Rodiac was the banker after having initially secured the position by putting up 250,000 francs as the opening bank. After winning five hands, the bank now totaled eight million francs. The other players were a little more hesitant to cry, *"Banco,"* which meant that one of them would cover the entire bank. Instead, the players might be more willing to bet against a portion of the bank—one might bet against 100,000 francs, another might bet against 500,000, and so on, until the entire bank was covered, or not. Only the amount of the bank that was bet against would be at risk.

Mathis watched carefully as an Englishman, after consulting with the woman sitting next to him, presumably his wife, called *"Banco."* Rodiac didn't flinch. The croupier repeated the amount of the bank as the Englishman slid chips totaling eight million francs on to the "Player" space on the table. Rodiac slipped a card out of the sabot. The croupier used the paddle to scoop it up and swing it over to the Englishman. The blind man then dealt a card for himself, then another for his opponent. Once the two cards were in front of him, the Englishman peeked under the corners to see what he had. He needed to get as close to nine as possible. Court cards were valueless and an ace counted as one. Rodiac's helper glanced at the faces of the banker's two cards and whispered in the blind man's ear. The Englishman indicated that he would take a card. Rodiac dealt it and the croupier turned it face up—a nine. According to the official rules, the banker had the option of drawing a third card if his total was three and he had just dealt a nine to the player. Rodiac hesitated, then dealt himself a card—an ace. Both hands were revealed. The Player's total was three. Rodiac's total was four.

Everyone at the table gasped and murmured. As for the blind man, he registered no emotion. He simply kept his head straight, as if he were staring through the croupier at the wall.

Mathis wondered the same thing that they all did. Had the blind man simply made a good guess in choosing to draw a card? Was it a lucky gamble? Or had it been some sort of trick? Had he known that the next card would be an ace? Mathis had indeed detected something before Rodiac had drawn the card. There had been something in the man's body language. He had *known* the card was good. But how?

Mathis carefully reached down to his belt buckle and activated a miniature camera that he kept there. He flicked the shutter twice in Rodiac's direction. With any luck, he would get a couple of good shots of the man.

"He seems to have a sixth sense about this game," Dominic said, shaking his head.

"I'm going to have a drink," Mathis said. They left the room and found the bar. Mathis got a Scotch and soda and went into the buffet room, which was relatively empty. The buffet room amused him because there was a painting on the ceiling that depicted a heavenly scene in which naked cherubs and angels were all smoking cigars. The room had once been the smoking area.

Dominic sat down with him and said, "I can't stay long, I must get back to my post."

"I understand."

"Monsieur Rodiac hasn't missed a Thursday night. He apparently comes in on his yacht and leaves it at the harbor. According to his identity papers, he lives in Corsica. His business address is in the town of Sartène. I haven't been able to find out exactly where he lives."

"Sartène?" Mathis asked. "Why, there's nothing there but devout Catholics and fervid penitents!"

"There are some vineyards in the area, sir."

Mathis raised his eyebrows, indicating skepticism. "Why would he want to live in such a remote area? He's obviously got a lot of money. If he wanted to be in Corsica, why not Bonifacio, Ajaccio, Porto Vecchio—one of the *nice* places?"

"I can't say, sir," Dominic replied. "I must get back."

"Very well." Mathis dismissed him with a wave of his hand and sipped his drink.

It had been a difficult four months. After his suspension he had been reinstated at the DGSE, and during the interim he had learned a thing or two.

To start with, the arms that had supposedly been stored at the Côte d'Azur Studios in Nice had actually been there. They had been moved out a day before the disastrous raid. Mathis hadn't been able to prove this to his superiors, but he knew it to be true. Secondly, he was becoming more and more suspicious of the studios' new owner, Léon Essinger. The man had made a lot of money from the fire insurance. He had to have ties with the Union.

More importantly, Mathis had discovered evidence suggesting that the Union was operating on a large scale in the south of France and in Corsica. Perhaps this meant that the current Union headquarters was somewhere in the area. Could it be on that mysterious little island in the Mediterranean that had more ties with Italy than with France? Corsica—the birthplace of Napoleon and the source of the concept of "vendetta"—it wouldn't surprise him if the Union had a base down there.

After Mathis went back to work in Paris, he had immediately been put on a new assignment that he believed to be Union-related.

The Americans had been experimenting with a new explosive material called CL-20. Supposedly, it was the most powerful non-nuclear explosive ever made. Described as a high-energy, high-density ingredient for both propellants and explosives, CL-20 looked like granulated sugar. When ignited by a detonator, it produced a massive explosion capable of leveling a building using a single warhead the size of a household fire extinguisher.

The US Air Force had loaned a supply of CL-20 to the French on a trial basis. It was being stored at the air force base in Solenzara, on the east coast of Corsica. A major strategic center for the French, Solenzara was a staging point during the Kosovo conflict.

The CL-20 had mysteriously disappeared under the very noses of the base commanders. It had somehow been smuggled off the base with the help of an insider, a lieutenant who had been in charge of the stockpile. When investigators arrived at the base to question him, the lieutenant was found dead in the barracks. His throat had been slashed, ear to ear, in the style of the Union. Working with the French military police, Mathis pieced together a possible scenario: the lieutenant had probably been bribed to pack the CL-20 in something innocuous, like laundry vehicles, or food vending lorries, then they were transported off the base to points unknown. Afterward, he had been killed simply to silence him.

Mathis followed the trail of money, but it led back to unidentified sources in Switzerland. The job had obviously been instigated by a superior organisation. Mathis would have bet his life that the Union was behind it.

Where did the CL-20 go? He had spent the last two months pursuing every lead. He turned Corsica upside down and found nothing. If anyone knew anything, they weren't talking. It was a strange country. Corsicans were rarely forthcoming when it came to secrets. Although the island was French, Corsicans firmly believed in their independence and considered themselves "separate" from the mainland. Being French, and an intelligence officer, Mathis was naturally treated with suspicion. It was difficult to get anything out of those people.

Mathis continued the investigation in the south of France. He thought that he might be on the verge of uncovering something when he got word from his man in Monaco. The report stated that a mysterious blind man from Corsica had begun appearing at the casino on Thursday nights and was making a killing. Casino authorities were perplexed by the man's good fortune. They couldn't spot any way that he was possibly cheating. Some people who had observed the blind man claimed that he had some kind of psychic ability. This was demonstrated when, one evening, the man held a total of three in his hand. He was expected to draw a third card and was about to when he stopped suddenly. "No," he said, waving away the third card. It was as if he had received some divine message in his head. Sure enough, he won the hand—his three against his opponent's two. The next card was revealed to be an eight, which would have given the blind man a total of one, and he would have lost.

Once Mathis learned about this blind man, this "Pierre Rodiac," he put the investigation of the CL-20 theft on the back burner and proceeded to unearth what he could about the stranger. His yacht, a superb Princess 20M, made the trip to Monaco every Thursday night, and back to Calvi, a port on Corsica's northwest shore. A black Rolls-Royce would then take Rodiac south, into the mountains. Where he went from there was still a mystery.

But when he reported all of this to his superiors at the DGSE, they admonished him and warned him not to pursue it any further. After the tragedy in Nice, they wanted no part of any "speculations about Union schemes." Mathis became angry and walked away, taking an indefinite leave of absence from his job. He decided to look into the matter on his own.

Mathis finished his drink and strolled back into the *Salon Privé*. Rodiac was still playing, and his pile of chips had tripled in size. Mathis shook his head, said goodbye to Dominic, then left the casino. He walked to the gardens behind the building and followed the path to the lift that would take him down to the harbor.

The smell of the sea was strong at this time of night. Seagulls were still out in force, crying loudly, looking for food in the water.

Rodiac's Princess 20M, a sleek, white modern motor yacht built by a British company, Marine Projects, looked to be about 70 feet long and probably came with all the modern amenities.

"She's a beauty, isn't she?" came a voice behind Mathis. It was the harbor manager, a salty Monégasque in his fifties with sea-brine white hair.

"*Oui*," Mathis replied. "Who owns her?"

"A blind man, he comes here every Thursday. He's up at the casino now," the man said. "He must be a wealthy bastard."

"May I ask where the boat is registered?"

The man frowned. "I'm not allowed to give away that kind of information, you know."

Mathis pulled out a 500-franc bill. "I'll pay for it."

The man scratched his chin. "Make it a thousand?"

Mathis slipped out another bill and handed it over. The man gestured for Mathis to follow him into the little office on the dock. He found and opened his notebook, then began to look through the pages.

"Here it is," he said. "It's registered in Calvi. Owned by a man named Cirendini."

"May I see?" Mathis asked, feeling his heart skip a beat when he heard the name. The man turned the book toward him. Sure enough, there it was. The yacht was registered to Emile Cirendini.

"*Merci,*" Mathis said. He left the office and walked back across the dock to the steps leading back up to the lift.

Well, well! he thought. Emile Cirendini . . . one of the most senior members of the old Corsican mafia—the legendary Union Corse! While the name "Union Corse" was no longer fashionable, the Corsican mafia was still very much alive, operating mostly in France and the Mediterranean. In the old days of the Deuxième, the Union Corse was the equivalent of the Sicilian Mafia, specializing in drug smuggling, prostitution, racketeering, arms sales and gambling.

Cirendini had been in and out of prison on various racketeering charges but always managed to produce sharp lawyers and a lot of money. He never stayed in jail long. Now he ran a supposedly legitimate shipping business out of Corsica.

So . . . the blind man Pierre Rodiac was using a yacht owned by Emile Cirendini! This was *very* interesting indeed.

Mathis decided there and then that he would make arrangements to follow the Princess 20M to Corsica—if not tonight, then next Thursday. From there, he would do his best to track Rodiac to his home and find out for certain if the man was who Mathis thought he was.

If it was true then Pierre Rodiac was in fact none other than Olivier Cesari, the man at the top of the Union, the man they called *Le Gérant.*

THREE

THE FILMMAKER

THE COCAINE BURNED THE INSIDE OF HIS NOSTRILS AS LÉON ESSINGER snorted and jerked his head back to savor the full effects of the drug.

He looked in the bathroom mirror at his shiny white teeth to make sure that none of his lunch was caught between them. As his heartbeat accelerated, he stared at his reflection. Not bad, he thought. His wavy brown hair, high forehead, dark eyes and full lips gave him a ruddy, Mediterranean look; he had been told that he resembled a famous rock star. At fifty-two, he was still considered good-looking. Women still came on to him, especially after his separation from Tylyn. He had everything going for him now.

Then why the hell was he so unhappy? Why did everything seem like a disaster waiting to happen?

Essinger was sure that Wilcox was wondering what could be keeping him. He said quietly, to himself, "You can wait, you American bastard."

He straightened his tie, stepped out of the bathroom and walked back through the corridor and out onto the bright terrace of the sumptuous Palais Maeterlinck restaurant in Nice. Most of the lunch crowd was still there. Sure enough, Wilcox was impatiently looking at his watch.

Essinger sat at the table. The lunch plates had not yet been removed.

"The reason you don't have any money is you spend it all on that crap," Wilcox said pointing to his nose.

Essinger didn't like Julius Wilcox. The man gave him the creeps. He was terribly ugly, what with that awful scar over the right eye, the hawk nose and greasy, slicked-back gray hair. He always appeared in a suit, but over that he wore a long duster, the kind of coat worn by outlaws in the American Wild West. It was an odd combination, thought Essinger, but it worked. The man oozed menace, and Essinger could tell that Wilcox had little regard for him. Wilcox was being cordial because he was following orders.

Essinger decided to ignore him and gaze at the Mediterranean. It was always a pleasure to come to the Maeterlinck when he was in Nice. It had a most interesting history. Originally conceived as a casino in the 1920s, the project was abandoned and later purchased by the author Maurice Maeterlinck. Recently restored and fashioned into a luxury hotel and restaurant, the Maeterlinck was the chic place to be in Nice, where Hollywood stars stayed when they were in town, where scenes from movies have been shot, and where they served the best truffles stuffed with lobster. Essinger felt *important* dining there. "We should be hearing from our man in LA any minute now," Wilcox said.

Essinger nodded. They had been there for nearly two hours. He had met Wilcox for lunch and they had completed the meal half an hour ago. At any rate, if the call came through there would be some consolation, Essinger thought. Perrin and Weil were thorns in his side that had to be extracted as soon as possible. The two rival producers had slapped a multimillion-dollar lawsuit on him recently for breach of contract. The litigation was holding up funding from an American studio for Essinger's latest picture. They had told him that the money would not be forthcoming until the suit was settled.

Sometimes Essinger wished that he were in another business. The motion picture industry had certainly made him what he was today but it had also corrupted him, turned him into a less-than-moral person. He admitted it, but he had few regrets. His successes were sweet enough to combat his failures. Unfortunately, lately he had experienced more failures and setbacks than successes.

As he took another sip of the *vin de table,* Essinger pondered the last ten years of his life. It had been a rapid rise to stardom. His early French films as a producer/director had established him as an *auteur* to be reckoned with, and he had spent nearly twenty years of his life making small films in Europe. Receiving the *Grand Prix* at the Cannes Film Festival at the age of twenty-eight had boosted his career considerably. As an experiment, he tried doing an action film when he turned forty and it was a major international success—one of those small-budget, big-business anomalies that are legendary in the motion picture industry. It wasn't long before Hollywood came calling, so Essinger packed his bags and left Europe. After moving to California and making two big-budget blockbusters for major studios there, Léon Essinger's fortune was secured. The first film featured a popular American actor in an action role that the public simply couldn't get enough of. Essinger quickly found that more money was to be made with that kind of pulp fiction than with art films. Some of the critics said that he had "sold his soul to Hollywood," but he didn't care. He was laughing all the way to the bank.

The second film built upon the success of the first one, and it nearly doubled the former's business worldwide. This film was even more significant in that it featured Essinger's wife, model Tylyn Mignonne in her first starring role. She had caused a minor sensation and, in the process, created a new career for herself.

The credit "A Léon Essinger Film" above the title began to mean something. He formed his own production company and produced other pictures under his banner. Some were profitable, others were *very* profitable. For ten years he lived the life of a Hollywood mogul, but it had cost him.

For Léon Essinger had a dark side. There was the cocaine bust that didn't help his standing in the Hollywood community. He also had a reputation for losing his temper in public, of throwing bottle-breaking fits in restaurants, exhibiting road rage, getting into scuffles, and beating his beautiful wife.

What nonsense, he thought. After Tylyn had left him, a ridiculous story came out that he had hit her!

But it was the special-effects accident that had really turned his life upside down.

He was in the middle of filming his third action picture in Hollywood and had decided to cut costs by using a less-than-adequate scenic material to absorb the heat of explosions on a set. The ensuing accident caused the death of a major Hollywood star and three young extras. The SFX man had been fired but that didn't keep him from telling the press that he had warned Essinger about the poor protection. A month later, Essinger faced criminal prosecution. In response he did probably the worst thing possible—he fled the States and returned to France. As long as he remained in his native country and continued to work there, he would be fine. But he could never return to America, which was unfortunate.

However, it wasn't long before he perceived that Hollywood had more or less turned its back on him. He found it more difficult to obtain studio funding. The calls stopped. He had been all but blacklisted by most of the major studios. Essinger had to rely on a small, independent art house, EuroClassics, to finance his last picture and the upcoming one. Unfortunately, he had made a mistake the night he had returned to Paris. Totally drunk and high on cocaine while dining at Maxim's, he made a deal with Joe Perrin and Craig Weil, two Hollywood fast-talkers who owned a company that made B-movies and teen horror and sexploitation comedies. They talked him into a contract that basically kept him prisoner to their company for life. He was forbidden to make any other deals.

When Essinger got funding for *Tsunami Rising* from EuroClassics, Perrin and Weil sued. EuroClassics withheld the money for his next proposed blockbuster, another action film starring international star Stuart Laurence. It was dead in the water until the lawsuit could be settled. Essinger had high hopes for the new picture, for *Tsunami Rising*, also starring Laurence, was scheduled to premiere at the Cannes Film Festival. Shooting on the new film, a sea epic called *Pirate Island*, was supposed to begin shortly in Corsica and on the Mediterranean. If production didn't begin on time, he could stand to lose what little money he had left.

When his wife left him things really began to turn sour. And to think that he had already cast her in *Pirate Island!* he thought grimly. He wished that he could fire her, but he couldn't. She was good for the box office.

The waiter asked if there might be anything else. Wilcox ordered a *café au lait*. Essinger waved the man away.

Essinger hated waiting.

Nine time zones to the west, the sun was not quite shining on Los Angeles. It was a kind of witching hour in the city—when it wasn't quite dark and wasn't quite light. It was the time of night when people are at their most vulnerable and unprepared.

The killer from the Bronx known only as Schenkman emerged from his discreet Volkswagen bug at the bottom of the hill where Maltman Street emptied into Sunset Boulevard. Traffic on the streets was light. Practically no one was about this early. Silverlake was unusually quiet.

He walked up the steep pavement, following the street as it curved up and around and met another hilly road called Larissa. Schenkman turned left and walked to the edge of a brown, stucco house that had been built in the thirties. He checked to make sure the two BMWs were parked in the drive, then paused to pull a 9mm Browning High Power from underneath his black leather jacket. Another hand brought out a suppresser seemingly from nowhere and attached it to the semi-automatic.

Light shone through two bedroom windows. Schenkman could hear music through the walls. The party was still going on.

Although they were based in New York, Joe Perrin and Craig Weil were native Hollywood players who kept a two-bedroom hideaway in Silverlake for business purposes. It was nothing fancy, but it was quiet and discreet. They also had flats in London and Paris. The apartments were the perfect havens for script meetings, deal making and orgies. They liked to travel often to get away from their wives.

They had arrived late the night before, immediately called their favorite escort agency, and proceeded to indulge in some serious partying. The festivities had begun around 1:00 in the morning and showed no signs of stopping.

When the buzzer rang, Joe Perrin had just turned over on his back so that the nineteen-year-old hooker could straddle his potbelly and get more leverage to move.

"Who the hell could that be?" he muttered. He called into the other room. "Craig? Are you expecting someone?"

Craig Weil was also in a compromising position. The girl with him was older, probably thirty, not as pretty, but she was definitely more experienced.

What the hell, this isn't supposed to happen, Weil thought.

"I'm not expectin' anyone," Weil shouted back.

"I dunno," Perrin said.

"Well, go answer it!" Weil shouted.

"You answer it!"

"Like hell I will!"

Perrin cursed and said to the girl, "Sorry, honey, you gotta get off," and pushed her roughly over on the bed. She said, "Hey!" as he got up, naked, and staggered to the bedroom door. He was quite drunk.

The buzzer sounded again.

"All right, damn it," Perrin called as he walked through the living room. "Who the hell is it?"

"Urgent legal papers from Europe, sir," Schenkman called from outside.

"It's kinda early, ain't it?" Perrin asked.

"I must have your signature, sir."

Perrin forgot that he was naked. He cursed again, unlocked the door and threw it open.

Phht!

The bullet caught Perrin in the head, throwing him back into the room.

Schenkman stepped inside.

"Joe?" called Weil from his bedroom. "Who is it?"

Schenkman began moving toward the sound when Perrin's hooker made an appearance. She took one look at the body on the floor and one at the man with the gun, then began to scream.

Phht! The Browning jerked again and the girl crashed into a glass table covered with half-empty drinks.

Schenkman kept moving toward the other bedroom.

"Joe?"

Schenkman threw open the door in time to catch Craig Weil slipping on a robe. His girl was standing by the bed, lighting a cigarette. When they saw Schenkman, they both opened their mouths in surprise.

Phht! Phht!

The girl slammed against the wall and fell to the floor. Weil spun around and collapsed onto the bed.

The intruder stood there for a few moments as the rock 'n' roll music coming from the stereo system filled the house. Blood began to seep onto the bed beneath Weil's body.

Schenkman put away his gun. He then produced a large regulation size bowie knife from a sheath attached to his belt on the left side of his waist and coolly slit Weil's throat, ear to ear.

Always let 'em know that this was Union business.

Schenkman went back into the living room and did the same thing to Perrin. He then cleaned the knife on the white sofa and returned it to its sheath.

As Schenkman left the house he encountered no one on the street. He walked back to Maltman, down the hill and hopped into his car. The killer drove onto Sunset, headed west and disappeared.

Wilcox's Ericsson rang. He removed it from his pocket and made a big show of flipping it open.

"Yeah?"

He listened for a few seconds.

"Right." He snapped it shut and put it back into his pocket.

"You know that lawsuit?" Wilcox asked Essinger.

"Yes?"

"It's been dropped," Wilcox said.

Essinger paid the bill and the two men got into the black limousine for the short ride back to the studio. He felt better, but he couldn't shake the feeling of impending doom.

The car went through the gates of Côte d'Azur Studios and passed the site of the tragic fire that had occurred four months ago. The place had been cleaned up, but the lot was practically deserted. Production had ceased after the disaster. Essinger hoped that it would begin again soon.

They got out of the limo in front of a stately villa that was used for administrative offices. Wilcox followed Essinger inside and into the producer's office. Essinger went straight to the cabinet and poured himself a double bourbon. He sat at his large glass-top desk and fingered a press packet for *Pirate Island* while Wilcox helped himself to a glass of vodka. The press packet was full of publicity photos. A gorgeous black and white head shot of Tylyn caught his attention; unconsciously he held it in his hands as he spoke, running his fingers along the edges.

"Thank you," he said to Wilcox.

Wilcox waved at him. "Nuthin' to it. When the Union wants somethin' done, it gets done, that's all."

The killer took a sip of his vodka and continued. "Now. It looks like the Union just did you a favor, right? Now you gotta do the Union one in return. That's the way it works. We scratch your back, you scratch ours, you know."

"I understand. We've been through all of this."

"Right. I, uhm, need to check your tattoo. Orders," Wilcox said, stepping behind the desk. "Stand up and turn this way."

Essinger sighed, stood, and turned his head. Wilcox pulled a cylindrical object out of his pocket and hit a switch. A tiny light shone on the end.

"Look over my shoulder," Wilcox commanded. The film producer did as he was told as Wilcox looked through the object into Essinger's right eye.

"Look up."

Essinger felt the slight warmth from the light on the ophthalmoscope.

"I'm no eye doctor, but I think you have an infection," Wilcox said. "Your eyes are bloodshot."

"I sometimes get conjunctivitis," Essinger said.

Wilcox switched it off and said, "Fine. It looks good. The procedure didn't hurt, did it?"

Essinger shook his head and sat down. "No, that doctor of yours made me very comfortable," he replied. "But I think you're right. I need to go and see my own eye doctor. I probably have an infection again. My eyes keep watering." He rubbed his eyes and squinted.

"Well don't cry too much," Wilcox said. "After our little job today, you should be able to rest easier." He moved to the couch and sat down.

"So!" Wilcox said. "You're one of us now."

Essinger swallowed. "I am honored," he said with a touch of sarcasm.

"*Le Gérant* has a lot of faith in you. If the outcome of the project is a success, and it will be, I assure you, then the benefits for all of us will be pretty damn great."

"I know."

Essinger already knew the gist of the plot. In twenty-five words or less—a lot of people would die, and he was going to help kill them. That was it. That was the pitch.

He took a sip of his drink and reflected on this, all the while looking into Tylyn's marvelous, cat-like eyes. She was so beautiful . . . how could she have left him? She was his treasure, his most valuable possession . . . Now she was gone.

The more Essinger thought about it, the more he felt angry. She was going to pay, like everyone else.

"Have you heard from her?" Wilcox asked.

Essinger was momentarily startled. "What?"

"Your wife. Have you heard from her?"

"Why do you want to know?"

Wilcox looked at Essinger and said, "Look, pal, she's a part of this thing whether you like it or not. Now. Have you heard from her?"

"No. We're to meet soon to discuss the separation and the so-called 'ground rules' for when we begin shooting."

Wilcox could see that the man was in torment over the woman. He liked to push his buttons.

"Do you think she will divorce you?"

"She wouldn't dare," Essinger said. "Not yet, anyway. Not while there is a movie to be made. It's a *trial* separation."

"I thought I saw a photograph of her in the newspaper, or some magazine. She was with some rich guy from America. A producer or director or somethin'."

Essinger sighed. "One of the benefits of a separation is that it entitles you to date other people without guilt."

Wilcox was enjoying this. "She seems to like her new-found freedom. She doesn't need you, you know. She's independently wealthy, right? You know, I think she's dating a *lot* of other people."

"Would you shut up?" Essinger snapped.

Wilcox laughed. "That's good! Jealousy is a perfectly healthy reaction."

"What are you, my therapist?"

"No, but I'm just trying to point out that you shouldn't have any doubts about what we're about to do, that's all." Wilcox stood and went back to the bar to pour himself another drink. Then he went over to the desk and held out his hand. "Are we on the same page?"

Essinger took a moment before responding. He had given Tylyn a starring role in *Pirate Island* because it would be great for the picture. But he did it mainly because he knew that she wouldn't dare divorce him before the movie wrapped. Wilcox was right. Tylyn was indeed dating again, modeling more than ever—her face and body seemed to be on every billboard in Europe. She was attracting the attention of every available bachelor in the world.

Essinger felt the rage building inside. He quickly slipped Tylyn's photo back in the press packet and took a drink.

To hell with her, he thought. When this was all over, she would be dead.

Essinger turned to grasp Wilcox's outstretched hand, and the deal with the devil was made.

FOUR

THE HYDRA

JAMES BOND STROLLED INTO HIS OFFICE AT SIS FEELING REFRESHED AND alert. In fact, he was fitter than he had been in two years. He had spent six months after the Gibraltar affair working hard to get back into shape. He had fully recovered from a serious head injury, improved his motor skills by doubling the repetitions in his daily workout routine, and sharpened his reaction time by participating in role-playing and puzzle-solving challenges offered by the firm.

When he got to his floor, he swiped his identity card and went though the sliding glass doors to the communal area shared by the various personal assistants. He was surprised by the presence of a young man sitting at the desk that had seen a succession of temporary secretaries since the death of his own assistant a while back. He looked to be about twenty-five, was tall and thin, had blond hair and wore glasses. Although he had a baby-face, there was something about the young man's demeanor—and even in his eyes—that immediately struck Bond, even before the fellow spoke. Bond recognized the look, for this man had seen some life or death action somewhere.

"Good morning," Bond said.

The young man blinked and said, "Oh, hello. You must be Commander Bond." He stood and held out his hand. "I'm Nigel Smith. I'm your new personal assistant."

"Are you?" Bond shook his hand. The boy had a firm grip.

"Yes, sir. I was recently transferred out of the Royal Naval Marines. I had requested MI6, so they put me here. I understand you've been looking for someone for quite some time."

Apart from his days in the navy, Bond had never had a male personal assistant before and he wasn't sure that he liked it.

"That's right, and no one's worked out," Bond said. "You're not with the secretarial agency?"

"No, sir, I was placed here under orders. The Ministry. Sir."

Was this M's idea? Was she trying to punish him by giving him a male assistant? Was it some kind of *message?*

Bond sighed and decided to make the best of it. The young man seemed capable. And since Bond had some rather outdated views on relationships with women in the workplace, it was probably for the best.

"Are you experienced with this sort of thing?" Bond asked.

Nigel shrugged and said, "I'm a quick learner. I do all the usual things: computers, typing, filing, phone, dictation, copying, posting, message taking, and takeaway ordering. What I won't do is fetch your tea, clean up after you or lie to your wife."

"I'm not married."

"I know. Just telling you how it is, sir. Actually I'm quite familiar with your CV, sir, and I must say that it's a pleasure to be working for you."

"Why were you transferred out of the marines?"

"Injury, sir. Bosnia. Got a piece of shrapnel in my back. Land mine. Lost a kidney. Was discharged on a medical, but I didn't want to leave the business, so to speak."

That explained the young man's rather hardened exterior. He obviously had the discipline of a naval officer and some tough experience to go with it. Bond was beginning to like him.

"What was your rank?" Bond asked.

"Second lieutenant, sir."

"Well, welcome aboard," Bond said. "By the way, I detest tea."

"I'm not too fond of it myself, sir."

"And what *do* you drink, lieutenant?"

Smith shrugged. "A soft drink suits me just fine, sir. Now, I've left something on your desk that I'm sure you'll want to have a look at. I know you're on the Union task force. I brought some material the Ministry just received from Mossad concerning *Le Gérant*. I think you're right, sir."

"Right?"

"That you believe *Le Gérant*'s real name is Olivier Cesari."

Bond was taken aback by Smith's knowledge of the case.

"I've read your reports, sir," Smith added.

"I see. Well, I'll have a look at what you brought. And please stop calling me 'sir.' "

"What would you like me to call you?"

Bond replied, "I'm sure you'll be calling me all sorts of names before long, but you can start with 'James.' "

Nigel smiled. "Very well, James. Call me Nigel. I'm sure we'll get on fine."

Bond nodded and slipped into his private office. Along with the usual memoranda and inter-office mail, there was an envelope and a videotape. Inside the envelope was the documentation for the tape, which had apparently been shot in the Rif Mountains of Morocco by a Mossad agent eight months ago.

He sat down and spent ten minutes catching up on bureaucratic paperwork and returning e-mails, then used the computer to open the most recent files on the Union. Thanks to his efforts, and to the endeavors of countless intelligence and law enforcement agencies around the world, a profile of the Union's leader, *Le Gérant,* had been pieced together.

He was believed to be one Olivier Cesari, a blind man who was half-Berber and half-Corsican. His father, Joseph Cesari, had made a small fortune in the perfume business in France. It was possible that Olivier had been born in the Rif Mountains and was raised in the Berber culture there until he was eight. At that point, Olivier's father came from Corsica and took the boy away from his mother. Olivier spent the next ten years with his father, living in both Corsica and mainland France. Olivier attended university in Paris, studied law and then economics, but after his graduation in 1970, no records of his subsequent movements exist. It was as if he had disappeared off the face of the earth.

Joseph Cesari had been dead since 1973, a homicide victim in Paris. Bond noted that the man's throat had been sliced, ear to ear. The senior Cesari's estate passed to his son, and in 1975 everything was sold—for a lot of money. Olivier Cesari was never present at the proceedings; it was all done through lawyers and private financial advisors. That was the last time anyone had heard a word from Olivier Cesari.

Why was he hiding? Bond wondered. Where did he go?

When Bond was in Morocco on a recent operation involving the Union, the SIS contact in Tangier claimed that he had known Olivier Cesari in Paris, and that he was certain that Cesari and *Le Gérant* were one and the same. Bond believed him.

He pressed a button on the desk. The wall above the lateral filing cabinets slid open to reveal a television. Bond put the videotape in the VCR and sat back to watch.

It was an interview with a Berber tribesman, a man in his sixties. His head was wrapped in a bulky turban and he wore a *jellaba*. He spoke Berber, but subtitles translated the words into English.

The man told a fascinating story. He described a man of near-mystical powers who came to live with his people for a while, probably thirty years ago. He was something of a folk hero—a man who had at one time lived with the tribe, as a young boy, but who had gone to the West to make his fortune. When he returned successful and wealthy, he rejoined the tribe and lived as they did—in the mountains, in tents, away from splendor for a few more years. He was very generous with the money he had made in the West—he gave it away freely to those who performed services for him.

The tribesman described the man's powerful charisma, how he could persuade any of them to do something. The fact that he also paid very well didn't hurt. Eventually he organized groups of loyal followers to do his bidding. Then . . . one day, he left, just as mysteriously as when he arrived.

The people from the Rif who knew him called him "The Blind Prophet," for he had an uncanny ability for sight when he physically couldn't see. The man *was* blind, the tribesman explained. Yet, he could move around easily in places he had never been before, somehow sensing the placement of objects around him. He was able to identify people he knew simply by their being in close proximity to him. He had prophetic dreams that he described to the tribe.

After the man went away the last time, "The Blind Prophet" became a legend among their people. They still hope that he will return some day.

Bond switched off the tape and returned to the computer. That explained where Olivier Cesari went when he disappeared from Paris. He went back to Morocco to see his mother and live with her people once again. But for how long? Just a few years? Probably no more than five, Bond guessed. Then, Cesari left again, and that's where the trail ended. That meant that the last known appearance of Olivier Cesari was at least twenty years ago. If this "Blind Prophet" really was Le Gérant, what had happened to him in the intervening years? According to what historical records they had on the Union, the organisation was taken over by Le Gérant within the last ten years. What was he doing during the ten years before that?

Bond wanted more information on the Cesari family. He punched in a password that allowed him into the database that MI6 shared with the DGSE. Bond searched through the files until he recognized Mathis' coded identity number on something filed two months ago. He opened it and found that it concerned the fire at the Côte d'Azur Studios in Nice—something Bond had tried hard to forget. The investigation had slowed to a standstill, but the French police had cleared studio owner Léon Essinger of any criminal activity regarding illegal arms. The French government had been forced to issue a public apology to Essinger. Mathis had noted that Essinger received a substantial payoff from an insurance company to help rebuild the damaged sections of the studio—so much, in fact, that major renovations were being performed on other parts of the lot as well.

Bond picked up the phone and punched in the number to Mathis' direct line. After several pips, the line was switched over to an assistant, who informed Bond that Mathis was away on leave and had been gone for two months. Bond left a message for Mathis to contact him, hung up, and then dialed Miss Moneypenny.

"Penny, dear, can you fit me in this afternoon?" Bond asked when Moneypenny answered.

"I suppose we'll never know unless we try, James," she said, suppressing a laugh.

"Look here, you naughty girl, I wanted to have a word with M."

"Oh, James, do you really think I'm naughty?"

Bond laughed. "Penny, you have a knack for cheering me up. When I retire and am old and arthritic, will you marry me?"

"In a heartbeat, James," Moneypenny said. "I thought you'd never ask."

"Well, I don't plan on retiring any time soon, so don't get yourself worked up."

"Oh, I know better than to do that. Now, what can I do for you?"

"M. Can she spare a few minutes?"

"She's locked away in her office but she's already mentioned that she wants to have a word with you. Why don't you come up at three o'clock?"

"Thanks, Penny. I'll be there."

He hung up and smiled. The on-going flirtation he had with Miss Moneypenny was sometimes worth every bit of the hell he went through for Her Majesty's secret service.

M looked up from a report that was marked "For Your Eyes Only."

"Come in, Double-O Seven," she said. "How are you?"

"Fine, ma'am, thank you." He closed the door behind him and sat in the black leather chair across from her desk.

"And how's the new assistant working out?" she asked.

"I've only just met him, but fine, so far," he replied.

"Good, then I assume he can stay where he is?"

So he had been right about it being M's idea! Bond smiled and played the game. "He seems efficient enough."

"Very well. I'll have Miss Moneypenny contact the Ministry. I suppose it's late enough in the afternoon—would you like something to drink?"

"If you're having something . . ."

She swiveled in her chair and poured two small glasses of Scotch and handed one to him. "Now, what can I do for you?"

"Probably not much. I think I just wanted a sympathetic ear," Bond replied. "I'm very frustrated with the lack of progress with the Union."

She nodded. "I can understand that. I'm frustrated too. We all are."

"What's happening with Yassasin?" he asked.

Nadir Yassasin, one of the Union's top commandants and its strategist, had been sitting in an English prison since the Gibraltar affair.

"Still awaiting trial, I'm afraid," she said. "Hasn't said a word. Interrogation is fruitless."

"I'd like to have ten minutes alone in a cell with him. I guarantee to make him talk."

"I'm sure you could, but that's not possible. Funny how once you've become a prisoner you seem to have more rights than the common person. They protect that man better than if he were Winston Churchill. At any rate, I'm glad you brought this Union business up. I think it's time that you move on. I can't afford having my best people floundering. I've decided to give you a new assignment."

Bond sat up. His pulse sped up automatically, a near Pavlovian reaction to the word. Perhaps he did need to get away from all of this academia and get back into the field, but he didn't feel that the time was right.

"Ma'am? A new assignment? Do you think—?"

"—that it's wise?" she finished. "I don't know. We're concerned about the reports coming in from Japan. Have you read the classified document on this man Yoshida?"

"I read the cover summary but haven't had a chance to read the full report," Bond said. "Goro Yoshida, a billionaire, the head of a conglomerate of industrial and chemical engineering firms in Japan and a suspect in organizing terrorists?"

"That's right. Foreign intelligence suspects that he may be involved with acts of terrorism against the West, mainly America and Britain. The American embassy was bombed recently, but no one was hurt. Two people were hurt at the British embassy bombing, one was killed."

"What do we know about him?" Bond asked.

"Only that he's extremely wealthy and commands the loyalty of a number of followers who would die for him if he asked them to. A few years ago he left the running of his company to others and now lives in some remote part of Japan. We're not sure what his political ambitions are. He may have ties with the *Yakuza*."

"Not much to go on, is there?"

"No, it's all on a hunch from the Americans. They believe that he could be raising some kind of army of terrorists. He's said to have very strong views on Japanese nationalism. He has been very outspoken about the way in which traditional Japanese culture and tradition have been corrupted by Western influences."

"And you want me to find him and see what he's up to?" Bond asked.

"That was the idea."

Bond shuffled in his chair. "Ma'am, with all due respect, I don't think I should leave the Union case. We *are* making progress, although I admit it's slow. I would like to dig deeper into Olivier Cesari's family background. The French provided us with a little, but I need to get back in touch with Mathis at the DGSE. The last time I spoke to him, two months ago, he said that he had a couple of interesting leads. He's obviously on the trail of something big."

"Or he's dead," M said.

The words cut him like ice. Bond sat back in the chair and admitted, "That's possible, too."

M took a sip of her drink. Bond continued, "If I know Mathis, then he'll be extremely thorough this time before blowing any whistles. Ma'am, if I could have two more weeks to follow up some loose ends . . . at least allow me to locate Mathis . . . then, if I've learned nothing new, you could put me on the Yoshida assignment?"

M drummed her glass with her fingers as she held it.

"Give me one good reason why I should do that," she said.

Bond thought a moment and said, "Because the Union have been too quiet. The New War has screeched to a grinding halt, as you will have noticed. In fact, we've had no Union activity that we know of since the incident in France. It can only mean one thing."

"What's that?"

"They're planning something."

M continued to drum her glass.

"I'm sure you are familiar with the myth of the hydra," she said. "Every time one of the heads was cut off, two more would grow in its place. That's rather a good analogy for the Union, don't you think? It seems that no matter how many times we've foiled their plans—that business in the Himalayas, or the affair in Gibraltar, for example—they always come back even more powerful than before. The FBI estimates that they have grown at a rate of 150 percent in two years. That's frightening."

"All the more reason why we need to concentrate everything we have on finding their leader, this *Le Gérant*. For once we have a very good lead on who this man might be—Olivier Cesari—and if the French aren't going to look into his background and try to find him, then somebody should."

"Very well," M said. "Two weeks. If you can produce substantial information regarding the whereabouts of this man, or any evidence of new Union activity, then you can stay on the case."

"Thank you, ma'am."

She stood and took the decanter of Scotch. She refilled her glass and then did the same to Bond's.

"Besides," she said, "I hate them as much as you do."

FIVE

THE TATTOO

NADIR YASSASIN WAS BEING DETAINED AT HER MAJESTY'S PLEASURE IN HMP Belmarsh, a Category A local prison that had become operational in 1991 in the London Borough of Greenwich. A Category A prisoner is one whose escape would be highly dangerous to the public, the police, or to the security of the state.

Despite the lack of freedom, the Union's most accomplished strategist found prison life not at all what he expected; in fact, he found it to be relatively pleasant. It didn't hurt that he was treated as a celebrity criminal, receiving special consideration when it came to his cell, his interaction with the general population, and personal activities. He was in the Seg Unit, separated from the rest of the prison, which suited him fine. His "peter," the cell he lived in, was comfortable for the most part, and he had been afforded certain luxuries such as books, a television and no pad mate. When he went to the hotplate for meals, the other prisoners perceived him as someone mysterious and exotic. A Senior Officer was assigned to him when he was out of his cell, more for Yassasin's protection than for keeping the peace.

The authorities had attempted to interrogate him about the Union for seventy-three days straight, but Yassasin never bent. Short of torture, there was no way that they were going to extract any information from him. Yassasin was thankful that he was in a civilized country. He had seen what the prison systems in some of the countries he had been to were capable of.

Yassasin finished a surprisingly satisfying bowl of vegetable soup in the hotplate, then stood and motioned to the SO that he was ready to go back to his cell. SO Evans, a burly bald-headed man from a working-class background, followed Yassasin out of the room as the other prisoners watched and whispered. The two men passed the latrine and Yassasin stopped, saying that he had to go.

"I'll wait here," Evans said.

Yassasin went inside and found himself alone. He looked into the mirror at his tall, dark reflection and decided that prison life had not done too much damage to his physique. He had not lost much weight, nor gained any for that matter.

Yassasin stepped to the wall of urinals and prepared to do his business when he felt a change in the air behind him. There was a rush of wind, and out of the corner of his eye he saw a Red Band—a uniform indicating that the wearer was a trusted prisoner who served as a messenger or escort without supervision in certain areas of the prison. Yassasin tried to turn in time, but something metal slammed against the side of his face. He felt as if lightning had struck him as everything went black, pain enveloped his head, and he crashed to the floor.

Belmarsh's healthcare center was a good one, designated Type 3, which meant that there were in-patient facilities and 24-hour nurse cover. Sixteen of the thirty-eight available beds were filled—one by Nadir Yassasin, who had suffered a severe concussion and damage to his right eye.

SO Evans had caught the Red Band responsible for the attack. He was revealed to be a prisoner who had wanted to prove to his peers that he was capable of violence. He had used a metal wastepaper basket as a weapon. Apparently, when the prisoner received Red Band status, he had been denigrated by the general population and had become an outcast. He was simply trying to gain favor with his friends again. The prisoner was stripped of his Red Band, received CC (confined to cell) for a week, and charged with assault.

Two days after the attack, Yassasin's headaches had improved but he was still having problems with his vision. An ophthalmologist was brought in from the outside to examine him as the prison doctors observed. SO Evans, feeling somewhat responsible for Yassasin's condition, was present as well.

The doctor used a Keeler binocular indirect ophthalmoscope with a 20-dioptre lens to peer into Yassasin's eyes after using a dilating solution on them.

"There are still some ruptured blood vessels back there," the doctor said. "That probably accounts for your vision not being perfect. I think it should get better with time. I also—wait, hold on . . ." The doctor peered closer at something in the right eye. "You have some kind of lesion on the retina. It appears to be laser scarring. Have you ever had any surgery on your eyes?"

Yassasin hesitated, then said no.

SO Evans asked, "What did you find?"

The doctor shrugged. "It's some kind of lesion on his retina . . . the same kind that is made by lasers. This one is not in a vital spot that would affect vision. It's almost as if it was put there on purpose, as some kind of signature. That's not unusual. I'd swear this is some kind of . . . design. Whatever it is, it was put there by man. It's not congenital."

The doctor put it in his report as the SO looked at Yassasin and frowned.

After the lights were out that night, SO Evans slipped past the nurse's station and moved quietly down the hallway to the main ward. The snores there were monstrously loud, worse than on the landings. All the better, Evans thought as he walked slowly and softly past the occupied beds.

Nadir Yassasin was sleeping quietly. He was lying on his back, head propped up on the pillow, with his arms resting gently on his chest. He might have been a corpse in the morgue, ready for viewing by family members and friends.

Evans took a pillow from one of the empty beds and stood over Yassasin. He reached into his pocket and removed a six-inch switchblade.

Evans looked around him to make sure that no one was watching, then quickly flicked the blade open. In three expert moves, he thrust the knife into Yassasin's throat, pulled it across, slitting it from ear to ear, and forced the spare pillow down over the victim's face. Evans held the pillow there, muffling the gurgling sounds and soaking up the blood. After a minute of minor struggling, it was over. Even Evans was surprised by how quietly he had done it.

He cleaned the knife on the pillow, put it back into his pocket, and turned to leave, lingering in the hallway long enough for the nurse to turn her back once more. The SO scooted past the desk and out of the healthcare center without anyone knowing he'd been there.

The murder of Nadir Yassasin sent shock waves through SIS. The Governor of Belmarsh was up in arms, steadfastly defending the security of the prison. A thorough investigation turned up next to nothing. The nurses on duty at the time of the killing claimed complete ignorance of the event. None of the other patients in the healthcare center knew anything had happened until the next morning. It was as if Yassasin had been killed by a ghost.

The ophthalmologist's report crossed M's desk not quite a week later. After she had read it, she called Bond immediately.

She thrust the folder into his hands as soon as he walked into her office.

"Read this and tell me if it rings any bells."

Bond sat down and read it twice. Both times he was struck by the discovery of the strange lesion on Yassasin's right retina.

"When I was in Spain last year," he said, "Margareta Piel inadvertently mentioned something about an 'operation' that Union members had to undergo, part of an initiation, I gather. Could this be it?"

"That's what I was thinking," M said. "I remembered that from your debriefing."

"Can we get a picture of this lesion? The doctor states that it's some type of pattern."

"I'm sure we can," M replied. "I have an idea—suppose that whoever killed Yassasin wanted to keep him from talking or something."

"A Union man on the inside?"

"Why not?" M asked. "It's happened before. I've already had a couple of chats with Belmarsh's Governor. Yassasin apparently had very little contact with other prisoners. The assault in the latrine was a fluke. Prisoners don't have access to the healthcare center without authorization."

"It had to have been a guard," Bond said. "A warder, someone on staff."

"Precisely."

Bond thought a minute. "If our theory is correct, this perpetrator would have the same lesion on his retina."

M nodded. "I'm going to ask the governor to hold mandatory eye examinations for the entire staff. Let's see if it smokes anyone out."

It was a tough two days. The governor had ordered the eye examinations on the pretext that they were part of a new medical regime that all civil servants, policemen, and government employees throughout England had to go through. Only three members of Belmarsh's staff refused the exam. One was a nurse who was told that she would be fired if she didn't submit to the test. She had second thoughts on hearing that and went through with it. The second was a warder who was planning to retire in five more years. He had been afraid that the authorities would find out that he was practically blind in one eye and would have to take an early retirement. Once the truth came out, he had the exam and was transferred to desk duty with his pension intact. The third holdout was SO Evans.

After extensive questioning, Evans could not come up with a satisfactory reason why he shouldn't have a simple eye exam. In the end, he agreed to do it. Dr. David Worrall, the ophthalmologist, was brought in and he confirmed that SO Evans also had the same, unique scarring on his retina.

The next day, Dr. Worrall was summoned to the SIS building on the Thames. Chief-of-Staff Bill Tanner ushered Worrall into M's office, where he found himself confronted by M, Bond, the Belmarsh Governor and two representatives from the Ministry of Defence.

"Dr. Worrall," the governor began, "we don't mean to alarm you, but you've stumbled upon something that could very well be a matter of national security."

"I guessed that it was about the retinal scarring I found on those men," Worrall said.

"That's correct. Could you please tell us, in laymen's terms, what it is you found?"

Worrall removed a color photograph from his briefcase. On first glance, it seemed to be a pink blur with a long dark spot in the middle; but on closer examination, one could see that the spot was a geometric pattern. It looked like three pyramids in a row, the middle one inverted so that the sides of the pyramids "fitted" together:

"This is the tattoo that was on Mr. Yassasin and Mr. Evans' retinas," Worrall said. "Believe it or not, marks like these are made by some retina specialists when they perform laser surgery. It's done with an Argon laser set at a very low wattage, say point one, and the mark takes up no more than five hundred microns . . . which is quite small. These lasers are used to perform all sorts of things—corrective surgery and the like. I know of at least two doctors who like to carve their initials on the retinas after they're done. Like an artist signing a canvas."

"Doesn't that affect the vision?" M asked.

"Not if it's in the right place," Dr. Worrall answered. "You see, there are areas on the retina that constitute a person's so-called 'blind spots'. We all have them. They're temporal to the area of sharpest vision—the macula. A doctor can see these areas by looking with an ophthalmoscope. As long as the tattoo is not placed anywhere near the macula or the optic nerve, then vision wouldn't be affected at all."

"Thank you, doctor," the governor said.

After Worrall had gathered his things and was escorted out, M asked, "What the hell does it mean?"

Bond took the photograph and studied it. "It could be something very simple. It's an illustration of a 'union'—note how the three objects fit together nicely. One is inverted, and yet it belongs with the others."

"Why would Union members have that? On their *eye,* for God's sake," M continued.

"The criminal mind works in mysterious ways. Perhaps I had better talk to this Evans fellow," Bond suggested.

"So far he hasn't said a word," the governor said. "When he was put into a holding cell, he made a phone call. He refused help from any lawyers, but said that someone was coming to help him from France."

"Then I had better talk to him before that," Bond said.

Thus, a few hours later, Bond found himself alone with SO Evans in a holding cell at Belmarsh. He spent thirty fruitless minutes asking questions and receiving no answers. Finally, Evans asked for a cigarette.

"If I give you one, you'll tell me what I want to know?" Bond asked.

Evans shrugged. "No Etonian pencil-pusher from SIS is goin' to push me around," he said.

Bond leaned forward over the table. "Look. You have a couple of options here. The first is that you'll tell me everything I want to know, and it'll be at your own volition. The second is that you'll tell me everything I want to know, and it'll be at my volition. Which is it to be?"

"You don't scare me. You can't touch me," Evans spat. "I know my rights."

"Rights?" Bond asked. "What rights? Have you been charged with anything?"

"No."

"And you've sent your lawyer away, is that correct?"

"That's right."

"You think the Union is going to come and rescue you?"

Evans shuffled in his chair. "Don't know anythin' about no Union. I jus' know someone's comin' to get me out of here."

In a lightning-fast move that toppled his chair and created a deafening noise that echoed loudly in the room, Bond suddenly jumped up, grabbed the man by his shirt and roughly pulled him to his feet. "Listen to me, as far as I'm concerned, you have no rights," he said through his teeth. "You're not a prisoner here. You have no lawyer present. We know you have no family, so no one would miss you. You're going to be charged with murder. You're withholding information that is vital to national security. If you think the Union are going to save you, think again. I don't give a damn about you. I enjoy squashing vermin like you." Bond locked Evans' head in his arm and began to apply some pressure. "I could break your neck with a twist of my arm, you know. The sound it makes—have you ever heard it? A man's neck being broken? There's this tremendous pull and then a sudden—SNAP! If it's done hard enough, the spinal cord is severed. If it doesn't kill you, then you're paralyzed for the rest of your life. Would you like to hear what it sounds like?"

"N-n-no, lemme go!" Evans cried in terror.

Bond released the man and he fell back into his chair. Evans was shaken by the sudden ferocity Bond had shown. He could now see that there was genuine cruelty lurking within the man standing over him. Evans, relying on the experience he had gained working at a prison, recognized a natural born killer. In the flash of a second, the man from SIS had completely changed his demeanor. Instead of the soft blue eyes he had seen earlier, they were now cold and steely. The mouth had curved into a grimace and the scar on the right cheek was more prominent.

Jesus, Evans thought. Why didn't I see this before?

"How . . . how about that cigarette?" he whispered.

Bond sat down across from him and removed the gunmetal case from his jacket inside pocket. He offered Evans one of his specially made cigarettes and then produced his Ronson lighter.

Evans took a couple of puffs and blew out the smoke, obviously taking comfort from the tobacco. "This is good, where d'you get it?"

"It's imported. Now . . . do we have an understanding?" Bond asked calmly, but maintaining the level of menace in his voice.

"What do you want to know?" Evans smiled.

"The tattoo in your eye. Tell me all about it."

Evans cleared his throat. "All Union members have it. Once you've been accepted, it's like you get a membership card, only it's on your eye. It's sort of a secret handshake, like. Each new member receives some money just for joinin' so nobody minds."

"Who does the procedure?"

"Depends on where you're located. I had mine done in Paris. There's a doctor there—I *don't* know his name, I swear—he does it for most of the Union people in Europe. He travels around."

"But why? Why a tattoo on the eye?"

Evans shrugged. "I wish I knew. Really! No one really knows. It's an order handed down from the big boss, that fellow they call *Le Gérant*. He has some kind of fascination wi' eyes."

"Have you met him?"

Evans shook his head. "I don't know anyone who's met him, except maybe that Yassasin fellow. But he never talked about the Union. He never talked at all."

"Why did you kill him?"

Evans hesitated. "I . . . I was ordered to."

"By whom?"

"I don't know. I get my instructions by phone. It's just a voice. It comes from France. That's all I know."

Bond stood and began to circle the room. "So, you reported to your superiors in France that Yassasin's tattoo had been discovered. And they told you to eliminate him before he could talk, is that it?"

Evans nodded. "Yeah, that's it."

"And what did you get out of it?"

"A little money."

"How much?"

"Two thousand quid."

"That's not a lot."

"It's a lot to me. You ever work for the bleedin' government?" Bond shot him a look and Evans realized his mistake. "Sorry," he muttered.

"One last question," Bond said. "Do you know where *Le Gérant* is now?"

Evans shook his head. "All I know is that the headquarters used to be in Morocco, but it isn't any more. They moved to Europe some-where. There's a Paris branch but I don't think he's there. I believe that's where my instructions came from. That branch controls all of the activity in Europe and the UK."

Bond circled the room one more time, quietly, staring at Evans, daring him to leave out something. After nearly two minutes of nerve-racking silence, Bond was satisfied that the man was too scared not to talk.

Bond moved to the door and said, "Thanks, old chap," and signaled for the guard to come and let him out.

The Kuril Islands form a chain of about thirty large and twenty small volcanic islands in extreme East Russia, separating the Sea of Okhotsk from the Pacific Ocean. They extend between north east Hokkaido, Japan, and South Kamchatka Peninsula, Russia. Settled by both the Japanese and the Russians in the eighteenth century, the islands at that time belonged to Japan. After the Yalta Conference during World War II, the islands were given to the USSR and today remain the property of Russia. Japan, however, has maintained a claim to at least some of the islands. No peace treaty had ever been concluded between Japan and the former Soviet Union, mainly because of the dispute over these "Northern Territories." As a result, there is also no peace treaty between today's Russian Federation and Japan.

Thus, the Kuril Islands remain a mysterious no man's land with regard to the two countries. While they are governed as part of Sakhalin Oblast, Russia, in many ways they are still culturally tied to Japan. The islands are heavily forested and contain many active volcanoes. Hunting, fishing, and sulphur mining are the principal occupations of the inhabitants, among whom are the Ainu, a primitive race indigenous to the area.

At approximately the same time that James Bond was interrogating SO Evans in Belmarsh prison, a black Kawasaki BK117 helicopter landed on one of the disputed Kuril Islands, called Etorofu by the Japanese and Iturup by the Russians. The helicopter was big enough for ten passengers, but today it carried only one. He had flown in from Tokyo, after having made a series of very long flights that began in Calvi, Corsica.

The helipad was on private property hidden amongst the trees. The owner was associated with a mining operation that worked a nearby quarry; but if anyone at the firm were questioned, they would have no knowledge of who that owner might be.

The helicopter touched down on the strip and its passenger looked out of the window at lush, green trees and a colorful mountain looming in the distance. Was it a volcano? He didn't know and really didn't care. He wanted to get his business done and go back to Corsica where he felt more at home. He wasn't suited to acting as an errand boy for the Union.

Emile Cirendini, carrying a briefcase, stepped out of the vibrating chopper and was met by two armed Japanese dressed in fatigues. One barked a greeting to him that he didn't understand, but he held out his hand and said, *"Bonjour."* The Japanese guard said something else and pointed to a jeep a few yards away. Cirendini wondered why Japanese people always sounded as if they were angry when they spoke.

Cirendini, a slightly overweight but otherwise healthy man in his fifties, was something of a giant compared to the two Japanese guards. He was a little over six feet tall, had short gray hair, a thick moustache, and deep brown eyes. He climbed into the back of the jeep and felt relaxed for the first time in twenty-four hours. But then one of the guards turned to him and said something. He held out an eyemask, the type used on transatlantic flights for people who want to sleep on the plane.

A blindfold? Cirendini took it and shrugged. He had been warned that something like this might occur. He put it on and the jeep began to roll.

The ride was bumpy as the vehicle drove over unpaved, rough terrain. Cirendini's backside was already sore from sitting so long in the airplanes; this certainly didn't help.

They drove for nearly twenty minutes. When the jeep finally slowed to a stop and the guard removed Cirendini's blindfold, they were in front of a modest army barracks. Cirendini looked around him and saw that he was in some kind of military camp. He could see a field where men were running through obstacles and conducting target practice. Camouflage netting covered several buildings. A group of soldiers were marching in formation. It looked like basic training for the Japanese army.

Cirendini knew that it was far from that.

After he was thoroughly searched, he was led into a dugout covered in camouflage netting. Steps went down into the darkness; a ten-meter passage emptied into a spacious, well-lit receiving room that was ornately decorated in traditional Japanese style. A sliding paper door opened as a guard ushered Cirendini into the next room.

But the guard stopped him and admonished him for something.

"What?" Cirendini asked.

The guard pointed to Cirendini's shoes.

"Oh, right," he said, removing them.

Cirendini was led into a room where a man was sitting on the floor at a low table, having dinner. A central ceiling fan provided a cool breeze and the smell of incense was strong. The man appeared to be in his fifties. He was handsome, had black hair sprinkled with gray and dark eyes. He was wearing a colorful kimono.

"Mister Cirendini," he said in English and bowing slightly. "Please sit. Have some sake. Forgive me if I don't get up."

Cirendini felt ridiculous sitting at the low table. His size seemed to dwarf everything in the room. A servant poured a cup for him and left them alone.

"You have a beautiful place here, Mister Yoshida," he said.

"Thank you. We try to keep it that way. The Russians have been most hospitable in allowing me to stay here. One of these days the island will be Japan's again. But for the moment, they are being quite reasonable. I suppose it helps that I pay handsomely for the use of the land."

Goro Yoshida took a sip of his sake and picked up his chopsticks to resume eating the sushi that was before him. "Would you care for something to eat?"

Cirendini was not fond of uncooked food. "No, thank you. I suppose we should simply get down to business."

Yoshida dabbed his mouth with a napkin and said, "Very well."

Cirendini opened his briefcase and removed a piece of paper. The text was written in English, only a few lines long. He handed it to Yoshida, who took it and read it carefully.

Then, without a word, Yoshida reached inside his kimono and took out a *hanko*. He stamped the piece of paper with a flourish.

"I will make the money transfer this afternoon," Yoshida said as he handed the paper back to Cirendini.

"Thank you," he said. "*Le Gérant* sends you his best regards."

"Tell him that it is a pleasure doing business," Yoshida said with an insincere smile.

Cirendini replaced the paper in the briefcase and stood. A guard opened the sliding door on cue. Cirendini walked out of the room, was blindfolded again, and taken back to the helicopter for another long series of flights back to the Mediterranean Sea.

SIX

THE SAILOR

After learning that "Pierre Rodiac" used a yacht owned by the Corsican mafia man, Emile Cirendini, Mathis took the ferry to Calvi to investigate further. When he had looked into the CL-20 theft from the air force base in Solenzara, Mathis had made several useful contacts. One of them was a man who worked on the marina in Calvi, which was one of the island's main shipping headquarters. Locals called him "The Sailor," and Mathis was unable to find out his true name. Nevertheless, the Sailor liked wine and money, in that order.

When the Sailor saw Mathis again, he smiled warmly and shook his hand.

"Hello my friend!" he said. He was a large man with long, curly black hair. His teeth were yellow and a front one was missing. He smelled strongly of fish and wine. "Come to spend more money on me?"

Mathis laughed and said, "I would be happy to if you are willing to have a little chat."

The Sailor put down a crate of salmon on ice, rubbed his hands, and said, "Let's go to the bar over there." He pointed to a pleasant-looking establishment with tables outside. Mathis appreciated the fact that the wharves in Corsica were well maintained, clean, and usually in close proximity to the tourist shops and restaurants.

It was the middle of the day. The sun was shining brightly in a clear blue sky, and the view from the harbor was always impressive. On one side spread the vast Mediterranean. On the other was a panorama of rugged mountains. Mathis noted that the highest peak still had a bit of snow on it. Corsica was indeed a place of hardy landscapes and a strong people to populate them.

All manner of small craft were docked at the harbor, and there was room further down the marina for larger cruise ships. Pierre Rodiac's Princess 20M was docked there as well.

The two men walked to a small café with outdoor seating facing the sea. Mathis ordered a bottle of *Domaine de Culombu,* a rich red Corsican wine, and asked the Sailor if he wanted lunch. The Sailor wasn't about to refuse. After a few minutes, a plate of scorpionfish with lobster sauce was placed in front of him. Mathis had langoustines grilled with basil sauce. Both dishes were Corsican standards.

"So, what brings you to our little island this time?" the Sailor asked.

"Do you know a man named Emile Cirendini?" Mathis asked.

The Sailor's smile vanished. He looked around to make sure no one was listening. Then he shrugged and nodded. "Yeah, I know who he is."

"What can you tell me about him."

"I believe you already know," the Sailor said. "Right?"

Mathis came clean. "I know that he's a shipping magnate but that he has ties with the mafia here."

"That's right! The old Union Corse," the Sailor said. "You don't hear much about them these days. The mafia today is not the same thing. At least in name it isn't."

"I know. Tell me, is Cirendini still involved in illegal activity?"

"How would I know? I'm just an honest fisherman. But I hear things, you know."

Mathis slipped the man a wad of francs. "I know that his shipping establishment is not far from here. Can you tell me anything interesting about him or his business?"

The Sailor pocketed the money so quickly that he might have made a good magician's assistant. "Yes, I can. I know that he imports and exports beverages, mostly to the mainland of France. That's his main business. He ships other goods, too—machine parts, electronics, that kind of stuff. All day long, every day. What he ships at night, that I don't know."

"At night?"

The Sailor raised his eyebrows. "Sometimes ships come and go in the dark of night, and they don't use any lights, either. Like he's *hiding* something."

"That's interesting. How do they keep from crashing into the rocks? The coastline is awfully treacherous around Corsica."

"Aha!" the Sailor exclaimed, building up to his punchline. "It's because there is a secret entrance to the shipping center. Through a cave on the coast!"

"You've seen it?"

The Sailor nodded. "I can tell you where it is. It looks like a harmless, natural cave, but it's large enough for a medium-sized boat to enter. Boats can slip in and out without the police noticing. I believe that there is access to the inside of the headquarters from the cave."

"That's excellent. Thank you," Mathis said. He ordered afterdinner drinks, a strong spirit called *Eau de vie de Corse.* "I have one more question."

"Go ahead."

"Do you know who sails on that yacht?" Mathis pointed to the Princess.

The man hesitated, then asked, "The blind man?"

Mathis nodded.

"The yacht is owned by your friend Cirendini," the Sailor said. "But the blind man and his bodyguards use it. They take it out every Thursday night. I don't know where they go—"

"Do you know the blind man's name?"

The Sailor shook his head. "A fancy car brings him here and picks him up when he returns."

"Do you know where they go from here?"

"South. That's all I know."

"I've heard that he has a business address in Sartène."

The man shrugged. "I wouldn't know. Sounds like you know more about him than I do."

Mathis smiled. "I don't know nearly enough, my friend. Not yet, anyway."

Mathis found Cirendini's shipping establishment east of Calvi, close to Cap Corse, the peninsula that jutted northward from the island. It was close to the small port of St. Laurent, a prime spot for diving enthusiasts.

Called simply "Corse Shipping," Cirendini's outfit was a large warehouse perched on the cliff overlooking the water. A dirt road went from the main two-lane paved highway to the building. A small gravel parking lot contained four cars. The building was once an old asbestos mine that had been closed years ago. Mathis eventually learned that Cirendini had bought the property and renovated it.

The most unusual thing about it was that a freight lift was built on the side of the cliff that went down to the docks. Cargo could be placed on the lift at the building level and lowered to the ships waiting below.

Mathis drove his rented Renault Mégane along the coast road that wound through the high cliffs. He went around a bend and pulled over to the side of the road, in a spot designated for snapshot seekers. From here, he could get a scenic vista of Corse Shipping, the cliff it was perched upon, and the docks and coastline below.

There it was, the cave that the Sailor had told him about. Mathis took some pictures with his miniature belt-buckle camera.

He drove back to Corse Shipping and parked his car. He went inside and found a middle-aged woman at the front desk. He could hear the sound of machinery back in the warehouse.

"May I help you?" she asked.

"Is Monsieur Cirendini available?"

She shook her head. "He is away on a business trip."

"Oh," he said. He produced a card and a fake identification that he had made up. "I'm with French Customs. I'm doing routine inspections of shipping establishments in Corsica. I had an appointment to take a look at your facility."

The woman frowned. She checked a book and said, "I don't have you down. When was the appointment made?"

"Weeks ago. It's all right, I don't need Monsieur Cirendini to show me around. I can just have a quick look inside. I won't be long. It's all very routine, I assure you."

The woman was obviously intimidated by the badge. "All right, go ahead."

Mathis went past her through big double swing doors into the warehouse. There were stacks of crates, boxes, and barrels all over the place. Large tarpaulins covered piles of goods. Another area held smaller packages and parcels. Some men were busy loading items onto forklifts. They looked at him suspiciously but he went about his business as if there was nothing wrong.

One area contained dozens of pressurized soft drink canisters, the type used in bars and restaurants.

Mathis noticed a caged area full of debris—probably rubbish waiting to be hauled away and destroyed. There were, however, many empty crates and boxes with shipping labels and markings still intact. He slowly made his way over to it. When the men weren't looking, he crouched to his knees to get a better look at what might have been contained in the crates and boxes inside the rubbish cage. He moved around to the other side of the cage to get a better view.

"What are you doing?" boomed a voice behind him. Mathis stood and was confronted by a huge, burly man with no shirt. His chest bulged with muscles and his skin was shiny with sweat.

"I'm an inspector," Mathis said confidently. He flashed the man his badge. "Do you have the key to this cage?"

The man was astounded at the question. "What? Yeah, I have it. Who the hell are you?" Mathis sized him up as the slow-but-strong type.

"I told you, I'm an inspector," Mathis said as he walked away. "I'm finished now, I was just leaving. Thank you very much."

Mathis walked away and shot around an eight-foot-high stack of cargo before the lumbering giant had time to react. "Hey you!" the man called, starting after him. Mathis pulled his weapon and flattened himself against the cargo. As the worker came around, Mathis swung the butt of his Smith & Wesson at the man's face. There was a huge *crunch* as the metal collided with flesh and bone. The giant fell backward like a brick, out cold.

Mathis peered around the cargo stack to make sure no one had heard. He then searched the man's pockets and found a set of keys. He quickly went back to the cage, examined the lock, and determined which key would be most likely to do the trick. He inserted it into the lock—and it worked.

Mathis squatted to examine the crates more closely. He pried off the top of one and found that it was empty, as expected. He rummaged through the boxes and came across a group of four ordinary wooden crates that were painted with a familiar French military green. And that's when he noticed it. On the corner of a crate, barely visible, was a marking that stated *"Propriété de l'Armée de l'Air."*

Solenzara? It had to be!

Mathis left the cage and locked it behind him. Instead of putting the keys back, though, he decided to throw them in a dustbin. He calmly walked past the still unconscious big man, smiled at the receptionist as he went past, and left through the front door.

Mathis chose to stay at the Hotel Corsica, on the road between Calvi and the airport. It was a secluded, recently renovated three star hotel.

When he got to his room, he took some hotel notepaper from the desk and sat down to write. Using a code that he had devised with Bond, Mathis wrote a short but direct message. He folded the paper, put it inside an envelope, and then addressed it to Bond at SIS in London. The next thing he did was pack and prepare to leave.

He went back downstairs to the lobby and checked out. He asked the receptionist where the nearest post office was. She replied that she could post a letter for him, so he left the envelope with her and went outside with his bag to his car.

Mathis drove into Calvi, past the looming citadel containing the old town, and parked his car a short distance from the marina. He got out and walked to the docks to look for his friend. He found the Sailor on a yacht, scrubbing the floor.

"*Bonjour,* my friend!" he said.

"*Bonjour,*" Mathis said. "If an Englishman comes here looking for me, please help him out. I'm going down south to see if I can find this Pierre Rodiac."

"No problem. I hope he likes Corsican wine as much as you and I do. By the way, I asked around about this Rodiac. I got some funny reactions from a few people. They told me not to stick my nose into his business. Apparently he comes from a very traditional Corsican family, one that abides by *vendetta.*"

Indeed, Corsica was the birthplace of the vendetta. Every gift shop on the island sold a selection of knives, for these were the weapons of choice among Corsicans. There was even a style with a long narrow blade and a thin wooden handle called *Vendetta Corse,* named after the centuries-old tradition.

"Rodiac supposedly lives near Sartène, but not in the village," the Sailor continued. "He goes there often enough for one to think that he lives nearby, maybe on a farm or something between villages. I would ask about him at restaurants and bars, I think."

"That's good advice, Sailor, *merci.*"

"So you're really going to Sartène, eh?" the Sailor whispered. "Be careful who you talk to. The people in that town take their heritage very seriously."

"Thanks for the advice," Mathis said. He shook hands with the Sailor, wished him luck, and left Calvi.

SEVEN

THE ASSIGNMENT

M HAD RETRACTED HER THREAT TO TAKE BOND OFF THE UNION CASE AFTER he had obtained information about the retinal tattoo and, further-more, she had given him another three weeks to find something more concrete about it and its relationship to Union membership. In the meantime, details of this bizarre Union "signature" went out to all the major intelligence and law enforcement agencies in the world. M was confounded by the Ministry's decision not to provide the infor-mation to ophthalmologists. Without them, she thought, there was little hope in identifying Union members.

Bond put in another call to René Mathis but learned from his assis-tant that his colleague was still away on leave. Christ, Bond thought, how long a leave was he allowed to take? Frustrated, Bond sat at his desk at SIS and wondered what the hell he should do now.

"Have you tried working with the Paris station on finding him?" Nigel Smith asked him.

"I never liked working with the Paris station," Bond said, grumbling.

"Do you know the new station head?"

"No," Bond said.

"He was assigned to the post during the last year. The entire operation is under new management, so to speak. Bertrand Collette's his name."

"I've never met him."

"Well, I know him," Nigel said. "We studied together at Oxford."

"He's French?"

"That's right. He spent a year at Oxford. Smart fellow. Very good with computers, the internet, that sort of thing. Why don't I give him a call and see if he can find out anything about Mathis?"

"Be my guest," Bond said, but he was skeptical. When Bond arrived for work the following morning, Nigel stopped him.

"I heard from Bertrand in Paris," he said. "He dug around the DGSE, collecting on some old favors. Mathis walked out of his job two months ago. This story that he's 'on leave' isn't true. He more or less resigned; I suppose the official line is that he's on 'indefinite' leave. He was on a case involving a possible Union-related theft of a new highly explosive material from a French air force base in Corsica. Some stuff the Americans cooked up, called CL-20. However, according to his last report to his chief, he thought he may have found a lead regarding the whereabouts of none other than *Le Gérant*."

Bond asked, "Where is he now?"

"That's the problem. No one really knows. He was last seen in Monte Carlo."

"Monte Carlo?" Bond rubbed his chin. "Good work, Nigel. Keep working on tracking him down."

"I will."

Bond stepped into his office and noticed the blinking red light on his phone. He picked up the receiver, pressed the message button and heard Miss Moneypenny's voice.

"M wants you as soon as you get in, James."

Bond punched the buttons and got her on the phone. "I'm on my way up, Penny."

He found M with Bill Tanner in her office.

"Morning, Double-O Seven," she said.

"Good morning, ma'am."

"Stroke of luck, I think," she began. "I've had a call from my opposite number at the DGSE. It seems that they were contacted by an ophthalmologist in Paris who was once in the French secret service, but has since retired. When he was an agent, his cover was an eye doctor, so when he retired from the service he simply went back to private medical practice." She nodded at Tanner, who continued the briefing.

"It seems that due to a bureaucratic error, this French doctor still receives reports sent to him by the DGSE so he read all about the tattoo. It interested him a great deal because he had seen the tattoo on one of his patients. He reported it right away."

"Who's the patient?"

"We don't know," Tanner said. "They won't tell us. I think after the débâcle in Nice a few months ago, they're not too interested in having us around."

"Whose side are they on, anyway?" Bond asked, shaking his head.

"I want you to go to Paris," M said. "You're to get in touch with our new Paris Branch head and work with him. You're to conduct the investigation with discretion. We don't want to upset our French friends . . . too much. But as far as I'm concerned, Double-O Seven, this is a war and we have to conduct it like one. Find out who this patient is and follow it through to wherever it leads you."

Bond told her what he'd learned about Mathis. She agreed that the information was important. "Keep on it," she said. "Who knows, maybe the two paths will cross at some point. Please make your arrangements with Miss Moneypenny and stop by Q Branch on your way out. Major Boothroyd has something for you."

"Ah, there you are, Double-O Seven," Boothroyd said as Bond walked into his office in Q Branch. He closed the door to keep out the noise from the workshop.

"You wanted to see me, Major?" Bond asked.

"I did, Double-O Seven, I did. Come in." Boothroyd got up from behind his workbench, went over to a table, picked up something inside a cloth bag, and brought it back to Bond.

"When this business with the retinal tattoos began, M asked me if I could come up with something that intelligence agencies could use to aid non-doctors in searching for these things. You're going to test the prototype. Go ahead, open it."

The bag contained an object that was small enough to fit in Bond's palm. Boothroyd's latest invention was heavier than he had expected.

"A camera?" Bond asked, turning it over to examine all sides.

Boothroyd seemed insulted. "It's not—oh, well, I suppose, it *is* a camera, it's a camera as *well*, and it takes damned good pictures, too, if I do say so myself . . . but that's not what it *is*, Double-O Seven."

"It's not?"

"No, it's an ophthalmoscope."

Bond looked at him blankly.

"You know," Boothroyd continued, "what eye doctors use to look through your pupils and examine the inside of your eye."

"But it's a *nice* camera," Bond insisted.

"Would you pay attention, Double-O Seven?" Boothroyd huffed. "Yes, it's an ordinary camera except when you depress this button . . ." He pointed to a tiny one located on the bottom of the device. Bond pressed it and the camera shot a thin bright beam of light from its lens.

"Do you know how to examine someone's eye, Double-O Seven?" Boothroyd asked.

"I'm afraid not, Major," Bond said, looking through the camera viewer at a blurry room. "I read your tutorial about it, though."

"Well that would have given you a rudimentary overview of how it's done. I'm pleased to hear that you bothered to look at it. Come closer to me with the device, Double-O Seven," Boothroyd said.

As the major's face came into view, the highly magnified images of flesh and hair surprised Bond.

"Focus on my eye, would you?" Bond got closer and found the major's eye. "The device inside is a Welch Allyn Coaxial-Plus ophthalmoscope with all the usual features such as superior optics for easy entry into undilated pupils, opacity settings, and twenty-eight lenses. Just be careful that you don't flick it over into the red zone."

"Why not?"

"Because that's the laser. It's not terribly powerful, but at very close range, say, two to three feet, it will cut through thin metal. At a distance you might be able to blind someone temporarily by pointing the beam at his eyes."

Bond instinctively found the correct dials to change lenses. As he advanced the selections in single dioptre steps, the major's eye began to exhibit remarkable clarity. Bond went into the pupil, and into the inside of the eye.

Boothroyd continued, "The camera is also equipped with a handy listening device. You pull out the earpieces from the sides and there's a suction cup—"

"Don't move, Major," Bond said as he pointed the light at the back of Boothroyd's eye, turning it into a strange, organic cavern. The blood vessels carved into the orange retinal walls were dark and red.

Boothroyd obliged him but continued talking. "The device is equipped with a Halogen bulb. Should last a long time. I also threw in a bonus—a UV filter that allows you to look at fingerprints!"

"Major, when was the last time you had your eyes checked?" Bond asked, focusing on an odd blood vessel.

"Why?"

"You have a blockage of a small vein. It's not too near the light sensitive area on the retina, but if the obstruction grows you might have a problem like retinal vein occlusion."

"*Thank* you, Double-O Seven, but yes, I know about that little vein. It's been like that forever."

Bond shut it off and said, "In that case, Major, then I'd say you have the eyes of a child."

"I'll take that as a compliment," Boothroyd said, taking the camera away from him. "Look here, if you release this mechanism, the ophthalmoscope separates from the camera housing." He pressed it and a cylindrical metal object the size of a lipstick ejected from the bottom. Boothroyd held it to his eye and turned on the beam.

"I see, so that you can use it as a legitimate ophthalmoscope instead of a camera," Bond said.

Boothroyd lowered the scope and said, "I don't believe you've *ever* used any of our equipment legitimately, Double-O Seven."

THE ALLY

B̲O̲N̲D̲ ̲E̲M̲E̲R̲G̲E̲D̲ ̲F̲R̲O̲M̲ ̲T̲H̲E̲ ̲E̲U̲R̲O̲T̲U̲N̲N̲E̲L̲ ̲I̲N̲ ̲H̲I̲S̲ ̲A̲S̲T̲O̲N̲ ̲M̲A̲R̲T̲I̲N̲ DB$_5$, THE one he had purchased from SIS when the company had auctioned off some of the company cars a few years ago. The extras had been removed and the cars were sold to the highest bidders and Bond had outbid Bill Tanner on this classic favorite. It still ran smoothly.

Bond had his eye on the new Aston Martin DB$_7$ Vantage and was hoping that Q Branch would purchase one for use as a company car. But for now, the reliable DB$_5$ was good enough. It still provoked the occasional stare from other drivers and could impress a girl or two.

He had made the crossing from Folkestone and entered the French traffic at Coquelles, some five kilometers southwest of Calais. Deciding to take the coastal road, Bond pulled into moderately heavy traffic on the A16 and drove toward Boulogne-sur-Mer. He eventually went through Amiens and headed south toward Paris.

Bond loved France, but he wasn't particularly fond of Paris. He found the French countryside gorgeous, its greener-than-green fields and hills—marked here and there with farms and villages—never failed to give him a sense of uncommon tranquility. He occasionally chose to visit Royale-les-Eaux on the north coast when he wanted to get away from England for a weekend without having to fly all the way to Jamaica to Shamelady, his winter retreat. He also enjoyed parts of the south of France, simply because he adored the Mediterranean.

Paris, on the other hand, he had never warmed to. His attitude probably harked back to his first visit to the city at the age of sixteen, when he had lost his virginity and his notecase in one evening. Although the sex had been explosive, the experience of discovering that he'd been taken for a ride had left a permanent bad taste in his mouth. As he grew older, Bond refused to buy into the myth that Paris was "the most romantic city in the world." No, his feelings for Paris hadn't changed with maturity. He still felt that the city had sold its soul to the tourists. Traffic was horrendous (he wouldn't have driven had he not thought that he might need the car later) and the women, while certainly beautiful, tended to be more aloof and haughty than in other European countries. They were almost as bad as the girls in London!

Bond smiled as he admonished himself for that one.

He got into the city by midday and drove deep into the center. As he made his way to the 9th arrondissement, where the *belle époque* splendor was thankfully only partially dominated by the busy traffic and pedestrians, he noticed a large billboard featuring an astonishingly attractive girl. It was an advertisement for a new line of women's clothing called Indecent Exposure, which seemed to flaunt the fact that whoever wore the clothes was actually wearing very little. The girl on the billboard was dressed in nothing more than a drape that ingeniously fastened onto a collar, swept around behind her back and under the right arm, across her breasts, flowed around her waist and back to the front where it ended, tied at the side of her left hip. What she may have had on underneath was left to the imagination. But it wasn't what she was wearing that struck Bond. It was her stunningly beautiful face. She had dark brown hair cut short and layered, amazing brown eyes that penetrated his solar plexus even from this distance, a sensuous mouth with full, red lips, a fresh complexion, and an attitude that dared anyone to look at her and not be mesmerized.

Perhaps there *were* some French girls worth pursuing! he thought.

Bond had never had a taste for fashion models. While many were extraordinarily gorgeous, he found that they lacked a certain presence of mind that was a prerequisite for him. Good sex was one thing and was fine for one night, but he also liked someone he could talk to if there was going to be any kind of longevity.

He quickly forgot about the billboard girl as he drove past the magnificent Opéra Garnier in the Place de l'Opéra, the setting for Gaston Leroux's famous horror story, made a sharp right onto rue Scribe, then pulled into the drive of his hotel.

Bertrand Collette at Station P had arranged for Bond to stay at the elegant Grand Hotel Inter-continental, certainly one of the finest hotels in Paris and probably in Europe. It was convenient since Station P, the Paris branch of Britain's secret service, was located close by.

In his younger days, Bond had preferred to stay at a hotel near the Gare du Nord, but it was long gone. The Intercontinental was expensive and chic, certainly not a place Bond would stay on his own, but since the company was paying for it . . . why not? He might as well enjoy the luxury. After all, this was *the most romantic city in the world!*

The six-story hotel was deemed the "best and most comfortable" of all known hotels when it first opened in 1862. Home of the equally prestigious Café de la Paix, the hotel was recently renovated so that its former elegance and architectural splendor were restored. Bond thought that all the superlatives were well earned as he walked into the brown and beige lobby. Its dark brown wood paneling gave it a decidedly masculine look, which he appreciated. The airy Restaurant La Verrière and lounge were directly across from Reception under a glass roof, adorned with potted plants and furniture of assorted colors. This atrium effect was quite striking. His suite was just as pleasing, done in beige and maroon.

This will do nicely, he thought as he tipped the porter. He quickly unpacked a few things and got on the phone to Collette.

The head of Station P spoke good English and sounded enthusiastic. He suggested that they meet in the hotel bar. Bond stripped, took some time to stretch and perform calisthenics, had a hot shower in the all-marble bathroom (after five minutes he switched the water over to ice cold), then dressed in a collarless black cotton shirt, a gray jacket and deep gray pleated slacks. Thirty minutes later, he sat down at one of the green marble top round tables in the small but comfortably refined Le Bar.

Bertrand Collette entered the place, looked around and spotted Bond smoking a cigarette in the corner.

"*Bonjour*, Monsieur Bond," he said, offering his hand. Bond shook it, noting the firm grip.

"*Bonjour*," he said. Since Bond spoke fluent French they conversed in Bertrand's native language. "Please sit down. What are you drinking?"

Bertrand shrugged. "Gin and tonic, thank you."

There was no waiter, so Bond got up and ordered the drinks from the bartender and got a vodka martini for himself. Sitting again, he offered Bertrand a cigarette.

"No, thank you, I don't smoke. I just drink like a Frenchman."

Bond laughed. "With all the wine you people consume here, it must be very hard on the alcoholics in this country."

"We're all alcoholics but we just don't admit it. Instead, we go to our meetings, stand up in front of everyone and say, 'My name is Bertrand and I am a Frenchman.' "

Bertrand was of medium height, blond and thin. In some ways he reminded Bond of his Texan friend, former CIA agent Felix Leiter. Bertrand was clean-shaven, but he had nicked himself and had a small piece of tissue stuck to his cheek.

"How do you like working for Britain?" Bond asked.

"It's fine. The pay is good. I have many friends in high places here in France, so I am capable of providing your country with good information."

"So what have you learned recently?"

Bertrand leaned forward and kept his voice low. "I'm still trying to track down Monsieur Mathis. He seems to have disappeared. I do hope he has not come to a bad end."

"Me too," Bond said. "We've known each other for years."

"I thought so. Don't worry, we'll find something soon. I have a friend in Monte Carlo who can find out things discreetly. The good news is that I've found out the name of the eye doctor who reported seeing the tattoo. His name is Didier Avalon and his office is over by the medical university."

"Can we see him today?"

"We can certainly try. He has patients today so he should be there this afternoon."

"Good. Listen, you wouldn't mind if I take your picture, would you?"

"*Pardon?*"

Bond held up the special camera. "Just look into the lens there and say cheese."

Bertrand wrinkled his brow. "I don't like having my picture taken." But he let Bond go ahead. The beam of light struck his eye and he flinched. "What the hell . . . ?"

"Don't move," Bond said, adjusting the lenses.

"Are you doing what I think you're doing?"

"Hold on . . . got it. All right, you're clear," Bond said, shutting off the ophthalmoscope.

"Where did you get that?"

"It's a prototype, but don't worry, they'll be in all the stores for Christmas. Let's go and see that doctor."

Dr. Didier Avalon's office was on rue de L'Université in the 7th arrondissement, very near the Université de Paris Faculté de Médecine. It was inside one of the two-century-old stone buildings that were prominent in the area.

"A lot of doctors are around here," Bertrand said as they parked his Citroën against the curb.

"What makes you think he'll talk to us?" Bond asked.

"Don't worry. I have credentials."

They went up the stairs to the first floor and found the doctor's waiting room. Three patients—an elderly man and two middle-aged women—were there, calmly looking at magazines. Bertrand told the receptionist that they were there on "police business" and needed to see Dr. Avalon right away. She went away, came back a minute later, and told them to wait a few minutes.

The doctor wasn't long. A nurse called Bond and Bertrand into the back, where Avalon had his private office. Like most European doctors, he also lived on the premises.

Dr. Avalon was in his sixties, had short white hair, a full white beard and glasses. Bond thought that he might make a good Father Christmas if he were fatter.

"How can I help you?"

Bertrand gave him a card. "Bertrand Collette with the DGSE. We spoke on the phone this morning?"

"Yes?"

"This is my colleague from England, Monsieur Bond."

"How do you do?"

Bond shook his hand.

They sat down. Bertrand continued. "I promise not to take up too much of your time. I realize that you've already talked to some of my colleagues. Monsieur Bond and I are on an international task force and we have reason to believe that the tattoo you found is indeed criminal in nature."

"Well, I thought it was. You don't get that kind of thing too often," Avalon said. "What happened to the other man I was talking to? Monsieur . . . oh what was his name? I have his card here . . ."

Bertrand quickly said, "He's still on the case here in *Paris*, but I'm handling it from an international standpoint. Two different committees, so to speak. Too much bureaucracy, if you ask me."

Avalon nodded as if he understood. "What would you like to know?"

"Just tell us what you told my colleague."

Avalon shrugged. "Well, a patient came in complaining of conjunctivitis. I examined him. He did have conjunctivitis and I prescribed an antibiotic ophthalmic solution for him. However, when I used an ophthalmoscope on him, I noticed a lesion at the back of his retina. I looked at it more closely and saw the pattern. Have you seen it?"

"Of course," Bertrand answered.

"Well, then, you know what I'm talking about. In this business it's not unusual for some doctors to make a mark with a laser when they operate—something like a signature—I don't do it myself. Anyway, I saw that this one was fairly elaborate. When I asked him about it, he became very defensive. I used to be in the DGSE, you see, and before that I was in the *gendarmerie*. I was trained to recognize when someone was lying, or acting suspiciously. This patient was definitely acting suspiciously. He wanted to leave immediately and even became abusive, telling me to mind my own business and such."

Bond asked in French, "He was a regular patient?"

"No, he was new. I wasn't his regular eye doctor."

"May we ask who your patient was?" Bertrand inquired.

The doctor hesitated. "That's confidential, you know. I told your colleague the other day only because I got a court order to do so."

Bertrand assumed a stern demeanor and said, "Doctor Avalon, that court order stands with us as well."

Avalon seemed surprised. "It does?"

"That's right. So please, it's best if you tell us everything."

Avalon didn't seem too put out by it. "Very well. He's someone pretty famous. That film producer, the director, you know, Léon Essinger."

Bond blinked. Well, well! he thought. Why was he not surprised?

Bertrand feigned astonishment. "Really? Léon Essinger?"

"That's right. He normally lives and works in Nice, but he has an office here at one of the television studios. Said that he was working on something here in Paris and couldn't go back to Nice just yet. Why, what's that tattoo really mean?"

Bertrand said, "Doctor Avalon, I'm afraid that's classified information. Just know that you did the right thing by coming forward to report it. So, doctor, will you be seeing Monsieur Essinger again?"

"Only if his condition doesn't improve. Those eye drops usually work, so I doubt he'll be back."

"Can you think of anything else to tell us?" Bertrand asked.

Avalon shook his head. "That's it, I suppose. I was afraid that perhaps I was overreacting, but I knew about Monsieur Essinger's—well, I knew about his reputation with the law, you know."

Bertrand nodded. "Yes, he's been on our list for some time. Well, thank you, doctor, you've been most helpful. We won't take up any more of your time."

As they walked back to the car, Bertrand said, "I'm way ahead of you. Essinger's office is at France Télévision, southwest of the city center. He just rents space there because his main office is in Nice."

"I've never met him, but I know who he is," Bond said. "Do you remember what happened at his studios in Nice a few months ago?"

"I sure do. The DGSE and the police took a beating for that one. Terrible tragedy. I wonder what Essinger is doing in Paris now. Making a movie?"

"Whatever it is, I think it's time for me to have a screen test," Bond said.

NINE

THE MAZZERE

MATHIS FOUND THE OLD WOMAN AFTER A CIRCUITOUS DRIVE FROM CALVI, down through the center of the island to Sartène, in the southern portion of Corsica.

Sartène is called "the most Corsican of Corsican towns." Legend has it that it is actually the birthplace of the *vendetta* because there is a long history of feuding families in the village. It is an austere, silent place perched on a mountain overlooking the gorgeous, green Rizzaneze valley. The inhabitants are very religious, and they take their Catholicism to extremes. Sartène is famous for a centuries-old tradition that is re-enacted annually. Every year on Good Friday, the entire town turns out to watch the spectacle of the *Procession du Catenacciu*, in which an anonymous, barefoot penitent is chosen and covered from head to foot in a red robe and cowl. He is then made to carry a large cross through the town while dragging heavy chains, followed by several more penitents (some dressed in black, others in white) and priests.

Mathis was amazed that the gift shops sold postcards depicting the *Procession du Catenacciu*, and tourists could even buy souvenir videotapes of the event. He wondered why any tourists would want to come to Sartène in the first place. It was a shadowy, severe town where even the stone buildings seemed to look upon strangers with suspicion. The atmosphere was oddly oppressive for no tangible reason.

Mathis left the gift shop and walked down the cobblestone street to the Place de la Libération, the town square. He sat down at an outdoor table in front of one of the four restaurants that surround the square and ordered Pietra, the Corsican beer. Directly across the square was the town's pride and joy, the *Église Sainte Marie,* a church built in 1766 and the center of activity in Sartène.

For a mid-afternoon, the town was awfully quiet. Where were all the people? Didn't they work? It was unnerving. Mathis felt strangely paranoid, as if he were being studied and talked about from behind closed doors. "Have you seen the stranger? He has been in town two days, asking questions, taking pictures. Who is he? What does he want?"

When he had first arrived in the village, he had gone straight to Pierre Rodiac's business address that had been provided to him by Dominic in Monte Carlo. Unfortunately, the building turned out to be abandoned. A shopkeeper next door said that no one had used the place in months. Next, Mathis visited the local *gendarmerie.* He showed the policemen his credentials and said that he was looking for a man named Pierre Rodiac. The men grew silent. After a moment, one of them said that they had never heard of him.

Rodiac obviously had some sort of power over the people here.

Mathis had prepared photos of Rodiac from the shots he had taken at the casino, so he spent the rest of the day visiting the shops and restaurants and showing the picture to the proprietors. "Have you seen this man?" Every time he was met by silence.

Now, as he sat and sipped the cold beer, Mathis wondered what his next step should be.

"I may know someone who can help you."

The voice was the restaurant owner's. Mathis had spoken to him a day earlier and shown him the photo, with no positive result.

"Oh?" Mathis asked.

"May I sit down?" the proprietor asked.

"By all means."

The man sat down and leaned in close to whisper. "Go into the church and look for an old woman dressed in black."

"Aren't they all old women dressed in black?" Mathis asked.

"Yes, but this one stands out. She wears a lot of jewelry and dresses like a gypsy from the old days. She has a scarf on her head and is very old."

"How can she help me?"

"She is a *mazzere*."

"A what?"

"Most people do not believe in the *mazzeri,* but they have existed on Corsica for centuries. Their gifts are passed down through the generations."

"I don't understand."

The proprietor looked around again to make sure no one was listening. Mathis thought that the man was being overly cautious, for the street, the square, and the restaurant were completely empty.

"*Mazzeri* are otherwise normal people who have the 'gift' of foretelling someone's death. This happens during a dream in which the *mazzere* assumes the body of an animal that ventures into the wilderness to hunt for prey. The prey is another human who is also in the form of an animal—but the *mazzere* can recognize its human identity. The *mazzere* kills the animal and returns home. Some time later, the person represented by the dead animal in the dream usually dies—by disease, misfortune or whatever. People respect and fear the *mazzeri,* because they don't want to hear if they're being dreamed about!"

"Fascinating," Mathis said, humoring the man.

"The *mazzeri* also have other gifts. They tend to know things that normal people don't. They are very wise."

"And you say this woman is one of these *mazzeri?*"

"Yes. You can ask her about this man you're looking for. Maybe she knows him somehow."

"Thanks," Mathis said, then added, "I have never heard of this superstition."

The man frowned and stood. "As you like," he said, and walked away.

Mathis paid for the beer and walked over to the church. He went inside and was simultaneously impressed and disconcerted by the

ultra-realistic depictions of the Crucifixion that surrounded the sanctuary. The cross and chains used in the *Procession du Catenacciu* hung
on one of the walls as well.

There were about two dozen old women in the church, all in
black, chanting softly to themselves. Mathis thought it was in Corsican, but he might have heard a Latin phrase or two. He scanned the
faces and had no trouble picking out the woman. She appeared to be
in her eighties and was sitting apart from the rest of them.

He waited until they were finished with their worship. The women
stood and started to mingle and chat as they left the church. The one
old woman didn't speak to anyone else and started to leave alone.
Mathis stopped her.

"*Pardon* madame, may I please speak with you?"

She looked at him with suspicion.

He introduced himself and showed her his card. "I have been told
that you might be able to help me. That you have certain . . . 'gifts' . . ."

The woman looked at him hard and said, "I don't know what
you're talking about," and she attempted to push past him.

"I can pay you," he said. She stopped. "Handsomely."

Her eyes flickered as she turned back to him. "I only talk about my
'gifts' in the privacy of my home. Come and see me there." She gave
him an address and told him to come after dinner. Without another
word, she moved toward the door and left.

Hours later, as the sun was setting, Mathis made his way through
the narrow streets and up a hill into the old town. He found the
address and knocked on a large wooden door. It creaked open, and
the woman invited him inside.

She introduced herself as Annette Culioli. Her home was modest,
containing very little furniture, but was decorated with all kinds of
plants and flowers. There were several cats of different shapes and
sizes roaming about. For someone preoccupied with death, Mathis
thought, she certainly surrounded herself with a lot of life.

Madame Culioli led him into her parlor and asked him to sit down
at a small round table. She asked if he wanted any wine.

"That would be lovely," he said.

She went into another room and returned with a bottle of the locally made red wine, *Fiumicicoli*. She poured two glasses and sat down.

"How may I help you?"

Mathis showed her Rodiac's photo. "I'm looking for this man. Have you ever seen him?"

She took the photo and studied it. A look of fear passed across her face. She handed it back and said, "Yes, I know him. But only in my dreams."

"Can you tell me anything about him?"

"Why do you want to find this man?" she asked.

"Because he is a bad man," Mathis replied.

She nodded. "He is a blind man."

"I know."

"He is of two worlds. He is part Corsican. His other half is very different." She got up suddenly and went into her bedroom. She returned, clutching a Bible. She crossed herself and sat down again.

"In my dreams he is always the wolf," she continued. "But the wolf isn't blind. It can see better than anyone else. In my dreams, I am the wild pig. I have run into the wolf several times out in the *maquis*. He protects his territory. We have fought, but I admit that I have run away from the fights for fear of being killed in the dream. It is bad luck to die in a dream."

Mathis knew that *"maquis"* was the term used to describe the Corsican wilderness.

"Where is his territory?"

She closed her eyes, as if trying to recall the dream. "Statues. Statues with faces. Old statues. And castles made of boulders. Prehistoric castles."

Mathis thought that he knew what she was talking about. The island was well known for its prehistoric archaeological sites, especially in southern Corsica near Sartène. The sites at Filitosa, Cucuruzzu, and Capula contained objects that matched her description. The phallic-like stone statues with carved human faces, or menhirs, dated back to the era of primitive man, and archaeologists were still pondering their significance and purpose.

"Do you think this man lives near Sartène?" he asked.

"The *mazzeri* stick close to home in their dreams."

"Are you saying that he is a *mazzere* too?"

She nodded. "He is. And he has other powers as well. He is dangerous. He is a man to be feared."

Mathis handed her a wad of bills and stood. "Thank you, madame."

She took the money, bowed her head, and said, "May God go with you." She crossed herself again, stood, and led him to the door.

The explosion at the British Embassy in Tokyo occurred at 5:30 in the morning, while the city was still asleep. In hindsight, embassy officials were thankful that the bomb hadn't gone off during peak hours of daylight. It could have been disastrous. As it was, there was only minor damage to one of the outside walls of the building at No. 1 Ichibancho. It was the second bombing attempt within three months.

The explosive had apparently been inside a van and a suicide driver had driven the vehicle toward the front gates. The bomb had gone off on impact, completely destroying the van and its driver and blowing a hole in the gate large enough for the flames to spill inside the grounds of the embassy.

For hours after the explosion, Japanese and British officials had attempted to determine who was behind the attack. There were no claims of responsibility, but a source close to *The Times* suggested that it had been the work of Goro Yoshida's followers.

No one could prove it, though.

THE STUDIO

On the afternoon of the following day, Léon Essinger sat in the office that he rented from France Television. He was staring at the associate producer of *Pirate Island*, refusing to believe what he had just heard.

"The boats will cost *how much?*" he asked, doing his best to contain his rage.

"Three times as much as we estimated," the young man said, swallowing hard.

"Get out of my office!" Essinger yelled. "What kind of producer are you? Your job is to bring the picture in *under* budget, not *three goddamn times over!*"

"I'm sorry, sir, I'll see what I can do," the associate producer stammered and quickly left the room, shutting the door behind him.

Essinger sighed and put his head in his hands. It was all becoming too much. Everything was piling up and he was fighting for air. There was the film, the most important thing, of course; that had to be a hit or his career was finished. There was Tylyn, his treacherous wife, the bitch who had left him for "more independence." There was the Union and what he was mixed up in with them. He wished that he had never heard of them.

His secretary, a woman named Madeleine, stuck her head in the door. "*Pardon,* Monsieur Essinger . . ."

"What is it?" he snapped.

"You said I could leave early . . ."

"Fine, go on. Get the hell out of here," he waved her away.

She made a face as she closed the door.

Essinger reached for a bottle of bourbon from a cabinet behind the desk. He always kept alcohol in his various homes and offices. He noted that he needed to have Madeleine stock up on the Paris office stash. There was just enough for a double. The phone rang, startling him. He let it ring again as he poured the bourbon and took a large sip. By the fourth ring, he was ready to answer it.

"*Oui?*"

"Léon."

Christ! he thought. It was Tylyn.

"Hello darling," he managed to say.

"How are you?"

"Fine. And you?"

"Fine," she said. "Listen, tell me again about this press thing in Monte Carlo."

He breathed easier. He thought she was going to bring up the subject of divorce. He had been dreading it for weeks.

"It's just a press junket, darling," he said. "All the major players on the film will be there. I'm counting on you to be there as well."

"All right," she said. "It's just that . . . well, you know . . . these reporters seem to only want to know one thing."

"And what is that?" he asked.

"Whether or not you and I are splitting up for good," she said.

"Are we?" he asked.

"Léon . . ." she said with a note of disappointment in her voice. "We agreed that we weren't going to talk about it while the film is in production."

"You brought it up, darling."

"Oh, never mind. I'll see you soon," she said.

"So you'll be there? I know how you hate press functions. But you can't be a star without letting the media have a piece of you. I would hate to pull contract on you . . ."

"I'll *be* there, Léon! Now, I have to go."

"Take care of yourself," he said with just a touch of sarcasm.

"That's exactly what I'm doing," she said and hung up the phone.

Essinger slammed the receiver down. "Bitch!"

He fumed for a moment.

She was *enjoying* herself! She was having a *good time* being alone and away from him. She *liked* this independence of hers.

It was over, he told himself for the millionth time. There was no goddamned hope.

The *Pirate Island* press packet was laid out in front of him. The actors' headshots were in a pile of their own. Essinger thumbed through them until he came to Tylyn's.

God, she was beautiful.

After a few seconds hesitation, Essinger slowly ripped the photograph in two.

He breathed deeply and started again.

He ripped it into quarters. He tore it again. And again.

When his wife's picture was in puzzle pieces, he scooped them into his palm and dropped them into the wastepaper basket.

Essinger got up, gathered his things, walked out of the office, and locked the door behind him. He was ready to go back to Nice and get busy.

It was the only way to bury the pain.

Bertrand Collette dropped James Bond off in front of the France Television building at Esplanade Henri de France. He looked at Bond and said, "Right, you go in and ask for Isabelle Vander, with Public Relations. You have the press card I gave you?"

"Yes, Bertrand," Bond said. He couldn't help but be amused by his French companion. Collette had nicked himself shaving again and was now wearing two tiny bits of tissue on his face.

"Call me on your mobile when you're ready for me to come back," he said. "I'll be close by."

Bond got out of the car and looked up at the metallic, marble and glass building that served as the center for France's stations 2 and 3 as well as other entertainment concerns. Security was very tight at the thoroughly modern, fairly new complex, just as it was at the BBC in London.

He was wearing a dark blue suit and tie, the Walther PPK tucked neatly underneath his armpit. The plan was that Bond would pose as a reporter from a popular British magazine called *Pop World*. It was a legitimate publication that focused on the entertainment industry, fashion and pop culture. SIS had connections with the magazine, but this was the first time Bond had used them for a cover. Nigel Smith had overnighted the fake credentials to Bond's hotel and now he was in business. Bond just had to play the role convincingly.

Bertrand had set up a meeting with the studio's Public Relations department. Bond was a visiting journalist doing a story on various European television production companies. The studio people were pleased to offer him a tour of the facilities.

The center lobby was a large atrium with glass walls. One could look up and see into the various floors on both sides. Several security guards were in the lobby—at the entrance, the way to the lifts, and near the reception desk.

Bond checked in at the desk, where they asked for his identification. He gave them his passport. In return he was presented with a key card that allowed him access past the lobby to the lifts. He was told that Mademoiselle Isabelle Vander would meet him there.

Bond swiped the card under the watchful gaze of the guard and went through the revolving glass door. He waited a minute or two for Mademoiselle Vander, who stepped out of the lift and approached him.

She was probably in her thirties, an attractive woman with blonde hair pulled back into a bun. She wore glasses and a business suit.

"Monsieur Bond?" she asked.

"Yes?"

"Hello, I am Isabelle Vander," she said in English. They shook hands. Hers was soft and warm.

"Why don't you follow me?" She led him into the lift and they went up two floors. "Is there anything in particular that you're looking for?"

Bond wanted to say, "The fourth floor," because that's where Essinger had his office. Instead, he feigned interest in the television studios. She brought him onto the second floor, where the main soundstages were set up for television news programs, a game show, and a soap opera, respectively. The game show was currently taping with a studio audience, so they had to be relatively quiet as they walked through the backstage area. Apparently it was some kind of dog show, for contestants had brought their pets with them to perform on the program. Bond and Isabelle stepped around three owners—one with a Chow-Chow, one with what looked like a black Labrador mix, and one with a Tibetan Terrier. Isabelle stopped to pat the dogs and whisper baby talk to them. She and Bond peered through the scenery to see an owner attempting to entice his Great Dane to dance. When the dog finally stood on his hind legs and circled to the music, the audience applauded.

Isabelle led Bond out of the studio and into the control room, where the *réalisateur* was busy directing cameramen and barking orders to assistants. Bond removed a small notepad from his jacket and jotted down some words so that he would appear authentic.

At one point they passed by the washrooms.

"Oh, excuse me, may I go in here for a moment?" he asked her.

"Certainly. I'll wait for you down at the end of the hall, in that alcove by Makeup."

"Fine," he said, and then ducked into the Gents. He waited a moment, then peered out the door. The hallway was clear. He slipped out, went straight to the lift, and took it to the fourth floor.

Once there, Bond found his way to Essinger's office, which was closed and locked. He stooped down so that he could access the false heel in his right shoe, a standard field accessory provided to all Double-O agents. Inside was a set of sophisticated lock-picks that were guaranteed to open 97 percent of the world's doors. He began to try them one by one.

The lift bell rang, indicating that someone would be walking his way at any moment. Damn! He tried another pick.

He heard the lift doors open and quickly stuck another pick in the lock. The door swung open and he jumped inside just as footsteps could be heard approaching at the end of the hall.

Bond waited until he heard the person walk by, and then he flicked
on the lights. He went through the empty outer office into Essinger's
private office. There were piles of papers on the desk, but they were
neatly organized by subject. A quick glance revealed that some dealt
with a new motion picture that was about to begin production,
another pile dealt with details of a screening of Essinger's newest film
at the upcoming Cannes Film Festival, and another concerning what
appeared to be miscellaneous expense records for Essinger's company.

Bond took a look at the expenses first. There were the expected
bills for office rental, utilities and employee payroll. There was extensive bills from various catering services, mostly a beverage company
called "Marseilles Bottling Company." Something struck him as odd
about the invoice. Apparently Essinger had arranged to import canisters of soft drinks from Corsica, using a shipping firm called "Corse
Shipping." Why would he want to import them from Corsica?
Weren't they made in France?

Bond turned to the production pile and examined it. A new film,
Pirate Island, was scheduled to begin shooting in less than a week.
Locations included Corsica and several spots on the Mediterranean. There were details on the cast and crew, the budget, insurance, and a production schedule. Bond removed the camera that
Boothroyd had given to him and focused the lens on the production schedule. He snapped pictures of it and of the cast and crew
listings. Who knows? he thought. Perhaps there were some known
Union people working on the film. Bond glanced at the pile of film
festival material. Essinger's film *Tsunami Rising* was going to premiere at Cannes in approximately two weeks. There were notes
indicating that the production of *Pirate Island* would halt for two
days so that Essinger and other members of the cast and crew could
attend the screening. The same director who shot *Tsunami Rising*
was at the helm for *Pirate Island* and the two films also shared the
same leading actor.

A trade ad announced the screening as an "out of competition,
gala charity event" that would benefit various causes. Someone had
scribbled in ink on the ad, "Royal family?" in French. Clipped to the

ad was a note from Essinger's secretary that read, "Léon—still waiting on confirmation of attendance by Monaco and Britain."

Meanwhile, Isabelle Vander became impatient waiting for "Monsieur Bond" on the second floor. He had been in the washroom for nearly fifteen minutes! What was keeping him? When a production assistant walked through, she stopped him and asked if he wouldn't mind having a look in the men's washroom to see if the visitor was all right. The assistant came out a moment later and said that the bathroom was empty.

Perplexed, Isabelle walked up and down the halls looking for her charge.

Bond spent another five minutes going through the filing cabinets and desk drawers but came up with nothing interesting. He wasn't sure if anything he'd seen in the office was useful. There was nothing that indicated that Essinger might be involved in any criminal activity. The search was fruitless.

He moved toward the door and noticed the wastepaper basket beneath the desk. On a whim, he looked inside and saw the torn pieces of photograph. He dumped them out on the desk and attempted to sort them. Bond could see that the photo was once the face of a woman, but there were too many pieces for him to complete the picture now. He scooped them up and put them in his pocket.

Isabelle gave up looking for Monsieur Bond and went back to her office to report a missing visitor. The security staff were alerted to watch out for an Englishman who was wandering about unescorted.

Bond turned out the office lights and opened the door a crack to look outside. The hallway was empty. He stepped out and shut the door behind him, automatically locking it. He straightened his tie and walked toward the lift. He pressed the button and waited. When it opened, he was confronted by a security guard.

"*Bonjour,*" Bond said.

The guard reacted, recognizing him as a visitor. He started to say something but Bond raised his right arm and punched the man in the nose. He fell backward into the lift, out cold. Bond got inside with him and pressed the ground floor button. Unfortunately, someone on two had called the lift and it stopped there.

When the doors opened, Bond shot past a group of men and women, all studio employees. One of the women screamed when she saw the unconscious guard.

Bond ran down the hall and saw the studio that Isabelle had shown him earlier. He rushed in, closing the heavy door behind him quietly. The dog show was still going on. The audience was laughing and applauding the antics of the Chow-Chow, which was jumping through a series of hoops set on the stage. Two cameras were moving around the action, capturing the best angles for the program. Bond moved around the scenery to try and get out another way, but one of the production assistants stopped him.

"Who are you? What are you doing back here?"

Bond waved his visitor pass. "I'm doing a story on your studio—"

He was interrupted by a loud bark. The black Labrador mix was behind him and looked as if it would take a bite out of him. Its owner whispered, "Hush, Spike!" but the dog must have sensed that Bond was an intruder. It barked again and growled.

"I was just leaving," Bond said to the assistant and started to go out through the door, but the dog broke free from its master. Bond held up his arm to prevent the sixty-pound dog from leaping onto his chest. The animal collided with him and Bond hurled it back. It yelped and barked furiously at him.

"Hey!" the owner cried.

Then, the Great Dane that was on the show earlier and had been watching the Labrador from the sidelines decided that it, too, would get into the act. It leaped from sitting position, taking his owner by surprise. The dog jumped on Bond, knocking him to the ground.

"Security! Security!" the assistant called into his headset.

The Great Dane grabbed Bond's right forearm with his huge jaws and held it tightly. Luckily, Bond's clothing was thick, but he could feel the teeth pressing against his skin. Then, the Labrador bit into his leg. Bond kicked hard, throwing the dog off, and then rolled as forcefully as he could with the Great Dane's head locked in his arm.

The huge dog did a somersault over his body and landed unharmed on the floor. Bond leaped to his feet and ran the most convenient way—onto the set.

The Chow-Chow had just jumped through a hoop as Bond emerged from the backstage area. His appearance surprised the dog in mid-air, throwing off its concentration. It landed right into Bond's arms.

The audience roared.

The director in the control room went nuts. "Who is that? What is he doing?"

The stage manager was calling frantically into his headset. "Security!"

By now, the Great Dane and Labrador had jumped through windows in the stage setting, which resembled the back of a house. Bond tossed the Chow-Chow at them and ran toward the audience. The three dogs crashed into each other, yelping with rage.

The stage manager attempted to tackle Bond, but he tripped over one of the camera cables. Bond ploughed into the seats, causing the audience to panic. The dogs were right behind him. Suddenly the entire soundstage erupted into chaos.

The members of the audience jumped out of their seats and ran toward the exits, crowding Bond from making an escape. Three production assistants tore off their headsets and chased after Bond. One of them grabbed him, spun him around and threw a punch and missed. Bond, who had carefully avoided hurting anyone except the guard, saw that he had no choice but to defend himself. He hit the man in the stomach, causing him to bend over. Bond then brought his knee up into the man's face. That took the fight out of him. When the other two saw what had happened to their colleague, they hesitated. After a moment's stare-down, they backed off, and then directed their energy elsewhere by yelling at the audience to remain calm.

But the dogs weren't afraid at all. They were barking furiously and knocking over the chairs in an attempt to catch Bond, who picked up one of the metal folding chairs and used it to hold them at bay, much like a lion tamer in a circus.

Then, four security guards pushed their way through the sound-stage entrance into the mass of people clambering to get out. One of them had a gun.

Bond tossed the chair at the dogs, temporarily blocking their advance, then ran back onto the stage. One of the camera cables went up into the catwalk some thirty feet above the floor. Bond jumped and grabbed it, then quickly pulled himself up, hand over hand.

"Stop him!" the stage manager cried. "This is expensive equipment!"

By the time the guards had reached the stage, Bond was on the catwalk. He had to crouch because the ceiling was so low, but he ran quickly to the nearest exit. He almost tripped over some lighting instruments attached to the grid, but he caught himself on a metal beam and used it to swing over a rail onto another catwalk that was nearer to his escape route.

There was a gunshot from below and a bullet whizzed past him.

"What are you doing?" the stage manager shouted at the guard. "Don't use that in here!"

Bond went through the little door into a lighting control room. It was full of electronic equipment, patch boxes and dimmer switches. He scanned the wall quickly and found the main power lever. He pulled it, plunging the soundstage into darkness. Then he climbed out of the light booth and found himself in a small corridor on the fourth floor. Apparently the soundstage was two stories tall.

He made his way to the stairwell and went inside. He was alone. Bond pulled out his mobile and punched in Bertrand's number.

"Bertrand get over here quick. I'll meet you on the street."

"Is there trouble?"

But Bond hung up. He ran down the stairs two at a time all the way to the ground floor. He stopped to catch his breath, then opened the door to peer outside. It was the lobby, and it was bustling with activity. Guards were looking this way and that and visitors were being kept from entering the studios.

Now what?

A group of two dozen Italians were making a fuss. They all had tickets to be in the audience of a talk show. A guard was telling them to stand back against the wall until the "problem" was taken care of. A stroke of luck—the guard ushered the Italians back against the stairwell door. As soon as the guard had turned his back, Bond slipped out of the door and joined the Italians. They were so busy chattering among themselves that they didn't notice the extra person.

He waited there for about five minutes, as there was no easy way to break away from the group and get across the atrium to the front doors of the building. Finally, a woman approached them and spoke in Italian. "I'm very sorry, but we have to cancel the show today. We can reschedule you to come back tomorrow."

One of the men protested angrily, but a woman in the group attempted to calm him down. They all began to walk toward the front doors, and Bond merely blended in.

"What do you think is going on?" one of the visitors asked him in Italian.

Bond shrugged. "Someone probably lost a dog," he replied.

The group filed out of the building. Bond got into Bertrand's Citroën and said, "Drive like hell."

Station P was located within a legitimate business on rue Auber, not a ten-minute walk from Bond's hotel. "Internet Works," as it was called, was an e-mail café where customers could check their e-mail or surf the net. The place also served snacks, coffee and soft drinks. They were open from 6:00 in the morning until midnight. Bertrand told Bond that they did *very* well.

"SIS lets me keep the money I make in the business, so I do okay," he said. "If I wasn't an agent, then I wouldn't mind running an e-mail café as my sole occupation."

"It's always important to be happy in one's job," Bond said with exaggerated enthusiasm.

Collette laughed as they walked into the back office of the café. With a flick of a switch, a false wall slid open, revealing something a little more private. All of Collette's communication equipment was inside. The room was full of radios, a couple of computers, and filing cabinets.

"Something to drink?" Collette asked Bond as he opened a small cupboard.

"Please." Bond sat down at one of the desks and dug into his pocket for the pieces of photograph that he had taken from Essinger's office. He spread them out on the desktop, face up, and began to put the puzzle together.

Collette set a glass of red wine in front of Bond. "Jigsaw puzzles, James?"

"Something like that," Bond said. There were thirty-two pieces, and he nearly had it done.

Those magnificent eyes, Bond thought. He'd seen them before. But where?

Thirty seconds later, the picture was complete.

Who *was* this girl? Bond knew her from somewhere. She was strikingly beautiful. She had a face that he had seen in a magazine, or on television—and then he remembered. She was the girl from the billboard Bond had noticed when he drove into Paris.

He was drawn to the mischievous half grin on her face that projected a dynamic self-confidence. This girl knew that she was beautiful and loved it. There was also intelligence in her almost cat-like eyes. The brown hair was cut short, just covering her ears and giving her a fringe. It was styled with a bit of layered shape that caressed her incredible face.

"Do I win if I know her name?" Collette said.

"You certainly do," Bond said. "Who is she?"

"That's Tylyn Mignonne," he answered, pronouncing her Christian name to rhyme with "smilin." He waited until Bond registered surprise, but got no reaction.

"Tylyn *Mignonne*," Collette said again. "The famous model and now actress?"

Bond shook his head. "I don't keep up with that world. Tell me about her."

Collette chuckled. "Be careful, James. She is married to Léon Essinger."

"No!" Bond said, aghast.

"It's true, *but* . . ." Collette paused for dramatic effect. "They're separated."

"So there's still hope. Do you have any tape?" Bond asked. Collette laughed again and got a roll of transparent tape out of his desk. Bond carefully taped the pieces of the photo together as Collette spoke.

"That's not her only claim to fame, you know," he said. "Ever heard of a Hollywood filmmaker named Jules Pont?"

"Yes." Bond knew who he was. Again, he paid little attention to the show business world, but Pont was a well-known French film director-turned-producer who had emigrated to America in the forties, made a number of popular and successful films in the fifties and sixties, created his own studio in the seventies, and then died. Some of Pont's comedies from the sixties were considered cinema classics.

"Tylyn's his daughter."

"Really?"

"Mignonne was her mother's maiden name, and that's how she goes professionally."

"So," Bond surmised, "she's probably a very wealthy girl."

"She is indeed," Collette said. "She is the heir to the entire Pont fortune."

"Which must be considerable. His studio is still running in Hollywood, isn't it?"

Collette said, "It sure is. Doing very well, too."

"Tell me about her."

Collette shrugged. "All I know is what the public knows. As she grew up, her parents brought her several times to France. She is an only child. Her parents were fairly old when she was born. She started modeling as a child and became a famous face before she was twelve years old."

"I had no idea," Bond said. "I don't think I've ever seen her before coming here."

"You need to read more women's magazines," Collette said. "Anyway, she achieved supermodel status by the time she was eighteen. She has her own clothing line, too. It's called "Indecent Exposure." Pretty sexy stuff it is. Recently she has started trying to be an actress. She's made a few films in France, one that was a big hit world-wide."

"What about the marriage to Essinger?" Bond asked as he finished repairing the photo. He looked at her again.

"They got married about four or five years ago. It was fairly soon after he came back to France."

"Why in the world would a girl like her marry him?" Bond asked.

"He's a celebrity, too. Has money. He's an artist. Don't all those show business types stick to each other like glue? It's a very incestuous world."

"I suppose so," Bond said. "She's in Essinger's new movie, so apparently there are no hard feelings."

"Is she? I would bet that Essinger cast her for the publicity. She's hot right now and he's capitalizing on it. That blockbuster she was in before was made by Essinger before they were married."

"Are they going to divorce?"

"Even the tabloids don't know," Collette said.

"I wonder . . ." Bond said.

"What?"

"If they do divorce, I wonder if Essinger will be upset about not being related to the Pont family fortune any more."

ELEVEN

THE HOUSE

Bond was convinced that Essinger was somehow involved with the Union's latest plot. Why would he have the tattoo if he weren't? What could they possibly want with a movie producer?

The night after Bond's visit to the television studio, he sat down in his hotel room at the Inter-continental to study the photographs he had taken in Essinger's office. Collette had blown them up to a readable size and they were as good as if they had obtained photocopies of the actual documents.

Bond studied the production schedule for *Pirate Island*. Even though it was difficult to say what the movie was about since he lacked a script, the locations gave Bond a pretty good idea that it was an action-adventure film to be shot mostly on water. The cost for special effects and second unit work was over half the complete budget. Bond found a sheet listing the salaries of principal players in the film—the stars, the director and the crew. Stuart Laurence, the star, was being paid $4 million. Tylyn Mignonne was being paid $1 million. The director was Dan Duling, who had directed Essinger's previous two pictures. He was being paid $1 million as well.

Bond saw something strange on the sheet, and at first he thought it might be a smudge. The second unit director and special effects coordinator, a man named Rick Fripp, was being paid $5 million!

More than anyone else on the picture. A London address was written beneath his name.

Bond got on the phone to London and spoke to Nigel.

"Hello, James, how is everything?"

"Fine, Nigel," Bond said. "Listen, can you look up a name for me? He's a movie special effects man, name of Rick Fripp. There's a London address." He read it aloud and asked Nigel to have him vetted.

Bond rang off and continued to look through the photographs. The taped-up picture of Tylyn Mignonne was set to the side, and he couldn't help glancing back at those bewitching eyes. He picked up the photo and sat back in the chair. Could she be involved in anything with the Union? Surely not. But one never knew . . .

The phone rang. It was Nigel.

"James," he said. "I ran Rick Fripp through the computer. He has a record. He served six years for manslaughter. Was released four years ago. Before that he had a long arrest record, mostly for petty crimes. There was an armed robbery charge, but he was acquitted."

"How is it that he can stay in the motion picture business?"

"I don't know. I suppose he's good at what he does. His record states that he is an expert in explosives, pyrotechnics. His work on films is primarily in that area."

"Thanks, Nigel. I'll be back in touch."

Bond hung up again and went out of the room. He went downstairs, bought a newspaper, sat in the Restaurant La Verrière, and had some strong black coffee. He thumbed through the news, noting that the bombing at the British Embassy in Tokyo was still a mystery. It had been a long time since Bond had been in Japan. He wondered if a trip to the Far East might not be in his future.

He continued through the paper and happened to come across the entertainment section, something he rarely looked at. His heart skipped a beat when he saw the photo, a full quarter page in size.

There she was, Tylyn Mignonne, dressed in a tantalizing wrap similar to the one she was wearing on the billboard. It was an advertisement for Indecent Exposure clothing. Next to the ad was a "personality profile" on Tylyn, accompanied by several other photographs depicting stages of her career: catwalk shots, head shots and fashion shots.

He read with interest that Tylyn had attended university in Paris after growing up in Hollywood with her famous father and mother. She elected to remain in France and become a model. After several very successful years at modeling, she tried her hand at design and created Indecent Exposure. Now her clothing line was sold all over Europe and she was hoping to open a retail store in America in the coming year.

Her acting career was jumpstarted with a small role in a French art film that had received good notices at the Cannes Film Festival a few years ago. A larger role for the same director followed that, and it proved to be a popular "foreign film" in America. Hollywood became interested and she eventually made an American blockbuster that did well internationally.

Although she hadn't made any films for a couple of years, now she was poised to co-star with Stuart Laurence in *Pirate Island*, a film to be produced by her husband, Léon Essinger.

There was no mention that they were currently separated.

The article went on to say that Tylyn enjoyed riding as a lifelong hobby. In fact, she owned a stud farm in the south of France, near Antibes. She was quoted as saying that she always went there, to her "home away from home," when she wanted to escape the hectic life of a supermodel and actress. Now twenty-nine years old, Tylyn said that she was actually looking forward to her thirties and that she hoped to correct some of the choices she had made in her personal life while in her twenties.

Bond looked at the Indecent Exposure ad again. It stated that there was an exclusive fashion show taking place the next day at the Louvre.

Bond grabbed his mobile and called Bertrand Collette.

"Internet Works," the Frenchman answered.

"I need a favor," Bond said.

"I will do my best. What is it?"

"There's an Indecent Exposure fashion show at the Louvre tomorrow at noon. Can you get me in? Maybe arrange for *Pop World* to interview Tylyn Mignonne?"

Collette laughed. "My friend, I think you have been struck by a thunderbolt. I will see what I can do."

Bond rang off and smiled. He hadn't looked forward to meeting a girl this much in a long, long time.

Mathis had parked the rental car on the side of the road, carefully climbed over the barbed-wire fence, and walked in the darkness toward the thick trees. Using a specially built pen light with a high intensity beam, he made his way through the thick of the *maquis* and found the menhirs.

In the moonlight, they were indescribably eerie. The limestone statues were phallus-shaped and stood between four and six feet tall. On the heads were rudimentary carvings of human faces. Erosion had smoothed them down considerably, so much so that what little carving had been done to the stone was barely visible. They were similar to the menhirs that could be found at the prehistoric site of Filitosa, one that was open to the public.

This one wasn't.

Before leaving the DGSE, Mathis had equipped himself with topographical and survey maps of Corsica. He had studied them carefully, pinpointing where the archaeological sites were located in relation to Sartène. He could see what pieces of land were privately owned and what was owned by the government or by villages. There were indeed a few patches of privately owned property north of Sartène and eastward on the road toward Levie. The prehistoric sites of Cucuruzzu and Capula were in that direction as well. Mathis figured that it was highly probable that other prehistoric artifacts existed on the private properties. After all, the Filitosa site was inhabited and still owned by the same family who had discovered it.

Which lot was *Le Gérant's?*

After making inquiries at the Cucuruzzu/Capula guest services center, he had learned that a strange rich man had taken over a nearby property and had built a house there. The land had been in one family for generations.

Mathis had waited until nightfall, then had driven close to where he thought it might be. Sure enough, a gate with the word *"Privé"* and a barbed-wire fence kept animals and the curious out. An unpaved road led from the gate up a hill, into the dense brush. Somewhere back there was a house.

Now, out of breath from the exertion of climbing the hill and fighting the thick foliage, Mathis finally came upon a clearing. There it was, some thirty meters away—a large two-story building, the silhouette of which, in the dark, looked like yet another Corsican old town citadel. There were ridges in the high walls, but the roof was flat, like homes in Morocco. Lights were on in two windows. Dark outlines of the mountains surrounding the property imbued the locale with a foreboding omnipresence. What was especially unusual was that the house was surrounded by a second wire fence. Mathis couldn't see the posted signs clearly, but he wagered that the fence was electrified.

He crept out of the woods and into the clearing. He couldn't see that anyone was about, so he kept going. When he made it to the second fence, which did indeed display warnings for "electrical shock," he lay flat on the ground to catch his breath again. From there, he could see that the building was made of stone and wood and seemed to reflect no particular style of architecture, except, perhaps, a blending of Arabic and French, like exquisite palaces in Tangier. The Malcolm Forbes Museum came to mind.

What should he do? Should he call someone and report his findings? Or should he try to get tangible proof that *Le Gérant* really lived here? If only he could catch sight of him.

Mathis crept silently around the fence, eventually coming to the side of the house where vehicles were parked. A garage was open and the Rolls-Royce was sitting inside. A 4 × 4 and two other cars were parked in the drive.

He could hear voices approaching.

Two men stepped out of the garage and lit cigarettes. They spoke in Corsican, looking up at the clear, star-studded sky. Mathis shrank into the shadows, willing himself to be as still as one of the menhirs that surrounded the property.

Then, Mathis' heart nearly stopped when he heard the sound of a car coming up the road toward the house. It would surely turn into the drive to park there with the rest of the vehicles. The headlamps would have to pass over him to do so.

He leaped to the ground just as the car, a sleek Porsche, pulled around, brightly illuminating the area. It stopped near the two men. Mathis looked up from the ground and saw another man get out of the Porsche.

"*Bonjour,* Antoine," one of the smokers said.

Antoine, a small, wiry man, greeted the two men and said something that made them laugh.

And then—horror!—Mathis noticed that a guard was patrolling the outside perimeter of the electrified fence and was headed his way. If he didn't move quickly, the man would surely notice him in a few seconds!

Mathis stayed perfectly still in the grass. The guard walked slowly, scanning the trees, looking away from the house. Closer . . . closer . . . then the man's boot grazed Mathis' side.

"What the—?" the man mumbled, momentarily off balance.

Mathis pushed the guard and did his best to get up and run.

"Stop!" he heard the man shout.

Mathis ran as hard as he could toward the trees, but the weight he had put on in recent years was a hindrance. Out of the corner of his eye, he could see that the guard was behind him, pounding the ground with large, muscular legs.

Ten more meters! Mathis ignored the pain in his chest as he mustered all of his energy, but it was useless. The guard tackled him and they fell hard on the ground. The impact knocked the wind out of Mathis.

The guard turned him over and slugged him hard in the face, stunning him.

———•———

He recovered his senses as they were dragging him to the house. Mathis attempted to struggle and get away, but the three of them held him. A quick kick in the ribs took the fight out of him.

He was brought inside and taken to a spacious room equipped with nothing more than benches, chairs and cabinets. It was some kind of waiting area, probably for the guards. They threw him on the floor.

A door opened and a man entered the room. He stood silently until Mathis was able to look up.

It was Pierre Rodiac. Aka Olivier Cesari. Aka *Le Gérant*.

"Monsieur Mathis," the blind man said. He didn't look at Mathis, of course. He simply stared straight ahead, his dead eyes focused on nothing in particular. "Welcome. You were successful in tracking me down. Yes, I knew you were following me the first time we were in the same room together in Monte Carlo. Don't you think that *Le Gérant* would know? Tsk tsk . . . I thought you were smarter than that, Monsieur Mathis. The question is who else knows that you are here?"

"Everyone," Mathis whispered. "They all know."

"Liar," Cesari said softly. "You have left the DGSE and are working as a renegade. The only person you are in contact with is a close friend of yours. Someone who works for another intelligence agency. Someone I would love to meet. Do you think you could arrange an introduction?"

"I don't know what you're talking about."

"Oh, I think you do," *Le Gérant* said. "Mister James Bond . . . Your friend and ally. Do you think you could direct him in our direction? Perhaps send him a note? Yes?"

"Go to hell," Mathis spat.

Le Gérant laughed. He circled Mathis, never once reaching out in front of him to make sure he wouldn't walk into anything. He knew exactly where the furniture was.

"Antoine?" he called.

"Yes, monsieur," Antoine said. He was standing by the door.

"There is a walking cane next to the bookcase over there. Would you throw it to me?"

Antoine found it. It was a black cane with a silver wolf's head handle. Jean threw it and *Le Gérant* caught it in mid-air. He never once flinched or moved his head. His hazy eyes were focused on the nothingness straight ahead of him.

"Now," he said to Mathis, "you are going to co-operate, isn't that right?"

"Never," Mathis said.

The cane came down hard on Mathis' back.

Le Gérant took two steps around Mathis and let the cane fly again. Mathis curled into a ball, attempting to ward off the blows.

"Take him outside and soften him up," *Le Gérant* said. "And then we'll let Doctor Gerowitz have a look at him."

The three men dragged Mathis outside. *Le Gérant* left the room, walked down a white, plain corridor, until he came to his own quarters, which were tastefully furnished with elegant furniture, a stereo system, bar, and other amenities of comfort. He sat down after pouring himself a cognac and putting on his favorite piece of music, Rimsky-Korsakov's *Scheherazade*. He closed his eyes as the lovely strains of the violins filled the room.

The music didn't quite drown out Mathis' screams.

TWELVE

THE GIRL

THE SPECTACULAR I. M. PEI PYRAMID ENTRANCE TO THE MUSÉE DU LOUVRE never failed to impress Bond. While it had its critics, the incongruous nature of a pyramid made of glass and steel tubing, surrounded by a structure that saw its origins in the thirteenth century, was the most impressive thing about it. The juxtaposition was not lost on Bond.

The museum was closed to the public on Tuesdays, so all special events were held on that day. The fashion show was scheduled to begin at 11:30 in the morning. Bond arrived at the Louvre entrance at 11:15 dressed smartly in a dark gray Savile Row suit. He joined the gathering crowd in the roped-off section in front of the pyramid to wait for the doors to open. A large banner had been erected across the entrance proclaiming, "Indecent Exposure—NOW!" The words were written in script over a faint reproduction of Tylyn's eyes. Bond thought that he might recognize them anywhere now.

The others in the crowd were journalists, fashion photographers and members of the elite who were lucky enough to receive an invitation. Several groups with television cameras were also preparing to descend into the museum for the event.

The sun was shining brightly, bouncing off the pyramid glass into Bond's eyes. He turned to avoid the glare and noticed several museum security guards conversing with another man in a dark green security uniform that was obviously from a different company. Bond couldn't hear what they were saying, but the man seemed to be trying to talk his way into the show. The museum guards were shaking their heads and looking at his credentials. After a moment, though, they allowed him over the barrier. The man went through the doors and disappeared inside the pyramid.

Finally, at 11:25, the guards removed the rope and ushered the people inside, checking invitations as they walked through. Bond got inside and stepped onto the escalator that descended into the spacious, bright reception area. The stage and catwalk had been set up just beyond the circular staircase that led to the ground floor. Numbered folding chairs surrounded the catwalk, which jutted out toward the CyberLouvre, the boutiques, and the Carrousel du Louvre. Bond thought it was a rather odd place for a fashion show, but apparently the museum was a popular spot for such events.

Shostakovich was booming out of portable speakers set up around the runway. A white tent, where the models could change and prepare to make their appearances, had been erected at the head of the catwalk and behind the stage. Another banner with the words "Indecent Exposure" hung over the curtained opening on the stage.

The audience was buzzing with the excitement in the air. Bond, too, felt twangs of anticipation as he found his seat, two rows back from the center of the catwalk. Not bad.

At 11:40, the lights dimmed slightly and spotlights operated by men on pedestals hit the curtain on stage. The audience applauded as the music switched to a sensuous, rhythmic jazz-rock piece accentuated by heavy bass and drums.

A tall blonde model stepped through the curtain wearing nothing but a black brassière, panties, and high heels. Bond thought that she looked more like a courtesan than a fashion model, but he wasn't complaining.

The expressionless girl walked down the catwalk as the cameras flashed around her. By the time she swiveled to head back to the tent, another girl, a shapely black woman, emerged wearing a red brassière and panties, but she had added a garter belt and stockings. The next girl, a brunette, had added a silk robe that flowed behind her as she walked. Each successive model added another piece of clothing. Bond got it—the girls were "dressing" before the audience's eyes. The sixth model in the set was fully dressed in a magnificent transparent evening gown that provided hints of all the various undergarments the other models had worn. The six girls returned to the catwalk and gave a slight bow, then slipped back into the tent.

The music and lights changed. It was time for something dramatic.

When she stepped out of the curtain, the audience went wild with applause. Bond actually felt his heart rate increase.

Tylyn Mignonne was arguably the most beautiful girl he'd ever seen, and he had certainly seen many. She was tall, naturally, with long legs that seemed to move like those of a sleek gazelle. Her dark brown hair was still cut short, the fringe swept to the side to reveal a bit of forehead. She was not terribly thin, like many models. She had a fine figure, a firm one that exhibited the physique of a girl who got a lot of exercise but managed to eat well too. Her breasts were not particularly large, but, in Bond's mind, they were perfectly adequate handfuls.

She was wearing the wraparound he had seen her in on the billboard, and it revealed much more than it concealed. The rounded, shiny tops of her breasts reflected the lights, and her undulating, flat stomach was completely bare. The wrap covered her waist and hips but just nearly screened the cleft between her legs, which were bare down to the high heels.

As Tylyn walked down the catwalk, the men in the audience whistled and cheered. She responded with warm smiles and waves. Her strong presence, her charisma and her self-confidence immediately struck Bond. Unlike the other models, who remained relatively humorless and stone-faced throughout the show, Tylyn was obviously enjoying every second. She loved being under the spotlights, having the flashes go off non-stop around her, and receiving the attention of the men in the audience. She had a rapport with the people that the others didn't attempt to create. Bond liked that. He had assumed that models never interacted with the audience while on the catwalk. However, she would pause every now and then to greet someone she knew, squatting down to give them a hug or accept a long-stemmed rose.

Tylyn completed the walk and went back into the tent as the show continued with a new set of fashions, beginning with the blonde in a chemise/panties combination. Bond now understood the allure of fashion shows and why they were always hot tickets. They were indescribably sexy, even when the models were fully dressed. There was something about watching a beautiful woman display herself to a crowd—not like a stripper, who teased her audience with nothing left to the imagination. She was a girl with a secret; a woman who tantalized men with the fantasy that she *might* be willing to show them something. She was the one in charge and would decide when and where that would happen.

The Indecent Exposure line was just what it promised—chic clothing that was sexy and revealing, yet tasteful enough to wear in public. Bond could imagine that much of it would be worn to things like celebrity parties, awards dinners, and the like. This wasn't run-of-the-mill boudoir wear. Tylyn was indeed a clever designer.

The entire show lasted about twenty minutes. Bond had counted ten different models who had changed clothes at least three times each. Tylyn, the last woman on stage, ended the event by leading the rest of the girls out onto the catwalk together. She received thunderous applause and cries of "Bravo!" as she accepted a bouquet of roses from two of the models.

A cocktail reception was held afterward in the Restaurant Le Grand Louvre, a small room next to the café. Glasses of champagne were handed out to every guest, along with a "goody bag" of Indecent Exposure promotional materials. Waiters circulated the room with plates of canapés as members of the audience mingled. The models joined the crowd a few moments later.

Bond stood to one side and waited until Tylyn made her entrance. When she finally did, she was dressed simply in black Capri pants and a white silk blouse that was open at the midriff and tied above her navel. Bond liked women in Capri pants because they showed off their calves and ankles whilst keeping the rest of the legs tightly outlined but under cover. He watched her with interest as she greeted people, kissing their cheeks and allowing hers to be pecked. She warmly embraced several members of the press, playing the consummate public relations rep for her company. She might as well have been royalty.

As far as Bond was concerned, she was.

Finally, he edged his way toward her and caught her eye. She looked at him and smiled brightly, momentarily distracted by his dark, good looks.

"*Bonjour,*" she said.

Bond greeted her in French. "*Bonjour.* It was a lovely show. I'm from *Pop World* in England. The name's Bond. James Bond."

"Oh yes, Mister Bond, we're supposed to do an interview, right?" she said, making no attempt to hide the fact that she was pleased.

"That's right."

"Let's see, where could we . . . ?" she thought a second and then said, "Would you like to talk over lunch? I'm starving, and these crackers and things won't do the trick."

"I'd be delighted," Bond said.

"Great! Let me finish here and perhaps we could take a walk, find a café nearby?"

"Take your time, I'll be right here."

She gave him a nod and a little wave, then turned to the others who were dying to speak to her.

Bond stepped back and picked up another glass of champagne. Out of the corner of his eye, he noticed the security guard in the green uniform standing near the emergency exit sign.

The man was looking at him, but when Bond's eyes met his, he turned and walked out of the room.

They left the Louvre under the scrutiny of the *paparazzi* and fans. Bond shielded his face the best he could as the cameras went off. He was uncomfortable being in the limelight like this and hoped that their picture wouldn't be on the front page of a gossip paper. "Tylyn Dating Mystery Man" . . . it was all he needed.

Nevertheless, he couldn't help but feel a slight thrill at being in the company of such a glamorous and high-profile woman. Normally he would have shunned the prospect. He didn't want notoriety, for in his business, it could be dangerous. Too many times the women he had grown close to had met with . . . bad luck.

But as they pushed through the crowd and walked onto rue de Rivoli and then turned east, they lost the crowd and were on their own.

"That's better, isn't it?" she asked, keeping a fast pace. She spoke in English now, but Bond noted that it was the American variety. "You never think you're going to get rid of them, but surprisingly you always do."

"How can you stand it?" Bond asked. "It would drive me mad."

She shrugged. "I'm used to it. It's part of the life, I suppose. You have to give up certain things, a bit of your privacy . . . Where would you like to go?"

"It's your city," he said. "But I do know a little place not far from here." Paris, of course, was heavily populated with sidewalk cafés.

"Lead on, sir," she said with a smile.

He escorted her to rue St. Honoré and further east until they came to a café called Le Petit Mâchon. It was a charming, quiet place painted yellow and brown. The day's specials were listed on a blackboard that stood on the sidewalk with the small square tables. Tylyn and Bond were greeted warmly by the hostess, who allowed them to pick a table at the end, away from the other parties.

Bond ordered them two kir royales made with champagne and *crème de cassis* for aperitifs and then took a moment to enjoy looking at her fresh, vibrant face. He hadn't realized how long her eyelashes were until now.

"So, Mister Bond, what would you like to talk about?" she asked with a knowing smile.

"You, of course," he replied. "How do you manage to juggle so many different careers?"

She laughed. "I don't see it that way. It's all one career, really, isn't it? Fashion design is probably my first love, and of course I like to model. It's how I made my name. But I want to branch out, get more involved in film."

"I understand you've got a starring role in a new picture?"

"That's right. It's called *Pirate Island*. My—well, my husband is producing it. We're separated, though."

"Léon Essinger, right?"

"That's right. Anyway, it's a chance to act with Stuart Laurence, whom I adore, and it's probably going to be a big movie. The director is someone I like. He's very good. I think it will be a boost to my career. I've only made one other movie in Hollywood and this one will bring me more work there, I hope."

"What kind of part is it?" Bond asked, writing down her answers on a small notepad.

"It's an action-adventure story set in the future," she said. "It's about pirates on high-tech boats. Stuart plays the hero, a man who's trying to save his island from being taken over by the pirates. I play his 'woman' ." She chuckled. "There will probably be a lot of bodice ripping. I'll get to do a little of the action, but they've hired a real stuntwoman for the hard stuff."

"Tell me what you remember of your father," Bond said.

"He was always there for me when I was a little girl. He encouraged me to go into modeling, and he got me my first horse when I was six."

"What was it like to grow up with such a famous father?"

"I never really paid it any mind. He was just 'daddy' to me. I mean, I knew he was famous and that he made all these great films and had Oscars and all that, but when I was little I just thought that's what all fathers did. He died when I was pretty young. It wasn't until I was a teenager when I fully appreciated the contributions he made to the business."

"What does knowing you're the heiress to a vast Hollywood fortune do to your psyche? It must make you deliriously happy."

She laughed. "I'm usually deliriously happy, most of the time anyway, but that's not the reason why. I never think about the money my family has. I've gone out and made my own money, you know.

When I model, I'm paid well. I don't just model exclusively for my own company. If the offer is good, or if it looks like fun, I'm there."

"What made you leave Hollywood?"

"I'm French, aren't I? I was tired of California. I feel more at home here. I suppose if my acting career takes off I'll have to go back, but then there are plenty of actors who manage to work and not live in Hollywood."

"How did you get your name?" Bond asked.

"Tylyn? Well, it's not French, is it?" She laughed. "My mother was expecting a boy and she already had 'Timothy' picked out. Naturally, when I came out it was a surprise to everyone! She had to scramble to come up with a name for a girl that began with a 'T'. She put 'Ty' and 'Lyn' together and came up with 'Tylyn'."

Bond thought that she was an amazing girl. She was outgoing, articulate, and intelligent. He could feel her energy and *joie de vivre,* and it was infectious.

"Tell me about your hobbies. What does Tylyn do when she's not working?" he asked.

"Horses. And then there are horses. Oh, and I also like horses," she said, then laughed. "You know I breed them? I love horses."

"I knew that. It's in the south of France, right?"

"Yes, it's a small equestrian center in Mougins, near Antibes. I live there when I'm not in Paris. I keep a small staff there who run things when I'm gone. I breed horses and sell them to various riding schools and so on. When I'm really stressed out I like to go there and get on Commander, my favorite horse, and ride for hours through the forests."

Bond mused that he knew a certain commander who would like a ride.

"How much time do you get to spend there?" he asked.

"More than you might think. I have a flat here, but if there's nothing happening at the Indecent Exposure studio then I go to Mougins. I have a workshop there and can work on clothing design if I need to. Oh, here's a card with the address . . ." She reached into her handbag, found a card, and handed it to him. "You should come around and take a look, you might find it useful for your article."

Bond glanced at the card and pocketed it. "Thank you. I might enjoy that. So other than horses . . . ?"

"I read a lot. There's always a book by my bed. I love mysteries and thrillers. I like to dance. There's nothing more romantic than a man who can dance. I enjoy sports, but I'm not very good at anything but riding."

"You were educated in California?"

She nodded. "Through high school, but then I went to college here. I studied languages here because for some reason in America they don't stress that. I think it's important to speak other languages."

"What else do you speak?"

"Besides French? English, German, and Italian. Some Spanish and a tiny bit of Russian."

"Impressive," Bond said.

She shrugged it off. "It's no big deal. What about you? Have you always been a journalist?"

Bond smiled to himself. "No. I used to be a civil servant. But my life is quite uninteresting compared to yours."

"Have you ever considered modeling?" she asked. "You have *killer* looks."

Bond almost laughed. "No, I've never considered it. But thanks, I think."

"No, really, you have this dark dangerous look that women just eat up," she said, reaching out to touch his hand. "But you probably know that already."

The blonde waitress interrupted them with the meals they had ordered. They both had mixed green salads with veal, croutons, tomatoes and goat's cheese. Tylyn had *côte de veau à la crème d'estragon* for the main course, while Bond had *quenelles de brochet fraîches à la crème d'étrilles*; pike with crab sauce. They shared a bottle of Pouilly Fuissé, which Bond found slightly disappointing, but it was adequate. The food, though, was superb.

As the waitress walked away, Tylyn giggled to herself.

"What's funny?" he asked.

"I just remembered a blonde joke. Want to hear it?"

"Certainly."

"A blonde's boyfriend gave her a mobile phone for her birthday. When she was out of the house, he decided to call her and see how it worked. She answered and was thrilled. 'Hi honey!' she said. 'The phone works great! But how did you know I was at the hairdresser?'"

They both laughed and continued eating.

She ate like a man, Bond thought. She wasn't dainty at all, but all she had to do to retain her femininity was blink those lovely eyes with the deliciously long lashes, lick her lips when she was tasting something, and smile—which she did a lot. In fact, she laughed quite a bit and Bond liked that. It seemed that everything amused this girl. She was damned attractive.

Careful, Bond told himself. She was way too famous to get involved with. Veer the conversation toward business. Find out more about her husband . . .

"You know, I'd like to interview your husband. He seems like quite the character," he said nonchalantly.

She snorted. "Léon? He's a pig. Why would you want to talk to him? I'm much more interesting." She laughed again.

"I have no doubt about that," Bond said.

"Besides, he rarely meets the press these days," she said. "Ever since the trouble he had in America. You know about that . . ."

Bond nodded.

"I suppose we're still friends. After all, I'm going to act in his movie," she said.

"Then I take it that the separation is temporary?"

For the first time she frowned. "I don't want to talk about that. Léon and I have an agreement not to talk to journalists about our separation."

"Fair enough. When do you start shooting?"

"In a couple of days. In fact, I'm going to have to leave soon, I hope you don't mind. I have to catch a plane to Nice in a few hours. I want to spend tomorrow at my home in Mougins. I need a good ride before I start work the following day."

She gave him a look that Bond could have sworn was an invitation.

When he didn't respond, she continued. "The next day we have to meet in Monte Carlo for some awful press event. I usually hate talking to the press, but somehow I don't mind talking to you." She laughed again so adorably that Bond wanted to hug her.

"Anyway," she said, "we start shooting the day after the thing in Monte Carlo. In Corsica. If you want to drop by the set, I think I could swing it."

She was after him! Bond thought. That was three times that she had been the aggressor. He simply couldn't resist this girl.

"Perhaps you'll see me in Monte Carlo," he said.

"I hope so." She wiped her mouth with the napkin and said, "This was fun. Did you get everything you needed?"

"Yes, for now anyway, thank you."

"I must run." They both stood and she held out her hand. It was soft, warm, and heavenly. "Thanks very much for the lunch. I hope to see you again, Mister Bond."

"Call me James."

"All right, James. *Au revoir.*"

And she was gone.

Bond sat back down and ordered coffee. He watched her back as she hurried up the street and waved for a taxi.

Somebody pinch me, Bond thought. She was simply too good to be true.

As he gazed out over the street, he noticed the gym across the road. And there he was—the man wearing the dark green security uniform was inside the gym, looking at him from the window. The same man from the Louvre.

What the hell do you want, you bastard? Bond thought to himself. Was he a flunky for Léon Essinger? Perhaps keeping tabs on his wife?

The man turned away and disappeared as Bond raised his coffee cup in salute.

THIRTEEN

THE FIRST VISIT

THE LETTER THAT RENÉ MATHIS HAD WRITTEN TO JAMES BOND HAD AN unfortunate unscheduled trip. The receptionist at the hotel in Calvi had forgotten about it and didn't mail it until two days after Mathis had given it to her. Then, a careless letter sorter in the Calvi post office accidentally dropped the envelope into a bin that was meant for mail traveling to Italy.

When Andrea Carlo, a postman in Milan, came across the letter more than a week after Mathis had sent it, he was in a destructive mood. His wife had just given birth to their sixth child, and he was worried about how they were going to make ends meet. His boss at the post office was a stingy crook and he had aspirations to quit his day job to become a writer.

He looked at the envelope and decided to play a little joke. Instead of dropping the letter into the bin meant for the United Kingdom, he put it in the one targeted for America.

It was only a matter of good fortune that when the envelope arrived in New York three days later, an efficient postal worker caught the error and immediately dropped it in the bag en route to the UK.

Unfortunately, the letter would arrive at MI6 nearly two weeks late.

The day after his lunch with Tylyn, Bond checked out of his hotel, left a voice message for Bertrand and drove south out of Paris. He took the A6 toward Lyons, a journey that he always enjoyed. He began to feel much better about France after he had left the bustling metropolis of Paris. It was a pleasure to go cross-country.

After passing through Lyons, the country's second largest city and the home of Interpol, Bond got on the A43, which in turn became the A48 to travel southeast into the mountains toward Grenoble. He probably could have avoided the French Alps by taking a detour south of Lyons, but Bond enjoyed the scenery. Grenoble was situated in a broad valley and surrounded by spectacular mountains—the Chartreuse to the north, the Vercors to the southwest, and Alpine peaks stretching east to Italy.

As he left Grenoble and headed toward the Côte d'Azur, Bond noticed a dark green van gaining on him. Bond increased his speed, passing several cars, but the van's driver insisted on keeping up with him.

Fine, Bond thought. Let's see who this is.

Bond slowed down so that the van was soon right on his bumper. The van could easily pass him if that's what the driver wanted to do. Sure enough, after a few moments, the van pulled into the left lane and sped past Bond. It was difficult to see inside, for the windows were tinted. But what surprised Bond was that the side of the van displayed the words, *"Securité Vert."* Bond was fairly sure that this was the agency that employed the man he had seen at the Louvre and at the gym across the street from the sidewalk café yesterday.

The van was now in front of him and the driver decreased his speed. Now it was Bond's turn to tailgate. What sort of game were they playing? Bond threw the car into lower gear and pulled into the left lane, almost wishing that the car still contained some of Boothroyd's extras. He accelerated and pushed past the van, then swung back into the right lane. He then increased his speed and moved way ahead of the van very quickly. The driver didn't show any inclination to follow him this time, leaving Bond perplexed as to what all that was about.

As he was approaching Grasse on the N85, Bond pulled over to fill up with petrol. It was a self-service facility, so he got out, swiped his card for 500 francs, and stood holding the nozzle while he surveyed the road.

From nowhere, the green van appeared and pulled into the service station. It stopped at the pumps directly across from the Aston Martin. The passenger door opened and the man Bond had seen at the Louvre stepped out. Bond thought quickly, analyzing the situation and looking at all his options should the man try anything.

He was large and tanned, with curly black hair and the broken nose of a boxer or wrestler. He still wore the security guard uniform. Up close, Bond thought that he looked vaguely familiar, someone from the deep past.

"*Monsieur,*" he said, then continued in English. "My boss would like a word with you."

Bond kept his hand on the petrol nozzle. "Is that so?" he asked. "And who might that be?"

"If you would be so kind as to follow us, he is waiting."

"Sorry, I was taught to never go anywhere with strangers," Bond said.

The man sighed. "I'm afraid I must insist," he said. He started to draw a gun, but wasn't fast enough.

Bond pulled the nozzle out of his car and doused the man with petrol, simultaneously bending to the side and kicking out with his left foot. The gun went flying. Bond dropped the nozzle, then gracefully spun around and kicked the man in the face with his right foot, knocking him to the ground. Bond then reached into his pocket, grabbed the Ronson lighter, and flicked it on.

The man lay sprawled on the pavement, looking up at Bond in terror. His shirt was soaked in petrol.

Bond held the lit Ronson in front of him and said, "Want to play catch?"

The man shook his head.

Bond reached down and picked up the gun. It was a Smith & Wesson .38. He emptied the cylinder and tossed the empty gun to the man. "Go on. Get the hell out of here. And tell your boss that if he wants to see me, he should make an appointment like anyone else."

Bond casually returned to his car, put the cap back on his tank, and got inside the Aston Martin. He pulled out of the service station, squealing the wheels as he sped out onto the highway.

That had felt good. Bond relished the electricity of danger. It was the best stimulant on the planet. He basked in the sensation for a while in silence, waiting for the van to reappear behind him. Surely they would continue the pursuit, and Bond was looking forward to a confrontation.

As expected, a few minutes later the van was behind the Aston Martin again. It was gaining on him, but Bond threw the car into low gear and shot ahead. He swerved in and out of traffic, putting some distance between him and the van. Soon he came upon another vehicle traveling slowly in his lane. It was another green van, identical to the *Securité Vert* van that had been following him all day.

He decelerated so that he wouldn't come too close to it. However, the van behind had gained on him. Now he was boxed in between the two.

If only he had the car's machine guns! Just a rocket or two!

The road made a sharp bend between two mountains, forcing the vehicles to slow down. Bond gripped the wheel and decided to take a risk. He pulled out into the left lane and stepped down hard. The Aston Martin roared ahead of the first van and was about to shift back into the right lane when a third green van appeared in front of him, headed straight for the car. Bond slammed on the brakes and spun the wheel to the right, knocking the first van hard so that it veered off the road and scraped against the rocks on the side of the mountain. Bond managed to pull over to the right as the oncoming van zoomed past him. The road continued to curve around the mountain, leading right into a tunnel. Bond accelerated again, hoping to lose them there. But as he approached the tunnel, he saw two sets of headlamps come on, aiming right at him.

There was no way out.

Bond screeched to a stop just outside the tunnel. He flipped open the compartment that held the Walther P99, grabbed the gun, and waited to see what they were going to do. The three vans, one slightly disabled, pulled up behind him. The doors opened and several armed men got out. Two were carrying sub-machine-guns. The man with the doused shirt gestured with his reloaded Smith & Wesson for Bond to get out of the car.

Bond aimed the Walther at the man's head as he got out of the Aston Martin.

"I'll take at least one of you with me," he said.

"We don't want anyone hurt," the man said. "Please, Mister Bond. Our boss is right inside the tunnel."

Bond didn't want to take his eyes off the security guard, but he dared to glance into the darkness. One of the cars inside started its motor and inched out into the sunlight. A black stretch limousine pulled up between Bond and the security guard, and then the window glided down.

The man in the back of the limousine had a brown, crinkled face shaped like a walnut.

My God! Bond thought.

The man had aged. The black hair had turned completely white, but the dark eyes hadn't changed at all.

It was really he, the head of the Corsican mafia, Marc-Ange Draco. Bond's former father-in-law.

Bond was flabbergasted, completely speechless, standing outside the Aston Martin on a road somewhere in France and facing a man he thought he'd never see again.

"Don't look like you've seen a ghost, James, it's really me," the man said, smiling.

"My God, Marc-Ange, I . . . we all—heard you were *dead! Years* ago!" Bond said in a half-whisper.

Draco laughed. It was a laugh Bond remembered from another time.

"Merely rumors," Draco said happily. "You'd be surprised what disappearing can do for you if you want to get away from it all. That's what I did. I got out of circulation for a while and no one ever saw me—so everyone *assumed* I was dead. How long has it been, James?"

"Forever," Bond said. There was a brief awkward moment as the two men were suddenly at a loss for words. Then they embraced as family.

When they parted, Draco asked, "How have you been, James?"

"I'm fine, Marc-Ange, and you?"

The smallish man shrugged his unusually broad shoulders. "Not bad."

There was another uncomfortable moment. Bond had never made a point of staying in touch with Draco after Tracy's death. After all, the man was a criminal. But the main reason for not doing so was because it brought back painful memories of a woman he had loved and lost.

Draco finally said, "Come sit in the limousine and let's talk."

Uh-oh. Bond felt a pang in the pit of his stomach. Are today's events a repeat of what happened long ago? The first time Bond had met Marc-Ange Draco, he had been forcefully taken to the man. Draco's charm had disarmed Bond, and they ended up talking as friends. Then Draco asked Bond for a "favor," and what a favor it was. He wanted him to marry his daughter, Tracy.

What was Draco going to ask him *now?*

It was cool in the air-conditioned interior, which was done up in expensive leather and sported a well-stocked bar. Draco still lived in his own brand of splendor.

"I know what you're thinking, James," Draco said. "You're wondering if I'm still in the, uhm, *business*. Once again, I must implore upon you to stay behind the Herkos Odonton with regard to what I'm about to tell you."

Bond smiled. "Herkos Odonton" was an expression Draco used to mean that the listener must keep what he heard a secret.

"The hedge of my teeth," Bond said, literally defining the term.

Draco twisted to the bar. "Drink?"

"Please," Bond said.

Draco dropped a couple of ice cubes into each of two Waterford pint glasses, then picked up a bottle of I.W. Harper bourbon and poured a generous measure into each glass. He set the drinks, a siphon of soda and a flagon of iced water on a small tray table that unfolded between them.

They clinked glasses and said, "Cheers," together.

"But before I get to business, first tell me about yourself, James. I follow your career, you know," Marc-Ange said. "I have my sources. You continue to be a credit to your service. I congratulate you."

"Thanks," Bond said. "I suppose I'm fine. There's nothing to tell. I haven't changed much."

"No, you haven't," Draco said. "The years have been kind to you. Me—I just keep getting fatter. For a while it was the hair. My hair kept getting whiter. Now it's completely white. So I complain about my weight now."

While Draco intended his comments to be humorous, Bond detected an intangible sadness about the man. The earlier laughing had been abrupt and was finished with quickly. The boisterous, interminably optimistic Marc-Ange Draco he had known years ago was different now. Bond surmised that he had undergone some kind of tragedy.

"So, you want to know if I'm still a crook, yes?" Draco asked.

"If you'd care to tell me, Marc-Ange," Bond said.

"Very well," Draco said, taking a sip of bourbon. "The short answer is 'yes', I am still a crook. Now would you like the long answer?"

"That's up to you."

Draco paused to down his entire glass, then poured himself another. Then he spoke slowly and earnestly.

"After Teresa's de—uhm, after Tracy's *murder,* I withdrew from public life. The organisation was run by my lieutenant, Ché-Ché—you remember Ché-Ché, James?" He pointed to the man outside with the broken nose. No wonder he had looked familiar to Bond! Ché-Ché le Persuadeur had been a long-time associate of Draco's. Ché-Ché had changed his shirt and cleaned himself up, but he didn't look particularly cheerful.

"Now I do," Bond replied. "Tell him that I hope there are no hard feelings."

"Don't worry about it. He did a fine job while I . . . went into hiding. I was not a happy man, James, I admit it. The loss of Tracy was quite overwhelming. At first I blamed you, and I was angry with you, but common sense prevailed. I completely understand that it wasn't your fault. And you exacted revenge for us both, and for that I am grateful. In many ways, it was my fault. I pushed her into the arms of a man who lived on the edge in his profession. Like me. But never mind that, it's the past.

"Around the time that rumors of my death began to circulate, there was trouble within the Union Corse. One of my lieutenants, Toussaint, left to form a rival syndicate. There was a war. I decided to let them fight it out, just to see who was stronger. I stayed completely away, which is why everyone thought I was dead except my most trusted associates. I have only a handful of them these days."

Draco offered Bond a cigar, but he refused, preferring to smoke one of his own specially made cigarettes provided by Tor Importers. They contained a unique blend of Balkan Yenidje and Turkish Latakia tobaccos that Bond craved, especially with bourbon.

Draco lit his cigar and continued. "About nine years ago, my life turned around. I climbed out of my depression. I met a woman . . . a girl, really . . . she was French . . . and we fell in love. It didn't matter that she had barely come of age. We got married in Corsica."

Draco wouldn't look at Bond now. Instead, he gazed out the car window at the French countryside.

"We had a child together. A daughter. James, I had found a new lease on life. I didn't want to be a crook any more. I let Ché-Ché run everything while I was happy again for the first time in as long as I could remember."

Bond saw the bomb coming before Draco dropped it.

"Earlier this year, they met with . . . an accident," Draco said in as steady a voice as he could. "My wife and daughter. Together. Killed. So I have been in mourning for the last several months."

"I'm sorry, Marc-Ange," Bond said. He didn't know what else to do.

Draco nodded, his eyes brimming with moisture. "Since then, yes, I have returned to my work. The business is not what it was. We don't call ourselves the Union Corse. My small group of men still run a Corsican mafia, if you really want to call it that. For me, it's just business."

Bond knew that Draco meant the "business" of common racketeering crimes—prostitution, money laundering, gambling, smuggling and sometimes murder.

"Don't get me wrong," Draco said. "I own some legitimate businesses as well. A security agency, as you can see, a real estate company, a chain of tobacco shops . . ."

"So it was you who had me watched yesterday in Paris," Bond said. He gestured to the green security vans.

Draco shrugged again.

"What happened to your other men?" Bond asked.

"Ah! That's why I invited you to have a talk with me. Toussaint and his merry followers joined a little organisation you know as the Union."

Bond felt a sudden burst of adrenaline. Of course! Draco had his fingers everywhere in France. As the Capu had once found a clue pointing to the whereabouts of Ernst Stavro Blofeld, Draco could possibly help Bond again.

"Marc-Ange, can you tell me anything about them? Do you know where their headquarters are?" Bond asked.

"Don't be so impatient, James," Draco said, smiling. "No, I don't know where *Le Gérant* is, but I certainly *know* him."

"Do tell," Bond said.

"His name is Olivier Cesari. I knew his father well. Joseph. He was one of my lieutenants in the old Union Corse."

Bond raised his eyebrows. "I thought he was in the perfume business."

"He was. That was his day job. He did quite well with it, too. In fact, our organisation financed his start-up. But he was also on my team and was quite useful. Joseph Cesari certainly passed on his ruthless qualities to his son. Whatever he wanted, he got. Anyway, I was quite close to both the father and the son. I adored young Olivier, and when he grew up, I could see that he was a fine, intelligent young man, despite his affliction of being blind. Now, he is the head of the most powerful criminal organisation in the world. He swallowed up my entire business after the war had torn us apart. The Union now operates where we used to. My small band of associates and I have had to work more in France rather than Corsica and have had to look for other means of doing business. So far, we have just squeezed out a living. Olivier Cesari keeps challenging my, er, territories. He has gone from being like a relative to becoming my worst enemy."

"This is extraordinary," Bond said.

"That it may be. But true. So, I am offering you, James, the chance to work together again. I want to find *Le Gérant* too. I know that he appears in public now, he has been seen in Corsica and in Monte Carlo. As I said, I don't know exactly where he is, but my sources tell me that he lives somewhere in Corsica now, and that's where the headquarters are located. I am still working on finding out where it is. In the meantime, I know for a fact that Olivier Cesari goes to the casino in Monte Carlo every Thursday night to gamble. He uses an alias, Pierre Rodiac."

Bond said, "Coincidentally, I'm going to Monte Carlo tomorrow and tomorrow is Thursday."

"Precisely," Draco said and beamed. "I thought that bit of information might be useful."

"Have you ever heard of a man named Léon Essinger?" Bond asked.

"Of course. Famous movie producer with a lot of legal problems," Draco said.

"I'm pretty sure he's involved with the Union."

Draco waved his hand and grimaced. "Forget it. You're—how do they say it in America?—you're 'barking up the wrong tree' with him."

"He is a Union member. I have proof."

"He may very well be. I wouldn't doubt it if the Union was helping him with his legal woes. Essinger is small potatoes. Go after the big fish."

"Perhaps you can help me with a related problem," Bond said. "I'm searching for a French colleague of mine, René Mathis. He disappeared not long ago while on the trail of *Le Gérant*. In fact, he was last seen in Monte Carlo."

"I know Monsieur Mathis, James. We met in the old days. I will see what I can find out for you. If he did find the Union headquarters, though, I doubt very seriously that he's still alive."

Bond nodded grimly.

"I'll be in touch," Draco said. "I'll also be watching your back, although you probably don't need my protection."

"Thanks," Bond said. "It will be interesting to meet Cesari face to face."

Draco reached into his pocket, pulled out a business card, and handed it to Bond. "Here is my number. You can call me from anywhere in the world, if you need to find me."

Bond pocketed the card and said, "Thank you."

"And now, I have another piece of information I need to impart to you." Draco took another drink.

"What's that?"

"The Union have just made a business deal with the Japanese terrorist, Goro Yoshida."

FOURTEEN

THE HORSES

BOND ARRIVED IN MOUGINS AS THE DAY TURNED FROM LATE AFTERNOON TO evening. He had consulted a road map and found the little road that led to Tylyn's home, which was located a few kilometers east of the village. He would have missed the turnoff had it not been for a small sign that said *Ferme Equestre—Privé*. Bond turned the DB5 onto the dirt road, rumbled over cattle grids, and drove the three kilometers to the house.

It was a lovely property in the forest, not far from Antibes, where the landscape was ideal for horse riding. The impressive main house looked like an inn, with two stories and numerous windows. It was mostly made of a dark, rustic wood and would not have been out of place in the American mid-west. Two smaller buildings of similar construction stood near the house, probably related to the horse business, and a large barn was behind. Bales of hay were stacked in front of the open barn doors, along with a forklift for loading and other equipment.

Bond pulled into a gravel parking area in front of the house and got out of the car. From here, he could see a path that led through the trees to the stables, which were built inside a large pen. The stables were quite large with blue and white striped roofs. There was probably room for at least ten horses. The paddock provided plenty of space for the horses to exercise outside.

A sign near the front door proclaimed *Ferme Equestre—Pension—Entraînement—Stages—Compétitions.* Bond knocked and waited until he heard footsteps on the other side. A frumpy woman in an apron answered it.

"*Oui?*" she asked.

Bond explained that he was looking for Tylyn and that she had invited him.

The housekeeper chattered a bit, then pointed toward the stables. Bond thanked her, turned and strolled down the path through the trees.

As he reached the paddock, he saw her. She was atop a beautiful Selle Français that was prancing around the fence. He was as fine a specimen as Bond had seen, with upright shoulders, a strong neck, compact body, and what appeared to be powerful hindquarters. The French saddle horse was completely brown except for white "sock" markings above its hoofs and a white "star" marking between its eyes. It was equipped with a black Western saddle and bridle.

Tylyn was attired, in part, in traditional dressage clothing—a canary waistcoat, white shirt with white stock, white breeches and black dress boots with spurs. All that was missing was a black tail-coat and top hat.

Bond stood and watched her as she took the horse around the paddock, performing various maneuvers—spins, rollbacks, flying lead changes and sliding stops. It was obvious that Tylyn was a pro. She handled the horse with self-confidence and a firm command, yet she was gentle and loving, speaking to him in French.

He finally made his presence known by stepping forward and standing by the gate. As Tylyn made another lap around the paddock, she saw him and beamed.

"James! What a surprise!"

"I decided to take you up on your offer to show me your home. I hope you don't mind," he said.

"Not at all! I was just giving Commander a little exercise. Perhaps you'd like to go riding? I was going to take him into the forest."

"I'd be delighted, although I'm not quite dressed for it."

"Don't be silly. You don't need to look like a jockey. Unlatch the gate there, and come on in. We'll see if we can find you a horse that's not too willful."

Bond opened the gate and closed it behind him as he walked into the paddock. Tylyn trotted the horse to him and swung her leg over and off. She landed on her feet and tied the reins to a pole. She murmured in the horse's ear and stroked him, saying that she would be right back.

"Did you drive from Paris?" she asked as they went into the stables.

"Yes, I parked in front of the house."

"That's fine. After our ride, I hope you'll stay for dinner. Chantal is a very good cook."

"That would be lovely."

There were several horses in the stables—black ones, white ones, brown ones. Tylyn ultimately picked a chestnut French Trotter.

"This is Lolita," Tylyn said. "She's fairly young, but she's well behaved. How are you on a horse?"

Bond shrugged. "I know how to make them go, turn, and stop. Changing gears can be tricky sometimes, but parallel parking is relatively simple."

Tylyn laughed. "I think you'll do fine." She deftly put the bridle and bit on the horse and led her out of her quarters. The horse nuzzled Bond as he patted her strong neck.

"Oh, Lolita likes you!" Tylyn said. "Actually she likes men, period. She's a little flirt."

"Then I'm sure we'll get along just fine," Bond said.

"Come on, help me saddle her up."

It was the glorious time of day. The sun was setting with finality and the remaining half-hour of daylight took on a mystical orange glow. Deep amongst the pine trees it was darker, but the light and shadow provided the two riders with a breathtaking scenic trip through the forest.

Bond conceded that she was a better rider than he was. In fact she was, quite simply, amazing.

Tylyn didn't have to show off. Every perfectly timed and flawlessly executed move that she made with the horse seemed effortless; it was completely natural to her. The horse was so well attuned to her commands that they truly acted as one entity, as if she were the upper half of a centaur.

Bond didn't embarrass himself though. He met the challenges with finesse. At one point, Lolita hesitated before jumping over a fallen tree. Bond had to urge her three times to go for it, and by then, Commander was nearly a half-kilometer ahead. Tylyn weaved in and out of the trees at a frightening speed, but Bond did his best to keep up. Even though Tylyn's horse was definitely stronger, faster, and more familiar with his rider, Lolita, Bond thought, was doing a damned fine job obeying him. As far as he was concerned, she was a terrific horse.

He caught up with Tylyn by a brook near the opposite edge of the forest. Commander was having a drink. Tylyn smiled broadly.

"How do you like her?" she asked.

Bond let Lolita trot over to the water so that she could drink as well.

"She's marvelous," Bond said. "A little shy at first, like most first-timers, but she became enthusiastic once I took control."

Tylyn laughed. "That's what I like! A man who associates riding with sex."

"Isn't that what everyone associates it with?"

"Only the right people." And with that she pulled on the reins. "Let's go, Commander!" Immediately, the horse bolted from the water and cantered back into the woods.

Bond sighed. "Come on, Lo, we had better go too." He had to pull on the reins twice to get her to move.

It had grown considerably darker. Bond couldn't see a thing, but Lolita trotted around the trees using her own sense of guidance.

"Tylyn?" he called.

In the vague distance, he heard Commander whinny.

"Go," he said to Lolita, urging her forward into the gnarly black and gray maze.

They were foolish to have stayed out past dark, Bond thought. Tylyn should have known better, unless it was her *intention* for him to follow her somewhere. Could it mean that she was a member of the Union, or that she really liked him?

Bond hoped that it would be the latter.

Commander whinnied again, and Lolita picked up speed. The horse did remarkably well navigating through the obstacles. At one point, she came too close to a tree and skinned her left hindquarter but kept going.

He found Tylyn's horse riderless, obviously distressed.

"Tylyn?" Bond called.

There was nothing. Just the sounds of the night.

"Tylyn?" he shouted again.

Then he heard the soft moan. It came from a clump of bushes to his left. Bond got off Lolita and tied her to a tree, then approached Commander, who was acting quite skittish.

"Easy, boy," Bond said soothingly. "Give me your reins . . ."

The horse hesitated and jumped away from Bond twice before he could get close enough to grab them. Once he did, the horse calmed down and allowed Bond to tie him to a tree next to Lolita.

Bond raced to where the moaning came from and found Tylyn, sitting up, rubbing her face.

"Ohhh," she said, dazed.

"My God, are you all right? What happened?" Bond knelt beside her, but it was too dark to really see what was wrong with her.

"Commander tripped and I went flying," she said. "It's my fault, I shouldn't have been racing him in the forest after dark. It's just that he *enjoys* it so."

"Are you hurt?"

"My eye hurts, there's something in it. I can't get it out. I might have a bruise on my left arm and shoulder, where I landed, but it's mostly my pride that's hurt."

"Can you stand? We should probably get out of here."

"I think so, it's just . . ." she stood and kept rubbing her eye ". . . . my eye really hurts. I can't open it. Do you have a flashlight by any chance?"

"Yes," he said. "Sit down again." She did so and Bond pulled the camera out of his jacket pocket.

He held it up to her and said, "My camera has special photographic lenses that work with certain kinds of built-in light sources. I'm going to use one on you, all right?"

"Sure, just get that awful thing out of my eye!" It was obvious that she was terribly uncomfortable but doing her best to maintain composure. Her beauty aside, it was Tylyn's willpower and spirit that continued to impress him.

He looked through the camera and flicked on the light. Tylyn's face was illuminated in a halo-like circle that centered on her eye. She was squeezing it shut.

"You're going to have to try and open your eye, Tylyn," Bond said. "Otherwise I can't see anything."

"Oh, all right, damn it," she said. "Help me, just go slow."

He put down the camera and used both hands to gently rub her face around her eye. With his fingertips, he gained a hold on the skin surrounding her eye and slowly began to flex his fingers, pulling open her eyelids.

Tylyn cursed like a man.

He held her eye open with his left hand while he reached for the camera with his right. He held it up, flicked on the light and shone it over her eye.

It was teary and red, all right, and Bond immediately saw the cause. In the anterior corner of her eye was a foreign object, a splinter, perhaps.

"Just hold still, Tylyn, I see it," he said. "You're going to have to hold your eye open, all right?"

"Okay," she said, and replaced his fingertips with her own, forcing the eye to stay open.

Bond put the camera in his left hand and removed the heel of his right shoe. The escape materials that Q Branch had provided were about to come in handy once again, for inside the kit was a pair of tweezers. As it was dark and Tylyn was probably in too much pain to notice, Bond retrieved them and focused his attention on her eye. He shone the light into the pupil and examined the retina. He looked up, down, to the sides . . . she had no Union tattoo.

With a quick and deliberate move, Bond reached into the corner of

Tylyn's eye with the tweezers and grabbed the offending splinter. He pulled it out smoothly and quickly, then surreptitiously replaced the tweezers. Tylyn felt no pain, just an overwhelming sensation of relief.

"Oh, *merci beaucoup!*" she cried and impulsively threw her arms around him and kissed him once on the mouth. This took both of them by surprise. Then, time seemed to stop as Bond and Tylyn concurrently worked out how they were going to react to that kiss. Should they laugh about it and move on? Should they say nothing? Should they do it again?

Bond leaned in and kissed her longingly, and Tylyn let him do it.

They emerged from the forest an hour later, after the sun was well on its way to the other side of the world. Their clothes were disheveled and there were twigs in their hair, but there was no other damning evidence of what had occurred between them. They had wrapped themselves in a blanket that Tylyn had kept fastened to her saddle, and there on the ground, they had made noisy, animalistic love. For her, it was a catharsis of sorts, as she had been mostly celibate since her separation. For Bond, it was the culmination of an intense desire that he had felt since he had first become aware of Tylyn's existence.

As they approached the house in silence, walking their horses and holding hands, Bond wondered again if he should take this any further. For one thing, he was being dishonest with her. He was no journalist. He would have to come clean, tell her what he really did for a living. He wasn't sure if he was ready to do that.

They had *salade niçoise* and wine by candlelight in her home, where they sat at a round table in the dining room and looked out of large French windows at a garden that was barely illuminated by the outdoor bulbs. A mixed-breed dog and a tabby cat sat quietly in the room with them, eyeing the couple intensely. Tylyn had put on a Billie Holiday CD, and it created a pleasant, mellow mood.

They spoke of horses, of how her business with them barely turned a profit but that she enjoyed it so much that she could never abandon it.

"I raise horses for riding schools, mostly. I sell them in France and some in Spain, too. I won't sell to racers, I'm not sure I like that," she said. "And never to circuses unless I personally know the people in charge of the animals."

"Why do you want to act, Tylyn? You have so much already," Bond said. "Your horses, your clothing company, your modeling career . . ."

She laughed. "I know, I know, it isn't as if I have nothing to do all day long. Why does anyone want to act? It's a thrill. It's a new direction. I'm ready for new directions." She sighed. "And tomorrow it all begins."

"What time do you have to be in Monte Carlo?"

"Pretty early. I'll be up before the sun."

"Then I shouldn't stay and keep you."

"Don't be silly," she said, starting. She put out a hand and laid it on his. "Don't go. Please?"

Bond looked into her magnificent eyes. He knew, as did she, that something had happened—not just the physical pleasure that they had experienced in the woods—but an awakening, the opening of private doors that were rarely unlocked. Poetry and mythology had cast labels on the phenomenon throughout history: "love at first sight," "finding one's soul mate," or "falling head over heels." Bond never set much store by such romantic notions, but he did know that there was something palpable between them.

Bond turned his hand over, took hers and said, "I hope you're not on the rebound from your husband."

She shook her head. "I'm not. Well, maybe I am. I don't know. You're not the first man I've slept with since we separated. You're not the first man I've slept with since we were *married*." For the first time since he had met her, Tylyn allowed Bond to glimpse her vulnerability. She said soberly, "Léon was not good for me. At first I thought he was, and the first couple of years were happy. But he has his dark side, you see. Me, I always look on the light side of life, whereas he always looks on the black side. I was more of a possession to him than a wife. And I think he always wanted to get his hands on my family's money, even though he knew he couldn't get near it."

"Did you have a prenuptial agreement?" Bond asked.

"Yes, and the deal was that he got nothing. He knew from the beginning that my money would always be my money. He never had a problem with that. He wouldn't get anything unless . . ."

"Unless what?"

"Well, unless I died or something. Then he would inherit it all. But after we're divorced, that's no longer a consideration."

Bond said nothing. He stroked the back of her hand with his thumb.

"I guess I'm not the marrying type," she said. "I'm too much like one of those horses out there. I like to ride with the wind and go wherever it takes me."

"You can say that again. I've seen it up close!"

She looked at him hard. "Have you ever been married?"

Bond was always reserved when it came to talking about that chapter of his life but this time the question threw him more than usual. She must have seen the walls go up, for she immediately said, "I'm sorry. That's none of my—"

"Yes, once," he replied. "It was another time, another place."

She nodded. "I suppose you have to talk about my marriage in your article?" she asked softly after a pause.

Oh yes, the article. How was he going to get around that?

"I don't have to mention it at all," he said.

"Good, because if you'll keep it off the record, I'll tell you something."

"You have my word."

She took a sip of wine, then said, "I'm going to divorce Léon. He just doesn't know it yet."

"Don't you think he has a pretty good idea that you will?"

"He's deluded," she said. "He believes that the separation is indeed a trial one, and that we'll be back together as soon as filming starts. He probably cast me just so he could keep some kind of hold on me, but I'm going to prove to him, and to the world, that I'm quite independent now. I'm not going to say anything until after filming is completed, but he's going to have to give me a wide berth over the next few weeks. In fact . . ." She looked at Bond with inspiration in her eyes. "Will you come and visit me on the set?"

"You really want me to?"

"Yes! Oh, it would help my cause enormously, you see. Léon will see that I am *not* his wife any more and it will make my decision to divorce him that much easier for him to swallow. Will you?"

Bond smiled. "I might."

"I can see that I'm just going to have to persuade you," she said, standing and pulling on his hand.

"Where are we going?"

"It's time for dessert."

"Dessert? Where?"

"In my bedroom," she said, leading him out of the room.

Bond woke to the sensation of a soft weight on his legs. He shifted beneath the sheets and saw that Tylyn's tabby cat was sitting on his thighs, on top of the covers.

Tylyn's side of the bed was empty, but there was a note on the pillow. Bond moved, nudging the cat to jump off the bed. He sat up and read the note.

> *"Dear James, make yourself comfortable. Ask Chantal for any-*
> *thing. I've left my mobile number. I hope to see you soon.*
> *Kisses, Tylyn."*

Naked, he slipped out of bed and found his clothes on a chair across the room. Once he was dressed, he left the bedroom and found his way to the dining room, where Chantal was already laying out break-fast for him: a feast of fresh scrambled eggs, a plate of assorted fruit, and yogurt. It couldn't get any better than that.

After thanking Chantal profusely, Bond got in his car and left Tylyn's home. He drove east, toward Monte Carlo.

All he could think about were the sounds she had made last night in bed.

Put her out of your mind! he willed himself. His usual method of detachment that normally protected his heart from the tumultuous hazards of romance was simply not working this time. Could this be love?

Whatever it was, he thought, he was hooked. The pursuit was on.

FIFTEEN

THE CASINO

TYLYN HAD CHECKED INTO THE HOTEL DE PARIS IN MONTE CARLO IN THE morning. She spent three hours in the spa, swimming pool and beauty salon, then had something to eat. She was preparing for the press reception that afternoon when there was a knock on the door of her suite.

"Who is it?" she asked in French.

"Léon."

She frowned and sighed. "What do you want?"

"I want to talk to you for a minute. May I come in?"

Shaking her head, Tylyn put on one of the hotel's terry cloth robes over her underwear, unlocked the door, and opened it. Essinger stepped inside, and kissed her on both cheeks. She returned the greeting, but only perfunctorily. He was dressed sharply in a silk white shirt with full, puffy sleeves, opened at the neck. His black trousers were tight around his buttocks.

"You look like one of the three musketeers," Tylyn said.

"Rather pirate-like, don't you think?" he asked, smiling. "I thought it fitted with the theme of our movie." He set a shopping bag on a table.

"What do you want? I'm busy getting ready."

"We have another press conference in Nice tomorrow before we set sail for Corsica."

"Oh, no, Léon, do we have to?"

"You're required by contract to do publicity, darling, so, yes, you have to. And . . . I'd like you to accompany me."

She shook her head. "I'll go, but I'm not accompanying you, Léon. We had an agreement. This is strictly business, this movie. You wanted me in it, and I wanted to be in it, and I'm working for you, but I'm no longer living with you."

He tried to grab her arm and pull her toward him. "But Tylyn—"

She broke free and walked away from him. "No 'buts', Léon. Where is the press conference tomorrow?"

"At the harbor, in front of our cruise ship. After the conference, we set sail."

"All right, I'll be there. Now go away."

He went to her and tried to take her into his arms. "Tylyn, don't be this way."

She turned to him and said, "Léon, how many chances did I give you? How many times did I say, 'if you don't change I'm going to leave'? How many times have you been caught with some young girl in your bed?"

"You're no saint, either, Tylyn. I seem to remember catching you as well."

"No, I'm not a saint, but I'm not a liar. And I don't hit my lovers," she said, rubbing her cheek. There was no longer a mark there, but the memory of it would remain with her always.

"Tylyn, I *have* changed," Essinger pleaded. "When we're together again, after the separation, you'll see."

"Oh, Léon . . ." She was tempted to tell him that she had no intention of getting back together, but it just wasn't the right time. "Please go."

"I see," Essinger said, releasing her. "You have another lover, is that it?" She recognized the change in the tone of his voice. It meant trouble.

"What are you talking about?"

Essinger went over to the shopping bag he had brought, reached inside, and pulled out a new copy of *Paris Match*. He turned to a page and showed her.

There were shots of the Indecent Exposure fashion show in Paris, including several flattering ones of Tylyn. Down at the bottom of the page was a photograph of her and Bond, leaving the museum. Bond had his face covered with his hand so that it was difficult to identify him. The caption read, "New Romance in Store for Tylyn?"

"Who is this man?" Essinger asked.

"Just someone I met. He's a journalist, for God's sake, Léon," she said. "He's with an English magazine. We had an interview scheduled and we went out for lunch to talk. It was arranged by my manager."

Essinger wasn't sure whether or not to believe her.

"You'll probably get your own chance to meet him," she continued. "I've invited him to the set. He's doing an extensive article."

"The set?" Essinger snapped. "All press of that sort must be cleared through Dana in publicity!"

"Then he'll come as my guest!" Tylyn said. "Now get out!"

"I think you should stay away from him," Essinger said.

"You can't tell me what to do any more, Léon."

He grabbed her roughly by the shoulders. "Listen to me, you little—OWW!"

Tylyn snapped her knee into his groin. He let her go and doubled up, falling onto the couch.

"I'm sorry, Léon," she said. "You seem only to understand things when they're directed at your wallet or at your genitals. Now, I'm going back into the bedroom to finish getting ready. As soon as you've recovered, please let yourself out."

With that, she left him in agony. After the door slammed shut, Essinger muttered to himself, "You'll get what's coming to you, you just wait and see."

After a few minutes, he rolled off the sofa and slowly got to his feet.

Bond phoned Bertrand Collette when he got to Monte Carlo mid-afternoon.

"I need you in Nice by tomorrow morning," Bond told him. "And bring Ariel with you." He was referring to something that Q Branch had shipped to several foreign stations a few months ago for testing purposes.

"Ariel?" Collette asked. "What for?"

"Essinger's film is shooting on water. She might come in handy."

"That won't be easy. I have to find a . . . what do you call it in English? A proper . . . hitch."

"Do your best, Bertrand," Bond said. "Just be at the harbor in the morning."

After checking in with Nigel in London, Bond spent the rest of the day keeping an eye on the casino and doing his best to avoid Tylyn's press reception, which was at the Hotel de Paris, next door. He thought it best not to appear too eager.

Later he ate dinner alone, put on an Armani dinner jacket, and stood outside the casino to smoke a cigarette and contemplate what might happen that evening. Was he really about to meet *Le Gérant* in person? Mathis had done so and had discovered something significant. Apparently whatever he had found was important enough to effect his disappearance.

The Monte Carlo casino was one of Bond's favorites. He knew the general manager and several staff members personally. He had both won and lost great sums of money at the casino over the years. Forget what anyone says, Bond thought. Gambling was not fun and games—it was serious business. Lady Luck could be a cruel mistress.

As he walked inside the elegant casino, Bond reminded himself that although he would be using the company's money, a limit on the amount available had been imposed this time and he couldn't afford to lose more than three hundred thousand francs. A tidy sum, but nowhere near the maximums in the *privé* rooms. He hoped that his prey would not be playing for the kind of extremely high stakes that could result in his being wiped out in one hand.

After his passport was checked and he had made the transaction for chips, Bond went into the main room. For a Thursday night, the casino was crowded early. There must have been a ship of tourists in town. From the look of them, Bond guessed that they were Americans.

He took a moment to admire the elaborate paintings on the ceiling that represented the four seasons, then went into the *Salon Privé*. A crowd had gathered at one of the *chemin de fer* tables, so Bond stepped over to see if this was where the action was tonight. Sitting at one end was a man wearing dark glasses.

So . . . was this *Le Gérant*? At last?

Bond scanned the rest of the faces. There were two bodyguards behind the blind man. A smallish bookkeeper type sat next to him and acted as his eyes. There were three other players sitting at the table—an Arab in a turban, an elderly German man and a fat, ugly American with a smelly cigar. The American, in particular, was in a foul mood. The blind man had taken him to the cleaners.

A group of at least ten other men, representing several nationalities, were standing around the table and observing.

As for the man who might be *Le Gérant*, he was broad-shouldered, muscular and tanned. His dark hair was slicked back, a little too oily. The man looked to be physically fit and Bond guessed that they were around the same age.

The croupier announced that the bank stood at 100,000 francs.

"*Banco,*" Bond said.

They all turned to look at the newcomer.

Le Gérant said, "Ah, new blood. Welcome, monsieur. Please sit down." Without moving his head, he raised his hand and snapped his fingers. One of the casino employees stepped up with a leather-covered chair and placed it at the other end of the table for Bond.

Bond sat down and placed his chips in front of him. Immediately he felt the indescribable rush that went with high stakes gambling. How many times had he been in this position, facing a ruthless opponent over cards? This was life or death played out on a green felt-covered table. Would tonight lead to death for one of them?

As the croupier counted the chips, Bond stared at the blind man. He never shifted his position; he kept his head straight, as if he was staring through solids into the next room. A slight smile was beginning to form on the man's face.

The cards were dealt. Bond received a three and a four. Seven—not bad.

The bookkeeper whispered in *Le Gérant's* ear after looking at his two cards.

Bond waved to signal that he didn't want another card. The hand was played out. Bond revealed his seven.

Le Gérant turned over a two and a six.

"Bad luck," the elder gentleman said to Bond.

"Yeah, join the club," the American said.

The bank stood at 200,000 francs. It was all that Bond had left. Was this the moment of truth? Would it be all over in two hands?

The croupier announced the bank's amount, challenging anyone present if they wanted to wager. If they had chosen to do so, several players could have combined forces to bet against respective parts of the bank. But no one desired to risk even a small part of his funds against a man who seemed unbeatable.

"*Banco*" Bond said, which meant that he was betting against the entire bank alone.

Le Gérant smiled. "I think this game is about to get interesting, eh, Julien?"

The bookkeeper whispered, "*Oui*, Monsieur Rodiac."

Le Gérant slipped the cards out of the shoe. Bond had a two and a queen, which was not encouraging. He watched the blind man as Julien peeked at their cards. He whispered to *Le Gérant*, who registered no reaction whatsoever.

Bond asked for a third card, the one that would decide the fate of the game. The croupier handed it to him on the paddle and flipped it over.

A seven. Bond had a total of nine. He was careful not to show any emotion, but inwardly he breathed a sigh of relief.

Le Gérant remained stone-faced, but the shock on Julien's face was evident. He had to draw a card. He did so, Julien whispered in his ear, and after a second or two, he turned over the hand.

A total of eight.

The crowd gasped. The blind man's luck had suddenly turned!

If Bond's perceptions were correct, then *Le Gérant* had known that he was going to lose. Bond had seen it in his demeanor. The man had realized it before he had drawn the third card. What was his secret?

There was a moment's pause as the bank and shoe were turned over to Bond. He was now a hundred thousand francs wealthier than when he had started.

Le Gérant said, "I hope you will allow me a chance to win my money back, Monsieur Bond."

The man knew who he was! But how?

"Of course," Bond said, doing his best to retain his cool. "I wouldn't just win and run."

Was he completely blown?

"*Banco,*" *Le Gérant* said.

The bank was worth 400,000 francs.

The identification had rattled Bond a bit, but he summoned his concentration and managed to deal the cards from the shoe with panache. It was important to appear confident and relaxed. Julien glanced at the cards and whispered in his employer's ear. Bond looked at his hand. He had a king and a five, which put him on shaky ground. A total of five could go either way.

Le Gérant sat a moment, pondering his hand. Should he draw? Finally, he nodded. Bond slapped a new card onto the table and the paddle carried it over to the blind man. Julien looked at it and whispered, then turned it over. An ace.

Damn! Bond was not allowed to draw. The rules stated that the dealer had to stand on a five if he dealt an ace as a third card to his opponent.

Le Gérant flipped over his cards, revealing a five, a ten, and an ace. Six.

He had won back the entire bank.

Bond turned over his cards. The crowd murmured enthusiastically, some shaking their heads in sympathy for Bond.

He shrugged it off and smiled to the crowd. "Easy come, easy go," he said.

But he was completely broke, so he set down a couple of chips he had held in reserve for a tip, stood, and said, "*Merci,* monsieur. I hope we will meet again soon." He passed the shoe back to the other end of the table.

Le Gérant smiled and said, "I'm sure we will, Monsieur Bond. It was a pleasure."

Bond walked away and went to the bar. He ordered a martini and nursed it while he reflected on what had just happened.

Le Gérant had swatted him away like a fly. Bond had never been bested so quickly. The man had been dealt a five and a ten, which gave him a total of five (since tens were worthless). However, he was entitled to draw on a five, or not. He had chosen to do so. Had he not done so, there would have been a tie.

Was it luck? A good guess on *Le Gérant's* part?

Bond could see where the legends about the man having a sixth sense might have come from. He certainly had a sense of power about him. He was confident, good-humored and obviously wealthy. This could really be the man who controlled the largest and most notorious criminal organisation on the planet.

Bond walked out of the casino toward the Hotel de Paris. It would be a while before *Le Gérant* finished for the night. He might as well look into other matters that were weighing heavily on his mind.

As he entered the grandiose lobby with its marble floors, high domed ceiling, stained-glass windows and a bust of Louis XIV, Bond felt a touch of apprehension. What was preoccupying his thoughts now was seeing Tylyn again. She was in the hotel somewhere. Should he phone up to her room? Was pursuing this girl really wise?

"James?"

His heart skipped a beat when he heard the voice. Bond turned, and there she was, an angel in a low-cut red dress, one that he had seen in the fashion show. She looked her best, which was saying a lot.

"It *is* you!" She beamed happily, embracing him.

"Hello, Tylyn," he said, kissing her cheeks. "Last night was lovely, do you know that?"

She nodded. "You don't have to tell *me*. I'm so glad you're here! Oh, but James, I'm leaving for Nice very soon. In an hour, I think. A car is picking me up. What are you doing here?"

"Looking for you, of course."

"Well, I wish you had come sooner! I was *so* bored at dinner this evening. I had to eat with the other actors, the director, and . . . well, Léon, too. I could have done without that."

"How was the press conference?"

"Nothing new there. A lot of patting each other on the back. More like a pep talk than a press conference. 'Aren't we great? Look at us, we're about to make a cool movie!' "

"Would you like to have a drink?" Bond asked.

"Let's go for a walk instead, what do you say?" she suggested.

"That sounds wonderful."

They walked behind the casino on Avenue de Monte Carlo, past the Bar Américain, and down broad stone steps to the gardens and terraces of the Casino. This was an ideal lovers' walk, as the gardens overlooked Monte Carlo's harbor and were stocked with all kinds of exotic flowers. It was a beautiful night, the sky was clear and the stars were out in force. The Mediterranean lay flattened out before them in the darkness and reflecting the moon on its surface. There were several other couples strolling through, as well as groups of tourists. All were exquisitely dressed, ready to partake of an evening's gambling at the casino.

The harbor down below was well lit and busy. One of the yachts there belonged to *Le Gérant*. Which one was it? As they walked, Bond noted that there was easy access to the marina from the gardens by means of a lift.

Tylyn spoke of her day and how she had missed Bond's presence. "I don't normally do that, you know," she said. "I realize that we, well, we jumped into bed on the first date and all, and I just don't want you to get the wrong idea about me."

"I don't believe it's possible to have wrong ideas about you."

"You're sweet." She leaned up to kiss him, but she didn't have to go far. She was nearly as tall as he was. "I wish I knew more about you."

"Tylyn . . ." he said.

She put her hand to his mouth. "No, don't. Not now. I know we're probably rushing things. Let's not. I'm not ready for a serious relationship, you should know that. Let's just take things day by day, all right? I'll learn about you in due time."

Bond nodded and kissed her again. She looked past Bond and frowned.

"Damn," she said.

"What?"

"It's Gérard, one of my husband's flunkies."

Bond casually looked behind him. A large man in a suit was some ten yards away, talking into a mobile.

"Your husband has you followed?" Bond asked.

"It doesn't surprise me," she said. "Look, I hope you're not going to disappear. Léon already suspects that I'm seeing you. I think a little jealousy is good for him. Will you come to the set to visit me?"

"You're just using me," Bond said, teasing her.

"No I'm not!" she laughed and pushed him. "Well, okay, maybe I am, a *little*. But I like you, too, James. I really do. Do you believe me?"

"Yes, Tylyn, and I like you, too. Let's give Gérard something to report to his boss."

With that, he kissed her passionately, holding on to her as if she were the last woman on earth. Tylyn lifted one leg behind her, bent at the knee. They stayed locked in the embrace for well over a minute. When they looked up, Gérard was talking animatedly into the phone.

"I must go now," she said. "I'll be at the harbor in Nice tomorrow at 10:30 for another press function. Then we set sail. Léon has chartered a cruise ship to carry the cast and crew out to sea. You're welcome to join me."

"I, uhm, have to *work* sometime, Tylyn," Bond said. "But I'll see what I can do. Besides, I'm not sure that I can stay away from you now."

She kissed him again, said goodbye, and ran toward the stairs. She turned, waved to him, then went up to the hotel.

Bond began to stroll back toward the casino when he heard a man's voice.

"Hey."

Bond turned to see Gérard standing with his hands on his hips.

"*Bonjour,* monsieur," Bond said, and attempted to move on. Gérard reached out to grab Bond's arm.

Bond reacted quickly by snatching Gérard's wrist, twisting the man's arm under and around to his back, and applying sufficient pressure to induce a good deal of pain.

"Why don't you mind your own business, my friend?" Bond whispered, then shoved the man to the ground. He then straightened his bow tie, brushed off his jacket, and continued to walk up the stairs to the Place du Casino.

Bond waited at the bar until *Le Gérant* was ready to leave. He and his entourage cashed in the blind man's impressive pile of chips, placed the cash inside a silver metal briefcase, and left the building. Bond followed them at a safe distance as they walked through the gardens to the lift. He noted that Julien would take *Le Gérant's* arm to guide him only occasionally. Most of the time *Le Gérant* was able to navigate the gardens without help and with no walking cane.

The party took the lift down to the harbor level, where they boarded a luxurious Princess yacht. Bond took a seat at the marina bar and ordered another martini. He watched the yacht's crew come and go, loading various bags from a van that was parked by the dock. After twenty minutes had passed, Bond saw two men appear on deck and walk across the bridge to the dock. One of them was Léon Essinger, and he was carrying the silver metal briefcase. Was it still full of money?

Bond recognized the other man, too, as someone very high up in the Union's bureaucracy. What was his name?

Of course—he was Julius Wilcox. The ugly one. The *commandant* with the reputation for being the cruellest man in the world.

Bond removed his camera from his jacket pocket and snapped a photo of the two men with the Princess in the background. Along with the retinal tattoo, this was further proof that Essinger was in bed with the Union.

He watched as the two men went up the stairs toward the casino, presumably to their car.

Now what? Bond asked himself as he lit a cigarette and stared at the dark sea. There were two courses of action open before him. One was to pursue *Le Gérant,* find out where he went, and ultimately discover where the Union's stronghold was located. The other was to stay close to Essinger and determine what the Union was up to. The latter was easily the more attractive, simply because of Tylyn's presence. Would both paths ultimately converge into one? Did it really matter which way he went?

While anyone else might have flipped a coin to help him decide what to do, Bond merely blew smoke rings in the air and chose to go with his gut.

SIXTEEN

THE MOVIE

NICE WAS ONE OF BOND'S FAVORITE PLACES IN FRANCE. CONSIDERED THE capital of the Riviera, it was a fashionable but relaxed city. Standing at the edge of the port, Bond could see one of these relics of this earlier era, the Château d'Anglais, a pink tiered building at the top of Mont Boron. Nice has one of the prettiest harbors in France, mostly because it is clean and surrounded by the hills and brown and yellow apartment houses, the spectacular veterans' monument cut into the cliff facing the water and the lovely expanse of Mediterranean.

The harbor was busy on this bright and sunny day. Camera crews were set up in front of a dock where the *Starfish*, a large luxury cruise ship, had put into port. A banner with the words *Pirate Island* had been hung over the side of the ship, announcing to the world that this was Hollywood come to the Mediterranean.

A long table covered by a white cloth had been set up on the boardwalk near the ship's dock. There were microphones on top of the table, awaiting the film's stars and major players. A crowd had already gathered and was becoming impatient.

Bond lit a cigarette and stood apart from the group, keeping his eye peeled for anything unusual. Right on time, a familiar face appeared in front of him.

"I just want you to know, *Mister Bond,* that I had *hell* getting here with your ridiculous contraption," Bertrand Collette said. Once again, the French agent had nicked himself shaving and his face was decorated with two small pieces of tissue.

"Bertrand," Bond said, "have you ever considered using an electric razor?"

"Very funny." He pointed to a small boat at the other end of the harbor. "I secured a boat for our use. It's nothing fancy, but it was still expensive. An outlaw Sportsboat with a ninety-five horsepower engine. Will that do?"

"How fast does it go?"

"They told me up to forty-five miles per hour."

"Fine," Bond said. "Thanks. And where's Ariel?"

"She's in the horse trailer I had to rent, along with the *four by four* I had to rent to haul her! I must say, I would hate to be the accountant at MI6. He probably suffers from a bad heart."

Bond laughed. "In truth, he does. Now, listen. This press conference is going to begin in a few minutes. I'm going to do my best to get invited along for the first couple of days of shooting. I have a feeling that it won't be too difficult."

Collette shook his head, smiling. "How do you do it, James? She is one of the most desired women in the world! You bastard!"

Bond shrugged and went on. "What I'll need you to do is follow the production company out to sea. I believe they'll be going to Corsica first. Bring Ariel in the boat. I may need her for some reconnaissance. I'll keep in touch by mobile. All right? Am I working you too hard?"

Collette shook his head. "I'm fine. Actually, this is the most excitement I've had since I took on the job for your government. Just do me a favor."

"What's that?"

"Next time you kiss Tylyn, please pretend that you're me."

The conference began soon after Collette went to arrange things with the boat. Léon Essinger, Stuart Laurence, Dan Duling, and Tylyn Mignonne got out of two separate black limousines and were ushered to the press table by security guards. Tylyn looked gorgeous. She was wearing black Capri pants again, and a colorful halter-top that made excellent use of her perfect breasts. As she passed by Bond, she greeted him warmly and gave him a big hug. Essinger, who was right behind her, glowered at them both.

Once they were all seated, a publicity director started the proceedings by introducing the participants and turning over the mike to Essinger.

"Thank you," he said in English. "We are all very excited and happy to be here, for today we begin production of my new film, *Pirate Island*. My good friend Dan Duling is directing from a brilliant script by Robert Cotton. We have a superb team of special effects people. Our stunt coordinator is one of the best in the business and he is with us today. Rick? Where are you?"

A stocky man with red curly hair stepped out of the small group of people behind the table. He waved to the cameras. Essinger handed him the microphone. "Rick Fripp, ladies and gentlemen," he said.

Fripp took the microphone and spoke in a thick, Cockney accent." " 'Ullo, it's a pleasure to be 'ere. I just want to say that *Pirate Island* will have the best damn stunts ever in a motion picture. If there was an Oscar for stuntwork, it would be ours. I guarantee it. You're gonna see things you've never seen before, even in 'Ong Kong movies. And the explosions! Wait 'til you see the explosions in this picture! We're gonna blow things up proper, I tell yer. 'Alf the bloody budget is going to me and my stuff, so we're puttin' it all on the screen. I'm the best, y'see, that's all there is to it." He handed the mike back to Essinger and stepped away.

What an arrogant ass, Bond thought. The man *oozed* smarmy egotism, and if anyone on the crew was a possible Union agent, it was most likely to be him. He had a criminal record, he knew explosives . . .

Stuart Laurence, the lead actor, said a few words next. He was a handsome, virile type, an American who had made a number of popular action films. He was definitely the biggest box-office draw connected with the picture. Tylyn spoke after him, saying that she was grateful for the opportunity to be in a big-budget film financed by Hollywood but made by a French production company.

The reporters began to ask questions. The first one was directed at the producer. "Monsieur Essinger, will you ever be going back to America?"

Essinger shrugged. "Hollywood has its charms, but I like working in my native country. Besides, if I went back there, my next picture would have to be a prison movie."

He got some laughs out of that.

"Can you tell us about the screening of your newest picture at Cannes?"

Essinger smiled. "I'm glad you brought that up. *Tsunami Rising* will have its world première in eight days' time, the second night of the Cannes Film Festival. We will suspend production on *Pirate Island* for two days so that many of us can attend the screening. Mister Duling directed it, and Mister Laurence is the star. It will be a very special charity event at Cannes, a screening out of competition, of course. I've just had confirmation that Prince Edward and his wife Sophie from the UK will be attending, and Princess Caroline of Monaco will come. It will be a splendid evening."

That explained the notations Bond had seen in Essinger's office in Paris!

After the conference, Tylyn found Bond and hugged him again. The cameras flashed, much to Bond's chagrin. "You're coming with us, right?" she asked him.

"I wouldn't miss it," Bond said. "If you'll still have me."

"Are you kidding? Come on, I'll introduce you to Léon."

She led him past the reporters to where Essinger was talking to Fripp.

"Léon," she said, interrupting, "I'd like you to meet Mister Bond."

Essinger poured on the charm. "*Bonjour,* monsieur." He shook Bond's hand. It was firm but a little sweaty. Bond noted that the man's body odor was particularly strong. Or was the smell coming from Fripp?

"So I understand you'll be joining us for a few days?" Essinger asked.

"Yes, and I thank you for allowing me to do so," Bond said.

"Don't thank me," he said, "thank Tylyn. *She's* the one who wants you here. Have you met your fellow countryman, Mister Fripp?"

Bond shook hands with the stuntman. The grip was strong and vicelike. The freckle-faced Fripp smiled, revealing two missing teeth.

Yes, the body odor was Fripp's.

"How do you do?" Bond asked.

"Fine, mate. It's a pleasure," he replied.

"Tylyn, I suggest you take your friend and get aboard," Essinger said. "We set sail in thirty minutes."

"Let's go," she said to him.

Bond grabbed a small bag that he had brought with him, then walked up the ramp with one of the world's most desirable women.

The *Starfish* was a floating hotel. There were rooms for fifty people, and the cast and crew took all of them. Accompanying the *Starfish* were several smaller craft carrying production equipment, costumes, and other supplies needed to support the production.

She docked at Calvi that evening. Under orders from the producer, late night partying was discouraged. First call was to be at the marina early the next morning.

Bond and Tylyn had a quiet dinner in town at one of the many sidewalk cafés off the main street. They had thin, crispy pizzas with a bottle of the local red wine. Afterward they strolled among the tourist shops, looking at the extensive displays of Corsican knives, T-shirts with the symbol of Corsica, "the moor," on them, and other arts and crafts souvenirs.

When they had grown weary of walking through the village, she turned to him without warning and asked that they go back to the ship. *"Faisons l'amour,"* she said.

That night they made love in her cabin aboard the *Starship*, basking in the warmth of each other's skin. It wasn't as wild and savage as that first time in the woods near Tylyn's horse farm. This time it was languorous and unhurried. The ebbs and tides of their pleasure were extended over several hours before they finally fell asleep in each other's arms, sometime after midnight.

The next morning the crew reported to the set on the harbor at sunrise. Art directors had been working through the night "ageing" the marina. Set pieces had been added to create the illusion that the harbor was the handiwork of a future civilisation, after the "apocalypse."

The harbor looked nothing like it had the previous day. All contemporary boats had been removed and replaced by strange, ultramodern sea craft.

"Oh, look, there's my stunt double," said Tylyn as they arrived.

She pointed to a woman who was conversing with Rick Fripp. She was the same height and weight as Tylyn, and she had the same hairstyle, but the face was nothing like her. In fact, Bond thought she had the face of a bulldog.

Bond followed Tylyn over to them.

"Hi, I'm Tylyn," she said.

The woman introduced herself as Betty and shook Tylyn's hand. She also had an English accent. Up close, Bond noticed that Betty was covered in scars.

Rick Fripp said, "Betty's one of the finest stuntwomen in the business. She'd take a bullet if the script called for it."

Betty said, "I *have* taken a bullet. It's not fun."

"Was that for a movie?" Bond asked.

"No, it was when I was arrested for armed robbery," Betty said.

What *was* this? Bond wondered. Did all stunt people have to spend time in prison before they were qualified for their profession?

Filming got underway after Stuart Laurence arrived. The scene involved Stuart's character, a fellow named "John Duncan," and Tylyn's character, a woman named "Sandra Jurinic," bartering with a boatman. Just as the deal was made, they were attacked by a group of pirates who had surrounded the dock. John and Sandra managed to fight their way out of it, jumped on a boat, and escaped.

There was a bit of dialogue between Stuart, Tylyn and a character actor playing the part of the boatman. The director, Duling, gave them minimal instruction and made a master shot from a wide angle. After a short break, they did four additional takes with more coverage. Bond watched from the sidelines, paying more attention to Rack Fripp than to the action. In his opinion, though, Tylyn did a more than respectable job in her short scene. She had a commanding presence, a good voice with strong timbre, and she looked absolutely marvelous.

After lunch, the shooting continued with the fight sequence. The "pirates," dressed in an odd mixture of period swashbuckler costuming and space age slickness, were choreographed to jump out of a "Trojan horse'-type of boat docked at the pier. As they took "John" by surprise, all sorts of mayhem erupted, including exploding grenades, fist fights, gunfire, and a hair-raising leap onto a traveling boat. Rick Fripp took over the direction and Bond was fairly impressed with his ingenuity and expertise. Perhaps the fellow was legitimate after all. Had he given up his bad-boy ways for good?

Bond doubted it.

Tylyn rehearsed the link between the earlier dialogue scene and her character's fight sequence. She was allowed to throw a couple of punches and kick one of the pirates, but the more complicated and difficult moves were given to Betty. After the director called, "Cut!" Betty would step in, find the mark where Tylyn had been standing, and take over.

When Tylyn was off camera, she stayed close to Bond.

"I wish they'd let me do more," she whispered. "Those moves aren't that difficult. I think I'm more limber than her anyway."

"They can't afford to have you get hurt, Tylyn," Bond said. "Besides, what would we do if you injured your back?"

She jabbed him in the side with her elbow, but she laughed. "Come here, you," she said, pulling his head to hers. She kissed him deeply, in front of everyone.

When she let go, Stuart Laurence said, "I hope you'll kiss *me* like that in our love scene, Tylyn."

Everyone laughed and whistled, and Bond, for the first time in his life, felt a bit embarrassed. He didn't like to flaunt his romances in public. He considered it in bad taste. Still, he was so taken with Tylyn that he went with the spirit of the moment.

Léon Essinger, on the other hand, was not pleased. He muttered to Fripp, "Journalist indeed. I hope he's getting one hell of a story."

—•—

In the small Chicago suburb of Buffalo Grove, Illinois, a national fast-food franchise was just changing its menu from breakfast to lunch. A steady crowd had been pouring in since the early hours, and the staff was prepared for the noon rush.

The smell of grilled hamburgers filled the restaurant as a potpourri of people formed queues to order food. There were mothers with their toddlers, men wearing greasy overalls from the road work up the street, and employees from the strip mall shops.

None of them noticed the Japanese man sitting alone, quietly eating his meal. After all, the dining area was already crowded. When he had finished, he slipped out of the chair, deposited his rubbish in the bin, placed his tray on the appropriate counter and left the premises. He was so inconspicuous that no one saw him leave a paper bag under his table.

The explosion that occurred fifteen minutes later blew out two walls and killed forty-two people.

The FBI spent the following three days at the site, attempting to piece together what had happened. They had very few clues, and not one of the surviving witnesses was able to identify the Japanese man. No one even remembered seeing him. In his preliminary report, the investigator in charge suggested that a radical anti-Semite had placed the bomb, for the village had a large Jewish population. But he was just guessing; there was no evidence to support this hypothesis.

It was a week later when the FBI head office in Quantico, Virginia, received an anonymous note that mentioned the bombing in Illinois. It was written in Japanese, claiming that followers of Goro Yoshida were responsible for the crime. It had been perpetrated as a strike against the "decadent and sin-ridden West."

The note also promised that the best was yet to come.

SEVENTEEN

THE TRAWLER

THE NEXT DAY, THE PRODUCTION MOVED OUT TO SEA. THE ART DIRECTORS had completed the preparation of a major action scene set some five miles out from the northwest coast of Corsica. The focal point of the scene was a large, disabled tanker that was rigged to be aflame when the scenes were shot. Other abandoned vessels were scattered about, floating on the water or half-submerged. A high-speed boat chase would occur in and out of this area.

The *Starfish* sailed to the point, followed by the smaller boats carrying the equipment. One particular ship interested Bond and that was a trawler carrying all of Rick Fripp's equipment. It was the largest of the accessory boats and it also seemed to be the best guarded. The cast and crew had strict orders to stay away from it, ostensibly because there were explosives aboard. Bond had decided early on that he would have to get a look inside it.

Tylyn had the day off, but they were stuck on the *Starfish*. The cast had the options of swimming in the ship's indoor pool, trying a little scuba diving in the sea, amusing themselves in the ship's cinema or game room, or simply relaxing on deck. Tylyn chose to lounge on deck, and Bond joined her. He watched over the rail as Fripp and his team sped from point to point in speedboats, supervising the rigging of the special effects.

Bond eventually found a moment to move away from Tylyn and make a call on his mobile.

"Bertrand?" he asked when it was answered.

"Hello, James. I hope you slept better than me."

"What do you mean?"

"I'm in this little sportsboat, remember? And Ariel isn't the most obliging of roommates. She takes up the entire back end of the boat. There's no place for me!"

"Sorry about that, Bertrand. Listen, we're approximately five miles out from the coast, do you see us?"

"I've been trailing behind, no problem," Collette said. "I'm keeping a safe distance."

"Good. Tonight I'm going to attempt to get over to Fripp's equipment trawler. Get some sleep today and I'll contact you after midnight."

"Over and out, James."

The day progressed uneventfully. Bond and Tylyn sunned themselves on deck, had dinner in the ship's dining room, segregated from the rest of the cast and crew. The rumors were flying about the couple, and Essinger, for one, was not happy about it. But Tylyn and Bond were oblivious to the gossip. Even though Bond was acting on a pretext, he found that he was enraptured with Tylyn. When two people are in the throes of courtship, when joy and sensuality overwhelm them, when they cannot possibly be happy if they are not with their new partner—then they are blind to everything around them.

As they walked back to her cabin after the late meal and bottle of champagne, Bond was lost in his thoughts. He had purposefully sought out Tylyn in order to get close to the film production. His aim had always been to investigate Essinger. However, he had done very little spying and much more lovemaking. In some ways, he felt guilty about it. Was he doing his job? Was he learning anything new about the Union? On the other hand, he felt perfectly entitled to enjoy himself with this wonderful girl. While he had experienced the love of many women, he rarely reciprocated with more than his body. This was one of those uncommon occurrences when he had to admit that he was falling in love. He was treading on dangerous ground, to be sure. Once again his brain attempted to warn him that Tylyn was far too famous for him to be involved with. And, once again, his heart told him otherwise.

When they were in bed, naked and entwined, Tylyn took his right hand and slowly licked and sucked on each finger. "You have such strong hands," she said. "Make love to me with just your hands."

Bond obliged her by first massaging her feet. He kneaded the heels, pressed hard on the bottoms of the big toes, rubbed the arches, and gently applied pressure to the soft spots below her ankles. Carefully, tantalizingly, he worked his way up each leg, one at a time, working the muscles and sending waves of pleasure up her spine. Bond purposefully avoided her sex and moved to her waist and hips. He massaged her there for a while, then navigated to her shoulders. He took each arm and squeezed the muscles all the way down to her fingers. He pressed his thumbs into the fleshy mounds in her palms.

As she moaned softly, closed her eyes, and parted her lips, he gently massaged her eyebrows and forehead. He rubbed her temples and cheekbones, then reached back and pressed on various points in the back of her neck.

Finally, he took a breast in his hand and used his thumb and forefinger to stimulate the nipple. When it was erect, he slowly and gently twisted it, pulled it, twisted it, pulled it . . . Tylyn squirmed under him as he alternated between the two breasts. Then, keeping his left hand on one breast and continuing the nipple stimulation, he slid his right hand down to the mound between her legs. Her hair was soft and thin there. She was wet, and his second and third fingers slid inside easily. Tylyn moaned loudly and arched her back as he used his thumb to circle the erogenous zone at the top of her vulva. He kept up this rhythm for several minutes, using her natural lubrication to slide his thumb up and down and around her clitoris, while keeping his two fingers deep within her. Tylyn's breath increased and the moans became louder until her stomach tensed and she gasped. Bond felt her contract spasmodically around his fingers as she writhed on the bed.

Later, after she had caught her breath and calmed down, she snuggled next to him, and said, "Don't you dare leave, James. Don't you dare."

She reached down, grasped him, and proceeded to return the favor.

But leave he did.

Much later, after Tylyn was sleeping soundly, Bond woke himself with that internal, trained alarm clock that allowed him to do so at any time, day or night. All he had to do was set his mind to it before falling asleep. It was second nature.

He slipped out of bed without disturbing her, and dressed in his swim trunks, black trousers, and a black T-shirt. He grabbed the camera and strapped it to his waist, along with one of the new Walther P99 Tactical Knives that he had brought along in his bag. It had a 5 1\2 blade and fitted neatly into a nylon sheath clipped to the belt. Bond then grabbed the spare key to Tylyn's cabin, slipped out of the room, and locked the door behind him. He crept down the hallway, purposefully avoiding the lifts, and took the stairs to the lower levels of the ship.

There were two gangplanks from the *Starfish*. Because cast and crew had to be able to get to various points in the water, a portable dock had been built at the site. Several speedboats and sportsboats were anchored there, ready to shuttle people to their desired locations. Two gangplanks led from the *Starfish* to the dock, one for passengers, and a larger one for crew with cargo to load or unload.

Bond went for the cargo area, not wishing to be seen by someone who still happened to be up. It was fairly well lit, but completely quiet. There was probably a night watchman somewhere, but Bond didn't see him.

He moved into the room, stepping slowly until he was able to peer around some stacks of cargo near the open loading door. The sky was dark, but the bridge and dock were well lit with strung bulbs. The water splashed and splattered next to the opening, rocking the bridge slightly.

There he was—a lone guard in a security officer's uniform, sleeping in a chair. He was armed, sitting right at the entrance and snoring like a sawmill.

Bond's training had included many hours of practicing stealth and he was particularly adept at it. His instructor had said that Bond "moved like a cat." He was able to walk, run, jump, swim, strike, and kill without making a sound. This ability was essential for someone in his profession to stay alive.

It was this skill that allowed Bond to run and take a shallow dive into the water without waking the guard.

The water was much colder than he had expected, but it felt invigorating. It made his senses come alive, totally alert and ready to work.

He swam slowly but steadily toward the trawler, which he estimated to be about one hundred meters away. No problem. By conserving his strength, he was able to pace himself and arrive at the trawler in ten minutes. When he got there, he found that the trawler had a similar entrance arrangement with a portable loading dock floating outside of the opening.

It was well lit inside and Bond thought that he heard voices. He climbed out of the water onto the dock, then slithered on his belly to the side of the opening, hugged the wall, and looked inside.

There were two of them. One was a security guard and the other was none other than Rick Fripp. They were laughing about something. Then, Bond heard Fripp say that he was going to bed.

Uh oh, Bond thought, that meant he would be coming this way and hopping into one of the boats tied to the platform. Bond shrank into the corner between the hull and the platform, but Fripp never showed. Bond looked inside again and saw that Fripp had left the room through a door leading to another part of the trawler. Where did he go? Bond wondered. Wasn't he sleeping on the *Starfish* like everyone else?

The guard, left alone, began slowly and self-consciously to pace the floor with his hands behind his back, lost in thought.

Like a cheetah, Bond bolted and rushed at the guard, striking him in the back of the neck with a spear-hand. The man noiselessly crumpled to the floor.

The place was like a warehouse, with crates and boxes stacked all around. Bond examined each pile and determined that most of it was legitimate production equipment. In one section, set apart by a rope, were crates of explosives. Bond took a look at them, assuring himself that there was nothing illegal there. He noted that they came from an address in Corsica rather than France. The label read "Corse Shipping," which Bond remembered as being listed on the manifests he had seen in Paris.

A door was behind the crates of explosives. He listened at it, hearing nothing. Bond tried to open it but it was locked. No time to go back to the guard and find the key on him.

He unhooked the camera from his belt and turned the dial to the laser setting. He squatted so that he was eye level to the lock, then aimed the camera lens at it. He pushed the shutter button and the bright white-blue laser shot into the metal. Bond held the camera steady until the lock was melted through. He shut off the laser and tried the door. It opened. Bond replaced the camera on his belt and went inside.

It was a small workshop. Tools were fastened to the wall, and there were two work tables where small pieces of props or machinery were assembled or repaired. On one table were the parts of what looked like a mobile phone. Bond knew that in fact it was some kind of radio transmitter. He leaned in closer to examine its exposed guts and found the tiny antenna.

Bond examined the other table and found two small crates with lids nailed on. The sides were marked with the warnings to "handle with extreme caution." Again, "Corse Shipping" labels were plastered on the tops. Bond unsheathed his knife and used it to pry open one of the crates.

Carefully packed amongst straw and padding were glass containers filled with a white crystalline material. It almost resembled cocaine, but it was much too sparkling for that.

Could this be the CL-20 that Mathis was looking for? The stolen explosives from the French air force base? If so, then they had ingeniously used the film production as a means of smuggling it out of Corsica.

He heard a door creak inside the warehouse. Bond cursed softly and moved back away from the table, flattening himself against the wall by the door.

It opened a few seconds later, and Rick Fripp walked in. Bond didn't hesitate. As soon as the man had cleared the doorway, Bond locked his fists together and brought them down on the back of the stuntman's head. Fripp fell to the floor, groaned, and attempted to rise. Bond kicked him with his bare heel in the back of the head. Fripp jerked forward and dropped into unconsciousness.

Bond took another look around the room to see if there was something he might have missed. Then he had a moment of inspiration.

Why not? He went to Fripp's body and pulled his head up. Bond removed the camera again and held it in front of Fripp's face. With his left hand, Bond opened Fripp's eye and turned on the ophthalmoscope with his right.

Fripp groaned, beginning to stir. What was that bright light in his eye?

Bond focused it into Fripp's pupil and found the retina.

Fripp moved slowly and moaned even louder. The muscles in his face started to resist Bond's fingers. His hands started to move. Any second he would recover sufficiently to be able to knock Bond away. So far, though, Fripp had not focused on Bond's face. He had not been recognized yet.

Come on! Bond willed himself. Find it! Is it there? The light scanned the retina, skipping over the red blood vessels and the macula until . . . yes! There it was, the Union tattoo.

Fripp regained his senses enough to groan with confusion. "Huh?" he mumbled as he looked at Bond, unable to focus his eyes.

Bond said, "Don't worry, Mister Fripp, you don't need glasses. I'm afraid your frequent headaches are being caused by something else."

With that, he grabbed Fripp's curly hair and casually banged his head hard on the floor, knocking the man out again.

He stood and left the workroom and stepped quietly past the still unconscious guard. As quietly as he had come in, Bond dove into the water and swam back to the *Starfish*.

Twenty minutes later, he crawled onto the bridge and peeked into the opening. The guard was still sound asleep. Bond stole past him and out of the cargo area, dripping water and unfortunately leaving a trail.

He moved into the corridor toward the stairwell, and almost made it when a voice stopped him.

"You! What are you doing?"

Bond turned to see none other than Julius Wilcox, the ugly Union killer.

"You're all wet! Who are you? What the hell are you doing?"

"Just felt like a swim," Bond said, then ducked into the stairway. He ran up the stairs to the next level and waited to see if Wilcox would pursue him. There was no sound. Bond kept going until he got to Tylyn's level. Using his key, he swept into her cabin, where she was still sleeping like a princess. Bond removed the wet clothes, hung them over the shower stall, dried off, and got back into bed.

Before falling asleep, Bond decided that he would phone Collette in the morning and have him position Ariel. He would then prepare to leave the *Starfish* for good. As Julius Wilcox must have recognized him, his life wasn't worth a penny.

"Wake up, you fool," Wilcox said, banging on Essinger's door.

When it opened, Essinger, his eyes full of sleep, said, "What do you want? Do you know what time it is?"

Wilcox pushed Essinger back into his cabin, entered and shut the door. He pulled Essinger up by the pajama collar and growled, "Do you know who that is that's sleeping with your wife?"

"Yes, he's some kind of journalist from England."

"What's his *name?*"

"Bond, I think. James Bond."

Wilcox released Essinger, shoving him to the bed.

"What's the matter with you?" Essinger spat.

"That man is an SIS *agent,* you idiot! We know him! We've had dealings with him before."

"You're joking!"

"You fool, why didn't you have him checked out when you learned that your wife was dating him?"

"I didn't really know she was *dating* him," Essinger said, huffily. "That was only evident once they got *here*."

"We have to take care of this immediately," Wilcox said.

Essinger sat up. "I'll do it. There will be a lot of dangerous stunt work at the shoot tomorrow—er, today. Accidents can happen. They're inevitable."

Wilcox nodded. They had an understanding.

EIGHTEEN

THE GETAWAY

BOND AND TYLYN WERE UP BRIGHT AND EARLY, BUT THE PRODUCTION CREW were awake before dawn. The spectacular boat chase for *Pirate Island* would begin filming today, and Rick Fripp had estimated that the entire sequence would take a week to shoot. Tylyn was needed only for close-ups, for Betty would be doing the rough stuff. The rusty tanker had been set on fire and was already burning on "low." On Fripp's orders the gas could be increased, turning the tanker into an inferno.

"It's full of explosives," Tylyn told Bond. "They've been rigging explosives all over the water. It will truly be something to watch."

They stood at the rail of the *Starfish,* observing the preparations. From what Bond could see, last night's little mishap hadn't affected Fripp's working capacity.

The entire "setting" was an area of approximately a kilometer in diameter. Dotted within the setting were the various disabled boats, the tanker and other obstacles that would figure in the chase. There were four Fountain powerboats that had been outfitted to participate in the scene: two forty-seven foot and two forty-two foot Lightning sportboats.

Stuart Laurence joined them, for a stuntman was doing most of his scenes in the chase as well. "Those are among the best racing boats in the world," he explained. "They bought a fleet of powerboats from Reggie Fountain's company in America—you know, he's a champion boat racer—and then the production designer created those futuristic hulls for them."

"How fast do they go?" Bond asked.

"Usually they're at the seventy to eighty miles per hour mark, but Fountain has outfitted them with extra boost that increases that speed. The two forty-twos have twin engines that'll push the speed up to one hundred and fourteen or so. The other two have triple engines that will kick the speed up to one hundred and twenty," Laurence said. "I'd love to get behind the wheel of one, but the insurance company won't let me. All the shots of me at the helm are done at, what, forty miles an hour?"

"I love speed," Tylyn said. "I've never been in a boat going that fast, but I'm sure I would find it thrilling, not scary."

"It's pretty dangerous," Laurence said. "Look, they've got rescue teams and a medic in ready." He pointed to a group near the portable dock with another powerboat displaying the international Red Cross symbol.

Two bulky men whom Bond recognized as a couple of Essinger's flunkies appeared on the deck and approached them. One of them was Gérard, the fellow he had met in Monte Carlo.

"Monsieur Bond?" Gérard asked.

"Yes?"

"Monsieur Essinger would like a word with you. Could you follow us?"

Aha, here it was. Well, better now than later.

Bond smiled broadly and said, "How nice. Tylyn, would you like to accompany me?"

"Just you, monsieur," Gérard said.

Tylyn squeezed his arm. "He probably wants to do an interview after all. Don't worry, he won't bite. Much."

Bond kissed her cheek and went with the men to the lift. Gérard walked in front, while the other man, a rough-looking man with a hawk nose, took up the rear. They took it to one of the higher levels, where Essinger had his luxury cabin. They escorted him to the door and Hawk Nose knocked. A voice replied, "Come in."

Gérard opened the door and held it for Bond. Bond carefully stepped inside, followed by the two goons. Hawk Nose quickly shut the door behind them.

Two more bodyguards—one wearing a baseball cap and another with an eyepatch—were standing in the middle of the room. They were both holding metal tactical side batons. A blow by one of those with the appropriate force could break a man's skull.

Gérard suddenly grabbed Bond from behind, pinning his arms to his sides. Hawk Nose moved around in front to frisk him, removed the Walther, then punched Bond hard in the stomach. Bond winced but had sufficiently tightened the muscles in his abdomen to lessen the blow. Springing into action, he jumped up and kicked Hawk Nose in the chest, knocking him back into Baseball Cap. Bond then brought back his foot hard, digging his heel into Gérard's shin. Gérard yelped and let go. Bond swung around and spear-handed the man in the neck, crushing the trachea.

A bolt of pain shot through his left shoulder. Eyepatch had hit him with the baton. The pain was so great that Bond fell to his knees, clutching his shoulder with his right hand. Eyepatch raised the baton to strike again, but Bond put his weight on his good arm, levered himself on the floor, and kicked out at Eyepatch's legs. The man lost his balance and fell into Baseball Cap, who was also attempting to hit Bond with his baton.

Hawk Nose leaped onto Bond and began to punch him, but Bond rolled and managed to get on top. He slugged Hawk Nose hard, then used a split second's reprieve to reach for the PPK that had been dropped on the floor. But Eyepatch was too fast. He kicked the gun out of Bond's hand, sending it flying across the room.

The baton came crashing down again, barely missing Bond's head. He had sensed it coming and moved an inch to the side; but still, the metal rod smashed into his neck and skinned his ear. He fell over but used the momentum to roll toward his gun.

"Hold him!" Eyepatch shouted.

Baseball Cap and Hawk Nose jumped on Bond and attempted to do just that. Bond deftly swept the Walther into his hand and rolled onto his back. He squeezed the trigger twice, blasting holes in Baseball Cap and Hawk Nose's chests. Hawk Nose catapulted into Eyepatch, who caught and held the screaming man in front of him for cover.

Bond fired again. The bullet zipped through Hawk Nose's shoulder but missed Eyepatch. But this gave Bond the time he needed to get to his feet.

Eyepatch, covered in the other man's blood, dropped the baton and reached for a Smith & Wesson that he had beneath his own jacket. Bond shot again, this time putting a bright red hole through Hawk Nose's neck. This one penetrated Eyepatch's shoulder. He yelled and fell back, dropping Hawk Nose and the handgun. Bond didn't stay to see what kind of damage he had done. He turned, jumped over Gérard's body, and ran from the room.

Bond took the stairs two at a time. He emerged on the dining level and darted through the restaurant, where a few of the cast and crew were having coffee. They gasped as they looked up and saw that the side of Bond's head was covered in blood and he was carrying a gun.

Bond heard a gunshot behind him and everyone in the room screamed. Bond leapt behind an empty table and pushed it onto its side. Peering over it, he saw that Eyepatch had followed him down. There was blood seeping through his jacket on his left shoulder, but he was fit enough to fire his gun. Eyepatch shot at the table, blasting a hole through it, too close to Bond's face for comfort.

Bond jumped from the table and ran through swinging double doors into the kitchen. Another bullet shot past him, ricocheting off the wall. As he ran through, Bond swept a dozen metal pots and pans off a counter with his arm, knocking them all over the floor behind him and creating a terrible racket. The cook was horrified and shouted something to him in French. Bond went out of the back exit just as Eyepatch burst in, hampered by the clutter on the floor.

As he came out of the kitchen, Bond ran into none other than Tylyn.

"James?" she said, panicked. "What was that noise? My God, your face! What's wrong?"

But he kept running.

"James!" she called after him.

He reached the deck rail and looked over it, down to a lower level. It wasn't too far, so he climbed over it. Before dropping down, he met Tylyn's eyes and said, "I'm sorry. Some day I'll explain."

Bond let go of the rail and dropped twenty feet to the next deck, crashing into a chair to break his fall and startling several people who were reclining in the sun. He got to his feet and rolled, then got up to run again. Tylyn ran to the rail above and called to him. "James!"

Then Julius Wilcox appeared from nowhere and was at her side, aiming a gun at the running figure on the deck below.

Tylyn, enraged, pushed the ugly brute. "What are you *doing?*" Wilcox reacted with a snarl and shoved her to the deck.

Bond ran to the edge and looked down at the water below. The portable dock was on this side, thank God. He climbed over the rail and prepared to dive into the Mediterranean. He holstered his gun and tore off his jacket.

Wilcox aimed and fired just as Bond performed a neat swan dive, sailing forty feet to the water.

He swam hard for the dock. Already the guards had been alerted and were swarming down the *Starfish*'s various staircases and ramps, ready to intercept Bond. But he made it to the dock first. He climbed out of the water, ran to the first 47 Lightning powerboat, untied it, and jumped in. It took him a few seconds to examine the controls and start the engine.

The boat's engines created a huge wake and a tremendous roar that could be heard over the entire setting. Bond maneuvered the boat away from the dock and steered it toward Corsica. However, two thirty-eight foot Lightning sportboats manned by guards came around the tanker and were headed in his direction. Bond made a hook, turning the boat sharply to the left. He sped back toward the center of the setting, where the director and stunt crew were just beginning to shoot part of the chase.

Duling called "Action!" as Rick Fripp sat at the controls inside a 42 Lightning sportboat near the burning tanker. He had access to the trigger mechanisms for every explosive he had planted. Two "pirates" in costumed 42 Lightnings sped out from another direction and started to chase a disguised 29 Fever piloted by Betty and Stuart Laurence's stunt double.

The guards made it to the dock and jumped into two of the remaining boats. They revved up noisily and took off after Bond, who was headed directly for the center of the action.

Bond bore down on the accelerator, increasing his speed to almost 100 miles per hour, sped into the scene, and started to gain on Betty's boat.

Duling shouted, "Hey! What's going on? Who is that?"

The guards' boats jumped into view and then the gunfire began. Bullets shot across the water, breaking the surface with dozens of jabbing spurts.

"This wasn't in the rehearsal!" Duling shouted into his walkie-talkie.

The assistant director asked if he wanted to cut.

Duling replied, "No! Keep the cameras rolling. This looks great!"

Bond sped forward, overtaking Betty's boat, but it wasn't long before Wilcox and one of the guards appeared in another powerboat. They zoomed in from the side, seemingly out of nowhere. Wilcox was now armed with a submachine-gun. He let loose a barrage of ammunition at Bond's craft, shooting several holes in the side and into the engines. The boat kept going, though, straight for one of the "derelict" boats that had been constructed for the movie. Bond increased his speed and prayed that he could remember how to perform a particular maneuver. He turned the wheel and his boat did a marvelous barrel roll, jumping out of the water and somersaulting at high speed in mid-air. The Lightning barely missed the top of the obstacle and then landed on its hull with a splash.

Everyone on the *Starfish,* who had by now appeared on the various decks to watch the scene, applauded. What a terrific stunt! Who was that driver? Excellent action choreography! It looked so real!

Fripp, now in communication with Wilcox by walkie-talkie, barked instructions to his pyrotechnics people, stationed in small rowboats at various stages in the setting.

"Yes, damn it!" Fripp shouted. "Fire them now! I don't care if he's too close!"

Bond steered his boat toward one of the obstacles, hoping that it would provide some cover from the gunfire. He got within thirty meters of it when it suddenly exploded with intense force. Bond hit the deck as shrapnel and burning debris flew over his head. Without looking he made another hook to the right so that the boat wouldn't sail right into the burning mess. Once he was clear, he stood and gained control of the boat again.

Fripp shouted more orders into his walkie-talkie. Explosives had been rigged in the water at various intervals to simulate cannon balls hitting the surface. These began to go off as Bond sped over them.

Christ! Bond thought. It's like going over a minefield. He had to get out of the setting as quickly as possible, but he was surrounded on all sides now. The other boats were closing in and there was nowhere else to go.

"Ha!" Wilcox shouted. "We've got him now."

Bond looked around for an escape route. The only possible place to go was into the burning tanker. Bond turned the boat toward it, prayed that Collette had followed his instructions, and stepped on the gas. The engines roared as the boat shot toward the tanker.

"This is better than I had hoped!" Wilcox said. Fripp thought the same thing, for he shouted more orders into his walkie-talkie.

"Yes! Blow the tanker! Blow it now!" Wilcox yelled.

Fripp pulled the lever.

Bond knew that he had to reach full speed before attempting this particular move and he didn't have a lot of room to do so. He accelerated, gripped the wheel, and concentrated on the water ahead of him. The speedometer was at 112. The tanker was meters away.

No time left. It had to be now.

Bond hit a wave with perfect timing and performed a flawless "stuff," a stunt in which a boat dives completely under the water.

The Lightning disappeared under the surface just as the tanker blew to pieces. It was a deafening explosion, causing all the spectators in the area to flinch and hold their ears. A huge fireball erupted as the tanker broke into a dozen pieces. Monstrous clouds of black smoke poured out of the wreckage.

Tylyn, aboard the *Starfish,* screamed as she saw Bond's boat vanish into that maelstrom. The other people gasped, certain that they had just seen a stuntman killed in action. Dan Duling was aghast and speechless. The tanker was destroyed and he never got the right shot. And who *was* that guy in the boat?

The next ten minutes were pure chaos. The rescue boat and medic sped to the scene to look for Bond, but they found nothing. His Lightning surfaced on the other side of the tanker, but Bond wasn't in it. The dive underwater had saved the craft from being destroyed, but it had been streaked and scraped by burning metal.

They searched for thirty minutes. Bond's body was nowhere to be found. Had he been vaporized in the blast?

Wilcox pulled his boat over to where Fripp was stationed.

"Do you think that got him?" Fripp asked the ugly man.

"It looks like it, doesn't it?" Wilcox replied. "Let's keep looking and make sure."

A half-hour later, Essinger had Wilcox in his office aboard the *Starfish.*

"What the *hell* gave you the authority to blow up my tanker? We *needed* that for the goddamned *movie!*" Essinger said through clenched teeth.

"Relax," Wilcox said. "The Union will cover your costs. We've been after that guy for a long time. Besides, I thought you said that *you* were going to take care of him."

Essinger fumed. "He . . . he got the better of my men."

"Apparently."

"It seems he got away from *you,* too, Wilcox," Essinger spat.

Wilcox didn't reply. He merely stepped close to Essinger and clutched the man around the neck with a strong grip. He squeezed, cutting off Essinger's oxygen and sending bolts of pain into his throat.

"Listen, friend," Wilcox whispered. "Don't *ever* talk to me like that again. If you do, I'll rip out your larynx and make you eat it. Do we understand each other?"

Choking and turning blue, Essinger managed to nod.

"I can't hear you."

"Ye-es-ss!" Essinger stammered.

Wilcox released him and the producer fell to his knees. The ugly man moved away and heard a commotion in the corridor outside.

"Get up, someone's coming," he said. "Be cool, Essinger."

Wilcox managed to stand just as Tylyn, near hysterics, burst into the cabin.

"What the *hell* is going on?" she demanded. "James is dead! Your goons just *killed* him!"

Essinger, a consummate showman, did his best to assume a calm demeanor, cleared his throat, and said, "My 'goons', as you call them, were merely trying to catch him, darling. I've been meaning to tell you something about your friend, Mister Bond."

Tylyn couldn't comprehend her husband's seemingly unconcerned attitude.

"What the hell are you *talking* about?"

He had to clear his throat and rub it again. "You see, dear," Essinger continued, "Mister Bond isn't a journalist. He never was."

"What?" she snapped.

"He's a criminal, Tylyn." He held her by the shoulders, attempting to talk sense into her. "He wanted to sabotage our production. He's one of those industrial spies who work for other movie companies. He was hired to cause *Pirate Island* to shut down. That's why he got close to you—so he could be in proximity to inflict a great deal of damage. I just got off the phone with Rick. He says that the tanker is destroyed and we never got the shot we needed for the movie. That's going to cost us a lot of money."

"I *don't believe you!*" she screamed. She turned to Wilcox. "And *you!* Who the hell *are* you?" She turned back to her husband. "Who *is* this man, Léon? Why has he been hanging around you so much? He doesn't *work* for you, does he?"

"Mister Wilcox is a . . . financial advisor," Essinger said. "Now darling, we must try to forget this and get on with making a movie."

"To *hell* with your movie!" Tylyn shouted. "James is *dead!*"

Essinger almost shrugged. "I know, it's a pity. Luckily we're insured. But that will teach the other studios not to go messing with Léon Essinger, eh, darling?"

"You're a liar!" she said with venom, struggling to get out of his grasp.

"It's true, Tylyn," he said. "The man was a killer. A hired gun. Whatever he promised you or told you, they were all lies. I'm sorry."

Tylyn broke away from him, put her arms around herself, and sobbed. Essinger moved toward her to comfort her, but she backed away, shouting, "Leave me alone!" She turned and ran out, tears streaming down her face.

After a moment, Wilcox said, "She could hurt us."

Essinger spat, "She won't be with us long."

Wilcox paused before suggesting, "You might need to make sure that she attends the screening in Cannes. At this point there's no guarantee that she will."

Essinger, still upset about Wilcox's threat, the loss of the tanker, and his wife's reaction to the spy's death, merely nodded.

"I've already taken care of that," he said.

As soon as the boat dived beneath the tanker, Bond used his arms and legs to springboard his body out of the boat. The trick was to stay suspended in the water so that the boat passed beneath his body without hurting him. Then, as soon as it was clear, he had to dive as deeply as he could to avoid the impact of the blast.

An impact it was. The force of the explosion was like a sledge-hammer, slamming into Bond with a fist of fury. Completely dazed, he floated motionless for a few seconds, then began to drift up toward the mayhem.

Snap out of it! Bond shouted to himself. *Swim!*

Summoning every ounce of strength in his battered body, Bond willed himself to paddle with his arms to halt his ascent. Then he straightened, aimed his nose downward, and swam toward the bottom of the sea.

Bond opened his eyes to the stinging, murky water. He swam harder, forcing his body to work on automatic while he concentrated on finding what Collette had conveniently dropped in the water on the perimeter of the setting just before sunrise.

He reckoned that it was a good forty or fifty meters to the land-mark, or rather, the watermark. A buoy floated inconspicuously at the perimeter on the north end of the setting, and that's where he and Collette had decided would be the safest place for Collette to bring his boat and get as close as possible to the *Starfish*.

Bond's lungs were burning like hell. How long had he been holding his breath? A minute or two? He had to have air soon. But was he still too close to the tanker?

When he thought that he had swum at least twenty meters away, Bond had no choice but to risk it. He surfaced and gulped a glorious breath of air and immediately dived back underwater. Bond hoped everyone would be focused on the tanker and would not have noticed him.

The oxygen energized him. He kept swimming toward the buoy, confident now that he would make it. The tide was much stronger than he had expected, but with a steady stroke he eventually reached the target. When he was able to grasp the side of the buoy, Bond sur-faced again and took some breaths. Resting momentarily, he looked back at the chaos. Boats were zipping this way and that, the perimeter was covered in black smoke and he could hear a lot of shouting.

How would he explain this to Tylyn? he wondered. Would he ever see her again and *have* a chance to explain?

Possibly not, thought Bond. And what good had he accomplished? What had he learned? Not much, only that they were carrying what he believed to be the stolen CL-20. Reporting it to the authorities was useless, for the Union would surely take care to hide it better. They were obviously attempting to smuggle it somewhere, probably into France. What he needed to do was regroup and formulate a new plan of attack. He had to discover what they were up to before he could credibly blow any whistles.

With a heavy heart, he turned his back on the destruction and began to work his way around the buoy with his hands until he was on the side facing the open sea. There, tied onto one of the buoy's handholds, was a rope, pulled taut into the water. The weight at the other end was not so much as to topple the buoy. Bond took another breath and descended the rope, hand over hand, until he came to the magnificent machine tied at the bottom.

"Ariel" was a K-10 Hydrospeeder, an innovative self-propelled diver propulsion unit that had recently been developed in America and was now being sold as an aquatic novelty to Caribbean holiday resorts. Bond had first seen one in Belize, where a diving colleague named Gaz Cooper sold and demonstrated them. Q Branch had licensed the technology and built a hydrospeeder with a few extras.

It was basically an underwater bicycle with a built-in re-breathing system. It was the size of a small motorcycle, but with no wheels. Instead it had two short wings that jutted out near the bow. The two motors were aft. The diver sat on a curved seat and leaned forward until his chest was resting on the top of the hydrospeeder.

Bond took the re-breather first and inserted it into his mouth. The lovely oxygen flowed when he turned the valve. Collette had been thoughtful enough to leave a facemask tied to one of the controls. Bond put that on next, doing his best to flush out the water. Then, he sat on the vehicle and started it. Finally, he untied the rope and he was off.

A man riding a hydrospeeder could stay underwater for nearly two hours. Seated on the vehicle, a diver's body hydro-dynamically completed the form of its design as his hands were used to manipulate the independently operated wings that controlled pitch and roll. The feet pushed on independent motor controls for the left and right motors, varying the yaw and speed. Embedded in the hydrospeeder was an oxygen tank. The vehicle had an electrical engine, delivering about 2000 watts for two hours. Dive data was available at a glance on the dashboard, which was flat in front of the diver's face.

Normally, it could travel up to five or six knots, but Major Boothroyd had increased that speed to ten with the aid of a turbo booster he had installed in-between the two original motors. Other extras included twin harpoon guns in the front, a mechanism for releasing small mines in the water below the vehicle, smokescreen capability, superior high-intensity headlamps and a second re-breather, although the hydrospeeder wasn't really built for two. Like most of the vehicles made by Q Branch, Ariel was also equipped with her own tracking signal and a self-destruct feature.

Bond studied the compass on the dashboard and the blinking light that marked the GPS coordinate of his destination. It would take him an hour to get there.

The hydrospeeder gracefully moved through the water, some fifty feet below the surface. It was an exhilarating feeling. He had enjoyed the thrill when he had first tested the hydro-speeder in Q Branch's tank at MI6. Now, out here in the wide-open sea, he was able to give her a full workout. He could roll and spin, dive up or down, or ascend and descend in a straight vertical line.

There were plenty of fish around, mostly grouper and painted comber, gliding along with Bond over the sponges that grew plentifully on the surfaces of rocks. The famous Corsican vibrant red coral was also abundant in the area. The bottom was covered with various types of seaweed. Some of it was brown, a lot of it was green, and a portion was red. As always, the alien landscape of an underwater vista never failed to mesmerize Bond. He was in his element.

Two dentex, carnivorous fish related to the sargo, appeared and swam behind Bond. Although they probably weren't dangerous, he didn't want to take the chance of one becoming curious and taking a bite out of him. He pushed a button and dark black smoke poured out of the hydrospeeder's tail. It was enough to scare off the fish.

The vehicle sped out of the dark cloud and sailed over a bed of ascidians, which resembled soft tubes and grew in violet and red with a little black here and there. They undulated back and forth, suggestively beckoning to Bond with their oval, open lips.

The GPS signal indicated that he was close. Bond began his ascent slowly, for even on a hydrospeeder, a diver had to compensate for the changes in pressure. On the way up, a beautiful rainbow wrasse swam near him and studied him curiously. It seemed to be congratulating him for making it. Eventually Bond saw the dark shape of Collette's boat above him and rose to the surface.

NINETEEN

THE INFILTRATION

NIGEL SMITH LOOKED AT THE PIECE OF MAIL THAT HAD ARRIVED FOR BOND. The envelope was addressed by hand, to "Commander James Bond." Whoever had written it had also used 007's subtle security code—a semicolon after the name and commas after every line in the address except the last one. This meant that the contents were "friendly" and/or "personal" and went straight to the addressee, going through only the obligatory X-ray upon its arrival in the post at M16 without being opened.

There was no return address, save for a single "M" with a circle around it.

Nigel knew that it wasn't from M. Could it be . . . ?

He was dying to open it but thought it best to contact 007 first. Nigel picked up the phone and dialed Bond's mobile number.

It went unanswered.

Bond had lost his mobile during his getaway from the film set. He was lucky to have his Walther, the Q-Branch camera, and the clothes on his back.

After loading Ariel onto the Outlaw and docking at Calvi, he and Collette spent the remainder of the afternoon resting at the Hotel Corsica, coincidentally the same establishment where René Mathis had stayed. Its location on the outskirts of town suited Bond nicely, just as it had his old French cohort.

"Bertrand, let me borrow your phone, would you?" Bond asked after he had rested, showered, and put on some clothes that Collette had brought with him. Collette tossed his mobile to him and Bond dialed M16.

Nigel was very relieved to hear from him.

"I was beginning to wonder what had happened to you," he said. "I was just about to leave the office."

"Everything is fine, I think. Bertrand Collette and I are in Calvi trying to decide how to proceed."

"Well, perhaps I have something that will help you. You have a letter here from an 'M', and it's not our inimitable chief. It was sent from Corsica, but it somehow got lost in the mail and just arrived here today."

"Christ, that's from Mathis!" Bond said. "What does it say?"

Nigel opened it and read it aloud. " 'James, I have tracked our friend to Corsica. I am going today to see if I can find his home. "Corse Shipping" near St. Florent is full of cobwebs, especially the cave below the cliff. If you do not hear from me in a few days, find the man they call the Sailor at the marina in Calvi. René.' "

"Full of cobwebs" was a code that meant the place was dirty, i.e., occupied by the opposition.

"What is the date on the letter?" Bond asked.

"Hmmm . . . over two weeks ago."

"Oh no. Thanks, Nigel. I'm going to look into this."

After he rang off, Bond and Collette looked at a map and pinpointed St. Florent and the best way to approach it.

"Corse Shipping figures in whatever Essinger is doing with the Union," Bond said. "The firm was mentioned in documents I found at his office in Paris. They've been providing catering services and the like. I also saw the name stamped on the crates containing explosives for the film in Fripp's trawler. If that was really the stolen CL-20 I found there, then Corse Shipping had its hands on that, too. I think we should take a look at the place."

"I figure we can take the boat and approach the place by sea, what do you think?"

"We'll go tonight, after dark," Bond said. "But first there's a man at the marina I have to see."

Bond went alone to the harbor. He asked someone where he might find "the Sailor," and the man pointed to a sailboat tied to the opposite side of the dock. Bond went over there and found the Sailor asleep on his boat.

"Pardon?" Bond asked, waking him.

"Huh? Who is it?"

Bond explained that he was looking for a Frenchman who may have befriended him a few days ago.

"Oh yes, Monsieur Mathis," the Sailor said, climbing out of the boat and standing on the dock. "Would you like to buy me dinner, too?"

Bond shrugged. Why not? "If you can help me, I'd be happy to do so."

Over pastis, a strong aniseed flavored aperitif and a couple of pizzas, the Sailor explained that Mathis had been asking about Emile Cirendini and the mysterious blind man known as Pierre Rodiac. The Sailor said that Mathis had traced Rodiac to Sartène and had gone down that way over two weeks ago. He hadn't heard from Mathis since.

"Did he say anything about Corse Shipping?" Bond asked.

"Apparently this Rodiac fellow has dealings with Emile Cirendini. Cirendini owns the boat Rodiac uses to travel to the mainland." He pointed to the Princess. "That's it. I know that your friend went to Corse Shipping to snoop around. I don't know what he found."

Bond bought the man a bottle of wine and bid him *adieu*.

After the sun set, Bond and Collette took the Outlaw back out to sea and sailed eastward toward Cap Corse. They passed St. Florent and soon found Corse Shipping on the coast. It was a forbidding place, perched high up near the coastal highway.

"There doesn't seem to be much activity right now," Bond said, studying the coastline with binoculars. "All the lights are off."

Then he saw the cave.

"Bertrand, pull in a little closer. Do you see that cave there?"

Collette threw the engine into gear and headed to shore. "That must be what Mathis was talking about. I'm taking Ariel into it," Bond said.

Collette stopped some fifty meters out, dropped anchor, and cut the lights. It took them a few minutes to drop the hydro-speeder in the water and for Bond to change into a black wet suit. He put on the facemask and jumped in.

"If I'm not back in an hour, call the marines," Bond said.

He climbed aboard Ariel and started the engine. Breathing regularly with the self-contained oxygen unit, Bond dived, manipulated the controls, and began traveling toward the cave some fifteen feet below the surface.

The inside of the cave was dark and ominous when he brought Ariel to the surface. Bond flicked on the high-intensity headlamps and pointed the hydrospeeder at the back of the cavern. At first glance, it appeared to be a natural cave big enough for a small tugboat. After a bend in the tunnel, the water passed between two stalagmites that stood like sentinels guarding whatever was beyond. Keeping low, Bond noticed that some machinery had been attached to the stalagmites. They were electric eyes, placed four feet above the surface. Trespassers would be caught before they could go any further. Bond submerged again and propelled Ariel forward through the passageway until he came to a larger cavern that was probably manmade. Sure enough, there was a dock there. Several speedboats were tied to it, as well as a craft that looked similar to a coast guard's patrol boat, but without markings.

Bond tied Ariel to a post on the dock and climbed up. Barefoot, but armed with his gun in a waterproof holster, his knife, and the camera, Bond stepped across the dock to metal doors that presumably led to a lift. There was an elaborate alarm system incorporated in the doors, so he pulled the camera from his belt and activated the laser.

He aimed it at the alarm box and made two quick cuts across the mechanism, burning it out and deactivating it. Bond replaced the camera and tried the doors. They opened freely.

A wide hallway led to a freight lift. It was open cage style, with a sliding mesh gate for a door. How noisy would it be? Bond slid open the gate, got inside, and pressed the top button. The machinery whirred and clanged, but it wasn't as loud as he had feared. Still, it was possible that the noise would alert someone.

He took the lift to the top level, deep inside the Corse Shipping complex. It opened to the warehouse, which was full of crates, boxes and barrels. He stepped out and got his bearings. He could see the outside lift, the one that faced the sea, on the other side of the warehouse. To his right he found the exit leading to the complex offices. He peeked into the brightly lit corridor and heard voices somewhere down the hall. Should he risk going farther?

Careful not to make a sound, Bond inched down the corridor until he found the office the voices were coming from. Next to it was another office. Bond listened at the door, heard nothing, tried the knob and opened it.

There was no one in the office. It contained a worktable and a desk. Bond switched on the light and locked the door behind him. He removed the camera from his belt again and pulled out the two earpieces that were attached to thin, flexible tubes. Bond flicked a switch on the bottom of the camera, out of which he pulled a stetho-scope-like suction cup, also attached to a flexible tube. He licked the cup and stuck it to the wall, then put the earpieces in his ears.

He could hear the conversation clearly, and, in fact, recognized one of the voices.

"Now that the bastard is dead, we don't have anything to worry about," Julius Wilcox said. "What a mess. They'll have to completely rebuild that damn tanker and film the sequence all over again. Essinger is pretty upset. But at least we got rid of the spy."

"Let's hope so. We've come too far to abort the project," the other man said. Emile Cirendini, perhaps?

"Oh, we won't abort, believe me. Once *Le Gérant* accepts a client's money, he goes through with the project, no matter how risky. Besides, this one will be a piece of cake. All of the parts are coming together nicely. Are you on schedule?"

"As soon as the detonator is completed, we'll be ready," Cirendini said. "I'll have the entire assembly shipped out by the usual method to the studios in Nice."

"Excellent," Wilcox said.

"Have you spoken to *Le Gérant?*"

"Yes, a few minutes ago. I'm sure he'll be staying put at his house until the project is completed."

"If you ask me, he's been very careless lately."

"How do you mean?" Wilcox asked.

"Gambling at the casino in Monte Carlo. Going out in public. It's not going to be long before someone figures out who he is."

"*Le Gérant* can do whatever the hell he wants to do. Nothing the Union has ever done can be traced back to him. He's perfectly clean. The man's a goddamned genius."

Bond glanced around the room while he listened. On the floor next to the worktable was a stack of large film cans, the kind that contained 35mm motion picture prints. Bond took a look inside the top one and saw that it was empty. Next to these were empty pressurized soft drink canisters, the kind seen in bars with hoses attached to them. A means of smuggling, perhaps? On top of the worktable was an odd-looking device that Bond was almost positive was the detonator Cirendini was talking about. By examining the pieces and the various small boxes that the parts came in, Bond determined that the device contained a servo receiver connected to an electric detonator, manufactured by a Canadian company. It was a high-strength unit designed for use in explosive initiation applications where there was no need for a delay between charges.

It was something that anyone could purchase over the internet.

What the hell were they planning to blow up? What was the significance of the film cans? What about the soft drink canisters? This must all be related to the radio transmitter he had seen on Fripp's trawler. Was Fripp assembling the transmitter to these devices, the receiver and detonator?

Bond was tempted to smash the pieces with the butt of his gun then and there but he froze when he heard a knock next door.

"What?" he heard Cirendini ask. There was activity outside the door.

"Monsieur, there is a strange boat not far from the cave. It's been there for half an hour."

Damn! They've seen Collette's boat.

"Well, get out there and find out who it is. Use your discretion," Cirendini said. "If you think that it's warranted, kill whoever it is and get rid of the boat."

"Yes, sir."

No time to lose. Bond pulled the suction cup from the wall, replaced the earpieces, and hooked the camera back on his belt. He listened at the door and waited until he heard the guards walk away.

The corridor was clear. Bond slipped out of the office and made his way back to the warehouse without being detected. He carefully looked inside the swinging doors before entering and saw that three guards inside were blocking his way to the lift.

So far, no one knew that he was there. If he could cause a diversion . . . ?

Bond drew his gun and peered inside again. Along one wall were stacks of more soft drink dispenser tanks. Perhaps these were full of pressurized soda? Bond took a bead and fired. One of the tanks burst, spewing cola in a steady, high-pressured stream.

The guards immediately snapped out of their reverie. One of them went over to the tanks to see what had happened. The two others walked toward the swinging doors, certain that the gunshot had come from that direction. As soon as they were two feet from the doors, Bond swung them open as hard as he could, hitting them both in the face. Bond spun inside, elbowed one guard in the stomach, leaned to the side, and kicked the other guard in the chest. He then grabbed hold of the first guard's arm and threw the man over his back into the second guard. They toppled to the floor.

Bond ran to the lift before the third guard could stop him. He got into the cage, slammed the gate shut, and pushed the button for the lower level. The third guard drew a handgun and fired down into the lift as it descended. Bond hugged the metal wall, just beyond the guard's aim. In just a few seconds, the lift had disappeared to a lower level.

Then the alarms went off.

When the lift got to the bottom, Bond could see several guards lining the corridor that led to the cave-dock. Luckily, they were facing the opposite direction and the alarms had covered the noise of the lift descending. Nevertheless, it was a thirty-foot gauntlet that he had to run through in order to get out of the place.

Bond waited a few seconds before opening the gate. He knew that timing was everything. Gun in hand, he sprang out of the lift and ran like the devil, firing shots above the guards' heads. The men immediately jumped for cover behind boxes and crates that lined the corridor, too surprised to react in any other way. By the time Bond got to the door he had disarmed earlier, one of the guards found the wherewithal to fire back. Bullets zinged around Bond's head, boring holes into the metal door. He dropped to the floor, rolled and shot back at the several guards running toward him. He hit the two men in front and they fell back into the others. That gave Bond the time he needed to get to his feet and open the door.

The "patrol boat" was gone. Bond rushed to the edge of the dock and was relieved to see that no one had discovered Ariel tied there underwater. He quickly got aboard, untied her and submerged.

Bond used minimal lighting to navigate his way out of the cave and into the open sea. Once he was clear of the cavern, he cut the lights and surfaced.

Oh no! Cirendini's patrol boat was alongside Collette's Outlaw, which was on fire and sinking fast. He heard the men on the patrol boat whooping and hollering as a burning figure, obviously bound, fell over the side of the Outlaw into the water.

Bond quickly dived again and sped at top speed toward the wreckage. It took him nearly three minutes—far too long, he feared. He put on the high intensity lamps and swerved the hydrospeeder back and forth, searching frantically for Collette's body.

There! The lifeless figure was floating toward the bottom, a weight attached to his feet. His arms were bound behind his back. When

Bond got close enough with the vehicle, the illumination revealed that his friend was badly burned.

Bond cut the engine and slipped off Ariel so that he could grab Collette. He immediately shoved the second re-breather into the Frenchman's mouth. Bond laid him over the hydro-speeder, started her up, and began to ascend.

When they broke the surface, Bond did his best to revive Collette. He removed the re-breather and laid Collette on his back over the vehicle. He then performed mouth-to-mouth resuscitation and CPR.

"Come on, Bertrand!" he whispered. Bond glanced up and saw that the patrol boat was headed back to the cave. They hadn't seen him. The burning Outlaw had all but sunk completely.

Bond continued working on Collette for another three minutes but his friend showed no signs of life.

Damn it! You're alive! I know it!

Bond blocked out everything around him and concentrated fully on Collette. He didn't believe in miracles, but he prayed for one now.

Was yet another ally going to die while serving with him? Bond had seen it happen too many times. It seemed to be a curse. He brought death wherever he went, which was why he preferred to work alone.

Come on, damn it!

When Collette unexpectedly coughed up water, Bond thought that there might really be a God.

TWENTY

THE SECOND VISIT

BOND DITCHED ARIEL IN THE BAY OFF ST. FLORENT AND RODE IN THE ambulance with Collette back to Calvi. Although the coastal port didn't contain a hospital, it had an emergency treatment center affiliated with the main hospital in Bastia. The Antenne Médicale d'Urgence handled all but the worst cases on site; otherwise a patient would be sent to Bastia by helicopter or ambulance. It was a small facility with three patient rooms, a treatment room, and an administration office.

A doctor and nurse took Collette into the treatment room and remained there for nearly an hour. Bond paced the small waiting area, feeling ridiculously helpless. Finally, the doctor emerged and approached Bond as Collette was wheeled into one of the patient rooms.

"Your friend has suffered many second degree burns and a few third degree burns. We've done what we can tonight, but he'll have to go to Bastia in the morning and spend some time in their burn ward," the doctor said.

"But his chances of recovery are good?" Bond asked.

"Yes, after some skin grafting and rehabilitation. He's very lucky to be alive."

"Should he go to Bastia tonight?"

The doctor shook his head. "It wouldn't do him much good to move him again so soon. We call this the eighth floor of the Bastia hospital. Our care here is just as good, and we can watch him tonight. Why don't you go home and get some sleep, monsieur? We'll be transferring him tomorrow around eight o'clock. You can check with the Bastia hospital staff after eleven to see which room he's in."

"Thank you," Bond said. "May I see him?"

"He's heavily sedated," the doctor said. "But I suppose it's all right. If he's asleep, don't disturb him."

Bond went into the room, which looked like any other hospital room in the world. Bertrand Collette was on his back, legs and arms bare and suspended. The skin was ugly and charred and was covered with a greasy ointment. His face was covered in bandages.

He bent over Collette's face and thought that he might be asleep when the Frenchman whispered, "The things I do for England . . ."

Bond laughed softly. "I'll make sure you get an OBE for this, Bertrand."

Collette groaned and said, "They really got me, didn't they, James?"

"It's not so bad," Bond said. "The doctor says you'll recover completely. It'll take some time, but you'll be fine."

"And I'll look like the Phantom of the Opera. What will people say?"

Bond said, "Just tell them that you cut yourself shaving."

That made Collette laugh.

"I'm going back to the hotel," Bond said. "Then I suppose I'll go to Sartène tomorrow. I'll give you a call when I can."

"James?"

"Yes?"

"*Merci.*"

Bond patted the top of Collette's head and left the room.

It was nearly two in the morning when Bond got back to the Hotel Corsica. Weary and discouraged, he took the stairs to the second floor and made his way to his room. As he put the key card into the lock, though, he sensed that something was amiss. Years of experience had fabricated in him a kind of organic radar, something inexplicable that pricked his nerves whenever trouble was around the corner—or behind a door.

Bond drew the Walther, dropped to a squatting position, and flung it open.

Marc-Ange Draco sat facing him, an open bottle of bourbon at his side.

"Marc-Ange!" Bond said, standing. "I might have shot you."

"No you wouldn't have," Draco said. "Your reflexes are too good. You would have seen that it was me before you pulled the trigger. Just as you did. Come inside."

Bond entered and shut the door. They were alone.

"Marc-Ange, what the hell?" Bond asked, holstering the Walther.

"Sit down, James," Draco said. "Have a drink with me. I'm well ahead of you. I think you need one, too, no?"

"As a matter of fact," Bond said, pulling up a chair. They sat around the coffee table that was a piece of standard furniture for the rooms.

Draco poured a tall glass of bourbon for Bond and handed it to him. "*Salut,*" he said, and they clicked glasses.

After the lovely fire coated his throat, Bond asked, "Now tell me, Marc-Ange, how did you find me?"

"Tsk tsk," Draco said. "Surely by now you know that I have eyes and ears all over this island. There are some people, you know, who believe that you are dead."

"Mmm," Bond said, taking another sip. "I suppose it won't be long before they realize that I'm not."

"I think you can bet on that. I apologize, James, but it appears that you were right about Léon Essinger. He *is* involved with the Union."

Bond said nothing.

"But I still think that he's not your primary concern," Draco said. "Our friend, *Le Gérant,* is hiding somewhere in the vicinity of Sartène."

"I know," Bond said. "I got a message from Mathis. It came rather late, I'm afraid. I'm going south after sunrise to look for him."

"Ah, I may be able to help in that regard," Draco said. "Since you last asked, my eyes and ears have been watching out for your DGSE friend. It seems that he was indeed last seen making inquiries in Sartène. After my man paid a very large bribe to a restaurant owner there, we learned that Mathis was directed to speak to a *mazzere* who lives in town."

"What the hell is that?"

Draco explained the legend of *mazzeri* and how they could foretell deaths in dreams.

"That sounds like a load of rubbish to me," Bond said.

Draco shrugged. "Being Corsican, I should take offence at that, but I tend to agree with you. I am very superstitious, to an extent, but I don't see dead people. At any rate, Mathis' trail stopped there. I was about to send my man to talk to this *mazzere,* but I figured that you would want to do that yourself."

"Do you know how I can find him?"

"Her. Her name is Annette Culioli." He gave Bond the woman's address.

They sat in silence for a few minutes, savoring the strong bourbon.

"The Union are up to something with Essinger's film production company," Bond said. "I found evidence that they've got some explosives. Something stolen from an air force base."

"Is that all you know?"

"Unfortunately, yes," Bond said. "Not enough to blow the whistle. I found what looked like a radio transmitter in the possession of Essinger's special effects man. I think I found pieces of its companion receiver at Emile Cirendini's place last night, and it was attached to a detonator."

"But for what?"

"I don't know. Yet."

Draco said, "Emile Cirendini used to be one of my most trusted colleagues. I gave him a lot of power in the old Union Corse, but he misused it. He defected years ago. Now he's with *the* Union. We are enemies, to say the least."

"Well, he's in this up to his neck," Bond said. "The Union are using his shipping firm to transport materials."

Draco nodded. "I tried to shut him down years ago, but the Union is much stronger than my little band of rebels. He damned near shut *me* down. I'm lucky to be operating at all on this island."

Again, Bond noted that Draco seemed unusually morose. His father-in-law had definitely changed. The once boisterous, life-loving pirate was now merely a shell of his former self. He seemed to be a broken man, someone who had been through too many tragedies.

"How many times have you been up against the Union?" Draco asked.

"What do you mean?"

"In an actual skirmish. Say, in a year."

"This past year? It's like the cold war all over again," Bond replied. "We hit one of their safe houses, they hit one of ours. They've been a thorn in our side for a few years now."

Draco looked concerned. "Tell me, have you had any particular fights with them in *France* this past year?"

"Yes," Bond said. "Just after New Year I was helping Mathis with a case in Nice. The DGSE thought that the Union were hiding arms at Essinger's film studios there. They set up a raid. It went . . . wrong."

"You were there?" Draco asked.

Bond nodded. "We had bad intelligence. They were waiting for us. If I hadn't have shot those barrels of petrol—but then they would have got away if I hadn't. I don't know how much you know about it."

"There was a fire," Draco said, bluntly. "Several innocent people died. It was all over the news. Of course I know about it."

Bond nodded and took another drink. They were silent again for a long time. Bond sensed that Draco wanted to say something else that weighed heavily on his mind. Instead, though, the broad-shouldered man stood abruptly.

"I must apologize again, James," he said. "I have become much too antisocial since the deaths of my wife and daughter. Forgive me. I had better leave you now so that you can get some rest."

"Don't go on my account, Marc-Ange," Bond said. "Is it something you'd like to talk about?"

"No," he said. "I *don't* want to talk about it at all." Draco held up his hands. "It is late. Good luck with your *mazzere*. I hope you find your friend. *Adieu*."

Without further ceremony, Draco walked out of the room without the obligatory embrace, or even shaking hands.

Odd, Bond thought. The man was very depressed. Not the old Draco at all.

Bond finished the glass of bourbon and crawled into bed. He was fast asleep in less than a minute.

When Tylyn Mignonne awoke the next morning aboard the *Starfish*, the emptiness and pain she felt in her heart were as heavy as ever. She clutched her pillow, and moved over to bury her face in the other one. She could still smell Bond on it.

Had she loved that man? she asked herself. Or was he merely, as he had playfully suggested, a rebound partner?

Whatever, she thought. The pain was real. She missed him.

Tylyn didn't believe a word that Léon had said about Bond. A film studio spy? Was he kidding?

She was convinced, however, that Bond was not who he said he was. He really wasn't a journalist. Was he some kind of policeman? Had he been investigating Léon? She knew that her husband had been involved with underworld types in the past. But Léon only associated with criminals, he wasn't one himself. That ugly man, Wilcox, now *he* was a crook if ever there was one. He looked as if he could easily kill someone.

The police had spent a day at the set, making inquiries. They had asked her many personal questions about Bond, but it was obvious that they didn't know who he really was either. The investigator in charge told her that the magazine he supposedly worked for, *Pop World*, confirmed his employment, but that was as far as they went. Since the body was never found, and from all the statements they took from witnesses, it appeared that neither Essinger nor anyone involved with the production was responsible for what had happened.

Oh, James, what *did* happen?

Had he been using her to get close to her husband? But his affections had seemed so real. Had she been a fool?

There was a knock on the door.

"Go away, it's too early," she called.

"Tylyn, I have some news for you!" It was Léon.

"Tell me later."

"I think you should hear it now."

She got out of bed, put on her robe, and opened the cabin door. He was dressed in "captain's" gear, smiling with exuberance. It made her want to throw up.

"What do you want?" she asked.

"I've just received word from Cannes," he said. "You have been asked to present the check to the charities on the night of our screening!"

She frowned. "What?"

Essinger was clearly taken aback by her lack of enthusiasm. "The screening at Cannes! At the end of the week. Remember? We're screening *Tsunami Rising* at a charity event."

"I wasn't planning on attending, Léon," she said. "That's your movie, not mine."

"But think of the publicity we can generate for *Pirate Island* if you're there. Prince Edward will be there! Princess Caroline will be there!"

"Oh, Léon, don't give me that crap. You just want me there so you can pretend I'm still your wife."

"You *are* still my wife."

"Not for long, Léon."

He stepped inside and shut the door. "What do you mean?"

"Get out of my cabin."

"*What do you mean?*"

"I didn't want to tell you until after we finished shooting the film," she said. "But I think we should divorce."

Essinger said nothing, but she could see his lower lip begin to tremble.

"Come on, Léon, you know it would be best," she said.

"I could fight you on this, Tylyn," he said finally.

"I was hoping that you wouldn't. It would be easier on us both if you didn't."

Essinger moved away, his back to her. "Then do this favor for me," he said.

"What?"

He turned to face her and put his hands on her upper arms. "Present the check at the screening. Show the world that we're still friends. It will do you good. You need to be there. Please."

She sighed. "You're saying that there will be no contest in the divorce if I agree to do that?"

He nodded.

"All right," she said.

He started to embrace her, but she held up her hands. "But everything else still stands. Our relationship from now on is strictly business. I don't accompany you, I don't sit with you, we are not photographed together."

"Very well."

"Now get out of my cabin."

"You're not still upset about that man Bond, are you?" he asked.

"Upset? *Upset?*" She turned on him, livid. "You and your thugs *killed* him! I don't care what you say he was, it didn't give you the right to do what you did."

"We didn't kill him! He brought it on himself!"

"Get out. I don't want to discuss it."

Essinger said, "Fine. I'll see you on the set later." He turned and left the cabin, slamming the door behind him.

Tylyn was furious.

That man was up to something. She knew him too well. He had something fiendish in the works, but she was too distraught and too involved on the film to attempt to find out what it was.

If only James were with her. He had possessed a kind of strength that she had found addictive.

But now she would have to forget all about him.

TWENTY-ONE

THE PRISONERS

"YOU ARE THE SECOND MAN TO COME LOOKING FOR THE DREAM-WOLF."

Annette Culioli set down a glass of red wine on the table and stood for a moment, looking at Bond with trepidation.

He thanked her for the drink and said, "Madame, I assure you that my intentions are honorable and that the main reason I look for this man is because my friend may be in danger."

"He *is* in danger," she said, sitting down across from him. "The dream-wolf told me so."

"Oh?"

"As I mentioned to your friend, the wolf and I are competitors in the dream world. However, be that as it may, we also converse from time to time. Even though he is a wolf, I can understand what he says."

Bond thought that the woman was on a plane of existence somewhere on the far side of Jupiter, but she was undoubtedly sincere in what she had to tell him. While he didn't believe one bit in the mumbo jumbo of dream worlds and the human-animals that inhabit them, he sensed that the basic details of her stories bore some resemblance to the truth. As long as she didn't break out tarot cards or a crystal ball, Bond thought, then he might be able to take her seriously.

"I cannot say where your friend is," she went on to say. "The dream-wolf has him in his den."

"Do you know where that is?"

"All I know is that he lives amongst the menhirs."

"The menhirs?"

"The ancient statues."

Right, Bond thought. He knew about Corsica's famous prehistoric sites and the ancient dwellings and artifacts that were plentiful in the southern part of the island.

"And this wolf," Bond asked, "do you think he is the blind man I spoke about earlier?"

The *mazzere* nodded her head. "The wolf can see, though. He can see very well. I interpret this to mean that the blind man can also see very well in his own way. He is a formidable person, someone who has great powers of intuition and control. He dominates my dreams when he is in them. Sometimes I cannot escape him. One day he will kill me in my dreams, and that will be the end of my life on earth."

Bond had heard the old adage that if one dreamt of dying oneself, then it surely would bring about a real death. He never believed it; but he had never dreamed of his own death. Not that he could remember.

"Is there anything else you can tell me?" he asked her. "Anything that might help me find my friend?"

"Look for the menhirs that are not on public property," she said. "Look in the vicinity of Cucuruzzu and Capula, but not as far east."

"*Merci,* madame," Bond said. He stood and turned to leave, but she stopped him.

"Monsieur, I warn you," she said. "This man is the devil. Even though his eyes do not see, he can look into your soul."

Bond nodded and left the house.

He stepped out onto the cobblestone streets of Sartène, still mystified by the strange, austere atmosphere of the place, and walked back to where he had parked his rented car.

Bond would have preferred to have his Aston Martin with him, but, having left it in a car park in Nice, he was forced to rent a vehicle from Europcar in Calvi. They had given him a modest Renault Mégane 1.6 16V. It was brand new, with less than 5000 kilometers on the clock, and Bond was pleasantly surprised by its performance.

After having driven it down the island to Sartène, he now left the village and traveled north again until he reached the D268 toward Levie, on the way to the tourist sites of Cucuruzzu and Capula. Filitosa had been another possibility, but he ruled it out after studying his maps. From what the old woman had said, the most likely place for Le Gérant's home was the stretch of road that traversed several lots of private property.

Unwittingly retracing Mathis' footsteps, Bond overshot his mark and found the reception area for the Cucuruzzu and Capula sites. He turned around and went back toward Propriano, drove a few miles, and suddenly had to stop when a small herd of wild pigs crossed the road. Huffing and snorting, the pigs took their time, unafraid of the giant, four-wheeled machine bearing down on them. As Bond waited patiently, he looked to his right and noticed the roof of a white building on a hill in the distance. It was barely visible from the road here, seen through a small opening in the trees; if he had been a few feet forward or backward, the foliage would have blocked it. Bond threw the car into reverse, made a U-turn, and drove back toward the Cucuruzzu and Capula center.

He parked the Renault in the gravel car park, locked it, and began to walk the two or three kilometers back down the road. The sun had nearly set, but there was enough light left to forgo using a torch—for now, anyway.

But by the time he had reached the spot where he had seen the pigs, it had grown quite dark. Bond carefully climbed over the barbed-wire fence and made his way through the thick brush toward the building.

It was as dense as a jungle until he came to a clearing of sorts. In the moonlight, he could see the building some forty meters away. A dirt road led to it through the trees from the main road, but there appeared to be yet another tall wire fence around the perimeter of the property. There were lights on inside, and he could vaguely see vehicles behind the house.

Had Mathis come this way?

Bond moved around the clearing, looking for a spot with more cover that might allow him to get closer. He made a half-circle around the property and came upon the menhirs.

On first sight, they were quite ominous. Phallic and imposing, the ancient stone statues had eroded faces that stared into the forest, protecting the grounds from God knew what. After finding the first one, Bond saw that they were spaced evenly around the perimeter of the land.

Finally he realized that the clearing circled the entire grounds. He would have to cross the exposed, open area to get to the second fence. Bond focused on a tree that stood alone on this side of the fence and made a run for it. He was there within seconds. He flattened himself against the trunk and peered around. There was no one about. He was safe for the moment.

Up close, Bond could see that the second fence was electrified. It was made of thick horizontal wires and was eight feet tall. Every ten feet or so were warning signs that were quite clear in their meaning. He studied the fence and could find no other easy access, but then he looked up at the tree he was hugging. At least three branches hung over the other side of the fence. Bond climbed the tree and inched himself onto a limb.

From this vantage point, he could see guards patrolling the grounds. There were two at the electric fence gate on the main dirt road leading to the house. Another man was in front of the home, and he figured that there were probably more on other sides of the structure.

Bond dropped to the ground, landing softly on his feet in the grass. He kept still and silent to make sure that no one had noticed him, then began to walk in a squatting position, like a monkey, toward the house.

Where would the best place be for him to gain entry? Should he take out one of the guards? What the hell was his plan?

Admitting to himself that he didn't have one, Bond kept going, hoping that an opportunity would present itself.

He was nearly at the house when a guard came around the corner with a large dog on a lead. It appeared to be a German Shepherd. The man was talking to it in Corsican, urging it to do something. The dog sniffed the ground for a bit, pulling the man closer to where Bond had flattened his body on the ground. The guard stood with his back to Bond, patiently waiting for the dog to finish his business. Bond lay perfectly still, willing the dog not to pick up his scent. At this point, he wasn't sure how bright the moonlight really was. If the guard looked this way, would he be seen?

The dog continued to sniff the ground. The guard tugged on the lead and said something. The dog refused to move. It began to growl softly.

The man questioned the dog and it barked.

Bond cursed to himself. *Pull the dog away, man!*

The guard tugged on the lead, ordering the dog to come along. It continued to growl, but it finally moved. They walked together back toward the house and Bond was able to breathe again. He waited a minute after they had disappeared around the corner, then raised himself.

Bond rushed to the side of the house and drew his Walther. Creeping along the wall, he came to the corner and peered around. It was the front of the house, brightly lit, with two guards standing in front, talking. One of them was the man with the dog.

Perhaps the other direction? Bond thought. Maybe he could get in through the back, where the vehicles were parked.

He retraced his steps along the wall until he came to the next corner and looked around. All clear. He kept going, inching along the wall and ducking under the windows.

When he got to the next corner, Bond sensed that he wasn't safe. He looked behind him and out toward the electric fence, but he couldn't see anything that might be a threat. He listened carefully and thought that he heard panting around the corner of the house.

He cautiously took a look. Sure enough, three German Shepherds were not six feet away, their leads tied to a pole near bowls of food and water.

That way was no good either. What was he going to do? He couldn't give up. If Mathis was inside, he owed it to his friend to do something.

Bond began to doubt the wisdom of storming the building alone. He should have called London, asked for back up. Did he think he was so invincible that he could walk into the Union headquarters alone and get away with it? The insanity of what he had done was suddenly all too clear. Then again, Bond justified, he knew that he probably hadn't much time. If Mathis wasn't already dead, then he was surely suffering. It wouldn't be the first time that he had walked blindly into a situation like this. He worked better by himself anyway. He had always believed that when he was killed, he would be alone, on a mission such as this.

A short bark interrupted his agonizing thoughts. There was a whine from one of the dogs, and he heard the sound of a lead scraping across the ground.

One of the animals walked out to the length of his lead and was in plain sight of Bond. It turned, sniffed the air, and saw him.

The ensuing barks from all of the dogs were so loud that they must have alerted the entire island to Bond's presence.

Bond broke into a run, electing to get out rather than fight his way inside. But as he was running, he realized that he wouldn't be able to get over the electric fence here. The branches that he had used before were too high to reach on this side of the fence. Frantically, he scanned the fence for the best possible means of escape and finally chose to run toward the main gate. He would shoot the guards if he had to.

The barking grew louder. The three dogs had been set loose and were chasing him across the clearing. They were strong, well-trained animals, and they were gaining on him much faster than he would have liked.

He heard shouts from the house as the guards began to give chase as well. Bond forced himself to run faster, but now the guards at the gate were headed toward him, guns drawn.

One of the dogs leaped onto his back, effectively tackling him.

Bond fell to the ground as the animal tore into his shoulder with its strong jaws. The Walther exploded once and the dog went limp, but by then the other two beasts had reached him. Instead of jumping on him, though, they squatted on either side of him, growling and barking, threatening to attack if Bond moved so much as an inch.

The guards surrounded him. One of them ordered him to drop his weapon and he did so. A guard approached him carefully, pulled off the dead dog, then kicked Bond squarely in the ribs.

It took four men to drag Bond, kicking and struggling, into the house. They brought him in through the back, a servants' entrance of sorts, next to the garage where three or four vehicles were parked. Bond noticed a Rolls-Royce and two 4 × 4s, but he didn't have much of a chance to get a very good mental picture of the area.

Here, the inside of the building was nondescript. The stone and plaster walls were white with no decoration of any kind. It was a room where the guards and servants could put their things, as there were cabinets, coat hangers and shelves, but the only other pieces of furniture were benches. Once they were in the room, two men held Bond upright, while another guard, a rather short but wiry fellow, stood in front and unleashed three hard blows to Bond's solar plexus. With the wind knocked out of him, they dragged Bond through a wooden door and down a bare corridor.

Bond must have lost consciousness for a moment, for the next thing he knew, he was being strapped into a black leather chair that resembled something a dentist might have in his office. Bond's arms were secured to the arms and his legs were locked into cuffs at the base. The room was small and there was a stand next to the chair with a slit lamp biomicroscope and other medical devices attached to it. A sink and instrument counter were near the chair, next to the wall.

What the hell was a doctor's office doing in this house?

Once Bond was secure in the chair, all but one guard left the room. The silence was unnerving.

He was still reeling from the blows to the stomach. The little man had known exactly where to hit him.

"Don't even think about offering me a bribe," the guard said in English.

Bond managed to say, "Sorry, I'm out of dog biscuits anyway."

The guard backhanded Bond across the face.

At that moment, a middle-aged man wearing a white coat and thick eyeglasses entered the room.

He said, "Good evening, I am Doctor Gerowitz." He spoke in English, but the accent was decidedly Eastern European. "I need to examine your eyes."

What the hell? Bond thought.

"Please look into the light," the doctor ordered.

Bond turned his head, refusing to co-operate.

The doctor sighed. "Either you do what we say and we get this over with painlessly, or we try other methods. I assure you that we will get the same results no matter what."

Bond reflected on his situation and decided that perhaps it would be better if he acquiesced. Bond turned back to the doctor as a light shone into his eyes. The doctor was using an ophthalmoscope, larger than Bond's, certainly without Boothroyd's additions, but very bright all the same.

After a few seconds, the doctor switched off the light. "He does not have the tattoo," he said to the guard in French.

"Did you really think he would?" the guard replied.

The doctor addressed Bond in English. "That's all for now. You can go." The guard stuck his head out the door and called his cohorts. The other three men came back into the room. One held a Glock to Bond's head as the others unstrapped him.

They took him down a hall and ordered him to walk down a flight of stone steps. The basement was cold and damp, furnished with a desk, lockers, and a cabinet.

The small guard who had hit Bond in the stomach earlier was sitting at the desk. He got up and addressed him in English.

"I am Antoine," he said. "I am head of security here. Take off all your clothes, please."

Bond didn't move.

The little man, who was probably no more than five feet tall, lashed out with his fist so quickly that Bond had no time to tighten his stomach muscles. He doubled over and fell to his knees.

The little bastard was strong, Bond thought, but his skill was in knowing where the vulnerable targets on a man's body were and repeatedly assaulting them.

"I will ask you again," he said, calmly. "Remove your clothes."

Bond got to his feet and did as he was told. He watched as another guard placed the Q-Branch camera, his knife, the Walther that they had taken from him earlier and the rest of his clothes into a locker. Another man handed him what amounted to prison clothes—gray loose-fitting trousers and a short-sleeved shirt with no pockets. They felt like pajamas with too much starch.

The next thing they did was shackle his ankles. There was a chain about two feet long between the two cuffs, allowing Bond to walk but not run. Next, they cuffed his wrists together in front of his body. The chain between these cuffs was only two inches.

"Follow me, please," Antoine said. He opened a wooden door behind the desk and walked into a dark stone hallway that smelled musty and moldy. A guard followed behind Bond, urging him forward with the barrel of a gun.

At the end of the hall was another heavy wooden door. Antoine unlocked it and held it open. The other guard shoved Bond through the door. He fell hard on the wet, stone floor. The door slammed shut and was locked from the other side.

It was fairly dark in the room, and the smell of urine and excrement was strong. A little light came from a single low-wattage bulb on the ten-foot high ceiling. Straw lay about the room, but there was no furniture.

It was a dungeon, pure and simple.

As Bond's eyes grew used to the dimness, he noticed a dark shape on the floor next to the wall. It started to move, and then it sat up.

It was a man.

"Is someone here?" he asked in French.

"René?" Bond asked.

The man gasped. "James?"

Bond rushed to the man and knelt. It was really Mathis, alive and well! He, too, was shackled in the same manner.

"My God, René, are you all right?"

Mathis uttered a slight, sarcastic laugh. "I guess. It's good to hear your voice. But it appears that you are in the same predicament as me."

"I'm afraid so," Bond said. Then he noticed that Mathis was waving his head around strangely.

"What have they done to you, René?" Bond asked.

Mathis swallowed and nearly choked. "I, uhm, I can't see a thing, James. They have blinded me."

TWENTY-TWO

THE ORDEAL

BOND FELT A SINKING FEELING IN HIS CHEST. WERE THEY GOING TO BLIND him too?

"What happened?" he asked Mathis.

"They used a laser, an eye laser, one of those things that eye doctors use to correct your vision," Mathis said. "It was horrible. They prolonged it over several days, burning me a little bit at a time. I didn't begin to lose my sight until three or four days after they started. Now I'm completely blind. Forever." He sighed. "I don't know why they did it. I certainly didn't know anything. They never really asked me any questions, except . . . well, they asked about you."

"Me?"

"They wanted to know if you would be coming this way to look for me."

"And?" Bond asked.

"After several days of torture, I told them that you would probably find me. They were waiting for you," Mathis said. "I'm sorry, James."

Bond put a hand on his friend's shoulder. "It's all right. They would have found out that I was coming by other means, I'm sure."

"Yesterday a guard said that you were already dead, but I didn't believe him."

"I think my little visit to Corse Shipping last night may have put an end to that particular rumor," Bond said.

"Cesari. *Le Gérant*, he's obsessed with eyes. I suppose it's because he's blind, too, but who knows? He keeps an eye doctor here on the premises."

"I've already met the good Doctor Gerowitz," Bond said. "He checked me for the retinal tattoo."

"That's another indication of *Le Géerant*'s fixation with eyes," Mathis said.

"A deranged mind works in unusual ways," Bond said. "Look, don't worry. I'll get us out of here, somehow. Perhaps another doctor can help you . . . someone in Paris . . . ?"

"It's impossible, James," Mathis said. "There is no way out. They have a guard outside the door at all times. We have to sleep, eat, and shit in here. It's a pigsty. Every day they come for you and torture you a little bit."

"Then that's when I'll make my move," Bond said.

"I wish I could have more confidence," Mathis said. "I'm afraid they have broken me. As for finding another doctor, that's of no use, too. My retinas are completely scarred."

Bond heard a rustling sound in a dark corner, near the straw.

"What the hell is that?"

"Oh, that's our only regular visitor," Mathis explained. "He comes in through a hole in the wall, scrounging for food."

Bond peered closely at the pile of straw and saw two red eyes. When the shape moved, he saw that it was a large, gray rat.

Bond jumped at it but it didn't scamper away in any hurry. The animal moved with little concern for the two humans in the cell with him. After sniffing the straw one more time, it slipped into a crack in the stone wall.

"The food isn't too bad," Mathis said. "They've been leaving a couple of meals a day, mostly stuff you can eat with fingers. No utensils."

Bond felt sorry for Mathis. His friend had lost his vitality and will to survive.

"Listen, René, I think the Union is about to do something big," Bond said.

"Tell me what you know," Mathis said. Bond related how he had discovered the substance he suspected to be CL-20, the detonator, and radio transmitter.

"From what you describe, that sounds like CL-20, yes," Mathis said. "It's quite volatile. The Americans developed it as a rocket propellant but some fool in the military decided that it would make an excellent explosive. What do you think the target is?"

"I don't know," Bond said. "But it's pretty clear that they're using Essinger and his movie production to smuggle the materials out of Corsica. I imagine that they will end up somewhere in France."

The sound of boots on the stone floor outside the door interrupted them. Keys rattled and the door opened.

Antoine and three other guards entered, guns drawn.

"You," Antoine said to Bond. "Let's go."

He got up and went with them, coolly and with no resistance.

After they had strapped him in the examination chair, one of the guards released a catch on the headrest. Hidden attachments for straps protruded from its sides with a click. Two guards held Bond's head as a third man strapped it down tightly. Two sliding panels were fitted onto the headrest and pushed inward, holding Bond's skull like a vice. These were tightened considerably, preventing any movement of the head.

Then all of them left the room, abandoning Bond to the eerie, antiseptic stillness of the place. A cold chill ran up Bond's back when he thought about what was going to happen.

Le Gérant entered the room alone and shut the door behind him. Keeping his head motionless, the mysterious Pierre Rodiac, aka Olivier Cesari, sat down on a swivel chair next to the desk. He was wearing sunglasses, dark trousers, and a short-sleeved polo shirt. He looked as if he were ready for a game of golf.

"No, I'm not your physician, Mister Bond," the man said, smiling. "I never got my doctorate, you see. Welcome. We've been expecting you."

"*Le Gérant*, at last," Bond said. "I should have killed you in front of everyone in the casino."

"But you didn't, now, did you?" Cesari said. "That's exactly where you and I differ, Mister Bond."

Bond waited for him to go on.

"You lack vision, Mister Bond," Cesari said, shaking his head. "You are a victim of your own stubborn, compulsive ways. You are a very good gambler, Mister Bond, I grant you that; and you have great courage when it comes to taking chances. However, you have no idea what the outcome will be for anything you undertake. To you, it's all a risk. Life is one big game. On the other hand, I never bet. I only act when I know with certainty what the consequences will be. And I usually do."

"What are you planning, Cesari?" Bond demanded. "What's the CL-20 for?"

Cesari chuckled to himself. "I'm impressed, Mister Bond, or should I say, Agent Double-O Seven? I didn't think you had uncovered so much."

"Cesari, if I fail to report, you're going to have the entire Ministry of Defence at your doorstep. They'll find you. We all know who you are now. It won't be so easy to blend into the scenery any more."

"By the time you fail to report and they *do* find this lovely house, I'll be gone. I never stay in one place very long, you know that. I rather like it here, though. It would be a pity to leave. I spent some of my younger years in Corsica, you see. This was my father's ancestral home."

"Stick to the subject, Cesari, what about the CL-20?"

"I remind you, Mister Bond, that I am sitting *here* while *you* are sitting *there*. You are not in any position to tell me what to do, are you?" *Le Gérant* had quickly lost his good humor and was snarling.

He paused a moment to calm down. "I finally have the great James Bond in my hands. It's a moment that I thought would have given me more satisfaction. Instead it's just, well . . . predictable."

Bond decided to gamble. "What is Goro Yoshida paying you? What does he want from the Union?" he asked.

"Ah, Mister Yoshida," *Le Gérant* said. "Let's just say that he made the Union a very good offer. You must remember that the Union does not take any sides in a matter. We are not a political organisation. What Yoshida wants to accomplish is of no importance to us."

"How many people will die this time?" Bond asked.

Le Gérant shook his head. "That doesn't concern me."

"How can it not? Are there innocent people involved? For God's sake, Cesari, what are you planning?" Bond persisted.

"I think you know, Mister Bond. You just haven't put it all together yet. We've even spoon fed some clues to you so that you would follow your nose here, right where I wanted you. Out of the way of our project. You have the uncanny knack of ruining our plans and I didn't want you near our latest one."

Bond thought a moment. All the pieces seemed so disconnected: detonators from Corsica, explosives from America, transmitters from France, a movie company carrying the parts . . . Was there something happening soon that involved crowds of people?

Then it hit him. "Cannes," Bond said. "You're going to blow up the film festival."

"Well, that's a bit of an exaggeration, Mister Bond," Le Gérant said. "Let's just say that we're providing the fireworks at a special screening with a lot of VIPs, exactly two evenings from tonight."

Christ, it was the charity event that was going to be attended by Prince Edward and Princess Caroline! Now it made sense. The pieces all came from different places. The explosive was stolen from the air force base in Corsica and then smuggled by the film company out to sea and ultimately to France. The detonating device was assembled at Cirendini's shipping firm and smuggled to the film set. Final construction of the bomb or bombs would probably be completed by Rick Fripp, the explosives expert, under the guise of "special effects" work on the film.

"Why? Why kill off a bunch of celebrities at a charity function? What's the point?" Bond asked.

"It's Yoshida's idea of a major strike against the West," Le Gérant said. "He believes that the festival symbolizes the decadence of the West. He has a big problem with that. The strike will also damage Japanese companies who are colluding with the West in the film industry. You know and I know that when famous entertainers die, it makes the news. Attacking the entertainment industry will hit the West where it hurts the most. People in the West love their celebrities more than their politicians. It will be a shocking, history-making terrorist strike. And the Union will carry it out."

"You're insane, Cesari," Bond whispered. "What happened to you that made you so indifferent to human life, to human feelings?"

Le Gérant was silent again, contemplating the question. Then he said, "Why should I reveal anything to you about myself? I must admit that there is no question in my mind that you are a superior human being and deserve a certain amount of respect. While I possess the greater intellect, you are undoubtedly the finest specimen of a man that I have ever encountered. You are a killing machine unlike any other. I wish that I could tempt you into working for the Union, but I won't bother asking. I know what your answer would be."

Bond told him where he would put his offer if given the chance.

Le Gérant smiled. "We are not too dissimilar, Mister Bond. We are both passionate about our work and our beliefs. We strike back at those who try to hurt us. We are cunning and skilful, albeit in different ways. You were orphaned at an early age, Mister Bond. I'm sure that has something to do with it. You see, I had a difficult childhood, too."

Bond, unable to move his head and limbs, listened with fascination to the story that Olivier Cesari began to tell.

"My father was a Corsican, born and raised in Sartène by strict Catholics who attempted to beat religion into him. When he was nine years old, his parents were killed as a result of a vendetta. He depended on the old Corsican mafia, the Union Corse, to raise him. He grew up to be a brutal and sadistic man, but someone with a very good business sense.

"Once when he was in Morocco on business, he raped a Berber girl who lived in the Rif Mountains. She became pregnant and gave birth to me. Some might say that I was born with a disability. I, however, consider my blindness fortunate. Nature compensated by enhancing my other senses. By the time I was seven, I realized that I had mental capabilities that my people considered somewhat . . . mystical."

He paused a moment as if he were savoring the image of a memory, then he continued.

"I lived with my mother in the Rif Mountains until I was eight years old, when my father returned and took me to Corsica to live with him. He ripped me away from my mother and her people and forced me to be almost like a servant to him. Even though I was blind, I had to learn to cook meals, fetch drinks for him, clean the house. My father was prone to losing his temper, so he beat me regularly whenever I displeased him, which was often. We lived in Sartène but we spent a lot of time in mainland France, especially Paris. My father had a mafia-backed perfume business, you see.

"While being a strict disciplinarian, he also demanded great things from me. In his own way, he loved me, I suppose. He spent a lot of money for an operation to restore the sight in my eyes, but it didn't work. He pushed me to excel in school, in my studies, and in day-to-day challenges I might face. He wanted me to overcome my disability, and in some ways, I am grateful to the bastard for pushing me so hard. Without the extra effort, I might never have risen above my situation.

"As a result, I learned everything I could. I read every book in Braille that I could get my hands on, studied mathematics and philosophy, learned foreign languages, and above all, mastered courses in law and economics. This education, combined with two cultural backgrounds—growing up first in the Moroccan mountains and then with the Corsican mafia as family—you can see how I might have developed into . . . a precocious young man."

"That's not the word I would use," Bond said.

Le Gérant ignored the barb. "I learned early on that I could predict things," he went on. "My grandfather on my father's side, I discovered, was a *mazzere*. As the ability is hereditary, I ended up with the skill. I could foresee events in my dreams even before I was old enough to understand what they meant. Gradually, though, I turned this skill into helping me with my blindness. I tap the same areas of the brain that are used for dreaming to boost my senses of hearing, tasting, smelling, and touching. As a result, I know exactly where this jar is sitting—" He reached over to the desk and picked up a jar of cotton swabs without turning his head. "I can *feel* the space it's sitting in without touching it."

"All right, you've proved you're a circus freak, Cesari," Bond said. "Let's get on with it."

Le Gérant stood and clasped his right hand around Bond's neck and squeezed, cutting off his victim's air supply.

"On my eighteenth birthday, my father was murdered," Cesari said, digging his fingernails into Bond's skin. "His throat was cut from ear to ear, the first appearance of the mark of the Union. I inherited his estate, which was considerable. As it was I who had brought about his demise, I gained a significant amount of respect among his peers, many of whom did not like him any more than I did."

He let go of Bond's throat. Bond gasped for breath.

So the man had committed patricide, Bond thought. That explained a lot.

Cesari sat down again. "I went back to Morocco after that. My mother had died shortly after my father kidnapped me. I lived with her people for several more years, until I was the master of two vastly different cultures. With my money, success, and psychic abilities, I quickly accumulated a following in Morocco. The rest, as they say, is history.

"The dreams continue to this day," he said. "I am always a wolf, hunting prey in the *maquis* of Corsica. Lately, I've been stalking a majestic stag. I'm going to kill it eventually, I know. And when I finally do, I'll be able to confirm that the stag is who I think it is."

He stood once more and placed his hand on Bond's shoulder. "The stag is you, Mister Bond."

He moved away and opened the door. He said something in Corsican, and a moment later Dr. Gerowitz and a guard entered the room.

"You've already met the good doctor, Mister Bond," Cesari said. "I leave you in his capable hands. I think it's high time that the Union receive some payback for all the times you've caused us trouble. Good day."

With that, *Le Gérant* left the room and shut the door behind him.

"What's the matter, Cesari?" Bond shouted. "Too squeamish?"

Bond turned his attention to Dr. Gerowitz, who approached the chair and stepped on a lever on the floor. The seat reclined so that Bond's torso and head were at a 45-degree angle from his waist. The doctor then held an eyedropper over Bond's eyes.

"This won't hurt," he said. "It's one percent mydriacil and two and a half percent phenylephrin. The solution will dilate your eyes."

Bond squeezed his lids closed.

"Come, come, don't act like a child," the doctor said. "That's what children do when they see the eye doctor." When Bond refused to open them, the doctor nodded to the guard. The guard forcefully pulled Bond's eyelids apart with his hands. The doctor managed to put a couple of drops in each eye.

"I'm going to leave you for a few minutes while those drops work on your eyes," Gerowitz said as he replaced the eye drops on the desk and left the room. The guard remained in the room, sitting behind Bond where he couldn't be seen.

Concentrate, Bond told himself. He had withstood great amounts of pain in his lifetime, and he could stand this, too. He would fight it every step of the way and he would endure whatever the sadist could unleash.

To be tortured for torture's sake. That was the worst. At least if the inquisitors were trying to find out something, a victim could always talk and perhaps be granted a reprieve from the pain. But to be at the hands of a sadist who simply enjoyed torturing someone . . . it was a sobering notion.

The twenty minutes that Bond sat helpless in the chair waiting for the doctor to return had to be among the most excruciating moments he had ever experienced. The anticipation of horror could be as bad or even worse than the actual torment.

The doctor came back in the room and said, "Let's get started, shall we? We're going to do a little at a time every day, per *Le Gérant's* orders. I could blind you with a single stroke of my laser and be done with it, but no, I'm afraid we have to draw it out. Now, to make sure you keep your eyes open—"

The guard helped the doctor place terribly painful retractors on

Bond's eyes. The devices were reverse-clamps that kept the eyelids open. Once they were on, Bond's eyelids were pulled apart and there was nothing he could do to alleviate the discomfort. The guard then stood by the chair and applied drops to Bond's eyes since he was now unable to blink.

"The drops our friend here is applying will keep your eyes moist while I work. Oh, are the retractors uncomfortable? I could have put some anesthetic drops in your eyes, but I elected not to. Now then . . ."

The doctor sat down in the swivel chair and pivoted the Coherent Novus Omni argon laser around in front of Bond's face. He looked through it at Bond's right eye.

"You'll probably feel a burning sensation," the doctor warned. "Usually we anaesthetize the eyeballs before this type of procedure, but . . . oh well."

The doctor flipped a switch and the laser shot into Bond's pupil. The sensation was bizarre and unnerving; it felt like a tiny needle had just entered his eyeball and was jabbing the back of it, but it wasn't terribly painful.

"This argon laser is set to point one watts," the doctor said. "As I inch up the wattage, I believe you'll feel a bit more pain."

The pricking sensation indeed began to change. Bond now felt heat in his eye. It was beginning to burn. He felt his heart racing as he clutched the arms of the chair, completely powerless.

"I'm at point two," the doctor said. "You feel that, don't you?"

Bond breathed in through his teeth, his jaw clenched in agony.

"Now we'll go up one more notch to point three," the doctor said calmly.

Suddenly, Bond's eye felt like it was on fire.

He couldn't help screaming, especially when he smelled his own eye burning.

TWENTY-THREE

THE RAT

LÉON ESSINGER SUSPENDED PRODUCTION THE DAY BEFORE THE SCREENING AT Cannes. Everyone had the next three days off so that many of the principals involved in *Tsunami Rising* could be at the event. There wasn't a lot that they could do on the film anyway. With the boat chase sequence completely derailed, the director had spent the last two days on pickup shots. The production was already several days behind schedule.

The *Starfish* pulled into Nice that morning. The cast and crew disembarked and scattered. Tylyn went home to Mougins, Stuart Laurence went to his rented villa in Nice and Essinger and his team went to the Côte d'Azur Studios.

After Essinger had settled behind his desk, Julius Wilcox and Rick Fripp entered the office. They grabbed bottles of beer out of the portable refrigerator and sat on the sofa.

"Make yourselves at home," Essinger said sarcastically. He was attempting to catch up on paperwork. "I can't believe these expenses. It's going to cost even more than I thought to rebuild that goddamned tanker."

"You worry too much," Wilcox said. "Put that stuff down and let's talk."

Essinger, frustrated, pushed the papers out of the way, got up, took a beer for himself, and joined the other men around the coffee table.

"Mister Fripp has some news for us," Wilcox said.

Fripp cleared his throat and held up his glass. "The bomb is finished, ready to go."

Essinger didn't say anything until they both looked at him. "What—" he said, "am I supposed to applaud?"

"I just thought you'd be pleased to know," Wilcox said. "Everything is in place to deliver it to the Palais tomorrow. Now we have to talk about our alibis. Mister Fripp and I shouldn't have a problem. It's you, mister big-time movie producer, that I'm worried about."

"What for?" Essinger asked. "I never attend my screenings, everyone knows that."

"We just don't want it to be too conspicuous that you're not at *this* one," Wilcox said. "Please go over the routine one more time."

"Christ, Julius," Essinger said. "After we arrive at the Palais for the screening, I am to be taken ill. I'll drink the castor oil in the men's room before the event begins. I'll make sure several people see me throw up."

"You guarantee it'll make you vomit?" Fripp asked. "If not, I can cook up something that will do the trick!"

"It'll work, trust me," Essinger said. "At that point, I will beg everyone's pardon and leave to have a lie-down. I'll go straight to my hotel room and make sure all the doormen see me."

"You know that the police will question you over and over and over . . . ?" Wilcox suggested.

"I can handle it," Essinger replied.

"Very well," Wilcox said. "I'm sure you'll be off the suspect list as soon as Yoshida's people announce that they were responsible for the act."

"Too bad we have to lose so many good people on the film," Fripp said. "Do you have a director in mind to replace Duling?"

"Are you kidding?" Essinger said. "*Pirate Island* will have to start again from scratch. We're losing our lead actor *and* director."

"And lead actress," Wilcox reminded him.

Essinger stiffened slightly. "Yes."

"But your insurance will cover it," Wilcox said. "The entire production is protected. You'll receive a shitload of cash, Léon. From your insurance company and from your wife's inheritance. I wouldn't mind being in your shoes after all this is over, fella." Essinger took a sip of his beer and nodded. Sure, it would be great. As long as he was able to live with himself.

When Bond awoke that morning, his eyesight had returned to normal. When they had finally taken him back to his cell, an agonizing, eons-long fifteen minutes after Doctor Gerowitz began working on him, Bond's vision was blurry due to the dilating solution he had received. At first he was alarmed that his eyes had been permanently damaged. But as the doctor had predicted, the laser had not harmed his vision. With no small amount of skill, Gerowitz had avoided the crucial sites at the back of the eyeball, namely the macula and optic nerve areas. Ironically, Bond was thankful that Gerowitz was good at what he did.

The only things that were sore were his eyelids, due to the retractors forcing them open. They felt as if they were made of sandpaper.

"I didn't start noticing a change in my eyesight until the fourth day," Mathis had told Bond. The idea, then, was to psychologically torture him as well as physically so. The day-to-day fear of becoming blind was almost too much to take. The good doctor would play havoc with areas in the eyeball that did not affect sight, pricking and burning him for a few seconds at a time without anesthesia. It was no wonder that Mathis was now so resigned. The ordeal would break anyone.

Bond was determined to find a way to avoid it.

They heard the keys rattle in the door at mid-morning. A guard came in with a tray of food—bowls of oatmeal and no utensils. Surprisingly, it tasted good, even scraped out by hand. The meal gave Bond the much-needed energy to formulate a plan.

He ate all but a small amount of the food. He carefully crawled to the hole in the wall and smeared the remaining oatmeal along the floor and into the straw.

Bond then moved closer to Mathis to tell him what he had in mind.

Tylyn Mignonne arrived in Cannes that afternoon and checked into the exclusive Carlton Hotel, *the* place to stay when at the film festival. In the past she had stayed at the Majestic and the Martinez, both first-class hotels, but the Carlton represented the top of the heap when it came to celebrity placement.

There was plenty about the film festival that Tylyn disliked. Mostly she felt that it had become way too snobbish for her taste. The organizers perceived it as a much bigger and more important event than it really was. She was constantly amazed by the lavish attention thrown at the Cannes Film Festival by the international media. There were more reporters and *paparazzi* at Cannes than there were film industry professionals. And even that inner circle was becoming more and more difficult to break into. She knew two journalists in Paris who were refused press accreditation simply because their publications weren't big enough.

What particularly irked Tylyn was the fans' behavior. She couldn't believe they could stand in the Riviera sun outside a hotel for hours just to get a glimpse of a celebrity. Even in Hollywood it wasn't that bad.

Because of the increase in media attention and interest from the masses, security had been beefed up considerably at the festival. Tylyn was more aware of uniformed guards everywhere. They were even stationed in front of her hotel, checking to make sure anyone who came in was staying there.

La Croisette, the main street that ran along the beach to the Palais, was already crowded and much of it blocked off from traffic. It was madness to get into a car anywhere near the festival grounds; it was easier to simply walk from one's hotel to the Palais. However, that meant fighting one's way through mobs of fans wanting a photo, an autograph, or even a kiss.

As Tylyn lay on the bed in her suite, she decided against going outside. The opening night screening was in a few hours—some film by a hot American director—and she felt obliged to go. She didn't really want to. If she could have her way, she would stay secluded in her room until tomorrow night, when she absolutely *had* to make an appearance at Léon's charity screening. But she had received scores of interview requests and she was under contract to give a few. She would be busy all day tomorrow up until the time of the screening, so why shouldn't she take today off?

Having made the decision, she phoned her publicist and told her to give away the tickets.

She turned on the television and—surprise, surprise—the program was coverage of the film festival. There was a clip of Prince Edward and his wife Sophie, Countess of Wessex, arriving in Cannes that afternoon. The reporter said that Princess Caroline of Monaco would be arriving tomorrow for a grand event screening of *Tsunami Rising*. A roster of the celebrities scheduled to attend included a glamorous headshot of her.

She ran through the channels with the remote and eventually turned it off. She lay back on the bed and stared a hole through the plain white ceiling.

Tylyn had spent the last few days in an uncustomary daze of distraction. At one point during a take, director Duling had to shout at her to concentrate. She knew that she needed to snap out of it, but damn it, she had a lot of questions! Tylyn *knew* that her husband was up to something and that it had to do with James Bond. She couldn't prove it, but it was the only possible explanation.

And what of James? Who was he really? Had what they experienced in the short time that they knew each other been real? No one could fake that kind of intensity, except perhaps a professional con man. If he had really lied to her about himself, it would break her heart. So far, she had been able to prevent that from happening because she refused to believe that he had been dishonest.

Instead, she concentrated on her memories of him: his steely blue eyes, the cruel mouth that had kissed her so passionately, his strong arms and hands, his expert and generous approach to lovemaking, his smile, his laugh . . .

She missed him deeply.

They came for Mathis at midday. He offered no resistance as two guards led him away, while a third kept an eye on Bond.

He was back thirty minutes later. Even though Mathis was already blind, *Le Gérant* had ordered the torture to continue simply to be cruel. Mathis looked deathly pale and was unable to speak coherently when they threw him down on the cell floor.

"Let's go," Antoine said to Bond.

Bond wondered how long the sadistic bastard was planning on keeping them alive. At this rate, he could torment them forever.

The second appointment with Dr. Gerowitz was half an hour of profound pain. From the moment Bond's head was strapped down and the terrible retractors were placed on his eyelids, he had rarely felt a more powerful sense of helplessness and fear. Not once did the doctor ask him any questions. Bond was never instructed to give away MI6 secrets. All they wanted, it seemed, was to hurt him.

Hours later, after the blurry vision had diminished, Bond heard the scratching sounds in the corner of the cell.

"James?" Mathis whispered.

"I hear him," Bond said quietly. He slowly raised himself from the floor and looked.

The rat had just come out of the hole and was sniffing the trail of now-sticky oatmeal that Bond had left. The rodent scampered along, scraping up the food and sniffing the straw around him.

Bond sat up and slowly crawled toward it. The cuffs around his hands limited his movements, but he managed to slide along without being too obvious. When he was within arm's reach of the rat, he stopped and waited. The animal, chewing on a chunk of oatmeal, eyed Bond but didn't seem to be afraid of him. In its tiny mind there was a belief that it was superior to the filthy human that left so much waste in the room for it to enjoy. The rat knew that it could bite the hell out of a man, so it didn't feel any need to be afraid.

With an unexpected lurch and the speed of a cobra, Bond grabbed the rat with both hands and clutched it around the neck. He squeezed as hard as he could, fighting the struggling rodent as its claws slashed his hands and wrists. He slammed the creature against the stone floor and continued to choke the life out of it. It took nearly a minute, but finally the rat was dead in Bond's hands.

"Are you all right?" Mathis asked.

Bond came back carrying the rat carcass. It was as big as a squirrel.

"A little scratched up, but I'll live," Bond said. "Ask me again after I'm done with the really disgusting part."

Before he could have second thoughts, Bond sunk his teeth into the rat's back. He needed something that the animal had—the only problem was that it was on the inside of the rat. Since Bond had no knife to cut the damned thing open, he had to take a deep breath and use the only other sharp objects he could find.

It was dark outside when the guard finally brought Bond and Mathis their dinner. The keys rattled in the door and it swung open.

"All right, stay back and I'll put these on the floor," the man said, but was surprised when he didn't see anyone sitting in the relatively clean section of the cell. He surveyed the room and saw two bodies in the straw. The man inched forward to get a better look. The one called Bond was face down. The other one was on his back, and there was blood and what looked like animal viscera all over his face.

What the hell happened? Had they killed each other?

The guard foolishly stepped closer, just as Bond had hoped he would. Bond lunged with the femur, puncturing the soft layer of skin beneath the guard's chin. The rat's leg bone, while brittle, had been whittled on stone to sharpen it. It served very well as a makeshift weapon—something that could take a person by surprise. The ploy worked beautifully.

The guard dropped the tray of food and screamed, but Bond didn't stop there. He propelled himself at the guard, tackling him. He took hold of the man's hair and slammed his head with tremendous force several times against the concrete floor. A pool of blood appeared underneath his skull.

Bond fumbled for the guard's handgun, drew it and aimed it at the open doorway just as a second guard came in to investigate the noise.

The gun kicked twice, knocking the guard into the wall. He slid to a heap, leaving a bloody trail on the stone.

Bond turned back to the first guard and searched the man's

pockets. Thank *God* he had the right guard! Bond took the set of keys and just managed to twist his wrist enough to insert the appropriate one into his cuffs. Free at last, Bond unlocked the shackles on his ankles and then freed Mathis.

Mathis took an old rag and wiped the rat's blood off his face. "We fooled him good, eh?"

"Come on," Bond said as he took Mathis by the hand and led him out of the cell.

THE BREAKOUT

IT WASN'T DIFFICULT TO BREAK INTO THE LOCKER WHERE THE GUARDS HAD put Bond's weapons and clothes. He dressed quickly, made sure his Walther was loaded, clipped the camera to his belt, strapped on the knife, and he was ready to go. Mathis stood by with his own clothes, waiting for Bond to help him.

"Come on, René," Bond said. "We had better hurry before someone else comes down here."

"You must go without me, James," Mathis said.

"Don't be ridiculous."

"I mean it, James. I would be a burden to you. By yourself, you just might make it out. If you have to drag me along, I will only slow you down and probably get us both killed."

"You're coming with me, now get dressed!"

"No, James." Mathis dropped his clothes on the floor. "I insist. Go on. Get out of here. I'll be fine. I'll just go back into the cell and wait for you to bring reinforcements."

Bond knew that Mathis was right, of course. He was loath to leave his friend, though.

"René . . ."

"Go!" Mathis said forcefully. "If you don't leave now, I'm going to start shouting. I mean it." He reached out with his right hand. "Good luck, my friend."

Bond clasped the man's hand and held it firmly. "I'll be back for you. I promise. Your job is to stay alive until then."

"I'll do my best," Mathis said. He smiled for the first time since Bond had been captured. "Now get the hell out of here."

Bond left him and climbed the stone steps to the ground floor of the château. He glanced at his watch and saw that it was after midnight. He silently stepped down the corridor toward the room where they had first searched and beat him. Luckily, no one was about at this time of night. He listened at the wooden door at the end of the hall and thought that he could hear movement.

The element of surprise was his only ace. He lightly tapped on the door and readied himself. When it opened, Bond let go with a solid punch to the guard's face. The man went tumbling backward into the room. Bond stepped inside, drew the Walther knife, and hurled it at the one remaining guard in the room. The blade pierced his chest with a dull thud. Bond rushed to him and covered the man's mouth before he could scream. Once he collapsed to the floor, Bond removed the knife, wiped it clean on the man's trousers, and made a quick examination of the first guard to make sure that he was still out.

The cabinets here were stocked with a variety of weapons. Bond took three hand grenades and a machine gun, then opened the door slightly to peer outside. Two men were talking to a man at the wheel of a delivery lorry. Markings on the side of the lorry indicated that it was a beverage supply vehicle. The motor was running; either the lorry had just pulled up or it was about to leave. Bond calmly walked outside with the PPK in hand, aimed it at the two men and said, "Hey!"

When they turned, the Walther recoiled twice.

Bond pointed the gun at the lorry driver. "Get out," he commanded. The driver, eyes wide, jumped out and held up his hands. "Lie on the ground," Bond ordered. When the man was face down, Bond said, "Don't get up until I'm gone."

He leapt into the driver's seat, threw the lorry into gear, and backed out. He turned onto the dirt road and headed for the electrified fence gate.

Olivier Cesari was sleeping soundly, enjoying a dream in which he had just stalked and killed a young fawn. He possessed such agility and skill as a wolf that Cesari never wanted to wake from these dreams. As in dreams in which people imagined that they could fly, the feeling was so exhilarating that the reality of the waking world was in contrast a complete disappointment. If Cesari could have had his way, he would have remained asleep forever. In his dreams, he was the king of his realm, the master of everything he touched.

And he could see . . .

However, something wrestled Cesari away from his newly killed fawn. He looked up from the dead animal and saw the stag—the one that he had been hunting for months—the beast that represented the British secret agent who had caused him so much misery.

The stag was staring at him, taunting him, and telling him that the war wasn't over by a long shot. Before Cesari the Wolf could run and leap at the wretched creature, the stag turned and bolted.

That was when Cesari woke and knew that James Bond had escaped. He reached for the phone and called down to the basement.

There was no answer.

Bond floored the accelerator, increasing his speed. The guards at the gate snapped out of their complacency and realized that something was terribly wrong with the lorry driver. They both pointed rifles at the vehicle and shouted for him to stop.

Bond ignored them.

The men jumped out of the way at the last second as the lorry burst through the metal gate. The electrified fence, now exposed, burst into flames at the breakpoint. One of the guards got on the radio just as the alarms went off in the complex.

Bond kept driving, eventually reaching the main paved road. Instead of turning right, to head toward Sartène, Bond went left toward the prehistoric sites that he had seen before he was captured.

Within seconds, a Porsche and a Land Rover were behind him. He heard gunshots, but the lorry was so big that Bond couldn't discern if the bullets had hit the back or not. Because of the vehicle's bulk, the damned thing would only do a maximum of fifty miles per hour.

The Land Rover swerved into the left-hand lane and pulled beside the lorry. Bond ducked as a bullet smashed the driver's side window, spraying shards of glass all over him. Bond drew the Walther and, with his left hand, aimed it out the open window and shot at the 4 × 4. The vehicle slammed against the lorry in an attempt to force it off the road, but the truck was too heavy. Bond tried the same maneuver by turning the wheel sharply to the left and banging the lorry into the Land Rover. The 4 × 4's tires screeched as it shot over to the far side of the road, scraping against the brush, but the driver managed to bring it back beside Bond. The guard in the passenger seat of the 4 × 4 aimed again and shot at the lorry. This time a bullet whizzed past Bond's face.

Damn!

Bond stuck his left arm out of the window again and squeezed the Walther's trigger. The round caught the guard in the face. He was thrown back into the driver, causing another near collision. The 4 × 4 slowed down and moved back into its proper lane.

Off with the kid gloves, Bond thought. He grabbed one of his grenades, pulled the pin with his teeth, and carefully tossed it out the window. It landed and bounced on the road behind him. If his timing were any good at all, then . . .

The Land Rover drove over the grenade just as it exploded. The 4 × 4 bounced into the air, riding a ball of flame and smoke, then veered to the right, landed on its side, and slid for twenty feet.

The Porsche's driver steered around the burning wreck and kept up the pursuit. He increased his speed and pulled up beside Bond in the left-hand lane. The passenger had a machine gun and proceeded to spray the side of the lorry with bullets. Bond stepped hard on the brakes so that the Porsche shot ahead of the lorry. He then aimed the Walther out the window and shot at the car's tail. He was successful in putting several holes in the boot, but couldn't get a good bead on tires or anyone inside. Firing a gun with his left hand out of a moving vehicle was not his strongest skill.

Bond remembered that the road curved around a gorge close to the prehistoric sites. He was nearly there. The Porsche had continued on, the driver probably thinking that he would turn around at the next opportune spot. Bond heard more gunshots from the rear and cursed to himself when he saw yet another 4 × 4 behind him.

He drove the lorry onto the curve that hugged the side of a high bluff. To the left was the gorge, probably two hundred meters down.

Since it was dark, Bond decided that this might be his only means of escape. Keeping his hand on the wheel, he scooted across the seat to the passenger side. He removed his foot from the accelerator, slowing the lorry down to about thirty. He opened the passenger door and prepared to make his move.

He took a second grenade, pulled the pin, and dropped it onto the floor. Then, he simultaneously turned the wheel to the left and leapt from the lorry cab. He landed hard on the road, rolled, and quickly made for cover on the shoulder. The lorry weaved unsteadily toward the edge of the gorge.

Come on, Bond willed. Had he forced the wheel far enough to the left?

The lorry's left front wheel went off the road, causing the vehicle's weight to shift and lunge in that direction. Finally, the back left wheel slipped off the road and the lorry was well on its way to hell. It toppled off the bluff and dived nose first into the trees just as the grenade exploded. The lorry exploded in a fireball that lit up the sky. Its bulk carried the vehicle over the tops of the trees as it somersaulted and collided into an outcrop of large boulders.

Bond didn't waste any time. He ran into the trees and climbed the bluff, looking for a safe place to hide above the road. He heard the 4 × 4 stop and the shouts of the men inside. He stopped to watch as the Porsche returned to the scene. Two men got out of the car and joined the others to examine the spot where the lorry went off the road. One of the men pointed to the wreckage as they pondered what to do. Was the escaped prisoner dead?

One of the men got a torch out of the car and began to shine it over the trees on the right side of the road. They weren't going to leave anything to chance. *Le Gérant* would have their hides if they hadn't searched properly.

Bond kept going. Once he reached the top of the bluff, he headed east. If they were following him, he couldn't hear them. He ran like a dog, tripping over fallen trees, cutting his arms and face on low branches, and tumbling down slopes. Fighting the forest was more difficult than he had estimated. After fifteen minutes, he was completely out of breath and had to stop.

He sat on the ground, willing his heart to stop pounding. As he breathed deeply, he listened to the night air and heard vehicles not far away. They hadn't given up the search.

Bond got up and continued to run. He rushed through the dense trees, over large rocks, and down a slope until he ran right into the barbed-wire fence that he had been looking for. He cut his hand climbing over it, but compared to everything else he had suffered in the last twenty-four hours, it was nothing but a scratch.

The archaeological site of Cucuruzzu and Capula was a major tourist attraction in southern Corsica. When Bond had been searching for *Le Gérant*'s home, he had studied the area and learned that the site contained stone man-made dwellings that dated from prehistory.

Bond found himself in a forest of chestnut trees. He removed the camera from his belt and flicked on the ophthalmoscope light, which served as something of a torch. At least it illuminated the ground in front of him.

The landscape around him was not only dense with the trees but was also heavily populated by granite boulders of varying sizes. They were in piles in some places, as if a giant had collected them and stored them at various points in the forest. Mostly they were in the shape of large round spheres, the result of erosion. Piled up in this way, the rocky masses created a kind of granite chaos.

Bond climbed over one pile and descended onto the path that tourists used when visiting the site. He breathed easier, knowing that he wasn't going to become completely lost in the dark woods.

Eventually the footpath led him to a shelf bordered on the left by the granite spheres, and on the right by a heavy wall of trees. He moved along the rocks past a menhir that presented on one side a bas-relief of a sword disposed vertically, and on the other side very stylized anatomical details of a man. Just beyond the menhir was the prehistoric castle of Cucuruzzu.

The *casteddu* was an amazing Bronze Age structure made entirely of stones, ingeniously placed one on another and affixed with lime mortar. At first glance, it might have appeared to be yet another pile of boulders, but closer examination revealed that there was order to the placements. This was a shelter for prehistoric man.

Bond climbed up and over the boulders and down a "staircase" of rocks into the enclosed space. There was no roof in this small castle. Instead, little cave-like rooms had been created out of the rocks. The rooms originally had their own purposes—one or two for sleeping, one for working, one for storing food . . .

Bond crawled into one of the shelters and found it surprisingly comfortable. The flat stone floor was smooth enough to lie on, no doubt made that way by ancient man. A nice, bear-skin rug would have made it more pleasant, but at this point Bond didn't care. He was exhausted.

He figured that if he could catch a few precious hours of sleep, he could get out before the site opened for business the next morning. He hoped he could find a ride to Sartène and from there he would call London and arrange for quick transport to Cannes. That was the most important thing at this point. He had to stop that bomb, and he had less than twenty-four hours to do it. If *Le Gérant* got away, then so be it. With any luck, the guards would give up the search and report that the escaped prisoner had died inside the lorry. The Union leader would then figure that there was no longer a threat of being discovered and stay put.

Lying in the dark hole, Bond was unable to escape a swirl of mental images. There was Dr. Gerowitz adjusting the slit scan machine in front of his face; *Le Gérant* relating his life story; Mathis fumbling for his food in the cold, damp cell; the torn-open carcass of the rat; and the inescapable vision of Tylyn Mignonne's sensuous eyes. Nevertheless, he fell asleep, safe for now, in a shelter built eons ago by men whose destinies lay in their dreams.

TWENTY-FIVE

THE SCREENING

THE SUN BOUNCED OFF THE SURFACE OF THE MEDITERRANEAN AND STRUCK Bond's eyes like a dagger. He flinched but was thankful that the glare was bright and uncomfortable, for another scenario might have dictated that he be unable to see the light at all.

The Aerospatiale Eurocopter SA 360 Dauphin soared over the sea, having left Calvi twenty minutes earlier. They would reach Cannes in forty-five minutes, shortly before sunset.

It had taken nearly all day for Bond to get out of Corsica. Early that morning he had emerged from the *casteddu* as the birds were dining on worms and insects. He made his way down the footpath, climbed over the fence, and found his rental car in the parking lot where he had left it. As he drove along D268 back to Sartène, he passed the gate leading to the Union's headquarters. His thoughts turned to his friend who was still inside. Was Mathis still alive? What had they done to him after they discovered that Bond had escaped?

First things first, he told himself. Bond turned his back on *Le Gérant* for now and focused his energy on stopping the Union's plan in France. When he got to Sartène, he went straight to the *gendarmerie*, presented his credentials and got on the phone to London. The efficient Nigel Smith immediately made arrangements for Bond to be picked up by helicopter, then transferred him to M. After Bond had explained what had occurred over the last few days and what was about to happen that night in Cannes, she told Bond to sit tight. She returned the call in ten minutes and explained that a British SAS force and a French RAID team would meet Bond in Cannes. The French would pick him up in Sartène and fly him in a helicopter to Calvi for a quick refuel, then on to Cannes. In the meantime, she would work on the American, French and Russian governments to help put together a strike force to raid the Union headquarters in Corsica, but that would certainly take more time.

Bond suggested that they should forgo contacting the other countries and simply hit them alone. M rejected that ploy as being too politically volatile.

"What about the bomb?" M had asked. "How will you know where to find it?"

Bond had thought long and hard about that. All of the various clues pointed to the pressurized soft drink canisters. He had seen them at every stage of his investigation—listed on the manifests in Essinger's office in Paris, empty ones in the back room at Corse Shipping, full ones in the warehouse—that had to be the answer.

They were going to fill up one or more soft drink canisters with the CL-20, attach their homemade detonators to them and deliver them to the theater. Then, during the screening, they would be set off with the remote control device Bond had seen in Corsica.

The trick would be to find the right canisters in time.

The Dauphin picked Bond up on a relatively clear plateau near the *gendarmerie,* and Bond said goodbye to southern Corsica. It was a quick ride to Calvi, but by then it was already late afternoon. To distract him from his own impatience, Bond made a phone call to the Bastia hospital and spoke to Bertrand Collette. His friend had already received a skin graft and was feeling poorly, but he wished Bond good luck and told him not to worry.

Now, as the helicopter approached the Riviera coastline, Bond felt his stomach tighten. While he possessed the ability to remain cool and calm in most situations, on the inside he could feel quite the opposite. His steely reserve was a façade that he had perfected with years of experience. The reality was that he was only human and was susceptible to pain, fear and anxiety like anyone else. What made him different was how he acted under the pressure.

He knew that the events of the next few hours would be yet another test for him.

Tylyn Mignonne also knew that something significant would happen to her that evening. She didn't normally believe in premonitions, nor did she suppose that what occurred in her dreams might possibly come true.

She had suffered a restless night in the hotel. Awful dreams of burning corpses haunted her when she did actually fall asleep. The projector in her mind kept replaying images of the Hiroshima mushroom cloud, pictures of radiation victims and buildings on fire. At one point in the middle of the night she had woken in a sweat. She turned to grab hold of her lover, James Bond, but then she realized that he wasn't there. He was dead.

As a woman who was usually happy-go-lucky, Tylyn didn't cry very often. But she had held back the tears for days and the dam finally burst. She cried for twenty minutes, sitting on her bed with her knees to her chest. Afterward, completely spent, she was able to go back to sleep but the disturbing dreams continued. One figure kept emerging as the protagonist in them.

James, where are you now? she had called to the void. And there was an answer—his voice, ethereally floating in the air, said, "Be careful tonight, darling."

Now, as she put the finishing touches her makeup, she felt apprehensive. It wasn't because she would be required to speak in front of hundreds of people, including members of royalty, but because something terrible was going to happen. The dreams had told her so.

She zipped up the black evening dress that she had designed herself. It was floor-length with a slit that went up to her waist, revealing a long, sexy-smooth leg. She had to wear a G-string instead of panties with the garment; otherwise anyone might see them. Instead, what they got was a flash of bare hip. The neckline was low but tasteful.

While her breasts weren't particularly large, they were certainly adequate enough to produce substantial cleavage. The crowning touch was the diamond necklace that Léon had given to her their first Christmas together. She had only worn it once and she somehow felt that tonight would be an appropriate occasion to display it again. She didn't know why.

She decided to walk to the Palais alone, not caring if the *paparazzi* followed her or if fans demanded a photo or an autograph. She craved the independence and she needed to remind herself that she was strong and resilient.

As she walked out of the Carlton through the gauntlet of onlookers, she switched on the million-dollar smile and waved as the cameras flashed. Someone yelled, "Marry me, Tylyn!" She blew a kiss to the man, then pulled him out of the crowd. She put her arm through his and asked him if he would walk her to the Palais. Flabbergasted, the young man nearly tripped and fell, but he quickly regained his composure and began a ten minutes that he would never forget.

Le Palais des Festivals was a grand structure that contained two cinemas and several floors of meeting rooms, press rooms, and other facilities to accommodate the huge event that the film festival had become over the years. A wide red carpet adorned the sets of steps leading up to the Lumière Amphitheatre, where all of the major screenings were held. Traffic had been blocked off and security barriers were set in place to keep onlookers back.

Evening screenings were always black tie affairs. Even the most famous celebrity could not gain entrance without a tuxedo. Tylyn had witnessed an incident a few years back in which a prominent, hot young American director was denied entry because he was wearing a turtleneck sweater. He was so enraged that he swore he would never return.

The parade of glamorous people usually began half an hour before the screening. No one was exempt from making the red carpet entrance. Everyone had to do it—the celebrities, the critics and the invited guests. The festival's organizers orchestrated it that way to make sure that all of the VIPs were seen at *their* event.

Tylyn said goodbye to her lucky escort at the edge of the red carpet, then proceeded to walk up the stairs alone. She continued to wave as the camera flashes exploded around her like fireworks. Other exquisitely dressed guests were also ascending the stairs. She recognized famous French actors Catherine Deneuve, Sophie Marceau, Jean-Louis Trintignant, Gérard Depardieu, Carole Bouquet, and Isabelle Adjani. Esteemed directors from all over the world were there: David Lynch, the Coen brothers, Roberto Benigni, James Ivory, John Madden, Jane Campion and Francis Ford Coppola. Tylyn assumed that the royal entourages had either already made their entrances or were being held back until last.

She found Stuart Laurence at the top of the stairs. She joined hands with him and they both waved to the crowd before going inside.

Tylyn thought the Lumière Amphitheatre was the ideal cinema. Despite the hassles and madness of the film festival, attending a screening at the Lumière was always a pleasurable experience. The acoustics were perfect and every seat in the house was a good one. She admired the purple and pink décor; the carpet and upholstery were kept in pristine condition, as if the cinema was a royal palace. The stage was black and there were large white panels in the ceiling that concealed lighting instruments. Usherettes dressed in white dresses with black polka dots greeted the audience as they entered.

Tylyn saw Léon in the lobby. She didn't want to speak to him, but he saw her and gestured for her to come over. Luckily, that ugly man Wilcox wasn't there. She took a breath, then pulled Stuart along with her to greet her soon-to-be former husband.

"Tylyn, you look beautiful," he said, kissing her cheeks. "Stuart, dashing as always." He noticed the necklace and said, "Darling, you have made me very happy by wearing that."

She shrugged. "I thought I should do something for you. This is your night, Léon. I hope this time you'll stay for the screening."

He shook his head. "I'm sorry to disappoint you, but no, I won't be staying for the screening. I'm way too nervous. In fact, my stomach is about to explode as it is. I feel very sick."

"Take it easy, man," Stuart said, clapping him on the shoulder. "Maybe you should sit down. You *do* look a little pale."

"Oh, I'll be all right, I think," Essinger said, stifling a belch. "We had a little scare this afternoon. I thought the film hadn't made it to the Palais. I used a new security firm to deliver it. They were late, but it's here now, thank God."

At that moment, the level of excitement in the lobby increased tenfold. All heads turned as Princess Caroline of Monaco entered with her group.

"I must greet Her Royal Highness," Essinger said. "Will you excuse me?"

"I'm coming with you!" Stuart said. "Tylyn?"

"You boys go ahead," she said. "I'll meet the Princess later."

They left her and she decided to avoid mingling in the lobby. She would have killed for a glass of champagne, but that would have to wait until the party afterward. Apparently Léon had arranged for a bash at one of the exclusive beach restaurants nearby.

Pretending not to notice some film critics whom she knew, Tylyn left the lobby and made her way to her seat inside the theater.

In the projection booth perched directly underneath the balcony, Julius Wilcox and Rick Fripp looked out of the small windows at the ever-growing crowd. Only Fripp was dressed in a tuxedo.

"I can't believe we're doing away with some of the most important names in show business tonight," Fripp said.

Wilcox dismissed the thought with a wave of his hand. "You've seen one goddamned movie star, you've seen 'em all."

"I understand you received some bad news this afternoon."

Wilcox nodded. "I spoke to *Le Gérant*. It appears that our English spy is alive and well. He's probably on his way here. We need to keep a look out for him. Shoot to kill."

"Right," Fripp said. "I could have sworn he had died in that explosion."

Wilcox said, "He'll wish that he had. Apparently he was at Corse Shipping the other night when I was there seeing Emile. We still don't know if he found anything out."

The projectionist entered the room and asked, "What are you doing here? Who are you?"

Fripp flashed his backstage pass and said, "We're with the film, my friend."

He looked at them suspiciously and said, "Oh. Well maybe you can explain something."

"What's that?"

"The film. I opened all of the cans except for one. It wouldn't open because there's a lock on it." He pointed to the stacks of metal film canisters on the worktable. All of them were open and the reels removed except for the one that had two padlocks affixed to the sides. The film had been spliced together onto two large reels for the projection system, as was the custom. "As far as I can tell, I've got the entire film loaded. But there's this one can that I can't open. What's inside it? Surely not more film?"

Fripp feigned interest, counted the empty cans, and said, "No, you've got them all. I don't know what this extra one is. Maybe it was stacked with the other cans by mistake. Just leave it and our people will take it back tonight."

"It's marked *Tsunami Rising,* Part Eight," the projectionist said. "But according to my notes, there are only seven parts."

"That's correct," Wilcox said sternly. "This eighth can is a *mistake.* Forget about it. Just do your job."

The projectionist looked at Wilcox as if to say, *Who the hell are you telling me what to do?* but the man thought better of it. This man was the ugliest and meanest looking person he'd ever seen. So he shrugged and said, "Fine."

Fripp and Wilcox left the projection booth and closed the door.

"You think he's all right?" Fripp asked.

"Yeah," Wilcox said. "Better give me the phone now. I've got to get out of here. I ain't wearing a tux."

Fripp gave him a mobile. "Here it is. You know the code."

"I'll hit the buttons one hour into the screening," Wilcox said, "and I won't be calling for a pizza. Are you all set to get out?"

"I'm leaving with Léon," he said. "I had better get downstairs. He's probably drunk his stuff by now."

Wilcox chuckled. "I wish I could be there to watch him puke."

TWENTY-SIX

THE RAID

"I'M COMMANDANT PERRIOT," THE HEAD OF THE FRENCH RAID TEAM SAID to Bond. "We have assembled twenty men, all armed and ready to go." He pointed to the two military vehicles that were idling near the helipad. The men inside were dressed in camouflage military uniforms and riot gear.

"Have you heard from the SAS team? Where are they?" Bond asked.

The man shrugged. "I just heard that they will be here in ten minutes. Do you want to wait?"

Bond looked at his Rolex. The screening would begin in ten minutes.

"No. Let's go."

They both jumped in the first truck and set off. The Dauphin had landed at the heliport west of the city. It would take them at least ten minutes to get into the Centre-Ville. With the traffic and pedestrian congestion, it might take longer.

"I have radioed the Cannes police," Perriot said. "Hopefully they have cleared the way for us."

"What have you told them?"

"Only that we have information that a terrorist act might occur at the festival this evening. I gave them no details, as per your instructions."

"Good," Bond said. "We don't want them to start evacuating the cinema."

"Why not, may I ask?"

"Because that would tip off the bombers that we know about the plan," Bond said. "If I'm right, the trigger-man can set off the bomb at his discretion. It's a radio-controlled device, so he could be anywhere in the vicinity. If we start evacuating, he'll know that the game is over and set it off immediately. Mission accomplished."

"What are we looking for, exactly?" the commandant asked.

"I'm guessing, but I believe the bomb is disguised as a pressurized soft drink tank," Bond said. "One of those that fits underneath a bar and has a hose attached to it for dispensing soft drinks. I think it's safe to say that it's in the cinema itself."

"Right."

The two trucks reached the Palais just as the last of the guests were ascending the red-carpeted stairs. Several Cannes policemen were gathered at the barrier to meet the RAID team. A young captain saluted Perriot and said, "Everyone is inside, monsieur. Do you want me to evacuate the VOs?" Bond knew that VO was a code that meant *"Visiteurs Officiels."* He pointed to two armored Rolls-Royces standing nearby.

Perriot turned to Bond. "What do you think?"

Bond shook his head. "Not yet. If they left it would arouse too much suspicion. Let us have fifteen minutes. If we haven't found anything by then, let's see if we can *quietly* get the VOs out of the cinema. As it is, just our appearance in the front of the building is sure to alert the terrorists to our presence."

Bond and Perriot, followed by the RAID team, ran up the steps in full view of the crowd and cameras. Immediately the rumor mill began to churn. *What's going on? Did something happen inside? Was Princess Caroline all right? I heard gunfire! No, you're crazy. It's probably terrorists from the Middle East. It's a publicity stunt.*

A news reporter approached the police captain and asked what was happening.

"Nothing, just extra security," he said, but he wasn't very convincing.

"Twenty armed men in riot uniforms?" the reporter asked. "Come on, sir, the people have a right to know. They're already talking. Has someone been hurt?"

"No, please, move along."

The cinema manager met Bond and Perriot at the entrance.

"Please take us immediately to the bar," Perriot ordered.

The manager looked confused. "But . . . there is no bar in the Lumière," he said. "The only bar in the Palais is Jimmy'Z on the third floor of the main building. It's nowhere near the Lumière Amphitheatre."

"No place where soft drinks are served to the audience?" Perriot asked.

"No, monsieur," the manager replied. "We keep our cinema clean."

Bond cursed softly. "Then I don't know what we're looking for," he said to Perriot. "I suggest that we start the search backstage, in the lobby and in the catwalks. Tell your men to use complete discretion. As far as the civilians are concerned, we're just extra security. After all, royalty is in attendance."

The team burst into the lobby and spread out. Several men went upstairs while Bond and others took the corridor that led along the left side of the house to the backstage area. The Lumière manager pulled Perriot to the side and asked, "If there is a bomb in the theater, shouldn't we evacuate?"

Perriot was explaining the problem with doing so when a tall American film critic walked by on his way to his seat after visiting the toilet. He wasn't fluent in French, but he thought that he understood the words "bomb" and "theater." Alarmed at the sight of the soldiers, he immediately went inside to tell his colleagues what he had heard.

Bond reached the backstage area and peered through the black curtains at the audience. He could see the special sections set aside for Prince Edward, Princess Caroline, and their respective groups, as well as for the celebrities involved with the film.

His heart skipped a beat when he saw her. Tylyn was sitting next to Stuart Laurence. Her diamond necklace caught the house lights and she looked magnificent even from this distance. When was she scheduled to speak? Before the screening?

He scanned the faces for Essinger, but didn't see him. It figured. If he were in on the plot, he would have found a way to be absent.

Bond turned from the curtains and rushed behind the huge screen, where the RAID team were busy searching behind and under every object. He looked up and noticed catwalks above the stage where the crew could hang lighting instruments or adjust the screen. He pointed them out to one of the men and directed him to climb the steel ladder and look up there, then he went out the door leading to dressing rooms and backstage offices.

As he stepped into the brightly lit corridor, he heard a voice that he recognized.

"Ohhh, I feel terrible. I really must go."

"Léon, it is such a shame!" a man said in French. "Was it something you ate?"

"It must have been. I just vomited all over the dressing room, I'm very sorry."

Bond peered around the corner and saw Essinger, Fripp, and several other people dressed in formal wear. The one speaking to Essinger was an older, bald-headed man that Bond recognized as Gilles Jacob, the President of the film festival.

"I had better take Monsieur Essinger back to the hotel," Fripp said. "Come on, Léon."

"But my screening!" Essinger moaned. "I need to be here! Ohhhhh!" He began to retch again and ran into the dressing room. Bond heard him gagging loudly. Everyone in the corridor winced.

"Poor man," Jacob said.

Bond drew his Walther and stepped into view. "Hold it right there, Fripp."

The stuntman froze.

"What is the meaning of this?" Jacob asked.

"Hands up, *now!*" Bond ordered. "Monsieur Jacob, please take your party and step back. Go into the theater. This is police business."

When they didn't move, Bond shouted, "GO!" They left immediately, frightened to death.

Fripp raised his hands but looked at Bond with a sneer. "You're not going to get away with this, Bond," he said.

"Get your friend out of there and let's go," Bond ordered.

Fripp stepped back two steps but kept his hands raised. "My friend is very ill. Can't you hear him?"

"Stay where you are!" Bond spat. "Where's the bomb?"

"What bomb?" Now Fripp smiled.

"No games. Either you tell me where it is or I'll blow a hole in your head." He pointed the Walther at Fripp's head.

Before Fripp could react, gunfire erupted from the dressing room door. A bullet barely missed Bond's shoulder. He responded instinctively and ducked, momentarily moving the gun away from Fripp. Essinger had the door ajar and was aiming a gun through the opening. He fired again, but Bond leapt out of the way, slamming against the corridor wall. This gave Fripp the opportunity he needed to run. Bond shot wildly at Fripp but missed him.

Fripp pulled a Browning Hi Power from inside his tuxedo jacket and fired at Bond, but the bullet missed completely and went into the wall. He continued to run.

Essinger slammed the dressing room door shut and locked it. Bond leveled his fire at the door, emptying his magazine. When he stopped to reload, Bond shouted, "Essinger? If you're alive you had better talk to me!"

"Go to hell you bastard!" the man shouted from inside the room.

A RAID officer ran into the corridor. "I heard shots!"

"Help me break this door down," Bond said. Together, they kicked it in and burst into the room. Essinger, his shoulder and arm bloody from a gunshot wound, stood with his hands in the air.

Bond held a gun to his head. "Where's the bomb, Essinger?"

"I swear I don't know," he said, trembling. His face was ashen. "Please, I have to sit down, I feel so sick . . ." He dropped to his knees.

"Talk, damn it!" Bond shouted, jabbing the gun barrel into Essinger's temple.

"They didn't tell me!" Essinger said. "I swear! They thought it would not be wise for me to know that particular detail."

Bond turned to the RAID man and said, "Take him outside and watch him. I'm going after the other one."

"*Oui, monsieur.*"

Bond left the room and ran back toward the stage, where Fripp had disappeared. A moment later, Essinger collapsed. The soldier knelt beside him and slapped his face. "Monsieur? Monsieur?"

He didn't hear someone step into the room behind him. An expert's hand grabbed the soldier's helmet and pulled his head back. In the time it took for the soldier to register that he was being attacked, the knife slit his throat from ear to ear. He fell over, blood gushing from his neck.

Julius Wilcox held out a hand to Essinger and helped him up. "Come on, let's *blow* this joint."

In the house, the audience was still buzzing, happily waiting for the moment when the festivities would begin. So far, most of them had not noticed the soldiers running around backstage. But the film critic who had overheard Commandant Perriot and the theater manager told his friends that there was a bomb in the cinema.

"I think we should leave," he said.

"You're mad," one of his colleagues said. "Sit down."

Unfortunately, a woman sitting behind them heard what was said and whispered to her husband, "That man said there's a bomb in the theater!"

Several rows behind them, in the VIP section, Tylyn Mignonne was becoming impatient. Let's get on with it! she thought. She was nervous enough as it was. Stuart Laurence had been talking non-stop but she hadn't been listening: her mind was elsewhere.

She perked up when she saw a man in a tuxedo run from the wings in front of the huge white screen. He turned and pointed a gun at something in the wings. It went off, frightening the entire audience.

"My God! It's Rick Fripp!" Laurence said.

No one moved. Was this part of the show? What was going on?

"Something's wrong," Tylyn said. She started to stand but Laurence stopped her.

"Wait," he said. "I'll bet Léon cooked up some kind of pre-show entertainment for us."

"I wouldn't bet on it," Tylyn said, but she settled uneasily in her seat.

Fripp ran into the wings on the other side of the stage and began to climb the metal circular staircase that led to the catwalks. Bond had run behind the screen and almost caught him, but the stuntman performed a surprise karate kick that kept his pursuer at bay. Bond chased him to the staircase and followed him up. He didn't want to fire his gun for fear of causing a panic.

When they reached the catwalk, the two men were nearly sixty feet above the stage. Bond tackled him and Fripp's Browning went flying. Fripp slugged Bond hard in the face, but Bond reciprocated with blows to Fripp's stomach. The catwalk was very narrow, perhaps three feet wide, so there wasn't much room for them to roll around. Nevertheless, Fripp leapt on top of Bond and attempted to push him off. Bond locked his foot around a metal beam and grabbed hold of a rail above his head. It was a matter of strength now. Fripp was very fit and obviously was used to working with heavy objects. Bond felt his trunk sliding off the catwalk despite his hand and footholds.

But Fripp made a fatal mistake when he bent one leg to obtain better leverage. He left himself wide open for Bond to drive his knee hard into Fripp's groin. Fripp yelled, immediately released Bond, and fell back onto the catwalk in pain. Bond punched him in the face and shouted, "Where's the bomb? Tell me!"

Even through his agony, Fripp remained defiant. He spat at Bond and laughed. Bond punched him again and then rolled him to the edge of the catwalk.

"Tell me or I'll push you over," Bond said.

"Let's go together!" Fripp said. In a surprise move, he grabbed Bond's neck and hurled his body over and off the catwalk, dragging Bond with him.

The two bodies fell together ten or twelve feet and collided with a bank of multicolored strip lights, which halted their fall, but their weight broke one of the support chains holding it up. The entire mechanism fell loose and hung vertically, in front of the screen where everyone in the house could see.

The audience gasped when they saw the two men hanging off the dangling strip lights.

Tylyn recognized Fripp again. The other man—he looked familiar too. She stood abruptly when she realized who it was. "James?" she gasped.

Fripp, fighting to hold on to the swaying bank of lights, grabbed a broken live wire. He screamed as the volts surged through his body and sparks formed a halo around him. He fried for nearly ten seconds before the wire broke and he fell. He landed with a loud thud on the stage, causing several women in the audience to scream. Bond still hung on to the panel, fighting for his life.

The tall film critic turned to his friends and asked, "Now do you believe me?" and then he stood and shouted, "There's a bomb in the theater!"

TWENTY-SEVEN

THE SEARCH

THE THEATER ERUPTED INTO CHAOS. THE ROYALTY VIPS WERE IMMEDIATELY ushered out through emergency exits by the efficient Palais security guards and handed over to the Cannes police. The respective parties from Britain and Monaco were then whisked away in armored cars and taken to safety.

Tylyn was caught in a stampede of people attempting to escape but she wasn't trying to leave at all. She wanted to get up to the stage.

"James!" she called.

Her voice barely carried over the clamor, but Bond heard her. He had a tenuous hold on the strip light panel and couldn't hold on much longer.

Tylyn forced her way through the crazed audience. A man knocked her over and she was almost trampled, but she crawled into a row of seats and stood on one. The shoulder strap on her dress broke and she could barely keep it up over her breasts. In desperation, she grabbed the nearest man and ordered him, "Tie this!" The man was in such a state of fright that he tied the broken strap around her upper arm without thinking. It did the trick, her dress stayed up.

Tylyn then lifted up her skirt so that she could step over the seats and get to the stage that way. She held on to the excess material with one hand and used the other to support herself as she climbed over each seat back, row by row.

When she got to the stage, Bond was slipping.

"Hold on, James!" she called. Looking around frantically for something to cushion his fall, Tylyn finally ran to the side of the proscenium and grabbed hold of the bottom of the act curtain. She pulled it toward center stage, in front of the screen. This formed a hammock-like canopy that curved beneath Bond's feet.

"Jump!" she called. "I've got it!"

Bond let go of the strip lights, fell twenty feet, and hit the curtain. The weight and force caused Tylyn to drop her end, but the curtain provided just enough of a break to his fall. He clung to the curtain and swung with it back to its original place, then dropped to the stage on his feet.

Tylyn ran to him and embraced him.

"My darling!" she cried, kissing him. "You're alive, you're alive!"

"Tylyn," he said, panting, returning her kisses. "You have to get out of here now. There's a bomb in here somewhere. Léon is responsible. I can explain later, but you must leave!"

"I'm not leaving without you!"

"Tylyn, I have a job to do here. I will find you outside. *Please!*" He grabbed her shoulders hard and pushed her away from him. He looked her in the eyes and said, "I love you, Tylyn. Now please go." Without another word, he turned and ran into the wings to continue the search for the bomb.

Tylyn stood there a second, her fingers to her lips. "I love you, too," she whispered.

Bond found the dead soldier in Essinger's dressing room and cursed. He followed the corridor to the end and came upon an emergency exit that probably emptied into the back of the building. He kicked it open and looked outside.

A white van was pulling out of a reserved parking space. As it turned to head toward the exit, Bond saw Julius Wilcox in the passenger seat. Bond leapt down to the pavement and ran as fast as he could.

The van stopped because the driveway was jammed with pedestrians. The panic had spread into the street as the audience came running down the steps. Now there were police sirens blaring all over the Centre-Ville and everything was chaotic.

"Run them over!" Wilcox shouted at Essinger, who was driving. The producer's shoulder was bleeding profusely from the gunshot wound and he was in terrible pain.

"I can't do th—" Essinger protested, but Wilcox had a gun to his head before he could finish the sentence.

"Go, you bastard," Wilcox said. He held the mobile phone in his other hand. "We have to get a few blocks away before I can activate the bomb. The blast will level the entire building and kill everyone around here. Running them over now won't make a bit of difference. Do it!"

There was a loud thump on top of the van.

Essinger looked up, his eyes wild with fright. "There's someone on the roof!"

"Drive, you idiot!" Wilcox shouted.

Essinger stepped on the gas and the van bolted into the crowd. There were screams as three or four people were hit. Wilcox aimed his pistol up and began shooting holes in the top of the van.

Bond, lying on top of the vehicle's roof rack, turned his body this way and that, gambling that the bullets wouldn't hit him. One came too close for comfort, searing the side of his face as it exploded into the sky. Temporarily blinded, Bond held on to the van tightly as it sped into the street.

Inside, Essinger asked, "Did you get him?"

"I don't know," Wilcox said. He set down the mobile, rolled down the passenger window, stuck his head out, and climbed up in his seat so that he could look. As soon as he did, Bond's foot smashed into his face. Surprised, he dropped his weapon and almost fell out of the window. Bond kicked him again but Wilcox managed to slip back inside.

"Knock him off, damn it!" Wilcox yelled.

Essinger swerved the van back and forth in an attempt to swing Bond off the top, but it was no use.

"We have to go faster!" Wilcox said. "Step on it!"

"I can't!" Essinger exclaimed, gesturing to the congestion on the street. "Where the hell do you suggest I go?"

Wilcox reached over and turned the wheel so that the van drove off the street and onto the pavement. Pedestrians jumped out of the way as the van crashed over several restaurant tables and chairs. Essinger took the wheel again and maneuvered the van off the pavement and into a side street, where it hit a parked police car, scraped the side of a limousine, and continued on into the crowded rue d'Antibes. There the congestion was even worse.

"Oh no!" Essinger said. "There's no place to go!"

"Run them over! Kill them all!" Wilcox shouted.

But by that time Bond had climbed over to the side of the van and was hanging on to the door handle. He managed to plant his feet firmly on the footstep there, then used every bit of strength he had left to slide open the door.

Essinger screamed when he saw that Bond had got inside. Wilcox got out of his seat and threw himself at the intruder, just as Bond managed to draw his Walther. The gun went flying as the two men fell into the back of the van. Essinger did his best to keep the vehicle moving, but when he heard a siren behind him, he panicked.

"The police!" he called back to Wilcox, but his partner couldn't hear him.

Clenching his jaw and closing his eyes, Essinger floored the accelerator and hoped for the best. The van lurched forward, hit three cars parked along the side of the road, swerved to the other side and onto the pavement, and into a large storefront window. The glass shattered and alarm bells rang with ferocity. Essinger was thrown forward into the windscreen, which cracked his head and rendered him unconscious.

The crash had little effect on Bond and Wilcox, who had their hands around each other's throats. Wilcox was an agile man but Bond was the superior fighter. He took a chance and let go of Wilcox's neck so that he could get in two quick punches to the man's face. But Wilcox wouldn't let go. He was squeezing hard, causing Bond to choke and gag.

Desperate now, Bond's right hand groped the floor of the van for a weapon—his missing Walther or anything that might even the odds. He felt a steel rod of some kind and grasped it. It was a tire iron. Bond swung it hard and fast onto Wilcox's head. The ugly man released his grip on Bond's neck and fell over, dazed. Bond hit him again, but this time Wilcox blocked the blow with his arm. He yelped like a dog at the pain, but that didn't stop him from rebounding. Julius Wilcox was no amateur.

Before Bond could strike him again with the tire iron, Wilcox kicked him hard in the chest. Bond flew back against the van wall and struck his head on the edge of the door. Wilcox, seemingly immune to the punishment he had received, pounced on Bond and began to pummel him mercilessly. Bond held his arms in front of his face for protection but the Union killer got through with several powerful blows.

Bond's head slammed against the floor; but through the haze he could see his Walther, a few feet away. There was only one thing to do. He allowed Wilcox to continue punching him unrelentingly so that the killer wouldn't notice him moving his hand toward the gun. Nearing unconsciousness, Bond inched his fingers a bit closer . . . closer . . . and he had it! Holding the barrel against Wilcox's stomach, he squeezed the trigger. The report was deafening inside the confined metal space as the bullet went through Wilcox's abdomen, exited out of his back, and blew a hole in the van roof. The expression on the killer's face changed from rage to disbelief. He stopped hitting Bond and froze for a moment.

Bond fired again. Blood dribbled from the ugly man's mouth as he coughed twice. Bond rolled him off and got up. Wilcox twitched and jerked for ten seconds, then lay still.

A groan from the front of the van got Bond's attention. Essinger was coming to. Blood streamed down his head, and his tuxedo was soaked from the shoulder wound. Bond stuck the Walther to the back of his head.

"Now," he said, catching his breath. "Where is the bloody bomb?"

Essinger nodded. "All right. Just a second." He was very woozy. "Let me get my bearings."

"Now talk!" Bond spat, shoving the barrel into Essinger's neck.

"All right!" Essinger reached over to the passenger seat and picked up the mobile phone. "I need to call the man who is supposed to set it off."

"What?"

He showed Bond the phone. "I need to call it off. He has to get the message not to detonate the bomb."

The fight with Wilcox had left Bond disoriented as well. Not thinking straight, he said, "All right. Call him."

Essinger switched on the mobile and punched a number. Then another.

Bond's mind reeled. *Wait a minute!* The detonator was built to receive a radio transmission.

"Go ahead," Bond said, shoving the barrel into Essinger's neck again. "Kill them all."

Essinger hesitated. His finger was poised to hit another button, but the hand holding the phone began to shake.

"Do it," Bond taunted. "Your friends and colleagues, the people who gave you a career, your *wife* . . . Kill them all."

Essinger closed his eyes and coughed.

"But if you do it, remember that I'm not there to die along with them," Bond whispered. "I'm right here."

With a whimper, Essinger dropped the mobile. Bond picked it up and shut it off.

Completely subdued, Essinger wilted in the seat. "It's in the projection booth," he said. "In a film can."

Bond lowered the gun.

"They put the CL-20 in a film can and rigged the thing with a radio-controlled detonator. The can itself serves as the antenna. It was enough explosive to kill everyone in the theater and probably a good many outside of it." The man began to sob. "I'm sorry. I didn't want to do it."

Bond left him and got out of the van. The police were just pulling up, followed by Perriot and two of the RAID officers.

"Are you all right, monsieur?" he asked.

Bond nodded. He pointed to Essinger. "Take him." He gave the mobile to Perriot and told him where they could find the bomb.

Bond refused to go to hospital, claiming that his injuries were superficial. He had certainly received worse. His face was battered, his eye was swollen and his ribs hurt, but there was nothing broken. He allowed a paramedic to treat his cuts and scrapes, then walked over to the command center that had been set up in the British Pavilion next to the Palais. This was a place where UK citizens attending the event could have a snack, a drink, check their e-mail, have meetings or simply relax.

The British SAS team had arrived ten minutes too late to participate in the search for the bomb, but now they were doing their best to interview witnesses and gather information about what had happened. The bomb had been found in the projection booth and carefully removed from the site.

Bond joined the commanders of the British and French teams in the tent after ordering a beer at the bar.

"Congratulations, monsieur," Perriot said. "You have done an exemplary job."

"Hear, hear!" said the rather stiff man in charge of the British. He lifted his own glass of beer to Bond.

Bond ignored the praise and said, "I want to know how they got that bomb into the building."

The Cannes police captain cleared his throat. "We were just going over that. It appears that the film production company, that is, Monsieur Essinger's company, used a private security agency to deliver the film cans. This is fairly standard procedure. The security personnel had clearance passes and were able to drive right up to the Palais and walk inside with the cans."

"Pretty cheeky, if you ask me," the British commander said.

A young technician with the French police who had been busy hooking up a VCR to a monitor said, "Excuse me, but I think I'm ready."

"Ah," Perriot replied. "We have tapes of everyone going in and out of the building. I got them from the Palais security team. There are cameras set up at every entrance." He turned to the young man and said, "See if you can find the service entrance tape. The film was delivered shortly after six o'clock."

"Yes, monsieur," the lad said and got busy reviewing the material.

Bond asked, "So what happens next?"

Perriot answered, "Well, for one thing, we're going to question every single person associated with Monsieur Essinger. They're being rounded up as we speak. I think that the real culprits, though, were Monsieur Wilcox and Monsieur Fripp. They are dead, of course."

"I have it, monsieur," the young man said. He switched on the tape and they all turned to the monitor.

The camera showed the back entrance of the Palais, shot from the inside looking out. A Palais security guard was standing by the door checking the badges of everyone who walked in.

"Fast forward, please," Perriot ordered.

The technician did as he was told until two men with film cans could be seen at the door.

"There. Stop please."

The tape resumed its normal speed.

When Bond saw who had delivered the film cans, his heart sank. He closed his eyes and rubbed his brow.

"Are you all right, Monsieur Bond?" Perriot asked.

He sighed heavily, and said, "Yes. It's been a long day."

Another young man in an SAS uniform approached him and asked, "Are you Mister Bond?"

"Yes?"

"There's someone here to see you. Outside."

Bond got up slowly, drained his beer, set the bottle on the table, and walked out of the tent. What he had viewed on the television monitor had thoroughly disheartened him, but when he saw who was waiting outside the tent, his spirits picked up.

"Tylyn," he said.

They fell into each other's arms and the entire world was lost to them.

———•———

They bathed together and then had a luxurious dinner in her room at the Carlton. Tylyn dressed Bond's wounds and kissed them, then gave him a thorough massage. They made love, and this time it was soft and gentle. Bond noted that their couplings had always been different, both in mood and intensity. He knew that this was a woman with whom he could find variety for the rest of his life.

Afterward, they lay in bed naked. He smoked a cigarette and she sipped a glass of cognac. Tylyn cleared her throat and said, "I have something to say and I'm not sure how to say it."

"Then just say it," Bond replied.

"All right." She took a sip and began. "You lied to me, James. You told me you were a reporter and I believed you."

"Darling, don't you see now why I did that? I was investigating your husband."

"And you used *me* to get to him."

He crushed the cigarette in an ashtray and sat up in the bed. "No. I didn't. At first, perhaps, I may have thought that I might get close to him through you. But after I met you all of that changed. I wanted to be with you, Tylyn."

She sighed. "And this job of yours. You're really a policeman. You carry a gun. You advocate violence."

"I don't advocate anything," Bond said. "Sometimes, yes, I have to use a gun. But only if I have to."

She nodded but didn't look happy.

He reached out and ran a finger along her smooth cheek. "Tylyn," he said, "don't think about that now. We're both alive. I'm desperately attracted to you, and I hope you still feel the same about me. I'm sorry I deceived you, but I promise to make it up to you. Tomorrow I have to finish this job in Corsica, but I'll be back tomorrow night and we can spend the rest of our lives together if that's what you want."

"Is that what you want?" she asked.

He hesitated. "I don't know. Perhaps."

"I don't know either," she said. "Let's not think about that."

"All right. Let's just enjoy each other tonight, shall we?"

She nodded and leaned over to kiss him. He placed a hand on her breast, gently laid her back, and made love to her once again.

Bond rarely dreamed, but he had a vivid one that night.

He was running through the Corsica *maquis,* the thick forest near the prehistoric sites. He was naked, but as he looked down at himself he saw that he wasn't human any more. He was an animal, some kind of stag.

He ran past the strange menhirs, and several of them turned to watch him go by. One even whispered that he should be careful.

That's when he realized that he was being followed. Looking behind him, he could see the silhouette of a wolf in the distance, running after him. He increased his speed, but the presence of the wolf was overpowering. The beast was getting closer . . . closer . . . until Bond could feel the animal's hot breath on his back.

He heard a horrendous, unearthly snarl as the wolf leapt for him—

And Bond woke up.

He got out of bed, careful not to disturb Tylyn, and took a bottle of Perrier from the bar. He drank it down quickly and sat in a chair to calm himself. His heart was pounding.

Tylyn stirred and noticed that he wasn't beside her. She looked up and saw him. "What's the matter, sweetheart?"

"Would you believe me if I told you that I had a bad dream?" he asked.

She smiled. "Yes. I would." She reached out to him. "Come back to bed. I'll make sure you get back to sleep safely."

He crawled under the sheets and felt her smooth, soft skin next to his. She reached between his legs and caressed him. In seconds, the aftertaste of the nightmare had vanished.

"*Fais-moi l'amour,* James," she said.

He was happy to oblige.

TWENTY-EIGHT

THE SHOWDOWN

INTERPOL OFFICIALS AGREED WITH M THAT COMMANDER JAMES BOND should be placed in charge of the strike against the Union headquarters in Corsica. During the night, Interpol worked feverishly with the governments of Britain, America and France to put together a team of professional soldiers culled from the countries' respective armies. The international force totaled twenty-six men, all SAS trained.

Bond learned that he had been chosen to lead the team when he awoke at sunrise. Nigel Smith had tracked him down by phone and told him to report to the airport in Nice at nine o'clock sharp. The ring had disturbed Tylyn's sleep, but she quickly dozed off again. Bond quietly got dressed, left without making a sound, was picked up by a military escort and taken to Nice.

The meeting took place at a hangar near Terminal One. A French air force captain provided aerial reconnaissance photos of *Le Gérant's* compound and made suggestions for an approach.

"The element of surprise must work in our favor," he said. "The Union must surely know that we're going to hit them, so what we need to do is make certain that we hit them before they *think* we're going to hit them. They just might be banking on the notion that a raid can't be organized overnight. That's why we're moving so fast. From the satellite films we have obtained, we can see that there has been activity for the last twenty-four hours. We estimate a force of twenty men, but that's difficult to say; at any rate it looks like they're moving out. If we don't get there quickly, they could be gone before the day is over. The raid is on now, gentlemen, and we want to be hitting targets no later than noon."

Someone asked what the objective was—to take prisoners, or what?

"Shoot to kill anyone that moves, except for two people," Bond said. "There is a hostage in the basement. You'll find his photo in the packet. My squad is going after him. Once the hostage is safe, we can blow the house to kingdom come. Secondly, everyone must be on the lookout for the blind man, the Union's leader. That photo in your packet was taken recently in Monte Carlo. He is our primary objective and is wanted alive. That said, if the rest of his men meet with unfortunate accidents, I'm not going to blink twice."

The French officer resumed speaking. "We're in three squads. Each squad will assault a different side of the building. Your squad leader will brief you on the specifics. We'll all be equipped with headsets so that we can communicate with each other. We leave in one hour. Good luck."

Bond checked his weapons—the Walther knife and the reliable P99, plenty of extra magazines, a bullet-proof vest and headset. As an afterthought, he clipped the Q-Branch camera to his belt. Commandant Perriot approached him and said, "I just want you to know, monsieur, that it will be a privilege serving with you. After witnessing your courage yesterday in Cannes, I would follow you anywhere."

"Thank you for volunteering," Bond said. "Before we leave, I need to make a phone call." He found Marc-Ange Draco's business card in his wallet and said, "I know someone who might be able to help us."

Le Gérant got off the phone with one of his most trusted colleagues and told Julien, the bookkeeper, "They are not going to be able to get together a strike force in one day's time, just as I thought. We've been given a reprieve. Tell the boys that they don't have to kill themselves to pack. Instead of being out of here by noon today, we have until midnight tonight. All right?"

"*Oui, monsieur,*" Julien said and marched out of the office.

But *Le Gérant* had a bad feeling in his gut. Something was wrong. Should he effect his escape now?

He stepped to a window, even though he couldn't see the view of the Corsican mountains around the property. Remember what the dreams have told you, *Le Gérant* said to himself. His last dream was a testament to his upcoming triumph, for in it he had slain the majestic stag. That meant that there was nothing to worry about. He didn't need to run so soon. The dreams had predicted that he would emerge victorious.

And dreams never lied.

The French army loaned them three Aerospatiale (Eurocopter) AS 565 Panthers armed with cannon pods, Matra Mistral AAMs, HOT AT missiles, rockets and torpedoes. Nine men in each chopper were quite comfortable as they made the journey from Nice to southern Corsica. As Bond looked down at the broccoli-like clumps of trees and the rough terrain of the rocky mountains, he thought again of the phone call he had made earlier and how it would affect the mission.

Never mind, he told himself. *Get on with it.*

The helicopters flew over Propriano and headed east toward Levie. Bond spoke into the headset, "This is it, gentlemen. Prepare for Phase One."

Every man in each chopper jumped up, checked their equipment, lowered the safety goggles on their helmets, and stood at attention near the open door. They were armed with M-4 A2 assault rifles, handguns, grenades, bullet-proof vests and knives.

"Monsieur Bond?" Perriot said on the headset.

"Yes?"

"I just received word that Assault Team B successfully raided Corse Shipping in St. Florent. Emile Cirendini has been arrested."

"One down, two hundred to go . . ." Bond said.

The choppers neared the property, split up, and flew to respective points of a triangle in the sky. Bond's helicopter would drop the men at the back of the house, where the vehicles were parked. Another would land in front, inside the electrified fence. The third would hover above the building and watch all sides of the property, attacking where necessary.

Bond looked out and saw the house and grounds—the strange hybrid of Moroccan and Corsican architecture, the circular field that surrounded the house and the fence. The gate looked as if it had been repaired.

There were a lot of men outside, especially in the back. A lorry was parked by the house and workers were busy loading things into it. Several other vehicles—4 × 4s, the limousine and a few cars—were sitting at the edge of the parking area, yielding the space to the lorry. At least four guards were in front of the building.

By the time the choppers were above the property, the Union men knew that they were under attack. Well trained and prepared, they dropped what they were doing, grabbed weapons and ran for cover or their defense posts.

"Hit them!" Bond commanded. "Go go go!"

All three helicopters let off rockets. One went straight for the front door of the house, directly over the guards' heads. The entire façade crumbled in a mass of flame and smoke. The second shot hit the side of the building, where Bond thought the barracks might be. The third rocket hit the lorry that was already nearly full of the Union's equipment. In Bond's opinion, it exploded with satisfying intensity.

The speed with which the return fire began surprised them all. The Union men were disciplined, well organized and they knew what to do. As many of them were former professional soldiers, each man could be a formidable opponent. An army of them was daunting indeed.

Bond's chopper flew within ten feet of the ground and he gave the order to jump. He went first, leaping out of the aircraft and landing on his feet. The others followed him, spraying the area with bullets. Bond ran for cover behind one of the parked cars and let loose a volley of ammunition at two men crouched behind the limousine. They were armed with what appeared to be Uzis.

Bond unclipped a grenade, pulled the pin and tossed it over to the limo. It rolled underneath the car. The men saw it and started to run but it was too late. They were caught in the blast, which was intensified by the limo's exploding petrol tank.

Bond and two British men ran through the flames and into the open garage. They were met with streams of gunfire, so they hit the ground and rolled, firing as they went. One of the British soldiers was struck. His body continued to roll until it lodged against a stack of tires. Bond and the other man concentrated their fire on the area of the garage where two opponents had found cover behind a 4 × 4.

On the other side of the house, things were not going so well. The Union managed to blow a hole in the hovering third helicopter with a twenty-year-old US M40 recoilless rifle that had been hidden on the roof of the building. The chopper wobbled in the air for a few seconds before it burst into flame and plummeted to the ground with a tremendous crash. All nine men inside were killed instantly.

"We've lost a third of our force," Bond heard Perriot say in his headset. "We're going to try to take out the gunner on the roof."

Bond shouted to the other man with him, "Cover me!" The soldier sprayed the 4 × 4 with his M16 while Bond rose and ran like the devil toward the open door to the house. The soldier's bullets punctured all four tires and riddled the vehicle with holes. This flushed out the two Union men, who made a desperate run for the open air. The British soldier picked them both off easily, then gave Bond the thumbs-up sign as he reached the door.

Bond entered the guards' quarters and found it deserted. He kicked the door to the corridor open and ran down the familiar, blank hallway toward the staircase leading downstairs.

There was no one about . . . it was too easy. Bond held the P99 tightly in both hands, ready to assume firing stance. He inched to the stairwell and peered down. Stepping quietly he went all the way to the basement and again found it empty.

He ran to the locked wooden door and banged on it. "René, are you in there?"

"James?"

Bond fired the P99 into the lock, demolishing it. He opened the door, ran inside, and found Mathis standing against the wall.

"Are you ready to get out of here, my friend?" Bond asked.

There was something about Mathis' joyless expression that Bond should have interpreted more quickly, but in his haste to free his friend he had been careless. Still, his reflexes were just fast enough to prevent grievous bodily injury.

The wiry little guard Antoine jumped onto Bond's back and attempted to plunge a knife into him but Bond used the man's own momentum and weight to throw him over his shoulder. In doing so, however, he dropped the P99. The gun slid across the stone floor and into the straw in the corner.

Antoine sprung off the floor with surprising agility and lunged at Bond again with the knife, a long and slender Vendetta Corse. Bond twisted and avoided being stabbed, then swung and kicked the Corsican with his right foot. The blow hit Antoine in the chest, knocking him back into Mathis. They fell on the floor, giving Bond the time to unsheath his own knife.

Antoine got back on his feet and held the knife in front of him.

"You want to dance, my friend, let's dance!" he said. He swished the knife in the air a couple of times. Bond, although adept at knife-fighting, knew that he was no match for a Corsican who had grown up with a knife as an extension of his hand.

"René, the gun, over in the corner!" he shouted.

Antoine leaped forward and Bond barely feinted in time. The blade sliced a bit of the material on the side of his vest. Bond spun and went into a crouch just as Antoine swung the knife over his head. Bond bounced forward with his knife pointed at the little man, but Antoine was like a circus acrobat. He performed a short leap, did a somersault in mid-air, and landed on his feet behind Bond.

How the hell . . . ?

Before Bond could turn around, the killer slashed the back of his neck with the blade. Bond felt a wrenching sting before falling forward, rolling out of the way and jumping to his feet.

Antoine stood across the room, grinning, his knife dripping with blood. Bond felt the back of his neck with his left hand. It was wet and there was a painful cut just below his hairline, but luckily it wasn't very deep.

Antoine gestured with his free hand, "Come on!"

Angered now, Bond rushed him with the knife, but Antoine was too fast. The Vendetta Corse hit home and made a nasty gash on Bond's upper arm. Bond twisted and retreated to avoid another slash, but he had backed into the wall—the worst possible position to be in during a knife fight.

Antoine raised the knife by the blade, ready to throw it at Bond. In that split second, Bond considered unsnapping the PPK but knew that he wouldn't be able to draw the gun before the Union man released the knife. He was done for.

A gunshot reverberated in the stone cell, its volume magnified tenfold by the enclosed space. Antoine recoiled as if he had been hit with a sledgehammer between the shoulder blades. The knife fell from his hand as he staggered a couple of steps toward Bond. His eyes glazed over and then he collapsed with a thud.

Mathis stood behind him, Bond's P99 in his hand.

"I hope that was him and not you, James," Mathis said.

"You did just fine, René," Bond said, immensely relieved. "You haven't lost your aim at all."

"They didn't tell me anything, James, but I knew you were coming soon. They started to pack up last night and move out of here. You are lucky that you got here before they left."

"That's because they thought we weren't going to be ready to hit them until tomorrow. They believed that they had another half day to clear out," Bond explained.

"How is that?"

"I'll tell you later," Bond said. "Do you know if *Le Gérant* is still here?"

"I cannot tell you, James," Mathis replied. "I've been down here in the dark the entire time. As a matter of fact, I would be in the dark no matter where I was, so I'm not the best person to ask."

"Don't worry about it," Bond said. "Let's get out of here." He took the gun from his friend and led him out of the cell.

On ground level, Commandant Perriot and his squad had successfully taken out the guards in front of the house. They rushed in
through the burning opening that had been created by the rocket and
were met with heavy resistance inside. Six Union men had barricaded
themselves in the foyer and they shot three RAID officers before the
latter could find cover. Perriot ordered one of his squad members, a
man carrying a flame thrower, to "Barbecue the bastards." The officer
readied the instrument and walked through the opening. He loosed
with a spray of fire that resembled a dragon's breath. The Union men
screamed as they were hit. Four of them panicked and ran, their
clothes ablaze. Marksmen shot them as they emerged from the house.
The other two were burnt to a crisp where they crouched.

Perriot led the rest of the squad further inside. It didn't take them long
to find the stairs to the roof, ascend them, and assume positions for an
assault. Two men bravely volunteered to go up first. They burst through
the hatch, firing their M16s as they climbed. The two men manning the
M40 pointed it at the hatch and sprayed it with bullets. One of the RAID
men went down, but the other successfully hit the two shooters. The rest
of the team emerged from the stairs and made a clean sweep of the roof,
making sure that no other Union men were hiding there.

Bond brought Mathis out through the back. He signaled his helicopter with the headset; it came down and landed in the field. Bond
helped Mathis get inside, told him to sit tight, and gave the pilot the
go-ahead to ascend to a safe position.

"Commence Phase Two," Bond said into his headset.

He re-entered through the back after verifying with Perriot that his
squad was accomplishing its goals. They had lost too many men, but
the Union force didn't appear to be as strong as they had expected.

Bond made his way through the war-torn building until he passed
the exam room where he had been tortured. Bond kicked the door
open and found Dr. Gerowitz cowering behind the exam chair. The
man raised his hands and screamed, "Don't shoot! Please! I am
unarmed! I was just following orders!"

Bond leveled the P99 at him and said, "I can overlook what you
did to me, doctor. This is for what you did to Mathis."

He squeezed the trigger and gave the ophthalmologist a third eye.

Bond left the room and continued into the bowels of the building. He approached the intersection to another corridor and peered around the corner. Two guards were waiting at the end of the hall in front of a closed, ornate wooden door, their guns aimed in his direction. Bond pulled the pin out of a grenade and tossed it at them. The blast shook the whole house.

He ran around the corner, stepped over the bodies, and kicked the broken door out of the way.

This had to be *Le Gérant*'s inner sanctum. It was an office, elegantly furnished with an unusual mixture of Berber rugs and tile work, yet there was also a Western sensibility to the place. Bond went through a door into a large bedroom that was similarly decorated. No one was there. There didn't appear to be any other way out of the room. He went back into the outer office and heard Perriot in the headset say, "Monsieur Bond, we have set explosives through most of the house. Just let us know when you are ready."

"Not yet," Bond said. "I'm still looking for the golden goose."

He made a cursory search of the desk for any clues that might point to where Cesari might be. Had he already left? Perhaps he had decided to abandon his home as soon as he had found out that the Cannes project had failed.

He went back into the bedroom and examined the walls. He opened the wardrobe and pushed back the clothes hanging there. The light caught the back wall of the wardrobe oddly, making it appear at an angle. Bond touched the wall and it moved. It was a secret door and it was ajar!

Bond opened it, revealing stone steps leading down into darkness. He unclipped a torch that he had on his utility belt, switched it on, and told Perriot where he was going.

"Let me send some backup to help you," the commandant said.

"No," Bond insisted. "I work alone. If I'm not back in ten minutes, that's a different story."

He descended the stairs and found himself in a dark, damp cavern. A path led between two stalagmites into a pitch-black tunnel. Bond entered the tunnel which, before long, began to twist and turn. Eventually it came to a fork.

Now where?

He gambled and took the path to the right. Soon, he ran into a T intersection.

The damned place was a labyrinth.

He went right again and noticed that the cavern floor was sloping down. It grew steeper and soon the tunnel spread into such a large chamber that Bond couldn't see the other side. As he began to traverse it, he had an overpowering sensation that he was being watched. He stood in one place and turned 360 degrees, shining the torch all around him, but he couldn't see a thing. He took a step, intending to continue walking across the chamber when suddenly a figure rushed toward him from the darkness. Bond raised the P99 and fired but a long, metal object slammed into his left shoulder. He dropped the torch and it rolled down the steep cavern floor and disappeared off a ledge.

The cavern was plunged into total darkness. Bond was completely blind. With the P99 pointed in front of him, he slowly turned around again, listening carefully.

He thought that he heard something to his right, twisted, and fired the gun.

The hard metal object struck him again in the back. He fell to his knees and felt the rush of air next to him in time to deflect a second blow with his arm. He turned and fired his gun in that direction, but it was no use.

After a moment's silence came the voice. "Here we are again, Mister Bond. We seem to meet under the most unusual circumstances."

Bond shot toward the voice, but then he heard Cesari laugh behind him. Bond twisted again and fired. There was silence and then the voice came from yet another place in the dark.

"You're in my habitat now, Mister Bond," Cesari said. "You can't see a thing, can you? Neither can I, but as I explained to you before, I *can* see. I know exactly where you are."

As Cesari spoke, Bond could hear his voice moving. He fired the gun into the darkness again, but the laugh came from a different direction.

The club struck him hard on the right shoulder blade.

"Was that your head or your shoulder?" Cesari asked. "Forgive me, I know where you are, but I suppose my aim isn't perfect."

Bond was in agony. If his shoulder blade wasn't broken, it was bruised as hell. He lay on the ground, clutching his arm.

"Have you had any strange dreams lately, Mister Bond?" Cesari asked. "You know what they say . . . never dream of dying. It just might come true."

Bond rolled over to face the direction of the voice and spray-fired the Walther. This time he heard an "Oompf," and a sharp intake of breath. Something hit the floor, probably the club Cesari had been using to hit him with. Bond fired again.

He managed to get to his feet and remove the camera from his belt. He ejected the ophthalmoscope cylinder, dropped the camera, and switched on the light. It gave him enough illumination to see shapes within ten feet around him.

There on the floor, a few feet away, he saw Olivier Cesari attempting to crawl away. He had been hit, but it was difficult to tell how badly.

"Hold it, Cesari, I see you now," Bond said. "Give it up. Hands above your head."

Cesari stopped moving and sat down on the ground. He held his side, which appeared to be soaked in blood.

But before Bond could make another move, he felt another presence rushing toward him. A powerful fist hit him in the face and a shoe kicked the Walther out of his hand. He dropped the ophthalmoscope as he fell to his knees.

Two torches switched on, flooding the chamber with light.

He looked up and saw the man known as the Sailor with a torch and a gun pointed right at his head. Next to him were Ché-Ché le Persuadeur, also holding a torch, and Marc-Ange Draco, who said, "You had better raise your hands, James. It's over."

TWENTY-NINE

THE FINAL VISIT

BOND WASN'T SURPRISED TO SEE HIS FATHER-IN-LAW.

The Sailor and Ché-Ché relieved Bond of his weapons, threw his headset on the ground, then resumed covering him.

"I was wondering if you would turn up, Marc-Ange," Bond said. He slowly raised his hands. He nodded to the Sailor. "Your 'eyes and ears', I presume?"

Draco replied, "Yes, the Sailor has always worked for me. You never cease to amaze me, James. When I got that phone call from you this morning, I thought that you were still in the dark, so to speak. I should have known that you might feed me false information. Stupidly, I trusted you at your word."

"We watched some security camera tapes last night, Marc-Ange. When I saw your security firm, the men in green uniforms delivering the film cans to the Palais in Cannes, I knew then that you were involved."

"*Securité Vert,*" Draco said. "Yes, they were my men. So that's how you caught me. Interesting. Now I understand why you called this morning and asked if I would be interested in helping you with a raid *tomorrow.* You said that it was taking more time than expected for the various governments to put together an assault team. Ha, and then you show up a few hours later and surprise us. Very clever, James.

You knew that we would have abandoned ship already had we not believed that we had more time. *Le Gérant* would have been far away from here."

"Why, Marc-Ange?" Bond asked. "Why join up with this poor excuse of a businessman?" He gestured to Cesari, who slowly stood and limped over to the Sailor.

Draco shrugged. "The money was better. Besides, blood is thicker than water. Olivier here is my nephew. His father and I were half-brothers. We shared the same mother, you see."

The news was like a punch in the solar plexus. That explained a hell of a lot, Bond thought. Christ, that would make him related, by marriage, to *Le Gérant*! Tracy and Cesari were cousins!

Draco continued, "When Olivier took over the Union from its American founder a few years ago, I was one of the silent investors who helped fund him. Needless to say, my investment has paid off splendidly. As the Union grew in power and size, I was happy to let it absorb the old Union Corse. It was a pleasure to let someone else be in charge for a change. I hadn't . . . been the happiest of men in many years."

It was all clear to Bond now. After the death of Tracy, Draco, once a criminal but a man with principles, had become a bitter, vengeful man. He was a totally different person from the man Bond once called his friend.

"It grieves me, James, to have to do this to someone who is family," Draco said. "You have to die today, my son."

"Marc-Ange, you have the power to walk away from all this," Bond said. "I cannot believe that you would have allowed that bomb in Cannes to kill so many people."

Draco shook his head. "Then you don't understand me at all, James. After what I have gone through, I didn't care what happened to a bunch of rich movie stars. Do you remember me telling you that I remarried and had a child?"

"Yes. You said that they died in an accident."

"It was no accident. My young wife was an actress, a beautiful young woman who had her whole life and career ahead of her. Our little girl, Irene, was a child actress. She had been on the stage a few times. She was making her first motion picture with her mother in Nice . . . when you killed them."

"Me?"

"Last January," Draco said. "The fire at Côte d'Azur Studios. You told me yourself that you had fired the shots that burst the petrol tanks. That fire killed a number of innocent people, James, and I'll bet that you had not one single moment of remorse."

"That's not true, Marc-Ange," Bond said. "I felt terrible about it. I'm very sorry about your wife and daughter, but it *was* an accident. You know I didn't set out to kill anyone inside that soundstage."

"Apologies are not accepted," Draco said. "I am Corsican, and we take blood vendettas very seriously. They can never be broken. I cannot let you kill my nephew, nor can I allow you to wreak any more havoc on the Union. The war is over, James, and you have lost."

Cesari limped to Bond and stared through him. With a sneer, he hit Bond in the stomach. Bond doubled over and fell to the floor.

"Ché-Ché, Sailor, take *Le Gérant* out to the helicopter," Draco said. "I'll wait here with our friend."

"Are you sure, boss?" the Sailor asked. "We can finish him off for you if you want."

"No, go on," Draco said. "Get him to a doctor quickly."

The two men led Cesari out of the cavern after giving Draco one of the torches.

"This tunnel leads to a hidden helipad in the hills behind Olivier's estate. It's a real pity that you destroyed the house. It was worth a lot of money," Draco said.

Bond started to get up but Draco pointed a Glock at him. "Even though you're my former son-in-law, James, don't think that I won't shoot you."

"Then do it, Draco," Bond spat. "Get it over with, or do you have any more speeches to make?"

Draco shook his head. "You were always impatient and petulant, weren't you, James? We're going to sit here and wait a few minutes. I have to give Olivier time to get out of here. You see, all of the

explosives your little assault team has placed in the house are superfluous. The entire complex is set to blow up in . . ." he glanced at
his watch, ". . . approximately five minutes. It will take out the
house, your men, and, unfortunately, this lovely cavern."

"What about you?" Bond asked.

"Oh, I'm cashing in my chips, James," Draco said with a sigh. "My
world just hasn't been the same without my wife and daughter. There
is no joy for me any more. I have decided to end my miserable life,
and I'm going to take you with me."

Ironically, Bond found himself faced with the opposite dilemma.
Could he kill his father-in-law? A man he had admired?

Then it hit Bond. "You were trying to put me in Cesari's clutches
the entire time, weren't you? You deliberately misled me, telling me
that Léon Essinger wasn't important. Instead, you threw clues at me,
advised me, pointed the way to this place so that your nephew could
get rid of me as he pleased."

"Yes, but you managed to escape," Draco said. "That complicated
matters. We nearly aborted the project, but Le Gérant had confidence
that it could still be pulled off. Now then. I suppose I should play it
smart and shoot you here and now."

Once again, Bond started to stand but Draco stopped him. "Just
stay on the ground, James. I feel safer that way."

Draco didn't notice that Bond had repositioned himself on the
cavern floor. He had sat down on the ophthalmoscope cylinder that
he had dropped earlier. Bond palmed it and stuck it in the elastic of
his sleeve.

"What difference does it make, Marc-Ange?" Bond asked. "If we're
both going to die in a few minutes, what's the point in feeling safe?"

"I want to keep you here long enough for Olivier to get away. I
don't care what happens to me."

"Then let's have a cigarette," Bond suggested. "I carry fine
Turkish—"

"Forget it. You'll only pull out one of your tricks," Draco said. "I
said stay down—"

Bond moved as if to reposition himself again but instead switched on the ophthalmoscope's laser and pointed it at Draco's face. The light surprised and blinded him momentarily, long enough for Bond to jump up and kick the Glock out of Draco's hand. The gun slid on the incline but lodged against a rock before going over the ledge. Bond stood, stepped in to Draco, and punched him across the face. The man fell backward and rolled until he stopped, face down.

Bond carefully moved down the incline and picked up the Glock. It was a shame that those other two had taken his weapons. Hopefully he could catch them in time.

He walked up the incline and started to run in the direction they had gone, but he heard Draco say, "James."

Bond whirled to see Draco with a miniature derringer, something he probably had kept up his sleeve. There was a pop as flame burst from its barrel and Bond felt a sharp, searing pain in his left shoulder. Instinctively, Bond fired the Glock, hitting Draco between the eyes. The former organized-crime boss jerked back and crumpled to the ground like a puppet.

There was no time to think about what he had just done. Bond turned, picked up his headset, and started to run as he spoke.

"Perriot, get all the men out of the building *now!* It's going to blow in two minutes! Move!"

"I read you, James! Evacuation commencing!" he heard Perriot say.

Bond followed the path through the cave, winding around fallen boulders and what appeared to be still active formations. The ground was very damp, the air was musty and there were more stalagmites to contend with. Eventually he came to a solid wall and could find no other way through.

Damn! He must have missed a turn. How much time was left?

He backtracked, studied the walls more carefully, and this time saw an opening to the right that he hadn't noticed earlier. He went through it and could smell fresh air. The light was brighter and natural.

He emerged from the cave on the inside of a hollowed-out hill. The sides of the hill adequately disguised the helipad and stone bunker that had been constructed there. A French Aerospatiale Astazou Alouette III was idling, its blades whirring around in anticipation of lifting off. Bond could see a pilot, Ché-Ché, the Sailor, and Cesari inside the elongated cockpit. Two Union men were supervising on the ground, their backs to Bond.

He aimed the Glock at the pilot and fired just as the helicopter began to rise. The windscreen shattered, the pilot recoiled and slumped in his chair. The Sailor's face registered surprise as he pointed at Bond. The two men on the ground turned and drew their weapons, but Bond swung his gun toward them and fired first. The guards fell back against the bunker wall and collapsed. Bond continued to fire at the figures in the cockpit, but he ran out of ammunition. He dropped the Glock and ran to the bunker, praying that there would be more weapons inside. Bond kicked the door open and rushed at a third guard inside the bunker. Before the man could react, Bond punched him in the stomach and threw him to the floor. He then kicked him in the chest, stamped on his face and kicked him again in the ribs for good measure.

Thank Heaven! There was a cabinet containing several rifles. Bond used his boot to break the glass doors. He reached in, grabbed a 40-calibre M203 grenade launcher, checked to see that it was loaded and ran outside.

The helicopter was destabilized, rising by itself. The Sailor had pushed the pilot out of the way and moved into his seat, desperately trying to get the aircraft under his control. The Alouette wavered awkwardly in the air but suddenly regained its balance and hovered some sixty feet off the ground. Bond raised the weapon and aimed at the rotors. He squeezed the trigger and felt a tremendous kick against his shoulder.

The helicopter started to shift direction as if it were ready to move from its stationary position just as the grenade exploded over the top of the blades. The flames engulfed the cockpit as the aircraft shook, completely disabled. The fireball appeared to swallow the helicopter whole as the craft shot out of Bond's sight. He could hear the roar though. The glissando from a high pitch to a low one indicated that they were on the way down.

He not only heard the crash but felt it as the ground shook.

Bond dropped the M203 then quickly climbed to the top of the hill and out onto its exterior. The only traces left of the Union and *Le Gérant* lay in the messy bonfire below.

Not quite thirty seconds later, the world convulsed as the hidden bombs in the house blew. There was a chain reaction, for the Union's bombs set off the explosives that Perriot and his men had been setting. The result was a destructive force nearly three times that which had been intended.

Bond hit the ground and felt the heat pass over him. Pieces of debris fell all around him, and he must have been at least a quarter-kilometer away from the house.

In a couple of minutes, it was all over. He could hear the surviving soldiers hooting with joy. Bond got up, held his shoulder, and walked back to the site of the devastation.

The strike team had made it out in time. Perriot helped Bond get emergency medical treatment for the gunshot wound and offered to ride with him to Propriano, the nearest village with decent medical facilities. Bond declined, but thanked him anyway. All told, the Interpol force lost nearly half its men, but there wasn't a single survivor from Union headquarters.

The battle, and perhaps the war, was over.

THIRTY

THE END

THE WAITER BROUGHT A BOTTLE OF NUITS-SAINT-GEORGES. AFTER HE HAD uncorked it and Bond had tasted it, the waiter poured the two glasses and left the couple alone.

It was early afternoon and they were sitting at one of the many sidewalk cafés in the old town of Nice, not far from the flower market made famous in Hitchcock's *To Catch a Thief*. Tylyn had worn sunglasses in the hope of avoiding recognition, but they were no use. An American tourist asked her for an autograph (on a napkin, no less— Bond wondered why anyone would bother) and some giggling French teenagers interrupted them to ask if she really was Tylyn Mignonne.

"If you'd rather leave, we can," Bond suggested.

"No, it's all right," she said. "I'm used to it. People recognize me all the time."

She took a sip of wine and sat quietly. Bond had never seen her so pensive.

"Tylyn?"

"I know," she said. "I'm not saying much. I think it's probably because I have so much to say."

"Then why not just say it?"

She looked away and rested her chin in her hand, elbow on the table, a posture that Bond thought of as "typically Tylyn." He had seen her do it on a number of occasions, and it made her look more like an inquisitive college student and so *unlike* a model or well-known actress that it was endearing.

"Because I don't know if it's the right thing to say," she replied.

Bond shifted in his seat and poured another glass of wine and topped hers up. The doctor who had extracted the .22 bullet had given him pills for the pain and the throbbing in his left shoulder was just beginning to subside.

But the pills wouldn't work with affairs of the heart. That kind of pain was more resilient.

"I served Léon with papers today," she said, as if to change the subject. "I'm almost sorry I wasn't there to see his reaction."

"I'm afraid that a divorce is the least of his concerns right now," Bond noted.

"Hmm. How long do you think he'll be in jail?"

"It's difficult to say," Bond said. "Depends on what the final sentence is. His lawyers will appeal, of course, and it could go on forever. But he won't be roaming the streets, that's for certain. He is accused of terrorism against his own country. Pretty serious stuff. He's liable to go to jail for the rest of his life."

"I would like to feel sorry for him, but I don't," she said. She took another drink. "And to think that I thought I loved him once."

"Don't be hard on yourself," Bond said.

"He wanted to kill me," she said. "He knew that bomb would kill me, along with all those other people. He wanted my money, my family's money, whatever he could get . . ."

"But that won't happen now," Bond said. "Try to put him and what happened behind you. You're an optimistic, life-loving girl. Don't let this ruin your sparkling personality."

She smiled. "You're teasing me."

He reached out and took her free hand. "What's next for you?" he asked gently.

She shrugged and said, "With *Pirate Island* cancelled, my agent will be sending me out for more auditions and such. There are a few scripts that have come in that I need to read. A producer in Hollywood wants me to go out there and be in something. I have another fashion show to plan for next fall. I need to approve a new line of clothing for my company. I have a photo shoot next week . . . shall I go on?"

"At least you'll be busy," Bond said. "That's the best therapy."

"And what about you, James? Are you off on another dangerous mission that puts you and your loved ones' lives at risk?"

Bond couldn't help detecting the sarcasm.

"Probably," he said. "And that is as good an opening as any for what I have to say. Perhaps after you hear what I'm going to tell you, then you may not need to tell me what's on *your* mind."

She looked at him through the dark glasses, took a sip, and said, "Go on."

"Tylyn, I know you're upset that I deceived you. But now you understand that I was working undercover. If I had not done it that way, Léon and his people might have been successful in killing hundreds of people. You do realize that, right?"

She nodded.

"I fell in love with you for a number of reasons," he continued. "However, someone in my profession simply can't turn his back on his job. I have been faced with the choice between Profession and Love before, and whenever I have chosen Love . . . it doesn't work out."

"What are you saying, James? That you can't see me any more?" she asked.

"Something like that. Another factor is your celebrity status. I can't afford to be recognized. If I were with you, both of our lives would be at risk. You are in the public eye a great deal. My enemies would try to get to me through you. I was married once, Tylyn, and that union proved fatal to my wife. I saw one of my in-laws recently, and that reminded me just how dangerous it is for a woman to fall in love with someone like me. At the same time, I can't be seen in glossy movie star magazines, accompanying you to awards shows. My life depends on my being anonymous. Do you understand?"

Tylyn smiled, but he knew that tears were forming beneath the dark glasses.

"I had a similar speech prepared," she said. "It basically amounts to the same thing, but for different reasons."

Bond poured some more wine in her glass and encouraged her to go on.

"I don't think I can have a relationship with someone in your profession, either," she said. "It's a profession built on deceit, and I just can't abide that. I'm not sure that I can forgive you for lying to me and masquerading as my lover."

"I wasn't masquerading—" he interrupted, but she put up her hand to stop him.

"I believe you," she said. "But I still can't forgive you. Our love affair was not what I thought it was, and I'm not so sure that it's salvageable. Even if you were to give up your job, which I'm not asking you to do, I don't think we could make a go of it."

Although he knew that everything she said was reasonable, Bond felt surprisingly rejected.

He took a sip of wine and smiled.

"What's funny?" she asked.

"Nothing's funny," he said. "I was just thinking that I haven't been ditched too many times in the past, and I'm not sure how I like it."

"We're ditching each other," she said. "It's mutual, isn't it? I mean, God, James, I would *love* to be with you. I'm mad about you and I know you feel something similar for me . . . but it would be *insane!* We would drive each other crazy with the demands of our respective careers and end up hating each other."

Bond squeezed her hand and said, "You're absolutely right, darling. I couldn't have said it better."

"But we'll be friends?" she asked.

Bond laughed. "I suppose. As much as that's possible."

She grew silent again, finished her glass of wine, and after a moment said, "I had best be going. I don't want this to be any more painful than it already is." She stood and said, "Please don't get up. Wait here until I'm gone, all right?"

Bond nodded.

She leaned over, took his chin in her hand, and kissed him.

"Take care of yourself, James."

"You too, Tylyn."

She walked away, leaving Bond alone with the wine and his thoughts. The waiter came by and asked if there would be anything else. Bond asked for the bill.

He looked to see where she had gone, but he didn't see her. He took the last drink of wine and sighed. It was time to bury the emotions once again, lock them away in the vault so that they could never escape and unwittingly reveal that he really did have a heart.

He would save all that for his dreams.

Bond left money on the table and stood. Once again he glanced down the street, but she had disappeared. He turned and walked in the opposite direction, retreating into the shadows of his life.

IAN FLEMING'S JAMES BOND 007 IN "BLAST FROM THE PAST"

BY RAYMOND BENSON

"MAY WOULD HAVE MY HEAD IF SHE SAW US NOW," JAMES BOND SAID TO THE naked girl draped around and across his own body. "And after decapitating me, she would certainly give notice. Head or no head, good help is hard to find these days."

He leaned on one arm and looked at her near-perfect form. She was all curves, with smooth slopes of exquisitely white skin. What had he got himself into? She was the daughter of his housekeeper's best friend, for Christ's sake! May, bless her soul, had all-too-naively recommended that young Kate take over the duties at Bond's flat off the King's Road in Chelsea while the elderly and fussy woman went on holiday to visit some ailing relative in Glasgow. May's friend and her daughter were also from Scotland. May liked to think of Kate as her "niece," and the girl couldn't have been more than nineteen-years-old, if that. He didn't dare think that she might be even younger.

"You can say that I forced you down and made love to you until you gave up all your little secrets," she said dreamily in a lovely Scottish lilt. "You can blame it all on me-s." The girl even *sounded* like May, insisting on adding that little 's' for 'sir' every now and then.

"I dare say that would shatter poor May's opinion of her friend's daughter. She adores you, you know. And please, after what we just did, there's no need to ever call me 'sir' again."

Kate sighed. "Auntie May is a dear, but she's very old-fashioned. She thinks sex is something that happens once on a wedding night, and in separate beds at that."

"Your Auntie May is a treasure, and I would hate to upset her," Bond said, sitting upright. He rarely felt remorse after a carnal encounter, but this time he wanted to kick himself—a bit. He had to admit that the girl was truly a jewel, and no warm-blooded man could have resisted her. It was true what Kate said. *She* had made it clear that she wouldn't leave him alone until he took her to bed. It was one of those pleasurable occasions in which Bond's protests meant nothing; either allow it to happen and enjoy it, or put up with a pouting, temperamental lass for the next ten days.

"All right," Bond said. "You're going to get dressed now. I'm going to exercise and then shower. We're going to forget this ever happened."

"Mr. Bond, I don't care what the bloody hell you do, but I'm *never* going to forget this happened," she said with a giggle. She sat up, wrapped her arms around him, and lightly ran her fingers through his chest hair.

"I think you've earned the right to call me James, too," he said, pushing her gently back down onto the bed.

Bond was between assignments, so he justified his liaison with Kate as a symptom of the restlessness and boredom he always experienced when there was nothing for him to do. Usually he spent this time reading, keeping his body fit, playing cards or golf with a select number of male colleagues and engaging in sexual dalliances with a select number of women who never demanded or required any sort of commitment. If he could forget that Kate was a friend of his housekeeper's, Bond could place her in that same compartment of female acquaintances and go on about his business. The problem was that every time she opened her mouth, he was reminded of May.

"Shall I cook your dinner now-s?" she asked, fluttering her eyes with a tease.

"Not yet, Kate, dear," he said. "And stop calling me 'sir.' "

Standing now, Bond allowed his eyes to explore her body again. She stretched seductively across the bed, her coal-black, shoulder-length hair covering a pillow. She had clear blue eyes that sparkled with mischief. She was a living centerfold, her arms beckoning him to join her once again.

"How about an appetizer, then, *James*."

Bond, being who he was, couldn't resist the invitation. One of the women he saw occasionally over the year had recently called him a "rake who was desperately behind the times." (She then added that at least was a *physically ageless* rake, and then proceeded to demonstrate her appreciation of that fact.)

Bond threw caution to the wind, shook his head, took hold of Kate's long legs, and pulled her closer.

"If it's exercise you want, my darling," she said as she thrust her pelvis forward, "I'll make sure you . . . oh! . . . uhm, work up a sweat."

The FedEx letter was delivered the next morning at 9:30. Kate was out shopping for groceries. Bond had completed his morning ritual of a cold shower, twenty slow pushups, as many leg lifts as he could manage (until his stomach muscles screamed), twenty reps of touching his toes and fifteen minutes of arm and chest exercises combined with deep breathing. Normally Bond rose with the sun, but with nothing pressing at headquarters and having the companionship of Kate, 007 allowed himself the luxury of a slow, lazy morning. Kate had prepared his favorite breakfast of two large cups of very strong coffee from De Bry in New Oxford Street (served black with no sugar), and one egg boiled precisely for three and a third minutes. That single egg was a very fresh, speckled brown egg from French Marans hens owned by some friend of May, and Bond insisted that it be served in a dark blue egg cup with a gold ring around the top.

Bond had lived in the same flat for many years. It was on the ground floor of a converted Regency house on a square lined with plane trees. It was private and comfortable, and Bond liked it that way. He had kept the same white and gold Cole wallpaper and deep red curtains that were present when he first bought the place, even though there was something distinctly dated about this decor. He was sitting and reading *The Times* at his ornate Empire desk in the sitting room lined with books when the bell rang.

Bond signed for the letter and took it back into the sitting room.

His brow creased when he saw that it was from "J. Suzuki" in New York, USA. He opened it and read—

DEAR DAD—TERRIBLY URGENT THAT YOU COME
TO NEW YORK! I NEED YOUR HELP! FAIL NOT!
WITH LOVE—JAMES

He rarely heard from his son,[*] who was now a young man working as a banker in the United States. James's mother, Kissy Suzuki, had died of cancer several years ago. The mere thought of his child born out of wedlock brought back a flood of memories, mostly painful ones. Bond had fathered the child while suffering from amnesia during a particularly tragic and dark period of his life. It seemed like ages ago when he lived as a simple fisherman with Kissy on that small island in Japan. Bond had eventually left her to search for his identity, unaware that she was pregnant with his boy. It was much later, after Bond had recovered from what could clinically be classified as a mental breakdown, when he learned of James Suzuki's existence. Bond had done his part to help Kissy support the child, even after she had re-married and moved to the States. Young James had always kept her surname. Poor Kissy had succumbed to her illness when the boy was a teenager and his stepfather had died a couple of years later. Since James Suzuki was one of the few people who knew Bond's home address, 007 knew the letter was authentic.

The memories of Kissy Suzuki and that island in Japan brought back other nightmares which Bond had pushed into the depths of his subconscious. M had sent him to Japan in the hopes that he would snap out of the depression he suffered after the murder of his wife, Tracy di Vicenzo, at the hands of Ernst Stavro Blofeld and his partner-in-crime, Irma Bunt. This was the main reason Bond had little contact with his son—the links in the chain of memories always led back to Tracy.

---

[*] See Ian Fleming's *You Only Live Twice*, Chapter 22.

Although they were buried deep within his psyche, recollections of the events of that era of his life were frequently featured in Bond's dreams. Sometimes he would wake in the middle of the night in a cold sweat with one of several recurring images lingering in the forefront of his mind: Blofeld's bulging eyes as Bond strangled him to death; Fräulein Bunt slumping to the floor after Bond hit her with a staff; the castle exploding as Bond watched from the air, clinging to a helium-filled weather balloon; and most often, the blood on Tracy's golden hair as he cradled her in the front seat of the Lancia that had spirited the couple away from their wedding.

Many years had past and Bond had lived through further adventures and dangers. He had managed to bury those painful scars by committing himself fully to his work. The women he encountered along the way were diversions, to be sure, but none had touched his heart the way Tracy had. He couldn't help but feel that there was something still unresolved, something he had to accomplish before he could exorcise those demons.

Bond waited until eleven o'clock before trying to phone his son. There was no answer at James's home number. A second call confirmed what Bond suspected: a secretary at the bank where James worked said that he hadn't been in for days.

Without a second thought, Bond picked up the phone and booked a flight to New York.

Bond arrived at Kennedy Airport mid-day and took a taxi into Manhattan. As it was a weekday, the city was alive with the energy that made New York the premiere cosmopolitan city. It was a sunny, unseasonably warm spring day, and the Manhattanites were out in force. Traffic was dense, horns were bellowing and endless swarms of pedestrians darted across intersections.

007 was dressed casually in a light blue cotton short-sleeve polo shirt and navy blue cotton twill trousers. He wore a light, gray silk basketweave jacket, under which he kept his Walther PPK 7.65mm in a chamois shoulder holster. Bond had recently picked up the Walther again after using an ASP for several years. The PPK was not standard

issue anymore, and he had a devil of a time convincing Major Boothroyd, the Armourer, to allow him to use it again. There was something about its history, its familiarity, that gave Bond a sense of security.

The taxi took him to the Upper East Side, where James Suzuki lived in a studio apartment at 75th Street and 1st Avenue, not far from the East River. Bond paid the driver and stepped out onto the pavement. The area was residential, made up of brownstones and eateries. James's apartment was appropriately above a Japanese restaurant. Bond surveyed the street before entering the building. A mother was pushing a pram and chatting with another woman as they walked. A toad-like homeless bag lady, dressed in rags and waddling behind a stolen shopping cart full of garbage and bundles, stopped in front of the door of James's building. Two black teenagers were throwing coins against a brick wall a few yards away. Someone was shouting in Spanish across the street. The traffic was terribly noisy. Bond wondered how anyone in an apartment facing an avenue could ever sleep, for the city never stopped.

Bond moved past the short bag lady blocking the door to the building and stepped inside. The woman never acknowledged his intrusion on her space. As he moved past her, Bond was perplexed by what he could see underneath the rags shielding her face. She had some kind of strange skin condition with a waxen look. Bond shrugged, turned away, and examined the building directory. He rang the bell marked "J. Suzuki" and waited. The intercom remained silent. He looked back out the glass pane in the front door and saw that the woman had gone. While London certainly had its own homeless problem, 007 found that New York's was by far the worst of all the western cities he had visited. Bond rang the bell again. Nothing happened.

One bell was marked "Super," so he tried that one. A moment later, the intercom blurted, "Yeah, who is it?"

"I'm looking for James Suzuki in 4A. I'm his father. Can you let me in?" Bond barked into the speaker.

He heard some grumbling, and then the lock on the inner door buzzed. Bond pushed it open and entered a dingy corridor facing a flight of stairs. The super's door opened at the back of the hall. A fat man in an undershirt and boxer shorts peeked out.

"You got I.D.?" the man asked. He had a thick Bronx accent and was most likely of Italian descent.

Bond showed him his Ministry of Defence credentials.

"You some kind of cop?" the man asked.

"You might say that."

"What, you from England?"

"Yes, could you please let me in my son's apartment?"

"The kid's a Jap."

"He's half-Japanese, and I'm his father," Bond said sternly. "Are you going to let me in or not?"

"Yeah, yeah, okay . . . just a minute." The man disappeared for a moment and returned wearing pants. He had a ring of keys with him. "It's up two flights."

Bond followed the man, who moved much too slowly for 007's thinly-worn patience. Finally, in front of the apartment, the man wrestled with the key ring and unlocked the door.

Bond recognized the foul stench as soon as the door swung open, and his heart began to pound. He bolted past the fat man into the small, one-room studio. "Stay out!" he shouted to the super.

James Suzuki was lying on his back in the middle of the floor, his body obviously in an advanced state of putrefaction. The poor boy's features were bloated and fluid had oozed from his mouth and nose and then dried. These were tell-tale signs that he had been dead a few days.

Bond knelt down beside his only son, not daring to touch him—but every nerve screamed with the longing to pick up the young man's body and grasp it close to his heart.

Agent Cheryl Haven scribbled in a small notebook as Bond spoke.

"You didn't touch anything?" she asked in a north England accent.

Bond shook his head. He was still stunned by the discovery. A man of lesser fortitude would have been in a state of shock.

Bond contacted the city's British Secret Service branch after convincing the super that there was no need for the local police and that his department would handle the situation. Within minutes, Special Agent Cheryl Haven and an American investigative team arrived at the apartment. The crime scene personnel—forensics specialist Dan Duling, photographer Paul Dantuono, and medical examiner Stuart Howard—were already at work on the body and the room. It was essentially one long room, with three distinct sections. James' sleeping area was at one end of the apartment, the kitchen and dining area was in the middle, and a living space with a television, stereo, and desk was at the other end. A small bathroom was adjacent to the living room. It was tastefully and cleverly furnished and decorated with a Japanese flavor. A framed portrait of James's mother, Kissy Suzuki, was prominent in the living room.

Bond gestured to the kitchen counter. "There's an envelope addressed to me. I haven't opened it."

Agent Haven said, "We'll make it top priority." She turned to the forensics specialist. "Dan? Could you dust the envelope on the counter so that we may see inside? Paul, could you take some photos of the kitchen before Dan dusts that envelope?"

Dantuono nodded and moved to the kitchen. The word "Dad" was hand-written in block letters on a number ten envelope Bond had found in plain sight.

Agent Haven said, "Your son was due to check in next week." Family members of all secret service personnel residing in foreign countries are required to contact the local branch once a month. "I know, because he usually spoke with me."

Bond's eyes moved to her. The woman looked at him with concern. "Yes, I knew him. He was a nice young man. I'm sorry."

Bond nodded abruptly and averted his eyes.

She quickly returned to business. "We still have time to go by his bank. I believe they're open late today. You have no idea why you received the FedEx?"

"No."

The medical examiner cleared his throat. "I have some preliminary results. We still need to do a post-mortem, of course."

"What did you find, Dr. Howard?" she asked.

"I believe he's been dead for four days, give or take twelve hours or so. From the looks of it, he was poisoned. Look at this wound on his arm here."

Bond and the woman stood and looked closely at the corpse. There was an incision an inch long on James's left forearm. It was swollen and dark.

"A very sharp, thin blade cut him, and that's where the poison entered the bloodstream. A razor blade, perhaps. You can see the edema around the wound there. There's dried blood on his shirt there, see? It must have been powerful stuff. He died of respiratory paralysis. It was some kind of inebriant, I imagine . . . something exotic."

"*Fugu,*" Bond said.

"What?" Dr. Howard asked.

"It's a poison from the glands of the blowfish that lives in the waters of Japan. The Japanese consider the fish a delicacy, and they have licensed *fugu* chefs prepare it in restaurants so that no mistakes are made. You're right, it's exotic."

"Are you sure?"

Bond nodded. "I had a dose administered to my shin a long time ago. I was lucky."

Agent Haven shrugged. "Well, the autopsy will tell us for certain, won't it . . ."

Duling finished dusting the envelope and handed it to Bond. Bond carefully opened it and emptied the contents onto the counter. A small silver key fell out. The number "366" was embossed on it.

"Paul, shoot this key, will you?" Duling asked. "Looks like a safety deposit key."

"You're right," Agent Haven said. She named a well-known Japanese bank. "It's got their logo on it."

"My son's employer," Bond said.

After the key was shot and dusted for fingerprints, she said, "Come on, Double-O Seven. Let's get you out of here. Let's take a trip to the bank and see what's in that safety deposit box. The boys will finish up."

Bond nodded. He needed to get out of that apartment and clear his head. He had to think. Who would want to kill his son? Was it an attempt to get at *him*? Bond rubbed his brow, forcing his mind to go back over the last few weeks. Had there been any kind of warning? Had he any reason to suspect someone? Anyone? He couldn't think of a single thing that was relevant. Maybe James really had been in trouble. What could his son have been involved in? Perhaps the contents of the safety deposit box would provide the answers.

The bank was located on Park Avenue, just north of the Pan Am Building. Arguably the grandest avenue in Manhattan, Park Avenue is home to many of the world's largest business concerns. It wasn't far from the apartment, but it was rush hour and traffic was heavy and slow. Fifteen minutes had past and the taxi had moved only four blocks across town.

"Come on, it'll be faster if we walk," Agent Haven said, gathering her purse. "We'll get out here, driver."

Once on the pavement, Bond and the woman walked briskly south on Park Avenue.

It was the first time Bond had actually looked at her, even though they had been in that wretched apartment together for four hours. She was in her late thirties or early forties but had the figure and complexion of a woman in her twenties. She was tall, with long, strong legs, revealed by the rather short, slim skirt of a Brooks Brothers glen plaid, lightweight worsted wool business suit. Her rather thin but silky blonde hair blew behind her as they walked, and her full breasts swung up and down despite the tight-fitting blue cotton blouse and the jacket that matched her skirt. Bond found her quite attractive.

"Blackpool, Agent Haven?" Bond asked.

"You got it right," she said, increasing the speed of her sprint. "Spent the first eighteen years of my life there. You can call me Cheryl, please, Mr. Bond."

"Only if you call me James," he said, continuing his stride. "How did you get to be station branch head in Manhattan? What happened to Forbes?"

"Alan got rich playing Lotto, can you believe it? He retired early and went to live in Texas somewhere," she laughed. "I was second-in-command and got the promotion. I'm surprised we've never met before."

"I am too," he said. "So tell me . . . about James. Was he all right? Did he ever indicate that he might be in trouble?"

The couple had to stop for a red light at a busy intersection.

"Never," Cheryl said. "He called on time every month and we chatted for a minute or so." She grinned. "He asked me out once. He was a flirt."

Bond smiled. Perhaps the boy inherited more of his genes than he thought.

"I never got any signs that he was into anything but his work at the bank, the girls he dated and the Knicks," she continued. The light turned green and they continued their gait.

Bond now felt curiously detached from what he had experienced since arriving in New York. Still somewhat numb by the cruel sight of his son, Bond looked at Cheryl Haven and could easily imagine that Tracy might have resembled her, had she lived today. He had to get hold of himself. If he was going to learn anything about what happened, he must be totally objective; yet James's death had shaken him, and he felt vulnerable. The old ghosts were at it again.

The couple reached another intersection, and the bank was just on the other side of the street. Immediately to their left, a street vendor selling hot dogs shouted, cursed at and waved away what appeared to be a homeless person. Bond noticed that it was another short woman dressed in rags and pushing a shopping cart. Was it the same woman that he saw outside James's apartment? Before Bond could verify this, she huddled over her cart and pushed it away from them. The vendor turned to Bond and Cheryl and said, "She's been here for two hours, I had to get rid of her!"

"Poor old lady," Cheryl said.

Bond felt intensely strange about the bag lady. He wasn't sure if his usually attuned instincts were playing tricks on him or not, but there was something oddly familiar about the woman—and it wasn't because she might have been the same lady outside the apartment earlier. Bond was staring at her back when he heard Cheryl say, "Come on, the light's green."

They crossed the street and went into the bank. It was 6:30 P.M.; they had a half-hour before the bank closed. Inside, they sought the bank manager, Mr. Nishiuye, to explain the situation and inform him of James Suzuki's death. Nishiuye expressed appropriate words of dismay and sympathy, then led them downstairs to the safety deposit box area. It was a small room protected from the public by a barred gate. There was a long table in the center, surrounded by four chairs on rollers. Number 366 was nearly eye-level amidst similar box fronts on the wall. The manager stood in the doorway and watched Bond insert the small silver key into the lock. Once engaged, however, the key wouldn't turn.

"Oh dear," Mr. Nishiuye said, apologetically, "I'm afraid we have been having trouble with some of those locks lately . . . that's the third one this week!"

Bond struggled with it, withdrew the key, and reached for his belt buckle. "I have a lockpick here, let me try that."

"From our old friend Major Boothroyd, I take it?" Cheryl asked. "I have one, too, but it's the ladies's model."

"Wait," the manager said. "We have maintenance man . . . he is locksmith. He opened the others easily. Let me find Sam."

"Hurry," Bond said. After he had left, Bond shrugged and said to Cheryl, "I probably could have had it open by the time he returns."

"Relax, Mr. Bo—I mean James," she said. "I don't think we're going to solve this in one night, and I'll make sure you're allowed to stay in the bank as long as you need."

Bond was still uneasy about the woman he saw outside. He sat down in one of the chairs and stared at the safety deposit box on the wall.

"What is it?" she asked. "You look tired. It's nearly midnight in London, isn't it . . ."

"Oh, I'm wide awake. A bit hungry, maybe," Bond said, lying.

"Well, we'll go somewhere for dinner after we're finished here."

"That would be fine," Bond said. "No, it's the homeless woman we saw outside. There's something . . . I don't know . . ."

"What?"

"I'm quite sure I saw her earlier outside James's apartment. When I first got there."

"Well, that was hours ago. She could have wheeled her little cart this far in that time."

"I know," Bond reflected, "but there's something else. She reminds me of something, or someone . . ."

Cheryl sat down beside him and placed her hand on his. He noted that it felt smooth and warm.

"Listen, James," she said. "You may not be allowing yourself to admit it, but you've had a shock—not that I don't think you're handling this remarkably well. But still . . . take it easy."

Bond knew she was right. Nevertheless, he was angry and his desire for revenge was stronger than his grief.

The manager returned with another man dressed in overalls and carrying a toolkit.

"Number 366, Sam." Mr. Nishiuye pointed to the wall of box fronts.

The man set his toolkit on the floor and removed a screwdriver.

"May I offer you anything?" the manager asked the couple. "Coffee?"

"No, thank you," said Bond, "but I would like to see my son's desk. Can I do that while your man works on the lock?"

"Certainly," the manager said. "Follow me."

James Suzuki's desk was neat and uncluttered. Another photo of his mother was framed and sitting on a computer monitor. Adjacent to it was a framed color snapshot of the boy with Bond. It was taken when James was about twelve years old, during a rare visit to London. They were posing in front of one of the Trafalgar Square lions. Kissy had taken the photo. It could very well have been the only photo James had of his father.

Bond did a quick pass through the desk and found nothing of interest.

"We can get someone to go through the files on his hard drive, but not tonight," Cheryl said.

"I think if there's anything to find, it's in that safety deposit box," Bond said.

The manager asked, "How is James's aunt doing?"

Bond looked at him. "What?"

"His aunt. She was here a couple of days ago and used the safety deposit box," the manager said. Bond stared at him, incredulous. "She . . . had written authorization . . ."

Before the man could finish, Bond and Cheryl bolted for the stairs and ran back to the safety deposit room and were stepping through the open barred door just as Sam was finishing his work.

"I think I have it," he said as he turned the lock.

The next instant, a tremendous noise and blinding flash of white light shook the room. The force of the explosion knocked Bond and Cheryl from the doorway and onto the floor of the corridor outside. Smoke filled the place as alarms blared.

"Are you all right?" Bond shouted to Cheryl.

"Yes!"

"Wait here!" He jumped up and into the room to get the maintenance man. Unfortunately, he was in several pieces amongst the flaming debris in the room. A large gaping hole was in the wall where the safety deposit box had once been. Again, Bond felt rage as he understood the significance of what had happened. That bomb had been intended for him, and whoever had planted it had used his son to get at him.

Bond returned to the corridor and took hold of Cheryl. "We have to get out of here or we'll suffocate," she shouted.

Bond nodded and together they found the stairs up to the ground floor. The bank had been minimally staffed that evening, so most of the employees were already outside. Mr. Nishiuye was helping a couple of others when he saw them. He looked relieved.

"I thought you were dead!" he exclaimed. "What about Sam?"

Bond shook his head. "He took the blast intended for me, I think," he said. He and Cheryl were both lucky to be alive, and only because Bond decided against picking the lock himself. For once, he would have to tell Major Boothroyd that he had survived by choosing *not* to use a Q Branch device!

They heard the firetruck's siren in the distance, but traffic was still heavy and there were dozens of people on the pavement in front of the bank. Bond and Cheryl moved out of the crowd where the air was better. They both had dark smudges on their clothes and faces.

Then he saw her. The homeless lady was standing on the other side of Park Avenue, watching. Bond could swear that she was not looking at the bank and the pandemonium in front of it—she was staring straight at *him*.

"Stay here," he said to Cheryl and started to cross the avenue.

As soon as the woman saw Bond approaching, she moved quickly around the corner onto a one-way narrow street heading west. Bond began to run. He reached the other side just in time to see the homeless lady step into the back seat of an idling black towncar! 007 rushed to it, leaped, and reached for the door handle. The driver stepped on the gas and the car screeched forward. Bond fell, but he immediately jumped up and chased after it. By then, Cheryl had crossed the street and was following Bond.

He reached Madison Avenue, but the towncar had already crossed it and was continuing west. He ran against the red light, dodging around cars moving up Madison. A taxi almost hit him and the horn blared.

"James! Wait!" Cheryl called as she caught up to him on the other side of Madison.

"She's in that towncar! We've got to follow it!"

"I'll call a car," Cheryl said, and grabbed the cellular phone from her purse, but the thing was smashed. "Damn, it must have happened when the bomb went off."

An empty taxi cab was idling in front of a delicatessen a hundred feet west of them. The "Off Duty" light was on; the driver had stepped out and gone inside the deli.

"I think we can take a taxi," Bond said.

"At this hour? You're mad," Cheryl said. "You'll never find one that's free."

"Want to bet?" He sprinted toward the cab and jumped into the driver's seat. She saw what he was doing, ran around and got in on the passenger side. As Bond drove off, the cab driver ran out of the delicatessen, shouting.

"I'm not sure what you just did was entirely legal," Cheryl said.

"Why not?" Bond said, speeding toward Fifth Avenue. "They do it in the movies all the time."

The towncar had crossed Fifth and was heading toward Sixth Avenue, but traffic congestion had brought it to a halt. Bond crossed the intersection and pulled into the line of traffic on the narrow street. Four other vehicles were between the cab and the towncar. Suddenly, the towncar tore out of the line of stalled traffic, pulled onto the pavement and sped along the shopfronts toward Sixth Avenue. Pedestrians screamed and jumped out of the way. The towncar pulled down a canopy in front of a shop as it raced recklessly toward the intersection.

Bond cursed and drove the cab onto the pavement as well. He floored the gas pedal and took off, following the towncar. Cheryl was too stunned to scream.

The towncar reached the intersection at Sixth Avenue and shot out into moving traffic. Another cab rammed into its back fender, but the towncar kept going. Horns were braying as Bond's taxi burst into the avenue. They managed to make it across without getting hit, but Bond was aware of squealing tires, horns honking, and angry shouts behind them.

They were still traveling west on a one-way, narrow street, and now there was nothing between the towncar and Bond's taxi. Bond bore down, gaining on it. Then he saw a figure lean out of the towncar window, pointing back at them.

"Duck!" Bond yelled just as the windshield shattered above his head. Luckily, the bullet only made a hole and didn't demolish the entire windshield. Bond never faltered and sped toward the towncar. He drew the Walther PPK, held it in his left hand out the window and shot at the towncar. He knocked out a tail light, but little else. Bond wasn't used to driving with the wheel on the left, nor shooting with his left hand.

At Seventh Avenue, the towncar turned left and headed south. Bond zoomed into the intersection doing sixty m.p.h. and almost hit an MTA bus. Cheryl gripped the dashboard and stared straight ahead, not saying a word. She was afraid, but she knew Bond was capable of handling the situation. After all, he was one of the Double-Os.

The towncar weaved in and out of traffic, scooting ahead and sailing through an intersection just as the light turned red. Bond, through his teeth, said, "Hold on!" He stepped on the gas and leaned on the horn of the cab. Cross traffic had already entered the intersection and another taxi cab pulled in front of Bond. He had to swerve to avoid broadsiding it, but nevertheless took off its back bumper and sent the cab spinning like a top in the middle of the intersection.

The towncar turned right onto another one way street heading west. Bond followed, hot on its tail. The figure leaned out of the towncar once again and fired at them, but missed.

Cheryl suddenly snapped out of her deep freeze. "All right, that does it," she said, and pulled a Browning 9mm automatic pistol out of her bag.

"Christ, Cheryl," said Bond, "*now* you think of that?"

"Sorry, I was enjoying the ride," she said, then leaned out the passenger window. She fired twice. The second shot hit the man who was aiming at them. He dropped his gun on the street and withdrew into the car.

"There're three people in the car," said Bond. "The driver, the woman and the man you just shot. Nice work."

"Thanks," she said.

"See if you can get their tires."

Cheryl leaned out again to fire, but the towncar reached Eighth Avenue. This time, it turned south *against* the one way traffic traveling north.

"They must be mad!" she shouted, but Bond followed them without batting an eye. Now they could hear police sirens in the distance behind them.

Both the towncar and Bond's taxi miraculously avoided accidents, but they left behind a cacophony of car horns. At 23rd Street, the towncar turned right and drove west again. Bond turned the corner and sped after it, wondering when and where this would all end. The chase continued across Ninth Avenue and on to Tenth. They were nearing the Hudson River.

Finally, the towncar slowed and turned into a driveway of an old four-story building on Tenth Avenue. Bond pulled in next to the curb a hundred yards away, jumped out of the cab, and took cover behind his open door. Cheryl did the same on the passenger side. There was no gunfire from the warehouse. Cheryl ran to the side of the building and flattened herself against it. Bond followed and stood beside her, watching and listening.

"What is this place?" he asked.

"Some kind of warehouse. No telling who it belongs to," she said. "You're in Chelsea. There's nothing here *but* old warehouses."

Bond snaked nearer to the driveway entrance, where a steel door had slammed down. It apparently led into a parking garage. There was no visible way in on this side of the building. The sun was sinking fast, and an orange glow permeated the streets. They didn't have many more minutes of daylight. The two agents suddenly felt very alone. The police sirens were lost in the distance, and this area of the city was surprisingly deserted.

There was a fire escape ladder on the side of the building. "I'm going to get in up there. Go find a phone and call for backup or whatever it is you do here," Bond ordered.

"I don't think you should go in there alone," she said.

"This is my fight," he said with determination, and then he leaped up and grabbed the bottom of the metal ladder. It rolled down with his weight. "Go on, please, Cheryl," he said, starting to climb the ladder.

"All right," she said, "but I'm coming right back after you." She looked around, located a phone booth on the opposite corner and ran for it.

007 quietly moved up the fire escape to the second floor. He tried the window, but it was locked or stuck. He went up another flight and tried the window there. It inched up a bit. Bond put all of his strength behind the effort and opened it wide enough for him to slip through.

It was very dark inside. He wasn't sure what kind of room he was in. He stood still a moment and allowed his eyes to adjust to the lighting. It was some kind of lounge area; chairs and couches dating from the fifties dominated the room. It was terribly dusty and dirty; obviously no one had disturbed the place in years. He listened to the stillness and could hear faint movement below him.

He slowly moved across the room to the open door, but the wooden floor creaked as he walked. Damn! If they didn't know he had already entered the building, they were aware of his presence now. He needed to find a hiding place in another room.

As soon as he stepped through the doorway, though, he felt a sharp pain on the back of his head and all light was extinguished.

The jolt of three slaps on the face brought Bond out of the pit of darkness. He was in a chair in a different room. It was some kind of old office, with junky furniture piled next to the walls. A single overhead light cast a dull yellow light over the floor.

The back of his head hurt like hell. His first reflex was to reach up with his right hand to rub his head, but the cold nuzzle of a pistol jabbed his temple.

"Don't move," a man's voice said.

Bond groaned, squeezed his eyes twice, then focused on the blurry figure standing in front of him. It was the bag lady, only she didn't look much like a homeless person anymore. The rags were gone, and she was dressed in a black shirt and trousers. Her face had a smooth, waxen, unreal quality to it. She was plump and short, probably no more than five feet and two inches, and had gray hair pulled back in a bun. The hair seemed fake—it looked as if she was wearing a wig.

"You don't recognize me, Mr. Bond?" she said. "Maybe this will help."

The woman reached up to her hairline and gently began to peel off something stuck to her skin. No . . . she was actually peeling off her skin! She worked carefully, removing what apparently was a thin mask of synthetic flesh that covered the right half of her face. Underneath was a grotesque skin condition that began on her right cheekbone and went up the side of her face and underneath the wig. It was the scarring of poorly-executed plastic surgery. She was a female version of the Phantom of the Opera.

"Hideous, Mr. Bond?" she said. "Take a good look. I want you to see what you did to me." She pronounced her w's as v's, like a bad horror film vampire—or a B-movie Nazi.

What the hell was she talking about? Who was she? Bond forced himself to look at her again, and this time the feeling of recognition that he had experienced earlier returned. He looked past the horrible fright mask and saw a square, brutal face with toad-like features. No! He felt his heart race when he realized who she was. A report claiming that the woman had been seen in Australia received some attention shortly after the Japanese affair, but this information proved to have been false. It was seemingly impossible, but there she was in front of him. She was supposed to be dead!

"Irma Bunt," he said.

"Oh, so you do recognize me after all!" she cackled. She carefully replaced the skin mask as she talked. "You thought I was dead, didn't you? Everyone thought I was dead. Well, I was. I was dead for years and years . . . until now." She chuckled to herself, then said slowly and with menace, "Now I am more alive than I ever was. It's a pity that you survived the surprise I left for you in the bank. Now I'll have to take care of you here, but that might be more entertaining after all."

Bond surveyed the situation. A man stood behind his chair and held a pistol to his head. Another man, the wounded one, was next to Irma Bunt. His shoulder was bloody, and he had crudely wrapped something around it. He was holding Bond's Walther PPK in his left hand. A third man was a few feet away, leaning against the wall. He was armed with what appeared to be an Uzi. Fräulein Bunt wasn't carrying a weapon.

"You are wondering how I am still alive," she said.

Bond hoped he could stall her and keep her talking until Cheryl could arrive with the cavalry.

"You're right, Fräulein, I am wondering. The last time I saw you, you were lying on the floor of that castle with a bump on your head."

Her mask was in place and once again the woman's features had a mannequin-like, waxen look to them. Bond couldn't decide which of her faces was more freakish.

"You thought I perished in the explosion, didn't you? I regained consciousness just as you were escaping on that balloon. I knew what was happening. I could hear the rumbling from below. I knew I had seconds to get out of there. You left poor Ernst in a heap on the floor, but there was nothing I could do for him. He was dead."

As she talked, the flood of nightmarish memories returned to Bond. Ernst Stavro Blofeld had become a fugitive from the law after the Thunderball affair and the business in the Swiss Alps. With the demise of S.P.E.C.T.R.E., he and his companion, Irma Bunt, had fled to Japan, where he had assumed the identity of a horticulturist named Dr. Shatterhand. Blofeld purchased an ancient, abandoned Japanese feudal castle and built a "research lab" for exotic, poisonous plants and dangerous animals. Mad as a hatter, Blofeld's true intention had been to entice Japanese citizens to commit suicide in his so-called "garden of death." Bond had infiltrated the castle's defenses, knocked out Irma Bunt with a staff, strangled Blofeld to death and rigged the underground geyser to explode.

"I was escaping in a small boat we kept for just such a purpose when it blew," Bunt continued. "I was hit in the head by debris and almost drowned. These men here saved me and have remained loyal. Like you, I lost my memory. I didn't know who I was. I was taken to a private German clinic near Kyoto, where I underwent several operations. There is a metal plate in the right side of my skull, and the skin on my face . . . well, my plastic surgeon could do very little with it. The damage was too great. I was in bed for a year, and rehabilitation lasted another two years of my life. It took another ten years for a psychiatrist to finally pull me out of the hole into which I had fallen. Then I remembered . . . I looked back at what I had lost, and the years of suffering ahead of me. That's a long time to ponder one's future, Mr. Bond. At the time I didn't know exactly how, but I knew you would play a prominent role in it. You English pig . . . I've waited so many years for this moment. And I promise you I am going to enjoy my revenge."

"Why did you have to kill my son?" Bond seethed.

"Ah, your son!" Bunt smiled. Her features were so distorted that the edge of her mouth lifted on only one side of her face. "My intelligence sources retraced your footsteps in Japan. I discovered your pretty little phony Japanese wife. There was a little boy living with her, about ten years old, when I finally found her. I kept watch and followed her movements, all the way to America. I watched him grow up, and I waited until the right moment. I wanted to kill her, too, but she saved me the trouble. It took a while, but I finally established that he had a link to you. After he was dead, it was simple to locate your address and send a letter."

She took a barber's razor and a small vial of liquid out of her pocket. "This is what I used on him. I lined the blade with a little *fugu* poison, and ever-so-subtly cut him one day as he was entering the building. Did you like my disguise? It fooled even you, Mr. Bond, didn't it?"

That explained the cut on James' arm. Bond hated her. He hated her with all his might.

"You killed my wife, too, you bitch," Bond said, "and if you think I'm going to let you live after today, you're as mad as ever."

"Oh, yes!" she gloated. "Your wife! The daughter of that criminal, the Corsican, Draco. That was an accident, Mr. Bond. Those bullets were meant for you. If you had died then, it would have saved us all a lot of trouble, no? It would have saved me my . . ."

Bunt's lower lip trembled. Her eyes grew fierce and she suddenly shouted, "LOOK AT ME! Look at what you did to me, English pig!! You destroyed my face!!"

"Fräulein Bunt," Bond said with venom, "you were never a beauty queen."

The woman stepped up to him and slapped him twice. She was shaking with rage and madness. Bond started to jump up from the chair, but the thug behind him roughly thrust the pistol into his temple.

"Don't move!" he commanded again.

Bond had to think. His hands were free. Surely there was some way he could gain an advantage . . .

Bunt stepped back, rubbing her palm. "My, my, Mr. Bond," she said, a bit more calmly. "You need a shave. You have quite a stubble. What do you think, Hans, don't you think Mr. Bond needs a shave?"

The man behind Bond grunted affirmatively.

Irma Bunt opened the vial of *fugu* poison and poured it along the edge of the razor. "Now hold still, Mr. Bond. I think you would hate for me to slip and nick you. You know how fast this poison works? In five minutes, you become disoriented. In ten minutes, you lose control of your muscles. In fifteen you stop breathing. I understand the experience is very painful and excruciating. Hold his arms, Hans. Adolf, cover him."

The man behind Bond holstered the pistol and grabbed Bond's wrists. He twisted them sharply behind the chair and held them in a vice-like grip. He was very strong. The other man with the Uzi stepped forward and held the barrel up at Bond. Irma Bunt stepped forward, holding the razor in front of her. Bond could see the syrupy liquid dripping from the blade.

Bond refused to close his eyes as the woman pressed the cold razor against his right cheek. He stared into her yellow eyes as she slowly scraped the blade down his face and cleanly cut his beard.

"It's a little rough without lather, is it not, Mr. Bond?" she said. "But you like close shaves, don't you?"

Bond held his breath, willing his facial muscles not to jerk involuntarily. The woman brought the blade down again, finishing the job on the right cheek. She fingered the age-old, faint scar there.

"Looks like you weren't so careful one morning, eh?" she said. "Now lift your chin, please. We need to do the neck now . . ."

She pulled his chin up and Bond stared at the ceiling. He felt the blade cut against the stubble. It was rougher going there, and he anticipated the sharp sting of getting sliced at any moment. The woman concentrated intently on her job, breathing heavily.

A bead of sweat rolled down Bond's forehead and into his left eye. He winced and almost flinched away from the razor. The woman's breathing became even more pronounced. Bond glanced down at her and saw that her free hand was rubbing her breasts as she applied the razor. My God, he thought, she was sexually excited by this! The sadistic woman licked her lips, her eyes focused on Bond's vulnerable neck.

"Now the left cheek, Mr. Bond," she said. 007 leveled his head and stared straight ahead, past the woman and Adolf, the man with the Uzi. To his amazement, Cheryl Haven was peering into the doorway of the room, gun in hand. Their eyes met. She gestured to Adolf with a slight nod of her head. Bond deliberately closed his eyes and opened them, a signal that Cheryl took to mean "do it!" Without a second thought, Cheryl quietly stepped into the doorway and assumed the firing stance.

The blast hit Adolf in the back and he fell forward. Bond simultaneously kicked up at Irma Bunt, knocking her away from him. Hans, the man holding his wrists, released his grip and went for his gun, but Bond leaped out of the chair and tackled him. Cheryl immediately turned her gun on the wounded man and yelled, "Freeze! Drop the gun!" The surprised man dropped Bond's Walther and held up his one good arm. Irma Bunt, however, managed to run out of the room before Cheryl could stop her.

Hans was all-muscle, and he delivered a blow to Bond's chin that knocked him down. With lightning speed, the man then drew his gun and pointed it at 007. The blast from Cheryl's Browning hit him in the head, splattering his brains across the dirty wooden floor.

"Thanks," Bond said, rubbing his chin.

"Not a problem," she said, training her gun back on the wounded man. "The lady ran out the door. My men will be here any minute."

"You watch him, I'll go after her," Bond said. He picked up his Walther and ran from the room and into a large, open space. What he saw startled him, and he was disoriented until Bond realized what he was looking at. The dimly lit warehouse was full of the ancient remains of what must have been parade floats. There was a storybook castle made of *papier mache* sitting on a flatbed with wheels. A large cartoon dog built out of wood and steel sat on its side, one leg broken off. Other dilapidated structures of varying subjects, from a giant hot dog to statues of American Presidents, were scattered about in a bizarre and other-worldly fashion. Bond suddenly felt as if he had entered a twilight zone of forgotten fantasy.

Where did she go? He listened to the room but heard no running footsteps. She was hiding somewhere—she couldn't have got far.

Bond ran toward the broken floats and began to search under, on and around them. She could be anywhere. The place was so full of junk that she could easily blend in with the debris and not be noticed. He needed more light.

He was looking around the body parts of a giant-sized *papier mache* Abraham Lincoln when a shot rang out. The bullet zipped past him and into Lincoln's head, shattering it into bits. The woman had a gun! Bond dove for cover, waited a moment, then peered out into the dark, open space. The shot had come from somewhere on the other side of the room. Bond fired the Walther in that general direction, hoping to smoke her out of hiding.

After a moment, a door behind one of the floats opened and a figure ran through it. Bond bolted and ran after her. It was a careless move, for she immediately leaned in and fired the gun at him. Bond dove for the floor and, with both hands on his Walther, fired into the open doorway. The figure had disappeared by then, running into the next room.

Bond leaped to his feet, ran to the door and flattened himself against the wall beside it. Commando-style, he swung in and crouched low, his gun ready. Again, his senses were assaulted by the surreal visuals in the place. This small room was full of naked, broken male and female mannequins—loose arms, legs, torsos, and complete bodies were piled together in a grotesque, frozen orgy. The image so confused Bond that he foolishly left himself wide open. The shot slammed into his left lower leg, shattering his fibula. Bond screamed and rolled over into a mass of plastic appendages. He unleashed a volley of ammunition toward the far side of the room, firing blindly at the mannequins. The noise was deafening, but Bond thought he heard a muffled cry.

His leg was burning like hell. He took a moment to examine the damage. Blood was pouring out of a wound a couple of inches above his ankle. He pressed his left foot against the wall to test his strength and tremendous pain shot through him. Was he crippled? Would he be able to walk again? He only knew that he would be unable to stand anytime soon.

Bond peered across the room at the mass of bodies and saw some movement. Pushing pieces of mannequins aside, Irma Bunt crawled out onto the floor. He had hit her after all. Her wig had fallen off, revealing a bald, scarred, horribly ugly specimen of humanity. The area where the metal plate had been implanted was clearly visible. The skin mask was loose and hanging from her face as if an epidermal layer had been sliced away. She must have dropped her gun, for she used both hands to pull herself along the floor like a snail. Smeared blood trailed behind her. Bond watched in fascination and horror as she got within a few yards of him and then stopped, completely drained of energy. She looked straight at Bond and snarled, "English . . . pig . . ."

And then she slumped forward and died.

Bond rolled over onto his back and drifted into unconsciousness, just as Cheryl Haven and a team of men entered the room.

James Bond gazed out the hospital window, enjoying another bright and sunny Manhattan spring day. His leg would be in a cast for the next few weeks. He had been in surgery for two hours the previous night. A pin had to be inserted to reinforce 007's broken fibula. He had no memory of the trip to the emergency room. Bond vaguely recalled the recovery room and a pretty nurse with a pleasant voice. He had been awake for just a few minutes, then drifted away for several hours. It was now late afternoon of the following day, and the grogginess was finally fading. He had eaten a half-portion of bland, intolerable scrambled eggs, drank a little tepid orange juice and picked at a cup of runny vanilla yogurt. Much to his surprise, the miserable meal had given him back some energy. He would have liked to stand up and walk around, but he had no crutches yet.

Bond mentally explored his mind and body, taking stock of the powerful instrument that had taken him so many times to the edge of disaster and back. All things considered, he felt good. Much of this, he knew, was due to the euphoria of victory. Seeing Irma Bunt die in front of him had been morbidly satisfying. He felt a closure on

a painful epoch in his life, and the relief was exhilarating. The occasional bad dreams about Tracy, Blofeld, and Japan would most likely
cease now. He thought of James, as well—the boy he never knew, the
son he never lived with. He hadn't deserved to die. Bond was aware
that he needed to grieve, and that it would happen sooner rather than
later. He wouldn't allow himself to dwell upon it too long, lest he
would start to blame himself. Save it all for another day, he ordered
himself. For now, relish the victory. Not only had his son's death been
avenged, but he had, hopefully, settled the score regarding Tracy.

"Well, look who's awake!" a familiar woman's voice said.

He turned his head from the window and was met by the lovely
sight of Cheryl Haven wearing a white, sleeveless T-shirt and a pair
of daringly short cut-offs. Her lack of a bra was obvious. Her golden
hair glistened in the sunlight which streamed in from the window.
Her smile was one of the most beautiful things Bond had ever seen.

"Good morning," Bond said. "Er . . . afternoon."

"How do you feel?" she asked, pulling up a chair beside the bed.
She crossed her long, shapely legs. She was in excellent shape.

"Now that you're here, I feel great," he said.

"So I hear they had to glue you back together."

"It wasn't necessary. A paper clip was all it needed."

She reached out and placed her hand on his arm. "I'm glad you're
okay. That was quite a night. You're going to have to come to New
York more often. I don't get many dates like that. You really know
how to show a girl a good time. You're cool as hell, you know that?"
She playfully squeezed his arm.

Bond laughed and then asked, "What have you found out?"

"The wounded man told us the whole story. They had entered the
country six months ago. We're still checking on how Immigration
missed them. All three of those men had been with her for years. The
way he talked, it was apparent that they had somehow been brain-
washed by her or that man, Blofeld. They were loyal to the very end.
They were actually living in that old warehouse. Did you know that it
used to be a storage center for Macy's? No one's ever cleaned it out."

"I want to thank you. You saved my life."

She laughed. "Oh, you don't know how many men I've longed to hear say that."

"I can't believe you don't have men lining up to say that," he said, taking her hand in his own.

"Oh, please stop it," she said, but her eyes betrayed that she liked the compliment.

"We never had that dinner," he said.

She chuckled again, "No, we didn't!"

"After the meal I just had, I'm ready to eat at the filthiest place you can recommend."

"Are you hungry now?" she asked, her tongue lightly licking her sensual lips.

"As a matter of fact, I'm famished," he said, staring into her warm, brown eyes.

Cheryl looked around, stood up, and closed the door to the room. Next, she pulled the curtain around the bed, giving them *a little* privacy. Without saying a word, she pulled off her T-shirt, revealing large, firm breasts. Her nipples were extended and the skin below her neck was flushed. She unsnapped her cutoffs, but kept them on. She climbed onto the bed next to him, carefully avoiding the injured leg.

Their mouths met, and for several minutes they just kissed, exploring each other with their tongues. Bond flashed on his last sexual encounter and remembered a very young woman—a girl, really. At the time, he had thought there was nothing better. Now, helpless in the hands of an older, more mature woman, he knew that there was no comparison. Cheryl Haven knew how to love. And he was going to let her show him what she knew.

"If you're hungry, darling," she whispered, lifting her right breast to his mouth, *"bon appetit."*

ACKNOWLEDGMENTS

HIGH TIME TO KILL

The author and publishers wish to thank the following individuals and organizations for their assistance in preparing this book:

Belgian Tourist Office (U.S.)—Liliane Opsomer
Carolyn Caughey
Tom Colgan
Dan Harvey
Hospital Erasme (Brussels)—Mrs. Laurence Taca
Captain Alexander Howard
Hôtel Métropole (Brussels)—Serge Schultz and Chafik Habib
Hotel Yak and Yeti (Kathmandu)—Richard Launay
Jaguar Cars (U.K.)—Fergus Pollock
Peter Janson-Smith
L'Alban Chambon restaurant (Brussels)—Dominique Michou
Madeline Neems
Roger Nowicke
Lucy Oliver
Louisa Parkinson
Police de Bruxelles (Brussels)—Lucien Vermeir
Doug Redenius

Dave Reinhardt

Moana Re Robertson

Dr. Patrick Sepulchre

Spymaster Inc. (U.K.)—Lee Marks

Stoke Poges Golf Club (U.K.)—Chester King,
    Ralph Pickering, and Nolan Edwards

Sulzer Intermedics Inc. (U.S.)—Julia Hsi Morris

Tor Imports (U.K.)—Mark Acton

Tourist Information Brussels—An Depraedere

Corinne B. Turner

Elaine Wiltshire

The heirs of Ian Lancaster Fleming

and, of course, Randi and Max, without whom, etc.

A special thank-you to the 1st Royal Gurkha Rifles for their invaluable assistance, and to Scott McKee, the first American to summit Kangchenjunga via the north face.

The Ian Fleming Foundation can be reached at P.O. Box 1850, Burbank, California 91507, or at the Web site Mr. Kiss Kiss Bang Bang at www.ianfleming.org

DOUBLESHOT

The author and publishers wish to thank the following individuals and organizations for their assistance in the writing of this book—

In Gibraltar
Andrew Bonfante; His Excellency the Governor, Sir Richard Luce and Lady Luce; Gail Francis—Gibraltar Tourist Board; Pepe Rosado

In London
Carolyn Caughey; Peter Janson-Smith; Corinne B. Turner; Zoë Watkins; The Heirs of Ian Lancaster Fleming

In Morocco
Said Arif, Bazid LaHoussine; Philippe Seigle and Reto Grass—Le Royal Mansour Meridien Hotel (Casablanca); Khalil Tass—Magic Carpet Adventures S. A. (Tangier); Rizki Mohamed Zouhir

In Spain
Victoriano Borrego Aguayo; Javier Conde; Felipe Paramio Alonso, Francisco Amorós Bernabéu, Agustin Lomeña, and Diana Serop—Costa del Sol Patronato de Turismo (Torremolinos); Pepillo de Málaga— El Ranchito Equestrian School (Torremolinos); Iwan and Margareta Morelius; Antonio Carlos Muñoz ("El Cuqui"); Francisco Rivera Ordoñez and Maria Eugenia, Duquesa de Montoro; José Antonio Guerrero Pedraza, and D. Alberto Urzaiz—Plaza de Toros (Ronda); Peña Juan Breva (Málaga); Restaurante El Chinitas (Málaga); Javier Rosenberg and Frederick A. Parody, Marbella Club Hotel (Marbella); José Navio Serrano—Parador de Ronda Hotel (Ronda)

In the U.S.
Paul Baack; Tom Colgan; Paul F. Dantuono, EC Tours; Sandy Groark—Bannockburn Travel (Chicago); James McMahon; Moana Re Robertson; Gary Rosenfeld; Dr. Michael Sergeant; Patricia Winn—Tourist Office of Spain (Chicago)

NEVER DREAM OF DYING

THE AUTHOR AND PUBLISHER WISH TO THANK THE FOLLOWING INDIVIDUALS and organizations in the preparation of this book.

IN CORSICA:
Antenne Médicale d'Urgence (Calvi); Astalla Taverne (Calvi); Jean Philippe Di Grazia—Agence du Tourisme de la Corse; Le Goulet Restaurant (Bonifacio)

IN LONDON:
Carolyn Caughey; Samantha Evans; Peter Janson-Smith; Corinne Turner; Zoë Watkins; the heirs of the late Ian Lancaster Fleming

IN MONACO:
William Ray—Casino de Monte Carlo

IN PARIS:
Blandine Bideau—France Télévision; Pascal Boissel—Le Grand Hotel Intercontinental; François-Xavier Busnel; Kevin Collette; Le Petit Mâchon Restaurant; Laurent Perriot; Daniel Pont—Musée de la Police

IN NICE:
Christian Duc—Riviera Studios; Sandra Jurinic—Office du Tourisme et des Congrès; Palais Maeterlinck; Pierre Rodiac

IN THE US:
Paul Baack; Gaz Cooper; Paul F. Dantuono; Fountain Powerboats; Dr. Ira Garoon; Dr. Rob Gerowitz; Isabelle Grasset-Lapiere—French Government Tourist Office; Sandy Groark—Bannockburn Travel; Tylyn John; David Knox; James McMahon; Gary Rosenfeld; and my wonderful wife Randi